ALSO BY CATHERINE COOKSON

NOVELS
Kate Hannigan
The Fifteen Streets
Colour Blind
Maggie Rowan
Rooney
The Menagerie
Slinky Jane
Fanny McBride
Fenwick Houses
The Garment
The Blind Miller
Hannah Massey
The Long Corridor
The Unbaited Trap
Katie Mulholland
The Round Tower
The Nice Bloke
The Glass Virgin
The Invitation
The Dwelling Place
Feathers in the Fire
Pure as the Lily
The Mallen Streak
The Mallen Girl
The Mallen Litter
The Invisible Cord
The Gambling Man
Miss Martha Mary Crawford
The Tide of Life

The Slow Awakening
The Iron Façade
The Girl
The Cinder Path
The Man Who Cried
Tilly Trotter
Tilly Trotter Wed
Tilly Trotter Widowed
The Whip
Hamilton
The Black Velvet Gown
Goodbye Hamilton
A Dinner of Herbs
Harold
The Moth
Bill Bailey
The Parson's Daughter
Bill Bailey's Lot
The Cultured Handmaiden
Bill Bailey's Daughter
The Harrogate Secret
The Black Candle
The Wingless Bird
The Gillyvors
My Beloved Son
The Rag Nymph
The House of Women
The Maltese Angel
The Year of the Virgins

THE MARY ANN STORIES
A Grand Man
The Lord and Mary Ann
The Devil and Mary Ann
Love and Mary Ann
Life and Mary Ann

Marriage and Mary Ann
Mary Ann's Angels
Mary Ann and Bill
Bill and the Mary Ann
   Shaughnessy

FOR CHILDREN
Matty Doolin
Joe and the Gladiator
The Nipper
Blue Baccy
Our John Willie

Mrs Flannagan's Trumpet
Go Tell It To Mrs Golightly
Lanky Jones
Nancy Nutall and the Mongrel

AUTOBIOGRAPHY
Our Kate
Let Me Make Myself Plain

Catherine Cookson Country

WRITING AS CATHERINE MARCHANT
House of Men
The Fen Tiger

Heritage of Folly

Catherine Cookson was born in Tyne Dock, the illegitimate daughter of a poverty-stricken woman, Kate, whom she believed to be her sister. She began work in service but eventually moved south to Hastings, where she met and married a local grammar-school master. Although she was originally acclaimed as a regional writer – in 1968 her novel *The Round Tower* won the Winifred Holtby Award – her readership quickly spread throughout the world and her many bestselling novels have established her as the best-loved of contemporary women writers. After receiving an OBE in 1985, Catherine Cookson was created a Dame of the British Empire in 1993.

CATHERINE COOKSON

UNABRIDGED OMNIBUS EDITION

THE LONG CORRIDOR
THE BLIND MILLER
KATE HANNIGAN

PATHWAY

TRANSWORLD PUBLISHERS LTD
61–63 Uxbridge Road, London W5 5SA

TRANSWORLD PUBLISHERS (AUSTRALIA) PTY LTD
15–25 Helles Avenue, Moorebank, NSW 2170

TRANSWORLD PUBLISHERS (NZ) LTD
3 William Pickering Drive, Albany, Auckland

Published in 1993 by Pathway
a division of Transworld Publishers Ltd

Copyright: *The Long Corridor* © Catherine Cookson 1965
First published by Macdonald & Co. (Publishers) Ltd.
The Blind Miller © Catherine Cookson 1963
First published by MacDonald & Co. (Publishers) Ltd.
Kate Hannigan © Catherine Cookson 1950
First published by MacDonald & Co. (Publishers) Ltd.

This edition printed in 1998 for County Bookshops

The right of Catherine Cookson to be identified
as the author of this work has been asserted in accordance
with sections 77 and 78 of the Copyright Designs and Patents
Act 1988.

All of the characters in this book
are fictitious, and any resemblance
to actual persons, living or dead,
is purely coincidental.

A catalogue record for this book is available from the British Library

ISBN 0593 03537 2

All rights reserved. No part of this publication may
be reproduced, stored in a retrieval system, or
transmitted in any form or by any means,
electronic, mechanical, photocopying, recording,
or otherwise, without the prior permission of
the publishers.

Typeset in 11/12 pt Monotype Plantin

Printed in Great Britain by
Mackays of Chatham, plc, Chatham, Kent.

THE LONG CORRIDOR

CONTENTS

PART ONE

THE FAMILY

'Aw, Doctor, I'm as fit as a fiddle. Go on now and sign me off.'

'Not for another week at least, Annie; you're in no fit state to go cleaning and scrubbing.'

'There's no scrubbing these days, Doctor; you're behind the times. I only wield one of them polishers. Magic, they are.'

'Well, be that as it may. To wield one of them polishers you have to get out of bed before six, haven't you? And that chest of yours doesn't take to the early morning fogs.'

'Doctor.' Annie Mullen's jocular face became straight, and her glance equally so as she looked across the broad mahogany table towards the doctor for a second or so before she said flatly, 'I can't stand another week in the house, Doctor. She wants me out of it, an' I want to be out of it. It's been sheer hell this last three weeks. Nothin' said directly to me you know. Oh, no, she's too clever for that. She talks at you. You know the kind. All day she goes at it until my Harry comes home at night, and then butter wouldn't melt in her mouth. It makes me sick, Doctor, so do me this favour, will you, and sign me off. I'll take a lot of killin', really I will, but when me time comes I hope it's short and sharp.' Leaning further across the table now, and her voice dropping to a whisper, she added, 'You promised me once that when I was goin' I would have no pain. Do you still mean that?'

'I do, Annie.' His voice was as low as hers. 'Never you worry about that, you've got my word for it.'

After a single nod the old woman straightened up and, the smile returning to her face, she said, 'That's good enough for me.'

She watched him writing swiftly, and when he handed her the certificate she rose to her feet, and as she buttoned her coat she glanced sideways at him, as he also rose, and said, 'My old man used to say that your father, God rest him, looked tough, and talked tough, but there wasn't a better stitcher in the land, nor a kinder heart . . . aw, an' you know what?' Mrs Mullen now laid the flat of her hand on the doctor's chest. 'He's passed everything he had on to his son. Goodnight to you now.' She turned abruptly away and made for the door.

The doctor did not call after her, 'Aw, I've heard your blarney

9

before, Annie'; he accepted her good opinion of him quietly, saying, 'Goodnight to you, Annie.' Then passing his hand over his chin he resumed his seat and pressed a button. And the door opened again and a man entered.

The doctor did not raise his eyes to the newcomer but consulted the card on his desk. Harold Gray, thirty-four years old. His eyes skimmed down the dates during which he had been treating the man over the last twelve months. Three weeks, five weeks, now four weeks. He looked up. 'Well, how are you?'

'Oh, you know, Doctor, not too bright.'

'Back better since you started taking those new tablets?'

'Well . . . well a bit, Doctor, but . . .'

'Ah, that's good, I thought they would do the trick.'

'But it's like this, Doctor . . .'

'Well now, I suppose you're ready to go back to work.'

'But, Doctor . . .'

'I gave you an extension last week that should have put you on your feet.' The doctor pulled a form towards him and began once again to write rapidly, and when he handed the certificate across the table to the man, Mr Gray, wearing a resigned and solemn expression, got up from the chair and looking down at the doctor, said, 'It'll only go again.'

'You'll have to chance that. But try to remember that the last time it went you had an X-ray and it showed nothing wrong with your back. And the time before that, when it went you had an X-ray and nothing wrong could be found . . .' He paused before ending, '. . . with your back. Goodnight.'

'Goodnight, Doctor.'

The salutation sounded like a threat, and Mr Gray closed the door none too gently after him.

The doctor now gathered a number of cards from his desk, patted them together and sat looking at them. They represented people, all sorts of people: among them old Annie, with cancer eating her stomach and he was treating her for bronchitis, and she wanting to work until she dropped, which would be the best way for her to end, and they both knew it. Then there was Gray. He wanted to spit. On the thought of this man he wanted to spit. He went out of the surgery, across a wide low waiting-room, pushed open a door marked 'Enquiries' and, throwing the cards on to a table at which sat a middle-aged woman, said, 'Anything else in?'

'No, nothing, not since Mrs Ratcliffe's call.'

'I've a damned good mind to make her wait until the morning . . . Neurotic individual.'

'We mustn't forget that the neurotic individuals pay on the dot, Doctor; and as you've said yourself, P.P.s are so few and far between these days we should pamper the ones we've got.'

A quizzical smile passed over the doctor's face, and, leaning his hands on the table, he bent towards his receptionist, saying, 'Your caustic memory will get you somewhere one of these days, Elsie; it's odd how you manage to remember all the wrong things I say.'

'I wouldn't call them wrong, Doctor.' Her smile was as quizzical as his own. 'Anyway, if I can remember all you say now after fifteen years I never will.'

'Fifteen years is it?' He straightened up and looked away from her back into the hall, with its big round table patterned with a criss-cross of magazines. 'Fifteen years you've been here? It makes you think, doesn't it?'

'Well, I wouldn't start and reminisce now if I were you. You haven't had anything to eat since one o'clock, so you'd better have something before you go to Mrs Ratcliffe. Then there's Mrs Ogilby. She's near her time; she might last till tomorrow, then again she might not.'

The doctor, still looking across the waiting-room, said submissively, 'As you say, Elsie, as you say.' Then over his shoulder he added on a sharper note, 'Leave that lot for tonight and get yourself home. If you ordered your own life as you do mine you wouldn't be so skinny.'

Elsie Ryan looked up at him and smiled her tight smile. 'Goodnight,' she said.

'Goodnight, Elsie.'

He walked across the waiting-room again in the direction now of a door marked 'Private'. Then almost as he was about to open it he turned slowly away, went past his surgery and out through another door into a courtyard. Here he stopped for a moment to look up into the star-studded sky. The moon was full and lit up the frost-coated tiles of the outhouses surrounding the yard. He filled his lungs with the sharp cold air, then sauntered over the wide square blocks of granite that paved the yard towards the open gates, and stood looking out into the square. It was utterly deserted at the moment, which was unusual, for nearly always there were figures going in and out of the Technical College across the road. He turned his eyes towards the right, where the block forming the top of the square was taken up by the refrigeration plant. It was funny how things grew. Pearson had started with a little butcher's shop in the heart of Bogs End – the vicinity alone would tell you what quality meat he sold – and now he had the biggest cold storage plant for miles. It was said he was a millionaire, a millionaire who couldn't write his own name. Old Pearson had been a patient of his father's for years, and of his too, until Mrs Pearson decided that they now needed a better setting for their wealth and had taken her coarse-mouthed, illiterate husband to the softer climes of the South. Still looking to the right his eyes passed over the Salvation Army barracks adjoining his own property. They, too, were quiet. No calling on God to come and jazz it up tonight. His lips moved into a tolerant smile. Did it matter how they called, as long as they had the desire to call, and the belief that they were being heard? Some folks looked on the Salvation Army with scorn and pity, but they weren't to be pitied. It was those who had thought themselves into the conviction that such simple souls were shouting to a deaf mute, it was these, he knew, who should be pitied. And he was one of them.

He looked to the left of him now, to the façade of his own house. Houses would be a better description, for Romfield House was really three houses knocked into one. Romfield House had begun when his grandfather, who had a taggerine business, made prosperous by the inhabitants of Bogs End, had bought the four-roomed, Georgian-fronted house in Romfield Square, which in those far-off days was on the fringe of Fellburn and not yet included in the vicinity of Bogs End. And it was in this house that his grandfather, the ambitious scrap dealer, had fostered his own son's desire to become a doctor. And when that son qualified he had bought him part of a practice in the best end of Fellburn. He had also, through time, bought the two houses adjoining his own – just as a business proposition this. But his doctor son had other ideas, and the outcome of these ideas was that the three houses were turned into one. And later, he brought his practice to the house in which he had grown up.

In due course Doctor Higgins did for his son Paul what his own father had done for him: he encouraged him in the way he wanted to go, and eventually, during the last years of his life, he had the reward of working side by side with his son and imbuing in him a love not only for his work but also for practising it from this house. But such loves have a way of dissipating themselves. Scanning the quarried stone façade of his house the doctor told himself it was well overdue for a clean-up, but he would have to see the Reverend Conway about getting those iron railings mended, where they were attached to his end wall. These iron railings hemmed in the dilapidated drunken-headstone cemetery, and the equally dilapidated but sober St Matthew's church.

This then was the Square. The Technical College along one side, the refrigeration plant along another; then the Salvation Army and the Church of England, with Dr Paul Hugh Higgins's house in between them. These formed Romfield Square, a part of Fellburn that had now become attached to the slum of Bogs End. Not a desirable residence, many thought, for a doctor. But although he dwelt more happily in its past associations than he did in the present, he still felt himself at one with its surroundings, rough, even grim though they were, and with the inhabitants who were herded, even in new council flats, beyond the Square – the inhabitants who were part rough, part gentle; cunning, honest; bad, yet good. He felt one with them because he knew he had every recognised trait within himself.

He inhaled deeply again, turned his gaze from where the moon was creeping behind the group of chimneys on the Technical College and went back across the courtyard, through the door marked 'Surgery', which he locked behind him, across the waiting-room and entered the house proper through the door marked 'Private'. Here he stepped into another hall; a smaller hall this one, oak-panelled and warm looking. The red carpet covering the floor continued up the shallow oak stairway that rose from the far end, and after the stark lighting of the waiting-room the wall lighting of the hall lent a mellowness which was reflected from the two gilt mirrors flanking a side-table and the various pieces of brass dotted here and there.

Having washed his hands in a cloakroom to the right of the staircase, he went into the room opposite which he called the drawing-room but which his wife referred to as the lounge.

His wife was sitting in a deep couch before the fire. She did not turn her head on his approach, nor did he look at her on his way towards the fire. Their lives had been separate for so long that each could pretend that the other wasn't there. But it was a pretence, and both of them were vitally aware of it, bitterly, irritatingly aware of it.

He leant his forearm against the edge of the high marble mantel-piece, the mantelpiece that she had wanted ripped out. He had stood firm against this as against most of the changes that would make the old house appear naked; you can't dress granite and oak up in pearl-grey paint and frills. He stood staring down into the fire for fully five minutes before, his irritation rising, he lifted his head and looked up at the large oil painting of his father hanging above the mantel and said, 'Well, what about the meal?'

'It's waiting for you; it's on the hotplate.' Her voice sounded controlled, like that of someone trying not to lose her temper.

Still looking at the picture he asked, 'Has Lorna eaten?'

'Yes, she has. It's too late to keep her waiting for a meal until seven o'clock.'

He didn't ask, 'And you?' for knowing that he hated to have his meals alone she would purposely have taken hers earlier.

Paul turned from the fire and looked at his wife. He looked at her deliberately, as if trying to find something that had escaped him. It wasn't the first time he had done this, and it wasn't the first time he had told himself that he had always disliked little women. There was something, to say the very least, irritating about them. They were like little men, pushing, forcing the issue. Anything to make themselves felt, making up in aggressiveness their lack of inches. But of the two, give him little men before little women, with their grim determination and their ruthlessness. Yet these qualities were, he supposed, what usually made little women the best mothers and enabled them to rear successful families.

From the couch Beatrice Higgins raised her eyes, then dropped her glance quickly away from her husband's scrutiny. She couldn't think of anything in this world that she detested so much as his face, his square face. Everything about it looked square; his mouth, his nostrils, even his eyes, the grey eyes that at one time had held a certain fascination for her. His strong sandy hair, as yet devoid of grey, did nothing to enhance his features. If she disliked anything more than his face it was his body, his big lumbering body. Big hands, big feet, chest like a bull. He was all bullish. A big, unthinking, uncouth bull. It was hard to believe that he was only forty-three, seven years older than herself. He could be twenty years older. Her thinking moved along a tangent – he could live another twenty years, perhaps thirty. Even the thought was unbearable and brought her upwards.

As she stooped to gather up her magazines from the couch she said, 'When you're finished put the dishes in the sink in some soapy water.'

'Put the dishes . . . What do you mean?'

Bett straightened up and, looking at him over her shoulder, said briefly, 'Helen's gone!'

'Helen's gone?'

'Yes. And for goodness' sake don't keep repeating everything I say.'

There was a dull red glow creeping up beneath his skin. Her manner of speaking to him had the power to infuriate him. 'Well, be more explicit.' His voice was a low growl. 'Then I won't have to repeat what you say. Why has she gone?'

'Because I told her to . . . Now go on and say, "You told her to?"' She moved her head further around and watched him grind his teeth. 'She used foul language to me, so I had no other option, she had to go. Her Bogs End education hadn't been neglected.'

'You were damned glad to get her. You never could keep a maid. And now when you can't get help for love or money you go and . . .'

'I go and dismiss her. Yes, and I'll do the same with your precious Maggie very shortly, so I'm warning you.' Now she was facing him, the pale skin of her face seeming to be pulled taut across her small bones, her blue eyes dark, giving evidence of rage.

'You just do that. You put your hackles on Maggie and that will be one time when you have gone too far.'

'If I catch her red-handed I'll dismiss her, and you can do what you damned well like. She's been robbing me for years, carting away stuff every night, packing it round her. Her bust is twice as big at night as it is in the morning.'

'Robbing you, did you say?' His voice was deceptively cool. 'Who pays for the stuff that Maggie takes, eh? I ask you that. Now you listen to me.' He was growling again as he stabbed his index finger slowly towards her. 'When my mother was alive she always saw that Maggie's basket was filled at night, but when you took over everything was changed. But with Maggie, habits die hard. She's always had it and she always will. She knows that I know she has her whack, so I'm warning you, leave her alone.'

They stared at each other for some considerable time in weighty silence. Then Bett, moving her head slowly and her features twisting as if in pain, said, 'My God, Paul, one of these days I'll get you where I want you. I don't know how but I feel sure in here – ' she placed her clenched fist on her breast, 'I feel sure that you'll be delivered into my hands some time or other, and then I'll make up for everything you've put me through. Remember that.' She gave a short, sharp bounce to her head, then turned from him.

As she made to leave the room there came the sound of the front-door bell ringing, and she went into the hall banging the door after her.

Paul turned and looked down into the fire. He was shaking slightly with the force of his feelings. He had no doubt that his wife meant every word she said, and did she but know it the weapon was ready to her hand. He turned his head sharply to the sound of her voice, high and pleasant sounding now, coming from the hall, exclaiming, 'Jenny. Why, where have you sprung from? Why didn't you give me a ring?'

When he heard the answering voice he made hastily across the room and, pulling the door open, he too became a different being.

'Hello, Jinny.' He always called his wife's cousin Jinny, never Jenny. 'Aw, it's good to see you. Why didn't you let us know? I'd have met you. Get yourself in.' He pushed the tall woman into the drawing-room.

'Give me your hat.' Bett spoke to her cousin as she extended her hand, and Jenny Chilmaid, laughing, pulled it from her head, saying as she did so, 'I'm going to burn it.'

'And not before time I'd say.' Bett looked down at the hat in her hand, and she rumpled it. Then almost skipping across the room, she cried, 'Come on, sit down. Sit down.'

Bett Higgins now appeared a pretty, vivacious creature, with sparkling blue eyes and a manner that seemed to set her whole body alight. She moved her hands when she talked, running them girlishly through her short, dark, glossy hair. The doctor's wife was acting at this moment as she always did when pleasantly excited. No-one seeing her thus could imagine any other side to her – no-one, that is, except the two people in the room, her husband and her cousin.

Jenny Chilmaid was the opposite in every way to Bett. To begin with she was five foot ten, and thin with it. Her clothes hung on her as they would from a wire coathanger. Her face, like her body, was long, but unlike it, it was in proportion in that it had a good bone formation. Her straight-lipped, wide mouth, a fine pair of deep brown eyes, and a head of tow-coloured hair, drawn straight back from her forehead into a bun in the nape of her neck, would undoubtedly have given her some claim to attractiveness, if it hadn't been for her main feature, her nose. This took the pattern of her body, being much too long and too shapeless to escape comment. When people looked at Jenny Chilmaid they looked at her nose. Bett was looking at it now as she said, 'Tell me, what's happened? Are you on holiday? Where've you come from today? From Havant?'

'Yes.'

'Well, why didn't you let us know?'

'Oh, well. It's a long story.' Jenny smiled from one to the other before pursing her mouth and adding, 'And I could do with . . .'

'A cup of tea.' Both Bett and Paul ended the sentence for her, and it appeared as if there was no dissent between them. As they all laughed, Paul said, 'And a cup of tea you'll have, Jinny. And in two shakes of a lamb's tail. That's if you keep all your news till I get back. I won't be a minute.'

He, too, was changed. As if a boy had come alive in his large frame, he hurried out of the room, and as he did so Bett sat down on the couch beside Jenny. Then emitting a sigh that relaxed her, she said, 'It's good to see you again.'

'And you.'

'Have you finished that job?'

'Yes,' said Jenny briefly.

'Good, then you can stay for a while.'

Bett sounded sincere, and she was, for Jenny was always helpful. She would be a godsend with Helen gone. And what was more, life was always easier when she was around the place. She had a way of anticipating your thoughts, at least about chores and the grind of running a house. Added to this she acted as a buffer between her and Paul. 'Come on,' she said now, 'tell me about everything.'

'Oh, I don't want to go over it twice, Bett. Wait until Paul comes back, eh?'

Bett raised one shoulder; then she looked from under lowered lids at her cousin. She fancied she sensed a change in her, but she couldn't quite lay a finger on what it was. She still had that quiet withdrawn look, not a reserve – there was nothing in her to reserve. She had worked out her cousin's character years ago: there was neither high passion nor low cunning in Jenny. She was a neutral; fitted for the things she did best; nursing people and doing tiresome odd jobs unobtrusively. Now and again she had thought it was a pity she hadn't married. But then she wouldn't, would she, looking as she did. Still it was an ill wind, and she was glad to see her at this moment. And the big fellow was always more civil when she was about. He always wanted to rate good with Jenny . . . the kind, considerate doctor.

'How are things with you?' Jenny rested her cheek on the back of

16

the couch and watched Bett reach out and take a cigarette from the box on the table to the side of her, and pat it on the back of her hand before saying, 'That's a silly question to ask.'

'Well, it's eight months since I saw you; a lot could happen in eight months.'

'What! Between me and him? Could you imagine anything good happening between us?'

'Aw, Bett, it could if you tried.'

Bett struck the lighter, then applied it slowly to her cigarette, and she drew on it once before she slanted her eyes towards Jenny, saying, 'I stopped trying years ago. I've told you before I'm not the humble type to go crawling. I tried it once and I was kicked in the teeth.'

Turning her head towards the fire, Jenny said very slowly, 'I've thought a lot about you both over these past few months, and you know, Bett, I'm sure if you had talked to Paul in the first place everything would have straightened—'

'Shut up, Jenny.' Bett bounced to her feet. 'Look, you haven't been in the house a minute, it isn't like you to bring this up. What's the matter with you? Anyway, you know better than anyone that the pattern was cut years ago and nothing can alter it. He goes his way, I go mine.'

'And Lorna?'

'Lorna is fifteen, Jenny.' Bett's voice was quiet now. 'In two to three years' time she could be married, and that will be the end of that.'

They held each other's gaze. Then Bett, her glance dropping away, reseated herself on the couch and there followed an awkward silence until Jenny said, 'How is she? I'm dying to see her.'

'Oh. In appearance pretty much the same as when you last saw her. I can see no change in her, outwardly at least, but she's reaching the difficult stage. Yet that's to be expected, I suppose. Her mind's on sex at the moment.' She thrust one slim leg out as if kicking something away. 'How anyone can want their schooldays back is beyond me. Talk about a breeding ground of false values. When I listen to her prattling on I could explode. But' – she gave a mirthless laugh – 'her dream-world was a bit shattered last week. One of the girls in the fifth form – not in the sixth, mind you – got herself pregnant. It's Fay Baldock. You know the Baldocks . . . the chemists. He's got a chain of shops now. Well you can imagine how Poppa Baldock reacted when the father-to-be was discovered to be a seventeen-year-old grammar school boy whose family live up in the Venus block, near the pit. Really, the Baldocks have my sympathy, for there's nothing to choose between the lot that live in the Venus block and the Bogs End crowd . . . Bogs End!' She screwed up her face. 'Oh, how I hate all the muck and squalor.'

'But there's no muck and squalor there now, Bett; most of the old streets have been pulled down.' Jenny was smiling gently at her cousin.

'That makes no difference, the people are the same. Some of them have twenty pounds a week and more coming in, but it hasn't changed them one jot. They look the same, they act the same. They have their cars now and go abroad for their holidays, but they just have to open their mouths. Do you know' – she leant forward and motioned her head in the direction of the kitchen – 'she, Maggie, she brags about her son earning thirty pounds a week and yarps on about him taking his family to Spain last year, and all the while she's helping herself to anything she can lay her hands on in my kitchen . . . Oh, it boils me up. And he won't do a thing about it. And you know that daughter of hers, Lottie, who used to spit when she talked, you remember?' She raised her brows. 'Well, she's married a fellow who's manager of the big electrical works, a new place. Can you believe it? . . . Her. And then there's . . .'

Jenny was looking at her cousin as if she was paying attention to her every word, but she was actually not with her at all, for she was thinking how odd it was that Bett should have such ideas about herself, and the width of the gulf between her own upbringing and that of Maggie's daughter, for instance. Also she began again to think of the freak storm, that spurt of nature which had been the deciding factor in their being brought up together.

It had happened on a day in nineteen-thirty-eight when she was twelve. The two families had decided to go to Wales for a seaside-caravan holiday, and for five glorious days the sun shone down on them and they lazed on the sands, or went swimming; sometimes the brothers, taking a small boat, went out fishing. It was on the afternoon of the day before they were to return home that the freak storm occurred. The sky became overcast making it like night, then the wind came with terrifying swiftness and what had been gentle waves were lashed into gigantic mountains of water. Jenny could recall how her mother, crouched on the floor of the caravan, had held her tightly in her arms as she prayed. And beside them had crouched Bett and her mother. She remembered Bett, who was only nine then, saying, 'Daddy'll get wet, won't he?'

The next morning they had found the remains of the boat on the rocks along the coast, and three days later the brothers' bodies came in with the early morning tide, and strangely they had lain only four feet away from each other, and about 200 yards from where they had set off in the boat.

After the numbness of the shock wore off and loneliness hit them, the two widows decided it would be better if they joined forces and pooled their small resources. So they rented a four-roomed downstairs-house, as it were termed, near the children's school, and Jenny's mother resumed the office work she had been doing before she married, while Bett's mother returned to the stocking counter in Weaver's Drapery store in the High Street, at which she had started years previously when she was fifteen.

The arrangement worked amicably enough for two years, until Jenny's mother, still lonely in heart and with not much will to live, gave in to a severe bout of influenza. And so Jenny, at the age of fourteen, was left with Aunty May.

Under the circumstances Aunty May had been kind to her, although she did take all the £300 that her mother had saved from her father's life insurance. But then, of course, Jenny knew, even without Aunty May giving her to understand, that she had to be fed and clothed until she could work. Jenny had learned one lesson very early in life. It was: if you made yourself useful, people put up with you. She had made herself useful to Aunty May, and also to Bett, and they had both accepted her usefulness without question. Should anyone at times, as they did, praise her for her industry her Aunty May, and her cousin Bett, would always say, 'Oh, Jenny's made like that.'

But Jenny knew that she hadn't been made like that. There had been lots of things she had resented doing, especially for Bett, for she knew that her cousin looked upon her as a kind of servant, at best someone who should make herself useful out of gratitude for a home. Deeply she had resented this, but she had the power to hide it. She also had the power to hide the pain that her reflection in the mirror caused her. And in her teens she had dared to protest against the reflection, for there was Bett, dark, vivacious, pretty, referred to as a live wire and a spark, attracting attention wherever she went; holding people with her bright chatter, apparently happy about everything in life that affected her, except her name. The name Chilmaid had become a source of irritation, even shame, to Bett from the time when she was fifteen and a boy, punning the name, had said, 'Bet you're a chill maid.' She had come home in tears that day, and from then onwards her name had taken on a kind of phobia. She wanted rid of it, and the only way to be rid of it was to get married. It was on this same day, when Jenny had tried to comfort her, that she had rounded on her, crying, 'It's all right for you, you look like a chill maid and always will.'

There are some things, silly things, that burn deep into the mind, and even when they heal with the years you can still feel the scars. Jenny hadn't realised how deeply she had resented, even the scars, until she had talked to Ben. Ben had been like a dredger cleaning her mind.

As her thoughts drifted over the years she was suddenly aware of Bett's voice.

'Jenny, listen. What's the matter? . . . You're nearly asleep. Are you tired? I don't believe you've heard a word I've said.'

'Yes, I have. You were saying that James Knowles had come to work in the new laboratory attached to the Burley Group and had called in last week.' Jenny smiled.

'Yes. Yes, it was that, but you looked miles away.'

'Is he still with his wife?'

'No, he divorced her.'

'You mean she divorced him.'

'Well, whichever way it was, they're divorced. You never did like him, did you?'

'No, I didn't. I could never stand a man who wanted to tell you a dirty joke before he'd been in your company two minutes.'

'Oh, don't be silly, Jenny.' Again Bett rose to her feet. 'James just does that to you because he knows it shocks you. I'm sure he doesn't do it to anyone else.'

'Shocks me!' Jenny's eyebrows moved into points, lengthening her face still further. 'Four years on hospital wards, and a good part of the last ten spent nursing men . . . I'll take some shocking. No, James Knowles talked to me as he talks to all women. He's dirty. There are men like that.'

'Jenny.' Bett was smiling tolerantly at Jenny now. 'You're so naïve; sometimes I think you're younger than Lorna.'

When Jenny made no comment on this Bett turned from her and threw her half-burned cigarette into the heart of the fire. And at this point Paul entered the room carrying a tray.

'There you are.' He put the tray on a table on the opposite side of the hearth from his wife, and sitting down beside it he poured out a cup of tea, and handing it to Jenny with exaggerated ceremony, he said, 'There you are, ma-dam. Cream off the top of a new bottle and two lumps, and if you take my advice you'll improve it with a little dash of whisky.'

'This is one time I'm not taking your advice.' Jenny took the cup from him. 'Thanks, Paul.' Her eyes smiled at him. Then looking him up and down, she said, 'I do believe you're losing weight.'

'I am.' He nodded at her brightly. 'I've lost half a stone this last month, down to fourteen two.' He pulled his trousers away from his waist. 'I'm terrified they'll drop off in the street, or, worse still, at the clinic. Not that the mothers would mind, but ooh! Sister Reilly. Imagine! How did that woman ever become a Sister, even a nurse? She should be in a closed order.'

Jenny had at one time worked with Sister Reilly, and what Paul had said struck her as so funny that she laughed with him loudly, until, seeing Bett's straight face, she let her laughter fade away. That was another thing she had learned. In a divided house you laughed with the woman if you wanted peace.

Yet need she bother now? Was caution necessary any more? Did it matter any longer if she annoyed Bett or not? Yes, yes it did. For it was true what Aunty May had said, she was made in a particular way. She had always wanted peace, and she had bought peace, and the price had meant the submerging of her own individuality, so deeply that bringing it to the surface again would, she imagined, be almost an impossibility.

'Well now, I'm waiting. Come on, let's have your news.' Paul pulled his coat sleeve up and looked at his watch. 'I've got half-an-hour. That includes my eating time; say ten minutes for that. Can you get through your lurid life story during the past months in twenty minutes?'

'I think so.' Jenny straightened herself, pressed her back against the corner of the couch, then wetted her lips preparatory to speaking again. But no words came, and after looking from one to the other and shaking her head she lowered it, and putting her cup down on the little wine table at her side she took a handkerchief from the pocket of her suit and blew her nose.

'What is it?' Paul asked quietly. 'Are you in trouble, Jinny?' He was sitting on the edge of his chair now, leaning towards her. Bett, too, had also moved towards her from the other end of the couch.

'Is Mr Hoffman worse?' Paul narrowed his eyes as he asked the question.

'He's dead.' Jenny again blew her nose. It had a loud sound as befitted a large nose.

'Oh, I'm sorry. But then' – he nodded – 'in a way I suppose it was best. He's been bedridden lately, hasn't he?'

Jenny inclined her head slowly. And now Bett put in, 'I've never seen you upset like this before. Somehow I thought you had got used to people dying.'

'You never get used to people dying.' Paul was not so much answering his wife as making a statement.

And Bett, going on as if she had not been interrupted, said, 'You're not worried about getting another post surely? Why, you're as rare as gold dust these days. If it's a job you're after there's one waiting right here any time you like, you know that.' Bett's smile was accompanied by an expansive movement of her head which indicated the whole house.

Jenny looked up at her now. 'I won't be wanting another job, Bett. You see . . . well, Benjamin Hoffman was not just my patient, he . . . he was my husband. We were married six months ago.'

'Jinny!' Paul fell slowly against the back of the chair, and he pulled his chin in and pressed his head to the side as if to bring Jenny's face into focus.

'Is it so surprising that I should marry?' She was addressing him pointedly, and the question brought his big head thrusting forward. 'No, no, my God, no. Only why didn't you tell us? It isn't like you to hold out on anything. You never said a word in your letters.'

21

Jenny picked up her cup and gulped quickly at the tea, and after she had swallowed she said, 'I . . . I meant to, every week I meant to, but somehow I just couldn't write it down. And then the time passed so quickly, and he became so ill.'

Paul stopped himself from asking the question, 'Were you happy?' It was unlikely that she was happy, other than in her job, being married to a partly paralysed bedridden man. And yet, who knew but that she was happy. It surprised him that in an odd kind of way he felt saddened by the idea that Jenny could be happy married to a total invalid, an old, total invalid, for in spite of her looks he knew that she was very much alive inside. If she had been happy it meant that she was reconciled at thirty-nine to middle-age and was becoming grateful for anything. It hurt him to think she had reached that stage; she deserved something better. She'd had no life.

'When did it happen?' he asked now.

'About a month ago.'

'A month ago?' Bett put in quickly, her voice high. You mean he died a month ago? Well, where have you been all this time?'

'Oh.' Jenny smiled weakly. 'There was a lot to see to. I sold the house and the furniture. I just kept a few good pieces. I did . . . I mean I'm going to do all that he wanted me to.'

'Had he money?' It was a soft enquiry from Bett.

'Yes, but—' Her face took on a stiffness. 'But I didn't marry him for that. I didn't know what he had . . . what he was worth before I married him. In fact I thought he was afraid I would leave him because his money was running out or something, and it was one way to keep me . . . At least that was how I thought for a little while, and then I found out that he . . . well . . .' She shook her head and lowered her gaze again. She could not say, 'He loved me'; it would sound too ludicrous to these two people who knew all about her, who were all the family she'd had until Benjamin had made her his wife.

'Well! He had money then? Go on.' Bett had screwed herself to the edge of the couch until she was almost sitting in front of Jenny. 'I mean real money?'

Jenny gave a little smile. 'I suppose you would call it real money; my share was forty-seven thousand.'

Bett did not repeat the sum, it was as if she had been stunned by the force of the amount. Forty-seven thousand pounds! A man had left that amount to this long, thin, odd-looking creature. Oh, granted she was kind, and good, and thoughtful, but what else could anyone be who looked like her at thirty-nine. You had to be something different to make up for a face like Jenny had. Yet a man had married her and left her forty-seven thousand. It wasn't fair . . . IT WASN'T FAIR. Bett remembered that when her own mother had died and left her five hundred pounds she hadn't offered Jenny a penny; and she could have done because it happened just after she had married Paul when she had the idea she was sitting pretty for the rest of her life. If only she had given her something . . . Oh, what was the use. She lifted her eyes up to her husband; he was standing over Jenny holding her hand, saying, 'If anyone deserves a slice of luck you do, Jinny. But tell me, what did he want you to do? You said he wanted you to do certain things. Aw, don't cry.'

Jenny was crying unrestrainedly but quietly now, the tears running unchecked down her unmade-up sallow cheeks. 'He . . . he wanted me to enjoy myself.'

'Good for him. I wish I had met him; he sounds like a man after my own heart. Had he any relatives?'

'A son. He came over from America for the funeral. He . . . he seemed pleased that I had married his father, ever . . . ever so pleased.' Jenny's head moved as if she still couldn't believe this fact. 'I . . . I thought he might question the will but no, he even seemed pleased about that an' all. He had the same amount but he doesn't need anything. He's got a big bacon-curing business of his own. He's a widower himself and no children.' She smiled as she cried, and her tear-drenched face looked odder still. 'He said that if ever he became ill he would send for me, solely on the recommendation of his father's letters. He . . . he made me laugh. In a way he was very like his father because we laughed a lot, Ben and I, and he said, I mean the son said, it would be a funny thing if I were to marry him an' all.' Her voice cracked, her face falling into painful lines, the tears spurted from her eyes, and from her throat were forced hard, broken sobs.

Paul, sitting on the edge of the couch, put his arm about her and drew her head against his chest, and looking towards his wife he said softly, 'Pour a drop of brandy out.'

Without demur Bett did as she was bidden. Going to the cabinet in the far corner of the room she poured a good measure into a glass and brought it back to the couch. 'Here, dear, drink this up,' she said.

Jenny gulped at the brandy, then drying her face with a large handkerchief Paul held out to her she said, 'I'm sorry; I didn't mean to go on like this.'

'You go on as much as you like, it'll do you good.'

'Your room's still ready for you,' said Bett now. 'I'll switch on the blanket and you have an early night; you'll feel better in the morning. Then you must stay and have a long rest.' She smiled sweetly down on her cousin, and Jenny, looking up at her, nodded and said, 'Thanks, Bett, but . . .' She hesitated. They were kind; they were both kind. Jenny's mind evaded the knowledge that Bett's kindness, in particular, was a self-seeking kindness. Also she didn't dwell on Bett's invitation for her to rest; there was no rest for anyone in this house. The emotions were too taut, but at this moment she would sooner have stayed than say what she had to say. 'I've . . . I've got to go up to town tomorrow, Bett. Thanks all the same.'

'Well, what's in that? You can come back in the evening.'

'Oh, I don't mean Newcastle, Bett; I mean London.'

'London!'

'Yes.'

'What are you going to do in London?'

'I've a bit of business to see to.' Jenny turned her eyes from Bett and glanced at Paul where he was still sitting on the edge of the couch, and he said, 'Is it the money? Isn't it settled yet?'

'Oh, yes, that's all right. It's . . . it's just something I'm going to do.' She dropped her eyes from his and muttered under her breath, 'Don't ask me what it is, it would appear so silly. I'll be back in three weeks and then you'll know all about it.'

'Is it such a mystery? Can't you give us an inkling?' There was an impatient note in Bett's voice, and before Jenny had time to answer, Paul, looking at his wife, said, 'It's Jinny's business. She says she'll tell us later, so we'll just have to wait, won't we?' He rose from his seat, his eyes still on his wife, and as he watched her face tighten he warned himself to go steady, not to start her off and Jinny not in the house five minutes; so changing his tone and forcing himself to smile, he said with weak jocularity, 'She's holding out on us. It's my guess she's going up there to open a night club.' He turned his smile on Jenny, and she, closing her eyes, said, 'Oh, Paul! A night club . . . Me!' Then again, 'Oh, Paul!' She sniffed on a laugh and blew her nose once more.

As Paul, about to carry the joke still further, bent towards her, the drawing-room door opened and a young girl came in, crying, 'Mammy, have you seen . . . ?' Her voice stopped with her feet, and then, her expression stretching her mouth wide, she cried, 'Aunt Jenny! Why, Aunt Jenny!' In a bound she was on the couch, her arms about Jenny, repeating all the while, 'Oh, Aunt Jenny.'

Jenny, holding her close, buried her face in the young girl's soft, jet-black hair. Then after a moment, pressing her away, she scanned the face that looked like a warm wax cameo. She had never seen anyone with skin like this girl's, nor a face like hers, a face that seemed built without the support of bones. The eyes were almond-shaped and grey, the upper lids full and smooth, lending to the whole an oriental look. The lips were not bow-shaped nor yet full as in young girls. They appeared somewhat shapeless, yet the mouth looked soft and fascinating. Jenny had always loved to watch Lorna talk, simply to see her lips move.

'They told me you hadn't grown,' she said, casting an accusing glance from Paul to Bett. 'Why, you've put on inches.'

'I have? You think so, Aunt Jenny? Coo! Good-o.' Lorna's vocabulary was girlish and her voice slightly husky. She galloped on: 'When did you come? Why didn't you come upstairs to my room? How long are you staying? . . . Ooh!' Again she had Jenny

24

enfolded in her fierce young embrace, and moving her cheek against her aunt's, she said, 'Aw, it's lovely, it's lovely to have you back.'

'Well, stop rumpling her like that,' Bett put in sharply; 'and get your feet off the couch.' She slapped at her daughter's legs. 'And you can stop kidding yourself that you're going to have someone waiting on you hand and foot during the next few weeks because your Aunt Jenny is leaving in the morning.'

'Aw, no!'

'Aw, yes.' Jenny was laughing now as she nodded back at Lorna's horrified expression. 'But I'll be back in three weeks or so.'

'Three weeks! Then you're not going on another job?'

'No, not this time, not for a while.'

'What do you think?' Paul had dropped on his hunkers by the side of the couch and taken hold of Jenny's hand. 'Your Aunt Jenny's married now.'

'Married? You? . . . Oh! I didn't mean it like that, Aunt Jenny. It's wonderful you being married. Fancy you married.' She opened her mouth wide, but emitted no sound. It was a gesture from her childhood. It usually followed amazement or surprise, and undoubtedly she was surprised now. Then she said, 'Does it mean that you'll not be able to come here like you usually do?'

'No, it doesn't. In fact it means that we're going to see more of her.' Paul thrust his other hand out towards Lorna. 'She'll likely be living with us, won't you, Jinny?' He wagged her hand as if to bring assurance from her, and she answered him rapidly, saying, 'Oh, now, Paul, Paul. We'll have to see.'

'Oh, yes, yes, Aunt Jenny. Oh, that would be simply marvellous. Oh, we'd have some fun . . . But . . . but what about your husband?'

'Well,' Jenny said, evenly now, 'he died.'

'So soon? Oh, Aunt Jenny!' She looked sad, and Jenny said, 'It's all right. We'll talk about it some other time . . . Now it's your turn. Tell me what you've been doing?'

'What's she been doing? I can tell you that,' put in Paul. 'Chasing the boys. At least, a boy. And not such a boy either, he's as tall as me. Brian Bolton. You know, the Mayor's son. Ah! ha! You didn't think I saw you. "Can I carry your school bag, Miss Higgins?"'

His teasing was checked by Lorna giving him a push, which caused him to overbalance on to the hearth rug, and as she went to pounce on him Bett cried, 'Stop it! Stop that horseplay!'

Her voice had the power to sober them all, and Lorna, hitching herself back on to the couch, took hold of Jenny's hand while Paul, straightening his coat as he rose to his feet, said, his voice flat now, 'I'm going to have a bite, and then I've one or two calls to make. I'll likely see you before you go to bed, Jinny, but if you want to get off early I'll see you in the morning. What time do you propose leaving?'

'I was going to get the twelve o'clock from Newcastle.'

'I'll run you there.'

'Thanks, Paul.'

He went out of the room, across the hall to the far end, and entered the kitchen; and there, taking a covered plate from the bottom oven of the Aga cooker, he placed it on the Formica-topped table by the kitchen window, where was set a knife, fork, and cruet, and slowly and thoughtfully he began to eat. And as he did so the pleasure of seeing Jenny again faded and he became filled with irritation.

He hated eating in the kitchen. He didn't mind occasionally, such as last thing at night when he would scrape up something for himself, but even then he often put it on a tray and took it into the drawing-room, for the radiator in the dining-room was always turned down after lunch. 'A waste of fuel,' she said. The new order was: meals after six o'clock would be taken in the kitchen . . . of course, provided Maggie had gone. He raised his eyes from the plate and looked around the kitchen. It had a clinical look, almost like the operating theatre. The big old easy chair with the sunken bottom was no longer in the corner, nor was the old pouffe that his mother had brought into the kitchen so that Maggie could put her legs up for half-an-hour after she had done the dinner washing-up. In place of the chair and the pouffe stood a washing-machine and spin-drier, and on the other side of the stove near the window stood a five-foot-high, naked-looking fridge. The old dresser had gone and in its place was a cabinet of frosted glass with drawers that stuck unless you used both hands to close them. And under the big working table in the centre of the room stood four plastic-topped stools.

The change, in the kitchen alone, since his mother had died was drastic. It was a wonder Maggie stuck it. Yet he thought he knew why she stuck it, and the knowledge warmed him.

He gathered up the dirty dishes and was on his way to the sink when Lorna put her head round the kitchen door. 'I thought you might have gone.' She came into the room at a run, adding, 'I've got a good Mrs McAnulty, Daddy.'

As he turned the tap on the greasy dishes he glanced at her and smiled, saying, 'I haven't time for a Mrs McAnulty now. I've got an important call; I should be there.' He continued to look at her. He thought she had finished with the Mrs McAnulty game, as she hadn't broached it for some time. It was a game that had started years ago when she had demanded he play patients with her. He had been quite willing to let it die a natural death as she was fast growing up, at least she should be, but she was still a very young fifteen for these days. And he was glad of it. Oh yes, yes.

'Aw, it won't take a minute. It's a good one.'

'When I come back,' he said.

'I'll be in bed.'

'All right.' He nodded, then lifting a detergent carton from the draining board he squeezed some liquid into the water, after which he reached for a towel on the rail by the sink and wiped his hands. 'Well now.' He turned to her and adopted an exaggeratingly long countenance, and in a sober tone said, 'Good evening, Mrs McAnulty.'

'Evenin', Doctor.' Lorna too had taken on a pose; she was now imitating the actions of what she imagined was an agitated patient.

'What can I do for you, Mrs McAnulty?'

'Am bad, Doctor.'

'I can see that, Mrs McAnulty. Tell me about it?'

'I've got hydro-ceph-alus.' She had difficulty in pronouncing the word, and as she finished Paul put his head back and let out a bellow of a laugh. 'Hydrocephalus. That's a beauty. Where did you come across that one?'

'Ah! ha! Ah! ha!' She was laughing up at him, wagging her finger in his face. 'There's more where that comes from. Just you wait; you've met your match at last, Doc-tor Higgins.'

'I should say I have. Well, Mrs McAnulty' – he resumed his stern pose – 'what are your symptoms?'

'Well, Doctor, me head's grown so big' – She demonstrated with her hands held level with her shoulders.

'You can say that again.' As Paul made this aside in a low voice, she cried, 'Aw, behave and listen. Listen.' Then slanting her eyes to the ceiling she concentrated her attention there as she went on, 'The disease made its appearance when I was six months old, and the water collected inside my head, and the bones not yet being set allowed it to form a kind of bag and it grew bigger and bigger until my head was as big as my body . . .'

'Poor soul.'

'Aw. Listen, will you? They thought at first it was only rickets, but it wasn't, I had dropsy of the brain, known to the uninitiated as water on the brain . . . Doctor.'

Paul thrust out a hand and gripped her chin, and, laughing again, he said, 'Very good. Very good. Where did you find it?'

'Oh, I've bought a gem of a book. It's called *The Family Physician*. I got it on Rankin's Bookstall for three shillings. It's got one thousand one hundred and seventy-six pages.'

'No kiddin'?'

'It's a gem. Mr Rankin said it might be worth a lot of money if I keep it a little longer. It's got a picture of St Thomas's Hospital in the front and a wonderful coloured paper skeleton. Well, it's not really a skeleton, it's the whole body in flaps right into the be-owels. Coo! Doc-tor, it's beautiful.'

'It sounds it. I'll have to have a look into this gem. But, Mrs McAnulty' – he was walking from the kitchen now with his arm around her shoulder – 'I wouldn't go searching for medical books

27

at present, not unless you have a consultation with Dr Higgins first. Understand?'

'But it's a gem, Daddy. Really, it's a scream. It gives you all the diseases and all the cures, and there's six frousty pictures of old men in the front between bones and things. One is Sir William Jenner, Bart., KCB, MD, FRS, and some. Oh he looks a holy terror. Some look sort of human but he looks as if he could eat you, like that Professor Wheelan you used to tell me about, remember?'

As he got into his coat in the hall he said to her seriously, 'The information is bound to be very dated, and quite a number of methods obsolete. We'd better look at it together some time, eh?'

'OK.' She wagged her head at him. 'But it's all practice. In one part it says a nurse should not be so young as to be giddy nor so old as to be useless. And you know, Daddy, it says a woman should stay in bed for three weeks after she's had a baby, and rest on a couch each day until the end of the month. It's a scream, isn't it? Mrs Price was out at the end of a week.'

'Ah, but then, don't forget Mrs Price is a doctor's wife.'

He laughed down on her. 'I'd better see this great find of yours. And I wouldn't look upon it as practice yet.'

'Oh, all right, but it's priceless, Daddy. Aunty Jenny'll laugh her head off. I was on my way to get it to show her. And oh, isn't it lovely to have her back? And fancy her being married.' Her voice dropped to a whisper now. 'Fancy Aunt Jenny being married, Daddy. She's lovely, but . . .'

In the act of picking up his bag from the side-table he paused and, turning and facing her squarely, said, 'Your Aunt Jinny is lovely, there's no buts; never judge by looks. Start early in this, Lorna, and practise it. Every time you see someone like your Aunt Jinny, say to yourself, she's only like that outside, and the outside doesn't matter.'

'Yes, Daddy. I didn't mean anything, I . . . I love my Aunt Jenny.' Her voice was sober.

'Good enough then.'

As he turned away she walked with him to the front door, and there she said, brightly now, 'Oh, I forgot to tell you, Daddy. Miss Charlton said I should sail through the exam. I came out second in maths in the mock. I could have come top if I'd paid more attention, I know I could, but I will in the real thing. I told her that I'd finally made up my mind to be a doctor and she's all for it. She's lovely is Miss Charlton.'

'That's fine. Keep it up.' He pulled his hat on, pressing the brim down over his brow. 'Now get inside or you'll catch cold; it's cutting out here.'

'Goodnight, Daddy. I suppose I'll be in bed when you get back.' She reached up, and he bent down and kissed her. Then she went into the house and he into the car, and as he started it up, and drove with less than his usual caution out of the Square, he repeated to himself, 'A doctor. She wants to be a doctor.' It was laughable really. Yet no, there was nothing laughable about it. It just gave you food for thought, a lot of thought.

PART TWO

IVY

It was ten minutes past eight when Mrs Ratcliffe's companion let Paul out of the front door. 'Thank you for coming, Doctor, she'll be better now,' she said.

He made no answer to the last, but jerking his head, replied, 'Goodnight, Miss Thompson.'

In the car he sat for a moment debating whether he should go straight to Ivy's or call in at the club. The thought of the club brought his teeth together. He didn't feel like the club tonight . . . Councillor Ramsay with his constant, 'Now this is 'ow I see it. Fair's fair like.' And the regulars. Parkins from his solicitor's platform looking down on Ramsay, despising him but needing him, for Ramsay's business siphoned money into his pocket. Then old Beresford with his weedy body and outdated medicine. Paul's mouth twisted as he remembered Lorna's find, *The Family Physician*, by the sound of it late nineteenth-century. He wouldn't be a bit surprised if old Beresford used a similar one as a reference book. But it was the thought of Beresford that told him he must visit the club first, that it would be policy to go there as often as possible in the near future if he hoped to get on the short list for the assistant physician's post at the hospital when Travers retired, which would be some time in the New Year. He hated the idea that he was nervous of Beresford, that some part of him feared his power. Beresford was near retiring, but until he died, Paul knew, the old man wouldn't get over the fact that twice he had failed to be selected for such a post. The first time, in Newcastle, he had been made to feel like a small fish in a big pool. The second failure was even worse, when they voted in favour of a younger man. He had never again applied but he had put his disappointment to use. He had turned it into a whip to flay his own kind. It was a well-known fact that there would be more than one happy doctor in Fellburn when old Beresford disappeared from the scene.

Paul had never liked Beresford, nor had his father before him, and he would have despised himself if he had felt the slightest inclination to butter him up now. Yet he warned himself not to antagonise him in any way, for the old man had power in his hands, the power of a

30

church-going moralist, the power of being a close friend of Bowles, the surgeon, who was on the Regional Board.

As he entered the lobby he met the Mayor on the point of leaving. Bolton was a man Paul liked, for he carried his mayoral chain with the usual quality of humility, which was likely one of the reasons he had been re-elected three times; this triple event had never happened before in Fellburn. Paul looked on Bolton as a scrupulously honest man, he did not think of him as 'a worthy man' – that was Parkins's phrase, and in an odd way, he surmised, it summed up for Parkins Bolton's worldly standing, which took the form of a double fronted stationer's shop.

'Hello, there, Doctor.' The Mayor had never called him Paul, nor had he himself called the Mayor Harry, and this in itself he felt engendered a deepened mutual respect. He did not take to the bandying of Christian names; Christian names were for friends, not for the acquaintance of an evening, as was often the case. Yet he would not have minded being called Paul by a man like Bolton.

'Hello, Mr Mayor.' It all sounded very formal, but they both smiled warmly at each other. 'Finished your day's grind?'

'No, not quite, I'm just going to collect Mrs Bolton. We have to look in at a dance . . . in aid of the old people's fund; but it'll only be a look-in, I've a full programme tomorrow . . . And you, Doctor, are you finished?'

'Just one or two calls. At least I hope so.'

'So do I for your sake. Well goodnight, Doctor. My regards to Mrs Higgins.'

'Thank you. Goodnight, Mr Mayor. Goodnight.'

He passed from the hall into the bar, then took his drink into the main club room.

Parkins was sitting to the right of the fire, in the chair of honour you might say. It was one of a pair of enormous brown leather chairs with outsize wings, a chair that forced you to walk to the front of it to see its occupant properly, and when Paul saw Parkins's thin body almost lost in it, he paused before saying, 'Oh, hello there.'

'Hello, Paul . . . Busy?'

'So, so. At least during the day. No epidemics at present. But there's been quite a lot of night shift these past few weeks.'

'I don't know how you do it; that would drive me mad getting up in the middle of the night.'

'You get used to it.' Paul looked around. 'Very quiet tonight.'

'Yes. There's a special committee sitting late, fighting that Labour bloke, Skiffings. He's for running up more blocks of flats in Bogs End. How in the name of God these fellows get on the council in the first place beats me.'

'By the same token that they want to put up the flats: they say they'll give the voters what they want, and in Skiffings's case he does

31

just that. Anyway, I suppose we need opposition to keep us on our toes.' Paul said 'us' but he didn't mean us, for he had almost voted Labour last time, and with the election coming off soon it would be a pretty near thing this time. In fact, he knew that, with the present set-up, Labour would be almost sure to have his vote. Yet there would have been no issue about his voting if Butler had become Tory leader instead of Home. A man gives his life to a cause and as payment gets a kick in the backside. He didn't like that. He himself always believed in paying well for services rendered.

'Here a minute.' From the depth of his chair Parkins motioned Paul to him with a lift of his thin chin, and when Paul stood over him he said in a low voice, 'Just a word in your ear . . . You know old B's assistant, Rankin?'

'I've never met him; I heard he had one.'

'Well, he's just down from Bart's. Bright boy; taken the lot, I understand, including your pet tangent . . . What is it?'

'Neurology.'

'Ah yes, neurology. Well, by old B's account he's swept the board with that and all the modern isms and ologies they're packing into them up there now. What I'm trying to say, Paul, is that old B's betting on him and is already singing his praises to the board, and Travers not yet with his notice in. But you know how thick he is with Bowles. I thought I'd tip you.'

There came into Paul's chest a restricted feeling that gave warning of his quick rising anger, and it was with an effort he said coolly, 'But the fellow hasn't been in the town five minutes, nor has he a practice.'

'I've got news for you.' Parkins deliberately reached out and took a sip from his glass of whisky, and returned it to the table before saying, 'Brace yourself.'

Paul waited.

'B's going to let him have his.'

'What!'

'S'fact.' Parkins jerked his meticulously brushed head and raised his eyebrows and showed a face full of concern, behind which Paul read the enjoyment his solicitor was experiencing in delivering this blow, this velvet-padded blow. Straightening up he looked hard down at him as he said, 'I think you're a blind jump ahead, Roy. You see Beresford can't hand over the practice to anyone he likes, that's decided by the local executive council. The days of selling practices are over. Since he was in practice before nineteen forty-eight he'll be compensated, but as for handing on his practice to whom he likes . . . Well, as I said, you're a . . .'

'Oh, I'm not a jump ahead, Paul, blind or otherwise. Oh, no. I know quite well, oh I know in ordinary circumstances you can't sell your practice now. But this is the point: you do know that there's only you and old B standing alone in this town, all the rest are working in twos and threes. Well, it's my idea, and I think I'm right, that old B's tactics are going to be in the form of a bluff. He's not quite due for retirement yet, but it's my guess he's suddenly going to give up, ill-health. That's why he has Rankin. There's not enough doctors in the town, as you know, growing as it is, and the three new factories going up, so what will happen? He'll propose Rankin and that, as I see it, will be that. So you'll need all your wits to get over that old codger. You'll have to keep on your toes, Paul. I'm just telling you. Thought I'd put you in the picture. And this isn't all surmise or hearsay about Rankin, no; I may as well tell you I'm speaking from good authority.'

There was a fury straining to burst from him. Parkins talking to him with that damned superior air as if he was giving advice to a sixth-former going out into the world. He forced himself to smile at him and say nonchalantly, 'Oh, I'm not worried, I think I'll manage. Beresford likes licking cubs; I consider I'm past that stage now.'

As he walked away Parkins put his head round the wing of the chair and asked, 'You off already?'

'No, I'm just going to have another, but I must be on my way soon, I've some calls to make . . . And then there's the night shift looming up.' He laughed, and had the satisfaction of seeing a puzzled expression on Parkins's face as it was slowly withdrawn behind the wing once more.

Five minutes later he was in the car again. His anger now spilling over, he swore under his breath as he drove out of the club yard. 'Damn and blast them, both Parkins and Beresford.' He wouldn't stand for it, he wouldn't. He had worked for years towards this appointment, and he was damned if Beresford was going to get the better of him now by pushing a pup under his nose. Yet what could he do?

The question was still with him when he drove round the perimeter of the market place, along by the park, past the foot of Brampton Hill, then up the long steep road that led to the cemetery, and beyond the slag heaps. He was now in the country, his headlights picking out the low stone walls, the hedges, the lone cottages. About two miles south of the town he turned the car into a narrow lane and brought his speed down to ten miles per hour, and when, after about half a mile of driving, the wheels went into the comparative softness of frost-covered turf, he drew the car to a stop. Before getting out he switched off the lights, then went towards the bungalow.

There was a light on over the porch and another in a window to the left of it, and as he entered the gate the front door opened and a young woman stepped into the light and greeted him.

She looked about thirty, of medium height and plump build. Her hair was brown and wavy and fell down each side of her round face onto her shoulders. Her face was pleasant, rather than pretty, and her smile wide and warm. Her voice too was warm, although thick with the northern inflection when she said, 'I thought you weren't going to make it.'

'I didn't get out until rather late; I was held up.'

As he went to put his arm around her she stepped back from him into the porch, and as he followed he looked down at her, his face crinkling with enquiry. But as soon as she closed the door she lay back against it and held her arms wide, and he went into them and pressed her to him, kissing her with a hard dry kiss. When it was finished and she rested her head back against his arm, he looked at her closely. 'Why did you do that . . . I mean move away just then?'

'Oh.' She wagged her head. 'It just struck me the other night that anyone behind the far hedge could see us.'

'Out here?'

'You never know. Arthur Wheatley, you know him who farms at yon side of the road . . . well, he comes over here shooting.'

'But he's no right; they're your fields.'

'Well, they're let to him for grazing.'

'But he shouldn't come into the paddock, that's not let.'

'Aw.' She took his hand and drew him further into the room. 'You can't stop these fellows wandering round. Farmers are like Peeping Toms; you find them in all odd places, and they always seem to have a right to be there.' She turned swiftly to him again and once more they kissed. Then as he moved his hands down her back he drew his lips from hers and said quietly, 'You've got nothing on underneath, you'll catch your death. It's freezing out.'

'I've just had a bath and you know I never catch cold. I'm as strong as a horse.' Her round blue eyes twinkled up at him. 'But if you like, I'll go and put some clothes on, Doctor.' She pursed her lips on the word doctor, and he jerked her to him and muttered, 'Oh, Ivy, Ivy.' When he buried his face deep in her hair she said softly, 'In a minute, in a minute, but look . . .' She pressed herself from him and pulled him to the couch that was drawn up before the red-stone fireplace, and pulling off his overcoat she said, 'Have you had anything to eat?'

'I had a bite around seven.'

'I've got some casserole steak in the oven. I just did it on spec. Do you fancy a bite?'

He looked up at her, then said meaningly, 'There's not much time.'

'There's time for everything.' She rubbed her finger gently across his lips, and he caught at her hand and put his lips to her broad, hard palm and muttered into it, 'Aw, Ivy, you're a life-saver.'

'Here, give me your shoes.' She bent down and undid his shoes, then swung his legs up onto the couch. Her hands were strong, her arms thick and as he fell back and she bent over him to undo his tie the lapels of her dressing-gown fell apart and exposed her firm full

34

breasts, and before she tightened her girdle he laid his fingers gently on her warm flesh. At his action they both smiled and, their hands gripping, they held fast to each other for a moment.

When she left him to go into the kitchen he lay still, letting out one deep breath after another until he had the feeling he was sinking through the bottom of the couch. This was peace, peace. What would he do without Ivy? Go mad. Stark staring mad.

'Were you very busy last night?' Her voice came to him from the kitchen.

'Yes, up till ten, and then I had a call at half-past three this morning.'

'No! You must be feeling dead.'

'I was, but not now . . . Oh, what do you think, Ivy? Jinny turned up today.'

'Oh, that's nice.' Ivy's voice was high. 'Oh, I'm glad; she's an oiler of wheels is Jenny.'

'You'll never guess what. She's married.' He twisted his head round the side of the couch as he heard her come to the kitchen door, and he looked at her from an almost upside-down position as she exclaimed, 'Jenny married!'

'Yes. It surprised me, but I was glad.'

'So am I. I always thought that when you got past her face she had everything. Mind . . . I'm not meaning that nasty like, about her face, you know I'm not, cos after a time you didn't notice her nose or how she looked, you just liked her. I don't think anybody could help likin' her.'

'That's what I think.' He lifted his head back onto the couch and Ivy returned to the kitchen. After a moment he called to her, 'And she's rich. Well, comparatively so. Anyway, I wish I had what she has, stacked behind me, with no calls on it. It would be good-bye National Health, thank you very much, sir.'

'Did you say she's rich?' Ivy was at the door again.

'Yes, forty-seven thousand. I suppose you'd call that rich.'

'He's given it to her?'

'No, he died and left it to her.'

'Well! Well!' She came walking slowly towards the couch, and when she looked down on him she said, 'It's romantic, isn't it? And fancy all that happening to Jenny. MISS Jenny.'

Paul raised his eyebrows and nodded. Then he spoke of the woman whose image had been evoked by the word 'Miss'. 'She's not pleased at Jinny's news. Oh, she pretended to be, but she's as green as grass. And she had another disappointment. She thought she was in for some free labour, but Jinny's off to London in the morning on some business and she won't tell her what it is. She didn't tell me either. But apparently her husband wanted her to do something and she's going up to town to do it and we'll know about

35

it when she comes back. It's all very mysterious . . . and nice for Jinny.'

'Good luck to her.' Ivy screwed up her face as she smiled at him; then added, 'Come on, sit up and have this, it's ready. I'm bringing it in.'

She brought the tray into the room and placed it on a low table before the couch, and she sat close beside him as he ate, and every now and again he would turn his big head towards her and nuzzle her or butt her forehead with his own. At one point he stopped eating, and with his voice devoid of all rancour he stated calmly, 'Old Beresford's all out to do me down over that hospital appointment, so I've just heard.'

'No! Oh, no! But what can he do?'

'Oh, he can do a lot. And Parkins is with him . . . You know.' He stopped eating and wagged his fork at her. 'I often wondered why I didn't like Parkins, and the reason came to me tonight as he was talking: it's because he doesn't like me. Simple, isn't it?' He smiled. 'Yet I liked his father; he was a nice old fellow, witty; should have been a barrister. His turn of phrase was lost on the locals. But his son is a different kettle of fish; there's a mean streak in him.' He was looking towards the fire now, the fork still poised in his hand, and he seemed to be talking to himself rather than to her. 'It's funny how often, when like meets up with like, whether they are good, bad, or indifferent; there's always a greater chance of harmony between them than if they team up with their opposites. People yammer on about the success of opposites, but they are only going by externals. It's the traits and characteristics that tell in the long run. That's why Parkins and Beresford hit it, and they'll queer my pitch if they can.'

'But what can they do?'

'Oh.' He brought his attention back to her. 'Oh, old Beresford has an assistant, a bright boy I understand. He's got him lined up for the post. Beresford's a vindictive old swine. He never liked my father, they were poles apart in every way . . . Liking again, you see.' He nodded at her. 'And he likes me less, but he's never been able to do much about it until this opportunity came up. He must be congratulating him. I can see him in church on a Sunday thanking God for giving him another chance to act as His deputy.'

He laughed, expecting her to join him, but her face straight, she said, 'But you've got the qualifications. Look how hard you've worked. I don't know much about how these things are settled, but surely they can see you're the right man for the job. Everybody wants to be on your books.'

He laid down his knife and fork and, cupping her chin in his hands, said, 'If they were all like you, Ivy, they would. But the ones who want to be on my books never get on committees. You know, it's one chance in a hundred when the right man for any

36

job gets it, Ivy, and in this town it's you scratch my back and I'll scratch yours. But even then you've got to be . . . my kind of fellow, you understand, before I'll scratch you.' He squeezed her chin, then picked up his knife and fork again and went on talking as he ate. 'This, they would have you believe, is the age of the classless society. Ha! ha! ha! God, people are more class-conscious than they were in my father's day, and more conscious of being class-conscious, if you follow me. I pity any fellow in this town who wants to get on in one of the professions unless he's a member of the right church . . . or the reigning body of councillors – thank God they can't stay put for ever – or a member of the Conservative Club . . . of which I am a member.' He bowed his head ironically to her. 'I know it's no use griping, the same kind of thing goes on in every town, but oh, they're so pie in this place, so holier than thou . . . Aw, old men who have forgotten they were ever young make me want to throw up.'

When he stopped speaking she made no response, and after a moment he pushed the table to one side. Then turning to her, he put his arms about her and looking into her face asked, 'What is it? What's the matter, you're quiet all of a sudden?'

'Nothing.' She was smiling broadly. 'What could be the matter?'

'You're not going to start worrying about what I've just told you.'

'Of course not, why should I?'

'Oh, I know you.' He took his hands from her and turned his body round and sat on the edge of the couch, his elbows on his knees, his hands clasped between them. 'I shouldn't tell you things, it only starts you worrying. I tell myself I won't . . .'

'Oh, darlin', give over, you can tell me anything. If not me, who else?' She was in front of him now, pulling him to his feet. 'Come on.' Her voice was tender and her smile warm as she led him to the bedroom, and there, her actions appearing natural and unembarrassed, she took off her dressing-gown and got into the big double bed. Within a minute he was beside her, holding her full, firm body to him. After a moment of relishing the feel of her he looked down into her open face and said, 'I mean it, Ivy. Every time I say I'd go round the bend without you, it's true.'

'And Doctor, dear.' She was laughing at him. 'I always say to that, there's another road round the bend, don't I?'

'You won't get tired of me, Ivy?'

'Tired of you?' She strained her face away from his. 'Aw, don't be silly. Me get tired of you!'

'But I feel I'm taking your life, your young life; you could marry. Any day in the week you could marry . . . What's his name?'

'I know that.' She wagged her head mischievously. 'That makes me think I'm giving you something worth while.'

'Oh, I-eevy.'

'Aw; I love to hear you say, I-eevy, like that. You know you've got a beautiful voice. That's what I fell in love with first, your voice.'

'You trying to. . . ? Aw, we're wasting time.' He pulled her to him fiercely . . . And fiercely she responded to him . . .

When, later, he lay with his head between her breasts, they were past talking, and as she had done so many times before she heard his breathing become deeper, and when he gave a gentle snort she knew he had gone to sleep, and as she had done before, she would let him sleep, for perhaps ten minutes.

She lay gazing over the top of his big rumpled head towards the orange glow of the table lamp. Her body was relaxed and at peace, but not so her mind. She had heard him say many times that the body was what the mind made it. But so often, as she had lain as she was doing now, her being satisfied, her mind would start at its niggling worrying, and it was never worry for herself but worry about and for him. And in this connection her worries were many and varied. She had no doubt that her body could hold him for many a long day, but she often wondered if the day came when a man wanted something more than a body, say a woman with a mind, one who could talk about things . . . But then, he had got a woman with a mind. My God and how. And look what they had done to each other. Although she loved this man as she had never imagined loving anybody in her life, she did not exonerate him from all blame for the situation that existed in Romfield House. He had never told her the beginning of it, the real cause of it, but there were times when, before she had come to mean something to him, she had blamed him for the separate rooms, for the body hunger in Bett Higgins's eyes. She had noticed the body hunger the first day she had started working there. It was odd how that had come about, her starting to work there. She had only been married three years when George had taken ill. It had started with pneumonia, brought on by working in all weathers, getting wet and the clothes drying on him, all in an endeavour to make a market garden out of four acres of poor land. And he was just beginning to see daylight when he went down with that cold; and that was the beginning of the end. He was dead within a year. All the time he was ill the doctor had attended him; not just when he should officially, but at all odd times when he thought he might be of help. And it wasn't because of her then; she wasn't in the picture, he didn't even see her. His one concern was to ease the pain of a man who had worked himself literally to death. He had said since, it had saddened him to the heart to see an effort like George's go for nothing. And then when the funeral was over he had come back and said, 'How are you fixed? What are you going to do, Mrs Tate?' And she had told him that the bungalow was hers, for George had taken it through an insurance, so she had a roof over her head, but no money. She had told him that she couldn't run the

smallholding herself, and anyway she wasn't inclined to gardening of
any sort, so she was letting the two cultivated fields to a man who had
a smallholding half a mile away. The other two fields she had let for
grazing. One of the farmers had been to see her about them already,
and the paddock she meant to hold on to, to keep the bungalow a
bit private like. As for the rest, she would get a job. It was then he
had asked her tentatively if she liked housework, and she had said
she didn't know about liking it but she was used to it, as she had
done it all her life. So it was on her twenty-sixth birthday that she
had seen the inside of Romfield House for the first time, and the
doctor's wife and that look in her eyes, which she recognised because
its cause was also in her own body. She had also summed her up as
being a bit of an upstart, and she guessed that her ah-la voice wasn't
her natural one. And this was proved before very long when, off her
guard or really annoyed, her mistress's vowels took their natural bent
and her Tyneside upbringing came over in her inflection.

Ivy's duties had consisted of doing the housework – and there was
quite a bit of it in that twelve-roomed, rambling old place – and
occasionally waiting on table. In her very first week she learned a
great deal about the members of that small household. She learned
it from the condition of their beds. Some mornings the doctor's
bedclothes were thrown neatly back; at other times the bedclothes
were rumpled and spoke of a disturbed night. In the child's room
the bed was merely untidy, but the wife's bed always appeared as if
it had been at the centre of a whirlwind.

As time went on and the pain of George's loss eased, the ache of
her body increased. She had had this ache before her husband had
died, because during that last year of his life he'd had no power to
alleviate it. It was when she had been working at the doctor's house
for fifteen months she decided to accept Arthur Wheatley's unspoken
proposal. Arthur had a small farm near by. He had twenty acres in all
and her bit of land was adjacent to his. She did not know whether he
wanted her for herself or for the two fields. He wasn't a bad chap, she
told herself; a bit quiet, but then that might be an asset. One thing
she knew was that no matter how much her body cried out at night
he wasn't going to get her without marriage. Once you started that,
marriage went up a gum tree, and she'd seen enough of people up
gum trees. She wanted marriage and respectability.

And then the doctor went down with a fever. At first they thought
he had the 'flu, and then it was decided he had a bug, and the bug
kept his temperature at sweating point. It had become evident to
Ivy within a very short time that Mrs Higgins was no nurse; even
if she had been in sympathy with the patient, she would have found
nursing an irritation. And as Miss Jenny was away on a case, and
the stairs taxed Maggie's breath and bulk every time she mounted
them, it seemed most natural that she herself, who had nursed her

husband, should also help to nurse this man who had been so good to him. Then came the day when he was very low and she was sponging his sweat-drenched body that he said to her, 'You've got kind hands, Ivy.' That's how it had started. In that moment as they had looked at each other they exchanged their need. In the following three weeks the look was repeated again and again, and on the day that the doctor resumed his work she gave her notice in.

She knew Bett Higgins had been both annoyed and surprised. She was well satisfied with her work, she said. Was it because of the extra running up and down stairs over the past few weeks? No. Then did she want more money? No. In the end she had told her she was going to be married.

She had left on the following Friday, and on the Saturday Paul had come to the house. When she opened the door to him she hadn't been surprised, it was what she wanted. She could see him now as she had that day, this big, burly, attractive man, this man of position, this highly respected doctor, standing with his hat in his hand looking at her and asking quietly, 'Are you going to be married, Ivy?' Without hesitation she had said, 'No.' And he had said, 'You are sure of this?'

'Sure as ever I'll be of anything,' she had answered.

He had come towards her and taken her in his arms, and as naturally as if they had been made for each other from the beginning of time they came together and had satisfied each other; and it had been the same every time it had happened over the last two years . . . Yet all the while she had worried, worried about what would happen to him if their association ever leaked out. In a town like Fellburn it could mean the finish of him, and with men like old Doctor Beresford and Mr Parkins he couldn't be too careful. She wondered at times, if he hadn't been in the position of a doctor and hadn't carried on his business in the old house which he loved, whether he would have thrown everything up and taken her away. She wondered . . . often she wondered, but she couldn't give herself the answer.

When the clock in the hall struck the three-quarter chime she ran her fingers through his hair, saying softly, 'Paul, Paul, it's quarter to.'

'Eh? Oh!' He drew in a long shuddering breath and, stretching his legs down the bed, muttered into her flesh, 'You shouldn't let me go to sleep. How long have I been off?'

'Just over ten minutes. Come on.' She shook him gently. 'I'll make you a strong coffee.'

He dragged his head from the warm valley of her and, having pulled himself up in the bed, stretched out his arms to their fullest extent and yawned. Then as he watched her pull on her dressing-gown he said lazily, 'Promise me that one night you'll let me sleep right through, will you?'

'I'll promise you no such thing. Come on now.' She smiled at him, and the smile covered the regret that she would never be able to do as he asked.

When she had left the room he rose from the bed and went to the wash-basin, where he slushed his face with cold water, then got into his clothes. A few minutes later he was standing near the table, fully dressed for outdoors, with a cup of coffee in his hand. She stood close to him, watching him drink, and when the cup was empty she took it from him, and going into his arms she returned his hard, fierce kiss. It seemed that the feeling between them would never be dulled with use. He said to her now, 'Look, I've been thinking. What about a day out? I'm due for a few days . . .'

'No. No.' She shook her head quickly. 'We've been over all this before; you know yourself it's madness, you know you do. I know why you're saying it, just because of me, but I'm all right. I'm all right. I don't want days out . . . jaunts. I've told you.'

'It doesn't seem fair, taking everything and giving nothing.'

She closed her eyes. 'Oh, be quiet. Be quiet . . . And look; go on or you'll be late back.'

'Don't come out' – he pulled on his hat – 'you'll get cold.' He kissed her again, then turning swiftly from her he went out, and as he passed through the gate he heard her locking the door. He had never said when he would be back and she had never asked. She knew he would come as often as he could.

When he entered the house he heard laughter coming from the drawing-room and he stopped in the act of taking off his coat, trying to distinguish who the company might be. It was now twenty to eleven; she usually got rid of her visitors before this – her young admirers from the Technical College usually came to tea. There had been a succession of them over the past years, one introducing another. They were rarely over twenty, except for that isolated case last year. He didn't want to dwell on that, but still he couldn't forget the ignominy of having to assure the parents that his wife's interest in their twenty-one-year-old son was purely maternal; was she not fifteen years the boy's senior? That business had made him sick, sick to the core. If she wanted a man why didn't she go for a man, not these gangling, pimply-faced youths. Why did she do it? He did not unlock the answer from within him and say because these slim youths were in all ways the opposite to himself. They were not, as yet, heavy of build, their necks weren't short, or their faces large and square. Nor would he say that his wife's obsession with youth was merely perverted sex, a safe outlet for a maddening frustration. When a similar case came before him in his practice he usually had a word with the husband, for nearly always, except if the woman was afraid of sex, the cause lay with him.

As he neared the drawing-room door and a rocketing bellow of mirth came to him he knew who the visitor was, and it was no youth. A frown brought his brows together and his lower lip jutting out – Friend Knowles, and the second visit in a week. Well, at least he was her own age. But he couldn't stand the fellow, and it wasn't because he was jealous, nor because Knowles was the slim, dapper type and the antithesis of himself. Why, he wondered, did you dislike more people than you liked? It was something that few faced up to. Most people, whether religious or not, hid behind the smoke-screen of 'Love thy neighbour', the while hating their guts. Look at himself tonight. Starting with Gray in the surgery; then Mrs Ratcliffe; followed by Parkins, and, of course, Beresford; and now Knowles.

When he thrust the door open James Knowles and Bett both turned and looked towards him. Then the younger man rose swiftly from the couch where he had been sitting beside Bett, and coming forward with outstretched hand he said heartily, 'Hello again, Paul. Oh, I am glad I've been able to see you before I left; I was just about to go.' He shook Paul's hand as if he were the host and Paul a hesitant visitor.

The handshake over, he stepped back and surveyed Paul, saying, 'Hi! You look tired, really fagged. You work too hard. Still' – he poked his head playfully towards him – 'just think of all the money you make.'

'Yes, there's that in it.' A flat response, the opposite to what James Knowles expected. It took the wind out of his verbosity for a moment; then coming back on the bounce he cried, 'Tell you what I came round for, Paul. I want you both to come to a dinner on Saturday night. My boss is giving a do up at his private house, Burley Court. You know, the big place that stands back off the top end of the new road. He hasn't been in it long.'

'But we don't happen to know your boss, or he us.' Paul was walking towards the wine cabinet as he spoke.

'Oh, that's all right; he told me I could bring a couple of friends, and immediately I thought of you both.'

'Thanks.' Paul lifted up a bottle of Scotch, where it was already standing on a tray on the top of the cabinet next to some used glasses, and he poured himself out a double knuckleful, and he sipped at it before he added, 'I'm afraid I've got a busy day on Saturday. Moreover, I've already made a dinner appointment at the club.'

'I would like to go.' Bett spoke for the first time since he had entered the room, but she did not turn towards him, nor move her position from in front of the fire, and he looked towards the back of her neatly waved head before he said, 'You go then.' He knew she would go in any case; it didn't matter what he said. He also knew that his presence was the last thing that either of them wanted.

42

'It's a pity, you would have enjoyed it. When our Mr Calvert Hogan throws his house open, he throws it open, and before the evening's out you can swim through it.'

'I dare say.' Paul drained his glass; then poured out another dose, and with it in his hand he walked towards the fire. And the indication that he was going to stay in the room gave impetus to the visitor's departure, for now, bending over the back of the couch, James Knowles addressed Bett with playful familiarity, saying, 'Well, little-un, I'll have to be on my way, but is it all right for Saturday, eh?' He lifted his gaze from hèr and looked towards Paul. And for answer Bett rose from the couch and walked towards the drawing-room door, saying casually, 'I'll be ready.'

'Fine. Fine. Well, goodnight, Paul.' Again there was the hearty handshake. 'Sorry about Saturday. Another time, eh?'

'Yes, another time.'

'Oh.' Knowles was half-way across the room when he turned, adding, 'Give my love to Lorna, will you? She was in bed when I arrived. Bye.' He jerked his head. 'You're a lucky chap. She's becoming a stunner. You're going to have some trouble with the boys in that direction, Paul.'

Paul said nothing; there was nothing to say. He just looked straight at the man and watched him turn about and leave the room.

When the lowered mumble of their voices came to him he could almost hear Knowles saying, 'He doesn't change. By God! He is a surly cuss I don't know how you stand it.' Then adding, 'Never mind, little-un, we'll make up for things on Saturday night, eh?' And then he would put his arm round her waist and give her a surreptitious hug.

His thinking urged him towards the cabinet again, where he poured out another measure of whisky, which he drained immediately. He had no room to talk, to criticise, had he? He hadn't a leg to stand on. Yet if he had ten women he could still not condone, even in his mind, her association with a fellow like Knowles. He was a nasty piece of work. It had nothing to do with sex; he was just a nasty piece of work, and it oozed through his veneer. That was, for anyone who had eyes to see.

He felt the best thing to do now would be to get upstairs without coming face to face with her again, at least tonight. He did not want any more words with her, any more rows. He had no desire to pick up where they had left off before Jinny had put in her timely appearance, yet he knew it could happen because he felt irritable, touchy. He had been like this for weeks now. He was tired, very tired. He wanted a rest; most of all a change.

He was still at the cabinet when she entered the room again, and as, without speaking a word, she began her nightly ritual of puffing up the cushions and straightening the chairs he asked, 'Any calls for me?'

43

She banged a cushion into roundness before she said, 'No; I would have told you, wouldn't I?'

'I don't know so much about that.'

She straightened up and by way of retort stared scornfully at him.

'It wouldn't be the first time, would it?'

'I've never done it deliberately; when that's happened it's because I've forgotten.'

'And forgotten to make a note of the call, too.'

Her lips moved hard, one over the other. Her face took on a pinched look and her body tensed. 'I'm not your receptionist; and in future if you want messages taken you can get somebody in to baby-sit to the phone.'

'You're only asked to do two evenings a week.'

'Two evenings, that's all. Well, it's two too many. And what do I get out of it? Damn all. You wouldn't put me on your books as receptionist, would you? Oh no, I might make a bit of money. Other doctors can employ their wives, but not you. Not the big fellow, the big above-board Doctor Higgins.'

'I told you' – his tone was even, 'I had no intention of dismissing Elsie to satisfy a passing whim – that's all it would have been.'

She stared at him as her face drained of colour; and then she said, 'Damn you! And Elsie. And your Maggie. The both of them are like old moth-eaten nanny-goats running round a dried-up Billy.'

He was holding the empty glass in his hand and he had the fearful desire to toss it straight into her face and see it splinter into fragments. He placed it quickly on the cabinet, turned, and went out of the room.

When he reached his own room he switched on the electric fire, and, sitting on a chair beside it, he placed his elbows on his knees and rested his head on his open palms. Something would have to be done; but what? One thing was certain: they couldn't go on like this, not for years and years. But the only way they could get a divorce, without it impairing his work, would be for her to petition him with cruelty. But she wouldn't do that because professionally it wouldn't harm him. The only way he could get free from her would be if it ruined him, if he was bereft of the work he loved, and through that this house, and his standing in the town. That would be her price for freedom. At least, in this direction, he knew exactly where he stood.

After a few minutes he rose and, going into the bathroom, that led out of his bedroom, he ran the bath, and as he lay in it he heard her come upstairs, pass over the landing and down the long corridor to the room that was hers. He tried to think back to the last time he was in her room; it must be all of five years ago. It was when she had 'flu and he had gone in with John Price when he had visited her, just to make things look normal. He shook his head at the fact that five years ago things weren't normal between them. They had been married

44

sixteen years and for fifteen of those years things hadn't been right. Yet for the first years, because of his parents' presence in the house, he had kept up the pretence, in as much as he shared a room with her, and sometimes, driven through necessity, a bed. He had done this until seven years ago when his mother had died. The day after the funeral he had taken up his abode in this room. It was, looking at it from a doctor's point of view, a terrible thing to do to a woman, to leave her physically alone, to ignore her body, and it was because of this he had made allowances for her attitude towards him. Yet the man in him attached no blame to himself . . . He felt justified in this attitude towards her, for no man likes to be made a monkey of.

Later, when he returned to his room, he immediately put the light out, and getting into bed he lay with his hands behind his head waiting for sleep. He'd had three broken nights in a week and he needed sleep. But the longer he lay the further it receded from him. And as this went on he told himself he'd have to have another glass. He'd had the equivalent of three already, besides what he'd had earlier on. The cure, he knew, could be worse than the disease. He was muzzy now, he'd feel like death in the morning. But it was either another drink or lie here staring into nothingness until the dawn, or until the phone rang.

He switched on the light and got out of bed and went to a cupboard in the corner of the room, and taking from it a bottle half-filled with whisky, together with a large glass, he returned to the bed, and, sitting on the edge, poured himself out a stiff drink. After throwing it back in one shuddering gulp he repeated the dose. Then putting the bottle and glass on the bedside table he got into bed again, switched out the light and waited for the cumulated spirit to have its effect. He reckoned that now he'd drunk nearly half a bottle since he'd come in. Well, if that didn't do the trick, nothing would. He waited for his muscles to relax, for his mind to become more hazy. But this time the spirit did not drop the curtain of sleep over him and obliterate the day. Instead, he found himself fixed on some half-way mental platform with suppressed irritations floating around him and an aggressiveness striving to escape.

And in this state of mind he imagined himself springing up from the bed, dashing out of the room and down the corridor, kicking open her door and standing over her. He could see the surprise on her face as he gripped her throat and yelled, 'You bitch! You dirty conniving little bitch!' He had always wanted to say that to her: 'You dirty conniving little bitch!' And if he had, perhaps things would have been better, because then she would have said, 'What do you mean? Dirty conniving little bitch?' And he would have told her. Aye, by God he would have told her.

But he had never said it, and the longer he put it off the less able he was to tell her . . . Years ago, when she first became aware that

45

he knew, she had retreated into herself, frightened that he'd expose her, frightened that the good marriage she'd brought off – oh yes, he knew she congratulated herself on the catch she'd made – was going to fall to pieces and she'd be out on her neck. And that's what he should have done if he'd had any sense, finished it right off, thrown her out on her neck. But what had he done? Not a blasted thing. And all because he couldn't bear anybody knowing he had been made a monkey of; especially his father . . . For two pins he'd get up now and go along and beat the living daylights out of her. He should have done that, too, yeàrs ago. When he felt his body heaving in the bed he chastised himself aloud, saying, 'Stop it, stop it.' He sat up now, holding his dizzying head. He shouldn't have taken any more of the stuff, not at this hour. Aw, to hell! He'd drink if he wanted to. Yet he'd eased up on it lately; he'd not drunk so much since he'd had Ivy. Aw, Ivy. Oh, if only Ivy were here. He turned on to his side and flung his arm across the pillow. Now if Ivy had been his wife. But they wouldn't have stood for Ivy being his wife. Nobody would have stood for Ivy being his wife, not even his mother. Because why? Because Ivy was an ordinary lass; she was without pretence. Ivy couldn't pretend to be what she wasn't, she couldn't put on the twang, so they wouldn't have stood for Ivy. What! Marry Ivy, who said, WAS YOU and THOSE ARE THEM. Tut! Tut! how shocking. How the doctor had let himself down. Bloody hypocrites. That's what people were. Bloody hypocrites. And he was living with the biggest of them, and she was driving him mad. Only yesterday she had said to him, 'You're going round the bend. YOU should see a doctor. Have your brain seen to.'

Perhaps he should at that. Perhaps he should see a doctor. Aye, he should go to a doctor. He started to laugh quietly.

'Doctor, I'm going round the bend.'

'Are you, Mr Higgins.'

'Yes, Doctor. Completely round the bend.'

'What's brought this on, do you think, Mr Higgins?'

'Me nature, Doctor, me nature; it's the way I'm made. Oh, I don't need a psychiatrist, I know all about meself.'

'That's good, Mr Higgins. That's a very good start. Tell me some more, Mr Higgins.'

'Well, Doctor, I was taken for a ride. When I was young I was taken for a ride by a clever little puss. Now it wasn't exactly all her fault, oh no. I'm fair . . . Fair's fair. Shades of Ramsay. Well, as I said, it's me nature. Doctor, I'm a big fellow, you see, and I'm the protective type – Sir Galahad on a white horse, you know the type. So protective and so galahadish that I tried to keep meself as pure as me white steed. Can you believe that? A bloke like me trying to keep himself pure. It's a fact, Doctor, it's a fact.'

'Are you Irish, Mr Higgins?'

46

'Not a bit of it. Begod, what made you think I'm Irish, Doctor? I'm talkin' like this because Maggie Swan talks like this. Maggie's known me since I was knee high to a dobble of spit – that's one of her sayings – and I always talk to meself at night like Maggie does; it's a comfortin' way, there's something warm about it. It was Maggie really who kept me pure. D'you know that, Maggie and hard work. I was always kept busy one way and another. You know, Doctor, there's something in this keeping everybody busy in boarding schools, filling up your time with games, prep, and eating; they make you so damned tired you haven't even any Sir Galahad dreams . . . "I pray to our Lady every night of me life for you," Maggie would say, and you know, Doctor, she did. She's the only one in me life who's ever prayed for me because me mother wasn't a praying woman. A fine woman, a broad-minded, grand woman, but no praying woman. So Maggie prayed for me . . . Here a minute. Here a minute, Doctor. Now I'll tell you something, an' it's the God's truth. It's just this. I never went with a woman until I was nineteen. It was at medical school; an' you mightn't believe it, but it's God's honest truth, Doctor. I wasn't taken with it, it made me feel a bit cheap like. Honest to God. That's a laugh, isn't it? You must remember, though, I was Sir Galahad, an' begod the first person I thought of – now would you believe it, Doctor – the very first person I thought of when I woke up the next morning was Maggie Swan, for her white steed had turned to grey, and its rider was black, as black as the coals of hell, and she knew all about the coals of hell . . . But I was trying to tell you, Doctor, there I was going along fine. Like yourself I came through on top, an' I walked the wards. Oh, I was a grand figure of a man, everybody said so. It was while walking the wards that I first saw Jinny. She was a young probationer and me eyes were drawn to her because she was the plainest creature I'd ever seen in me life, and she had the biggest neb on her, you could have poked a drain with it, and the thought crossed me mind that God had done a dirty trick dishing out a dial like that to a girl. A man might have got by with it, but not a girl. And then one night, it happened like this. I was on duty and I got talkin' to her and found she was the nicest creature that Himself had ever made. It came over in her voice, and it shone out of those big eyes of hers, whose beauty was lost in the contortion of her face. And, begod, do you know what I found out besides? I found out that she was from this very town. So wasn't it natural like that later when I started up I should bump into her? And wasn't it natural like that she would introduce me to her cousin? And that's how it began. That's how it all began. And as you know, Doctor, her cousin was just a wee, wee thing, an' I was a big hulking fellow with traces of Sir Galahad still clinging to me cloak, and she got hold of those traces, Doctor, the wily little bitch got hold of those traces and she climbed up them, and into me life. You know yourself, Doctor, I never liked little women, and

Maggie never liked little women, and she said to me, "Think, boy, think. Don't be rushed, don't let yourself be rushed." But I wanted to be rushed, Doctor, and little Bett wanted to be rushed. By God, aye she did that, an' we galloped like hell towards the church.'

'And what happened then, Mr Higgins?'

'Aw, what happened then? Well, that's my concern, Doctor. I'm a big fellow, I've got a big head inside and out, an' I've got an opinion of meself, at least I had, and nobody's going to make a monkey out of me and sit on their backside and laugh.'

'Well, shall we talk about it, Mr Higgins, bring it into the open . . . Put it into words? Shall we, Mr Higgins? Shall we? Shall we follow the advice you gave Mrs Ratcliffe to ease her nerves? Confiding in someone is a great easer of nerves. You spout that at least once a day, don't you? So what about a small dose of your own medicine?'

'You mind your own bloody business. Do you hear, Doctor? You mind your own bloody business.'

'It would be better for you, Mr Higgins.'

'I know what's good for me, I don't need to be told. Go on now, get yourself away, go on along to her and ask her to talk about it. Aye, that's where you should be, along of her, she's the one that should do the talking. Go on, have a try . . .' He swung out his arm and the bottle went flying off the table, but he didn't hear it.

'Doctor, Doctor, do you hear me now? Wake up. Come on, wake up.'

'Aw. Aw. Oh, it's you, Maggie. God!' He turned on to his side and put his hand to his head. 'What time is it?'

'Just turned half-past seven, I've only just got in. Here, drink this cup of tea. You've got to get up, there's a call for you.'

'Aw, God.'

'You been at the bottle I see?'

'Yes, I suppose you could call it that.'

'Aye, well, it's your own look-out.' She thrust the pillow up behind his head. 'An' nobody suffers for it but yourself. But it'll do you no good in the long run, you know that. Well now, shall I get you a couple of tablets?'

'Yes, do that, Maggie.'

When she came from the bathroom with a glass of water and the two tablets in her hand he said to her, 'Who's the call?'

'It's for a Mrs Ogilby. She's on her time. The husband came to the door just a minute afore I let myself in.'

'Ogilby.' He nodded. 'Well, the district nurse will be there.'

'He seems very anxious for yourself.'

'Huh!' He rubbed his hand through his hair. Ogilby. Ogilby. Aw yes. Yes. He remembered he had promised to be there and he'd better be, too. They should have made a place for her in hospital. But still, she had wanted to have the baby at home.

He swung his legs out of bed, then sat on the edge for a moment screwing up his eyes against the light of day as Maggie drew the curtains. And when she turned from the window she stood looking at him like a mother at an erring son. She appeared a big woman, because of her breadth, for she was below five foot six in height. She had a round face, the skin lying in folds at each side of her mouth. Her lips were thick and pale and held in fullness at the front by four teeth, top and bottom. Her eyes, too, were round and small and dark, and sunk well back in the sockets. They were keen eyes with a youthfulness that belied the rest of the face, for every pore gave evidence of age. Yet emanating from the whole face and body was a suggestion of strength, a protective strength. Again she said, 'You shouldn't do it. It does you no good, serves nothin', an' only puts years on you – you look fifty if a day. Will I run your bath?'

'No, there's not time, I'll have to get going. Look.' He squinted up at her. 'Make me a large, strong coffee, black.'

'Aye, I'll do that.' As she went to pass him she put her hand out and patted his shoulder, and he remembered he had been dreaming about her, or something connected with her. It was all so hazy.

Five minutes later he was downstairs in the kitchen drinking her coffee. She had brought his bag from the surgery, and his coat and hat from the hall, and she stood with the coat in her hand ready for him to get into it.

'How long are you likely to be?'

'God knows. If it's going to be a long job I'll slip back and see Elsie. If not I should be here in time for surgery. Oh, by the way.' For the first time since he had got up, his features moved out of their grimness as he explained. 'I nearly forgot to tell you, Jinny's here.'

'Oh, begod, is she now? When did she come?'

'Last night, after you left.'

'Aw, that's nice. Well, that'll lighten our day.' She nodded at him. 'She's always good to have in the house is Miss Jenny.'

'I'm afraid her stay is going to be short this time. And that reminds me an' all; I'm taking her to Newcastle to catch the twelve o'clock.'

'Aw begod, that's hail and farewell all right. What's sending her off at that speed?'

'Look' – he bent towards her – 'she'll tell you all about it. You take her a cup of tea up. Tell her that I haven't told you anything, that I haven't had time, and she'll give you all her news and something that'll surprise you.'

'I'm past surprises, as you know yourself.' She followed him to the door. 'But that won't stop me from goin' up this minute. Button that coat up now, it's an awful mornin', the drizzle goes through to your marrow. I'll cook you something on spec. Take care now.'

49

As he backed the car from the garage he saw her still standing at the kitchen door, not worrying about the effect of the drizzle on herself. Thank God for Maggie. Yes, indeed, thank God for Maggie. And she threatened to get rid of her. Well, just let her, that was all, then the fireworks would fly. Whoever was leaving Romfield House it wouldn't be Maggie, for Maggie was the only sane, natural being in his life. She had always been there and she always would. At this moment he thought neither of Ivy nor of his daughter . . . nor yet of Jenny.

PART THREE

JENNY

As the train ran into Fellburn Jenny looked at herself for the last time in the mirror of the first-class compartment. Her heart was thumping against her ribs, but its beat, she knew, was nothing compared with what it would be like when she entered the house.

When the train stopped she opened the door and lifted out on to the dimly lit platform three strikingly new pigskin suitcases. She then beckoned a porter in the distance, and when she saw him coming near and recognised him, she said, 'Hello, Mr Harris.' At one time she, Bett, and her Aunty May had lived near Mr Harris.

'Why . . . why, hello, Jenny. Why, I didn't know you.' He scanned her face, evidently puzzled. 'You're looking grand.'

'I'm feeling grand, Mr Harris.'

'You want a taxi?'

'Yes, please.'

'Going to the doctor's?'

'Yes, Mr Harris.'

'Hooker's outside. That's if he hasn't been snapped up.' He nodded at her. 'He's got a brand-new car, just suit you.'

He moved his head down to her feet, then brought his eyes up to rest for a moment right in the centre of her face. 'Aye, yes. Well, glad to see you looking so well, Jenny. The wife was only talking about you the other day.'

'Yes, Mr Harris?'

'Aye, she was sayin' she didn't envy you; nursing wasn't every-body's cup of tea.'

'No, I suppose not.' Jenny smiled quietly; she knew why Mrs Harris didn't envy her, and it wasn't because of nursing.

Mr Harris's son-in-law was disengaged, and when Mr Harris had ushered her into the back of the car as if she had suddenly become someone of note – and evidently he thought she had from the size of the tip she gave him – she settled back, telling herself to take advantage of the next few minutes and relax, yet knowing at the same time this was an impossibility.

The taxi-driver deposited her cases at the front door and she stood for a moment before ringing the bell. Within the radius of the street lamp to the left of her she could see people coming and going in the courtyard, which meant that Paul was still taking surgery.

It was Maggie who opened the door to her. 'Yes?' she demanded, peering out from the lighted hall into the darkness.

'Hello, Maggie.'

'In the name of God! Come in. Come away in.'

Maggie lifted a case over the step, and after putting it down by the side of the two which Jenny had brought in, she looked up into the face that for many many years she hadn't really seen, for Maggie, like her master, had never been one to lay any stock on looks. But now she peered into Jenny's face because it was different, the whole long being was different. She put a hand up to her lined mouth and whispered, 'Miss Jenny. Why, Miss Jenny. Mother of God! Who would have believed it.' And now she laid her other hand gently on the lapel of Jenny's coat, and Jenny, as if clutching at support, gripped it and held it pressed tightly to her as she asked in a whisper, 'How do I look, Maggie?'

'Fine, Miss Jenny. Grand. Why saints alive! It's a transfiguration.'

Jenny wanted to let out a howl of laughter, even at her own expense. Transfiguration! Well, that was one up on transformation. 'Oh, thanks, Maggie.' She pressed the hand tighter. 'Where is Mrs Higgins?' She always gave Bett her correct title when speaking to Maggie.

'Oh, she's in the drawing-room with Miss Lorna. And what . . . ? You'll never guess.' Maggie grinned up at her. 'The child's got a lad, or 'twould be better to say a suitor. A suitor indeed, and a fine-looking one at that. Oh, himself was tickled to death. He caught him hanging round one night a while ago, outside, and he did the right thing; he asked him in. He told him if he wanted to see Miss Lorna then to come openly. An' begod! the young cock's never been off the doorstep since.'

Jenny looked slightly disappointed at this news. She blinked as if wondering what to do, then said hastily, 'Look, Maggie, I'll go into the morning room.' She nodded her head in the direction of the door. 'Would you tell Mrs Higgins I'm here? Do it on the quiet . . . you know, I'll leave it to you.'

'Aye. Aye, I'll do that. Don't bother with them cases.' She wafted Jenny away. 'I'll see to them afore I go.'

'No, no, they're too heavy for you to hump upstairs; just leave them.'

'Well, never bother now. Away to the mornin' room and I'll get herself to you.'

The morning room was cold and Jenny shivered, and her shivering increased when she heard the drawing-room door open, and as the laughter came to her, together with the sound of Bett's running steps, she knew her cousin was in high spirits, and being girlishly girlish.

52

When the door was thrust open and Bett cried, 'Why, Jen-ny!' the name was split, and the last syllable left her mouth hanging agape. Like Mr Harris, she was staring into the middle of Jenny's face; then her eyes flicked up and down the length of her only to come to rest again at the telling point.

'What – on – earth . . .'

Jenny knew that she was blushing, that the whole of her body was blushing, in fact sweating now.

'We-e-ll!' The word had a tremulous sound. 'So that's it. The big secret.' Bett's voice was strangely flat. 'You've had your nose done.'

'Yes, I've had it done.' Jenny swallowed; then swallowed again. 'That among other things.' She took off her hat.

'And your hair off?'

'And not before time. Nothing's before time, I should say.'

'And you've had it bleached. You've certainly gone the whole hog. Well.' Bett folded her arms across her chest; it was an attitude she took up when she was going to pass judgement, damning judgement, and she said now, 'It isn't you.'

'No, I know it isn't.' There was a touch of sharpness to Jenny's voice and she was trembling no longer. 'I've been stuck with the lot since the day I was born, and now I'm rid of it; well, as much as I can get rid of.'

'And this was all his idea?'

'Yes, it was. But it wasn't the first time I'd thought of it.' Jenny turned her face away from Bett's hard scrutiny. 'Many a time I've thought, if only I had enough money . . . Well.' She lifted one shoulder and it drew up her bust and brought Bett's gaze to rest on it now; and after a moment Bett raised her eyelids until they seemed to disappear into the sockets, and to the question they asked Jenny said, 'Oh, this part was easy.' She put her hands gently under her breasts. 'I could have worn falsies years ago but they wouldn't have gone with the rest of me.'

Bett's smile was slightly derisive, and she rocked her head from one side to the other as she said, 'I only hope it makes you happy.'

'It will; it has. I've had the best three weeks I've had in my life.'

'And what are you going to do now?'

'I've plans.'

'I bet you have.'

'What do you mean, Bett?' The light in Jenny's face had dimmed.

'Oh, I only mean that if you planned all this and kept it dark then you're bound to have other plans . . . Where are you going to settle?'

'Here, in Fellburn, I think. I'll have to get a flat. I'll . . . I'll have to have some place to put my clothes seeing as I've three cases full, and a trunk coming on.'

'My, my! We have been busy.' Bett could no longer keep the bitterness from her tone, and turning to the door she said, 'Well, we've got company, but you'd better come in and see Lorna.'

'I'd rather wait until later, until she's by herself.'

'Oh, I thought the new set-up would have given you all the confidence in the world.'

'Are you being nasty, Bett?'

The question was really unnecessary; this is what she had feared all the journey down, Bett's reaction, yet it said something for her new façade that she had dared to voice the question.

'No, of course, I'm not being nasty, only I think it was quite unnecessary to make all this mystery about what you intended to do. And I don't suppose his lordship will be very pleased either; he'll likely get professional pip thinking that you might have said something about the operation . . . because it was an operation, wasn't it?'

'I suppose you could call it that.' Jenny had never thought of Paul being annoyed about her doing this off her own bat, but now the possibility presented itself. Apart from Bett's reactions she had imagined everybody being kind, even pleased. She was under no illusions; her altered nose hadn't made her into a beauty, but it had taken the focal point from people's eyes, and in doing that had literally removed a weight from her body and a burden from her mind. It had also, as Ben had said it would, made her want to dress up. Oh, Ben, Ben. Of all the wise men in the world Ben had been the wisest. Why should she have been so lucky as to meet Ben? If only he had lived; that deep, hidden pain that was always in her would have been soothed, and the dreams to which her mind escaped at night would have faded; they must have done under Ben's kindness. But here she was now, without Ben but as Ben had always seen her. But how would Paul see her? And what if he was annoyed? One thing she did know; it would please Bett if he was.

Jenny did not answer Bett's last remark but said instead, 'I'll go in and see Lorna. I hope she survives the shock.' She laughed nervously and waited for Bett to make some comment, and when she didn't, but continued to appraise her coolly, she became embarrassed. And this increased when Bett swung round and without further words went out into the hall. There was nothing for Jenny to do but follow her, and for the first time in weeks she felt flat, and the feeling didn't lift when she entered the drawing-room.

Jenny had never ceased to be amazed at the mercurial changes Bett could bring about in her attitude, and here again she was witnessing just such a change, for Bett, on pushing open the drawing-room door, assumed an entirely different character. 'Look who we have here,' she cried to Lorna, ushering Jenny in as if she were an exhibit.

'Why, Aunt Jenny.' Lorna turned from the long record-player in the far corner of the room where she was standing near a young man, and flinging her arms wide with youthful gusto she darted

54

across the room, only to come to a sliding stop on the carpet some feet away from Jenny. Her arms dropping slowly to her sides, she gaped for a moment at this smartly dressed woman who was, yet who wasn't, her Aunt Jenny. The face was the same yet different; her nose was gone, the big hooked nose with the wide nostrils, and in its place was a straight affair, still largish but rounded at the end, a nose that was part of the face and no longer protruded from it as if trying to free itself from its base.

'Why, Aunt Jenny!' Lorna's voice was just a whisper, and what else she might have said was checked by the sound of the young man's voice answering her mother, and she remembered they had company, and her arms flinging upwards she embraced Jenny, and Jenny held her tightly.

'Don't be silly, child; leave your aunt alone.' Now Bett's voice separated them and went on, 'This is Brian. Brian Bolton. Brian, my cousin . . . Mrs Hoffman.' She inclined her head deeply towards Jenny as she gave her her married title for the first time.

Jenny shook hands with the tall fair boy, Lorna's first boy, who had looks and undoubtedly charm, perhaps a little too much, Jenny thought, as he said, 'How do you do, Mrs Hoffman. I feel I know you very well; Lorna is always singing your praises.' Then to her slight annoyance he turned her round and added, 'Do you keep your wings under your coat?'

'Oh, really!' Jenny flicked him away with her hand and walked to where the tea things were still on the trolley to the side of the fireplace. She hadn't much room for slick young men, slick men of any age.

'Go and ask Maggie for a pot of fresh tea, Lorna.'

'OK, Mammy.' Lorna skipped to the trolley and grabbed up the teapot, and, laughing towards Jenny, darted from the room.

Bett now looked towards the boy where he stood examining some records on the side-table and called in a high voice, as if he was at the other side of the house, 'Put another record on, Brian.'

'A dance one?' He turned his head, his wide grey eyes laughing at her. It was as if he had been coming to the house for years, he seemed so at home.

'Yes, let's have "Twist and Shout" again.' With a few movements of her hips Bett demonstrated the record, and the young man laughed out loud, and she with him.

Jenny, her face unsmiling, stared at Bett. What made her do it? Why must she act like a girl? Granted she was still young, only thirty-six, but she was no longer a teenager, she was a woman with a fifteen-year-old daughter. As the raucous cries from the record burst upon them, Bett, hips, arms, and feet twisting, moved towards the young man, and he, his tall body wriggling with the mobility of a snake, came towards her until they faced each other.

As she watched them Jenny became warm with embarrassment. Yet why? Why? She could do the twist. She guessed that most housewives could do the twist. What woman, listening to Housewives Choice, hadn't done a wriggle? She herself had made Ben laugh until he was sore when she'd had a go. Anybody who could stand could do the twist, so why should she feel so embarrassed now? It was certain that neither of the dancers felt embarrassed. Yet a moment later it became plain to Jenny that Lorna too, when she returned to that room, felt something akin to what she herself was experiencing. She had come in laughing, the teapot balanced on a stand, but by the time she had placed it on the trolley the smile had gone, to return fleetingly as she said, 'Will I pour, Aunt Jenny?'

'No, I'll see to it. You go and have a dance.'

'No, I don't want to. I . . . I've been dancing for the last hour.' But as she went to sit down Brian called, 'Come on, Lorna, beat it up.' And immediately the cloud lifted from her face and she was around the couch and facing him. Jenny watched her as she started to dance, her movements slower than her mother's, more flowing, less intense; naturally graceful, nothing forced. As if this fact had made itself evident to Bett, she suddenly stopped her prancing, and coming to the couch she flopped down, helped herself to a cigarette, then lay back panting gently as she blew out the smoke in quick nervous movements.

Without looking at Jenny she said, 'You haven't had any tea.'

'I'll help myself.' Jenny rose to her feet and went to the trolley.

'How long are you going to stay this time?'

'For a week or so if you'll have me; over Christmas, perhaps, until I find a flat.'

'You can stay as long as you like, you know that.'

'Thanks.'

'Have you thought of what you are going to do with yourself?'

'What was that?' Jenny screwed her face up against the heightened noise of the record, and Bett spoke louder, 'I said, have you thought what you are going to do with yourself?'

'Not really.' Jenny returned to the couch with the cup in her hand. 'I feel I'd like to make a home, just a little home, somewhere to come back to after I have a holiday. I'd like to go abroad for a time. But I know that I couldn't live without working; I'll very likely take up nursing again later on.'

'You must be barmy.' Bett slanted her glance towards her. 'I know what I would do if I had it.'

'Yes, so do I, Bett; so it's a good job you haven't, because your place is here.' Jenny had turned her head to meet Bett's gaze, and as she held it she said distinctly and slowly, 'I could give you half of what I've got, and I could do it quite easily because I don't need very much. I know I don't. Just enough to give me a little security – I can always work. But what would happen to you? You'd go mad. I know you, Bett. And what about Lorna and Paul? So . . . so I'm not going to give you anything to help you lose what . . . what you've got.'

'Who's asking you?' Bett's voice was harsh and rasping. 'It's time enough for you to refuse when I ask you for anything, and that'll be a long time, I'm telling you. As for losing what I've got; you can have it . . . anybody can have it . . . God, what I've got!'

'I'm sorry, I'm sorry.' Jenny, her voice full of contrition, put her hand on Bett's arm, and Bett, as if suddenly deflated, sat forward on the edge of the couch and dropped her head on to her chest.

'Bett, listen.' She moved closer to her. 'I'm going to get you a little car; you've always wanted a car. Do you hear?'

Bett's head sank lower, and she appeared to be on the point of crying. It was as if she had forgotten the dancers and had become oblivious to the sound of the thumping of the record, but when it stopped she lay back again and composed herself, the only evidence that she was upset showing in the constant nipping of her lips.

Into the silence that followed the noise of the record, Brian's voice, although low, came clearly to them, saying, 'There's a beat session on at the Ricco Club tonight, what about it? The Howlers are topping the bill.' After a short pause Lorna said, 'Oh, I'd love to, but I've got homework . . . But' – her voice lightened – 'I could do it after. Mammy, can I go out? Brian wants to take me to the Ricco Club?'

Bett pulled sharply on her cigarette. 'You just said you've got homework to do.' Her tone was flat, uninterested. 'Anyway, I don't think your father would like you going there.'

'It's quite all right, Mrs Higgins.' The boy was facing her now from the hearth rug, bending slightly towards her, a strand of his fair hair drooping across his forehead to his left eye. He looked a mixture of sophistication and gauche youth. 'We just all sit round; there's turns, folk songs, community songs, and "The Howlers" do some of the pops. It's all very nice.' He stressed the last words, speaking like a man who was trying to assure a doubting mother as to the propriety of the club. And then his blue eyes widening, as if the thought had just come to him, he exclaimed, 'Why don't you come along, too? You would love it. It would just be up your street.'

Jenny watched Bett being lifted on to the plane of careless youth by this young man, who hadn't, she thought, much to learn. She watched the eager, hardly submerged girl in her rise to the invitation and grab it with a technique so thin that it was pitiful.

'Oh, you don't want me trailing along with you. Goodness gracious . . . And her mother came too!' She made the high infectious sound that she could do so well, it was a cross between a laugh and a giggle.

'Don't be silly.' He bent further towards her. 'You're not like her mother.' He lifted his glance above the couch and smiled at Lorna

57

standing exactly where he had left her in the middle of the room. 'You're not even like sisters, you're more like twins. Come on, what about it, eh?'

It was as if he had thrown both his hands out to her, for she wiggled on the couch and brought herself towards its edge and him, saying again, 'No, no, it can't be done. Anyway, this is one of my nights on; I've got to stay in and receive calls. You see, our cook goes shortly after six and I'm without a maid.' She glanced at Jenny now, a quick questioning glance.

Jenny looked down at her hands, lying slackly, one on top of the other in her lap. She knew that if Bett didn't go to the club then Lorna wouldn't be allowed to, yet she wondered at the same time if it wouldn't be better like that rather than Bett impose her false youth and gaiety into the natural element that was growing between these two young things. Her voice sounded prim as she said, 'I'll not be going out, I'll take the calls.'

'Would you, Jenny? Oh, but it would be an imposition to ask you.'

'Why?' Jenny could not resist making the blunt statement. 'I've done it before, haven't I?'

'Yes, yes, but . . . Oh well, I'm not going to look a gift horse in the mouth. Thanks, thanks, Jenny. I'll go and get ready then. What time does it start?' She turned her head back towards Brian.

'Seven o'clock, but we must get there early if you want a seat; it's generally packed.' He straightened up and pulled at his tie. He looked pleased with himself, as if he had brought something off.

'Give me ten minutes.' As Bett laughed at the tall, smiling youth, Jenny was forced to look away, and her eyes were drawn to Lorna where she was bending over the record-player. Lorna, she noticed, hadn't said anything one way or the other, and when her mother called to her gaily as she went from the room, 'Come on, dear, and get ready,' she replied, 'I am ready. I just need to put my hat and coat on.'

She might have said, Youth is its own dresser, it needs no adornment, for Bett stopped abruptly. Her face straight now, her voice sharp, she said, 'Don't be silly; you can't go out in that get-up.' She indicated with a wave of her hand Lorna's pleated skirt and bulky pullover.

'I'll have my coat on.'

'Oh, well!' She raised her shoulders and her eyebrows together. 'If you want to look a mess that's your business.' Then turning about she closed the door after her.

The boy was looking towards Lorna now, but made no effort to join her, and Jenny looked at him and she didn't know whether she liked him or not. In any case she felt he was a bit too old for

Lorna, at least for her first boy. To make conversation she said to him, 'Do you work in Fellburn?'

'Yes, I'm at Boyes, the engineering works, and I do half-time at the college.' He motioned his head in the direction of the Square.

'You're going to be an engineer then?'

'I hope so.'

As they spoke, Lorna came to the fireplace, and lifting her narrow foot on to the raised tilted fender she started to tap it, a sure sign that she was upset. And apparently the boy realised this for now turning to her he said quietly, 'I think you look fine in that.'

Lorna cast a sidelong glance at him. 'I don't really.' Her voice, although holding its natural attractive huskiness, sounded dull.

'It doesn't matter, it suits you. That goldy brown of the sweater is your colour . . . isn't it?' He appealed to Jenny, and Jenny said, 'Yes, I think it is, but then Lorna can wear almost anything.'

'Aw, Aunt Jenny.' The set look slipped from Lorna's face and, coming to the couch, she dropped with a plop beside Jenny and added, 'You always say nice things, Aunt Jenny.'

'Me?'

'Yes, you.' Leaning towards Jenny, she dropped her head on to her shoulder and hugged her arm. It was as if she had forgotten Brian's presence for the moment. 'And you look lovely, Aunt Jenny. I meant to say it. And you smell nice. What is it? What's it called . . . The scent?'

Jenny laughed down at her. 'You'd never guess, not in a month of Sundays. It's called . . . "Snake Charm". Did you ever hear such a name for such a nice smell?'

'Snake Charm! Good Lord! But it's lovely. Was it expensive?'

Jenny closed her eyes and moved her head slowly. 'The earth. Four pounds for a small bottle. I expected to get a cobra with it for that money.'

'Oh, Aunt Jenny.' They were laughing together when Lorna, raising her head from Jenny's shoulder, looked up at Brian and said, 'I told you so, didn't I?' Brian seemed to understand this enigmatic remark, for he smiled down on Jenny; then said, 'Lorna tells me you're going to live here.'

'Oh, not here.' Jenny shook her head. 'Not in the house. I'm thinking of taking a flat, and I want someone with good taste to help me furnish it.' She doubled her fist and pressed it gently against Lorna's nose, and Lorna cried, 'You mean it? You really mean it . . . I could help you choose things?'

'Well, I'll have to have help from someone; I've no artistic sense, although I've got an eye for colour, quiet colours, like flaming red, purple and orange. Oh, I like flaming red, purple and orange, and nicely mixed.'

'Oh, Aunt Jenny, you don't, you don't. Don't believe her.' Lorna shook Jenny as she spoke to Brian, and Brian, playing the gallant, looked Jenny slowly over before saying, 'Your choice of clothes belies that statement.'

The compliment and the way it was said brought a straight look to Jenny's face. No, she didn't like this boy when he was playing the man. She thought again he was much too old for Lorna. She was saved from trying to make any reply to his gallantry by Bett entering the room.

Bett was wearing a grey coat with a broad half-belt at the back and a high collar, and perched jauntily on her hair was a white fur toque. It was a youthful-looking rig-out, and together with a skilfully made-up face, which gave the impression of no make-up at all, she could have passed for twenty-five or under.

'You're not ready yet.' She looked at Lorna, and Lorna rising slowly from the couch said, 'I told you, Mammy, I've only to put my hat and coat on, they're in the hall. Bye-bye, Aunt Jenny.' She bent and kissed Jenny. 'See you later.'

'Yes, dear.'

'Goodnight, Mrs Hoffman.' He remembered names.

'Goodnight,' said Jenny.

Then Bett was standing in front of her, pulling on her gloves. 'You don't mind . . . you're sure?'

'Of course I'm sure.'

'Bye then.'

'Bye-bye. Oh, what time will I tell Paul you'll be back?'

'You can tell him to expect me when he sees me.'

Jenny turned her head away impatiently, and when she heard the front door bang she rose slowly and walked about the room. She had come home, as she thought of this house, full of her new self, but now it didn't seem to be of the slightest importance. As usual, she felt swamped by the needs of those around her, by Bett's in particular. What was going to be the end of her and this constant warfare with Paul? What was equally bad was her obsession with youth. Didn't she realise even yet she'd get talked about, laughed at? It had happened before. Well, she couldn't do anything about it, she knew that, because although Bett was in no way as mature as herself, she was stronger, for being selfish and self-willed she was less amenable.

But she was glad in a way that Bett had gone out, for this would enable her to meet Paul alone.

She sat down again, and opening her handbag took out her mirror, and for the thousandth time in the past few days she scanned her face. She still couldn't believe she was looking at herself, that this ordinary, normal-looking creature was her.

When she heard the surgery door close she put the mirror quickly back into her bag and snapped it closed. She waited. She paced his steps to Elsie's room. After this she had to wait a further five minutes, and when she next heard his feet crossing the hall she was in such a state of agitation that beads of sweat were resting on her upper lip. The steps came to a halt some way from the drawing-room door and in the silence there came the distant blare of the Salvation Army's band. Being Friday night, and money night, and club night, the army was off to do battle in the centre of Fellburn. The sound was cheery, rousing. She wondered if Paul was standing listening to it. The band nor the players never aroused his ire, as it did Bett's. He had been brought up on the sound of it. Such was her agitation that when the drawing-room door eventually opened she gave a start. She hadn't heard him come in.

'Why, Jinny!' His deep rumbling voice was loud, pleased. 'When did you come?' She turned slowly towards him as he rounded the couch.

'About half-an-hour ago, Paul.'

'Jinny! . . . Jinny!' His big face seemed to be spreading even wider. His head was moving in small, almost imperceivable little motions.

'Well, Paul?'

'Jin-ny!' He took a slow heavy step towards her; then taking her hands, his eyes still on her face, he said, 'So this was it?'

She gulped and nodded. 'What do you think?'

'I . . . I don't know. Honest, I don't know. I . . . I liked you as you were, Jinny.'

'Well, I'm still me. But . . . but I always wanted to get rid of it and . . . and Ben said I must.'

'Ben did?' He jerked his chin to the side, and it gave emphasis to the question.

'Yes; he was the only one I ever spoke to about it. He wanted me to go and have the operation when he was still alive, but I wouldn't. He didn't want me to do it for – for his sake, but for my own.'

Paul's face crinkled now into painful lines, and he said under his breath, 'But, Jinny, I didn't know it worried you so. I could have arranged something, but . . . but I would never have thought of putting it to you.'

'No, I understand; it had to come from me. But still' – she leant away from him – 'what do you think? Does it make any improvement?' Her lips were apart, there was a beseeching look in her eyes, and he too leant back from her, still holding her hands, and surveyed her from head to foot before saying, 'You're all changed, right from your feet up. Yes, Jinny, I suppose it does. In fact there's no doubt about it. I suppose I should say you look extremely smart, and you do.'

'But . . . but you're not really in favour of me having done it, Paul, are you?'

'Yes, Jinny, yes.' His voice was loud now, like a gentle roar, and he shook her two hands up and down. 'Yes, I am, and it's going to

61

make you happier. Not that I ever thought you were sad, but . . . but some time later on, when I get thinking about it, I know I'll be flaming mad with myself for not having proposed it.'

It was in a way as Bett had said, but only in a way, for she could see that he was still flabbergasted at what she had done, at the complete change in her. Well, she was flabbergasted herself.

'Where did you go?'

'To Belling's Clinic.'

'Oh, he's good, he's got a name. You went to the best place. Come on, sit down and tell me about it. I mean the whole thing, all you did.'

So with one hand still in his she told him about the operation, about Doctor Belling himself, about all the contacts she made from the clinic, the beauty specialist, the dress shop with the private room and the two women hovering over her; and she finished with, 'And you know, Paul, altogether I spent five hundred pounds . . . five hundred pounds on me.' She thumped her chest.

'You couldn't have spent it on a better person. Good for you, Jinny. And now what are your plans? What are you thinking about doing?'

'Well, I thought of getting a flat, perhaps on Brampton Hill; they're turning the big houses into flats there.'

'Nice; that's nice. I'm glad you'll be near. You're a comfort; you know that, Jinny, don't you? You've always been a comfort.' Letting go her hand now and getting to his feet, he added, 'How is it you're cousins and there's not a spark of you in her? I've looked for it for years; but no, you're poles apart.'

'You're too hard on her, Paul.'

'Huh!' He swung his big body quickly round and his voice was accusing now. 'You mean that? You really think that, Jinny?'

'Yes, I do, Paul.'

'But you know how she goes on, you know she's unbearable.'

'Yes, but . . .' Jenny shook her head, she couldn't say, It's unbearable for her too, isolated at the end of the corridor. She wished she didn't feel that Bett had a point in her favour; she didn't want to feel any sympathy for Bett. 'It's none of my business,' she went on. 'I don't want to get involved, Paul. What I mean is, I don't want to take one side against the other.'

'I don't understand you . . . at least with regard to Bett, Jinny. I know she's as fond of you as she can be of anyone, yet she's used you at every opportunity; all her life she's used you.'

'Perhaps I wanted to be used, Paul. Free agents, and I'm a free agent, are not often made to do things. If they do them it's because in some part they want to do them. We were brought up together; she and her mother were the only family I had. I suppose that's the explanation really; they were my people. And I've always wanted her to be happy, because in spite of everything, her looks

62

and her gaiety, she's never been happy, not even when she was young.'

He made a sound in his throat, then turned from her as if tired of the conversation, and looking at his watch he said, 'I've got a full evening; I'd better be off.'

'Have you had your meal?'

His mouth twisted in a semblance of a smile as he said, 'No. Anyway, I've never liked eating in the kitchen. You know that, Jinny. And the new order is, the kitchen or the cold dining-room.' He waited for her to make some comment, but when she didn't he went on, 'I could put my foot down and turn every blasted radiator in the house to the top of its bent; I could put every electric fire on, every gadget; but what would that lead to? Anyway,' he wrinkled his nose, 'it's getting to mean less and less. Everything's getting to mean less and less.'

'Oh, Paul; don't sound like that.'

'It's a fact, Jinny. Aw, well, I must be off.' He bent quickly towards her now and, touching her cheek gently, scanned her face for a second before saying, 'Don't change inside, Jinny.'

'There's not much fear of that.'

'Aw, you never know.'

'I'm set in me ways.' She laughed at him.

'I'm glad. Goodnight, Jinny.' He tapped her cheek.

'Goodnight, Paul.'

When he was gone she sat with her chin drawn into her neck, her eyes fixed on her hands gripped together in her lap. And she sat like this until she heard the sound of his car moving out of the yard; then she rose heavily from the couch and went up to her room.

Her new cases were standing by her bed. She did not look at them but walked towards the wardrobe mirror and there, gazing at herself, she asked her reflection, 'And for what?' All the excitement of her transformed being was gone; she felt flatter, more desolate, more alone than she had ever done in her life before. Addressing her new self in the mirror, she said, 'Get yourself out of here as quickly as possible.' And she watched her head nod slowly in answer . . .

It was around nine o'clock when the front-door bell rang. There had been no calls during the evening, and Jenny knew it wouldn't be them back from the club, because Bett had her key. When she opened the door she expected to find someone from the vicinity, who found it quicker to come to the doctor's house than to phone, but she actually fell back in amazement as Lorna dashed past her into the hall.

'Where are the . . . ?' She didn't finish the question but, putting her head out of the door, she looked into the Square. There was no-one to be seen; so, closing the door, she hurried after Lorna into the drawing-room.

'What's the matter?'

Lorna was standing in the centre of the room, the fingers of one hand pressed tightly across her mouth.

'What is it, dear?' Jenny approached her slowly and put her arms about her; and Lorna, as if she had been holding her breath for an unimagined time, whipped her hand from her mouth and as her body deflated cried, 'I hate Mammy, Aunt Jenny, I hate her!'

'Oh, Lorna, Lorna. Don't say such a thing. What's upset you?' She drew her to the fire. 'Here, take your coat off and sit down.' She threw her hat and coat to one side and asked again, 'What is it? What's upset you like this?'

'Oh, Aunt Jenny, Aunt Jenny.' Lorna collapsed against her and began to cry noisily.

'There now, there now. Don't go on like that. Come on, come on, dear. Sit down and tell me what it is.'

Slowly the crying ebbed away; and then Lorna, pulling herself upwards, looked through her streaming eyes at Jenny and said quietly, 'I do hate her, Aunt Jenny, I do really.'

'Lorna, you mustn't say things like that.' Jenny's voice was stern. 'Now don't; it's a dreadful thing to say, no matter what she's done . . . But what has she done?'

Lorna moved slowly from the couch on to the pouffe that was near the fire, and she crouched on it like someone on a rock trying to evade the incoming tide, and with her head hanging she began, 'We couldn't get in at the club, it was full, and there was a dance on at the Borough Hall. She's always looked down her nose at the Borough Hall, yet when Brian said what about it, she went all girlish.' A slight repulsive shiver went through her body. 'She pretended she was going slumming, and Brian met a boy he knew and he joined up with us. And I didn't like him, and he saw I didn't like him, and after the first dance he didn't ask me again. But Mammy' – her head jerked violently – 'she didn't give Brian a chance, she danced with him nearly all the time. She made him dance with her. She kept teasing him and laughing and joking, and showing him she could twist better than anybody else . . . trying to beat the young girls. I – I felt sick. I couldn't watch her any more so I just walked out.'

The room became very quiet, until Jenny said, 'You know, Lorna, you must realise that your mammy isn't old, she's only thirty-six. It's not old.'

'But she's a mother.' Lorna twisted quickly round on the pouffe and confronted Jenny. 'She's my mother. Queenie Price's mother doesn't act like that, she – she acts properly . . . like a doctor's wife should. And Rhona Watson's mother doesn't act like her, and she's pretty. Nor Phyllis Bell's; nor any of the others I know . . . She wants Brian, Aunt Jenny.'

'Don't say that, Lorna.' Jenny sounded shocked.

'I will say it; yes, I will say it, Aunt Jenny. I'm no longer a child, I know about things. I read, I read a lot. She's never told me anything that a mother should tell a daughter, and I can't talk to Daddy, not about that. But I've read all about it.' She lowered her eyes. Then lifting her head sharply, and her husky sounding voice coming from deep within her, she said bitterly, 'Mammy wants Brian, and he knows it. He's only been coming to the house for about three weeks and he's changed. I've known him for a long time; he used to meet me on and off coming from school. He had other girls. I know two he went round with. Paula Bradford. She left last year; he used to go with her. And then Mary Weir. But every now and again he would meet me; and then one night he came to the house and waited outside and Daddy saw him and told him to come in. That was the first time she had met him, and she went silly, ab-so-lute-ly silly . . . Oh, Aunt Jenny, it makes me feel terrible when I watch her.'

'Come now.' Jenny leant over and pulled her gently from the pouffe, and when she was seated on the couch again she cradled her in her arms and said soothingly, 'You're in love for the first time and everything is larger than life. It's a very nice state to be in, but you tend to exaggerate lots of things when you're like that. Now, have you looked at it this way? Brian is being nice to your mother because he wants her on his side, because he's in love with you.'

'Yes, I thought that at first; but then you see, Aunt Jenny, that's not Mammy's side of it, she'll not see it like that. I tell you she's gone all shot about him.'

Suddenly Jenny pulled her to her feet. 'Come on; you'll see everything clearer in the morning. The time's getting on. You get to bed and I'll bring you a hot drink up, and we'll sit and have a natter. I've got lots of plans for the future, about my flat and everything, and I want someone to listen to me. Go on now.'

As if her light body was held down by weights Lorna went slowly from the room, and Jenny went into the kitchen, and here she stood resting against the edge of the table for a moment. Paul would do something desperate if Bett started that again. Was she mad altogether? Well, not altogether, only a part of her, the part that was starved of physical expression. And who could blame her? You couldn't say to Bett that she should sublimate it. No, that kind of thing was only expected of nurses with big noses. As her thoughts turned bitter she went hastily to the cupboard and, taking out a pan, she warmed some milk.

A few minutes later, when she mounted the stairs with the tray in her hand, she saw Lorna coming out of the bathroom. She was dressed now in her pyjamas and she looked like a slim boy, a beautiful, dark, oriental slim boy, and the sight hurt her, and she wondered if it hurt Paul.

She had been sitting on the edge of Lorna's bed for about ten minutes when she heard the front door open. On the sound she stopped talking, and leaning towards Lorna she said, urgently, 'Now don't be nasty. Just say you came home because you felt tired.'

At this Lorna lowered her lids and pressed her lips together, but said nothing. There was the sound of the drawing-room door banging, then footsteps on the stairs, followed by the bedroom door being thrust open. And there stood Bett, an enraged Bett, no semblance of the girl visible now.

'What do you think you're up to, madam?' She came quickly towards the bed, ignoring Jenny, her eyes fixed hard on her daughter. 'We've searched the place for you. Frightening the life out of me, going off like that.'

'I didn't think you would notice.' Lorna's voice sounded cool.

'What do you mean, you didn't think I'd notice? I went to the trouble of going to that beastly dance hall just so that you could have a dance – you're always on about going to dances – and then what happens? You sit like a stook, and then you just go off without a word to anyone. Well, it won't happen again; I'm not going to waste my time . . .'

'Oh, stop kidding yourself, Mammy.' Lorna had pulled herself swiftly up in the bed, and now her face was on a level with her mother's.

'How dare you speak to me like that!' Bett's face was scarlet.

'Well, you've asked for it. You are kidding yourself. You kid yourself all the time . . .'

The force of the slap overbalanced Lorna and knocked her head against the wall. And Bett, leaning over the bed, would have repeated it if Jenny hadn't gripped her by the arms, crying, 'Bett! Bett, stop it! Pull yourself together. What's come over you, woman?'

'I'm not having her speak to me like that. How dare she. How dare she. I won't stand for it.' One arm was flaying the air now. Then all of a sudden it dropped; and Bett's voice dropped, too, and, her small body crumpling, she burst into tears, loud hysterical tears, and tearing herself from Jenny's hold she rushed out of the room.

Jenny didn't follow her, except to close the bedroom door. Then, returning to the bed, she gently drew Lorna to her and held her shivering body tightly in her arms. Yet strangely it was Bett she thought of as she comforted Lorna, Bett who had now lost her daughter, for this thing would always be between them. She wished she hadn't to be sorry for Bett; oh, how she wished that.

'Boxing Night. I used to love Christmas at one time, but it's like everything else, it changes. Hand me your glass.'

'No, no. No more for me, Paul.' Jenny laughed up at him while she put her hand over the top of the empty glass. 'I've had three.'

'Come on; give it to me here.' He pulled it from her hand. 'What's three on Boxing Night! And you Poppet?' He turned to Lorna. 'Tonic water? lime? orange?'

'Can I have a sherry, Daddy?'

'No, you can't; you've had one tonight, me lady, and wine with your dinner. My, what's the world coming to . . . well?'

Lorna screwed up her face at him. 'Oh, I suppose it'll have to be a tonic water then.'

'Yes, you suppose right.' As Paul went across the room to the wine cabinet, members of a party that was well under way on the television began a Scottish recl, and as the bagpipes' wail filled the room Paul, dropping the glasses on to a table, cried, 'Come on, Jinny. Come on, Lorna. Let's swing our kilts. Come on, we'll show 'em.' Watching the screen, he took the pose of the dancers, right arm cocked high, left arm on his hip, and with surprising agility went into the dance, and with each step he cried 'Foot up; heel, toe, foot up; cross feet, cross feet, a-roll-of-the-body; heel, toe, foot up . . . Come on, get on your feet, the pair of you.'

'Oh, Daddy, Daddy.' Lorna was leaning over the side of her chair doubled up with high laughter, and Jenny held herself around the waist to ease the pain of her mirth, until he danced round to her and scooped her up from the couch with a lift of his arm, and then she was spluttering through her laughter, 'Oh, Paul, Paul, I can't.'

'Come on with you. Heel, toe, foot up; heel, toe, foot up.'

When Jenny tried to follow his instructions and all out of time, Lorna threw herself onto the couch and her laughter rose, and as if in agony she cried, 'Oh, stop it, Daddy! Give over, Aunt Jenny. Oh, stop it! You both look . . . look . . . oh!'

Paul was now leading Jenny in a comic form of the lancers. He would turn from her, bow to an imaginary partner, then gripping her by the waist swing her round. With the change of each figure he would do the bowing act. The music stopped at the same time as they knocked over a small table, and they hung together, panting and laughing. Then Paul, taking her to the couch, bent over Lorna and demanded, 'What's funny about our dancing, eh?'

'Oh, Daddy!' Lorna turned on her back and gazed up at him; her face was streaming, and her mouth wide. 'Oh, I've never laughed like that for ages. Oh, Daddy, you did look funny. And you, too, Aunt Jenny.'

'She's saying we're old, Jinny.' He nodded solemnly at Jenny. 'That's what she's saying. I'll show her.' He reached down and thrusting his hands under her armpits lifted her to her feet, nearly overbalancing them both in the process. 'Look,' he indicated the television, 'they're doing the tango. Now this is my cup of tea. Come on, miss; I'll show you.' Dragging her, still shaking with laughter, into the centre of the room, he now did an exaggerated form of the tango. He was contorting and twisting his big bulk when Lorna brought the exhibition to an end by falling against him, crying, 'Oh, Daddy! Daddy, stop it! Stop it. You're like a big cart-horse.'

'What do you say?' He glared down at her in mock anger. 'I'll have you know, miss, I took the prize for the best tango dancer at the students' ball . . .'

'Oh, stop it, stop it!' She actually sounded as if she was in pain.

And Paul stopped it. He leant his chin on her head and, looking across to Jenny, said quietly, 'I'm drunk.'

'Well, it's a good job you know it.'

'But . . .' He now thrust his daughter from him, and shaking her by the shoulders until her head wobbled while she still laughed, he cried in threatening tones. 'But not so drunk, madam, that I can't do the tango. I can do the tango on my head. Watch me.'

When he went down on his hands and knees and tried to hoist his great lumbering body into the air, Lorna once again collapsed. Throwing herself on Jenny she cried, 'Oh, Aunt Jenny, stop him, stop him.'

And Jenny, the tears streaming down her own face, looked to where Paul, violently kicking his great legs backwards, was endeavouring to stand on his head, and she thought, I wouldn't stop him for the world. She'd never seen him act the goat like this for many a long year. In fact she'd only seen him act like this once before. It was the night before he married Bett.

'Aw, to the devil with it.' He straightened his body up and adjusted his coat. 'I used to do that every morning before breakfast.' He went to the fire and flopped into the big chair; then putting his head back and looking up at the clock, he said, 'Good Lord! Quarter past one.'

'Yes, quarter past one,' repeated Jenny. 'It's time I was going.'

'Why don't you stay the night, or what's left of it?'

'Oh no, I must get back, Paul. Don't forget I've got a do tomorrow night and I must be on the spot in the morning to get an early start.'

'Would you like me to come and help you, Aunt Jenny?'

'I would, I would,' said Jenny. 'I've still got umpteen fiddly things to do. You know, I think giving a dinner would have been easier than a buffet affair with all the tit-bits.'

'How many are you expecting?' asked Paul.

'Twenty. It'll be a crush.'

'Oh, I don't know; the rooms are not skinty. You were very lucky to get that flat.'

'Yes, I was.'

'I think I'll go to bed.' Lorna stretched out her arms and pulled herself upwards. 'Goodnight, Daddy.' As she bent forward to kiss him she added, 'Me Highland laddie.' And they laughed again. Then turning to Jenny, she kissed her, saying, 'I'll be along about ten, Aunt Jenny. How's that?'

'Fine. I hope I'm up. Goodnight, dear.'

When Lorna had closed the door behind her, Paul, his eyes still fixed on it, rubbed his hand over his mouth before he said, 'That's the first time I've seen her like herself for weeks. There's something worrying her, Jinny. You any idea what it is?'

Jenny looked away from him. 'No, Paul; not really.'

'Not really? Then you have some idea?'

'Well, she's going with Brian, and it's her first affair. Well, you know what they say, it never runs smoothly.'

'Aye, yes. Do you think she's still seeing him? He hasn't been near the house for over a fortnight. And we're in the middle of Christmas, and no parties.'

'She was at one last week.'

'One! What's one party at Christmas. Even her mother's been to three. Huh!' He dropped his head back against the framework of the chair. 'I wonder if she's enjoying herself?'

'Now, now, Paul, stop it. You know you could have gone with her, you were both invited.'

'. . . And Mr Knowles?'

After the silence that followed this remark Jenny said briskly, 'Well, Paul, I really must be off. And look' – she rose and stood over him – 'it doesn't need me to tell you you're in no condition to drive, so I'll ring for a taxi.'

'A taxi! You damn well won't.' He jumped to his feet. 'No condition to drive! Jinny . . . Jinny, I'd have to be very drunk before I couldn't drive my car. Come on, get your coat on and I'll show you.'

With a resigned smile Jenny went upstairs and into the room which she always thought of as hers. It was at the opposite end of the landing from Bett's, and next to Lorna's, and as she stood before the mirror adjusting her hat there came to her the sound of muffled crying, and with her hand still to her head she paused and listened. She wasn't at all surprised to hear Lorna crying; her laughter all evening had been

69

too high, too forced. Again she thought of Bett, but, almost for the first time, without any sympathy. She felt that if she was near her at this moment it would be she who would do the face slapping, and the cause would be more justified.

Bett had gone with James Knowles to a dinner-dance, a special invitation dance, to which the Mayor and Mayoress and their son, Brian, would undoubtedly have been invited. Without ever having seen them together, or any concrete evidence to justify her feelings, Jenny knew that Bett was seeing young Brian Bolton, and the fact made her sick. She also felt sick, but in a different way, for Lorna.

She made no attempt to go into Lorna's room but went straight downstairs, and Paul's voice called to her from the waiting-room door, 'Look at this, Jinny.'

She went out of the smaller hall and into the larger one and saw him standing on the steps of the courtyard. He was pointing to the ground and saying, 'It's like glass; the sleet's frozen; it's a black frost. You're right, I'd better not take the car out in this.' He laughed a thick laugh. 'And you'll get no taxi tonight, either, Jinny, so it'll be shanks's pony.'

'I can manage on my own, Paul, it's only fifteen minutes' walk.'

'Jinny . . . Jinny, what do you think I am to let you walk through the town in the dead of night?'

'I've walked through it many times before, Paul, and alone in the dead of night.' She laughed at him.

'Well, this is one time you're not going to do it.'

'But Lorna; she'll be in the house by herself.'

'Oh, she'll be dead asleep by now. And anyway,' he looked at his watch, 'if the other one's not going to make a night of it she should be back soon.'

'Shall we wait a little longer then?'

'No, no. I don't want to set eyes on her. This is as good a way as any for us to miss each other. You see, Jinny.' He pulled her gently over the step, then locked the door. 'You know I haven't got much control over this temper of mine at the best of times, but when I've knocked off the bottom half of a bottle then I'm not accountable for anything I might say, or do . . . to anyone. So come on, Mrs Hoffman.' He gripped her hand and pulled it through his arm. 'I'm escorting you home. Not because I'm thinking of your safety in the streets but because I want to be looked after during the next hour.' He squeezed her arm. 'The dangerous hours before the dawn, the hours during which you ask yourself questions. Why were you born? Where are you going? And why has this to happen to you? Such daft questions as that. But anyway,' he gave a hick of a laugh, 'it's been a nice night, Jinny. I've enjoyed myself tonight, just the three of us. What about you?'

'Oh, I've enjoyed myself, too, Paul. I've had a grand time.'

'Ups!' Jenny slipped on the icy surface of the path and would have fallen if he hadn't hoisted her upwards. Then they were both slipping, and clinging to each other, and as they laughed aloud the echo came back from the dead Square.

'Let's get into the road. Ah, this is better. You can still feel the grit here.' He kicked at the loose gravel. 'You know what, Jinny. I think everybody should get drunk on a frosty night. How can they say you are drunk and incapable when the road's like glass, eh? Funny thing about people being drunk, Jinny. I've noticed it time and again. Some only need a few whiskies and they trip over their words; but now myself, I've got to be almost blind before I fuddle my tongue. You couldn't tell, could you?' He pulled her arm into his waist. 'You couldn't tell by the way I speak, now I ask you, could you . . . could you tell that I've got a load on?'

'No, Paul; nobody would ever tell.'

'And my walk, it isn't bad, is it? Look, I could do a white line.' He let go her arm and demonstrated with one foot before the other.

'Oh, Paul, you're a fool. Come on, come on. If a policeman does come along you'll have a job to talk yourself into being sober.'

'Who's afraid of a pollisman?' He used the northern idiom. 'Who's afraid of anything or anybody?' He had hold of her again. Then his voice changing, he said slowly, 'Aw, this is nice, Jinny. Me and you walking in the night together. A hoar frost around us and the sky studded with stars. I'll remember this night, Jinny.'

He became quiet and she let him be quiet. She had thoughts of her own to think, and she too would remember this night.

When they reached Brampton Hill they found the going more difficult, and a number of times they nearly fell. So when they reached the drive that led to Farley Court, a one-time gentleman's residence which was now turned into four flats, they were laughing again. But as they neared the house Jenny warned, 'Ssh! We'll wake them up.'

'I thought the others weren't in?'

'One lot are, in the upper flat. Not above me; the other side.'

With exaggerated caution Paul now tiptoed into the hall, and when she opened the door of the flat he still tiptoed. He switched on the lights, and he tiptoed across the room, and switched on the imitation log fire set in the strikingly new fireplace; and then he whispered hoarsely, 'Do you think anyone saw us?'

'Not a soul,' she whispered back at him. Then pulling off her hat and coat and holding out her hands she went towards the fire. 'It strikes a bit cold. I think I'll get central heating in – the electric kind, you know.'

Paul was looking about him. 'I like this room. You know, Jinny, I never thought I'd like modern furniture, but you've done something with it. And all these colours. Yet they blend and are restful. I was always under the impression that I wouldn't be able to live with modern furniture, but this looks good; it's nice . . .' He sighed now.

'There's room for improvement.' She was standing by his side, she, too, looking about her; and her voice dropping, she said, 'You know, Paul, this is my first home, my first real home.'

'I suppose it is, Jinny.' He had turned his head towards her. 'It means a lot to you, doesn't it?'

'Yes, yes, it means a lot to me. You don't know how much . . . But there.' She brought her face round to his and her tone lightened. 'I suppose I should offer you a drink, but do you think you could carry another one?'

'Madam!' He thrust out his chest. 'You put the plumb line down, an' you'll find there's another three feet afore it touches bottom.'

'Oh, Paul.' She pushed at him with her hand. 'Well, what is it to be? The usual?'

'The usual; I rarely mix my drinks.'

'I have tonight. I've had a little of everything.'

She walked from him towards a cocktail cabinet standing at the side of the fireplace, and added airily, 'And it makes you feel nice; you forget everything for a time.'

It wasn't until she brought the glasses back to the fireplace that he questioned her last remark. 'What have you to forget, Jinny?'

'You'd be surprised . . . Is that right?' She handed him the glass of whisky.

'Oh, that's a dose, that's a very good dose. What have you got there?'

'The same.'

'Tut! tut! tut! You are mixing them. Well, here's to you, Jinny.' He raised his glass.

'And to you, Paul.' She drank. And to you, Paul. And to you, Paul. And to you, Paul. The words were dizzying in her head. Everything for you, Paul. Everything for you, Paul. All my life for you, Paul. Nobody else but you, Paul. Here's to you, Paul. Damn Bett. What has she ever done to deserve you? Has she ever given you a day's happiness? And she wants to get rid of you. Why hadn't she ever said to her, 'All right, get rid of him; I'm waiting . . . why? Was it just because she had been brought up with her and they were like sisters? Perhaps. Perhaps. But it was more than that; it was the knowledge that Bett needed an anchor; on her own she would go to the dogs. Well, she wasn't on her own and she was still going to the dogs, wasn't she? So to hell with Bett.

'What is it, Jinny? You look so sad all of a sudden. Come on, drink up.' He put his arm round her shoulders, then drained his glass. 'Go on, finish it up and don't look so sad. What is it? What's troubling you, Jinny? Tell me.'

She stared into his big face, into the brown eyes that at this moment looked so kind. He had asked what was troubling her and she gave him the answer. She gave him the answer that she had dreamed of giving him for years and years. The dream had had no place in her working day; it had been successfully covered by Bett, and loyalty, and long absence. But now it was night again, and her body was warm with a mixture of cherry brandy, sherry, advocaat, and whisky, and she fell against him, her arms about him now, her face buried in his neck, crying, 'Oh, Paul! Oh, Paul!' And she pressed her body to his as she did in her dreams, pressed it until she felt the warmth of his flesh.

He was well aware that he was carrying a heavy load, but he had always been able to carry a great amount of whisky, and even when he was very drunk there was always a small section of his mind seemingly immune from the influence of the spirit, and now this section shouted at him, screamed at him. God blast it, man, not with Jinny. No! No! But the shock of the revelation of her feeling for him dulled the voice, yet even while he responded to her it kept crying, 'Give over. Stop it, for Christ's sake, man.' But he held her more tightly. She wants me. Blast it, she's always wanted me. I can see now. She wants loving. She's lonely . . . What about Ivy? Oh . . . Ivy! Yes, Ivy. But she's lonely. God damn it, she's lonely, an' I didn't know, I never guessed. Thirty-nine, she is, and I'd like to bet me bottom dollar still a virgin . . . Stop it, you'll regret it for the rest of your life. Stop it. Her mouth was in his. Stop it. Stop before it's too late, you're both drunk. Isn't Ivy enough? There's the morning, as Maggie says; don't forget there's the morning.

With a thrust he pushed her from him and she staggered back as if indeed she was drunk; and now turning and resting his arms on the mantelpiece and dropping his head on to them he muttered, 'I'm sorry, Jinny, I'm sorry. I shouldn't have done that . . .' That was the line to take, take the blame. Make it easy for her. It was a dreadful thing to throw a woman off. He had thrown Bett off. Aye, yes, but for a different reason altogether. There was no comparison. He said aloud again, 'Aw, Jinny, I'm sorry, I'm drunk; that's what it is, I'm drunk.' When he received no answer he turned slowly round to see her sitting with her face in her hands, and he went to her and dropping on his knees he said, 'Jinny, Jinny, forgive me. I'm sorry. I'm so blasted drunk I've lost all sense of shame. Look at me, Jinny.'

'Oh, Paul, Paul. It was me, me . . . It was me.'

'What d'you mean . . . you? Don't you believe it. Don't you believe it for a minute. I've had it in mind for a long time, even before . . . even before you had that done.' He touched her nose with his fingers and her tears ran over his hands. 'You're so good, Jinny, so nice, so nice inside. Will you forgive me and forget it?'

Her head drooped low onto her chest.

'We'll both likely have forgotten it by tomorrow morning, anyway. Your mixing your drinks made your load as big as mine, but I'm more used to it. Come on now, get off to bed and I'll let myself

73

out.' He rose from his knees, then pulled her up to face him. And now he said softly, 'Can I kiss you, Jinny? It'll be the last time, for I'd better not play about with this.'

She gave him no answer, nor did she move when his face loomed nearer, but she shivered when his mouth touched hers. Otherwise she made no response.

'Goodnight, my dear. Try to forget it, eh?'

He left her standing limp in the middle of the room, and when he reached the drive he unbuttoned his great-coat which he had just done up, unloosened his scarf, then slackened his collar and tie. He felt he was about to go up in flames. My God, that was a near thing . . . Jinny! Jinny! He'd been a blasted blind fool, hadn't he? But how was he to guess at a thing like that. And she wasn't drunk, not even tipsy. She'd had four drinks since seven o'clock last night. Four drinks in seven hours. It wasn't drink that had made her give way. It was hard, even now, to associate passion with Jinny, yet she had held him as even Ivy had never held him. In those brief moments she had poured herself over him . . . Aw, Jinny, Jinny. Well, if he was so sorry for her why hadn't he responded, gone the whole hog, for she had needed him; at least she needed something, someone . . . no, not someone, or anyone . . . him. Why hadn't he seen it before? All these years she had been handmaiden to Bett. Was it because of him? He saw again the look in her eyes, bare, stark; offering him all she had, all she was; and from Jinny that would be no small thing, even without the passion thrown in . . . God! One thing he was thankful for, she had a place of her own. It would have been unbearable if it had happened in the house. Yet somehow he felt that it would never have happened in his house. He wished daylight was here, for when he was sober all this would be blurred and would fade like a dream. But if it didn't, what then? Well, he'd have to keep up the game, the game of shouldering the blame, of being a bit of a skunk, and he'd have to play it well if things were to continue as they had always been between him and Jinny.

As he walked down the slippery hill he realised that he wouldn't have to wait for daylight to sober him up – he felt stark sober now.

PART FOUR

BETT

It was towards the end of February, on a Monday morning, that Paul, looking at his engagements for the week, decided to visit Ivy that night because there didn't look much chance of him having any free time until the week-end, and he didn't want her to sit at home each evening waiting for him.

Tomorrow night there was a Conservative dinner; on Wednesday he had to go to a medical meeting in Newcastle, which meant him getting back late for surgery and doing his visiting afterwards. He could have got over this by asking John Price to fill in for him, but he didn't like to impose; John was too willing. Of course, being one of a four-way partnership gave him an easier time. Still, that wasn't the point. Then Thursday was clinic day and there wouldn't be a spare minute between getting out of bed until getting into it again . . . And Friday. Well, Friday was the day for sweeping up so to speak, getting things tidy for the week-end if he hoped to have a half day clear on Saturday, and he wanted Saturday clear. He wanted the week-end clear so that he could get down to some study, revising. It was only ten days before the Board sat, and he wasn't sure what questions might be thrown at him. He was worried about going before the Board, there was no use hoodwinking himself.

By the second post that morning a letter came from Doctor Beresford. Elsie gave it to him when he called in from his rounds to phone the hospital about getting a patient in. It was the first letter he had received from the doctor and it puzzled him, puzzled him greatly. The letter was written in old-world phraseology, and to the effect that Doctor Beresford would like him to call at his house at seven o'clock that evening. The matter for discussion was something that warranted a private meeting, otherwise the letter would not have been written. The whole tone was that of an order, and it both angered him and made him apprehensive, for he linked it with Friday and the selection committee.

During the rest of the morning the letter loomed large in his mind, and one period he almost phoned Beresford; his intention being to say he would be unable to call on him this evening and would he state his business now. But this action, he knew, would be nothing more or less than the outcome of his fear . . . But fear of what?

In the afternoon of that particular Monday Bett went to see Jenny.

Over the past weeks Jenny had curtailed her visits to the house. She had made various excuses for her absence and some of them seemed very thin. When she ran out of them altogether she decided that she must do what she should have done weeks ago, get herself away from the agonising proximity of Paul, for once having dropped the barrier of sisterly affection, try as she might, she couldn't raise it again.

On the day after Boxing Day he had come with the others to her house-warming, and, taking her aside, he had apologised, telling her that everything about last night was a bit hazy, but, having remembered bits here and there, he felt he had overstepped the mark and would she forgive him?

She had wanted to believe that this was really how he had thought it had happened. Oh, how she wanted to believe it to ease the shame; not of what her feelings had led her to, but of what they had not achieved. If only he had loved her, just that once, she would have lived on it for the rest of her life . . . or would she? Would it have been the beginning of something unbearable? Because in the light of day it was unbearable that she should have an association with Bett's husband. If only she could have believed him her mind would have been easier, but knowing his innate kindness, she had no proof but that he remembered everything as it happened, and was helping her to shield herself.

And this personal matter was not the only worry she had. She was and always had been very, very fond of Lorna, and she knew there was something wrong with the girl. The boisterous enthusiasm, the heritage of all youth, had fallen from her, leaving her quiet and tired looking, or glum and stubborn, the latter always when in the company of her mother.

And there was Bett. She felt that in some way she had betrayed Bett. In moments of logical thinking she knew that this was ridiculous, more so when she gave thought to the fact of the number of times that Bett must have been unfaithful to Paul. You don't go out often with a man like James Knowles and expect to eat tea and buns, so to speak.

Anyway, she would soon be far away from them all . . . although what she was going to do by herself in a hotel in Switzerland she didn't know. She could have taken a holiday in England but she wanted to put distance, long distance, between herself and those nearest to her.

She was actually packing her last case when the doorbell rang, and the sound made her hope it was Paul, then hope it wasn't. But on opening the door and being confronted by Bett, the colour flooded guiltily to her face. She saw at once that her cousin was definitely agitated, worked up to a high pitch about something. It was in her manner, in her walk, and the fact that she didn't come to the point straight away. Also she didn't look well, she looked as if she had a heavy cold. Her face was red and her voice was hoarse as she said, 'Well, if Mohammed won't go to the mountain . . .'

Jenny followed her into the sitting-room, saying, 'I'm sorry I haven't been round these last few days but I've been so busy. I've had to keep trotting back and forwards to Newcastle about passports and this, that, and the other.'

'You're lucky you can trot back and forwards to Newcastle about this, that, and the other.'

'Aw, Bett, don't keep on. I offered you the car.'

'I didn't want the car, I told you, I wanted the money. But looking back now, I could have taken the car and sold it, couldn't I? I'm a damned fool.'

She turned from Jenny and walking the length of the room looked out on to the tangled garden that surrounded the house before she said, 'You've always done everything in your power to tie me to that house and him, haven't you?'

'Don't talk rot, Bett. I've only thought what was best for Lorna and you, and I didn't want to be the one to give you the chance or egg you on to do something foolish.'

'Foolish! That's funny, that's a ha-ha-ha. Do you know something?' Now she swung round and walked quickly towards Jenny. 'It's the do-gooders of this world that cause all the trouble. If I'd left him years ago we'd both have had some chance of happiness. But no, the respected Doctor Higgins couldn't bear the thought of anyone walking out on him. And then there was you, yarping on all the time, telling me that my place was with him and Lorna. Well, now, as you're going off tomorrow . . . it is tomorrow, isn't it?' Jenny didn't answer and Bett went on, 'I thought I'd tell you that your efforts have all been in vain, because very shortly Fellburn will know Doctor Higgins no more; neither will the house. I've always told you that I'd get him where I wanted him, haven't I? Well, the day has come.'

'Don't talk wild, Bett. What's the matter with you?'

'I'm trying to tell you what's the matter with me.' She went and stood by the hearth, and from there, with her head resting almost on her shoulder, she said, 'You were always for the big fellow, weren't you?'

Jenny's heart seemed to stop and she muttered faintly, 'I don't know what you mean.'

'Oh, you know what I mean all right. He could do no wrong in your eyes; even when I was left at the other end of the landing you

77

thought it was no more than I deserved, now didn't you? . . . I'd been a naughty girl.'

Jenny drew in a long breath, partly of relief; then slowly and flatly, she said, 'Look, Bett, I've tried for years not to take sides, you know I have. I've tried to be fair.'

'Oh, yes, I know you have.' Bett flicked her fingers in the air. 'Oh, you've been fair . . . Yes, and all the time you've been blaming me for the way things were. I was the wrongdoer. Well now, listen to this . . . But perhaps' – she moved her head in a sweeping half-circle – 'it may not be news to you, you may even be in his confidence.'

Jenny waited, moving one dry lip over the other; she stared at Bett and waited.

'Is it news to you that he's got a woman, that he's been keeping a woman for years, is it?'

The pain went through her like a red-hot blade; she even took a sharp shuddering breath from the impact.

'Well, did you know?'

Jenny made a slight movement with her head; then walking to a chair she sat down.

'And you know who it is?' Bett made a quick grab at another chair and, pulling it forward, sat on the edge and bent towards Jenny. 'Ivy Tate.'

'Ivy! You mean Ivy who was . . . ?'

'Yes, Ivy who was . . . Ivy who was working in my house for three years. What do you think of that? It must have been going on under my nose. I . . . I' – she squared her lips and showed her small white teeth clenched tight – 'I could kill him, I could throttle him. Ivy Tate, a common, cheap, sloppy looking individual, Ivy Tate. But then, when you come to think, would you expect him to choose higher than the likes of her? As I've said before and to his face, he's got his scrap-iron, rag-gathering grandfather in him. Why do you think he wouldn't go to the other end of the town and set up practice? Because he's not at ease with civilised people, that's why. Under the veneer of the doctor he's more at home with the Bogs End crowd, and the likes of Maggie Swan, his dear, dear Maggie. Well, I've told her where she can get off, too. She's going, even before he does . . . Oh, I'll see to that . . . Maggie! Maggie Swan . . .'

'What . . . what proof have you?' Jenny's head was lowered now; her words were slow; she felt tired, weary. She also had an odd feeling of being naïve, even stupid. A big virile man like Paul. Of course he would have to have someone; all these years he would have to have someone. She hadn't thought of it that way. Well, she was a nurse and she should have, shouldn't she? She'd been a fool . . . all these years he'd been having a woman and yet he'd pushed her away.

'Proof! I've got proof all right. Three times recently I've phoned the club to pass on a call, and each time they said he'd been left some

78

time, and on each of these occasions there were no calls on the surgery board, and yet he never got in until eleven or later. I never thought much about it at first, then something that James said . . .'

'Oh, James! If you're going to believe James Knowles—'

'Yes, I believe James Knowles. I'd believe him before I'd believe the big fellow. But that's no matter; I can believe my own eyes, can't I? You see, I've watched him, I've followed him. What James said was quite innocent. "Paul's got a patient out of town," he said, "Beckley way, up Moor Lane. I've seen him up that way a few times." It was Moor Lane that struck a bell. I'd never been to Moor Lane, or Beckley, but I remembered Ivy Tate lived there and that he used to go visiting her husband. He attended him for over a year, and it was after that that he brought her to the house. Then he must have felt he'd better go careful. It was about the time that he thought of going in for the assistant physician's post and he began to work like stink. So back home she goes supposedly to be married, and from then he visits her. She's on his books – I looked her card up, but there's not an ailment down there. So I watched him; I watched him three nights last week. I waited for his car to come out of the drive. They were cold nights but I wasn't cold; it's a wonder he didn't see me glowing red. I tell you I could kill him.' Her hands were like claws now grabbing at the air.

'What are you going to do?' asked Jenny dully.

'What am I going to do? I'm going to wait and watch the goose being cooked. I lit the fire this very morning. There's one thing he wants more than anything in life, and that's to get that hospital post. Well, I've put paid to that for him.'

'No, no, Bett.' Jenny bounced up. 'You couldn't do anything to harm him in that way.'

'Can't I? Can't I? Just you wait and see.'

'But what do you hope to gain? You'll be cooking your own goose while you're cooking his. Don't you see? If he hasn't got a practice and a house, what's going to happen to you?'

'Do you know he was offered twenty thousand pounds for the house by Pearsons? They want to put up another refrigeration plant. And then the town wants to extend the Technical School, so they're playing against each other. He turned down Pearsons' offer of twenty thousand for that rambling, freezing mausoleum. But he'll reconsider now; oh, he'll reconsider all right.'

'But what is twenty thousand pounds if he hasn't got a job, Bett?'

'He won't only have twenty thousand. He's got ten thousand coming next year from a big insurance his father started for him. Then the old boy left him about fifteen thousand in shares which must have doubled by now. But it isn't only the money I'm after. No, it's to see him stripped, that's what I want. I've promised myself for years I'd see him out of that damned house. I didn't think I'd be able

79

to get him out of the practice though, but after a divorce through another woman, and her a patient . . . Well. Not to mention years of cruelty . . . I picture him at nights standing before the medical council . . . God, with his big head you'd have thought he'd have had that much about him not to take up with a patient. Well, there's one thing I know, he won't be going to his dear Ivy tonight, I've made other arrangements for him.'

'What kind of arrangements?'

'Oh, you just wait and see, as I said.'

'You're mad, Bett. And what about Lorna in all this?'

'What about her?'

'How is she going to react?'

'I wouldn't know, Jenny, and I don't care very much. That shocks you too, doesn't it? She's been on her high horse for weeks . . .'

'. . . And you know why she's been on her high horse, you know why, Bett?'

'What do you mean?' Bett's face had had a vicious look, and now of a sudden there was superimposed on it a look of fear.

'You know what I mean, I don't need to go into it. I don't want to make you feel worse than you are now, but for God's sake, Bett, why don't you grow up?'

Bett let out a long, slow breath; then getting up from the chair she took a step backwards before she spoke. 'You know sometimes, Jenny, I hate you more than I do him. Do you know that?'

Jenny shuddered; she shuddered not only at the statement and what it implied but at the tone in which it was said and at the look on her cousin's face.

Bett now turned from her, and as she went to the door she said, 'I hope you have a nice holiday, Jenny. I don't expect to see you at the house again, nor do I expect you to interfere in my affairs. And don't think you can do anything to alter this situation, because the wheels are already in motion. I saw to that before I told you; I wanted you to have something to take away with you.' She turned before she went out of the room and bounced her head once in Jenny's direction, which gave emphasis to her last words. Then she banged the door after her.

Jenny sat down again, groping at the chair as she did so. Dear, dear God. Bett was mad, mad with hate and frustration. What had she done? What was this thing she was going to do which would ruin Paul? She tried to think of all she had said. Platitudes, terrifying platitudes, such as: she had cooked his goose. But what actually had she done? She said she had made sure that he wouldn't get the hospital post, but how had she gone about it? Had she told someone about Ivy, someone in the town who had power? Or was she only bluffing? . . . No. No, she wasn't bluffing. And whoever she had told would spring it on Paul.

If he could only be warned. Perhaps he could make a stand of some sort. In her heart she doubted it. What could anyone do against such hate? And Bett had said there was nothing she could do, she was contemptuous of her . . . Well, she would see about that; hate was contagious.

The next minute she was running towards the hall where, grabbing up the phone, she dialled the house. When she heard Elsie's precise tones at the other end she said, 'This is Jenny, Elsie. Is the doctor in?'

'No, Jenny, he's out on his rounds.'

'Have you any idea when he'll be back?'

'Oh, not until five.'

'Elsie, listen. I must find him. Can you give me the addresses where he's likely to call this afternoon? And don't let on . . . Do you know what I mean?'

'Yes, Jenny, yes. I know what you mean. Just a minute.' After a pause her voice came again, saying, '124 Fowler's Road, a Mr Smith there. 26 The Avenue, child name of Bailey. Got that? Then 14 Preston Mews, a Mrs Caldwell. Then there's four calls in Creasy House, Bogs End. The big block of flats, you know. I'll just give you the numbers: 8, 17, 24, and 25. Got that?'

'Yes, thanks, Elsie. And listen . . . Don't . . . don't let on to anyone I've phoned. But when he comes in ask him if he's seen me. And if he hasn't, tell him to come straight round here, will you? Tell him it's very important.'

'I'll do that, Jenny.'

'Thanks, Elsie. Good-bye.'

Jenny now phoned for a taxi, and when it came she gave the driver the address of 124 Fowler's Road.

It was nearly half-an-hour later when she reached the block of flats. The doctor had been and gone from all the previous addresses, but when she enquired at the first flat she was told he hadn't been yet. Also, that if he didn't get his calls in at the flats in the morning he often didn't come until after evening surgery; that was unless it was urgent.

This last information set Jenny a poser. It was now four o'clock. If he wasn't in the habit of visiting the flats until after surgery where would he go? Not to the club in the afternoon; and he rarely returned home until five, when he would have a cup of tea before starting with the evening patients . . . Ivy Tate's. The significance brought her teeth on to her lower lip, and as she stood pondering she became aware that the taxi driver was watching her. Under his stare she considered for another minute. She couldn't go to Ivy's place, she couldn't. To see them even standing together would be a form of torture, for in this she had to agree with Bett, he had let himself down. Yet where would she find him if not there? But one thing was dominant in her mind, pressing everything else aside at the moment: she couldn't tolerate the idea of his exposure being sprung on him. It was going to be dreadful enough in any case, but if he was warned he might be able to put up something of a defence. She had very little hope of the latter, but the important thing was to let him know that the ice was cracking beneath his feet and that all that meant so much to him, his practice and his house, was going to be swamped. There crept in the thought that Ivy Tate might matter too, but this she disregarded. Getting into the taxi again, she said hastily, 'Moor Lane. Do you know where it is?'

'Yes, I know it; it's on the outskirts, near Wheatley's Farm.'

Fifteen minutes later the car bumped its way up the narrow lane, and when abruptly it emerged from the shelter of the bushes on to the wide grass verge she whispered hoarsely, 'Stop! Stop!'

She sat staring out of the window. There was no other car ahead of them, nor to the side of the house, and further on was a dead end, but in the garden beyond the gate Ivy Tate was standing. She had apparently been weeding. Jenny, as if unable to move, watched her open the gate and cross the grass. Then she was standing opposite the open window, facing her. Her face had lost all its high colour; it looked greyish, her eyes were stretched wide and she was visibly trembling as she said, 'Why! Miss – Miss Jenny . . . Is anything wrong?'

Jenny now looked at the back of the driver and then to Ivy again before she asked, 'May I come in a minute, I'd like a word with you.'

'Yes, yes.'

As she got out of the car the driver said, 'You want me to wait?'

'Please.'

'OK.' He nodded at her.

Jenny had hardly entered the bungalow before Ivy, closing the door, turned and whispered under her breath, 'What is it? Something's wrong . . . The doctor?'

'I . . . I thought he might be here. I have to see him, it's important.'

'You knew a-about him coming here?'

'No . . . I mean, not before today.' Jenny watched Ivy put her two hands up to her face and press them against her cheeks, until her mouth formed a button. 'Something's happened. What is it?'

'I've got to find Pa . . . the Doctor. Are you expecting him?'

'No. No. At least not yet. But look.' She thrust out her hands now towards Jenny. 'Tell me, tell me what's happened. I'm concerned, aren't I? It's about me? For God's sake tell me, please.'

Jenny looked at this homely, ordinary-looking young woman. In attractiveness she didn't seem to have anything more than she herself had, at least now, except that she was plumpish and a little younger. Yet this was the woman Paul had chosen to come to night after night. For how long? It was two years since she had left the house, and as Bett said it must have started long before that. For years Jenny had known she had been jealous of Bett, but she had never let it get the upper hand; in fact, she had hardly let the emotion breathe. She had told herself it was enough to see Paul now and again, to know that he was fond of her and appreciated her presence in the house. And sanctimoniously she had imagined it was part of her path in life to ease the tension in which he lived. But as she looked at Ivy she knew no such restraint on her feelings, and she cried bitterly within herself: I should have been in your place, I should, I should. And if I'd known as much as I know now I would have been too. As she stared at Ivy there returned to her mind the incident on Boxing Night and she became hot yet again with the shame of his refusal. He had known all right – oh, she was more convinced than ever now that he had known – and he had refused her because he had been faithful to this woman.

'Don't look at me like that, Miss Jenny. I did what I had to do; he needed me and me him. I was lonely, but he was more so. If it hadn't been me it would have been somebody else. I made him happy in a way. Just in a way, the only way I knew. But I also knew that there would be an end to it.' Her voice had lost its tremor and sounded calm now, and she walked towards a chair and, sitting down, she motioned Jenny to a seat opposite. Then she asked, 'How did you find out?'

'She knows; she's been watching.'

'Oh, no.' Ivy groaned out the words, and her head sunk on to her chest.

As Jenny looked at this beaten woman she remembered she had always liked Ivy, she had always got on with her, and she endeavoured now to waive her personal feelings. Leaning towards her, she said hastily, 'She means trouble, Ivy. I don't think she's quite right in her mind where he's concerned. She's going to use her knowledge to stop him getting the hospital post. But what is worse, she'll make a case of it, proving that you're a patient of his, and then his career'll be finished.'

'Oh, my God!' Ivy began to rock herself, her head still down, her body swaying backwards and forwards as if trying to ease a physical agony. Then slowly the rocking stopped and, lifting her head, she looked at Jenny and said, 'She'd have to have proof of that, wouldn't she? I mean legal proof. Has she had us watched, privately?'

'No, no, I don't think so. She just came herself.'

Ivy now straightened her shoulders. 'You have to have proof in these things, eye-witness accounts so to speak. I could say he had been attending me for my allergy . . . I've got an allergy. Certain foods I eat bring me out in great weals and I feel off colour.' She stared at Jenny for a moment in silence before saying, quietly, 'It may not be too late; there is something I can do. Would you wait a few minutes more?'

Jenny inclined her head, and Ivy turned slowly away and went into the bedroom, closing the door after her.

Jenny looked about the room. The furniture was cheap and

ordinary, there was not a vestige of taste in anything; the only comfortable thing in the room was the couch. It would be. Her mind tried to move away from the couch and its comfort but failed. Even when she had been running helter-skelter round the town trying to find him, there had been in her a feeling that the whole thing was nasty, that he had let himself down. Ivy Tate, who had been a servant in his house. She knew these things happened and always would. It was more prevalent today than ever, but she hadn't associated Paul with promiscuity, and if she had she would have imagined him picking someone in his own class. Yet had he taken a wife out of his own class? Bett liked to think of herself as having been brought up superior, but the truth was she had been an ordinary working girl, a typist, not old enough when she met Paul to have reached the post of secretary. And then, when she came to think of it, had he, in taking Ivy, stepped so far out of his own class when only two generations ago his grandfather had been a man of Bogs End? There was a lot of truth in what Bett said, and his association with Ivy Tate proved it.

She began to walk round the room as if to get away from her critical thinking. She didn't want to think like this about him. It was as if she hated him too, and she had to admit that the relationship between him and this woman wasn't as nasty as she would like to think. There was really nothing nasty about Ivy Tate. In the local idiom, she was a nice lass; you could see it in her face.

When the door opened and Ivy came out of the bedroom she expected to see signs of her crying, but her face wasn't wet, nor were her eyes red, but there was in her expression a look of painful resignation, and it touched Jenny more than anything else could have done.

'Will you give him this yourself?' She held out a letter. 'And if he should still try to come, stop him, will you? Because it'll be no use. An' the less he's seen coming here the better.'

'I . . . I doubt if I'll be able to stop him coming, Ivy; he'll want to see you.'

'I've . . . I've explained it all in the letter. I won't be here. An' when I do come back things'll be different. It . . . it won't be any use him coming then. It's all in there.' She pointed to the letter Jenny was holding.

The two women looked at each other; then Jenny said softly, 'I'm sorry, Ivy.' And she was sorry, really sorry.

'So am I.' Ivy's lids blinked rapidly. 'But I'm not surprised at this, I'm only surprised it went on so long.' She moved closer to Jenny until she had to look up at her, and her slow words expressed the pain she was feeling. 'I'd sooner die than anything should happen to him, anything, and through me.'

Jenny at this moment felt very small. She had imagined that in hiding her love for Paul all these years she had been doing something noble. She had imagined there were only two people in the world who really knew Paul, and loved him: one was herself, and the other, Maggie Swan. Lorna's love she didn't count; it was that of a child for its father. But this ordinary woman's love, she saw, was something big. It was an utterly unselfish love. And this was borne out as Ivy said softly, 'He's . . . he's very fond of you. Will you do what you can for him? He'll need somebody calm like, for if he loses his temper with her God knows what'll happen.'

Calm like. She was very far from being calm like. When Ivy turned towards the door she followed her, and she paused in front of her on the step and said, 'I'll do my best, Ivy. Good-bye.'

'Good-bye, Jenny.' Ivy now omitted the 'Miss'.

Jenny was aware that the door closed immediately behind her, and as she went towards the waiting car she had the impression that Ivy was standing with her face pressed tight against it.

In a few minutes they were on the main road again. 'Where to now?' asked the driver laconically.

'Romfield House,' she said. Bett had told her in plain words that she wouldn't be expected there again, but she was going.

It was a quarter to five when she reached the house, and even as she stood on the pavement paying off the driver the sound of the raised voices penetrated the thick walls. She did not ring the front-door bell but went into the courtyard, and there, immediately, Bett's high screaming tone met her, answered by Maggie's thick, loud, coarse twang. When she passed the kitchen window she saw Paul's back blotting out the room and its occupants. She let herself in through the waiting-room door. There was no-one about – Elsie had two hours off in the afternoon and wouldn't be in until five when the patients started to arrive. Quickly crossing the waiting-room, she went into the private hall, and here the voices filled the house, seeming to make it vibrate with their anger.

'Quiet, woman! Quiet! Do you hear me?'

'Don't tell me to be quiet. I've told you, she's going, and now, this very minute.'

'And how many more times have I to tell you she'll go when I say, and not before. And that won't be as long as I'm in this house.'

'Ha! Ha! Ha! God Almighty man makes big joke . . . As long as you're in this house! Well, let me tell you, big fellow, your time's running out, and fast.'

'You're crazy, woman. There's been times in the past when I've doubted your sanity, but now . . .'

'Crazy, am I? Well, we'll see who's the craziest before the next twenty-four hours is over. But the point in question at the moment, doc-tor, is that I'm dismissing my cook. I'M DISMISSING HER HERE AND NOW. Get that into your thick skull. And you, or no-one else, is going to stop me. Her time, like yours, is short anyway, but I'm going to have the pleasure of seeing her going through that

85

door, her bust flat. And it'll be the first and last time, won't it, Maggie, for you've got the most fluctuating bust in the human race, haven't you?'

'I know what you're after suggestin', Madam, but I've told you afore I take nothin' away up me jumper. But if I did it wouldn't be yours I was takin', an' that I've told you afore an' all. An' I'll tell you this, I'll come back to the door each mornin' and himself will let me in, an' I won't stop comin' till he says with his own lips that I've got to. Not that it's any pleasure workin' in this house. Sheer hell it's been for years now, for you're no more fit to be a doctor's wife and have a place like this than any slut from Bogs End. But then you were born and bred not a kick in the backside from the place itself, an' you went to what was in my day the council school, an' you stand there darin' to put on your airs to me . . .'

At the sound of splintering china Jenny was impelled into the kitchen, there to see Maggie pressed against the fridge door and to her side the shattered remains of a heavy glass water jug which had fortunately missed her and hit the wall.

At the centre of the kitchen Paul stood holding Bett. He was gripping her shoulder with one hand, while with the other he slapped her face.

Jenny herself screamed as she ran in between them, and when she caught the deflected blow from his open palm he stopped, but still held Bett, who, her face now scarlet with inward rage and the slapping, continued to kick out at him and claw his jacket – which was as far as she could reach the way he was holding her – as if bent on tearing him to shreds. Like an enraged bull he swung her about and, gripping her around the waist, hauled her ignominiously from the room, across the hall and into the drawing-room. There, throwing her bodily onto the couch, he stood over her, glaring down at her as he panted for breath.

Bett lay still now, rigidly still. Her eyes and lips looked colourless and stood out from the rest of her face, and the hate that was in her came up like vapour and enveloped him.

When he could speak he said, 'This is the finish, do you hear me? It's the finish. I'm divorcing you.'

Jenny, standing with her back to the closed door of the drawing-room, could not see Bett's face but she heard the strange noise she made. It was an unreal, inhuman sound. Then she saw her head slowly appear as she pulled herself upright on the couch.

Bett hadn't taken her eyes from Paul, and now they bored into him, seeming to screw each word home. And they were more impressive because they were spoken quietly. 'You! You are going to divorce me? Oh, no. No, you've got it wrong. It's me who's going to divorce you. I'm not only going to divorce you, I'm going to ruin you. I always said

I would and that's just what I'm going to do. The wheels are already moving and you can do nothing to stop them. This is final, final, big fellow, do you hear? Oh, you've got something coming to you, and I won't spoil it by telling you.'

Glaring back at her he wondered if she really had become unbalanced. He imagined that if she'd had any real evidence on which she could get a divorce, such as knowledge of Ivy, she would have spurted it out. He didn't give her credit for enough hate to make her diabolically cunning. All this was an act coupled with wishful thinking. But there was one thing clear in his mind: he couldn't go on. A little more of this and he might do her an injury. He said now, 'Who divorces who doesn't matter as long as it comes about.'

'You think so? Oh, but I see it differently. As I told you, you're going to learn a lot within the next few hours. And in a very short space of time I'll see that you own just what you stand up in. You'll be so fleeced you'll feel the wind through your clothes. And you'll have no chance to earn more.'

No chance to earn more? What was she up to? Unblinking, he returned her glare before he said, 'Well, you must remember that if I have no practice I have no money.' He sounded tired now.

'You'll have what this house brings and all your other odds and ends. Oh, I've got it all worked out. It'll be enough to keep Lorna and me going for a while.'

'Lorna?' It was a question.

'Yes, Lorna. You'd forgotten about her, hadn't you? Lorna will be going with me, for you've no claim on her, have you? You won't, like an ordinary father, be able to claim her for part of the time.'

'Shut up!' He bent nearer to her, and she, thrusting her face towards him, cried, 'No, I'm not going to shut up, I'm going to bring it into the open, air it at last. Say it, YELL IT, SCREAM IT . . . Lorna isn't yours . . . That's what's tormented your load of flesh, isn't it? It's been like sandpaper under your vest for years, never letting you rest . . . She isn't yours. You were a bit puzzled by the look of her from when she was born, weren't you? And, of course, she was a premature baby, she had to be. And then the day when Arthur Dressell came looking for me and you saw him holding her, you knew then, didn't you? Arthur's mother's maiden name was Haiyakawa. Very Japanese, don't you think? Anyway, he gave me a baby, and that was something you couldn't do; for all your brawn you're as ineffectual as a—'

As his hands gripped her throat Jenny reached him. Silently now she pulled and tore at him, and when at last she got his hands free they both staggered back, and she fell lopsidedly into the armchair. Remaining where she had fallen, she watched him with his hands held out before him, as if they had been burnt in some way, walking across the room.

When she saw the door close she looked at Bett. She was lying with her hands on her neck gasping at the air. Slowly Jenny got up and went to her. Her body was trembling, so she could hardly stand. As if she herself had almost been choked she gasped, 'Why . . . why did you have to—?'

'Don't . . . you . . . start. You . . .' Bett suddenly closed her eyes and put her hand across her stomach. Leaning forward she said feebly, 'I'm going to be sick.'

Without a word Jenny hastily helped her from the couch and out of the room and up the stairs into the bathroom, and there she held her head while she vomited.

A few minutes later, when they were in the bedroom, Jenny said, 'Come on, get your things off and get into bed, and I'll get you a drink.'

'Leave me alone.' Bett pushed her to one side. 'I told you you weren't wanted, didn't I?'

For answer Jenny said, 'You'll feel better lying down.'

Bett slapped her hands away. 'I can take my own clothes off, just leave me alone. For God's sake! I'm all right. Don't you worry about me.' She wagged her head airily now.

Jenny looked down on her, and her voice held a perplexed note as she said, 'I wonder why I always have, and still do, because you're not worth it.' On this she turned quickly away and went out of the room.

When she went into the kitchen Maggie was sitting at the table, her head resting on her hand, and she looked slowly up, and after a moment said, 'I never thought I'd see this day. He's broken, broken entirely.'

Jenny didn't know how much Maggie had heard, but very likely she knew it all. Maggie, like many a privileged servant, gave herself the licence to hover outside doors.

'I'm worried. I'm worried to the soul of me. An' I would leave this minute if I thought it would do any good, but who will he have with me gone? And then there's yourself off the morrow. Oh, I wish you weren't goin'.' She moved her head in wide sweeps. 'I wish to God you weren't goin'. I've a feeling on me that always spells trouble. I'm worried, Miss Jenny, I'm worried.'

'Where is he, Maggie?'

'In his surgery. He wouldn't let me near him. He's not fit to work the night.'

'Would you mind making me a pot of tea, Maggie?'

Maggie didn't ask who the tea was for; she simply answered flatly, 'I'll do that.'

As Jenny went into the waiting-room she saw Elsie behind the partition at the far side of the room, where the patients' filing cabinets were kept. Already there were four people standing in a queue waiting for the numbered round discs that would ensure them their correct turn.

When she knocked on the surgery door and received no answer she opened it slowly, to see Paul sitting behind the desk. His hands were resting on the arms of the chair, the fingers hanging limply over the edge. She had always thought that he carried his age well, not looking anything near his forty-three years, but at this moment he looked fifty and over. She came slowly forward and sat in the patient's chair. Except for her hat, which had been knocked off when Paul accidentally struck her in the kitchen, she was still in her outdoor clothes. Her handbag was again in her hand, and inside of it was the letter, but how, she asked herself, could she give it to him after what had happened. Yet perhaps this was the best time; let it all come together. One shock might cancel out the other, at least in part. She said softly, 'Can't you get out of surgery tonight? Maggie could tell them you've been called away. Or why not phone Doctor Price?'

He stared at her for a full minute, and then asked, 'Did you know about Lorna, Jenny?'

She dropped her gaze from his.

'All the time?'

Her head moved lower still.

'You made a monkey out of me, too?'

'No, Paul. No.' Her head was up. 'I couldn't do anything, it was too late. I didn't know before you were married, but afterwards I remembered she had been friendly with Arthur Dressell when he was a student, and when he went back to France, where his people were, she was in a state. Then almost immediately . . . there was you and . . . and she . . .'

'And she chased me. Say it, Jinny. Huh! How that girl chased me . . . Did she ever mention it to you that she knew I was on to her when Lorna came early?'

'No.'

'I love Lorna, Jinny. Do you think that strange?'

'No, Paul, no.'

'It's funny but I couldn't bear the sight of her after I saw Dressell. Then one day, she was about two at the time, she cried when I pushed her away, and after that, well . . .' He brought his limp fingers into the palms of his hands but seemed to have no strength to clench them. 'What will happen when she tells her, Jinny?'

'She'll still love you. She'll always love you.' She did not say she hates her mother. 'And you'll be able to see her. She can't stop you from seeing her, no matter what she says.'

He rose heavily from the seat, and, standing with his hand on the corner of the desk, he said, 'First thing tomorrow I'll see Parkins and get the proceedings started.'

'Paul!' She glanced up at him. 'Bett knows.'

'Knows?' He screwed up his tired face at her. 'Knows what?'

Jenny could not continue to look at him as she said under her breath, 'About Ivy.'

From the level of her lowered gaze she saw him seat himself again. His hand on the desk, his body bent towards her, he whispered, 'She knows? She can't; she would have said; she would have hit me with everything she's got.'

'She's already done that.'

'What do you mean?'

'I don't really know, but she's done something, and the result, when it comes about, will mean your ruin. Your practice and everything, but I don't know what it is.'

He drooped his head forward, his eyes moving over the desk, darting from one thing to another, as if trying to read an explanation somewhere. And then his head jerked upwards again and he said, 'How did you come to know, Jinny?'

'She told me this afternoon.'

He shook his head violently now as a swimmer does when breaking the surface of the water. He couldn't make it out, her knowing, and not saying a word about it. It wasn't her type of reaction. He had imagined that should she ever find out she would pounce on him with it.

'How long has she known?'

'I don't know, Paul, but she's followed you a number of times.'

'God almighty!' He strained his lip through his teeth. 'Ivy . . .'

'Paul,' Jenny leant towards him. 'I tried to find you this afternoon. I went all round the town, and . . . and when I couldn't get you I – I went out to Ivy's.'

'Jinny!'

'I – I told Ivy. I had to, because at the sight of me she guessed something was wrong. She thought something had happened to you. She – she gave me a letter for you, Paul.' She opened her bag and slowly handed him the letter. And slowly he took it from her hand, and more slowly still he picked up a paper knife and slit it open. After taking the folded sheet from the envelope he held it for a moment and looked again at Jenny before unfolding it.

The change was so sudden that it startled her, making her body jerk and causing the chair to scrape backwards on the polished tiles. He was standing before her, his body stiff, seeming broader and taller than he already was. There was anger in his face, but of a different kind from that which had been brought there by Bett, and through gritted teeth he spoke to her as he had never done since the first day they met. 'You shouldn't have done this, Jinny. You should have minded your own business. This is my business, and my business alone. You know what you have done?' He bent nearer. 'Do you?

90

You've spoilt a good woman's life and Ivy's a good woman.' He threw the letter on the desk. 'You've made her sacrifice herself when there wasn't a damn bit of need. What's the practice and any other damn thing compared to peace and happiness? And Ivy gave me peace, and I made her happy . . . Oh, Jinny.' He ran his hand over the top of his head and round to the back of his neck, and he held it there, pressing his head forward as he still stared at her.

She could say nothing; she felt as if he had hit her, blow after blow. And not the least painful was the knowledge that if it came to the push and he had to decide between his practice and Ivy, he would pick Ivy. He would do in this matter what he had thought right, right to Ivy. A good woman. You could go on all your life doing good and you got no thanks, but you could become a man's mistress and through that you claimed the title of a good woman. There was a bitterness in her that was new.

As she pushed the chair further away from him so that she could rise he grabbed at her limp hands. 'Jinny, Jinny. I know you did it for the best . . . you did it for me, but oh! Oh! how I wish you hadn't. Believe me, I'm not thinking of myself so much in this, but of her. I'll miss her, God knows, but I'm not so besotted that I don't realise that I'll get over it in time; but for her, it's her whole life . . . You see she's – she's going to marry Wheatley. He's a farmer. I've closed my eyes to it for a long time but I knew he was after her, and not as she always said, because she's got a bit of land.' He turned his head towards the desk where the letter was lying, then asked, 'Do you think there's any chance of stopping her, or is it already too late?'

Jenny pulled her hands from his and her voice cracked as she said, 'Don't ask me. Don't ask me any more.'

'Oh, I'm sorry, Jinny. I'm sorry I've upset you.'

As she moved towards the door he said softly, 'Don't go like that. I'm at my wit's end. Don't you take the pip at me, Jinny . . . please.'

She looked at him over her shoulder. 'I'm not taking the pip at you. Anyway, I'll be off tomorrow and . . .'

'Aw, yes.' He stepped hastily towards her. 'I'd forgotten. Your holiday. Oh, Jinny.' He only just prevented himself from adding, 'Don't go.' He needed her at this time, needed her balancing influence. 'I hope you have a good time; you deserve it.' Again he took her hand, but this time she didn't allow him to hold it. Instead, withdrawing it quickly, she said, 'We rarely get what we deserve. I'll be seeing you, Paul.'

She went out into the waiting-room that was now half-filled with people and made her way to the kitchen. Maggie was at the stove and she jerked her head towards a tray on the table which held a teapot covered with a cosy, milk jug, and a cup and saucer. 'It's ready.'

'Thanks, Maggie.'

Jenny picked up the tray and went upstairs. Bett was half sitting up, leaning against the bed head. She had her hand to her throat, and Jenny, after putting the tray on the table, asked quietly, and somewhat stiffly, 'Does it hurt?'

'Yes, it hurts.' Bett went on stroking her neck. 'And inside too. I've had a throat for days, and nearly being throttled to death hasn't helped in any way.'

Jenny, her own nerves frayed and still harbouring a feeling of bitterness, wanted to say, 'You only got what you asked for,' but Bett, she saw, was in no condition for home truths; she looked shaken, even ill; and she was trembling so much she could hardly take the cup of tea Jenny offered her.

'Are you cold?'

'Yes, I feel shivery.'

'I'll switch the blanket on.'

'Jenny.' Bett put out her hand and gripped Jenny's wrist as she went to move away from the bed, and her tone softening now, she said somewhat grudgingly, 'I'm sorry.' Then she asked, 'Are you going tomorrow?'

'Well yes, I told you all my arrangements are made.'

Bett closed her eyes and a shudder passed over her body, communicating itself to Jenny through their joined hands. When the cup in her other hand began to rattle on the saucer, Jenny took it from her and put it on the table.

Bett was now gripping the front of her nightdress, and to Jenny's astonishment she began to whisper, 'Don't go, Jenny. Don't leave me, I need you.'

Never, in her long acquaintance with Bett, had she heard her speak as she was doing now, nor had she seen her look like this. She had seen many facets of her cousin's character but never had she seen her looking really frightened and her whole body shaking as if with fear. She said gently, 'It'll be all right. You can make it all right with him if you go the proper way about it. Everything could be . . .'

'Oh, him! It isn't him . . . It isn't that.' Her voice had again assumed the tone she always used when speaking of Paul. 'It's—' She stared up into Jenny's face. Then her head drooping slowly, she screwed her eyes up until they were lost in their sockets.

'Oh, my God! Bett. Bett, look at me. You're . . . you're not pregnant?'

Bett opened her eyes, but with her head still hanging she said slowly, 'No, I'm not pregnant. It's funny' – her face moved into a twisted smile – 'people always think that's the worst that can happen to a woman . . . for her to be pregnant.' She turned her face away, and then her body, and fell heavily onto her side.

92

'Well, tell me what it is.' Jenny leant over her.

'It doesn't matter, it doesn't matter. Forget it.' She had stopped trembling and her voice was controlled now. 'And forget that I asked you. You go tomorrow. It's this cold; it keeps hanging about, it's making me lose my grip. Go on, leave me alone; I'll likely go to sleep.'

Jenny stood looking down on the small, huddled body. She had never seen Bett like this. 'Will I send Lorna up to sit with you for a while?'

'No, no.' The answer came quickly, jerking her body into a different position. 'I don't want anyone; I just want to be left alone.'

'Drink your tea while it's hot then.'

'I will in a moment . . . Go on.'

Jenny went slowly from the room; then stood on the landing. There was something wrong with her. What was she frightened of if she wasn't pregnant? It certainly wasn't what she had done to Paul or what she was going to do to him; there was not a vestige of remorse in her on that score. Her mind lifted to James Knowles. But if she wasn't pregnant what had she to fear from him, or anyone else? But one thing was certain: she was afraid of something. If she knew her cousin, she was very much afraid of something.

She found herself walking towards what had been her room and passing it and knocking on Lorna's door. Lorna was in the habit of shutting herself away when her parents battled in the open. She had never been able to stand them rowing.

There was no response to Jenny's knock, and she pushed the door open to find the room empty. She stood with her hand on the door knob gazing about her. Then turning, she ran down the stairs and in and out of the rooms on the ground floor. She was still running when she entered the kitchen again.

Maggie hadn't seen Lorna. Not since she came from school, she said. She wiped her hands on her apron. 'What is it?'

'She's not in the house. Has she been in?'

'Aye. Yes, I've told you. She came in at quarter past four as usual an' had a cup of tea an' a cake. She took it out with her; she often takes it up to her room an' gets on with her homework right away. What about the playroom? Have you looked there? She's got a lot of books stacked up there. Her . . . her mother won't have them in the bedroom.'

'I've been in the playroom. Perhaps Elsie's seen her. She may even be with her.'

She forced herself to a walk as she entered the waiting-room. It was full now, with some people standing. She passed through them and into Elsie's office. 'Have you seen Lorna, Elsie?'

'Yes, she went out just a moment or so after I came in. Just before you went in with the doctor. Why, what's the matter?'

'Nothing, nothing. Did you speak to her?'

'No. I didn't get the chance; she was running, kind of helter-skelter.'

Kind of helter-skelter. Yes, she would have run helter-skelter if she had heard the conversation in the drawing-room. She was likely still running now. She hurried from Elsie and into the kitchen again. Maggie seemed to be waiting for her.

'Where were you, Maggie, when all that was going on in the drawing-room?'

Maggie jerked her chin as if trying to remember, and she said, as if to herself, 'Now where was I?'

'Maggie, were you in the hall when they were going at it?'

Maggie now looked her straight in the face. 'I was.'

'Did you hear all that was said?'

'I did. I did, and God forgive her because I never will, even if himself does.'

'Did you see anything of Lorna at that time?'

'The child? No. An' would I have let her stay there an' that goin' on? You know me better than that, Miss Jenny. But why do you ask?'

Jenny put her hand to her brow. 'Elsie says she went dashing out of the house just after that. I believe she must have heard. I feel sure of it.'

'She couldn't have; there was no other place for her to be down-stairs unless . . . unless she was in the mornin' room. But then she never goes into the mornin' room; it's as cold as charity in there, as you know, even on the best of days.'

'But if she was in there, Maggie, she could have heard every word, because there's only a wooden partition filling the archway that used to divide the room.'

'Don't say that.' Maggie put her hand behind her and dragged at one of the stools from under the table and sitting down she mopped her face with her apron. 'That child adores the ground he walks on. He's all she's got, an' she's always known it. She's always known that her mother had no time or feelin' for her.'

'Maggie!'

'It's no use; you can't stop me tongue from sayin' the truth. She's had no love for the child from the day she was born, an' it's all clear now why. She jumped into the marriage to save her face, and she hated the cause of it and the cause of it was the child. An' she also hated the face-saver, himself. Aw, how she's hated him. There's lots of things clear now, though it isn't to say I hadn't me doubts from the beginning. But I smothered them because I couldn't bear the thought of himself being taken for a ride by the likes of her. An' now this . . . I'm tellin' you, if that child knows he's not her father she'll be lost entirely.'

94

'But after this she would have known sooner or later, Maggie. You've got to look at it that way. What I'm afraid of is the way she's learned it.'

'What are you going to do?'

'I don't know.'

'Should you tell himself?'

'Not for a while. Let him get his surgery finished; she might be back by then. She might walk it off, although something makes me doubt it.'

'And me too. Anyway, I'll not budge till I see her home . . . Did you have a drop of tea?'

'No, Maggie.'

'I'll make you a cup then and bring it in to you.'

'Do you mind if I sit in here?'

'Do I mind?' Maggie stopped in her journey across the kitchen. 'I'll be only too glad of your company. I never mind pleasures, and they are few and far between in this house.'

There was hardly a word exchanged between them while they waited for Paul to finish the surgery. And it was turned half-past six when the sound of a car starting up in the courtyard took Maggie to the window, and as she peered through the fading twilight she exclaimed: 'He's off!' She swung her head round to Jenny, and Jenny, behind her now, knocked sharply on the window, but the noise of the car must have drowned the sound for he did not turn his eyes in the direction of the kitchen.

'Well, what are we going to do now?' Maggie spread out her hands, palms upwards.

'I'll go and ask Elsie where he's visiting.'

'He had no visits,' said Elsie. 'He had got them all in during the afternoon. Yes, even the flats.'

'Do you know where he's gone, then?' asked Jenny.

'I haven't a clue. He generally tells me when he brings the cards across, but he didn't bring them tonight. He just went straight out after he'd finished the last patient . . . What's up, Jenny?'

'Oh.' She shook her head. 'There's a bit of trouble in the house.' It was no use trying to hoodwink Elsie.

'Bad for the doctor?'

'It could be, but I hope not.'

'So do I. Has no-one in there any idea where he's likely to have gone . . . the missis or Maggie?'

'No, I don't think so . . . I'll be seeing you, Elsie.'

Jenny turned away. No, they mightn't have any idea, but she had. She could see him speeding to Moor Lane.

The bungalow was in darkness. Both the front door and the back door were locked and there was no key on the shelf among the paint tins inside the shed. Ivy had done what she had said she was going to do in the letter. He knew she would have done it but he'd had to come. He didn't know how far away she was, whether she was over at Wheatley's, or miles out of town, but he knew for a certainty that she had gone from him for good and all. He felt the loss of her weighing on him as if she were dead. It was impossible to think that he would never hold her in his arms again, feel the warmth and response of her kind body, and have those moments of oblivion and perfect rest with his head between her breasts . . . But it was over.

On the main road once again, and driving towards Fellburn, it came to him that although his association with Ivy was finished the consequences were only about to begin. When he had received Beresford's letter this morning it had puzzled him, but now it puzzled him no longer. It had come to him during surgery that Beresford was Bett's secret weapon. Working through Beresford she would, as she had said, see him where she had always wanted to see him, outside the medical profession, outside of Romfield House. And it went without saying . . . you couldn't be a consultant if you were no longer a doctor. Yet somehow at this point of emptiness the vital issue of his livelihood didn't seem so important. He was a little tired of medicine, National Health medicine, jumping like a frog from one human being to another; he had been tired of this way of practising for a long while; this was why he had laid so much stress on getting the assistant's post and so specialising a bit. Now he was in danger of losing the lot. Yet nothing would have mattered all that much, he supposed, if Ivy had been waiting for him and they could have disappeared into some backwater, and there lived out their existence together . . .

He swung the wheel violently about and turned into Melbourne Road. Why was he kidding himself like this? He would have gone into no backwater with Ivy, nor would she have wanted him to; she would have wanted him to fight, fight to keep the place he had won through hard work. And hadn't she given him the chance to fight? He had said to Jenny that Ivy had sacrificed herself, and she had done just that. Well, he would take it from there. If he sank, he sank, but he wouldn't go down without first trying to swim.

Mrs Beresford opened the door to him, and as he looked at her he was struck yet again by the fact that happily married couples grew more alike as the years gathered on them. Mrs Beresford was sparse-framed, prim behind her smiling façade, and swathed in invisible garments of moral righteousness. The Beresfords were church-going people. And so were many other doctors in the town, but the Beresfords were pie and sanctimonious, of the type that got under his collar and made him sweat. The Beresfords had found each other early in life. Each had what the other required; the marriage had been perfect, as perfect as marriages can be after forty-one years. They had three children, of whom they were proud. The eldest son was a medical missionary; the youngest son was a schoolmaster in a public school; and their only daughter was headmistress of a girls' school. None of them was married except to their vocations. Doctor Beresford and his wife knew that they had been blessed with such a family only because of their own good living and example.

Mrs Beresford, still smiling, ushered Paul into her husband's study, saying, 'Doctor Higgins, George,' and left them immediately.

The atmosphere of the room was foisty as if the windows hadn't been open for years. Like the old fellow's mind, Paul thought.

Doctor Beresford was sitting behind a long mahogany desk which was covered with letter holders and papers of various sizes, together with a number of books, two heavy brass ink-wells, and a totem-pole paperweight. He did not rise to his feet nor offer his hand, but inclined his head and said, 'Good evening.'

'Good evening.' Neither of them had named the other; it was like a declaration of war. But this war was old, Paul knew, and dated back to his father.

Doctor Beresford now indicated a chair with a wave of his hand.

'Thank you.' Paul made his tone light; he refused to be put in the position of a boy in the headmaster's study, which was the attitude his colleague was taking up.

'You received my letter?' Doctor Beresford had his elbows on the arms of his chair now, his finger-tips tapping slowly together. It was a position that some actors adopted when playing the doctor, and it looked just as much out of character in this instance.

'I'm here, aren't I?' It was impossible to maintain the light tone.

'Yes, yes, of course.' The head bounced in time with the tapping fingers. 'It was merely an opening, merely an opening. In a business like this one has to start some place.' His eyes had been roaming over his desk as he spoke, but now they seemed to jump on Paul as he demanded, 'You follow me?'

'I'm afraid I don't.'

'I've never considered you a stupid man, Doctor.'

'Thank you.' It took all his willpower not to add, 'I cannot return the compliment.'

'So we will stop fencing, eh?'

Paul, deliberately now, put his elbow on the desk and leaning just the slightest bit towards Doctor Beresford said slowly, 'I'm afraid you'll have to be more explicit. I really don't follow you.'

'You're making this very awkward for me, Doctor, so don't blame me if I speak openly. I'm a doctor and also a man of the world . . .'

'Your own particular world.' He shouldn't have said that.

'What do you mean to infer by that?'

'Just that the phrase is rather outdated; men no longer make the grand tour to become men of the world. We're all men of the world now, particularly, as I said, of our own small worlds.'

Doctor Beresford closed his eyes for a moment, wetted his thin lips and said, 'We're fencing again, Doctor.'

'Then it's up to you to come into the open at once, which will do away with the need for further fencing, won't it?'

Doctor Beresford sighed patiently. 'I sent for you, Doctor, in the hope that I would be able to help you.'

You did like hell. Again it was difficult not to put the thought into words.

'This is a delicate matter, and it has always been my opinion that men of our profession should be men of integrity; however, there is always the odd one who runs amok and besmirches the nobility of our calling . . .'

God in heaven!

'. . . When this happens I feel that our dirty linen should be washed in private; that is, as much as possible . . .'

'Doctor Beresford, what are you accusing me of?'

'I am not accusing you of anything, Doctor Higgins. I am merely going to bring to your notice the penalty attached to having a liaison with a patient.'

The two men stared at each other.

'I hope you know that you are laying yourself open to an action for slander, Doctor Beresford.'

'Now, now, Doctor, don't get high-handed. I've told you, I'm trying to help you.'

'Like hell you are.' It was impossible not to say it.

'Control yourself, Doctor.'

'Oh, for God's sake, Beresford, stop this cat-and-mouse game and come into the open . . . or should I get straight on to Parkins . . . Yes' – he nodded – 'I think that would be a very good idea. Parkins is my solicitor. Is he yours?' He watched the thin nostrils draw inwards, the eyelids waver. For the first time the old man was wondering if he had been put on the wrong track.

Doctor Beresford's altered tone conveyed his feelings as he said, 'Now, look, Doctor, don't get heated. I've done this in good faith. I received certain information which left me no alternative but to follow it up, yet I didn't do so; I thought it only fair to see you first.'

'You thought it only fair to see me first! You knew if you followed any such information up where it would land you if you were wrong, and your implication is going to land you in exactly the same place . . . Court, because I'm not going to let this pass, Beresford; this is serious. You know what you're doing, don't you, what you're insinuating? This is my career . . .'

Doctor Beresford brought his fist gently into the palm of his other hand and wagged them for a moment under his chin. Then grabbing at a letter to the side of him, he demanded, 'Look. What am I to do when I get a thing like this? Send it to the authorities?' He thrust the letter at Paul. 'That is what I could have done; but no, as I said I wanted to help you . . . Read it.'

Paul's hand was steady as he took the letter, but as he saw the writing he had to hold it in both hands to stop the paper from fluttering. Although it only confirmed what he already knew it still came as a shock to him.

'Dear Doctor Beresford,

Knowing you as a man of integrity I feel bound to bring before your notice the unprofessional conduct of one of your colleagues. This doctor has for a number of years been having an affair with one of his patients, a woman named Ivy Tate, of Moor Lane. She also worked as a maid in his house for three years. He is in the habit of visiting her in the evenings two or three times a week, and on Thursday evening of last week entered her house at half-past seven and did not leave until eleven o'clock.

As I understand that this doctor is applying for the post of Assistant Physician in the local hospital I think it only fair that the Regional Board should be made aware of the circumstances. I have no need to draw to your notice, Doctor Beresford, that this man has already got a wife and daughter.

I know you will act according to your conscience.'

The letter ended here.

The bitch! The vicious, vicious bitch!

He drew in, through his teeth, a long filtered breath, and over the top of the sheet of paper he met Doctor Beresford's eye. 'Do you believe it?'

'Now what do you expect me to say to that? I can only ask you, is it true?'

'It's true that I know Mrs Tate, and I knew her husband before he died. I attended him for a long while. And as this states' – he flicked the letter disdainfully – 'she worked in my house; I gave her the work to help her. It's also true that I have visited her on many

99

occasions.' And now leaning well over the table until his face was only a foot from the old man's he went on, 'It's also true, Doctor, that she's about to be married.'

They were staring hard at each other, eyes unblinking, and Paul kept the situation like that for some seconds before he went on. 'I don't usually visit her three times in one week, but there was a lot to talk about last week. She was very excited' – God forgive him – 'for I suppose you could say she's making quite a good match. You see, she's marrying a well-to-do farmer.' Slowly he straightened his heavy back, and it was heavy, heavy as Judas's. It didn't lighten the weight to know that this was how Ivy would have wanted him to tackle it. He finished with, 'A little knowledge, Doctor. The old adage is right once again.'

There was a slight pink tinge to Doctor Beresford's sallow complexion and it was a full minute before he said, 'In my place what would you have done? And a further question.' He picked up the letter from where Paul had thrown it on to the table. 'What would you do now?'

'I'll leave that to you, Doctor. As it says, whatever your conscience dictates. But I'll tell you what I'm going to do, I'm going to get in touch with Parkins first thing in the morning . . . Take that and present it to the Board by all means, but understand' – here his voice dropped to a growl – 'I'll defend my name and not only before a medical council but, Doctor Beresford, in a public court. Goodnight to you.'

'Now just a moment, just a moment.' The old man pulled himself upwards, his hand extended across the desk, and Paul, now at the door, turned his head over his shoulder, not sufficiently far enough to look at the old man, but just enough to indicate his contempt. And again he said, 'Goodnight, Doctor.'

On leaving the house the cold night air hit him and made him conscious that his whole body was bathed in a lather of sweat. As he drove the car towards home the sweat ran into his eyes, and once he actually pulled up to mop his face. As he alighted from the car in the courtyard he saw that the curtains of the kitchen window were drawn aside. That meant Maggie was still there. But he didn't want to see Maggie, or anyone else; he wanted to be by himself and think. The bluff he had used on Beresford would only get him over a short space of time, for if Bett named Ivy as co-respondent that would be that. Ivy's marriage would do little to save him except perhaps stop Bett from proving her case. But the smear would stick, and he'd be lucky, damned lucky, if he kept his practice.

As he crossed the waiting-room towards the surgery Jenny came hurrying through the house door.

'Paul! Just a minute.'

He kept his eyes turned from her. 'I'm going to be busy.'

He had the surgery door open and she was close behind him. 'Paul; you must listen a moment; it's important.'

He continued into the room, his back still towards her.

'It's about Lorna.'

'What about her?'

'I – I think she must have heard you and Bett . . . in the drawing-room. She ran out of the house after that. Elsie says she saw her running through the waiting-room here. She – she hasn't come back.'

He stopped. 'But she was up in her room. She always dives up there if we have—'

'She must have been in the morning room.'

He rubbed his hand round his face leaving traces of moisture along the edges of the pressure, then walked to his desk, round it, and came to confront her, saying flatly, 'Anyway, she would have known sooner or later. It would have only been a matter of hours before her mother let her have the full story, if only as a means of taking another shot at me . . . By the way, Jinny.' He pulled his nose between his finger and thumb. 'I've just come from Beresford; she'd written to him.'

'Oh, no!'

'Oh, it doesn't matter. She's out to destroy me, but she'll likely destroy herself in the effort. It wouldn't surprise me if the woman doesn't go mad. She's been neurotic for years . . . But enough of her.' He jerked his head backwards as if throwing Bett and all her works away. 'Where do you think Lorna's got to? Couldn't she be with some of her friends?'

'I phoned the Watsons first, then the Bells, and then Doctor Price's house. Queenie said she hadn't been there, but as I was talking to her the doctor came on to the phone. He asked what time Lorna had gone out and I told him. He said it was most odd, but when he was coming along Sunderland Road at yon end, about four miles out, he picked up a girl in his headlights. She was walking on the grass verge and he was so sure it was Lorna that he pulled up: but when he called to her she took to her heels and ran on to the waste land. He – he said it puzzled him for a bit but he could understand the girl running away if it wasn't Lorna. He said if she wasn't back shortly, to contact him again.'

Before Jenny finished speaking he had picked up the phone and dialled a number. 'Hello. That you, John?'

'Yes. Yes, Paul. Has Lorna turned up?'

'No . . . I'm worried. About this girl you saw. Where abouts exactly?'

'Well, you know the waste land near Braithwaite's factory. Just there.'

'You think it was Lorna?'

'Paul, I'm sure of it now. I was sure of it then, but when she ran . . . well, you understand.'

'How long ago, John, exactly?'

'Oh, an hour and a quarter to an hour and a half I should say.'

'She could be anywhere by now.'

'Was there any trouble?'

'Yes . . . yes.'

'What are you going to do?'

'At the moment, I don't know. She might turn up, but on the other hand if she was that far out who knows, she might be going straight on. I think my best bet would be to inform the police. What do you think?'

'Mine, too. Look, I'll come straight over.'

'Thanks, John.' He put the phone down, held his hand on it for a minute, while he looked at Jenny, then dialled the police station and asked if Sergeant Cooper was on duty.

The sergeant came on the phone and his voice was more than affable. 'Anything I can do for you, Doctor?'

Paul told him what had happened, finishing with, 'It might be nothing; I might be making a mountain out of a molehill and I'll feel a bit silly if she walks in within the next few minutes but . . . but, you see, she was in a bit of a temper when she went out.'

'I understand, Doctor, I understand; I have three of my own. Leave it to me. I'll get things moving right away and I'll keep you informed.'

'Thanks, Sergeant . . . By the way, I'm going out to have a look round myself, I'm just waiting for Doctor Price to join me.'

'There'll be someone in the house?'

'Yes . . . yes.' Paul cast a sideways enquiring glance towards Jenny.

'Very good, Doctor. I hope I have news for you shortly. Don't worry. She couldn't have got very far, unless of course she took a lift. But . . . but likely somebody will have seen her. Don't you worry, sir.'

Paul put the phone down and resting his two hands on the desk repeated, 'Don't you worry, sir.' Then glancing sideways at Jenny he said again, 'Don't you worry. I feel I'm going mad with one thing and another and I'm told not to worry . . . How often I dish out that advice myself.' He turned round and leant his buttocks against the edge of the desk and asked her, 'Will you get me a drink, Jinny?' But as she turned away he said quickly, 'No, no, better not; I'd better keep my head clear.' As he glanced at his watch she looked at him and said tentatively, 'Paul,' and her tone brought his head round to her.

'Yes?'

'There's something else I – I think you should know. I've just come down from Bett. She isn't well, she's running a high temperature . . .'

'Jinny.' His big body reared upward away from the support of the desk and he seemed to expand as he growled at her. 'Don't

102

you expect me to show the slightest concern about my wife's condition. I don't care if she's got a fever so high it melts her bones. At this minute Bett could be lying dead at my feet and I would step over her and walk out . . .'

The colour drained from her face. He had every reason to be wildly angry, but it seemed that he was also blaming her; this was the second time he had gone for her in a matter of hours. The Paul of her acquaintance was an impatient, sharp-tempered, slightly arrogant individual, but at all times so very human; not so the man facing her.

'. . . And don't mention Bett to me again, not for a long, long time. Tomorrow we part company, and if she doesn't go off of her own bat, I'll put her out. She'll drain me dry when it comes to a settlement, and if my throwing her out goes in her favour, so be it, but out she goes . . .'

Not a little to her own surprise, Jenny found her anger rising swiftly against him. There wasn't another soul in the world she really cared two hoots about, except perhaps Lorna, and it didn't seem possible that she could go against him in anything, but now she cried at him and her voice wasn't low, 'All right! all right! You needn't go on. But when you can forget your personal feelings remember you're still a doctor. And don't forget also that I'm a nurse, and as such I know she's in need of help. Her throat is infected, and this hasn't just started today. She must have been feeling off colour for some time. Now if you don't want to give the order perhaps you'd have no objection to me asking Doctor Price to look at her?'

He had been glaring at her as she went for him, but now his face relaxed just the slightest, and in a semblance of his ordinary tone, he said, 'You know you could have been sisters, you and her, Jinny, for when it comes to a balance between us you always tip the scales to her side . . . Well, you do what you like, only don't tell me about it . . . There's John, now. Look.' He turned back to her. 'I suppose it's a kind of nerve to ask you after that to stay on until I get back . . .'

'Aw, don't be ridiculous.' She blinked her eyes and jerked her head away from him. 'Go on.' Her voice softened. 'And for God's sake find her.'

As he went across the hall to the front door he saw Maggie standing just within the kitchen door as if she was waiting for him, but all he did was to pause slightly and exchange a glance with her.

John Price was a tall, thin man, a few years older than Paul, and the father of two daughters and two sons. He had been friends with Paul for many years, even before he had been asked to attend Bett, but he knew as little, or as much, about either of them as did any outsider. He knew, for instance, that they had separate rooms, but so did a number of people, because the daily helps and maids had been numerous over the years. And then it wasn't anything new for a couple to have separate rooms, particularly a doctor who was liable to be disturbed any hour of the night. Who knew; it might be out of consideration that he had a separate room; yet in this particular case John Price had his own opinion. The only thing he knew that was perhaps not public knowledge was the situation between the Higginses had been tense for many years, and he was sorry for them both because he liked Paul and in a way he was fond of Bett. When defending her to his wife he had often said, 'She's never really grown up, and whatever you say, you've got to admit she's always cheerful.' His wife had had varying answers to this kind of comment, but they all suggested that Bett was only cheerful in the company of men. And she had now and again commented on Lorna's strange oriental look; she hadn't much use for the theory of throwbacks.

But he was worried about this business of Lorna. He could still see the frightened face of the young girl in the headlights. He blamed himself now for not giving chase, but if he had been wrong he could have scared the girl to death.

He said on greeting, 'Hello, there. Any news?' What was the trouble, anyway? 'Queenie said she was all right when she left her after school.'

'Aw.' Paul put his hat on and tugged on the brim before saying, 'We had a few words.' He did not mention Bett.

'Oh, well, I can understand that upsetting her. I could never imagine you and her having words. It's funny, but whenever Queenie and her used to fall out Queenie used to do a mime of her talking about you. The little devil used to call you Lorna's Big Chief Daddy Doctor.'

Paul jerked his chin. It was meant as a light movement, in place of a laugh.

'Where do you intend to look?'

'Well, I think it would be a good idea if we went along to where you saw her and we worked from there. She might be miles away; on the other hand she might be hiding among the buildings around there. But I think I'd better call at the station first and tell the police where we are going.'

Before John Price got into his car he turned to Paul and asked, 'How's Bett taking this?'

Paul was pushing his bag and some files along the seat; his body was bent and his voice came muffled in reply, 'She's under the weather. A bit of a cold, I think. She's in bed.'

'Oh, I'm sorry to hear that; I'll look in on her later.'

Paul's car door banged shut behind him. Then Doctor Price's door followed suit, and the two cars moved swiftly out of the Square.

Maggie sat with her slippered feet pressed close to the bottom of the Aga cooker, while her hands gripped the towel rail. She had a feeling on her of impending doom. If anything happened to the child it would be the finish of him, seeing that it had come about because of the two of them warring. She had known all along right in her bowels that the child was no blood of his. She remembered the slant-eyed little fellow coming to the house and the tizzie herself had got into. She had known then all there was to know, and the old doctor had known, and the mistress, too. Ah, yes, she had known . . . And then himself . . . It was from that day that that look had come on to his face. Aye, they had all known, yet nobody had said a word because it was a thing best left buried. And the little snipe had played it off with a high hand, defying the lot of them, saying as plain as if she had bawled in their faces, 'You prove it. Go on, prove it.' Well, there was one thing to be glad of: it had burst into the open at last. They couldn't have gone on much longer as they had been doing these past years, with the hate growing atween them so thick you could cut it with a knife.

Then look how the little upstart had treated her, like so much muck beneath her feet. Before the mistress had died young mistress Higgins had minded her p's and q's, but from the day the mistress had been carried out of the house she had done her best to get rid of her. And begod! two seconds she wouldn't have stayed if it hadn't been for himself. No, she wouldn't that. But there was nothing she wouldn't put up with for him, for he was to her like a son; in fact if there was anything closer than the flesh of your flesh then he was that. Never had she had the same regard for her own boy, and let's face it, he hadn't it for her, for at no time in his life had he shown her half the consideration that young Paul had. The mistress had given birth to her only son six weeks after her own Monica had been born, and from when her daughter was six weeks old she had lain during the day in a clothes basket in the corner there while she herself had gone about her duties, and later on wasn't it natural, when the mistress wasn't feeling too good that she should nurse them both on her knees and that they should often drink from the same font. Perhaps that was why she loved him so, for she had suckled him like a mother. He was supposed to have been bottle fed and everybody exclaimed at his thriving and the wonders of the patent food, and she had smiled quietly to herself and went on giving him the mixture as before, and in after years as she saw him broaden and grow she had taken credit to herself. She knew in this moment that if her three children, who had gone from her, should die altogether from one blast she wouldn't feel it half as much as if anything should happen to himself. She sometimes felt that she hadn't very much to live for. When she left this kitchen at night and went back to her empty house, all she thought about was getting her feet up and getting her rest to enable her to carry on another day. She knew that in ordinary circumstances she would have given up work long ago, for she was past it; she was old – how old only herself knew. Most people when they guessed her age were out by ten years or more. But for the remainder of her time she was determined to spend it near him, for she knew that if during some part of the day she didn't see him then it wouldn't be much use her going on.

When the kitchen door opened and Jenny appeared, she turned her head slowly towards her and said, 'If that phone doesn't ring soon they'll have to cart me away. Another night it would be deafenin' you. I've never known it so silent. Isn't it just like the thing?'

Jenny came slowly towards the stove. 'Well, in one way it's a good job it isn't ringing, for he wouldn't be able to see to anyone tonight.'

'No, you're right there; he wants no calls the night. With one thing and another he's had his bellyfull the day, and I've a feelin' inside me it isn't finished yet.'

'Oh, Maggie, don't say that.'

'Aw, Miss Jenny, I come from a race that can smell disaster from afar off, an' I wish to God you weren't goin' the morrow.'

'At the present moment I can't see myself going tomorrow, Maggie.'

'Have you told her' – Maggie jerked her head upwards – 'that the child's gone?'

'No, no, I haven't, Maggie, she's in no fit state to be told. She's partly hysterical as it is.'

'Well, she hasn't far to look for the cause of her trouble. She deserves all she's got an' more. Not that I'm holdin' it against her for tryin' to brain me with the water jug. No, no; that's a natural sort of response, an' it's many the time I've done the same meself, let fly at my Frank with what came to me hand when he came in bottled, God rest him. No, I'm not holdin' that against her . . . Has that clock stopped? It must be more than quarter to ten.'

Jenny looked at the wall clock, then at her watch. 'It might be a minute or two out, but that's all; the time hangs heavy.'

'Aw, well, I wish to God somebody would use that phone. That's all I ask.'

As if in answer to Maggie's plea the phone shrilled from the hall and Jenny, darting out of the kitchen, picked up the receiver.

'Is Doctor Higgins in?'

'No, but can I take a message?'

'Yes. This is a report to tell him that a girl who answers the description of his daughter has been picked up in Newcastle. She is being held at Pilgrim Street Police Station. But she won't give her name. Will you ask him to go there?'

'Oh, yes, yes. Thank you. Thank you very much. As soon as I hear from him – he's out searching – I'll tell him. Thank you; thank you very much.' Jenny's hand remained gripping the phone after she had replaced it on the rest, and for a moment she rested against the wall by the side of the table, her whole body slumped.

'Maggie, Maggie.' She burst into the kitchen now. 'They've got her. At least, someone of her description. But there's not two Lornas.'

'Aw, thanks be to God.' Maggie was standing holding on to her chair, and she crossed herself. Then drawing in her thick wrinkled lips she sucked at them for a moment before saying, 'I'll make a cup of tea.'

Jenny began to pace the floor, talking all the while. 'It must be an hour since he rang; he could be miles away. Oh, if only he'd call. But anyway she's safe.'

'There it goes.' As the phone rang again, Maggie's voice almost drowned it . . .

'Hello. Oh, Paul. Paul, listen. They've found her. She's at Pilgrim Street Police Station, Newcastle . . . Paul, are you there?'

'Yes, yes.'

'But where are you?'

'We're in Low Fell. John and I arranged to meet here. We'll . . . we'll get off now, Jinny. Thanks. Thanks.'

The phone clicked and she put the receiver down, then she stood looking across the hall and up the stairs.

She should now be able to think. Well, that's that. I can leave tomorrow as arranged, but in her mind she was looking along the upper landing and to the end of the corridor, to where Bett lay tossing and turning in distress, both mental and physical. What would happen to her if she was left with Paul and Maggie? Paul who wouldn't go near her, and Maggie who hated the sight of her, while the fact of being visited by either of them would, Jenny knew, increase her mental distress. And then there was Lorna. The gulf between them would be greater than ever now. Why, she asked herself, as she returned slowly to the kitchen, was she pulled from all sides by the emotions that filled this house.

'It was himself?'

'Yes, Maggie; he's going straight there.'

'Thanks be to God. An' sit yourself down an' have this cup of tea; you look as white as a sheet. And you'll have to content yourself to wait, for it'll be an hour afore they are back. So sit down, sit down.'

It was nearer two hours before they came. The sound of the car coming into the courtyard brought Jenny to the door, while Maggie busied herself at the stove, knowing that it was better at moments like this not to make too much of them.

From the light of the kitchen door Jenny saw Lorna and Paul standing beside the car. Then from the street came Doctor Price. Like Maggie, she told herself to act calmly and make no fuss, and so she waited. At least for a short time until she heard Paul's voice curt, commanding, saying, 'Now stop this, Lorna, and come inside.'

'Come on, Lorna, that's a good girl.' Doctor Price's tone was low and persuasive.

'I – I don't want to. I'm not going in.'

'Lorna!' Paul was shouting.

'I'll go to Aunt Jenny's.'

'I've told you your Aunt Jenny's here. Look, there she is.' He twisted her round and pointed towards the light of the doorway. Jenny came forward. She held out her hand, saying, 'Come on. Come on inside.' But Lorna remained stubbornly firm, pressing her back now against the car. 'I want to go to your place, Aunt Jenny.'

'All right, you can in a minute, but come inside first or we'll all be frozen.'

'Will you let me stay with you, Aunt Jenny?'

Jenny did not look towards Paul but she paused a moment before saying, 'Yes, yes, of course you can. You know you can.'

'Well,' Lorna jerked her chin to the side, turning her head full away from Paul, 'I'm only coming in for a minute, so there.' She sounded different, older, brittle. It was as if she had been away for years.

In the bright light of the kitchen she stood with her head down, and Maggie, coming from the table with a cup in her hand, said, 'Sit yourself down a minute an' drink this cup of chocolate; it's just how you like it.' She spoke as if everything was ordinary, but Lorna exploded the myth by saying loudly, 'I don't want any chocolate, Maggie; I want nothing, nothing.' Her throaty voice was high, cracking.

'Jinny.' Paul sounded tired. 'Take the doctor into the drawing-room and give him a drink, will you?' He glanced at John Price now and added, 'I'll be with you in a minute.'

When they had gone he stood looking at Lorna, but she wouldn't look at him; her head was still hanging when he reached out and firmly taking hold of her hand drew her forward, saying, 'Come with me.'

As she pulled against him he said, 'Just for a minute, come along.'

She resisted him all the way to the surgery, but when he had closed the door behind them she flopped down on the edge of the patient's chair and, her head bowed again, she waited.

Bending over the ruffled black shiny head, he said softly, 'Lorna, look at me.'

For answer she jerked her body away from him.

'It's no use evading this, Lorna; we've got to talk about it . . . clear it up.'

He was slightly startled when she swung quickly round and looked up into his face as she demanded, 'Is there any way we can clear it up, Da . . . ? You see, that's the point; I was going to say Daddy, and you're not, are you? You're no relation. She said you were no relation . . .'

'But that's where you're mistaken.' He dropped on his hunkers before her and, gripping her hands, went on hoarsely, 'I'm your father in the real sense of the word, in the only sense of the word I'm your father. I love you . . . I love you, Lorna.'

'When you knew you weren't my father did you love me then?'

Her eyes bright and dark were looking straight into his, demanding the truth, and he gave it. 'No, not at first. At first I was wildly angry and hurt and . . . and I pushed you aside, literally pushed you aside, till one day when I did that you cried, and we looked at each other, very much like we're doing now, and it was done. I knew you were mine in all that mattered, I knew then that I would never have a child by your mother and you were the only child I wanted. I loved you then, Lorna, and that feeling has increased with the years.'

'But you're not my father.'

He gulped in his throat, and as he searched for words he watched slow painful tears fall over the dark line of her lower lids, and when, haltingly, she began to voice something of the agony of mind he himself had carried for years he felt he couldn't bear it.

'My father was a Japanese wasn't he? Wasn't he? . . . Years ago a girl at school said I looked a bit Chinese and I hated her for it. But . . . but of the two I'd rather be Chinese than Japanese. I – I think they're filthy.' Her face became awash with tears, and her head bounced up and down as she pulled her hands from his.

Dropping onto his knees, he took her in his arms and soothed her for a moment before saying softly, 'Your father wasn't all Japanese, just one of his parents. And they're a very talented race; there's nothing to be ashamed of being Japanese . . . What?' He put his ear closer to her to catch her spluttering words. 'In the war . . . in the war people said . . . they were terrible.'

'Every nation was terrible in the war. And, Lorna, listen to me.' He lifted her face to his. 'Your father looked a nice man. I – I only saw him the once, but I remember thinking how good looking he was. And you have his looks. I – I think that's been the hardest thing for me to bear over the years, you being so beautiful—' When she dropped her head onto his shoulder he pressed her more tightly to him and went on: 'Because if you had looked like us, what I mean is a combination of me and your mother, it wouldn't have made for beauty, I know that.'

'Oh, Daddy! Daddy!'

On the sound of his name coming easily to her lips again he took in a long, slow breath. After a moment she raised her head and between gulps she asked, 'What am I going to do?'

'Do?' His brows went up slightly.

'I can't stay here. I can't, I can't. I couldn't look at Mammy, I just couldn't.'

'Would you like to go away to school, or some place?'

'Perhaps.' She thought for a moment. 'Perhaps. Yes, later on, but in the meantime can I stay with Aunt Jenny, please? Please, Daddy.'

'But your Aunt Jenny is leaving tomorrow; she's going on holiday.'

She put out her hand and picked at the lapel of his coat, and she kept her eyes on her jerking fingers as she said, 'Would you ask her to take me with her?'

'Oh, but, Lorna . . .'

'Please, Daddy, please. I'll have to go some place. I can't . . . I can't stay with Mammy. It isn't only about tonight's, it's . . . Oh!' She twisted her body from side to side.

'What is it? Tell me?'

'No. No. Only I want to get away. Go and ask Aunt Jenny. Just ask her. Please, Daddy, please.'

'Very well.' He pulled himself up. 'Come into the kitchen with Maggie and have your drink and I'll have a talk with your Aunt Jenny.'

At the kitchen door he pushed her gently inside and nodded over her head towards Maggie; then went to the drawing-room, there to find Jenny alone. She was standing looking down into the fire, and she turned her head swiftly towards him.

'Where's . . . where's John? Has he gone?'

'No.' She looked away from him. 'I asked him to have a look at Bett.'

When she finished speaking he went towards the wine cabinet, and as he poured himself out a drink he said, 'Jinny, can I ask you to take Lorna with you?'

'What do you mean? Home, tonight?'

He came towards her, the glass in his hand. 'No, to Switzerland. There'll only be trouble if she stays here. In fact, I don't think she will stay. I think she'll repeat tonight's performance again, I'm sure of it.'

'Yes, of course I'll take her.'

'You won't really mind? Oh, I say, you won't really mind, when I know it's a bit thick, in fact it's an imposition.'

'But I don't mind taking her; you know how fond I am of her. But there's another point. I'm wondering whether I should go at all . . . I've got to speak to you about this, Paul, whether you like it or not. Bett is ill, and if she's left with you and Maggie who's to see to her?'

'Jinny.' He lifted his glass and drank most of its contents before he went on. 'Who I'm concerned about at the present moment is Lorna. She's had a shock tonight and if we don't want repercussions later on she's got to get away.' Again he lifted his glass, and drained it and placed it on the table before he said, 'I'll get a nurse in if she's bad enough. And I'll go and see about getting more help for the house tomorrow. But, Jinny' – he walked up to her – 'you'll do me the biggest favour of my life if you'll take Lorna away, and now. Let the scales weigh in my favour this time . . . please, Jinny.'

She stared at him without speaking; then turning from him, she said, 'All right.'

'Thanks. Thanks, Jinny.' His hand went out and gripped her arm, but she did not turn towards him again, not even when the pressure deepened. When he let her loose she went down the length of the drawing-room, saying, 'We'd better go now; I can get her things tomorrow.'

They were crossing the hall when John Price came down the stairs. He came down slowly and they both stopped and watched him, and when he reached the foot Jenny went towards him and asked, 'What is it?' She was a nurse and the countenances of doctors weren't inscrutable to her. She saw that something was amiss and again she said, 'What is it?'

'I'm not quite sure yet, Nurse.' Although John Price had known Jenny for years he had always addressed her as nurse, and she had addressed him as doctor. He turned to Paul. 'I'd like a word with you.'

There was a short silence before Paul said, 'Lorna's spending the night with Jinny. I'm just going to run them over.'

'Oh, well.' John Price nodded his head. 'Go ahead. Go ahead.'

'Do you mind waiting?'

'Not in the least. Go on, go on. But I'd like a sedative for her. If you'll give me your keys I'll see to it.'

'They are in the desk in the surgery.'

'I won't be a minute.' Jenny glanced at Paul. 'I'll just pop up and see her before I go.'

It was Doctor Price who answered her. 'I wouldn't, if I were you, Nurse; I'd leave her as she is for tonight.'

Jenny, her eyes on the doctor, wanted to remind him that first and foremost she was a nurse, but she didn't. She went towards the kitchen, leaving the two men again looking at each other. It was John Price who turned away first, and Paul stared after him as he went out of the hall and into the waiting-room towards the surgery.

What now? In God's name what now? John looked shaken. Was she really ill? Something serious? He hoped to God not. He wanted this business over, no delay. He knew that he was quite prepared to lose his livelihood rather than continue life with Bett.

In the kitchen he put his arm around Lorna's shoulders and led her towards the door where Jenny was already waiting, saying, 'Have you said goodnight to Maggie?'

Lorna turned and, looking back at Maggie, said, 'Yes, and good-bye; she knows I'm going with Aunt Jenny.'

'It isn't good-bye, me bairn. You go and have a good holiday, have the time of your life. Go on now.'

'Bye-bye, Maggie.'

'Bye-bye, hinny.' Maggie shuffled forward, saying, 'An' good-bye again, Miss Jenny. An' you enjoy yourself an' all. Have a fling. Go on, have a fling.'

Jenny gave the old woman a weak smile. 'You'll be seeing me again, Maggie, I'll be round in the morning,' she said.

'Stay where you are till I come back, Maggie, and I'll run you home,' Paul called from the yard, and she answered, 'Aw, never you bother, I'll be in me bed by the time you get back.'

'Now look.' He came back to the doorway. 'I've told you. Stay put; I'll not be more than a quarter of an hour.'

'All right. Have it your own way.'

Not until the car had left the yard did Maggie close the door. Then, as she went to sit down, she heard the distant sound of a man's cough, and she remembered that Doctor Price was still in the house and was likely waiting for himself coming back, so she decided to make a pot of coffee. This done, she took the tray into the drawing-room.

The room was empty, and when she returned to the hall she glanced towards the stairs. Then her eyes were drawn towards the morning room door which was open. What made her go towards it was the reflection of a glow in its dark panelling. The fire had been left on. The child had evidently switched it on when she was in there, and in her flight and shock had forgotten to switch it off again. If milady had been about it wouldn't have been left on. Oh, no. You could freeze to death to save a shilling or two. She stood looking about her. She had never felt the room as warm as this for years. It was a nice room and she would have liked it but for the fact it was as cold as an ice-box; but at the moment it was like toast.

She sat down on the deep couch against the wall to the side of the fire. It was an old couch but still in good condition. The mistress had been wont to put her feet up on it in the afternoons. Her own feet were the size of two pairs, she could do with getting them up herself. And why not – why not indeed, until himself came back? The other one wouldn't likely be stirring the night if she was so bad she needed a doctor. She went and closed the door. Then returning to the couch, she slowly raised one swollen leg after the other and lay back. Her body felt as heavy as her heart; but aw, this was nice; aw, she hadn't realised how tired she was; she could go to sleep, she could, she could that. An' if she wasn't careful she'd be out for the count.

Twenty minutes later when Paul returned and didn't find Maggie in the kitchen, nor receive an answer to his quiet call from the hall, he clicked his tongue with impatience.

When he entered the drawing-room John Price was standing on the hearth-rug, supporting an elbow in one hand while tapping the index finger of his other against his teeth. It was an agitated gesture. Moving slowly towards the fireplace, Paul kept his eyes on him, and when he reached the couch he stopped and said, 'Well?'

'Paul,' John moved uneasily, 'I'm in a bit of a fix. I've got something to say and I . . . I don't know how to say it, or where to begin.'

'In that case, John, you'd better come straight out with it.'

'It isn't as easy as that.' John glanced sideways at him. 'I'm – I'm knocked, I just don't . . .'

'Look,' Paul lowered his head and said slowly, 'spit it out. There's something wrong with her, is it cancer?'

'No.' The older man pressed his shoulders back and stretched his chin out of his collar. 'I could say at this minute I wish it was. Paul.' He went closer to him and, his voice rapid and low, he spoke to his averted face. 'I know that things haven't been quite right between you and Bett, not for a long time. Even if I hadn't been your friend and known a little about you, and was just visiting her . . . well, I would have sensed things weren't quite normal. Do you follow me?'

'I follow you.'

'Paul, I . . . I must ask you something . . . pointedly.'

'I'm waiting.'

'Have you been together lately?'

'That's easily answered.' He turned and faced him. 'No. But what do you mean by lately?'

'I mean . . . well, within the last few months, the last year.'

'Multiply that by twelve and you'll be nearer the mark.'

'Aw, man.' John Price's hand went to his face and rubbed it in evident agitation, and when Paul said, 'Look, what is this? Spit it out,' he inhaled deeply and his voice now sounding calm, even disinterested, he said, 'I suspect she has syphilis, secondary stage . . .'

113

What happens to a man when he is told that his wife has venereal disease and he knows that he hasn't given it to her? The normal reaction would be hate, disgust, a loathing of the woman and the dirt with which she was impregnated. A feeling of being cheated, of his manhood being indelibly stained. But Paul experienced none of these emotions; what he did experience was a feeling that he had been winded by a kick in the stomach, and that the blow made him want to retch. As if his wits had become dulled with the kick he heard John Price's voice, his words hesitant and limping, coming as if from a distance, saying, 'Of course there's a chance I may be wrong, but I don't think so. Still . . . well, you can see for yourself. Her throat's very sore, but a sore throat could be a symptom of anything. It was the papules on her arm that gave me the first indication. It . . . it happened when she lifted her hand above her head, and . . . and the sleeve of her nightdress fell back. There were two, and one or two brown stains which speaks of recrudescence. I . . . I might even have had doubts of my own powers of observation, but when she realised that her arm was bare, and she saw my eyes on it, she covered it immediately and became very agitated, even hysterical . . . Paul, it's awful, man, it's awful, but she knows, she knows all about it. She didn't want to see me in the first place. When I went in she called Nurse everything for telling me. I thought her attitude was surprise at seeing me so late at night. Then after a while she calmed down; but once she knew that I suspected what was wrong she really did become hysterical . . . Well, there it is. I've given her a hefty dose of chloral. She should be well away in a little while, and with your permission I propose to do a Wasserman . . . Paul, man, look.'

Paul went to the couch and sat down.

'Will I get you a drink?'

After a space of time, during which he sat staring straight before him, he made a small movement with his head.

The glass of whisky in his hand, he looked at it. Syphilis. Bett and syphilis. Of all the people he had to treat it was those with this disease he pitied most. Altogether he hadn't many on his books, not more than three or four. It was a secret disease. People had it, and hid it, and passed it on; and the receivers had it, and hid it, and passed it on. As was sometimes the case, they didn't actually know they had it, they just had spots and were feeling off colour; and of course they didn't connect the rash with the person with whom they had been cohabiting. As one young fellow had said to him, oh, he couldn't have got it from his girl, she was nice. The boy was seventeen and the girl was his first girl. He'd had to convince them both that they needed treatment. That had been a piteous thing, but it was imperative that they had treatment at once, for this thing, this vile thing, could lie dormant for years then spring on them with frightening consequences, terrible consequences. Very often the only way he could

114

get patients to have treatment was to send them to Newcastle, for they couldn't bear the shame of attending the special clinic, although treatment was carried out everywhere with the greatest privacy.

'Drink it up. Come on, man, drink it up.'

Obediently he put the glass to his lips, but only sipped at it.

John Price sat down on the couch beside him. 'Look, I can arrange for her to go away and have treatment. Not a soul need be any the wiser, so don't worry.'

'Don't worry?' There it was again, that useless, ineffective phrase. He turned his face full towards John and there came the sound of a laugh from his throat while his features remained as stiff as if they had been set in cement. Only his lips seemed to have the power of movement. 'Don't worry, you say. Would it surprise you to know that's all I've done since we married? From the very beginning our nerves have screamed at each other. And just tonight, a few hours ago, I decided that it was the finish, and tomorrow either she or I put in for a divorce. Although I know I stand very little chance of getting it against her, for I won't use the proof I've got, for that concerns Lorna, she has enough on me to knock me flat, finish me.'

'What do you mean? A divorce isn't the end.'

'It will be for me; but at the moment I don't give a damn.' He lay back against the couch and closed his eyes. 'I've had a mistress for the last two years and she's found out about it.'

After concentrating his gaze on Paul's mouth, John Price lowered his lids and said with a laugh, 'Well, it won't be the first time a doctor has done that. She can't hang you for it.'

'She can in this case, she's a patient.'

'Aw, Paul! You above all people.'

'Aye, me above all people.'

'Has she absolute proof?'

'Pretty near. But in any case the mud would stick.'

'And the Board next week, and you on the short list. Aw, Paul.'

'It'll be short all right, if Beresford has anything to do with it.'

'But how? Why him?'

'He knows all there is to know. He received a letter to the effect that I was having an affair with Mrs Tate, Ivy Tate, who used to work here. Do you remember?'

Paul watched the effect of this last piece of news on his friend. He didn't know why he was telling him all this except that in some way it eased the shock of the disclosure concerning Bett. It was as if in exposing himself he was lessening the disgrace attached to her. Yet he couldn't explain to himself, feeling as he did towards her, why he should do this.

John Price rose from the couch and walked to the fire, where he stood looking down at it before saying, 'This is awful. You should have told me. Look.' He swung round now. 'We'll have to go into this. You're not going to lose everything because of something that happens every damn day of the week to other men. You know this has always incensed me about our job . . . Mustn't have anything to do with a patient. God! You see them stripped, you examine them, and you're supposed to view them as a skeleton in the lecture room. The damned stupid thing about it is, that if the woman concerned is not your patient she's somebody else's. It has always annoyed me that . . . Ethics, unprofessional conduct. Taking advantage of someone under your care . . . taking advantage. That's funny. Talk about raising a laugh . . . when they sit at the other side of the table and rape you with their eyes, and go out disappointed if you don't ask them to strip off for an examination. Look, Paul.' He bent over him. 'Fight this. Anyway, Bett hasn't got a leg to stand on now . . .'

Paul made no response, he knew why John was letting off steam like this. In the ordinary way Doctor John Price would have supported every maxim in the professional book because he was a good doctor, a good husband, a good father, and a moral man. He was talking as he did to make him feel that what had happened was really of no account; as he had said, this kind of thing happened every day, it was part of the usual routine. But it wasn't true and he knew it. The women who raped you with their eyes were few and far between, and except for the odd one here and there they disliked stripping off. And the odd one would have stripped off for anybody; doctors weren't exceptions in this case.

He said now under his breath, 'How long is it since you gave her the chloral?'

John Price looked at his watch. 'Just over an hour; it should have taken effect by now.'

He pulled himself up from the couch, and slowly they went from the room. He let John precede him up the stairs and along the corridor to the door at the end, and as he entered his wife's room he clenched his jaws and felt the cords of his neck and the muscles of his stomach tighten against the final evidence.

5

It wasn't until Paul saw the side of the Salvation Army Hall with 'The Citadel' painted in large letters upon it, that he realised it was morning and the dawn was coming up. He remained standing at the window until the pale grey light turned to pink and the sun, visible somewhere beyond the roofs, sent its rays like spilt paint into the sky; then he turned and looked about the room. His bed had not been disturbed; his coat lay across the foot of it. On the table to the side of the bed the standard lamp was still alight and looked conspicuously alone in that there was no bottle and glass standing near it. He hadn't touched a drink since John had given him that glass last night. Somehow he hadn't the taste for it; not that he didn't need fortifying, but what he needed more was the power to think clearly, to get this thing sorted out. Except for one instance his feelings had remained at the same shock level of last night. The instance had been when they were standing in the hall after they had come downstairs, and John had said, 'Have you any idea who it is?' and he had answered, 'Yes, I've an idea.' At that moment he'd had the desire to rush out of the house, burst into Knowles's flat, take him by the throat, and worry him like a bull terrier does another dog.

But later, when he began to think somewhat rationally, he had to admit that Knowles was not all to blame. Knowles could have got nowhere without encouragement, without sanction. Yet this fact did not resurrect his hatred of Bett. It was an odd thing, but not once since he had confirmed without a doubt that Bett had the disease had he felt his rage rise against her. His main reaction still was the feeling of nausea following a shock.

As the night wore on and he had alternately paced the room and sat with his head in his hands, he began to question why there was still no condemnation in him towards Bett. Yesterday, when to him she was, besides being the woman who had tricked him into marrying her, a vicious, unbalanced creature, his hate of her had been something consuming and mighty. Yet now, when he had more reason for hate, it had not increased by one jot. It slowly became apparent that what had happened to Bett was having a cathartic effect.

So, by the first light he faced the unpleasant truth that most of the responsibility was his. He realised that had he tackled her with Lorna's parentage years ago things might have straightened themselves out, her confession might have brought from him forgiveness and pity. The excuse that being the kind of man he was he couldn't bear the slur her deception placed on his manhood seemed thin. The fact that he had withheld himself from her, even while sharing the same room; and when his mother had died he had unhesitantly put the length of the corridor between them, filled him with a deep shame now.

He knew this morning that he had reached the hill of decision; he was on the summit. Whether he was to fall from it in his own estimation depended on what action he was going to take.

Somewhere along the line he knew he had to do something right. He, the supposedly moral man – and he had been a moral man until he took Ivy, for the bottle had been his mistress during the previous years – had to act morally. Bett was frivolous, petty, vain. She had a mania for young fellows, but only, he imagined, to give vent to her skittishness. She would never, he felt sure, have gone with Knowles if it hadn't been for the long corridor. Whatever Bett was fundamentally, she had been, and was still, his wife, and, his conscience continued to tell him loudly, she hadn't deserved the loneliness he had thrust on her. Years ago she had made a mistake, and as a frightened young girl had grabbed at him to hide that mistake. Had he not sympathised with a thousand women in his time because they were frightened of having made that same mistake, of the disgrace it entailed? He had been kind to them, even tender in his commiseration, but when the disgrace touched himself he had seen it as a different kettle of fish.

Anyway, he knew now what he would have to do. Bett was still his concern. She had tried to break him because she thought there was no humanity in him towards herself. Well, he would have to show her she was wrong. He would have to show to her the consideration he gave even to the least worthy of his patients. It wouldn't be easy but he must try. He must think about life with her as something to be lived a day at a time, and no more. Looking at time as the future which meant months and years ahead would get him down. Life as he saw it with Bett could only be taken in small doses.

And there was another thing he must do. As he went to a chest of drawers and took out a clean shirt his stomach muscles knotted on the thought that he must contact Knowles. This in a way would be even harder than facing Bett. But as a doctor he must do this. He stood with the shirt in his hand. Why must he? Could he count on this calmness of mind lasting when confronted by Mr Knowles? Wouldn't it be better to ask John to deal with it? No. No. This was his concern, and his alone.

After a bath and changing into a different suit, he went quietly downstairs, and there to his surprise he found Maggie with the kettle boiling and the teapot standing ready to hand. She turned at his entry, saying, 'You're early.'

He stood looking at her. 'Why have you come at this hour?'

'Aw, I couldn't rest. I thought I might as well be doing something.'

'You should have waited for me last night.' He peered at her. The permanent bags under her eyes were swollen still further; her old face looked drawn.

She made no mention about having spent the night in the breakfast-room, but said, 'Do you feel like something to eat?'

'Oh, no.' He closed his eyes and shook his head. 'Just make the tea strong.'

'I'll do that.'

Some time later they sat at the table facing each other and drank the hot tea in silence.

'Maggie.' He rubbed his hand across his eyes, then pressed the eyeballs with his first finger and thumb. 'I'll have to have help in the house. Do you know anyone, anyone decent, to be housemaid?'

Maggie looked down into her cup. 'They're like gold dust. If they can get three and nine to four shillings an hour in the factory they're not doing housework for two and six to three shillin's, it stands to reason.'

'But I'll pay anything.'

'Well, that'll be different, for they never got more than half-a-crown.'

'It doesn't matter about the wage, Maggie. Do you know anyone, some woman with a husband out of work? There's a good few of those knocking about now.'

'Yes, yes, I know one or two meself, but as I said, they're all for the factories an' the bigger money. But there's Alice Fenwick. She doesn't like the factory; she'd sooner do housework if it pays. Now I think there might be a chance of gettin' her.'

'Where does she live?'

'In Kibble Street.'

'That's quite near. Do you think you could see her before she goes to work?'

'I'll have a try.'

'Thanks, Maggie.'

As she rose from the table she looked up at him and said, 'Things goin' on as before then?' Her tone was apprehensive.

His head was turned from her when he replied, 'Yes, Maggie, I'm afraid so.' As he walked towards the door he paused and added, quietly, 'Can I ask you to take a tray up later on, Maggie?'

'You can ask.'

'And will you?'

'I will.'

'Thanks.'

He went out into the hall, through the waiting-room, and into his surgery, and sitting at his desk he picked up the telephone directory and found James Knowles's number.

It was just turned eight o'clock when the front-door bell rang and Paul went to open it. On the sight of the pale, smiling, self-assured face all the reasonableness, born of the self-analysis during the night, fled and he had an almost uncontrollable urge to answer Knowles's greeting by bashing his fist between his eyes.

'Hello there.' Knowles had stepped into the hall. 'You want to see me? I didn't know Bett was ill.' His voice had no trace of nervousness, yet there was a wary look in his eyes as if he knew that this visit was not going to be classed under the heading of social.

'Come this way.'

There was a deep indent between Knowles's brows as he followed Paul across the waiting-room and into the surgery, and as he closed the door he said, 'Is it serious? I didn't even know she was bad.'

With a slight movement of his hand Paul indicated the patient's chair, then slowly made his way behind the desk to his seat, from which point of vantage he hoped he would be able to deal with the situation in a professional way. But immediately he answered Knowles it was evident that the professional attitude in this case was beyond his power, for he found himself spacing his words in a deadly cold, ominous tone.

'Yes . . . I . . . suppose . . . you could . . . call it serious.'

Knowles was puzzled. He screwed up his eyes as he asked, 'What is it? Why take this attitude with me? What have I done?'

What should be a man's answer to this, a man's, not a doctor's? His whole frame began to shake; it was most noticeable in his hands. There was a pile of bulky correspondence lying on the table, the majority of which, he knew, was from drug firms. He pulled it all towards him as he said, 'I think it's got a lot to do with you.'

'Oh. So there's more in this than meets the eye, is there? Well, come on, come on, spit it out. I don't know what it's all about but I'm willing to listen.' Knowles's voice sounded brittle, cocksure.

The nerve of the bloody swine! But he would have nerve; his type always had; the lady-killers were well equipped. The fury was rising in him. Like a red tide it flooded up to his eyes. With a sweep of his hand the mail went sprawling all over the desk, and bending half-way across it, his anger causing him to splutter, he growled below his breath, 'Would it surprise you to know that she has contracted syphilis?'

Still leaning over the desk, his body rigid, he watched the colour rise into the pale face. He watched the eyes blink, then stretch, as if the man had just woken up. Then what followed took him definitely by surprise, for Knowles, springing up from his chair, thrust his face almost into his own as he barked, 'And you think I gave her that? Me?' He gripped the lapel of his coat. 'By Christ! As big as you are I'll ram that down your throat. Who the hell are you to sit there like some bloated god and say that to me? . . . Me give Bett syphilis! Let me tell you, I haven't got syphilis; nor have I ever had it. As for me giving Bett anything—' He drew his head back and screwed up his whole face as if the sight of Paul was distasteful to him, as he went on, in a bitter low tone, 'I suppose it's news to you what I'm going to say, but the fact is I've never been with Bett ever . . . Now what do you make of that? Because we've had a laugh together, a bit of a joke, and yes, a bit of slap and tickle, you have to see something else in it. But let me tell you this.' His face was thrust forward again. 'Whatever has happened to Bett there's one person to blame for it, and it's not the one who's passed it on to her, but you . . . Oh, she's told me some things about you, big fellow, and nothing that's good. And I'm telling you this: I'm sorry for Bett, always have been, for the simple reason she's had to live with you. She could talk to me and she has, we're pals. Always have been, but nothing else.' He now wagged his fingers about an inch from Paul's face, and Paul, unable to stand any more, took his hand and gave him a push that sent him reeling.

When Knowles regained his balance, he stood glaring across the room as Paul said, 'All right, all right, I've made a mistake, and you've had your say. You don't like me and I don't like you, and I believe you when you say you've never been with Bett, but speaking as a doctor I think that you've found more satisfaction in spewing your filthy stories into her ears than you would have if you had been with her.'

Knowles, his face a dark purple red now, adjusted his perfectly knotted tie and sneeringly he replied slowly, 'Bett always said you were a sanctimonious, big-headed swine, and by God! she was right. But you weren't so sanctimonious that you couldn't do a bit of homework on the side. Your kind make me sick.'

Paul swallowed deeply. 'I think we make each other sick, Mr Knowles.'

'Ivy Tate! And in this house, under Bett's nose.'

The urge to use his fists was rising again and he had to give himself time before he could say, 'Just to put you right, Knowles, I will tell you that nothing went on in this house under Bett's nose. Also I would advise you to guard your tongue in case you might have to substantiate what you say, not only to my solicitor but to Farmer Wheatley.'

As Knowles narrowed his eyes Paul went on, 'Mrs Tate is being married shortly; the wedding has been in the offing some time . . . Now I'll let you out.'

When they reached the front door he said, 'I won't expect to see you here again,' and Knowles, turning on the step and looking at him, replied, 'You got me here, sure in your own mind it was me who had passed it on to her, and if you had been right, tell me, what would you have done then?'

'I would have advised you to have treatment.'

'Oh. Oh God! It's as Bett once said, you're as cold as a dead jelly fish. Advise me to have treatment! . . . I can't believe it. You know what a man, a real man would have done? He'd have wiped the floor with me, bashed my face in, not just give me a push. No matter what he thought of his wife, he'd have wiped the floor with me. So you would have advised treatment, and now you've got to find out who to advise, haven't you? Well, I can see you'll have to do some detective work . . . Doctor; but I'll give you a clue, not in order to help you, but in the hope that it'll worry your guts out. How about starting in the Mayor's Parlour, eh? Good-bye and I wish you luck.'

Paul watched him get into his car before he closed the door, and then he stood supporting himself against it with his outstretched hand. From the moment that Knowles had convinced him that he was speaking the truth he had been shocked into an acute awareness of the

121

magnitude of this thing that had fallen upon him. Behind all the talk with Knowles he had been asking feverishly, Who then? Who? Who? And now the Mayor's Parlour? The Mayor's Parlour? Somebody on the Council? But who? Who? . . . The Mayor's Parlour? There wasn't a man younger than himself on the Council. Somebody in the offices? . . . The Mayor's Parlour? The Mayor? The Mayor, Arthur Bolton? ARTHUR BOLTON! Don't be ridiculous . . . Brian . . . Brian Bolton? BRIAN BOLTON, the youngster . . . Lorna! He recalled the night he had come in and had heard the rumpus upstairs and Bett clashing about and Jinny sitting on the bed rocking Lorna. What he had made out of this, and only through Bett's tearful yelling, was that Lorna had walked out of a dance because her mother danced with Brian. Then there were the times he had come home and found him in the drawing-room. He had thought he had been waiting for Lorna coming back from school. At these times he said that he had just finished over the road at the Technical School and called in. And then there were the nights Bett was out he had thought she was with Knowles. But Brian . . . he was only a boy, nineteen, if that.

No! No!

Now he was really sick.

He was half-way up the stairs on his way to his room when he stopped. On the thought that came crashing into his mind he gripped the banisters. Just suppose! Just suppose . . . Lorna had been very distraught of late. She had been sick several times, and she, too, had had a throat. She also had a herpes on her lip. But it could just possibly have been a chancre.

He swung round, dashed down the stairs, grabbed his hat and coat from the hall, went through the waiting-room so as not to give any explanation to Maggie, and out into the garage. Within minutes the car was roaring towards Jenny's.

He rang the bell three times before there was any answer, and when Jenny opened the door, the sleep was still weighting her eyes.

'What is it? Something wrong?'

'No, no, Jinny; I just want to talk to Lorna.'

'She's asleep. She's in the spare room. Will I wake her?'

'No, I'll go in, Jinny.' He went swiftly past her.

'But, Paul, something's wrong . . .' He had already gone into the room and closed the door before she had finished speaking.

Lorna was lying on her back. Her face, although swollen from her crying, looked beautiful, painfully so. He stood staring down at her for a while before gently touching her shoulder. 'Lorna, Lorna,' he said.

'Yes? Oh! Oh!' She opened her eyes, closed them again, then sat up with a jerk. 'Daddy!' Her tone was high, frightened. 'What is it?'

'Nothing, nothing.' He sat down on the bed and forced himself to calmness. 'I just wanted a little talk.'

'You're not going to stop me going with Aunt Jen . . . ?'

'. . . No, no.' He moved his head widely. 'Nothing like that. You're going on a holiday but . . . but, there's something I've got to ask you. It's very important and it's very delicate.' He took hold of her hand and smoothed it before saying, 'It's about Brian.'

Her fingers jerked within his, and she muttered quickly, 'I've finished with Brian, ages ago.'

'I know that, dear, but . . . but what I want to say . . . what I want to ask you is about the time when you used to go out together.' As he felt her hand stiffen, the sickness deepened in his body, but he went on, 'You know I wouldn't do anything to hurt you, or upset you, not intentionally, and why I'm asking you this is because I love you and wouldn't want the smallest harm to come to you. You understand?'

She was leaning back against the pillows and she stared at him blankly when she said, 'What do you want to ask me?'

This was terrible, terrible. He could ask this of patients, of young girls who denied ever being with a man when he had to tell their mothers they were three months pregnant. He had got used to talking tactfully, easily, soothingly, but none of his past experience helped him now. He looked down at her hand gripped into a fist within his. 'I'm going to ask you a question and you can answer yes or no . . . Did Brian ever try to do anything to you that wasn't very nice?'

'Yes.' The answer came short, sharp, and coolly, and brought his startled eyes to hers.

'Lorna!' Her name sounded like a pain spilling from his wide-lipped mouth.

'Well, you asked, Daddy.'

'Yes, yes, it's all right, my dear . . . Can I ask you something else?'

'I can't stop you, can I?' She sounded adult, not at all like a young girl, not at all like his Lorna, and he had to drop his eyes from hers when he put the next question. 'Did you submit to him?'

'No.' The answer came as quickly as the previous one, and the relief caused his body to slump.

'Why did you ask that?'

'Oh, it doesn't matter, it doesn't matter any more.'

'But it does. Why do you want to know that? Why did you ask such a question if it doesn't matter?'

'All I can say is, dear, that Brian isn't a boy you should associate with.'

'Not even to play tennis with? Or go dancing with? Or to the pictures?' The enquiry sounded ordinary.

'No, not even that. I would rather you didn't see him again.'

'Oh, you needn't worry about that, Daddy.' Her small nose wrinkled as if with distaste. 'I haven't seen Brian since before Christmas. Didn't you know that?'

123

'No, I didn't, dear, I knew you weren't seeing much of him, but I didn't know that you had stopped seeing him altogether.'

'Oh, yes. He's got someone else.' Her head was tossing now, and if he needed further confirmation of Bett's association with the boy he had it. My God! And how much did she know? Too much. That was evident, and it might only be a short time before she knew the whole of it. It was imperative that she should be got away.

As he rose from the bed he wouldn't have been surprised if she had said, 'Shall we do a Mrs McAnulty?' and then gone on, 'I'm bad, Doctor. I've got something with a funny name; it's got three stages and the third stage mightn't happen for years and then it can drive you mad or blind or affect all your bones, and it can be passed on to babies and they can be born blind . . .'

'Daddy. About Mammy.'

He bit hard on his lip. 'What about her?'

'Well, I don't want to see her before I go. Can Aunt Jenny go and get my things?'

He actually smiled, at least his lips stretched, as he said, 'Yes, dear. Aunt Jinny will come and get your things. And you'd better not go back to sleep; you've got a long journey before you.' He went swiftly back to the bed and, bending over her, took her in his arms and held her tightly for a moment, and when she returned his embrace, he sighed deeply, kissed her, then left her without further words.

In the sitting-room Jenny said, 'I've made a cup of tea.'

'Thanks.' As he watched her pouring the tea out he said, 'Don't let anything stop you getting away as early as possible, Jinny, will you?'

'What's the matter, Paul? What's the matter with Bett?' She kept her attention on what she was doing as she asked him this.

'She's got VD.' His voice was level and low and he looked straight at her.

'Oh, no. No-o!' She put down the teapot and placed her two hands over her ears as if to shut out the sound. And she rocked her body backwards and forwards in the fashion that Maggie would have done under stress. Then, becoming still, she said, 'Who? Knowles?'

'No.' His head was bowed. 'That's who I thought, but I've seen him. No, it isn't him, but it could be . . .' He found difficulty in speaking the boy's name, for when he linked it with Bett his mind presented him with something indecent. It had nothing to do with sex as such; sex would have covered his wife's association with Knowles, with Brian Bolton it appeared more like incest. 'It could be young Bolton.'

Again Jenny said, 'Oh no. No-o!' Then, 'Lorna?'

'That's what I was afraid of, and that's putting it mildly. I nearly went mad when I thought . . . Anyway, it's all right, she hasn't been with him, and she doesn't know about Bett.'

'She knows they've been seeing each other, that's what's been upsetting her.'

'Perhaps, but she doesn't know about . . . about this other business. I'm sure it would have a dreadful effect on her if she did. In any case her attitude towards men will always be coloured by her mother's attitude, but if she was to know the whole of it . . . well! So the sooner you're away the happier I'll be . . . You see?'

'But I can't go. I just can't walk out and leave her like this.' Jenny's tone was incredulous.

'You've got to, Jinny.' He came and stood close to her. 'Listen. Listen to me.' He took hold of her arms. 'I'm going to see to Bett, for I realise, now it's too late, that this is mostly my fault. So don't worry. I know where I stand and what I've got to do. I should have done as you said years ago and had the whole business out. But there's no need for you to stay. Maggie's getting me someone for inside the house, and John's going to see about having her sent away for treatment. It will all be done very diplomatically; she'll just be going away on a holiday. And when she comes back . . . well then, well, I'll have to try to make amends, won't I?'

'You know I could laugh, I could laugh at you, Paul, I really could. You mean to say you think you can make amends after this? You think you can take up a normal life with Bett or, what's more to the point, she with you? Aw, Paul . . .' Jenny moved her head in derision.

'Well, I can but try.' His tone was stiff and on the defensive.

'It won't work. I know Bett. It won't work. I've got to say this now, Paul. Bett will never forgive you until the day she dies. You can turn over all the new leaves you like and try to make up to her with everything you think possible, but even before this last, awful, awful business she had worked up a hatred against you that was terrible in its intensity, and now, do you think she'll feel any better towards you knowing what she's got? Why yesterday, when I mentioned your name, she nearly had hysterics; in fact she did; that's why I wanted Doctor Price to see her.'

'You never wanted Bett to leave me, or me her, did you, Jinny? All these years you've tried to keep us together, so what's made you change now?' She could have answered him truthfully and said, 'I worked to keep you together because deep inside I wanted you separated. Work that out, and what's the answer? My conscience was too much for me; it was stronger than my desire for you.' But what she said was, 'I never wanted you to separate before last night, but after that explosion I knew it was too late and that you'll only destroy each other.'

'Well, under the present circumstances what would you have me do, walk out on her?'

'I don't know, I don't know. But what I do know is that, because you've made up your mind to forgive her don't expect her to fall into your arms out of gratitude, because it won't work.'

'Jinny, Jinny, you know me better than to think at this stage of our lives I'd even want that. I just want to do the right thing now because I'm admitting my responsibility for the plight she's in. I expect nothing in the future, Jinny. Nor do I want it . . . sufficient unto the day . . .'

'That's a very reasonable state of mind.'

'Jinny, don't sound like that.' He took hold of her hand and made her face him. 'Don't you turn on me; I couldn't bear it.'

'I'm not turning on you. I couldn't, even if I wanted to, because, well . . .' She shrugged her shoulders and her smile held all the bitterness she was capable of. 'You know all there is to know about me, don't you? You know how I feel about you; you always have.'

When she bowed her head, his hands touched her arms, and as he went to draw her gently to him she pulled away, saying sharply, 'Oh, no. That would be the end, wouldn't it? If Lorna saw you holding her Aunt Jenny . . . Oh . . .' She pushed her hand through her thick loose hair. 'I . . . I didn't mean it like that. I . . . I know it meant nothing. Oh!' She covered her eyes for a moment. 'It's as you say, I think I'd better get away and quick.' She looked at him now standing mutely regarding her. 'Aw, Paul, I'm sorry.' Her manner softened with her voice. 'You're going through the mill with one thing and another, and I'm not being much help. Go on home.' She moved towards the door. 'I'll come as soon as I can and get Lorna's things together, and perhaps you'll run us to the station; then there'll be two less in your hair.'

She was about to open the sitting-room door when he stepped quickly forward, and keeping it closed with one hand he drew her to him with the other. Putting his back against the door he held her pressed fast for a moment; then, lifting her face to his, he kissed her. When next he looked into her eyes they were large and soft and startled.

'Go on liking me, Jinny, please.'

She had difficulty in making out his muttered words. He had not said, 'Go on loving me,' but that's what he meant. She nodded dumbly at him, and he released her and, opening the door, went out.

He was going across the drive to his car when he asked himself why in the name of God had he done that? Why, when his mind was in all this turmoil, when there seemed nothing more that could happen to him had he to go and kiss Jinny like that? He supposed he had done it because she had wanted him to; perhaps because he himself had wanted to. But God hadn't he enough on his plate without getting involved with Jinny in that way? Some part of him must be slightly unbalanced . . . It must be. What he should be concerning himself with at this moment was Brian Bolton. Yes, Brian Bolton. He rammed in the gears of the car and drove it full pelt down the drive and into the main road, hardly stopping to check whether the way was clear or not . . .

There were already a number of people in the waiting-room when he passed through it and into his surgery. Again he consulted the telephone directory, and then he dialled the Mayor's number. It was Mrs Bolton who answered the phone and replied to his question, 'Oh, Doctor, he's just left the house this minute; this is one of his days for the Technical College. He'll be there in a couple of minutes. Was it anything important?'

It was nothing important, he assured her; he was doing a bit of writing and wanted some technical know-how; he thought that Brian might be able to help him.

Mrs Bolton assured him, too; Brian would be delighted. She asked after Bett, and Lorna, and remarked on it being a lovely morning.

He replied that indeed it was and then rang off.

Passing through the waiting-room again, he went down the courtyard and stood at the outer door. The square was busy. Three lorries were being loaded up with carcasses outside the Pearsons' factory. Across the road opposite the Technical College the cars were parked tightly against the kerb. A number of motor-cycles came whizzing into the square and went round the side of the college where there was parking space. Young men, in twos and threes, came hurrying up the street and went up the steps into the building. And then he saw Brian in company with another young man. He was wearing a leather jacket, drainpipe trousers, and painted black shoes. His apparel seemed to emphasise his youth and stamp him as of another world.

Stepping quickly into the roadway, Paul called, 'Brian! Hi, there!' And he had to call again before he brought the boy's attention to him.

Brian had been laughing and demonstrating something with wide gestures of his hands, and when he heard his name called and saw the doctor his hands became stationary in mid-air for a second, and the smile slid from his face. As Paul beckoned he left his companion and came across the square. But not until he was close to Paul did he speak, and then he asked, 'You want me?' not 'Good morning, Doctor,' or 'Hello, Doctor,' but, 'You want me?'

'Yes, I want you. I would like you to come to the surgery for a moment.' As he spoke Paul was forced to turn away, but after taking a few steps he stopped and looked over his shoulder to where Brian was standing, straight, stiff, and unsmiling.

'I can't come now, classes are about to start.'

'You can make your excuses about that later; I will leave that to you; but at the moment I would like to speak to you.'

Paul had turned fully round again and they were staring at each other. If there had been any doubt in his mind as to whether he was on the right track in following Knowles's lead of the Mayor's Parlour it was gone. In the face of the young man before him was a mixture of defiance, fear, and guilt.

'We get into trouble if we're late.' Brian's voice was surly.

'You'll find yourself in greater trouble if you don't come with me, and at once.' He was growling at him now, his words muttered and thick. 'I haven't much time to waste on you. I phoned your home. Your mother asked me what I wanted. I said I was doing a paper and wanted some technical advice. It's up to you. If you come into the surgery now we can leave it like that, if not, then I must advise your parents of my real reason for wanting to see you.'

He saw the boy's face turn grey. He heard him utter something that sounded very much like, 'To hell with you!' He remained still while Brian passed him, his step slow, and defiance emanating from him. Then he followed him to the house, through the courtyard and into the waiting-room.

The sight of the number of people waiting seemed to take Brian aback slightly, for after glancing behind him he allowed Paul to pass him, then followed him into the surgery. And when he had closed the door he stood just within the room.

Going to his desk, Paul said, 'You'd better sit down.'

'I don't want to sit down.'

'I think you'd better; I may have to shout if you stand at that distance, and perhaps you wouldn't want the patients out there to hear what I have to say.'

Slowly Brian moved towards the desk. His body still looked stiff with defiance, but there was open fear on his face now, and as Paul looked at him he found that he couldn't sustain the fierceness of his own anger. He almost saw the boy as a patient. Perhaps it was the chair, and the desk between them, and the atmosphere, but he wasn't seeing him as his wife's lover; at least not until Brian, poking his head out and speaking below his breath, hissed rapidly, 'It's about her, isn't it? Well, it wasn't my fault, she kept chasing me. I tried to push her off but it was no use, she kept on.'

'Be quiet!'

'I won't. That's what you got me here for, isn't it? Well, this is my side of it. She was determined from the word go. She broke Lorna and me up . . .'

'That's about the only thing I'm thankful for; I'm grateful to my wife that she accomplished that.'

'What d'you mean?'

'Have I got to put it into words for you, or are you going to do the talking?'

'I don't know what you're getting at. I did nothing to Lorna.'

'That wasn't your fault, was it?'

'Now look here . . .'

'No, my boy . . . you look here. If it had to be either my wife or my daughter I would prefer it as it's happened, and that it was my wife who contracted your disease and not my daughter.'

128

As Paul took out his handkerchief and wiped the sweat from his face he watched the boy's jaw sag, and his eyes widen. His expression was very much like that of James Knowles, and for a moment it brought a feeling of horror to Paul with the thought that he might be making a mistake for the second time . . . But no, as he watched Brian's hands go up to his face he recognised the confirmation of the boy's fear.

'I . . . I've got nothing wrong with me. I couldn't have given her . . .' The finger that came out and pointed towards Paul was trembling. 'You can get into trouble for saying a thing like that; it's taking a fellow's character away. Look. Look, I admit to being with her, and I've told you how it was, but there's nothing wrong . . . I tell you there's nothing wrong with . . .'

'You have syphilis, Brian.'

The quiet tone in which this statement was made and the look on the doctor's face, which at this moment was not that of an enraged husband, deflated the boy. His body sagged like a punctured tyre and he pressed his hand over the lower part of his face and bent his head over the desk.

'How long have you had this?'

It was a full minute before Brian spoke. 'I . . . I thought it was gone. Honest, honest, Doctor.' He raised his eyes to Paul's. He was seeing him no longer as Bett's husband, or Lorna's father, but just as the doctor, his doctor, for he was on his panel, and he began to gabble: 'I was a bit off colour about a year ago, spots and things, and then . . . then they got better. I didn't know it was anything, and then a few weeks later they came back. I had a sort of cold. I was going to come to you, but I happened to tell a fellow about it and he said . . . well, he said I'd caught it. I felt bad, awful, then it passed away and . . . and this fellow said if it cleared up like that I was all right, I wouldn't have it again.'

The face before him was dead white, the eyes were full of a mixture of fear and shame, and when the boy's voice, almost a whimper now, said, 'I'm clear again, no scabs or anything,' Paul replied softly, 'You have syphilis, Brian; it's in your blood. But we'll have your blood tested and that'll make sure.'

'Can I . . . can I be cured?'

'Yes. Yes, you can be cured.'

'But . . . but my father; he'll go mad, he couldn't stand it. He couldn't live in the town, the Mayor and all that, you see . . .'

Yes, Paul saw; he saw what effect news such as this would have on Arthur Bolton. It would break him, and his wife . . . Oh yes, it would surely break her up. Their respectable lives would be shattered. Bolton himself was an honest, conscientious, good man, but he was an ordinary man, and as such this would hit him as a terrible, shameful catastrophe, magnified a thousandfold because of the position

129

of honour he held. It would still matter if no-one else in the town knew a thing about it; once he possessed the knowledge of his son's condition that would be enough. He said slowly and emphatically, 'Your father needn't know, he need never know. I – I couldn't inform him, anyway, without your consent.'

'But he'll – he'll get to know somehow if I have treatment in this town.'

This was indeed true, although there was a social service making contacts with VD patients and this was done with the utmost tact and secrecy, so much so that contacts didn't often realise at all that they were being investigated for VD. Yet in the case of this boy, whose father was the Mayor and whose family life was open to the public, greater caution than ever would be needed. He said, 'I'll make arrangements for you to go to Newcastle, after I've taken a blood test. You needn't worry; everything is strictly confidential. I will be kept in touch with your progress, and when you come to visit me here you can be coming to give me information for my paper.'

He watched the boy's chest expand and his head droop as he muttered, 'I'm sorry, I'm sorry about . . .'

There was a short silence before Paul said, 'Well, you can prove that.'

'How?' His head came up a little.

'You can tell me how many girls . . . or women, you have been with since you first knew you had contracted this, and . . . and, by the way, do you know from whom you got it?'

He watched the boy straighten his shoulders and swallow a number of times, then smooth his hair back.

'I was with a woman in Newcastle.'

'Do you know her name?'

'No . . . No. Well, she was just one of those . . .'

Paul wetted his lips. 'You're sure it was from her you got it?'

'Yes.'

'Before you noticed anything wrong with you were you with anyone else?'

Brian's head drooped again. 'Yes.'

'Can you give me her name?'

'I . . . I couldn't do that.' Brian wagged his head from side to side. 'She lives in the town; she would get . . . Well, her people would go mad.'

'We can approach contacts in a very diplomatic way. She may be on my books or a patient of one of my colleagues . . . Don't worry, don't worry.' He put his hand up as he saw the boy's agitation. 'No-one will know from where I got this information, I promise you that. But in the course of taking an ordinary blood test, or an examination, we could perhaps accidentally discover if this girl has been infected. You see what I mean? Now give me her name.'

'Fay Baldock.'

'Fay Baldock!' Paul repeated the name in a whisper. 'But she's going to have a baby.'

'Yes, yes, but that wasn't me, she's been around with a number.'

Paul leaned back in his chair. A girl still at school was going to have a baby and perhaps already she had given it an inheritance that might cause it to be blind and a thousand and one other things.

'Are there any others?'

Brian shook his head wildly. 'Aw, I can't remember . . . Yes, yes, one. Susan Crabb. She lives in Bogs End, although she's all right.' He jerked his head upwards. 'Quite decent.'

Quite decent! 'Was there anyone else?'

'No, no, I don't think so.'

'Think hard. It's very important that the girls you've been with should be traced, because it's more than likely they don't know they have anything the matter with them, anything serious that is.'

'There's nobody else.' Brian's head was lowered again, and as Paul looked at him he knew that he was not telling the truth, but he supposed that this was enough for the time being.

He said now, 'I'll take a blood test, then I'll want you to come back tomorrow morning. By then I'll have made arrangements for you to begin treatment . . .'

'Where are you going to take it from?'

'Your arm; just a little prick.'

Brian sidled up from the chair, his head still hanging. 'You'll promise you won't tell my father?'

'Your father won't know, or anyone else who matters, if you follow my instructions.'

It was strange but he felt no reluctance when he touched the boy. 'There, that's done.' He dabbed at the small puncture; then went towards the door, and as he put his hand on the knob Brian looked at him and said again, 'I'm sorry. Believe me, I'm sorry for – for everything.'

'I believe you.' He opened the door and the boy went into the waiting-room, pushing his shoulders back as he did so, erecting the façade once again.

After closing the door Paul stood looking around the room. He felt like a man who had been in an earthquake, dazed, slightly stupid, knowing that it was impossible to attach the blame for the eruption to anyone, yet knowing that if Lorna had been concerned, vitally concerned, his reactions would have been totally different. Yet that boy had cohabited with his wife. He had, in doing so, infected her with a filthy disease. Shouldn't he, as Knowles had said, have wanted to bash his face in, wipe the floor with him? Did being a doctor make you less of a man? The truth was, doctor or no, if he had loved Bett in the slightest he would likely have done all that Knowles required as proof of a man. Yet had he loved her he couldn't have borne to live with her after this. It was because his feelings were mainly compassionate now that he could tolerate the thought of staying with her. And there was something more. He had never been able to satisfy Bett. Even at the very beginning, when he had thought he loved her, he had still been incapable of satisfying her; he was, as she had so often said and in so many ways, ineffectual . . . But look at Ivy. What had been the cause of the physical barrier that he couldn't surmount with Bett? Was it the deep rooted illogical feeling against small women? Big men were supposed to be attracted by small women, yet since he was very young he had always felt an antipathy towards them. Had he allowed himself to be married to Bett to prove something? He didn't know.

He went out now and across the waiting-room again, and noticed with a feeling of irritation, even aversion, that it was almost full.

In the kitchen Maggie said, 'Sit down and have a bite.'

'Nothing to eat, Maggie.' He shook his head at her. 'A strong coffee, that's all.'

'You won't last long at that rate, you've got to eat. Look, it's ready for you an' they can wait.' She nodded towards the surgery. 'I do believe it's a form of entertainment with some of 'em, especially the afternoon lot, the ones that have nothing to do. It's a meeting place for 'em to exchange their symptoms with their pals.'

She went on talking as she busied herself about the kitchen, until he broke in on her, saying, 'Did you take a tray up, Maggie?'

There was a pause before she answered, 'Aye. Didn't I say I would? She was asleep. I spoke three times, but she didn't let on, so I left it there. I didn't know whether she was awake or not. An' about Alice Fenwick. I caught her, an' she'll be round to see you in the dinner time.'

'Thanks, Maggie.'

He finished his coffee, pulled down his waistcoat, and went out to begin the business of the day.

6

Jenny arrived at the house about half-past nine. She could see that Paul was still in surgery so she entered by the kitchen. When she saw Maggie wasn't about she went through the hall to the playroom, and there, collecting two cases, she took them upstairs to Lorna's room. It didn't take her more than ten minutes to fill the cases; and this done, she placed them outside the door, and as she did so Maggie's voice came from the bottom of the stairs, saying, 'Who's that up there? Is it you, Miss Jenny?'

'Yes, Maggie.' She leaned over the banister. 'I'll be down in a minute.'

'All right, all right. It's just that I heard somebody above me head in the child's room.'

Jenny now turned and looked towards the far end of the corridor. What was she going to say to Bett? Well, whatever she said she couldn't appear other than callous in leaving her. And what was to be her attitude? Was she to let her know that she was aware of her condition? Or pretend that she was just leaving her with a cold?

It was Bett herself who decided this. When Jenny knocked at her door and pushed it open she saw her sitting propped up in the bed. Her face was white and pinched, yet on it there was a look of determination that hadn't been there last night. It was as if she had made up her mind that nothing was going to floor her, not even this detestable state.

'How are you?' said Jenny softly.

'Well, how do you think I'd be, eh?' Bett raised her eyebrows with the question. 'And you needn't look so shocked; you know all about it, don't you?'

Jenny turned her head towards the window. She couldn't find anything to say, but Bett didn't leave space for an embarrassing silence. 'I'm not the first one it's happened to; half of them in this town are rotten with it. All very quiet and hushed up, special clinics, but I know. I could burst a few balloons if I liked, and in some very respectable residences at that . . . All right, I was unlucky and I'll have to put up with it, I suppose. And nobody's going to say, you're too small, and too nice, and too respectable for this to happen to you. Besides, you're a doctor's wife and it couldn't happen to a doctor's wife . . . Look at me, Jenny. Jenny!' She was leaning over the side of the bed now, her tone demanding, and when Jenny turned her head towards her she said, 'When you're busy blaming me, ask yourself, would this have happened if I'd been treated right? If I hadn't been kicked to one side? . . . Now if in the beginning he'd ignored me because I'd got this then it would have been understandable, but he kicked me to the end of the corridor because I had committed the great sin of having a baby . . .'

'. . . No, no, be fair,' put in Jenny quickly. 'What you did was to hoodwink him into marrying you. You know you did. But if you had told him the circumstances, even after you were married, he would have got over it. But no, you kept it up. And from the beginning you pretended you wanted him because you were in love with him, mad about him, couldn't live without him, when the only thing you were mad about, Bett, was to get a wedding ring on your finger . . . I'm not defending him from any blame but . . .'

'. . . Huh! That's news. You're not defending him you say; why, you've done it with every breath and every look for years. You've always been daft about him. I knew that the day you introduced us.'

Jenny, staring down at this cousin of hers, experienced a feeling akin to that which Bett's tongue had engendered in Paul over the years, a feeling that urged the hand to come out and strike.

'Not that I mind a damn. And when the divorce is through the way will be open for you. And why shouldn't you try your hand now that you've been remodelled? And he'll likely fall into your arms by then; anyway, he'll need a nurse to help tend his wounds and somebody to keep him, so your money'll come—'

'Stop it! Bett . . . Stop your bitchiness. Oh, if you weren't ill I would tell you some home truths. I've been tempted to many a time in the past but—'

'Well, why didn't you, eh? You know why you didn't? You didn't because you couldn't risk having any rows with me. You wouldn't do anything that would stop you visiting the house, would you?'

Jenny's eyes were as hard as Bett's now, and her tone more deeply bitter as she said, 'The only thing you know at the present moment is that you're hurt and that you're determined to hurt in return. When I came in I was sorry I was going away; I had the idea that you might need me; but I see now that you don't and it'll make things easier.'

'You know, Jenny, you're so naïve. You always have been. But now for you to be surprised that I'm kicking out, that I want to hit back, well!'

'I'm surprised at nothing you do, Bett. You've always done what you wanted to irrespective of what anyone felt. And you've used me for years, you've always used me, and I was willing to let you go on using me . . .'

'Oh, come off it. You're like him, holier than thou, and, like him, you're a damned hypocrite, for you've had your fun on the side. You can't tell me a man's going to leave someone like you – like you were – forty-seven thousand for giving him blanket baths. He might have been paralysed and incapacitated . . .'

Jenny did not listen to the rest; she had never banged a door so hard in her life before. She was shaking so much that she had to put her hand out against the corridor wall to steady herself. Her whole body was sweating as if from a high temperature; it was in her eyes blurring her vision. When she saw the bulky outline of Maggie before her she blinked rapidly and wiped her eyes; then she allowed Maggie to take her arm and lead her to the landing. Neither of them spoke, not even when at the top of the stairs she looked towards the cases and, Maggie leaving go of her arm, she went to them and picked them up, and slowly followed the old woman down the stairs. But when she put them down on the kitchen floor, she bowed her head and, her long body shaking again, she began to cry.

'Aw, lass, lass, don't. Don't give way. She's not worth it, she's not worth your little finger. She's an ungrateful sod, and I'm not asking God to forgive me for saying it, for that's what she is. Sit you down an' I'll make you a good cup of tea.'

'No, Maggie, no thanks. The – the taxi will be back at any minute; I said in half-an-hour.'

'Well, sit down till he comes; you look like a piece of lint.'

As Jenny went to sit down, the taxi came into the yard, and she said, 'Here it is, Maggie.' She wiped her face quickly and, picking up the cases, went to the door which Maggie opened for her.

'Good-bye, Maggie.'

'Good-bye, Miss Jenny. And don't you fret. Don't fret, I tell you. Try to enjoy yourself.'

For answer Jenny said, 'Tell the doctor I've been, will you, Maggie? He's coming to pick us up later.'

'I'll do that, I'll do that.' Maggie remained standing at the door until the taxi left the yard. Then going slowly through the kitchen and the hall, she stood at the foot of the stairs and, looking up them, said to herself, 'The Devil found habitation the day you were born, and he won't be without a house until the day you die, for you're neither good for man nor beast.'

It was twelve o'clock when Paul saw Jenny and Lorna off from Newcastle. He did not indulge in the usual platitudes, exhorting them to have a nice time and to enjoy themselves, but when he had found them seats he took Lorna in his arms and kissed her, and was again grateful for her response. Then taking Jenny's hand he held it for a moment as he looked at her, and there came a softening to his face when he said simply, 'Thanks, Jinny.'

She let him go along the corridor without a word, but when she saw him alight onto the platform she called, 'Paul! Paul!' and hurried after him. Looking down on him she said what was usually said at partings: 'Take care of yourself'; but her tone wasn't light and her words were heavy with meaning.

'I'll do that.' He smiled again.

'Let me know what happens, won't you?'

'I'll write. But don't worry; I don't think anything more can happen. Good-bye, Jinny.'

It was as if the incident in her sitting-room had never taken place.

As he passed down the platform he saw Lorna standing at the corridor window and he paused and looked up at her, then moved on.

When he got outside the station he knew a sense of relief – relief that Lorna was going away – yet the relief was coupled with a sense of loss. But the loss wasn't attached to Lorna, it was attached to Jenny. Sometimes he never saw Jenny for months on end, as during the period of this last post of hers; yet he knew now that it had been a comfort to him that she was always within reach, within a car ride or a phone call. Well, he could still phone her; distance was no object to phoning. Yet now it was different. This morning had made it different. He would never phone Jenny or contact her in any way.

When he returned to the house at lunchtime he was struck immediately by the silence. There was no banging of doors and running feet and swirling into rooms . . . That was Lorna. Yet she hadn't swirled, or dashed about the house so much of late, which he had put down to her growing. How blind you could be to those nearest to you. He even missed Bett's high voice reprimanding or criticising someone or other.

As he took his hat and coat off in the hall his eyes were drawn to the stairs. He had to face her some time.

He walked slowly into the kitchen, and Maggie, turning from the stove, said, 'They got off then?'

'Yes, they got off.'

'Doctor Price has been. He said to tell you he'd be back later.'

'Oh!' He paused, then asked, 'Has she had anything?'

'She had a drink around eleven.'

He was about to walk out of the kitchen when she said, 'I'll serve you now.'

'Hold it a minute, Maggie. I'm going upstairs.'

'Take my advice and have somethin' to eat first.'

'I won't be a minute.'

Outside Bett's door he braced himself before knocking. When there was no answer he knocked again; and when there was still no answer he slowly opened the door and went into the room. She was lying well down in the bed. Her face looked swollen, hot, and sweaty. What could he say? How could he begin? How could he convey to her that he wasn't repulsed by her, that he understood, that he had to share the blame for what had happened to her? He forced himself to look at her kindly as he would at a patient who was frightened and ill, and he said, as if to that patient, 'How are you feeling?'

'Huh!' She stared up at him over the rim of the bedclothes. Then again she said, 'Huh!' And the sound was rough and rusty and told him of the soreness of her throat. 'How do you expect me to feel? But then you wouldn't know how I feel, would you?' Her voice was uneven, the words cracked.

'You . . . you can soon get well.'

'You think so? You think I can ever be the same again? Go on, tell me, tell me how I'm to go about it?'

'We'll talk later, when you are feeling better.'

'Oh, for God's sake come off your pedestal.' For the first time her body moved, and bringing up her hands she covered her eyes as she went on speaking, 'I could bear you shouting, storming, better than this sanctimonious front. And it doesn't cover up anything, I can see through it. Oh, I know you . . . I know you would like to kill me.'

'Strangely enough, Bett, I wouldn't. I've been wrong and you've been wrong. I mean it when I say we've both got to bear the consequences.'

'Oh, for God's sake go away. Go away! I tell you I can't bear you like this. It's worse than when you are your natural big-headed self.' She took her hands from her eyes and glared at him. 'Look, we don't change, we're still the same under the skin.'

Striving to keep the seemingly calm demeanour, he picked his words. 'We can try. At least in our attitude.'

Her body became quite still again, and looking down the length of the bed, she said, 'I don't want you to forgive me, not about anything, you understand? I couldn't change towards you, not in a hundred years, ever. It's over, finished. As soon as I'm able I'm going away. As I said yesterday, when everything's settled I'll have enough money to live on. Even if you bring this out in the divorce you'll still have to stump up, because what's happened to me now is through your neglect, and judges are sympathetic to women, especially wives who have been neglected.' She raised her bright, hard eyes to him. 'You see, I couldn't change. I'll feel this way about you till the day I die.'

Gazing down at this fragile-looking woman, he again thought of the compressed fierce driving power of small women. Their frames never seemed big enough for their emotions, and when the emotion was hate . . . She was right, she could never change.

He turned from the bed and walked towards the door, and as he opened it she said to him, 'Where's Lorna? I haven't heard her.'

'She's gone away for a holiday.'

'What!'

He turned and looked at her again. She had raised herself up on her elbow. 'She's gone with Jenny to Switzerland. They left on the twelve o'clock from Newcastle.'

'Damn her!'

He watched her drop back on the pillow; then he went out, closing the door softly. It wasn't Lorna she was damning, he knew, but Jinny, who she had used all her life, Jinny who had always taken her side. And now Jinny had left her when she most needed her. Not only that, she had taken Lorna with her. He pondered at this moment that Jinny, who must have always loved him, had for the first time in their long acquaintance tipped the scales in his favour.

As he went down the stairs he heard the bedroom door being pulled open and the next moment Bett's voice came croaking loudly at him. 'You and her won't get away with this. She's mine. You have no claim on her and she's coming back here. She'll take a holiday when I say so. D'you hear?'

He heard.

Paul awoke to Maggie's voice saying, 'Come on now, sit up and have this cup of tea. Come on now.'

With an effort he pulled himself up through the thick layers of sleep; then turning on to his side he forced his eyes open and grunted, 'What's the time?'

'It's turned eight.'

'Turned eight!' The sleep slid from him and he sat up and pressed his two hands over the top of his head.

'How far turned eight? You shouldn't have let me lie so long.'

'Aw, just about ten past. I'll run you a bath. Get yourself into it an' you'll be as right as rain. Drink that tea first.'

His hand shook as he lifted the cup from the side-table, just as if he'd had a skinful, yet he had got to sleep last night through sleeping tablets, not the bottle. He had needed that sleep. He rested his head against the bed panel, and as Maggie went towards the door he said to her, 'Did you have a good night?'

'Aye, I didn't raise me head until after seven, that old couch is better than a bed.'

'Were you warm enough? That morning room's like death.'

'Aw, warm as toast. I left one bar of the fire on.'

'Maggie . . . have you taken a tray along?'

'Not yet.' She had her back to him as she spoke. 'I'm just after setting it. I'll get your breakfast first, then see to it.'

'Take it up now, Maggie, will you? See to it now.'

She made a movement with her shoulders which said she would do as he wished, then went out.

Slowly he got out of bed; he still felt a bit dopey. After his bath he had a cold shower and a brisk rub down, and he was naked when he went back into the bedroom, there to come to a dead stop when he saw Maggie standing with her back to the door. She looked as if she was leaning against it. As he grabbed at his pants and pulled them on he asked quickly, 'What is it? Are you feeling bad?'

He went to her and took hold of her arms and watched her trying to speak. 'Maggie! Maggie! What is it?'

'Put . . . put something on,' she said. She pointed to his trousers. 'You'd . . . you'd better come.'

He glanced to the side of her, towards the wall, in the direction of Bett's room; then pulling on his things he went hastily along the corridor, Maggie following slowly.

Bett's door was open. Bett herself was lying sprawled across the floor. The bedside table was overturned and on the floor was a travelling clock, a glass, and a bottle. He knelt down and turned her over and felt her heart; then reaching out he picked up the bottle. It was the one from which he had taken his two sleeping tablets last night. The same bottle that he had locked up in the medicine cupboard in his surgery. That was after he had handed John two tablets to bring upstairs to her.

He looked down at his wife. Her features were contorted as if she had died in an agony or struggle. Oh, the pity of it. Oh, the waste, the waste of energy and temper, of bitterness and resentment. He wanted to lay his head down on her small breast and cry. He knew all about the remorse that comes with death. Remorse for not having done enough for the one who has gone. This happened to people who had no need to feel such remorse. But now he himself was filled with it, justifiably filled with it. Oh! Bett, Bett. This was what was meant by the irrevocability of the last chance. He knew, as he knelt there looking at this girl who had been his wife – and she looked a girl, for the years had not turned her into a woman – he knew that until the day he died he would carry with him fragments of the feeling that was in him now.

He lifted her onto the bed; then turned about to see Maggie standing, not in the room, but out in the corridor. He went towards her and they stood looking at each other in guilty silence. He had no doubt that she, too, was experiencing some of his own feeling, for she had been against Bett from the beginning. He saw that her old body was shaking, and so, taking her arm, he led her down the stairs to the hall, and after sitting her in a chair, he went to the phone and got through to John Price.

It was forty-eight hours later when John Price, standing in the drawing-room and facing Paul squarely, said, 'I know you'll think it a callous thing to say, Paul, but, between you and me, it's the best thing that could have happened to her . . . and you.'

'Perhaps.' Paul held his hands out to the fire as if he were cold, and it was some seconds before he added, 'But I can't get rid of the feeling that she must have been in a dreadful state of mind to do it; it wasn't like her. You know yourself self-preservation was her slogan, and although she was ill she was full of life, aggressive life, when I last spoke to her. She was still determined to go through with everything she had set her mind to.'

'That was likely just a front she was putting on. A thing like that happening to her was bound to affect her. The very fact that it might become known must have worried her.'

'Will . . . will it have to come out at the inquest?' He slanted his glance towards John.

'No, of course not, you know that. Not publicly anyway, but

. . . well,' John Price bit on his lip, 'I think there's one man in particular who should be told of it.'

'One man? Who?'

'Beresford.'

'Beresford! Good God, no. No! Anyway, why him, him of all people?'

'You mentioned self-preservation a minute ago. Well now, this, to my mind, is a vital matter of self-preservation. You see, Paul, I was talking to Beresford yesterday, and if I hadn't known already about that letter, the letter Bett sent him – oh yes, she told me it was she who did that – I would still have thought his manner slightly odd when speaking of you. But as it was I could see him putting two and two together. He's got a good idea now who sent that letter . . . if he hadn't before, and he's just got to say a word in the right quarter and what will happen at the inquest? There'll be an investigation. Wait a minute, wait a minute, Paul.' He held up his hand. 'You were, let's face it, having an affair with another woman; your wife found out about it, and she wrote to your colleague; the colleague in turn spoke to you about the matter and you were furious . . . Moreover, and what is much more important, you were the only one in the house with her who had access to the medicine cupboard; in fact there was no-one else in the house that night except Maggie, and I think we can rule her out . . . Now you see what I mean. You see how one thing can lead to another? Now what I propose to do is to go and have a talk with Beresford. As Bett's doctor I can do this. And once he has the facts he'll see things in their right perspective. He'll have the reason why she took her life . . . You know the first thing he asked me was had I informed the police, and I told him of course I had. And what you must realise too, man, is, that if such a rumour started it would put paid to your chances of getting that appointment.'

'That's been put paid to already, for the simple reason that I'm not going before the Board,' Paul put in quickly.

'Don't be a damn fool, Paul. This time next week when the inquest's over you'll feel differently. You've got on the short list and you're going before that Board, if I've got to drag you there.'

'It's no use, John.' Paul began to pace the floor between the window and the couch. 'Beresford's had it in for me for a long time. I would rather lose my practice than you go to him, I'm telling you.'

'Paul, look, you don't seem to have understood me. It'll be more than the practice at stake if I don't go. Now you leave this to me. But with regard to the appointment you lay too much stock on Beresford; he's really very small fry in that quarter. You talk as if he were actually on the Board.'

'He might as well be, he's a pal of Bowles, and his son trained under Bowles too. Oh, don't underestimate Beresford's connections. Do you think his locum would have got on the short list without

Bowles's aid? . . . But look, John, don't think I'm ungrateful. I'm grateful in all ways, for I don't know where I'd have been these past few days without you, but I'm just not bothered any more about the appointment. A few days ago it was important, I meant to fight to get it, but now I don't feel that way, it just doesn't matter, so I'm going to withdraw my application.'

'You're a damned fool, Paul.'

'Maybe, but there'll be other posts, if not here, in some other place.'

'You know what Beresford will think? He'll think he's frightened you off.'

'Well, let him have that satisfaction and then he can go to church and give thanks to God for his benefits to a just and moral man.'

'Well, I suppose you'll have it your own way. Look, let me take surgery for you tonight. Crawford will do mine.'

'No, no thanks, John; you've done more than enough this week. No, I've got to start some time, the sooner the better.'

'By the way, when are you expecting Jenny and Lorna back?'

'I'm not.'

'You're not? What do you mean?'

'I haven't told them and I'm not going to.'

'But, man!'

'Look, John, I think it's too soon for Lorna to come back. She's got to do a bit of thinking on her own, to adjust herself to the new relationship with me, and Jinny is the right person to help her. They were to be away for a month, so I'll leave it like that. I'll tell them just before they return, that's if they don't see anything in the papers. But I doubt it, out there.'

'There's always the possibility of someone telling, someone from these parts on holiday.'

'Well, I'll have to take that chance, but that's the way I want it, John.'

'It isn't right you being left here on your own; it isn't good for you.'

'I'm not quite on my own, there's Maggie. She's a rock is Maggie.'

'Well, just as you say. But I don't agree with you; I think you should let them know. Now I must be off. I'll look in tomorrow . . . You wouldn't like to come round for a drink after you're finished?'

'Not tonight, John, thanks.'

'All right. I'll be seeing you.'

'Thanks for everything, John.'

'Oh, be quiet . . . Until tomorrow then.'

After John Price had gone Paul stood in the drawing-room staring before him. His mind was taken up at this moment with a question which centred around Beresford and the selection committee. What, he was asking himself, was the real reason he wasn't going before the Board? Was he really afraid of Beresford and what he might say about the circumstances of Bett's sudden death? To this he gave an emphatic no. Then what was the reason, if not fear? He could find no answer to this except to say he was tired, tired of it all.

He looked around the room. The cushions in the two big armchairs were rumpled; they would never have been like that if she had been here. Nor would the evening paper be lying on the table; it would have been in its correct place in the paper rack. Her finickiness in this way had always annoyed him, yet at this moment he had a longing for her to walk in, and in her maddening way put the room to rights. His world was suddenly empty; everyone that mattered in one way or another, for good or bad, had gone from him. Ivy, Lorna, Jinny, Bett. He had a sudden longing for company, not company outside his house as he would have had if he had gone to John's, but company inside, family company. As the loneliness weighed on him he began to think of Ivy. Had she heard about Bett, and what did she think? Did she wonder if he would have married her? Would he? He didn't know. But she'd be committed now. Ivy was as dead for him as Bett was. He had a sudden impulse to go and phone Jinny. He had only to phone her and she would be home like a shot. But as he had said earlier to John, he had Lorna to consider. This news coming so soon on top of the revelation of her birth might affect her adversely; she wasn't ready to receive another shock so soon, because she, too, would suffer in the same way as himself. She, too, would be filled with remorse, for she hadn't loved her mother, she hadn't even liked her. He had been long aware of that. In a way he had taken Lorna from Bett. It had been a form of retaliation for Bett's deception, subconscious perhaps but nevertheless real.

The clock in the hall struck the quarter hour. It would soon be time to start surgery, but he would go in the kitchen and have a cup of tea with Maggie first. .

In the kitchen, Maggie said to him, 'I would like to slip into Newcastle; it's me niece, she's bad. There was a letter waitin' for me at the house when I slipped along a while ago. I could be back by nine or so.'

'You go on, Maggie, and do what you want to. And look, I'm all right here, get yourself home to bed tonight.'

'I'll do no such thing. I'll stay here until Miss Jenny and the child comes back. And if you want my opinion I think you're mad not to let them know.'

'Perhaps I am, Maggie, but I've worked it out it's better that way.'

'Have your own way then, but don't tell me to go until they're in the house.'

He put his cup down, patted her shoulder as he passed her, and went to his surgery.

Elsie as usual had placed the patients' cards on his desk, and he began to look through them. Annie Mullen was the first. He hadn't seen Annie for months. It came back to his mind the very night she had paid her last visit; it was the same night as Jinny had come back and said she was married. It was also the same night that Bett had told him that one day she would get him where she wanted him. He shied away from the thoughts that might lead to renewed recrimination of his wife. She was gone; let her rest. He felt nothing but pity for her now . . . Was that all he felt? Wasn't his big body really light with the feeling of release? He quickly passed on to the next card. This read: Harold Gray. Well, Gray was due for another visit. He looked back at Annie Mullen's card and saw that he had signed them both off the same evening. Funny how things link up. He pressed the bell on his desk, which would show a light outside his door. The next minute there was a tap on it and Annie Mullen entered.

'Hello, Annie. Sit down. How are you?'

'Middling, Doctor, just middling.' She sighed. 'But before I start yapping on about meself I would like to offer you me condolences. 'Twas sorry I was to hear of your dear wife's passing. It was tragic, tragic.'

'Thanks, Annie.'

'The mind can only stand so much, that's what I say. You know I often think, Doctor, that the body is stronger than the mind. At least, I can stand pain in me body but I can't put up with the naggings at me mind.'

'Has she been on again, Annie?'

'She's never stopped, Doctor. Anyway I'm after thinkin' I won't have to put up with her much longer.'

He looked at her grey, drawn face and said, 'Now, now, Annie, you mustn't get despondent. Come along, tell me what the trouble is.'

'It's me stomach.'

'You've had pain?'

'I could say so.'

'A great deal?'

'I'd be tellin' a lie if I said no.'

'Go and take your things off' – he nodded towards the screen in the corner of the room – 'and get on the couch.'

She nodded back at him and went behind the screen, and as he listened to the rustlings of her undressing he looked back over her case history, to which he added hard work, worry, and sorrow, which had brought her to where she was now, and at sixty-nine she was about to die. He knew it, and she knew it.

A few minutes later, when he came from behind the screen and returned to his desk, he talked to her as she dressed again. 'I'm going to get you a bed in hospital, Annie. Now you mustn't worry; you'll be under Doctor Fenner, he's a grand man. I know him well and I'll have a word with him about you. You might be in for a week or two and when you come out I'll make arrangements for you to go to a convalescent home.'

To all his talking she made no answer until she was seated opposite to him again, and then, looking him in the eye, she said, 'Do you believe I'll ever come out, Doctor?'

'Mm! It's an even chance, Annie,' he said. He should have put the percentage at ninety-five but truth was cruel and age had to suffer enough cruelty. 'It all depends if you put up a fight.' He put his hand out and patted her broken-nailed, blue-hued fingers, where they lay on the edge of the desk.

'Well, we'll see, Doctor, eh? We'll see about the fight . . . But about what you promised me.' She brought her face nearer to his. 'You won't be able to do anything for me if I'm in the hospital.'

'Don't you worry.' He picked up her hand and pressed it. 'They'll see to it. You'll be in much less pain than you are in now. You know, Annie, you should have spoken about this years ago when you first felt the pain.'

'Aw, Doctor, if I kept runnin' to you with every pain and ache I would have been camped on your doorstep for years.'

He came round the desk and put his hand on her shoulder and led her to the door, and looking down at her he said, 'They don't come like you today, Annie; they're made in a different mould.'

'Will I be seein' you again, Doctor?'

'Good gracious, Annie, of course you will. Now goodnight, and don't worry; you'll be hearing from me very shortly.'

'Goodnight, Doctor, and God bless you. And thanks for all the kindness you've shown me all these years.'

When he was seated behind the desk he did not immediately press the button. Poor Annie. Poor Annie. And when she was in hospital he wouldn't be able to visit her, at least not professionally. It wouldn't be in his province; that kind of thing was the privilege of the consultant, or assistant physician.

He pressed the button and there was no tap on the door before Harold Gray entered. He didn't look at the man but went on writing as he said, 'Good evening, Mr Gray. What's your trouble now?'

'It's me back again, Doctor. I'd be all right if it wasn't for this back.'

'Oh, yes, yes. Well, I've been thinking about your back, Mr Gray.' He raised his eyes. 'It came to my mind when I was down in the physiotherapy department. Now I think I'll send you for some massage. Since the X-rays have failed to find anything we'll try some massage. How about that?'

'It's up to you, Doctor, it's up to you.'

Yes, it was up to him . . . and old Peter Willings. Old Peter could spot a phoney a mile off. He wondered why he hadn't thought of

144

him before in connection with Mr Gray. He said now, 'I'll give you a note making an appointment. Mr Willings will give you a good do over.' . . . 'And how!' he added to himself. He'd like to gamble that Mr Gray's back would be better in a fortnight. He wrote rapidly on a sheet of paper, put it into an envelope and sealed it. If Mr Gray decided, as he very likely would, to steam the envelope open, he would find only some medical terms which he wouldn't be able to translate.

'There you are.' He handed the letter and certificate across the desk to Mr Gray. 'You take that letter to the hospital, to the physiotherapy department, and ask to see Mr Willings. Ask to see him personally.'

'I will, Doctor.' Mr Gray stood beaming down on Paul. His smile said there was one born every minute, the secret was to know how to handle them. 'Goodnight, Doctor, and thank you.'

'Goodnight, Mr Gray.'

He sat looking at the closed door. It took all kinds. The world was filled with the Annie Mullens and the Mr Grays, but how he loathed the Mr Grays . . .

It was five past seven when the last patient left the surgery and, gathering up the cards, he went across the waiting-room and into Elsie's office.

'Anything in, Elsie?'

'Yes, two calls, but I put them through to Doctor Price.'

'Now why did you do that?'

'Because he told me I had to.'

'Yes, for the last two nights . . .'

'. . . And for tonight. He got through to me just after he left here and he gave me my orders.' She bounced her head at him. 'And now you go indoors and get yourself something to eat and sit down and have a rest.'

There was a faint smile on his face as he answered her, and in the same vein as she had spoken to him, 'And you get yourself away home and leave that lot until the morning. I'm always telling you. Goodnight.'

'Yes, you are. Goodnight, Doctor.'

Elsie's tone was crisp and normal sounding. Everything had returned to normal; at least it would appear so. He crossed the empty waiting-room and stood on the step above the courtyard looking up into the sky. The long northern dusk was creeping over the Salvation Army building. The figures he could see crossing the Square through the open gate were dim, mist-shrouded.

He shivered and turned indoors, and going to the door marked 'Private' he entered the hall. Once inside, the silence and emptiness of the house hit him. He was instantly conscious that Maggie wasn't in the kitchen. He walked slowly across the hall and down the length of the passage that led to the playroom. He switched on the light and looked inside. It had been his nursery, and Lorna's nursery, but now it was full of discarded pieces of furniture and old books. Why had he come here? He closed the door, walked back down the passage and into the morning room. It had always struck cold, this room; it was too big for a morning room. Bett had been right there, but he had opposed her, even to the extent of not letting her take the old couch away. The couch now was made up as a bed for Maggie. She had refused to sleep upstairs, either in one of the spare rooms or in Lorna's. He bent and switched on the electric fire; it would be warm for her coming back. Next he went into the dining-room. He had always liked the dining-room, always liked to eat here, but of late years it had been used less and less. It was a good-shaped room with good furniture, the oval dining-room table surrounded by Hepplewhite chairs. The glass-topped sideboard with the wine cabinet built in. The china cabinet ornate but beautiful, which Bett had considered a monstrosity. He would like to use the dining-room more. He closed the door after him and went into the drawing-room. Here the emptiness of the house was more telling The easy chairs, the couch, and no-one sitting in them. The baby grand in the corner with the top closed, the music stacked neatly in the cabinet. But then the piano wasn't often used; he hadn't played it for a long time. He had the urge to go to it now and open it up, but the thought seemed indecent. He put some coal on the fire and stood with his back to it; then slowly he began to inhale, deep, deep breaths that expanded his chest and pressed out the muscles of his stomach. And do what he might, he could not check the feeling of release and relief from rising in him. All day he had been pressing it down, pushing it away, ignoring it, telling himself it was too soon for that, she was hardly cold yet; it wasn't decent. Wasn't he full of genuine remorse for the part he had played in her life and the awful end it had brought her to? Yes, yes, he was. And there was part of him just as vitally aware now, as it had been when he saw her lying on the floor, that always he would carry the deep secret feeling of guilt within him. But it was a guilt bred mostly from things undone, and not the big things, such as lack of understanding and not being able to forgive her for using him, but the small things, small unkindnesses like preventing her from moving the couch out of the breakfast-room, although he himself had always considered it an eyesore . . . Yet all this apart, he had to face the fact that the feeling of remorse was being overwhelmed at the moment by that of release. He began to pace the floor. Be as conventional as he liked, wear a face of mourning, yet to himself he knew he must own to the truth. This feeling was telling him he was free; after sixteen years he was free. It went further: it told him he was just turned forty, that he could start another life, that he was still young enough to achieve something . . . Here he stopped in his pacing as the words of Annie Mullen came back to his mind. 'But you won't be able to come and see me in hospital, Doctor.' He began to walk again, but more slowly now. There'd be more Annie Mullens and more times when he'd know the frustration of not being allowed to follow a case to the end. Once patients went into hospital they were on an island and he couldn't make contact with them until they returned to the mainland and came under his jurisdiction again . . . Did he want to be able to follow them to the island? Again he stopped, and the answer was almost verbal. Yes, he did. It wasn't true what he had said to John, he still wanted that appointment, but he knew he didn't stand a chance in hell of getting it if Beresford told Bowles about the letter. Even if they didn't connect it in any way with Bett's death he wouldn't have a chance, for Bowles too had his cronies. Sir David Cooper, for instance, who was also on the Board. And you only need two such men to give their heads an almost imperceivable shake and it would be over. There was the reason for his fear; being ignored or overlooked, being considered unfit to fill a post of responsibility. The humiliation would be too much.

There came a pause in his thinking, and he turned his steps towards the hearth again and stood looking down into the fire, and as he stared into the flames there was borne right home to him, and it came in the form of a shock, the fact that unless John made Bett's death clear to Beresford there would, as he had said, be more than the post of Assistant Physician at stake, more than even his practice; there could be his liberty. There was only Maggie's word to prove that she'd heard someone moving about around twelve o'clock, and thinking that it was himself she had got up from the couch in the morning room and gone to the door, and when she saw her mistress going up the stairs she went back to bed.

Of a sudden he began to sweat. They could question whether Bett would have been able to come downstairs if she had taken the two sleeping tablets prescribed for her. John had said he had left them on the side-table, together with a glass of water. But if she had intended to acquire more of the tablets she wouldn't have taken them, would she? He recalled the moment when John had told him that he had left the tablets on the table. He'd had his back towards him and his voice had sounded odd. He could recall it now, muffled, muddled . . . Was all this imagination? Had John really given her the sleeping tablets? If so, it would have taken a mighty effort of will for her to keep awake until twelve o'clock. But then Bett had had a mighty will . . . And what was John thinking?

He began to breathe deeply again, but it brought no feeling of relaxation now. He was imagining all kinds of things, but what he mustn't imagine was that John suspected him of doing Bett in.

This is what came of being alone in the house. He wished Maggie were back or that someone would call. He went and poured himself

147

out a large whisky, and after drinking it at a gulp he again made an inspection of the house, upstairs too now, all except Bett's room. For although her body was no longer there her presence would be heavy in it.

He stood on the landing looking about him, seeing things that he had forgotten were there. The black Chinese dragon-carved chair, which, taking into account its sloping back, had never been made to sit in. The set of Chinese prints along the landing wall. His father's tastes had run to the Chinese, and he had done quite a bit of collecting in his later years. He stood on, pondering, as if undecided what to do with himself; then releasing his lip, which had been held tightly between his teeth, he ran down the stairs and went straight to the phone and rang John Price.

'Hello there,' he said. Then, 'Oh, hello. Is that you, Muriel?'

'Yes, Paul. How are you?'

'Oh, not too bad. I just wanted a word with John.'

'Oh, he's out, Paul, he's gone along to Doctor Beresford's. Some consultation about a patient, I think . . . Why don't you come over? Now, why don't you?'

'Aw, I'm not fit company for a dog, Muriel, not tonight at any rate, but I'd be glad to keep you to your invitation tomorrow, say.'

'Any time, Paul. Just suit yourself.'

'Will you ask John to phone me when he gets in, Muriel?'

'Yes, yes, of course.'

'Goodnight, Muriel.'

'Goodnight, Paul . . . Take care of yourself.'

'I'll do that. Goodnight.'

When he replaced the phone he kept his hand on it, and as he stood thus he became conscious of the tick of the hall clock. He had never heard it so loud before. It seemed to boom through the empty house. Many a time over the years he had longed for a period of peace and quietness. Well, now he had the quiet, utter quiet, and it was terrible.

When the door bell rang his hand jerked on the phone, almost lifting it from its rest, and before going to the door he wetted his lips and pulled his collar straight. And when he opened it and saw the white face of Brian Bolton looking at him, he again wetted his lips and after a moment said, 'Yes?'

When the boy did not speak but moved his head from side to side, Paul said briefly, 'Come in.'

In the hall, his head hanging, Brian still made no effort to speak.

Paul, his tone even, asked, 'You want to see me?'

'Yes . . . but . . . but not about that.' His head was slightly raised now but his eyes were still downcast. 'I haven't been able to sleep since I heard. I . . . I can't get it out of my head that she did it because . . . Oh God!' He turned sideways and leant against the wall and buried his face in his hands.

Paul remained apart, standing looking at him. It was strange, but he had hardly given this boy a thought since Bett had died. It hadn't really entered his mind that if this boy hadn't infected her she'd be alive today. Why hadn't he thought like that? Because, he supposed, there were more factors than her contagion that had led her to take her life. The disease had merely been the last straw. Not having blamed the boy in his own mind for Bett's death he was finding it somewhat of a surprise that Brian himself should have taken on the responsibility. He hadn't given him credit for a conscience.

He found it easy to put his hand on his shoulder and bring him from the wall. 'Come along,' he said. 'Let's talk this out.'

He did not lead him into the drawing-room, for he did not know what memories that room might evoke for the boy, but went through the waiting-room and into the surgery.

After Brian was seated in the patient's chair Paul rested against the edge of the desk within arm's length of him and said, 'Well now, tell me about it.'

Brian wiped his face with his handkerchief, then blew his nose before saying, 'I've . . . I've got the feeling that I've killed her. I . . . I can't get rid of it. If she hadn't got this . . . contracted this . . .' He closed his eyes and shook his head frantically. 'Well, if she hadn't got it she would never have taken her own life, would she?' He looked up at Paul and went on under his breath, but rapidly, 'She was so full of life, so jolly. I know she was older, a lot older, but she wasn't like other women. She was like a girl; she sort of . . . well' – his head was shaking again – 'loved living, and I . . . I can see her face all the time, laughing as she twisted. She always used to laugh as . . . she . . . twisted.' As his voice trailed away his body slumped until his head was in line with his knees.

As he looked down at him, Paul realised, with a sense of pity, that youth had fled from this boy. He also remembered that it was he himself who had first brought him into the house, and, what was more, that he had thought at the time that this was the kind of boy he would like for Lorna: open-faced, clean-looking, manly. How wrong could you be? He prided himself on being a judge of character – he'd had enough practice in that line – yet when he had first seen this boy and passed his opinion on him, Brian Bolton had already been with a number of women, and infected them. How, just how could you tell what was below the skin? And could you blame yourself for not being able to tell? As he stared at the dejected figure he knew he had the power to mar this boy's future. He had only to let him assume all the blame for Bett's suicide and it would remain with him, and with what dire reactions, for the rest of his life.

As he made a swift decision, he knew, as he had done two days ago that his magnanimity was possible only because Lorna was not involved. Had she been, he had not the slightest doubt but that his attitude would have been ruthless. He said now, 'You mustn't blame yourself. She didn't take her life because of that, not entirely.'

'How do you know? Did . . . did she leave a letter or anything?' There was fear in Brian's upturned face.

He shook his head. 'No, nothing.'

'Then how do you know?' His tone was despairing, insistent.

Paul looked down, and gripping the edge of the table with his hands, did a sort of swaying motion with his body before saying, 'It's a long story. There were many things that led up to her taking her life. All her laughter and high spirits were a form of cover up. She . . . she was really very unhappy.'

'Bett unhappy?' Brian's face screwed up in disbelief.

'Yes, she was unhappy. She was unhappy because . . .' How was he going to put this? How was he going to give this boy something to hang on to, something feasible that would bring him back on balance? He had no intention of telling him about the impending divorce, yet to be convincing he must give him part of the truth. He blinked his eyes rapidly and rubbed his hand over his face. 'Well, she was unhappy because she liked youth. You see, my wife was thirty-six years of age, but she was still a young girl in her mind, and I was perhaps' – he jerked his head – 'too old for her.'

This latter statement had no truth in it, yet he could see that the boy had grasped it and was holding it fast. His expression said that he could comprehend this, and this was made evident as he said, 'Well, you're not all that old.'

'I'm turned forty.'

'Aw yes.' It was a telling sound, and the single upward movement he made with his head gave it emphasis. And this was followed by a deep intake of breath.

'I am past being frivolous. My wife liked the company of young men, so our life wasn't entirely compatible, you understand?'

'Yes, yes.'

He saw that the boy's breathing was easier.

'She was very dissatisfied with life. Although her death came as a shock, it . . . it wasn't entirely a surprise.'

'No? Then you don't . . . you don't think it was because of the other?'

'As I've been trying to tell you, not entirely.' The eagerness in the boy's attitude here warned him that it might be wrong to take all responsibility from him. It might be better to let him carry some of it, if only as a deterrent against passing on his crippling gift. 'We all do things we're sorry for,' he went on, 'but very often if we face up to ourselves these very mistakes help us to be more sensible.' The triteness of the remark, the smugness that it conveyed, checked him from following this line.

As he brought himself sharply up from the support of the table

Brian, his head low again, muttered, 'I'm going to get away. I've got a cousin in the South. He's . . . he's got a good car business; he's offered me a job.'

'What about your career? Couldn't you carry that on from some place else?'

'I don't want to; I want to make a complete change.'

'What has your father to say about this?'

'We – we've had words, a row yesterday.'

'And your mother?'

'She's terribly upset. She – she senses something's wrong and if I don't get away I'm afraid I'll blurt it all out.'

'You mustn't do that. That would upset them both much more than your going away. They'll get over you going away but I doubt whether they'll get over the real reason for your going.'

'I know, I know.'

'And what about the treatment?'

Brian rose to his feet and buttoned his coat, and he kept his eyes on his hands as he replied, 'I mean to see about that, I do.' Now he was looking at Paul and after a short silence he repeated, 'I do. I'll see to it.'

'It'll be wise, if only for your own sake, for, remember, this thing can rear its head twenty years from now. Well now,' he moved towards the door, 'you go home and try not to worry.'

He led the way out of the surgery, across the waiting-room and unlocked the door leading into the courtyard, and when he stood aside with the door in his hand, Brian paused, and, looking up at him from under his lids, said in a shamefaced way, 'Thanks. You've been kind when you needn't have been. All along you've been kind. I feel a bit better than when I first came, yet – yet I know now that I'll always feel that somehow I'm to blame for what she did.'

'That feeling will wear off with time. If it's any comfort to you, I feel the same way.'

Brian remained a moment longer looking at him; then briefly he said, 'Goodnight, sir.'

'Goodnight.'

Paul closed the door. The boy hadn't said 'Goodnight, Doctor' but 'Sir'. It put him into focus somehow. It was like a pointer to the boy's future life. It seemed to foretell that he would make an all-out effort to regain his self-respect, yet at the same time Paul knew that Brian might never succeed, for, as the boy had said, he would always feel responsible for her death. If he was inclined to be pie he could say that it was only justice that he should carry the weight with him for life, but who wanted justice? Justice was an over-estimated quality. It was odd that this last thought should bring James Knowles to his mind. He'd had no word from him, and he'd been expecting some word either through a letter or a phone call, and either form to convey abuse.

It was very unlikely that he hadn't heard, the whole town knew. He had no fear of him mentioning Bett's contagion, for Knowles was sensible enough to know that other people would link it with him. One thing Paul knew was that Knowles would place the full responsibility for Bett's death on him. Well, whatever move he made he felt capable of meeting it. He wasn't afraid of anything Knowles could do; at least he was sure of this.

As he went through the door marked 'Private' the phone rang again and when he lifted it he heard John's voice, saying, 'Hello there! That you, Paul?'

'Yes; yes, it's me, John.'

'I've just got back from Beresford's.'

There followed a pause. 'You shouldn't have done it, John, but how did it go?'

'Very well, very well indeed. I think putting him in the picture will have made all the difference.'

'You do?'

'Yes, indeed.'

'But . . . but what do you mean, John, by putting him in the picture? You didn't tell him everything?'

'As much as was necessary.'

'You didn't mention about Bri – about the boy?'

'No. Well, not exactly. What I mean is: no names were mentioned.'

Paul ground his teeth lightly, then said, 'What if he talks?'

'He won't. I can answer for his discretion. And after all, Paul, no matter what you think about him he's a doctor, and in his old-fashioned way he's a good one; and you know this won't be the first secret he's kept.'

'I'll take your word for it, John, but I'm not easy in my mind. But . . . please don't misunderstand me, I'm most grateful for what you've done, but well, knowing old Beresford, I suppose I'm prejudiced.'

'Well, you're not the only one who is prejudiced against him. I'll give you that – he's got more enemies than friends in the town – but I've always seen his good side, and he has one. By the way, I tapped him about the post.'

'You did?' Paul waited.

'Yes, we had quite a natter about it. Naturally, he's backing Rankin, but by what he said he still expects you to stand. And there's another bit of news I've got for you. Sir David Cooper is off the Board, resigned, ill-health so I understand, and Baxby's in his place.'

'Baxby? You mean from the Royal?'

'The same.'

'Oh, I know Baxby very well.'

'Good. Well, what do you say now? You're going to take a chance?'

There followed a lengthy pause before Paul said, 'Yes, John, I'll take my chance. I've done a good deal of thinking since you left and

I know I must do something besides the ordinary grind.'

'Fine, fine. Oh, I'm glad . . . Now you're sure you won't come over and have a drink?'

'No thanks, John, not tonight. I told Muriel, Maggie's gone out for a while and I'll have to stand on call. And by the way, I'm on full duty from now on. It'll do me good to keep going; it'll keep my mind off things. But thanks again, John. I can't put into words what I feel. I'll look in tomorrow.'

'Good. And I'm delighted you've altered your mind about the other business. Goodnight, Paul.'

'Goodnight, John.'

He walked slowly from the phone towards the drawing-room, but before he reached it he turned about and went into the kitchen. Of a sudden he felt hungry. He hadn't had a proper meal for days. There was a tray all nicely set on the table, and he knew there would be something tasty in the oven. Going to the Aga he opened the bottom door and lifted out the covered dish and set it on the tray, and when he raised the lid his mouth watered: curried chicken. Maggie was a dab hand with curried chicken. There should be a bowl of rice in the oven too. Bending down he pulled a dish from the back of the oven and placing this too on the tray, he carried it into the drawing-room.

When some twenty minutes later he brought the tray back into the kitchen as from habit he put the dishes into the sink and ran the hot water on them, and as he stood with his back to the sink drying his hands his eyes roamed round the familiar room. The plastic-topped stools under the table offended his eyes. He looked to the corner where Maggie's armchair used to stand but which space was now taken up by the washing-machine. Then his eyes settled on the corner near the stove where stood a small chair which would not have held one of Maggie's buttocks. Slowly he went out of the kitchen and down the passage to the playroom, and there he selected from the discarded furniture the larger of two armchairs. This he carried to the kitchen and placed it to the side of the stove. Then sitting down in it he tested it for comfort. It felt good, easy; it was a chair made to take a lot of weight. Maggie would be pleased about this. He stretched out his feet until they came opposite the lower door of the oven. Yes, Maggie would appreciate this. He must see that she got off her legs more from now on; he must get extra help in the house. She'd had it pretty tough of late years. It was a wonder she had put up with it, even taking into account her loyalty to him. Bett had been a swine to work under. It was no use trying to varnish that truth. She hadn't had the remotest idea of how to control a staff. Of course, it must have been irritating to her when Maggie loaded her blouse each night. But then, as he had said time and again, who was paying for the stuff Maggie took? In his mother's day she hadn't needed to help herself, her basket had been packed for her. During the hard times she had brought up

153

her family on what his mother had given her. Looking quietly back now, he was amazed at the patience Maggie had shown since Bett had taken over, for she had a tongue of her own and would use it at times; but what Bett had never seemed to understand, what he couldn't get her to understand, was that underneath Maggie's rough exterior lay a thoughtful, kind creature who wouldn't hurt a fly.

It was at this point of his thinking that the door bell rang once more.

He did not wonder who the caller might be as he approached the door, there was just someone at the door, so when on opening he found himself enfolded in Lorna's thin arms he stood helplessly, his own arms hanging slack, looking over her head to where Jenny, carrying only a small case and her handbag, went past him into the hall.

'Oh, Daddy! Daddy!'

He put his hand on Lorna's head, while he looked at Jenny, and he said weakly, 'Why didn't you tell me?'

Jenny's back was towards him and she turned her head over her shoulder but did not look directly at him when she answered, 'Tell you? Why didn't you tell us?'

He put out his hand and closed the door. Then leading Lorna, who was now crying unrestrainedly, past Jenny towards the drawing-room, he muttered below his breath, 'I had my reasons.'

In the drawing-room, his arm still about Lorna, he pressed her to him, saying, 'There now, don't cry.'

'Aw, but, Daddy, Daddy, it's awful.' She raised her tear-stained face to his and, shaking her head slowly, she repeated, 'Awful, awful.'

'We all feel that way. Come along, take your coat off.'

He now took her hand and led her towards the fire, and, pulling a chair forward, said, 'Sit down; you're frozen. When did you leave?'

'First thing this morning, around ten.' She sniffed and her head bobbed each time.

'How . . . how did you find out?'

Lorna did not answer but turned her drenched face to where Jenny was entering the room, and she left the answer to her. But Jenny did not speak until she had seated herself stiffly in a chair to the side of the couch, away from the fire and Paul, and then looking at him she said flatly, 'We were going into breakfast when we met the Turnbull family, the accountant. They had just arrived last night. They seemed surprised to find Lorna there and they sympathised with her about her mother's death.'

Paul lowered his gaze and bowed his head. 'I'm sorry. I did it for the best.'

Jenny gave a little sigh which took some of the tenseness from her body and her voice sounded less stiff as she said, 'I suppose you did. But it would have been better, I think, if you had let us know.' Again she sighed. Then turning to Lorna she said, 'Do you think you could make us a cup of coffee, Lorna?'

It seemed a surprising request to make of the girl, the state she was in, and Paul said immediately, 'No, no, sit where you are, I'll see to it.' As he made to move from the hearth Jenny said quickly, 'Let Lorna do it, please.'

Lorna looked from one to the other, and when her eyes were held by Jenny's she rose and went past her father, and as she rounded the couch Jenny touched her gently on the hand, saying, 'Just make it in the cups, as long as it's hot it'll do. All right?'

'Yes, Aunt Jenny.' Lorna's voice was submissive. She was aware that her Aunt Jenny wanted her out of the room, and she knew why.

The door had hardly closed behind her before Jenny, leaving her chair, went to the fire and resting her forearm on the mantelpiece stared at the frame of the picture as she said, 'Now tell me what happened.'

Paul stood looking rather helplessly at her back. He didn't know where to start. Jenny seemed alien. Whatever her attitude when they were to meet he hadn't expected it to be like this. 'Well,' he began, 'I don't know whether they told you or not, but she took her own life.'

'They told us all right. Mrs Turnbull has a flair for shock tactics. I couldn't believe it at first, I couldn't take it in. But that wasn't Lorna's reaction; she took it in immediately and has hardly stopped crying since. You know something.' She swung round and faced him. 'She blames herself for Bett's death.'

'Nonsense.'

'No it isn't not with her way of looking at it. Not when she remembers what she's been wishing on her mother for a long time now. Do you know she'd been wishing that Bett would die, that she would drop down dead, or be knocked down – anything as long as she was out of the way?'

'She told you this?'

'Yes. She's talked of nothing else the whole journey.'

'Well,' he hunched his big shoulders, 'it's not unusual for children to wish death on their parents, not unusual at all.'

'But she's not a child, Paul. Don't you realise that? She's a child no longer. And what's more she's older than her years . . . Oh,' she put her hand up to her head, 'why didn't you get in touch with us and bring us back?'

'It wouldn't have made any difference, would it, if she thinks like that? I can't see that it would have helped in the least.'

'Of course it would. It would have been different coming from you. But having it shot at her in that strange hotel miles away, and then to face that awful journey feeling like that.'

'I'm sorry, I'm sorry.' He sat down on the couch and leant his elbows on his knees and supported his forehead with his hands. 'It wasn't that I didn't want you back. I – I thought, coming so close on everything else it might affect her.'

'You would really have let us stay there a full month and not told me? I cannot understand it.'

'No, perhaps not.' He shook his head wearily.

She stood looking down intently at him for a moment. Then slowly she lowered herself into a chair to the side of the hearth and asked, 'Who found her?'

'Maggie.'

'That Mrs Turnbull said she had taken a full bottle of sleeping tablets. Is that right?'

'Yes. She came downstairs around twelve and went to the surgery cupboard. It was the easiest thing in the world; she knew where the keys were.'

'And it wouldn't have happened if I'd been here.'

He brought his head up quickly. 'What! Now don't you be silly, Jinny.'

'I'm not being silly. I know for a certainty in my own mind that if I hadn't gone away she would never have done it. I knew I shouldn't have left her. She was ill, almost demented – yes, almost demented, and I left her with you and Maggie, and neither of you had a grain of sympathy for her.'

He looked at her steadily before saying, 'But there you are wrong. I felt more kindly towards her that last day than for many a year, and I told her so as best I could. But it didn't make the smallest difference to her; she was determined to break me.'

'If that's the case, what made her take the tablets?' Her mouth now fell slightly agape and she eased herself up from the chair by gripping the back rail. 'Paul, you . . . you . . . ?'

'. . . No, no, I didn't, Jinny.'

'I'm sorry.'

'You needn't be, for I won't say there weren't times I didn't think about it. But my opinion is she took her life because she couldn't bear the thought that she had contracted the disease.'

'Yes, that's what I think too, and that's why I'll never be able to forgive myself for leaving her.'

'Now, now don't be silly.'

As he made a move to go to her, Lorna came into the room carrying a tray, and after placing it on the table she silently handed Jenny a cup and then one to her father, and taking the other cup she sat down on the edge of the couch and slowly and methodically she began to stir her coffee.

They were sitting now like three strangers in a waiting-room, quietly ill at ease, waiting as it were for a signal to move. When

156

the silence of the room became unbearable, Paul, leaning towards Lorna, said, 'Are you very tired, dear?'

'Yes.' She nodded, still looking down into her cup.

'Have an early night, eh? You'll feel better in the morning.' Again she nodded.

'We'll all have an early night. I'll go and switch the blankets on.' He was in the act of putting his half-empty cup on the table preparatory to leaving the room when Jenny said, 'I'll be going home, Paul.'

Before he could protest, Lorna exclaimed loudly, 'Oh no, Aunt Jenny!'

'Yes, Lorna, I think it's better this way, but I'll be back in the morning.'

As Paul stood looking helplessly at Jenny's profile he sensed in her face the beginning of a battle that would be harder for him to fight and win than the straightening out of the relationship and re-establishing the love between himself and Lorna. Just a short while ago he had pictured what it would be like to have them both in this room. Now the picture had come alive and the reality held no promise of happiness, not even contentment, it simply posed another problem. How had he expected Jinny to react? He had known that she would be upset, but not that she would take the blame for Bett's death on her own shoulders . . . Brian, Lorna, Jinny, and himself, all feeling responsible for Bett's death . . . And she wasn't worth it. The thought appeared blasphemous, but he held on to it and attacked it by repeating, no, she wasn't worth it. In life she hadn't done one good thing that he was aware of, and in death she had the power to rob four people of their peace of mind. Well, he wouldn't let her. He had already done what he could for the boy. He was positive he could explain Lorna's guilt feelings away. For himself he was damned if he was going to let her get the better of him after all; he would deal with his own conscience . . . But could he deal with Jinny's? He would have to talk to her. It suddenly became the most important thing in life that he should get things straight with her. But he must go careful.

When he heard Lorna say, 'I think I'll go up, Daddy,' he answered quickly, 'Yes, yes, dear, I think that's the best thing you can do. I'll come in and see you in a little while. Go on now.' He went to her and kissed her gently and said softly, 'It'll be all right, it'll be all right.' Then he watched her go to Jenny and cling to her for a moment before turning swiftly away and running from the room, not like an adult as Jinny had suggested, but, to him, like a very young girl. And he saw this as a hopeful sign.

When the door had closed he did not turn immediately to Jenny and say, 'Why do you want to go home?' It was some seconds before he spoke, and then he forgot all about going careful for he said outright, 'You're going to hold the whole thing against me, aren't you? I can see by your face you are.'

157

It was a full minute before she said, 'No, not against you, against myself.'

'Oh, that's nonsense. You did everything possible you could for her for years. You did more for her than anyone else.'

'Except when she needed me most.' She turned and faced him fully now. 'Paul, I knew that morning I shouldn't go. I almost didn't take the plane; I had a dreadful feeling on me. I might as well tell you now that we quarrelled bitterly before I left the house, but when I'd time to think I realised it was because she was ill and lonely and frightened. I phoned twice and couldn't get through; I wanted to say to you I was coming back. I tell you I had a premonition that something was going to happen. And now,' she spread out her hands, 'it's with me for life.'

He moved slowly towards her and when he was within touching distance of her he stopped. 'Jinny.' His voice was soft and had a note of pleading in it. 'I know how you feel, believe me, for there's part of me eaten up with remorse, but we're human beings and time will bury these feelings. Later on we'll be able to look to the future . . . we will, Jinny.'

'You think so?' She was staring into his face. 'You really think so? I wish I could feel the same.'

'You will.'

'I doubt it.' Her lips were trembling and she began to pluck at the front of her suit with her fingers, and when his hand came over hers she screwed her eyes tight and the tears pressed from beneath her lids and rolled down her cheeks.

'Jinny. Jinny, don't. Please.'

'You . . . you know how I feel.' She was sobbing and gasping now. 'There's no need to go into all that, but as impossible as the situation was for me when she was alive I felt nearer to you . . . But . . . but now, well now, her going has made a gulf so wide that I can never see myself crossing it.'

He brought her hands to his breast and held them tightly and he looked at her long, still ordinary-looking face, drenched with her tears, and he knew that in her and her alone lay his future peace and what happiness there still remained for him. He knew now that he had always needed her, but he needed her most at this moment. Yet he also knew that if he were to press that need he would lose her, perhaps for good.

'When is . . . when is she to be buried?'

'Monday.'

She withdrew her hands from his, and turning slowly from him she walked towards the door, saying, 'I'm going back to work as soon as I can.'

Again he took the opposite course from that which his mind and caution prompted. He knew this was neither the time nor the place,

158

but he had to say it. 'Jinny. There's a job waiting here for you if you want it.'

She stopped but she didn't turn round. 'Thanks, Paul.'

He stood still as he said, 'You don't consider taking it? I mean, just to look after the house . . . and us?'

'I couldn't. But thanks all the same.'

He warned himself again, but it was no use, he had to ask her. 'Do you think you would later on?'

'I don't think so, Paul. I don't know. Don't ask me now . . . the way I'm feeling . . .'

When he moved to her side and took her arm she looked at him and all the hidden sadness of her life was in her face. For years and years she had dreamed of what it would be like to be loved by this man. She'd had to fight her jealousy and envy of Bett. She had thought that if he would only love her, take her once, just once, she'd live on it for the rest of her life. And here he was, offering her everything and she couldn't take it. She doubted whether she'd ever be able to take it, for what he didn't know, and what he wouldn't lay much stock on, if she were to tell him, was that she, like Lorna, had wished Bett out of the way. That it had been a deep hidden wish, and that she hadn't really acknowledged it until Lorna had blurted out her feeling for her mother, she didn't alleviate her guilt. She felt almost buried under it. She doubted if Paul would ever understand how deep her feeling of responsibility for Bett's death went.

'No-one knows the weight of a conscience except the owner.' She'd heard that somewhere and now she knew just how true it was.

'What did you say?'

'Nothing. I – I was just thinking.'

'Try not to think too much, and don't judge anything on the way you're feeling now. I won't press you, I'll leave it to you. But the job will always be there, Jinny. I just want you to know that.'

She bowed her head deeply; then turning from him, she went into the hall. And as he watched her there came to his nostrils a scent, a scent that he had always associated with Bett, a particular perfume she used; it was as if Bett herself were crossing the hall, passing between them. And now the scent was a smell and he actually felt Bett's presence. For a moment he imagined he heard her laughing as she turned his own phrase, indicating her victory: 'She's tipping the scales towards me again.'

Dead or alive, it seemed that Bett would win. The hell she would! At this instant there came the sound of movement from the kitchen. Maggie was back.

As if attacking the still warm bitter spirit that stood in the space between him and Jinny he gripped the door and flung it wide, bouncing it back against the wall.

159

When Jenny turned her startled face towards him, he advanced to her, smiled, and, taking her arm firmly in his hand, led her towards the kitchen saying, 'Maggie's just come in. Let's go and have a natter with her, eh? Her home-spun wisdom has a habit of clarifying things. Oh, to be as uncomplicated as Maggie! What do you say, Jinny? Wouldn't life be simple if we could accept things like Maggie does?'

Jenny, seeing him through her blurred vision, thought that at the moment he looked boyish, and that there was even something child-like about his way of thinking, as child-like as his Maggie's.

PART FIVE

MAGGIE

It was many years since Maggie had been in Newcastle and she
felt slightly lost when she walked out of the Central Station, but,
she reasoned, Northumberland Street would still be in the same
place, and St Clement's Church wasn't likely to have moved itself.
Nevertheless, she noticed, as the bus took her towards St Clement's,
that there had been some changes over the last few years, and also
that some were desperately needed still. She alighted from the bus
and went along a street that she remembered well, and when she
saw the old iron and taggerine heaped up in the little railed gardens in front of the houses she thought to herself, 'It's a bulldozer
they want along here; you would have thought that they'd have
pulled such streets down years ago.' But still, she had to concede
when she came to a square that held towering blocks of new flats
that they were getting on with it.

St Clement's, as she surmised, was still in the same place. It had
always served the poorer quarters and would likely go on doing so,
new blocks of flats or no. They had always held confession here on a
Thursday night and she hoped to God they still continued to do so,
or her journey would have been in vain.

When she entered the dim church and saw half-a-dozen people
scattered in the pews before the confessional to the right of the door
she thanked God; then taking a seat she slowly lowered herself onto
the wooden kneeler and prepared herself for confession.

By the time her turn came there were at least another eight people
waiting to go in after her, and for this she also thanked God.

When she entered the confessional box she had to grope for the arm
rest and the kneeler and when she was settled she raised her eyes and
saw the outline of the priest's hand that was cupping his face. His nose
protruded beyond the stub of his little finger; it was a fleshy nose as
far as she could make out, with wide nostrils. The rest of him was
all in shadow, beyond the light of the solitary candle.

'Father, I want to make a confession.' It wasn't the set type of approach to the making of a confession, which usually began along such
lines as, 'Pray, Father, give me your blessing for I have sinned.'

'Make your confession, my child.'

Child is it, she thought. It was nice to hear that again. It was many, many years since she had heard that phrase.

'Make your confession, my child.' Aw yes, it was nice, sort of comforting. So she began: 'I haven't been inside a church for years, Father.'

'When did you last make your Easter duties?'

'Oh—' She stopped herself from saying begod! 'Oh, many a long year since, Father; I've lost count.'

'Ten? Twenty years?'

'Oh, I've been about twice in that time I should say, but I've done no harm to anybody in my life up to recently. I've got a sharp tongue, I'll admit, but I'm loyal, aye, I'm loyal in me way.'

Maggie stopped here and the priest waited. This certainly wasn't the usual line he had to listen to. When the penitent didn't go on he proffered in a whisper, 'And now you've done some wrong to someone?'

'Aye, in a way, Father. Aye, yes, that's it. To tell you the truth I've poisoned a woman.'

The priest's middle finger knocked sharply against the end of his nose, and then, his voice lower still, yet the words piercing, he said, 'You mean you've committed a murder?'

'You could say that, Father, but I don't look upon it like that. It was somethin' I had to do.'

'Nobody has to commit murder; it – it's the greatest of sins to take a life.'

'There are different ways of killin', Father. You can watch someone being killed slowly each day. An' you can see them bein' driven to the limits of their endurance until you expect them in their turn to kill . . .'

'Was she old?'

'No. No, she was youngish, but she was bad. And she'd got a disease.'

'And you killed her because of that?' There was the sound of horror in the young priest's voice.

'No, not because of that, but because her husband had been goin' to divorce her because he couldn't stand any more. And then she goes and gets this thing from goin' with other men. And I could see him sacrificing the rest of his life to her because he blamed himself for what had happened afore, or what hadn't happened for years atween them. It's all the way you look at it. You see, they hadn't been like man and wife from shortly after they were married, and I could see him goin' on until he was an old man tryin' to make amends an' being broken on the wheel of her. I just couldn't let it happen.'

There was a long pause before the priest asked, 'How did you do this?'

'I got some sleeping tablets and I mixed them up in a glass, and I

162

woke her out of her sleep – she'd already had a few of them – and I made her drink it.'

'This is terrible, terrible.'

'Perhaps you bein' a priest of God may think like that. It's understandable.'

'Don't you? Aren't you laden with remorse?'

'Truthfully speaking, no, Father.'

'Then why have you come to confession?'

'Well, I thought I'd make me peace with God, because this is atween Him and me entirely. He knows the rights and wrongs of the case, He knows me motives. He knows that there was no personal feeling in it at all, for although I didn't like her, I wouldn't have got rid of her on me own account. He knows the real reason why I did it, that's why I've come.'

The priest was stunned by this logic. He knew that the person on the other side of the grid was no longer young, over middle-age, perhaps old, yet the voice gave no indication of age, for it was strong and vibrant. He had a duty here that was clear; he must make her see that this crime, for crime it was, was not only between her and God, but between her and man, her and justice. He said to her, 'I must talk to you further about this. Would you be willing to see me after confession?'

She paused for a moment before saying, 'Yes, Father, as you will.'

'Then go out into the church, go to Our Lady's altar and begin on the sorrowful mysteries. I'll be with you shortly. Now make a firm, firm act of contrition.'

She hadn't said an act of contrition for years, but the words came back to her mind as if she had only used them yesterday: 'Oh, my God, I am very sorry that I have sinned against Thee because Thou art so good and by the help of Thy Holy Grace I will not sin again. Amen.'

'Thank you, Father.'

She went out of the box and made straight for the church door, and from there she hurried up the dark street. She was no fool, she told herself; that was why she was glad there had been people going in after her, it would keep him occupied for a time. She had done what she had felt compelled to do, and her conscience was at rest, and that was all there was to it. He might look in the paper to find the suicides. Well, there was never a week went by but there was a number of them . . . Death from Misadventure. Death while the balance of the mind was disturbed. He had served his purpose. She wasn't goin' to have him haunt her for the rest of her life, however long or short that was. What she had done was, as she had told him, atween her and God, and she would do it the morrow again if called upon. And now she must get back to himself for he'd be feeling lost in the house on his own. It wasn't good for a man to be on his own . . . Yet better that than have his brain turned and have him do something he'd suffer for.

As she got out of the bus and went towards the station the thought came to her that if by accident she should happen on Miss Jenny's address there'd be no harm in droppin' her a line to ask if she was enjoyin' her holiday, and to say what a great pity it was about the missus. She had always known that the poor plain body was a bit taken with himself, and she'd had proof of it when she'd gone and got her nose done, but she hadn't imagined for one minute that that little snipe had been aware of it. And then for to throw it in the poor soul's face as she had done the morning she left . . . Well, she was where the good God pleased at this minute and she'd try to think no more ill of her. Her concern now was with the living, with one human being, to see him settled and happy afore her time came. She had always seen to his needs as far as it lay in her power. Hadn't she manoeuvred Ivy into his bed? She had made the excuse that she couldn't do the stairs, knowing that a full-blooded young widow like Ivy couldn't wash a man down and remain cool; an' hadn't she been right? She only wished to God Ivy had come into the house years ago. But now from what she could gather Ivy was no longer in the picture, and all things considered it was just as well, for he could never have married her. No, that would never have done. An' she herself wouldn't have stood for it . . . Ivy as mistress of the house! That would have been more intolerable than seeing him sacrifice himself to a dirty disease-ridden woman. But with Miss Jinny . . . well, she was a different kettle of fish. She would know her place and realise that the kitchen, particularly the larder, was a very minor part of it.

As she gave the porter her ticket she said it was a nice evening and it was good to see the days drawing out, and he said in reply, it was indeed. And he told her to be careful how she went for she seemed a little unsteady on her feet. It was thoughtful of him to tell her to be careful; people were kind. Oh, aye, people were kind.

As she sat in the train she wished she was home; she didn't think she'd ever visit Newcastle again, and she told herself she wouldn't miss much.

At Fellburn station she hailed a taxi to take her to the house. And why not, why not indeed! The circumstances, she felt, warranted such a luxury; it wasn't every day in her life that she went to confession.

When she entered the house by the kitchen door she sensed immediately that there was company in; the kettle wasn't in the place where she had left it, and there was the coffee tin on the table and three cups missing from the rack.

She had just taken off her hat and coat, put on her apron and made her way to the stove when the door opened, and as she turned and looked at Jenny and himself standing side by side, there entered into her a beautiful feeling. It was as if her body was filled with light; it was a good feeling and she took it for a sign of God's utter forgiveness; that Miss Jenny was back in the house at this time showed that the Almighty, like herself, was working towards one end. And she thanked Him as she went forward, her hands outstretched towards Jenny, for she said, 'Thanks be to God.'

THE BLIND MILLER

'Though the mills of God grind slowly, yet
  they grind exceeding small;
Though with patience He stands waiting, with
  exactness grinds He all.'

HENRY WADSWORTH LONGFELLOW

PART ONE

CHAPTER ONE

'I should have known.'

'Why should you?'

'Me mother should have told me.'

'How did she know that they were going to give you fruit with your tea? And, anyway, you said you used the fork all right.'

'I felt clumsy. It was awful . . . awful.'

'What's up with you, our Sarah, worrying about using a fork to fruit? Lord, if I was in your shoes I'd be thinking about what they thought about me . . . along that line.'

'Well, I am . . . that's what I'm doing. What'll she think about me using a fork as if it was a pick shovel?'

'Look, forget about the fork and tell us what it was like, the house and everything.'

'Oh, it was lovely, lovely. You've no idea, Phyllis.'

The two sisters sat on the edge of the bed, their thighs brought together by the sagging mattress. They looked at each other, one bursting to unload her experiences over the hump of humiliation brought about by a new venture in table manners at a Sunday high-tea, the other waiting to be warmed in the glory that had befallen her elder sister.

'There was a beautiful linen cloth on the table; everything was to match, china and all that, and tea-knives besides the knives and forks. I knew what they were for all right.' She pulled a face; then her features flowed into a quick smile that illuminated her surroundings like a light through a dirty window. 'And they've got a proper dining-room, they don't eat in the kitchen.'

'That's because it's a corner house, it's double like.'

Sarah nodded quickly. 'And there's a carpet in the front room, and there's a whole suite; and a piano, and a cabinet – glass-fronted you know, with best china in it. Oh, Phyllis, is was lovely.'

'Did you get upstairs?'

'Yes, she took me up to take me things off.'

'All of them?' Phyllis pushed Sarah in the shoulder and they swayed from each other before the bed brought them close together again.

'Don't be nasty, our Phyllis.' Sarah's eyes were blinking; her face was straining not to laugh now. 'That's what they do. An' you know something . . . they've got a flush lav.'

'No!'

'Yes, truly.'

'Coo! Did it wet your things?'

'Don't be silly.'

'I'm not; I sat on one once and pulled the chain, Ooh, lor! I was wringing.'

'You are a fool you know, our Phyllis; you don't pull it till you get up.'

'I know now. But go on. Did they leave you in the front room to do your courtin'?'

Now it was Sarah's arm that shot out, and so quick was the thrust that it knocked Phyllis from the edge of the bed on to the floor. Within a minute they were back into position again, holding each other as they rocked silently together.

When they were sitting upright once more, their faces wet with their controlled convulsions, Phyllis said, 'I wouldn't have been surprised if they did, you know. Coo! He's not slow on the uptake, is he? You've only been going with him for three weeks and he asks you home. There's May Connor, she's been going with Harry Willis for six months and never darkened his mother's door, and they're supposed to be goin' strong.'

'That's different . . . I don't suppose Harry's particular for May to see inside the house.'

Phyllis wriggled her buttocks on the bed, which brought her feet from the floor, and she lifted them upwards and looked at them as she said, 'They're talkin' about you next door. Old Ma Ratcliffe had her head over the wall the minute you went round the bottom corner. She said to me mother: "Sarah's looking bonnie the day".' Phyllis nudged Sarah with her elbow and stuck her tongue well out. 'That was a sure lead-up to the old snake sticking her fangs in. Will I tell you what she said?'

The eyes of the two girls were now slanted towards each other. 'I'll likely have heard it all afore,' said Sarah.

'You haven't, not this bit . . . we're all one family now.' Phyllis drew her upper lip to a point, showing her large white teeth, and, thrusting her chin out, brought her face into a good imitation of that of their neighbour as she said, ' "Well, Annie, you know nothing can ever come of that, we being at the bottom end." We, you note . . . we're all one big family now . . . no looking down her nose the day. "Stink-pots like the Hetheringtons couldn't be expected to walk this way with wedding rings." That's what she said.'

'Who's talkin' of wedding rings?' Sarah's voice sounded hoarse and threatening.

'Well, I'm only tellin' you what she said. And she didn't forget to rub it in an' all about them being chapel. And then she fired her last gun afore saying she had to get the tea ready. "You'll be having the priest sitting on the doorstep from now on," she said.'

6

'Damn her!' Sarah got to her feet and walked the two steps to the window, and Phyllis, looking at her straight back, said, 'Eeh! our Sarah, fancy you sayin' that; I thought you had said you'd promised Our Lady never to use a swear word in your life.'

Sarah did not turn her head but stared through the lace curtain to the row of chimneys opposite. Her whole being was flooded with an anger that was not just the outcome of the moment, but stemmed from years of puzzled thinking, of probing and groping blindly to know the reason why. She had been protesting constantly for ten years now from a particular day when she had seen, as if in a revelation, the whole of her life being spent in the lower end of the Fifteen Streets. She'd had a bad cold and her mother had given her nearly half a bottle of cough mixture. It had knocked her silly, and she'd seen funny things, most of which she had forgotten. But she hadn't forgotten the mud picture, as she now thought of it. In the picture she not only saw her mother and Phyllis and her new step-father, wallowing, choking, in a sea of mud, mud like that which filled the huge timber pond at Jarrow Slacks, a mile down the road, but all the people of the Fifteen Streets, all of them, were choking in the mud; there wasn't one of them who wasn't up to the neck in it. And she knew that they all knew there was no hope of getting out. Yet they still struggled. Some upheld others, but some, like Mrs Ratcliffe next door, put their hands on the heads of those nearest them and pushed them under.

'I hate that woman.' She was glaring down at Phyllis now. 'She's never so happy as when he's goin' for us. But I'll show her. I'll get out of here, you'll see.' She bounced her head at her sister, and Phyllis nodded back, saying under her breath, 'An' the day you go I'll be on your heels.'

Again they were seated close, and Sarah's voice, stripped now of all anger, asked softly, 'But what about me mother?'

Phyllis, sitting straight on the iron frame, eased her hip to one side before she said, 'She wants us to go, an' as soon as possible. There'll be no peace until we get out.'

'She told you that?'

'No, no, of course she didn't, but she could manage him if we were out of the way.' Phyllis sighed now, and tossing her head back and her long fair hair from her shoulders, she supported herself with her hands, gripping the iron frame of the mesh base as she looked up to the ceiling, and said dreamily, 'I wish I had a bust like yours.'

This remark brought from Sarah a quick downward jerk of the head. The movement showed impatience and an effort to crush down laughter. She got up from the bed, and with her back against the narrow window-sill she looked down on Phyllis, and once again tried to understand this mercurial sister, who could change not only a conversation but her manner so quickly as to leave you bewildered. She said, 'You can have it, and welcome.'

7

'That's what they go for, a bust.'

'Don't be nasty, our Phyllis, I've told you.' In embarrassment Sarah gathered the frayed end of the lace curtain in her hand and laid it in a bunch on the sill.

'I'm not. I tell you I've watched you going past the bottom corner. An' I've seen the men. Some of them look at your legs sometimes, an' others at your face, but their eyes nearly always finish up on your bust.'

'Our Phyllis!' Sarah was now kneeling on the bed with one knee; pinning her sister down by the shoulders with her hands as she hissed, 'Stop it! Stop such talk! And you only seventeen. You're as bad as the women up the street standing round their doors.'

The bed began to shake and once more they were enfolded together, their arms tight round each other, rocking from side to side, the springs making a zing-zing sound as they moved, until Sarah choked, 'Stop it! You'll have me mother up.'

'I can't help me bust.' They were lying quiet now, their faces wet with their laughing.

'Don't try, you've got something there.'

Again their arms were round each other; again the springs were zing-zinging.

'Do you know you'll have to go to Confession?'

'What for?'

'Well, talking about such things.'

'Oh, our Sarah! You know you are a bairn in some ways. Do you mean to tell me you'd tell Father Bailey about your bust?'

Sarah pulled herself off the bed; a battle was now going on inside her. This too was an old battle. She wanted to laugh loudly at Phyllis's suggestion, but she knew that it was no laughing matter, for if she had been guilty of bringing up the conversation about her bust she would definitely have had to confess to bad thoughts.

As she stood up there came from below the sound of a door banging, and the sound brought Phyllis from the bed too.

'Better get in.' They were whispering.

Quickly they began to undress, standing where they were in the two-foot space between the wall and the iron bed. As they bent down to pick up their clothes their buttocks bumped and this brought a suppressed giggle from Phyllis, but Sarah, swiftly hanging her things on a hook behind the door, motioned her to silence. Then almost simultaneously they knelt down side by side and, crossing themselves, said their prayers.

Sarah, holding the spring taut with gripped pressure from her hands, waited for Phyllis to crawl cautiously to the far side of the bed, and not until her sister was settled did she take her hands away. Then, sitting on the edge of the bed, she slowly allowed her large frame to sink towards her sister; and when they were close once again

Phyllis whispered, 'He'll be disappointed that we're in; he'll have to find something else to yell about.'

Sarah nodded, then whispered, 'Goodnight.'

'Goodnight,' said Phyllis.

They both turned slowly on to their backs and lay looking up at the flaking ceiling, fading now in the light of a summer evening.

It was ten o'clock on this Sunday evening. It was warm and nice outside; couples would be strolling up in the country still, yet here they were packed off to bed as if they were still bairns. Well, Sarah supposed Phyllis wasn't much more being just seventeen. But she herself was nineteen, nearly twenty. It couldn't go on; it mustn't go on. She thrust her long legs down the bed, and when her toes caught against the iron rail she bit tight on her lower lip and screwed up her eyes and in the bright sparked-off pain patterns in the depth of blackness in front of her lids she saw pictured in vivid detail the tea-table in the Hetheringtons' house. And once again she was overwhelmed with shame about the fork business, until the shame was suddenly flicked away and her eyes sprung wide with the thought, It'll come to nothing, them being chapel.

All along she had known it would come to nothing – what hope was there for a Catholic and a chapelite? It was a greater barrier than a social one. The Hetheringtons might live in the Fifteen Streets, but the gap between her family and them was as wide as between a prop man in the docks and one of the managers living in his big house down Westoe end in Shields. The fact that the four Hetherington men all went to work in collars and ties and that three of the men living in one house were actually in work, whereas her own father – as her mother had insisted she call him – hadn't done a batt for the past seven years, and would have fought shy of it now if he had the chance of it, even this barrier, the difference which meant living with bugs behind the wallpaper or without them, could, with a miracle, have been surmounted, but not even time or death could alter the religious difference. And yet here she was, yarping on to herself about making a mess of using a fruit fork. That's what she did, she told herself heatedly: she never faced up to things, always started worrying about some little thing that didn't matter a damn, trying to cover up the bigger issues, like trying to cover the sky with a blade of grass. If you held the grass or anything else close enough to your eyes you could blot out what was behind it. At least for a time, then your arm got tired, so to speak. She had to face up to things in the end, but it was always in the night that they caught up with her, which was why she was so tired in the morning.

Well, she had known who he was from the word go, hadn't she? When he had stood outside the shop waiting for her she had known he was from the posh house at the end of Camelia Street. Everybody knew the big house at the end of Camelia Street because it wasn't

9

divided into two. It had seven rooms and a brass knocker on the door, and the curtains were always beautifully white.

He had said to her 'Hello', and she had answered 'Hello', while sweat had suddenly burst into her oxters and the palms of her hands.

'I hope you don't mind.' He had stopped, as embarrassed as she was, and then she had answered. 'No, no, not at all', in the swanky tone she tried to adopt at times. She had got it from the people who came into the sweet shop – some talked swanky. But they didn't get many like that, although it was a good-class shop.

He said, 'Can I walk home with you?'

The shop was in Ocean Road in Shields and she always took the tram from the Market Place to Tyne Dock and there changed to the Jarrow tram. In the mornings she usually walked part of the distance to save the fare, but at night, her feet were nearly always swollen with so much standing, and her heavy build didn't make them any better, so she was glad to sit down in the tram. But this first night they walked all the way from Ocean Road to Tyne Dock, then up through the arches, past Simonside Bank, which led up into the country, past the respectable New Buildings flanking the Jarrow Slacks, past the dark jumble of houses built on a rise and called Bogey Hill, and on to the Fifteen Streets. It was a long walk and she really only came to herself as they neared his street, Camelia Street, and she stopped as if she had been pulled to a halt with a rope and said, primly, 'Thank you, but I can see me own way now.' It was such a silly thing to say and she blushed with the stupidity of it, but he smiled and said, 'Can I see you tomorrow night?'

To this she merely nodded shyly.

'The same time?' he said.

'Yes.' She was on the point of moving away when again she was halted, by the fascinating sight of a man raising his hat to her, a trilby hat.

She had tried to walk straight because she knew he was still standing watching her, but her legs were tired, and they felt wonky, just as if she was slightly tipsy.

There were men grouped at the bottom of all the streets past Dudley Street – Dudley Street was the sixth street from the top end. The men looked at her, they always did, but none of them spoke until she came to the corner of their own street. There were about a dozen men here; some were on their hunkers, some leaning against the wall, all with their coats and caps and mufflers on, although the night was stifling. The older ones hailed her, while the younger ones just spoke with their eyes.

'Brought any bullets with you the night, Sarah?'

She smiled, and with a feeling of gaiety answered them, saying, 'There was only a box of chocolates over, and I knew you wouldn't like them so I gave them away to the bairns.'

10

'Oh, aye!'

'Well, Aa never liked chocolates,' said another; 'acid drops is more in me line.'

'Sherbet dips for me.'

'I like suckers, oh! I'm very fond of a sucker.' She was well past them when this remark was made; it came from a man who lived three doors down from her, a nasty man. She heard one of the older men saying. 'That's enough, shut tha' gob.'

The man who had spoken in the pitmatic was Mr Ferris and lived opposite to them. He had often slipped her a ha'penny when she was a bairn. They had no children of their own. She liked Mr Ferris . . .

So that had been the beginning, only three weeks ago, and every night at half-past eight he had been waiting for her when the shop closed and he had walked her home. He had wanted to take her to the pictures, but she had refused. When at the end of the second week he had again asked her to go to the pictures and she again refused he had seemed puzzled. How could she tell him it was because she felt shabby and hadn't any Sunday things. It was different being met coming from work, you weren't expected to be dressed up then. Then last Saturday night he had asked her if she would come to tea on the Sunday, and she had stayed up late washing and ironing her skirt and blouse.

The odd thing about all this was her father had never mentioned the matter. If he had known that she was seeing a lad of any kind the place would have been raised; he simply went mad if he saw her talking to a lad. He had belted her when she was sixteen because he had seen her coming up the road three nights running with the same lad. None of the lads around the Buildings made up to her – perhaps because she kept herself aloof, but she also knew that they were slightly afraid of Pat Bradley. This had puzzled her in her early years because her stepfather was an undersized, insignificant-looking man, but lately she had come to understand people's fear of him, for there was an innate vicious strength about him that had nothing to do with his stature.

Of one thing she was sure: if he had known about her meeting with David Hetherington she would have heard about it. There were a number of people who had seen her with David, Mrs Ratcliffe next door for one, yet none of them had split on her. She felt a warm feeling towards the whole population of the Fifteen Streets. But the warm feeling fled with the thought. Perhaps the longer he's in the dark the bigger the bust-up there'll be, and that's what they're waiting for. Her father was known as a know-all, and likely a lot of the men were laughing up their sleeves at the way she was hoodwinking him. They would think of it as hoodwinking although she had done nothing on the sly.

11

Her mother had said last night, 'There'll be murder when he finds out; I would drop it if I were you.' And to this she had answered, 'I will after tomorrow night. He's asked me to tea, I'll tell him then.' Her mother's answer had been, 'My God! And them chapel!'

She turned on her side now and began to pray: 'Holy Mary, Mother of God, pray for us sinners now and at the hour of our death, amen. What am I going to do? Make him turn . . . don't let him be bigoted, Holy Mother. Oh, Queen of Heaven, the ocean star, guide of the wanderer here below.' Her praying trailed away and slowly she turned her face into the straw pillow and pressed her nose until it was pushed to one side and her mouth bit on the rough ticking. Was she mad altogether? She had only known him three weeks and here she was thinking he would ask her to marry him. Yet why had he asked her home? Why was he meeting her every day if there wasn't something in his mind? You didn't ask a girl home unless it meant something. Yet he knew where she came from, he knew she came from the bottom end – in fact the bottom, bottom end, for they lived in the last street, the last habitable street. Beyond, the houses were so dilapidated, so overrun with bugs, that they were only inhabited now and again by flitters, and there was talk of them being pulled down any time. Yes, he knew where she lived, and his mother must know too. She had been afraid of meeting his mother; she hadn't been afraid of meeting his father, or his brother, or his uncle. She wasn't afraid of men as she was of women; not really, except perhaps her father. But his mother had turned out to be . . . well, all right in a way. Cautious; oh yes, very cautious. Scrutinising, looking her over from the side, and quizzing in her talk. How long had she worked at Bentons?'

Since she was fourteen, she had said; it was her first job.

How long had her father been out of work? What was he when he was in work?

He had been a platelayer, but that was before the War, and then he had been in the Army, but could only get odd jobs since he came out. Work was very scarce. She had said this as if they didn't know, and found the eyes of the three men on her – the father, the uncle, and David. The other son wasn't there. He was married and lived in the next street.

Where did her sister work?

She worked in a café in Shields.

She was glad they didn't ask where the café was.

David sat opposite her through the tea, and every time she became slightly overawed or embarrassed she would look at him. His eyes were always waiting for her. She thought he had the kindest eyes she had ever seen in a man. They were clear grey. They were his best feature, although he had a nice mouth too. All his features were nice, yet they didn't make him good looking. She supposed that was because of his skin. It was rough, with red veins high on the cheeks, like a man who had worked in the blast furnaces all his life. His face was more suited to what she classed a working man than a man who worked in the dock offices. But his voice was not that of a working man. He had a lovely voice; soft, warm, kindly. She liked his voice and his eyes; she liked him altogether.

His father must have looked pretty much the same at David's age, but now his hair, instead of being brown, was wispy grey and he had a twitch in one eye. But he, too, was nice. Then there was the uncle. She had laughed when she was introduced to the uncle. David hadn't called him uncle but Dan. 'This is Dan,' he said. 'He's really my uncle, but he's only six years older than me so why should I call him uncle? And he's a rogue, so you look out for him.'

She had been at home with Dan right away, more than with any of them, even David. Dan wasn't as tall as David, who was close on six feet, but he was broader, much broader, with a big square face. You could call Dan good looking. And from the start she had seen that Dan was what was known as a joker. He could keep the conversation going and make you laugh. And yet there was something about Dan that she couldn't fathom; it was linked up in some way with his sister's attitude towards him, the sister being David's mother. She had noticed right away that Mrs Hetherington's manner towards her brother was different altogether from the manner she used to either her husband or her son. Either she ignored him, or when she was forced to speak, as when she thanked him for passing something across the table to her, she did not look at him and her voice took on a prim sound as if she was displeased, like a teacher's attitude towards an erring pupil. Sarah hadn't realised this fully until now, when she was going over the whole scene in her mind.

But there was one thing she was sure of: all the Hetheringtons were wonderful; and if only David would ask her she would die of happiness.

And so with another prayer to Our Lady to get him to turn, she dropped into fitful, dream-threaded sleep.

CHAPTER TWO

The last customer was a boy about seven years old. He couldn't decide whether he wanted jube-jubes, everlasting strips, or walnut-tray toffee. Sarah said as gently as she could, 'We're closing, hinny; come on, make up your mind.'

The child thought a little longer, then, looking up, he asked, 'Can I have a ha'porth of each of two of them?'

Sarah sighed, 'Which two?'

13

Again there was some consideration and Sarah raised her eyes from the top of the boy's head to the glass door and to the figure walking slowly past.

As the boy's mouth opened on his decision a voice from the back of the shop called quietly, 'It's time, Sarah.'

'Yes, Mrs Benton.'

She flung the sweets into a bag, then pushed them at the boy, who had the temerity to say, with no small indignation, 'Why, you've put them in the same bag? The jube-jubes'll stick to the taffy.'

'Go on,' she hissed at him now.

Having pushed him out of the door, she stooped quickly and shot the bolt in while keeping her eyes averted from the street beyond.

She was getting into her coat as she said, 'I'm all locked up, Mrs Benton. I'll away then.'

The elderly woman smiled quietly. 'Yes, get yourself away . . . I wouldn't like to have to pay for his shoe leather.'

The colour flooded up into Sarah's face. She hadn't imagined that Mrs Benton had noticed David.

'Is he a nice boy?'

'Yes, very nice, Mrs Benton.'

'Be a good girl.'

Sarah said nothing to this, only her eyes widened a little as she turned away with her head bent. She felt she should laugh, but she couldn't, for she was slightly annoyed. The admonition hadn't been spoken in a jocular way, as one of their neighbours might have said it, but more broadly, more casually. 'Divn't dee what I wouldn't dee unless ya want the priest after ya.' No, Mrs Benton's words had sounded like a warning and they made her feel hot. And so, when she came out of the side passage and he was standing there facing the alleyway, his first words were, 'You look warm.'

She stood in front of him, smiling widely now. 'I am . . . I've just finished a big deal . . . a shipping order.'

'Yes?' His smile too was wide as he waited.

'That bairn you saw coming out. He couldn't make up his mind how to spend a penny. He wanted jube-jubes, everlasting strips, and walnut toffee. He just couldn't make up his mind.'

'What eventually did he plunge for?'

'A ha'porth of walnut taffy and a ha'porth of jube-jubes, then he went for me because I put them in the same bag.'

Their heads back but their eyes holding, and still laughing, they turned away and walked as one, not touching, yet their bodies joined through the rhythmic swing of their limbs. But at the corner of Fowler Street, where it branched off Ocean Road, he stopped and said, 'We'll get the tram here.'

She turned her head quickly towards him. They had done the journey on foot every night since they had first met. It was the only time they had together. She watched his eyes flick down towards her ankles as he said, 'You've done enough standing for one day.'

She had the desire to crouch down, covering her feet with her clothes, as she had done when a child, when they had played mothers and fathers in the back-yard and she had always wanted to be the baby which had occasioned her doubling herself in two. But now she looked down at her ankles and she hated them. They were the only part of her body that she hated; in her opinion they spoilt her. For she could not help but be aware that her body earned her the northern compliment of being 'a strapping lass'. In the morning her ankles were as thin as her wrists, but they always swelled if she stood on her feet for any length of time. With her build she supposed she should have tried for a sitting-down job. As it was, there wasn't even a stool behind the shop counter.

'They get like that with standing.' She didn't want him to think that they were always swollen.

'I know; Dan's swell too.'

Dan, she had been surprised to learn, worked in a grocer's shop in Jarrow. She imagined that he would have worked in the dock offices, seeing that David and his father did. She didn't know where the other son worked; she supposed it was in the dock offices too.

She said, 'But I don't mind walking, they don't pain.'

'Nevertheless we're taking the tram.' His voice sounded firm, nicely firm. 'Here it is; come on.' He took her arm and hurried her across the road.

As they were going up the gangway of the tram he spoke to a workman sitting in the back, saying, 'Hello there, Fred.'

'Hello there, Mr Hetherington.'

The distinction in the form of address pleased Sarah. She felt proud, as if she was bathing in the glorified reflection of a title; the workman had called him Mr Hetherington.

David's hand was on her arm now, pulling her gently back, and he ushered her into the seat in front of the man; then, twisting round, he asked him, 'Did you get it, Fred?'

'No-o.' The word was drawn out, it was a long deep thick syllable. 'There was about thirty waiting for it. It's no good, man; even a bit of influence isn't any good any more.'

'I'm sorry.'

'Oh, don't you worry, Mr Hetherington, man. It was good of you to put me on to it.'

David turned to give the conductor the fares, then he looked at Sarah and said under his breath, 'It's frightful, this business, trying to get a job.'

Sarah didn't catch all he said because of the rumble of the tram-car, but she gauged he was speaking sympathetically about the man. Then he turned again and, looking over his shoulder, said, 'Try

15

Fullers, Fred, first thing in the morning. There might be something doing, you never know. You'll find our John somewhere in the yard.' His voice dropped. 'If you can get a word with him on the quiet, tell him I sent you.'

'Oh, thanks, Mr Hetherington. Thanks, I'll do that. I'll be up afore the lark. Man, this life gets you down.'

'Good luck, Fred.'

'Aye, good luck, that's what we want. And good luck to you, sir.' His eyes flicked to Sarah's profile and back to David, and the jerk of his head was an open compliment. He rose to his feet, jabbed at the bell pull, as the conductor was upstairs, and brought the tram to a stop.

David did not look at her as he now said, 'It gets me down, to see them standing about, rotting away. I remember him as a big man when I first started in the dock office. Now he seems to have shrunk to half his size. It has effect on all of them in the end: it shrivels up something inside of them, I suppose.'

Sarah glanced sharply at him, her face quite grave. She had heard all he had said and somehow she didn't like it; she didn't like to think of him associating with workmen, talking to them as man to man. He was from a different world, from the top end. He worked in an office. She wanted to keep him, at least in her mind, secluded, away from all contact with labourers, riveters, platemen, propmen, trimmers, pitmen, and the like.

And then he said, 'My brother's a foreman joiner, it's a small firm, but he'll set him on if it's at all possible.'

His brother a joiner? This news came in the form of a blow, even with the title foreman before it. She hadn't imagined one of the Hetheringtons working in the docks, actually working among the rough-and-tumble. Oh, she wasn't an upstart, she wasn't, and she didn't want to be an upstart, she didn't. Her mind reiterated the phrase as if she was answering in agitated defence some voice that was spitting scorn at her, and her environment-encumbered mind, being unable to put forward any argument to uphold her snobbishness, ended helplessly. Oh, I just want to get away from it all.

She was looking at her hands encased in thin cotton grey gloves – an outward sign of gentility. And from her hands her gaze dropped to David's feet. He was wearing nice brown shoes, very highly polished. He had worn black ones last night, but then he had been wearing a dark suit. Fancy having different shoes to go with different suits. She had seen him in two different suits besides grey flannels and a tweed coat.

'Have you dropped something?'

'No.' She jerked her head up to him. 'I . . . I was only looking at your shoes.' She hadn't meant to say any such thing.

'Oh . . . the polish?' He brought his lips tightly together and his
eyes twinkled as he bounced his head before saying, 'My mother.
She polishes all our shoes. You would think she had been trained
in the army.'

She answered his smile, but weakly. It was as her mother was so
fond of saying . . . you got everything in batches. And it was true in
every aspect of life. He had talked to the workman as if he was on
the same level as the man. Then he had told her his brother was a
fitter, and now he had pricked the illusion of the exclusiveness of his
family, by telling her his mother cleaned all their shoes. Why, even
her father, as bad and as lazy as he was, cleaned his own shoes.

The tram was rumbling its way down Stanhope Road now, and
as it passed the Catholic Church, the church that she had attended
from when she first went to school, she bowed her head deeply in
obeisance to the Sacred Heart that was ever present on the altar. It
was an involuntary, almost an unconscious movement.

That the action had not been lost on David was given to her just
after they alighted at the bottom of the dock bank and had crossed the
road, beginning the walk through the arches towards East Jarrow.

'Are you a regular attendant at church?' he asked, smiling quietly.

'A regular attendant?' She repeated his phrase as if muttering a
foreign language, and then said hastily, 'Yes, yes, I go every Sunday.
We have to.'

They walked on in silence for a few minutes before he said, 'I
used to go every Sunday too. To chapel, that was.' He smiled, rather
apologetically, following this statement.

'Don't you go now?'

'No . . . no. I've never been since I was eighteen.'

There came a lightness to her mind. This could make things easier,
oh, so much easier. 'Why?' she asked.

He moved his head slowly. 'I just couldn't stand it any more. The
narrowness, the idea that God belonged to the Baptists and he would
shoot you down sort of business if you didn't think along the particular lines they laid down appeared mad to me. Of course I didn't see
it all in a flash, I had a long time of troubled thinking to go through.
But now I think people are quite bats, almost insane, to believe that
if there is a God he's there just for them and their particular way of
thinking, while the rest of the community – and not only the community but the world – is damned if they don't come in with them.'

Her mind for a moment was devastated. If he thought that about
the Baptists what did he think about the Catholics, for the Catholic
religion was the only one true religion, and every Catholic knew
this and maintained it. They might stay off mass, they might get
drunk, the men might knock their wives about, but when they went
to Confession and their sins were absolved, they knew that they
were receiving a privilege given to no-one except a Catholic . . .

The devastation moved its dull sickening weight to allow for a ray of brightness. Didn't his attitude make things easier? The very fact that he was no longer a chapelite made the battle half won. But even as she thought this she said, 'But you believe in God?'

'I just don't know.' He shook his head. 'Sometimes I know positively that I don't, at others . . . well, I just don't know. I could cry for the greatness, the simplicity, the naïveness, in Jesus. I could wring his hand for his detestation of the holier than thous. I could walk beside him as he smiles on the publicans and whores. But I can't see eye to eye with him when he tells me that the slow, slow force that urged a seed into a tree, then compressed it into fuel for firing for man it had not yet conceived – is my Father. But does it matter all that much? Does it matter much?' He was walking close to her now, his face, long and serious, turned towards her, and she did not look at him as she answered quite untruthfully, 'No, no.'

Again they were walking in silence, and now they were on a quiet stretch of the road bordered by high stone walls that ran between Simonside Bank and the Saw Mill, and it was at a spot where no-one was in sight that he suddenly took hold of her arm and brought them both to a stop. His hand still holding her, his eyes roamed round her face, and in a way that she termed quaint he said, 'Hello, Sarah.' She had the desire to giggle; it was funny the way he said it, as if they had just met, and her lids began to blink as his eyes slowly picked out her features. It was as if he were detaching them from her face and examining them. When his eyes came to rest on hers again he said, 'What about it, Sarah?'

She didn't know how to answer. She wetted her lips, which were trembling, and, like the fool she told herself she was, she remained dumb, and he went on speaking. 'I've never spoken your name before. We've come up this road twenty-five times. I've kept count – and I've never called you by your name. And tonight is the first time I've touched you, when I helped you on to the bus. You know something, Sarah . . . you're very beautiful.'

'O . . . oh!' It was an inarticulate sound, like a groan.

His eyes flicked from her now up and down the road and then he said softly. 'May I kiss you?'

Still she could make no answering sound, but her whole body spoke for her and the next moment they were close and his lips were on hers, gently, softly, as if afraid of what they were about. It was over in an instant, and then silently again they were walking up the road, their arms rubbing every now and again. Her body felt light, there was no longer any heavy tight pressure around her ankles, she seemed to be afloat. They passed the open space of the Jarrow Slacks. The tide was high and there were children playing on the timbers. They passed the tram sheds. They passed Bogey Hill. And not until they

18

walked up the bank that led to the plateau of the Fifteen Streets did he break the enchanted silence.

'Will you come to Newcastle with me tomorrow night, Sarah, to a show?'

'Ooh!' It was another groan, but a different kind of groan. Go to Newcastle and do a show. That would be living indeed; hitting the high spots. Oh, if only she could say yes. She had her pay in her pocket, eighteen and six; it was good money and she could have been dressed up to the eyes if she had been able to keep at least the eight and six, but no, she had to tip up fourteen shillings each and every week. Then there was two shillings out of the remainder for her clothes club. That left half a crown and she wouldn't have had that if she hadn't stuck out for her bus fare each day. If only she could have managed a five-pound club she would have been able to rig herself out. Well, she would get a club. Her chest moved upwards on the decision. She would get a five-pound club and get herself a new coat and shoes . . . But that wouldn't fix tomorrow. Her chest moved downwards again, and she answered, 'I'm sorry, I can't tomorrow.'

'Why? You said last week it was your early night off this Saturday . . . Sarah.' Again they were standing facing each other, 'There isn't somebody else?'

'Somebody else!' Her voice was high, right up in her head, and she laughed as she repeated, 'Somebody else?' Then, putting her head on one side, she dared joke. 'And where do you think he's been every night for the last three weeks?'

They laughed together, his head back in his characteristic style. And when he was looking at her again he asked, 'Then why won't you come?'

Now her eyes were steady and travelling over his face. It was a good face she was looking into, a kindly, honest face, and as she stared at it, it came to her that this man had no side. The knowledge was warming. She felt wise, even superior, being able to appraise his character. She knew it was because of his lack of side that he was to the workmen one of themselves. That was why he could talk about his mother cleaning their shoes and his brother being a fitter. He had no side. Her revealed knowledge of him supplied her with the courage to touch the front of her coat, lifting it outwards, and say, 'I haven't any clothes.'

'What!' His eyebrows moved up in genuine surprise. Then his long face seemed to crumple into agitated concern and the end of his nose twitched with a rabbit-like movement before he went on, 'Oh, my dear. Why, fancy you worrying about that! I've never even noticed what you've got on.' His features spread outwards again into an amused smile. 'Nobody will ever notice what you're wearing, Sarah. You carry your clothes like . . . well, like someone who doesn't have to have clothes to make her out. You know what I mean,' he finished swiftly.

Her lids were lowered. 'It's nice of you to put it like that, but a girl needs clothes. It does something to you to have nice clothes . . . new clothes.'

'I tell you people will never look at what you're . . . Oh, come on.' He swung her away now, holding on to her, laughing. 'You're coming to Newcastle tomorrow night and the dames in their rabbit skins won't be able to hold a candle to you.'

Her chin was on her chest, her large body was shaking with a gurgle of intense happy laughter. Then abruptly it stopped. She was looking ahead, speaking quietly. 'You know what?'

'No.'

'I think you're the nicest man in the world.'

'Oh, Sarah!' She was about to be pulled to a stop yet once again when she said hurriedly, 'Eeh, no! Look, we're nearing the streets. There's people about.'

She was blushing all over; she hadn't intended to say anything like that, about him being nice. It was a bit forward at this stage, she supposed, like pushing herself, throwing herself on to his neck. But he wouldn't take it like that, he wasn't that kind, and she had meant it – he was the nicest man in the world. And he was a man. He looked a man, not a lad, or a chap; he was a man. She wondered how old he was, he had never said. He appeared about twenty-five or twenty-six. She seemed to have no control over her tongue tonight, for she heard herself asking quite boldly, 'How old are you?'

'What do you think?' There was laughter in his voice again.

She cast her eyes slantwise towards him as if taking a measure of his age, and then she said, 'Twenty-six.'

'Twenty-six?' His eyebrows went up. 'Three years out.'

'You're not twenty-nine?'

'No. Are you disappointed? I'm twenty-three.'

No, she wasn't disappointed, but he looked older. She was startled now as he said, 'And you're nineteen.'

'How do you know?'

'Oh, I know when you left school.'

'You do?'

He leant near her and whispered menacingly, 'I've had my eye on you for years, Sarah Bradley.'

Again she was flooded with a happy gurgling feeling, an unusual carefree feeling. Fancy now, he'd had his eye on her for years . . . But if that was so, why hadn't he come forward sooner? Perhaps because she had never looked at him. Now and again she had passed him on the road but had always averted her gaze, knowing he was from the top end.

As they were passing Camelia Street two women came round the corner, and he said to them, 'Good evening, Mrs Talbot. Good evening, Mrs Francis.'

'Good evening, David,' one of them said, while both of them nodded, with their eyes tight on Sarah.

A coolness touched her warm body. What were they thinking? Oh, she knew what they were thinking: that he was mad. Well – she bridled inside – he wasn't the only one that was mad, she was mad in her own way too.

She stopped at their usual place of parting.

'Why don't you let me walk down with you?'

She looked straight into his eyes. 'Do I need to have to tell you?' It was a relief to be honest. Since she had told him about her clothes she felt she could tell him anything.

'Don't be silly.'

'I'm not being silly, but you know what it's like down there.'

'Well, I'll have to come sometime.'

The coolness was pressed from her body, she was warm again. She dropped her eyes from his.

'I'll call for you tomorrow . . . that's fixed.'

Her head was up. 'No, no. Please, oh please.' She was pleading now. 'Don't come to the door, I'll meet you here.'

He was about to say something when a group of boys who had come tearing down the roadway now raced round them on the pavement, and one of them, as he swung away from a pursuer, grabbed at Sarah's skirt. As she almost overbalanced David's hand went out to steady her, and he cried at the boy, 'Here! Here! Let up on that, will you?'

The boy scrambled back into the road again, but the one who had been doing the chasing stopped in the gutter and peered up at Sarah, and without a preliminary lead-up remarked. 'There's hell going on in your back-yard, Sarah. Yer da's taken the belt to Phyllis. She's been screaming blue murder and he's locked yer ma in the netty.'

Sarah's lips moved without any intention of uttering words. For a moment they were like the lips of a very old woman chewing the cud of unformulated thought; only Sarah's thoughts were not unformulated. In a matter of seconds the faint sweetness of life that she had tasted was smudged out with the picture conjured up by the boy's words. She could not bear to look at David but turned away and with a swing of her body sped from him and raced up the road. Then he was by her side running with her, and she was forced to stop. Gasping, she almost barked at him, 'No, no! Don't come, please. I don't want you to. Don't you see?'

He remained still, saying nothing, and once again she was running past the street corners. There were no men standing at the bottom of her own corner tonight, nor were they in the front street. The street was strangely bare, except for Mrs Young, the neighbour on the right-hand side. She was coming out of her house as Sarah hammered on the front door, and she said quietly, 'I doubt you'll not get in that way, hinny; he's been at it for the last half-hour. You know, something should be done with him. I would go to the Cruelty Inspector, I would an' all, if it wasn't for your ma. He's belted that poor lass within an inch of her life. Sam Ferris just got over the wall in time. He's mad, you know, vicious and mad when the fit takes him. I wouldn't care if he did it in drink, but for a man who's tee-total and acts the way he does there's somethin' radically wrong with him.'

'But what'd she done, Mrs Young?'

'Aw lass, it's none of my business, you'll know soon enough. But I'd go round the back if I was you.'

Running again, Sarah entered the back lane. There were groups gathered together all along its length, the men mostly by themselves, the women likewise. Outside of their back door were four men standing and a woman. The woman turned and said, 'Oh, it's you, Sarah.' And one man, taking hold of her arm, said, 'I wouldn't go in for a while if I was you, lass; let him cool down. Your mother's with him now.'

'He's not all to blame,' another man was addressing her, his head bouncing as if on wires. 'You've got to do something when it comes to that, you know.'

'What are you talking about, Mr Riley? Comes to what? What's happened? . . . Leave go of me.' She turned to the man who was holding her arm, and when he released her the other man said, 'Arabs, to put it in a nutshell.'

'Arabs?' Sarah was aware that she was showing all her teeth, that her lips had moved back from her gums as if the word itself smelt.

'Aye, that's what I said, lass. Young Phyllis's been with an Arab. Now your da's no angel, we all know that, but I would have done the same in his case.'

'No bloody fear you wouldn't; he's a maniac!'

As the woman spoke, Sarah pushed past the group and went through the open back door and up the yard. There was no sound coming from the kitchen, the whole place appeared quiet. She opened the door and stepped into the little square scullery and noted that the tin dish, which usually stood on the cracket behind the door and in which they did the washing up and used for everything that required the use of water, was lying against the wall end up, and that the floor surrounding it was covered with soapy suds. She opened the kitchen door and stepped quietly into the room. Her father was sitting at the corner of the table. His thin sour face looked yellow, and the red marks that always streaked the whites of his eyes seemed to have spread completely over them. They looked a bloodshot blur except for two dark jets pointed at her from his narrowed lids. His short wiry body and equally short legs were held taut; he looked as if he were jointless.

She glanced quickly from him towards her mother, who was standing with her hands gripping the mantelpiece, her head hanging forward, gazing down into the low fire in the bottom of the deep grate between the black-leaded oven and the pan hob. Her mother was a big woman, almost twice the size of her father. She had been bonnie too at one time, with a fine figure and a laughing face, but Sarah hadn't seen her really laugh for years. A thought that she had asked herself countless times she asked again now. Why did she do it . . . marry him? A man ten years younger than herself. Perhaps, as she had told herself before, it was just because he was ten years younger and she had been flattered.

Her words came out on a stammer as she asked, 'W-what's the matter?' She couldn't believe what they had said in the back lane, that Phyllis had been with an Arab. Her father would jump at anything that would give him the excuse to use his belt.

'So you've come in, have you?'

Ignoring his words, she said again, addressing herself pointedly to her mother, 'What's the matter?'

Pat Bradley was on his feet, glaring at her now from his bloodshot eyes. 'You're goin' to make on you know nowt about it, that's what you're going to do, aren't you? There's a pair of you. Oh, aye, there's a pair of you. What she doesn't know you'll put her up to. Not that she needs much coachin'.'

Her mother turned from the fireplace, speaking for the first time, her voice heavy with a dead kind of weariness. She said, 'Go on upstairs, Sarah, and see to Phyllis.'

'She'll go when I give the word.'

'Leave her alone.' Annie Bradley turned on her husband, towering over him, threatening now. 'You've done enough for one night, I've told you. You've gone too far this time. I told you what would happen if you lifted your hand to one of them again, didn't I?' She turned from the staring eyes of the man and said again to Sarah, 'Go on up to Phyllis.'

Sarah turned away slowly. She wanted to go up to Phyllis and yet she didn't want to go, at least not yet. She wanted to face up to this man too, to tell him what would happen if he dared raise his hand to her. She knew that she had been waiting for a long time for this opportunity and praying for the courage to use it, but she obeyed her mother. Moving between the square wooden table and the leather couch, she opened the staircase door and, groping for the rope balustrade, she pulled herself up the almost precipitous staircase. One step across the four-foot square of landing and she was in the bedroom, standing by the bed looking down at Phyllis.

Her sister was lying on her side. Her jumper lay in shreds across her back; there were two rents in her skirt from waistband to hem, and the seat of her bloomers were all black as if she had been dragged around the yard. Sarah brought her face closer to the torn blouse. There was no sign of blood, but, lifting the shreds of material apart, she saw a criss-cross of rising dark-blue weals.

'Oh, Phyllis!' She put her hands gently on her sister's shoulder, but Phyllis did not move or speak, and Sarah said, urgently now, 'Phyllis, sit up. Phyllis, do you hear me? Come on . . . Phyllis.'

Phyllis moved slowly; then with an effort, as if her body was tied to the bed, she turned on to her hip. Her eyes were closed; her face, except for a dark weal that started at the top of her ear and came down across her cheek to the corner of her mouth, was a sickly white. But Sarah was not looking at her face, she was looking at her breasts, the small undeveloped breasts that Phyllis was forever trying to enlarge. They were bare and criss-crossed with lines, similar to the one on her face.

'Oh, my God!' Sarah sat down on the edge of the bed and gently enfolded the slight body within her arms, rocking her like a mother with a child. And again she said, 'Oh, my God!' She stayed like this for some time, gently rocking and making sounds that expressed pain; and then she said, 'I've got some Pond's cream; I'll rub it on, Eh?'

Phyllis still did not speak, but when Sarah released her she moved her legs and sat on the edge of the bed. She looked as if all life had been whipped out of her, not a protest left. But this impression was shattered as Sarah went to apply, with gentle fingers, the first dab of cream on to the weal on her sister's cheek, for Phyllis's hand came up and gripped her wrist and in a whisper, cracked and hoarse but laden with a fierce strength, she said, 'One day I'm going to kill him, Sarah.'

Sarah did not reprimand her for the statement, but, sitting close to her, she whispered. 'Why did he do it?'

'He said I'd been with an Arab.' Phyllis's eyes were looking straight into Sarah's.

'But you hadn't, had you? Not an Arab.'

'He said I'd been WITH an Arab . . . not just speaking to one . . . WITH him.'

'But you've never even spoken to an Arab, have you?'

'Of course, I have.' Phyllis's eyes did not drop away. 'They come into the café every day, you've got to speak to them.'

'Yes I know, but not outside?'

'Yes, I've spoken to one outside.'

'Oh, Phyllis!'

'Don't say "Oh, Phyllis!" like that. He's a decent enough fellow; in fact he's better than them around these doors, I can tell you that.'

'Oh, Phyllis . . . but . . . but an Arab. You know you'll get your name up. You'll be hounded out of the place. Remember Betty Fuller? You mightn't, but I do. She married one, and when she came back to see her mother, Mrs Baxter emptied the chamber-pot on her out

24

of the upstairs window. I was only about ten, but I remember. The whole neighbourhood was raised.'

'What do I care? Anyway, I hadn't BEEN WITH him and I've only spoken to him twice outside the shop. Once, when I was crossing the ferry, Mr Benito had sent me to North Shields with an order and he was on the ferry and we got talkin', and I can tell you' – her voice now hissed at Sarah with a strength born of anger – 'I can tell you he spoke to me better than the lads around this quarter do. He talked just like any Geordie, but he had manners.'

Sarah did not say anything; she was bewildered, amazed. Phyllis talking to an Arab! Everybody knew what happened to girls who went with Arabs; they were ostracised, never again could they come back into the clan. Their families knew them no more – at least not around this quarter, they daren't. Most of the white girls who married Arabs lived in the Arab community in Costerfine Town and East Holborn way. Those who made a break and took houses in other parts of the town only stayed for a short time, the neighbours saw to that.

Even among their own kind Sarah knew that class distinction was strong. The top and the bottom of the Fifteen Streets knew their places; they didn't mix . . . or at least they hadn't until she had broken – or, more correctly, David Hetherington had broken – the hoodoo. But this distinction of class, which took its pattern from the even stronger sense of distinction that prevailed in Jarrow and Shields, even crippled as each town was with unemployment, was nothing to the distinction between a white girl of any class and an Arab.

At this point Phyllis's face screwed up with pain and she pressed her hands gently over her chest; then, turning her head slowly to Sarah, she said, 'You don't believe me?'

'Yes, yes, I do, Phyllis. But tell me, how did he' – she nodded towards the floor – 'get to know?'

'It was this afternoon; it was only the second time I'd spoken to him outside, as I told you. I'd just finished and I was comin' up into the market when I thought I would like to bring me ma something home; you know she likes mussels, and so I went to that shop, you know that sells the mussels and the brown bread and beer, and he was inside. He was having a plate of mussels and he asked me if I'd have one. I said no thanks, I'd just come in to take some home, and when I came out he came with me and we walked along the street and up into the market. I couldn't say "You can't walk along of me", could I?' Her eyes, painfilled yet rebellious, asked the question, and Sarah said, 'No. No, of course not . . . And that was all?'

'Aye, that was all; atween me and God that was all. But you know something?' Phyllis brought her face to Sarah's. 'It won't be all from now on. You bet your bottom dollar it won't be all. He's done something to me the night, broken something. He's belted me afore but not like the night, and I swear I'll get me own back. An' I

25

know how I'll do it an' all. By God! Aye, I'll get me own back!'

'Oh, Phyllis, you're feelin' bad, don't talk like that.'

'Aye, I'm feelin' bad, I feel awful.' Phyllis now moved her head in a desperate fashion. 'I feel I'm gona die, but I'll not die.' Her head wagged quicker now. 'No, I'll not die, I'll live just to spite him. Oh God.' She joined her hands tightly together. 'Oh God, I'll get out of here and quick. You'll see, you'll see. I'll be gone afore you; you'll see, our Sarah.' She was talking as if Sarah was opposing her. And Sarah said, 'All right, all right, don't excite yourself. Go and lie down; let me put some of the cream on your back.'

Like a child now, Phyllis lay on her stomach, and when Sarah had treated her back she turned over slowly and said, 'I feel bad, Sarah; oh, I do feel bad.'

'You lie still, I'll go and get you something.'

Sarah smiled compassionately down at the slight figure, and her fingers touched the white cheek, the one without the weal.

But when she closed the bedroom door behind her she stood leaning against the wall for a moment. There was in her an over-powering feeling of rage. Such was its strength, it filled her with apprehension, for she had the desire to rush down the stairs, pick up the shaving strap that hung below the little mirror to the side of the fireplace and lash his thin body with it until he cringed for mercy; and she knew she could do it, she knew she was big enough and tough enough to do just that. Then why didn't she? Perhaps because she had never raised her hand to anyone in her life. She tried to force herself to carry out the urge, but all she did was to say, 'Holy Mary, Mother of God.' Then, as she groped her way down to the room below, she ground out at herself, 'You're big and soft. Why don't you do it? If you did he'd never use that belt again.'

There was only her mother in the kitchen, but a signal from her indicated that her father was in the scullery. She said to her, 'I'm going to get the doctor.'

'What's that you say?' The small tousled head came round the scullery door.

'I said I'm going to get a doctor.'

'Be God y'are! You bring a doctor here and he'll be attendin' to two of you; I'll give you a taste of what I've given her. I intend to in any case, me lady. An' if I hadn't come across her the night with her chocolate-coloured fancy man you would have had it first. But it isn't too late.'

'I've told you I'm having no more of it.' Annie had moved towards her husband.

'You save your breath, woman. If you're satisfied to have a couple of tarts for daughters they're not staying under my roof.'

'Well, let them go!' Annie was shouting now.

26

'They'll go when I'm ready and not afore. But I'm not keeping a roof over a pair of bloody prostitutes.'

Sarah took two rapid steps and she stood leaning forward, gripping the edge of the table as she cried, 'Who you meanin'? You'd better be careful, because I'm telling you, after what I've seen upstairs it won't take much for me to turn the tables. You've had it your own way too long, everybody scared to death you've had. Well, it's finished. If you as much as raise your hand to me or anybody else in this house I'll use your belt on you and flay you live I will! I will, I'm telling you!' Sarah was yelling now, almost screaming the words, and her mother was standing to the side of her, pulling her away from the table by the shoulders, as she tried to drown her voice by shouting, 'Give over! Give over! Do you hear me?'

As if she had been galloping down the road, Sarah leaned back, drawing in great gasps of air. And this was the only sound for some moments, then Pat Bradley, pushing the door back to its fullest extent, came into the room. He began talking, but his voice was low, even calm. 'Huh! We're talkin' big now, aren't we, since we've rubbed shoulders with the top end?'

'What about the top end?' Sarah was glaring at him over her mother's shoulders. She watched him saunter casually to the fireplace and stand with his back to it, the palms of his hands pressed against his small buttocks.

'Nothin'. Nothin' at all, if you know where you stand. But when a fellow from Camelia Street picks up someone from the midden end it's not with the idea of turnin' her into a respectable woman. Is it now? Plain thinkin', all round, is it now?'

'Well, you're wrong then.' She was barking at him again. 'You, with your sewer mind, you're wrong then, because I'm going to be married, see . . . SEE!'

She felt her mother's body start, and it acted like an injection on her own. She slumped against the table. My God! What had she said?

There was silence in the kitchen again, until the alarm clock on the mantelpiece gave a rheumaticky whirring sound as it passed the hour.

'Well, well, we're movin' fast, aren't we? What's all the hurry for, eh? You haven't known him a month.'

She was gasping again. He had known all the time? No, no, he couldn't have; he would have been at her before if he had. But somebody had told him.

'Has he put one in your oven already.'

Before she realised what she was doing she had grabbed the teapot from the table. It was only Annie's strength against hers that forced her arm downwards and the big brown china pot fell with a dull thud on to the mat, where the lid rolled off and the tea spewed outwards.

This unusual retaliation coming from his stepdaughter seemed to tell Pat Bradley that he no longer had any domination over her – not physically, anyway. But he did not rely solely on physical force to gain his ends; he had other methods. And now he put them into action. Buttoning up his coat and pushing the knot of his muffler upwards towards his prominent Adam's apple, he hunched his shoulders and marched towards the scullery door, saying, 'Marriage is it, atween a Catholic and a chapelite? And him in the dock office and his faather a boss there an' all. Don't make me laugh. Anyway, there's only one way to find out, and that's to go and ask him, isn't it?' He turned and faced them from the doorway, his thin features splitting into a wheedling grin. 'Will you kindly tell me your intentions towards me daughter, Mr Hetherington . . . sir?' He cut his mimicking short and ended, 'There's no time like the present for gettin' at the truth, is there, me girl?'

As the door banged behind him Sarah held her face tightly between her hands, repeating aloud, 'Oh no. Oh no. Oh no. Oh, my God, no!' Then she was gripping her mother's arms. 'He's going down there . . . stop him! Stop him, will you?'

'It's no use, lass. He may not go; when he gets outside he may think better of it. If I try an' stop him that's the one thing that'll send him pell-mell to their door.'

'Oh, no, no, no!' Sarah went to the mantelpiece and laid her brow against it. 'I want to die . . . I want to die. Oh God, I want to die.'

'Has he asked you?'

'No, no. I just said that.'

'A . . . aw, lass!'

'Yes, I know – aw, lass!'

'Well, you've cooked your own goose. You shouldn't have said a thing like that, not if the fellow hasn't said anything . . . he hasn't hinted?'

'No, no, not really. Even if he had this would have killed it.' She brought her head slowly up and then, turning and facing her mother, she said dully, 'You've got to get a doctor to Phyllis, she's bad.'

'I'm not gettin' the doctor, lass. If a doctor was to see her it would mean the polis.'

'Well, don't you think it's time somebody took a hand?'

'I don't want no polis here. Anyway, I haven't paid his club for months; I'd have to pay on the nail and I can't. I'll go up and see to her. I'll bathe it in her own water, it's good for bruises.'

Sarah's nose wrinkled in distaste as her lips moved apart. She felt weak, tired and weak; all the verve had gone out of her. What was the use? She looked round the darkening kitchen. Well, she had known it couldn't last, hadn't she? But the shame of it . . . the shame of it. What would he think of her? And his mother and the rest of them? If she could only die.

She stood looking down at her feet, her mind curiously blank now, numbed with pain. Then once again she opened the staircase door and pulled herself slowly up to the landing, and when she entered the bedroom the blind was down and her mother, by the light of a candle, was bathing Phyllis's back with a flannel rag that she was dipping into the chamber.

CHAPTER THREE

The round-faced stark-looking clock on the wall said one minute to twelve. David eyed the man at the end of the long-counter-like desk as he began quietly to clear his allotted portion. First, he closed two notebooks and put them into a drawer; next, he cleaned an ordinary narrow-pointed pen. This he returned to the groove next to the inkwell. The pointer on the clock had moved thirty seconds. Slowly he closed the ledger, screwed up some dirty blotting-paper, and dropped it into a basket where his feet were under the desk. Then, standing up, he pulled down his coat, adjusted his tie, pushed the legs of the stool over the wastepaper basket, then moved towards the man who was still writing in a ledger. The clock struck twelve.

'Will it be all right if I have a word with my father, Mr Batty?'

The man raised his eyes upwards, not towards David, but towards the clock, and his tone was significant as he said, 'Oh, it's twelve.'

The colour deepened around David's cheekbones and his tones were apologetic as he answered, 'I've got a bit of business to do . . .' His voice trailed off.

'Aw, well, go on along . . . He won't be finished yet.'

This remark, with a stress on the he and a raising of the eyebrows, was a reprimand on clock watching, and as David went along the corridor he wondered what his reaction would be to old Batty if he weren't afraid of losing his job. Very likely the same as it was now, because he hated disturbances, rows, unpleasantness. He wished at times he had a bit of their John in him.

As he neared the door at the end of the corridor it opened and two men, one about his own age, and one well into his fifties, came out. The younger one said, 'Going to the match this afternoon, David?'

'No, not this afternoon, I can't make it.'

When he entered the room that held three desks his father looked up from a ledger in which he was writing and said, 'Hello there. Are you off?'

'Yes.' David stood in front of the desk looking down at his father, and he rubbed his hand across his chin before saying, 'Will you tell Mother that I won't be in for a while, not until about two?'

'You know what she is about spoilt dinners?'

'I can't help it.'

29

Stanley Hetherington took off his glasses and peered at his son. His eye was twitching rapidly. 'You're going through with it then?' he said.

'Yes. Yes, of course.'

'There's no of course about it, you've been rushed into this. I don't believe you asked that girl to marry you and neither does your mother. In fact, she's positive that you didn't. Bradley's a little snake of a man. I've known him for years; he'll neither work nor want. I knew him when he was in the docks here, a mischief-making little rat if ever there was one, and a toady into the bargain. The only thing he doesn't do is drink, and that makes it worse. You can forgive a man what he does in drink. But there's a bad streak in Bradley. Now look.' He wagged his finger slowly at his son. 'Don't you be driven into anything . . . Oh, I know.' He closed his eyes and flapped his hand before his face before going on, 'She's a fine looking lass, but if you marry her don't forget you're marrying her family, and is it fair . . . is it fair to your mother?'

'You know what my mother thinks, don't you? This is the lesser of two evils. Don't let's hoodwink ourselves about that.'

'Yes, yes, I suppose so.' The older man dropped his head; then, bringing it up sharply, he demanded. 'There's one thing you won't do, will you; you won't go over?'

'No, I won't go over. Yet I can't see, Father, why that should worry you.'

'My belief or lack of it has nothing to do with this present business really; all I know is, if they get you into the Catholic Church, under whatever pretext, you're finished, you won't be able to call your soul your own. No, my God, you won't.'

'But I'm not . . .'

'Yes, you say that now, but wait till the priests get at you. I've seen some of their tactics, I'm telling you. From all angles you've got to look at this thing with open eyes. She's from a bad home, she's a Catholic. Then there'll be the gossip; there's enough already, for, let's face it, David, to take up with somebody from the bottom end isn't the right thing to do. I can't see it working, although on the surface I must admit she's a nice enough lass, but she's got too many reins tied to her, holding her down to that end!'

'I'm going to marry her.'

Stanley closed his eyes; then, opening them again he wiped his glasses and put the wires slowly behind his ears before saying, 'Well, there's nothing more to be said, is there?'

'I'm sorry, Father.'

'Look, don't be sorry for hurting me or even your mother, although she's taken this better than ever I imagined . . .' He jerked his head. 'But, as you said, I suppose she's doing it because she can't bear the thought of anything coming of the other business. But it's yourself you've got to think about in this case. Marriage is a long and difficult business no matter which way you take it. You're in love with somebody one minute and you hate their guts the next . . . Aw, go on. Get yourself away or I'll say too much. Go on.'

David turned and went slowly from the room. He collected his raincoat and his trilby hat and went out of the main door of the dock office, and he stood for a moment on the pavement. The Saturday bustle was all around him; men coming out of the dock gates, those who were fortunate enough to be in work; men going into The Grapes, into The North-Eastern, into one after the other of the bars that lined the street opposite the dock wall and part of the bank that led to the station, the bank which always looked black, black with the figures of men standing against the railings or in groups on the pavement, waiting, waiting, and hoping, some cursing, some even praying to be set on, to get a few shifts in; even one a week would be something to help tide things over and take away the feeling of utter uselessness.

David never stepped on to this pavement but he imbibed this feeling that was sapping the moral fibre of the men of the docks, and of Jarrow, and of the whole Tyne, and many parts of the whole country. But today the feeling, although present, was subordinate. Covering his mind was the thought of Sarah and of getting to her and speaking to her, and comforting her.

He threaded his way across the road to where the tram was halted for its usual five-minute break, and as he went to mount the platform his arm was gripped and he was pulled round on to the road again.

'Where you off to?'

'Oh, I'm just going into Shields.'

'At this time? What about your dinner?'

David stepped back on to the pavement and looked at his brother in silence for a moment. John Hetherington was two inches shorter than David but he was almost twice his breadth. Like his uncle's, his face was nearly square, his eyes wide and of a deep brown colour, with a brooding quality in them. His mouth too was wide, as were his nostrils. His nose could be said to mar his face; it forbade the term handsome to be applied to it but made place for the word attractive, or perhaps arresting, for people always gave this man a second look. He now brought his heavy fringed lids together as he said, 'You look under the weather. Feeling off-colour?'

'No, no, I'm all right. I'd better tell you what's happening though . . .'

As David wetted his lips John said, 'Happening? Aye, well, go on then, but look slippy, I want to catch the tram.'

'I'm going to be married.'

'You're what?' The question was low, easy sounding and full of disbelief. Then, his tone changing swiftly, he said under his breath,

31

'Aw, no! You're not going to be such a bloody soft-headed fool. Man, it'll be suicide. And you know how me mother . . .'

'It's not Eileen.'

'Not Eileen.' The eyes were screwed tighter. 'O . . . h! No?' He thrust his fist out and punched David in the shoulder. 'Not the missy from the bottom end that I've heard about? Why, man, you've only known her a couple of weeks.'

'I've known her longer than that, much longer.'

'Well, well!' John took a deep breath that pushed open his coat, 'Why all the hurry-burry?'

'Look, I've got to go. You'll hear all about it if you call in home . . . at least what happened last night.'

'Aye, aye, I suppose I will. But look here, Davie, don't let yourself be rushed into anything.' John's face was straight now, there was no lightness of any kind in the brown eyes. 'Look, lad, you be warned by me, and I'm speaking from experience. I've never said anything to you or anyone at home before, you know that, but I think you can put two and two together for yourself as far as my case is concerned. You make your bed and, by God, you have to lie on it! There's no truer saying than that in the whole world. Marriage can be hell, sheer bloody unadulterated hell. Oh, aye.' His voice was very low now. 'I know, I know there are wonderful marriages that go on for ten, twenty, thirty, forty, fifty years. You hear about them, in fact you see them; but, you know, you've got to ask yourself, have either of them done a day's thinking in their lives? Most of them are together because of the house and the sticks of furniture; they exist together, but they don't live. You know what most men are? A bread ticket . . .'

'Look, John, I'll have to go now; I want to catch this tram.' He motioned to where the conductor was mounting the platform. 'I'll see you later.'

'All right, all right.'

They stared at each other a moment longer, then David swung round, leaped on to the platform, and took the stairs two at a time.

When their John started talking nobody could stop him; he could make an issue out of anything. He was always probing and dissecting the whys and wherefores of even the simplest things . . . But he had just said that marriage was hell. It had been his own marriage he was speaking of sure enough. He hadn't realised that he had felt about it like that. He had known that he and May went at it, but then May had a mind too. There was a pair of them in that way. May argued against politics and strikes and the dole, because, like half the women in the town, she was worried that the next pay-day might be the last.

Sheer bloody unadulterated hell.

He could never imagine his own life like that, not if he married Sarah . . . Sarah was no May. Yet what about his father saying you could love them one minute . . . Oh, my God! He wished they would

32

all hold their tongues and let him do what he knew he must do . . .

Half an hour later he stood gazing into the shop window until there was only one customer left, then he went in.

Sarah saw him as she passed the woman her change and she started visibly, and the woman, turning and looking at David, smiled knowingly to herself.

He stood facing her in the valley between the hills of glass jars. He saw immediately that she looked ill; her eyes, although not red, were puffy, and her face, which he held always in his mind as representing a bright light, looked dull, even brow-beaten. The fact that this girl, this well set-up girl who was going to be his wife – yes, she was going to be his wife – should show an emotion that held the ingredients of intimidation, raised in him a rare and answering emotion of anger; and so his voice sounded stiff to her ears when he said, 'What time do you finish?'

She could not look at him. More than ever now she wanted to die, just to sink through the earth and be swallowed up. Humiliation had stripped her of any small pride she had clung to in desperation to keep herself afloat in the bog of her section of the Fifteen Streets.

'Do you get out for dinner? Sarah, speak to me.'

'One o'clock.' It was a mumble coming from the region of her chest.

He whispered now with gentle insistence: 'Sarah, Sarah, look at me.'

She did not raise her head but turned it aside, and her hands did something with a box, pulling out pieces of crinkled paper and rolling them up into balls.

'It's ten minutes to, I'll wait outside . . .'

At three minutes to one Mrs Benton came downstairs from her flat above and Sarah, stacking empty boxes in the corner of the back room, said nervously, 'I've got a bit of shopping to do. I'll take me sandwiches and have them in the park the day, if you don't mind.'

Sarah felt Mrs Benton looking down at her. Mrs Benton didn't like serving in the shop. Sarah guessed that she thought it slightly beneath her, her being the owner, and it was rarely that she served the full hour. Very often at a quarter to two she would come into the back room and say, 'There's nothing doing; I'll just pop upstairs. Call me if the bell rings.' Sarah never called her. It was a good job and she wanted to keep it. Not many girls were getting eighteen and six a week and not soiling their hands. Of course a twelve-hour day was a long stretch, but she wasn't grumbling.

Without looking at her employer she knew she was annoyed. Mrs Benton was always annoyed when she didn't speak. Sarah grabbed up her coat and pulled her hat on without looking in the glass, and with a mumbled 'I won't be long' she went out of the side door and into the alley.

She had her head down and she did not stop in her walk as she saw David's legs coming towards her across the pavement but kept on moving down the road towards the sea and the park.

'Don't be like this.' He was walking close to her, his head bent down to hers.

'How should I be?' Her muttered words were not only a question but an answer in themselves.

They went on in silence until they entered the park and found a seat, which was easy, as the place was virtually empty at this time of the day. It was Sarah who spoke first, her head still down, looking at her fingers as they plucked at each other. She said, 'I'm sorry.'

'Sarah, look at me.' He had hold of her hands now, pulling at them with small tugging movements, trying to get her to raise her head, but she wouldn't, and he said, 'I've watched you for years going up and down the road, and I knew from the first night that I stood outside that shop that I was going to marry you. The only thing was I was too blooming shy to get it out, and you know you weren't very helpful.'

'Don't, don't.' The tears were raining down her face now from beneath her closed lids.

'Oh, Sarah, Sarah.' He pulled her forearm against his chest. 'Oh, my dear, my love. Oh, Sarah, dear, don't.' He took out his handkerchief and gently dried her face, all the while murmuring, 'Don't, Sarah, dear. Don't, Sarah, dear.'

'He . . . he said you were t-taken aback. He . . . he . . . said you got the surprise of . . . of your life.' She gasped out the words now as if wanting to be rid of the burden of them.

'Who did? You mean your father said that?'

'Yes.'

'Aye, well, I was taken aback. But just at the sight of him and the way he blurted it out. But I said straight off the bat that I wanted to marry you. I did, Sarah.' He shook her arm once. 'Believe me, I did.'

'Your mother was there an' all.'

'Yes, she was there. She came into the hall.'

Her head drooped lower as she put the question, 'Did he raise the house?'

'No.' David's voice was high. 'No. He was very quiet; in fact, I thought he was most reasonable. If I hadn't heard about him and was meeting him for the first time I would have thought he was a reasonable kind of man altogether. But things get about, you know, even as far as our end.'

'What did you say to him?' She had her head up now and was blinking away the still running tears.

'Well, when I opened the door . . . well, you see it was all so sudden. He said, "What's this I hear about you going to marry

34

my daughter?" And quite honestly I couldn't say anything for the moment.' He gripped her hands tightly and once again brought them to his chest. 'He was putting into words something that's never been out of my mind since I met you, but at that moment it was such a surprise I couldn't say anything. And then he said, "Have you asked her?" It was then I sensed there was something wrong – I linked it up with what the boy said he was doing to your sister – so I said to him, "Will you come in?" And when he stood in the hall he repeated, "I asked you a question," and to that I said, "Yes . . . yes, I've asked her to marry me." It was then my mother joined us. He was very civil to her, very polite. He said, "I've just come round because my girl said that your son here asked her to marry him . . ."'

'And your mother didn't say anything did she?' Sarah licked the tears from her lips. 'She was so flabbergasted that she didn't say anything, for she knew if you had asked me you would have told her.'

'But listen, listen to me. I told her that I had asked you and that I was going to tell her . . . but later. I told her I had every intention of telling her and then bringing you round this evening for tea.'

'But she didn't believe you?'

'Why do you keep saying that?'

'Oh' – she screwed her body away from him, trying to pull her hands loose from his grip – 'I had it all word for word, nothing left out.' She shook her head slowly now and the scene of last night returned to her with all its ignominy; it returned for its hundredth showing in the few hours since it had been enacted. She had been lying in bed with Phyllis when the door had been kicked open and he stood on the threshold yelling into the darkness. 'Surprised to bloody death he was and frightened out of his bloody skin, an' all. Oh yes, yes, he said, he had asked you . . . But he only said that because . . . because why? Because he knew I'd tell his mother what he'd bloody well been up to, an' I was right. No bloke like him is gonna be taken for a ride up the aisle by the likes of you unless he's gone in by the back door, you big-bellied sod, you!'

The street had been quiet; there was no sound coming from the Youngs' house or from the Radcliffes', for they were all listening and would be able to hear without any straining of their ears, as would the neighbours down the road. And those who had missed anything would be given it in detail, she knew, before the sun shone without shadow tomorrow.

Eternities of suffering later, when the flesh of her body seemed to have melted with shame and her large frame was twisted with the force of the humiliation that had beaten upon her, she heard the distant chimes of a clock, somewhere in the town, striking three. It was then that Phyllis, her own pain forgotten, her arms about her tightly, whispered, 'Don't let him take the gumption out of you. That's what he's after, to break your spirit, to have you crawl. You

35

know why he's goin' for you, don't you? It's because he wants you himself.'

Her crumpled body had shuddered and straightened itself as if by an electric shock. But Phyllis still held her and went on whispering, fiercely, 'Me ma knows. What you want to do is to pack up an' get away. Don't think of how me ma'll manage, he'll have to stump up if there's nobody here . . . You know something? He had three pounds in the lining of his waistcoat yesterda' mornin'. He must have forgotten it, his waistcoat I mean, and left it on the chair downstairs. I went through the pockets when I was down early, and felt this paper in the lining. He's been running for a bookie this week. I'd like to bet he's got money tucked away somewhere . . . You stop worryin' about me ma and get yourself out of this, our Sarah, because I'm going to . . .'

'Sarah, look at me!'

She looked at him, into the eyes that were soft and glowing with love and kindliness, and her heart was sick at what she was losing.

'I love you, Sarah; I love you so much I just can't find words or ways or means of telling you . . . Now answer me one thing. If when we were going home last night I had asked you to marry me what would you have said? Truthfully, Sarah, what would you have said?'

'I'd . . . I'd have said yes.'

'Because you love me?'

'Yes.'

'Oh, Sarah, that's wonderful, wonderful. You know I just can't understand what you see in me. I've no push, no go.' He smiled. 'If you had fallen for someone like our John it would have been understandable, but me! I'll never be anything. I'm quite content to stay in my little rut until I die . . . that is as long as I have you.'

He was changing the atmosphere, subtly threading it with the description of his own character, making it slightly jocular, ordinary; and under this influence her bones seemed to straighten and the flesh on them fill out again. Her whole being was becoming saturated in enervating relief. She wanted to slump forward on to him, lay her head on his shoulder and rest; that's all she wanted to do for the moment, just rest. And then she thought of his mother. She wouldn't be able to face his mother; his father and his uncle, yes, but not his mother. She said now with candour borne of dead hope, 'There's your mother . . . I couldn't face your mother, it's no use.'

'My mother!' He screwed up his face until it looked comical. 'Why, she's the one who understands most. Look, Sarah.' He had her by the shoulders now. 'My mother wants me to marry you; there's a particular reason why she wants me to marry you. I won't tell you it now, but she wants it in spite of your father.'

'My stepfather.' It was the only thing left she had to be proud of, that there was no blood relation between her and Pat Bradley.

'Your stepfather. I'm glad he's your stepfather. Well, in spite of him and his barging in last night . . . although I maintain he came in quietly and left quietly; but in spite of all this she still wants me to marry you. You know, I think she's taken to you. She doesn't take to many people. She's what you would term a close woman, reticent, difficult, but she's been a very good mother, and, as I said, she's taken to you. I know her so well, better than my brother; better, I think, than my father, and I can vouch for what I say. Now . . .'
He brought his hands from her shoulders to her cheeks, and, holding them, raised her face towards him. 'We were going to Newcastle tonight, remember? But instead we'll go home. I've told her I'm bringing you, and she's expecting you. I'll meet you when you're finished and we'll go straight there.'

'Oh, David . . . David!' She was leaning against him, her head in his neck, shaking both their bodies with the convulsion of her weeping.

Then once again he was drying her face – under her eyes, round her nose, round her lips. His eyes remained on her lips, fixed as if he had become lost in a dream. Then with a suddenness his hands were clamped to her ears, and when he pulled her face towards his her hat fell backwards on to the grass. And then they were kissing. In the open on a bench in the Marine Park and on a Saturday dinner-time, they were kissing. It was enough to get your name up. You could cry on a bench but not kiss. Something of this ran through her mind. But what did it matter? What odds? What odds? Nothing, nothing in the world mattered at this moment except this man, this man David who wanted her.

CHAPTER FOUR

His mother opened the door to them. 'Well, you've got here,' she said. She was smiling faintly.

David pressed Sarah before him up the two steps and into the hall. 'Give me your coat,' he said.

His mother opened the sitting-room door now. She put her head inside; then, withdrawing it, she looked at Sarah. 'There's a fire on; it gets chilly at nights, especially when it's drizzling.'

'Have we kept you waiting?' David was straightening his tie.

'No, no, there're all in the living-room. Tea isn't quite ready yet. Go on in.' She held out her hand and touched Sarah's arm with the tips of her fingers, halting her as she crossed the threshold into the room and adding quietly, 'There'll be plenty of time to talk later.'

When she turned away and walked across the small hall and into the room, from where came a buzz of voices, and the high gleeful shriek of a young child, Sarah, standing stock still, gazed after her. She felt unnerved; she didn't know if it was with relief because the talking had been put off, or because it was to come.

'Don't look so mesmerised.' David was pulling her into the room and towards the couch.

'Oh! If I get over the night I'll live to be a hundred.' It was her first attempt at jocularity, and he pulled her swiftly into his arms and held her tightly for a second. Then, releasing her as quickly, he whispered, 'They'll all be in in a minute.' And as if working along the lines that attack was the best form of defence, he said, 'Would you like to come into the living-room now and get it over with?'

'No, no.' Her tone was low and rapid. 'Give me a breather.'

'Do you mind if I leave you for a minute, then? I . . .'

He seemed hesitant to tell her why he had to leave her. It could be that he had to go to some place like the lavatory, she thought, then dismised the idea. No, he wanted to have a word with them, or likely with his mother.

'Go on.' She pushed him gently, playfully. 'I've only got to die once.'

He laughed at this. His head back, in spite of his evident nervousness, he laughed. Then, clasping the palms of his hands for a second over her ears, an action of endearment she was to find that had its drawback, as it dimmed her hearing, he whispered, 'We're going to have some times together, Sarah, good times; you were made to laugh, you know.'

He left her on this, and the sound rushed back into her ears again. She sat down on the edge of the couch thinking, I was made to laugh. Funny that; there's been so little laughter in me life. But he's right, I love a good laugh. Fancy him knowing that. She looked round the room. To her eyes it was a beautiful room, beautiful in its arrangement, in its prismatic brightness, and the absence of litter of any kind; not a paper or a book to be seen, nor clothes lying about, not a cap or a coat dropped carelessly. No packets of Woodbines on the mantelpiece. She looked at the gleaming white-painted wooden frame that surrounded the pale-blue tiles. She couldn't see anyone daring to lean a finger on that edifice, except to dust the marble clock and the two pink vases with the pictures on the front of ladies in old-fashioned dress. She turned her head and looked over the back of the couch to the piano. It wasn't cluttered either; it held only two photographs, one at each end. They were both of boys. One of them was David, when about six. His eyes hadn't changed, nor yet his smile. She sat gazing at it with a warmth of feeling that was yet threaded with awe. She was going to marry that boy. She was really going to marry that boy.

Her head jerked away as the door opened and she looked at the man standing just within the room, and he looked at her. He still held the door in his hand, and after a second, when he went to close it, he did so without taking his eyes from her. Then he shook his head as he exclaimed, 'Good Lord! Fancy seeing you.'

Sarah had sidled to her feet. She couldn't remember seeing this man before. She guessed this was John, the brother. But he didn't look at all like David. Just as she was an oversize of a girl, he was certainly an outsize of a man.

'Well, well.' He was standing in front of her, holding out his hand now. 'I'm John, your future brother-in-law.'

His hand was hard, his grip was tight. 'I've seen you going up and down the road for years, but I didn't know it was you our David was after.' He jerked his head to the side. 'Well, I must say he knows when he's on a good thing.'

Sarah hadn't spoken. She was standing smiling weakly, as she thought, it's hard to believe they're brothers. The only thing she recognised as similar in both of them was their voices. Yet even these were different because this man used his words in a way that made his voice seem ordinary, in fact even like the voices of the people from her own end. Although he wasn't broad Geordie there was no refinement in his speech as there was in David's.

He dropped her hand and pointed to the couch and said, 'Sit down and don't look so worried.' The last words brought his chin out and his head and shoulders towards her. He was speaking like a kindly conspirator. 'In a few weeks you'll wonder why you ever felt nervous and you'll kick yourself.' He stood looking down at her, his hands on his hips, and he brought the side of his face into his hunched shoulder, which action laid stress on the enquiry, 'You can talk; you're not deaf and dumb, are you?'

'Yes . . . No.' Now they were laughing.

'I . . . I said to David if I get over the night I'll live to be a hundred.'

He did not answer for some seconds; his broad face took on an expression that puzzled her in its implication of aggressiveness until his words explained it when, bending down to her, his face not more than six inches from hers, he said tersely, 'Look, you set out with the idea that you're not going to be frightened of anybody, in this house or anywhere else. If you think you're going to be frightened you'll be frightened. If you let people put the wind up you you've had it, you're finished.'

'Yes, yes, you're right there.' What else could she say. She could feel the heat from his face. She looked at his mouth. It was well shaped, broad, but not kind like David's. He was better looking in all ways than David, handsome she would say, but he wasn't like David. She was feeling disturbed, nervous under the pressure of his eyes, when the door opened once again and Dan entered.

'Oh, hello there.' He looked past John towards Sarah, and Sarah took in a deep breath and smiled. There came a slackening of her muscles as if she had been relived from an ordeal and answered, 'Hello.'

'Oh, of course, you two have met before.' John cast his glance between Dan and Sarah, and Dan, tossing his head and winking, said, 'Yes, I've got one up on you there, lad.'

'Mind, I'm going to tell you something.' John was standing on the hearthrug, his back to the fire, his hands rubbing his buttocks, his body bent forward towards her again. 'You look out for him there.' He motioned towards Dan with a sideways tilt of his eyebrows. 'A proper Casanova we've got in this family. It's a fact. He'll be after your blood.'

'Enough of that, John, enough of that.'

Sarah saw that Dan's face was slightly flushed and he looked put out, not really annoyed but just a little put out; she could almost have said a little hurt.

'You know he's my uncle?' John's arm went out and gripped Dan around the shoulders and they stood pressed together looking at Sarah.

'He doesn't look old enough to be your uncle.' Sarah looked at Dan as she spoke, and Dan said, 'I don't feel old enough to be their uncle. It's one of these odd situations, I was born late . . .'

'You said it, chum, you said it.' John rocked them backwards and forwards for a moment until Dan put in laughingly, 'Stop acting the goat, Sarah'll think you're barmy. She knows what I mean.' He nodded towards her. 'I was just a baby when Mary, their mother' – he indicated John – 'was married. We were all brought up together, so to speak. Mind you' – his voice dropped to a confidential whisper – 'they wouldn't have been my choice of relatives; but there, I didn't have any say in the matter . . . Davie's all right, but this one . . .' He tried to pull away from John, and now John's two arms were around him crushing him to his chest, and Dan was crying, 'Leave over, man. Look, you don't want to start a rough-and-tumble. You'll have your mother on us like a ton of bricks; leave o-ver.' With a sudden twisting jerk he freed himself and the two men stood apart, laughing at each other.

'See what I mean?' Dan sat down beside Sarah on the couch. 'Anyone would think by the look of him and the size of him he was grown-up, mature-like, but not him, he's still in the puppy stage.'

'Puppy stage! That's right, that's right.' John was standing on the hearthrug again, his hands once more behind his back and his expression and tone reverted with a suddenness to what it had been before Dan had entered the room. 'That's funny, that is. Not grown-up! When I'm the only one among the lot of you that sees straight. Davie with his head in the clouds . . . no offence meant, it's a compliment.' His tone was slow and flat, and he accompanied each word with a movement of his head towards Sarah, then went on, 'Father with the spunk beaten out of him.' He looked towards the door, then his eyes moved towards Dan, 'And you not caring a damn except . . .' He stopped abruptly and screwing up his eyes, asked loudly, 'Why did you set me off?'

'Aw! You don't need much setting off; and Sarah might as well know the worst from the beginning. What do you say, Sarah?'

Sarah turned and looked at the man sitting beside her, and before she answered she thought, this one could be David's brother, there's a kindliness about him. With sudden daring gaiety she replied, in broad Geordie dialect, 'Aa've summed him up, shockin' lot. He'd never get past the dock polis, him.'

This retort was daring in the extreme. She was joking as if with her equals, her equals down at the bottom end. Yet she had never thought of the inhabitants of the bottom end as her equals, and had rarely, if ever, joked with any of the neighbours and never with the men. But if she had done so her remark would have been similar to the one she had just made. And now she was amazed, and a little apprehensive at the reaction to it, for the two men, their heads back – this seemed to be a characteristic of the Hetherington family, to laugh with their heads back – were now filling the room with their laughter, and the sound seemed out of place in the atmosphere of gentility.

'Well, well! And what's all the noise about?' Mary Hetherington came into the room, followed by David and a thin dark young woman with a child in her arms.

'You know what? You've picked a cheeky monkey.' John's arm was out, the finger extended, stabbing in the direction of David, and David's face, with a bright relieved smile, said, not without pride, 'I have?'

'Yes.'

'Well, that's good.' He went and took up his place beside the couch, putting his hand on Sarah's shoulder. Sarah was looking at Mrs Hetherington now; fear and nervousness had leapt back into her system again. She hadn't liked it, coming into the room and finding them all laughing. Perhaps she thought she was being forward. But she was speaking to her now, stiffly.

'This is May, John's wife.' She nodded towards her son. 'And this is their child Paul.' She took the child's hand from its mother's shoulder as she spoke. The introduction had a formal sound and no-one moved in the room while it was being made. Then Sarah attempted to rise to her feet, but Dan, heaving himself upwards, said, 'No, no, sit where you are; you come and sit here, May.'

May sat down, the child still in her arms. Neither she nor Sarah had spoken to acknowledge the introduction. The child was between their faces now, gurgling and bouncing, and as Sarah lifted a finger to touch it its plump hands shot out, and with startling suddenness and the power and demoniac tenacity, which in all infants is a contradiction to their helplessness, its fingers entwined themselves in Sarah's hair, dragging and pulling her sideways, bearing her head towards its mother's shoulder.

Although the diversion was painful, Sarah was thankful for it. The attention was on the child and amid cries of, 'Oh, you naughty boy, let go. Naughty Paul. Leave go, you rascal. Would you believe it, isn't he a little beggar?' she was eventually released.

Sarah laughed as she combed the thick waves of her long chestnut hair back into the bun with her fingers. 'It's all right; my sister used to do that. My scalp is tough.'

The baby was now in its father's arms, kicking its toes into his flat and seemingly unfeeling stomach, and as Sarah looked at him she became aware, as if she had not noticed it at the time, that they were his fingers which had prised the child's hands from her head.

'Well, now, that rumpus is over and we can have tea.' Mary Hetherington threaded her way through her family towards the door, adding as she went into the hall, 'Come on, Father is waiting.'

One after the other they followed her, David coming last, his hand extended, cupping Sarah's elbow. Before her went May, and with the perspicacity that lends itself to intuitiveness Sarah thought, I'm not going to like her, she's sour.

And when they were all seated round the tea-table and she found herself right opposite to May, she said to herself, 'She looks uppish and discontented.' Her eyes moved to John sitting to the right of his wife, the child on his knee, and she thought, What's she got to be discontented about? He seems a nice enough fellow, a bit noisy. And then she's got the child.

It was strange, and Sarah was aware of this, that all during tea her thoughts were on the slight, dark, thin girl opposite to her. Her mind was occupied so much with this new acquaintance that for the time being she forgot about Mrs Hetherington; and although she did not fail to notice that Mr Hetherington was very quiet and had hardly spoken to her, she did not worry about it. Perhaps he was always quiet. It was not until they were rising from the table to return once more to the sitting-room that it came to her that John's wife, as she thought of her rather than as May, had not opened her mouth at all during the meal; in fact she hadn't heard her speak at all. And yet nobody had seemed to notice it; nobody had remarked on her silence or pulled her leg about it.

'Let's have a sing-song. Come on, the occasion calls for it.' They were in transit between the living-room and the sitting-room when John, in a loud voice, made this announcement, but his mother's voice came quickly in answer, saying, 'Don't be so rowdy, John.'

'Look . . . my God, it's an occasion. Davie's going to be married . . . Oh, all right, I'm sorry.'

As John came into the sitting-room, his head lowered, he said in an aside to David, 'I wish she'd put a notice up, No blasphemy, no swearing, then I'd remember.'

David turned to his brother, punching him gently in the back as he said, 'Come on, big fellow, forget about it. She's a bit up . . .' He pulled himself up abruptly, but not abruptly enough. Sarah knew he was going to say she's a bit upset.

She was again seated on the couch, and once more she was alone with the men. There were present now not only the brother and the uncle but Mr Hetherington. He was sitting to the side of her in an armchair, his hands resting idly on his knees. It was perhaps the idleness conveyed by his motionless hands that made her realise that not one of the men were smoking. That was strange, nearly all men smoked.

A rolling chord of notes brought her body twisting round towards the piano. She was looking at David's back; it was David who was playing, her David. The thought added dimension to her body.

'Oh, not Chopin, not tonight. Let's have something we can sing to . . . You don't want Chopin, do you, Sarah?' John's big head was turned towards her, then away again in a second before she would have been called upon to stammer her ignorance of Chopin.

' "Blue Heaven". Come on, let's have "Blue Heaven". Where's the music? That's appropriate: "Happy in my Blue Heaven".' John was singing now in a deep resounding bass voice. 'Here it is, and "All Alone on the Telephone", and "Yacky-hoo-lah, Hicky-doo-lah".'

Sarah wanted to get up and go to the piano. She knew the songs and she could sing them too. She was told she had a decent voice – she would have gone in for a singing competition before this if it hadn't been for her father. But she had better be careful. Yes, she had better be careful. She'd better not sing too loud, or push herself. At this point she thought, I should have asked her if she wanted any help with the washing-up. She leant forwards towards Mr Hetherington and said under the cover of David's playing and John's voice, 'Do you think Mrs Hetherington needs any help with the washing-up?'

For the first time Mr Hetherington smiled at her. He smiled slowly, a considered smile, as if it was the outcome of thought and a decision taken, and he brought his hands from his knees and joined them together as he leant towards her, saying, 'Mrs Hetherington can cope. And don't worry, don't be nervous any more. What has to be will be. I hope you'll be happy and make him happy.'

It was the first time that anyone had made any direct reference to her marrying David. It was in everybody's mind, but they were all doing different things, it would seem, so as not to have to mention it. She looked at the older man, his eye twitching every few seconds, and

43

she had an almost uncontrollable urge to clasp his hands and bring them to her face and cry over them and pour out her thanks to him. She felt gratitude towards him equal to that she had for David. But all she could say was, 'Thank you, thank you, Mr Hetherington.' And then, her voice trembling and her eyes lowered, she finished, 'I'm very grateful.'

'Aw, lass.' He shook his head and his tone conveyed the same meaning as John's had done; it was telling her not to humble herself, not to crawl.

'Come on, up you get.' John's arms came over the couch under her oxters, pushing her upwards. Then, grabbing her hand, he pulled her round towards the piano stool and David, saying, 'Stand yourself there, next to your intended, and raise your voice in joyful song, something soft and harmonious. Come on: "Yacky-hoo-lah, Hicky-doo-lah".'

'Stop your clowning.' It was Dan speaking across David now. 'Go and fetch May in.'

'Aw, May knows the way. And, anyway, we're not speaking . . . There you are, there you are . . .' John was wagging his finger at Sarah. 'You're being let in on family secrets already: my wife and I are not speaking.'

The music stopped. David's hands became still on the keys, and, turning his head slowly upwards, he looked at his brother and said quietly, 'Stop it, John, and put the ego under lock and key for tonight, eh?'

Sarah watched the brothers. They were looking at each other, their faces strained, slightly tense. Put the ego under lock and key. What did David mean? What was an ego? Something to do with the way John was carrying on, but what was it? She must get a dictionary; she had always promised herself a dictionary.

'Sorry, let's sing. There . . . he's strapped down.' John's hands made the motion of tying a knot across his chest.

David touched the keys again and then they were singing. John and Dan and even Mr Hetherington. Mr Hetherington was singing with an odd-looking smile on his face as if he were laughing at himself. But Sara found she could not join her voice to theirs; they were singing 'Blue Heaven' and she was finding it embarrassing.

Just Molly and me and baby makes three,
We're happy in my Blue Heaven.

She had a feeling almost of horror in case John should change the Molly to Sarah, but John was apparently behaving himself. The chorus finished, David's fingers changed the key almost imperceptibly into the ballad 'Parted', and at this her eyes brightened. Oh, she knew 'Parted' – she loved 'Parted'.

44

Dearest, the night is passing,
Endeth the dream divine,
You must go back to your life,
I must go back to mine.

She forgot her embarrassment. In a moment she was singing softly, as if to herself, and then, when David turned his glance towards her, nodding in approbation and encouragement, she let her voice rise. But not to its full extent; even so, it impressed them. She felt herself glow because of this, her one accomplishment: they liked her voice. She saw Dan signalling to John to stop, but John was already stopping, and when there was only her voice carrying the song she looked from one to the other and her words faltered and died away.

'I can't sing by my . . .'

'Come on, come on,' said John. 'Start again, David. You're going to sing that right through. You've got a voice, my girl.'

'Come on, Sarah, let's hear it right through from the beginning.' David's voice was quiet, even firm. It steadied her. He seemed, when sitting at the piano, masterful, in command as it were. Perhaps that's how he felt; he played beautifully, lovely.

She stood ready to sing, telling herself not to let her voice go . . . to do it gently.

Dearest, the night is passing,
Endeth the dream divine.

She was singing with only part of her mind, analysing the words with the other. She hoped . . . oh, she prayed that her dream divine would never end.

You must go back to your life,
I must go back to mine.

David and she would have no life separate from each other. She would love him until she died, she couldn't help it; even if only out of gratitude she would love him until she died. But she did not feel only grateful to him for wanting her; oh no, she loved him, she loved him because he was David, somebody different.

Back to the joyless duties,
Back to the ceaseless cares;
Living and loving parted,
All through the empty years.
How can I live without you,
How can I let you go,
I whom you love so well, dear.

You whom I worship so . . .
You whom I worship so.

There was a short silence when she finished, and it was Mr Hetherington who broke it. He said, 'Very nice, very nice. You could do things with that voice, you know.'

David was looking at her, not speaking, his eyes tender and proud.

And Dan was looking at her. He was smiling with his head on one side, and he said, 'I would like to hear you let rip.'

But John was not looking at her, nor did he say anything. He was at the fireplace carefully lifting a piece of coal from the scuttle, carefully because one hand was poised underneath the coal in case it fell from the tongs. Sarah had not noticed him moving from the piano, but she did notice that he made no comment on her singing. Well, he can't have thought much of it, she said to herself; then added, he's a funny fellow, I can't really make him out.

'Play "Fur Elise".' Dan was sorting some music on a table by the side of the piano as he spoke, and then the front-door bell rang. 'Aw, who's this now?' His voice held a touch of impatience. It gave Sarah the impression that he was enjoying the present gathering and did not want it extended in any way.

She turned her head towards John. He was standing to the side of the bow window. It was the note of apprehension in his voice that brought her attention to him. He was squinting through the narrow aperture of the curtains looking into the street, and at the same time he was speaking directly to David. 'It's Eileen,' he said, 'and . . . and her mother.' Now his head turned quickly about and he looked over his shoulder to where David had moved from the piano stool to face him.

'Well, what about it? Let them come in, they've got to some time.'

'Not tonight, man.' Now all of them were looking at Dan. His head was still bent over the music. 'Here it is,' he went on as he lifted up a dog-eared doubled sheet and handed it to David, nodding at him. 'Go on, play.'

Whatever all this was about Sarah couldn't understand, but what impinged itself on her notice was that Mr Hetherington was sitting quietly in his chair and he had made no remark whatever. It could have been that he was stone-deaf.

David was now holding the music, and after rolling it backwards he placed it on the stand, manoeuvring it to keep it upright; and while he was doing this there was a movement in the passage and the front door was opened. There filtered into the room an exchange of voices, and then the room door was opened.

Instantly Sarah saw that all the men were disturbed, even Mr Hetherington, for he was now on his feet.

46

Standing to one side, with the door in her hand, was May, and past her came a short plump woman with fair hair. She was well dressed; as Sarah explained to herself, well put-on. Behind her came a tall girl. She was also fair and she had the most beautiful face that Sarah had ever seen, and it wasn't the first time that she had seen it. She had on occasions seen this girl when coming round the Stanhope Road way, and she had thought, By! She's beautiful, that girl.

Her skin was the colour of thick cream and her eyes were the deepest blue of any eyes that Sarah had looked at. Her features were perfect, too perfect. She looked – and Sarah was again colloquially explaining this to herself – the girl looked – too good to be true.

The two visitors were staring at Sarah, but before any remark could be made there appeared behind the girl the tall dominating figure of Mary Hetherington. Her face was flushed, her eyes bright, and her voice had lost the coolness that Sarah associated with this woman's whole demeanour. The tone was now brittle, nervous. She began talking straight away. 'Why, Ellen, I didn't expect you . . . And you, Eileen, how are you?'

'Oh, I'm very well, Auntie.'

'Well now, well now, you must come into the living-room and have a cup of tea. I was just making a fresh one. I never manage to get a decent cup when I'm looking after this horde. Oh, by the way, this is Sarah, Sarah Bradley.' Mary Hetherington paused here, took a deep breath, then brought out in slow meaningful tones, 'She's David's young lady; they've become engaged today.'

Sarah was looking at the girl, and the girl was looking at David, and David was now looking at 'Fur Elise'.

'Oo . . . oh!' The sound seemed to be acting in reverse, as if it had started outside the elder woman and was sinking down into the depths of her stomach, for she held her arm across her waist as if in pain. She was looking at Sarah now with a look that made Sarah want to exclaim, Don't take it like that. The woman looked hurt, shocked, and angry, but most of all she looked hurt. Sarah watched her take hold of her daughter's arm and push her past Mrs Hetherington into the passage, and as May went to follow them and close the door, Mr Hetherington, his eye twitching at twice its usual rate, went hastily across the room, and, pulling the almost closed door out of May's grasp, went into the hall, from where the visitor's voice came clearly into the room, saying in broken tones, 'You're cruel, Mary, cruel. You've had everything and you're still not satisfied. You're cruel, cruel.'

As the door closed on the voice John seemed to spring across the room, and pulling it open, he thrust his arm outside, saying, 'Here a minute you.' And in the next second he had pulled May into the room.

'Leave go. What are you playing at?' May jerked her arm from

47

his hand. It was the first time Sarah had heard her voice, and to her surprise it sounded refined.

'Why couldn't you have shown them into the other room?' John was hissing at his wife, his face hanging menacingly above her.

'Why should I?' Her voice was cool, aggravatingly cool. 'They always come in here, don't they?'

'You're a bloody mischief-making little bitch. You're never happy unless . . .'

'Here! Here! John, steady on!'

'Steady on?' John turned his head towards Dan. 'Steady on, you said?'

'Yes, that's what I said, steady on. And keep your domestic differences for your own hearth.'

'Now you're asking something.' May was nodding her head while her eyes stretched themselves into large circles. 'You're asking something, aren't you, Dan? Did you ever know him to use tact or discretion, the big fellow. The great I am.'

Sarah, standing apart, was experiencing a feeling of shock, and the shock in this case could almost be classed as severe. That the Hetherington family, this family from the top end who lived in the best house in the Fifteen Streets, who were the best people among the two thousand or more who filled the houses, that they could quarrel, that one of their members could swear, could even look as if he was going to hit his wife, the wife who appeared as aggravating as any other working man's wife did when having a row, was a shock.

In this moment she saw all the Hetheringtons struggling in the mire beside her, and the effect was distressing in the extreme.

Only one thing was clear in her mind – and her reasoning on this point surprised her. She knew that she understood why John had lost his temper, and she could understand and even condone his attitude towards his wife. She watched him now screw up his eyes as if someone had suddenly thrown acid into them, clench his teeth as if the pain was unbearable, and with his head down, like a charging bull, dash from the room.

'Well! Nice conduct, isn't it?' May looked from Dan to David, then her eyes settling on Sarah, she spoke to her directly for the first time since they had met. 'You want to be thankful there are no two people alike in one family,' she said.

'Oh, May, May.' Dan moved towards her. 'You know what he's like; he'll be over it in no time.'

'Yes, I know what he's like, Dan. And as you say, he'll get over it in no time, but that will make no difference to me.' She tilted her chin on this statement and, turning slowly and deliberately about, she left the room, closing the door behind her, and this with quiet deliberation too.

David turned on the piano stool and, facing Sarah, he bowed his head as he said, 'I'm sorry about all this. I was going to explain it all to you later, but there's been so little time. It's all so very simple, Sarah.'

'It's all right, it's all right. It doesn't matter.'

But it did matter. Again Sarah was feeling afraid. Nothing ever went smooth in life, did it?'

'You go into the kitchen, David, and have a word with them, and then you and Sarah take yourselves out for a walk. Go on.' Dan pushed at David's shoulder. 'I'll do the explaining to Sarah.' He laughed here. 'I've an idea I can do it better than you. Go on now.'

'I won't be long.' David, his face tense-looking and sad, touched Sarah's hand, and again she said, 'It's all right.'

'Here, come and sit down.' Dan put the tips of his fingers lightly on her arm and drew her towards the couch, adding, 'And don't look so worried, there's nothing going to happen. Look, I'll make it brief and put you out of your misery.' He smiled again and patted her hand while she waited, sick with anxiety, to hear what he had to say.

'It's just like this. Eileen's always been sweet of Davie, but he's never returned the sentiments, if you follow me, not in the same way. Now her mother wanted to make a match of it. She had her own reasons.' He smiled widely here. 'You see, years ago her and Stan . . . you know, David's father . . .' He nodded towards the kitchen. 'Well, they were as good as promised to each other; nothing in the open or anything like that, but a sort of understanding between them. And then he goes and meets Mary and that was that. But Ellen's a nice woman, a forgiving woman, and over the years the two families have kept in touch, with the precise idea on Ellen's part that Eileen and David should make up for her lost romance. You see the pattern?' He raised his eyebrows at her. 'But then Mary didn't see it like that and she had every reason. And they were good ones, I must say that much, because . . . well' – he wagged his head – 'you would know, anyway, sooner or later; but Eileen's father's in Harton, in the mental block. He's had three trips inside these last few years, and Eileen, poor lass, has the curse of fits on her; not very bad, but nevertheless she has them. And she is also cursed, as you've seen for yourself, I'm sure, with a beautiful face. It's out of this world, isn't it . . . Now, look . . . look. You're not going to cry, are you?'

'No, no.' Sarah swallowed. 'But it's sad, very sad.'

'Yes, it is, I grant you. But you must believe this. Davie had never any intention of marrying her. Yet him being a soft-hearted chap . . . and you know he is soft-hearted, and it's nothing to be ashamed of . . .' Again his eyebrows went up. 'Well, his mother was always a bit afraid that he would sink under the pressure both from Eileen, her mother, and Stan. And now . . . well, she's relieved. But I must tell you that his father doesn't see it in the same way as she does. In fact, I'm sure Stan would have welcomed Davie's match with Eileen.

I think at the back of his mind' – he was whispering now – 'he thought that in some way it would make up for the dirty trick he had done on Ellen. You know, we're queer cattle, we humans. We'd sacrifice somebody else, our nearest and dearest, to our conscience. Anyway, there's the tale. And David picked for himself, and a very very good choice he's made, I'll say that for him.'

He was smiling at her, and she should have felt warmed by his evident sincerity and the fact that David had never any idea of marrying the girl, but instead she felt afraid because her thoughts were now taken up with Mary Hetherington . . . That was why she had been welcomed into this higher stratum; why she had been welcomed by this woman who evidently ruled and dominated her family. It was a case of any port in a storm. She thought of the little woman's voice saying, 'You're cruel, Mary, cruel. You've got everything . . .'

If things hadn't happened in such a whirlwind of hurry she would have asked herself before why this woman had stooped from her high perch and welcomed her. But she had the answer now: she was the lesser of two evils. Pehaps his mother had thought too that if she opposed her son's choice he might become more pliable under the silent pressure of his father and the desire of both the girl and her mother. It was as Dan had said.

'Don't look so sad. I've told you there's nothing more to it than that. Come on, smile . . . laugh.' He put his fingers out to touch her cheek but withheld them before they made contact. Then with an embarrassed laugh he withdrew his hand, saying, 'You know, you look the kind of lass that should laugh a lot.'

Everybody thought she should laugh, just because she was big. But he was nice, this young uncle of David's, so nice. He should have been the brother and John the odd man out. She smiled sadly at him now, saying, 'I've never had very much to laugh at.'

'We'll alter all that. You know, before John was married we used to have some good nights in this room. All except Sunday.' He pulled a face. 'David's a fine player, you know. He's passed all his exams and could teach if he liked, but there's nothing in it, he says. And his mother plays the fiddle; she's a grand hand with the fiddle is Mary.'

'Do you play anything?' she asked quietly.

'Me? Oh yes, yes.' He nodded his head quickly. 'I've got me diploma, first grade; mind you, it took some getting. There was a big do at Morgan's Hall the day it was presented.'

Morgan's Hall! That was at East Jarrow near the New Buildings, a big gaunt empty place. She never knew they presented prizes there. She asked politely, 'What do you play?'

'The comb. But mind' – he held his finger up – 'I have a special kind of paper on it.'

She was laughing; her body shaking, her hands pressed over her mouth, and her face turned into the corner of the couch. And Dan was laughing too; lying back, he too was holding his mouth.

'Oh!' Sarah groaned inside. He was funny, dry; he had her believing him. She slanted her wet eyes towards him and he was looking at her, his face alight.

'We needed that, didn't we?' His whisper was as one pal to another.

At this moment the door opened abruptly and David entered the room with Sarah's hat and coat in his hands. He looked to where she sat wiping her eyes and for a moment a lightness spread over his face and he drew in a long breath as if of relief. Then on a note he attempted to make jocular he said, 'What was it? Dan been telling you about the time he fell in the rain-barrel, or when Father was on the roof and he took the ladder away?'

'No.' Sarah shook her head. 'About him passing the examination for playing the comb.'

'Oh, that's a new one.' David nodded at Dan, then added, 'You are a fool, you know.'

Sarah was in her coat and hat now, and David said, 'We won't bother going into the other room, we'll come back later.'

'Goodnight, Mr . . .' Sarah turned to Dan.

'Plain Dan, Sarah.'

'Goodnight, Dan.'

'Goodnight, Sarah.'

When she reached the front door she heard Dan's voice, soft sounding and careless, call, 'Here a minute, David.' And as she stood waiting she heard him say, his tone changed now, low and earnest, 'Macdonalds are moving from next door, they'll be out before Christmas. It mightn't be the most suitable place, so close, but empty houses up this end are few and far between as you know. I would get things settled as soon as possible, the wind might change at any time, understand?'

'Yes, Dan . . . thanks.'

Out in the dark street he took her arm. It was a firm possessive hold, and when they came to the main road he said, 'You heard what Dan said?'

'Yes.' Her voice was low and she kept her eyes ahead.

'Well?' The pressure tightened on her arm. 'Would you marry me before Christmas, Sarah?'

Her heart began thumping against her ribs, knocking like a small wooden mallet. It checked her answer for some seconds. Then she stopped and, looking fully at him in the dim lamplight, she said, 'I'll marry you any time you like, David.' Then she added. 'Thanks.' The last word had a silly sound. She wondered why she'd had to say it like that; it made her feel cheap, common. She didn't want to feel cheap or common. She thought of what John had said about being afraid of people. But she wasn't afraid of David, only grateful to him, so very grateful.

51

Sarah stood just within the kitchen door. She still wore her hat and coat. The kitchen was warm with the heat from a blazing fire piled high in the grate, but she still felt cold, and her body seemed to become stiffer as she looked at the priest, and he at her.

Father O'Malley was seated at one corner of the kitchen table, her father was seated at the opposite corner, and her mother at the corner nearest her. They formed the usual triangle of persuasion. One using threats – her father; one using cool fear-filled reason – the priest; one using the weapon of superstition – not the least strong of the three, her mother.

'Good evening, Sarah.'

'Well, don't stand there as if you were struck. You heard the Father speaking to you.'

'Yes, I heard, I'm not deaf.'

As she glared at Pat Bradley there arose in her, yet again, an acute feeling of hate. She had always hated this man, but the feeling had become stronger during the past weeks during which he had done everything in his power to break up her association with David and the family at the other end. The weapon he used was her religion, and his natural ally was the priest – at least this priest.

Father Bailey, on the other hand, had been understanding, even nice. He had asked her to bring David to see him, and David had gone and told him in a quiet way his reasons for not wishing to become a Catholic. He had pointed out to him that it wasn't a case of changing his religion because he wasn't of any particular denomination, he was an agnostic. She had felt proud that David was able to talk to the priest as he had done, and she felt that Father Bailey liked and respected him. He had said, 'Well, the Bishop, under certain circumstances, gives permission for a mixed marriage . . . they are not popular.' Father Bailey had smiled as he had said this. 'But nevertheless permission is given on the understanding that you will allow the children to be brought up in the Catholic faith.'

Sarah had felt embarrassed at this point, yet had waited eagerly for David's answer. It hadn't come immediately, but when he did speak she had let out a long slow breath, for he had said, 'Well, as I'm no longer speaking for myself on this point . . . It won't be a matter of personal opinion but what Sarah thinks too. I'll leave it to her, Father.'

He had buried deep into her heart when he had called the priest, Father. Oh, David was so reasonable, and Father Bailey was reasonable . . . Father O'Malley kept saying that he too was reasonable, but he wasn't – he was adamant, fanatic. By the things he said anyone would think she was marrying a leper.

Yet this same priest spoke civilly to her father simply because he attended Mass every Sunday. It was a wonder, she thought, that the church didn't fall round about his ears. This undersized man who looked what he was: a dirty-minded swine.

'Have you thought over what I said last week, Sarah?'

'Yes, Father.'

'Then you know you can expect no happiness or peace through a mixed marriage.'

Sarah remained silent.

'Can't you answer the Father?'

'Be quiet, Pat.' The priest lifted his hand in temperate admonition, then went on, 'I understand from Father Bailey that this man has no intention of changing his views, now or at any other time.'

Still Sarah did not answer.

'So in that case you must see your position clearly. Surely you cannot contemplate damaging you immortal soul by joining in a union with this man . . . If you do you will be damned, and your children will be damned, and you will be held responsible. Do you understand that?'

Sarah's throat was swelling, her eyes were widening. All the pores in her body seemed to have taken on separate lives and were rubbing one against the other, jangling her whole being. Looking into the priest's eyes, she saw the loss of her immortal soul. It took the shape of agony brought on by misfortune after misfortune as he had prophesied during the past weeks. If she married David bad luck would dog her. The penance for her crime while she lived would come in the shape of every disaster . . . But no disaster that her brain could conceive would be equal to the loss of her immortal soul and the immortal souls of her children, so his eyes told her. She turned from their penetrating stare and the eyes of the others and, tearing open the staircase door, she crawled frantically like some wild animal up to her room, there to find Phyllis waiting for her.

'What's the matter? What's he done?'

Sarah turned from her sister and, pressing her hands over her face, leant against the door.

'What is it, Sarah?' Phyllis was tugging at her. 'Look, what did he say?'

The hands still covering her face, Sarah whimpered, 'My immortal soul . . . He said . . .'

'Oh, my God!' Phyllis's sharp retort came as if from an older woman. 'Don't be a blasted fool, our Sarah, and let him scare the daylights out of you with that talk. Immortal soul! Tell him he can have your *immortal soul*, and stick it . . . Tell him to take my dear father's . . . there's an immortal soul for you. I bet if

53

Father O'Malley hadn't taken up the priesthood he'd have been twin brother to Pat Bradley.'

'Ssh! Don't talk like that, Phyllis, not about the priest.'

'Look, our Sarah,' Phyllis was whispering again. 'I thought you had some guts. You don't mean to tell me you're going to let him get you down, not at this stage.'

'No, no, I'm not.' Sarah sat on the bed and, tearing off her hat, flung it into the corner of the room, repeating, 'No, I'm not! David's not going to turn and that's that. He's even willing to be married in the church, but he's not going to turn. No, they won't get me down.'

'Look, Sarah.' Phyllis was kneeling by Sarah's knees now, gripping her hands, looking up into her face with an urgency that seemed in excess of sisterly interest in this matter. 'Why don't you do what the uncle said, the Dan one? Why don't you get married in the registry office, then there would be neither Baptist chapel as his mother wants, nor the church?'

'I couldn't . . . No.' Sarah shook her head wearily. 'Not in a registry office; I wouldn't feel married somehow.'

Phyllis pulled herself back on to her haunches and, looking up at Sarah, said, 'You know, our Sarah, you're a big softy; you let people play on your feelings, first one side then the other. When the only one you've got to think about is David. Now I'm telling you, our Sarah, things can happen, things that'll put the kibosh on you marrying him altogether.'

'Nothing'll stop me marrying him. The only thing I want is to be married in church, and he's for it.'

Phyllis looked at Sarah for a long moment now before turning and walking to the window. The paper blind was down but she stared at it as if she were looking through the glass, and her tone was fierce as she whispered, 'I expected you to be married afore this. Now I'm waiting no longer.'

'Afore this?' Sarah repeated in a harsh whisper. 'Well, we've only been going together just over two months. And what do you mean, you can wait no longer?'

Sarah was sitting on the edge of the bed now, her hands gripping the iron frame. Something that she had dreaded but forced down under the pressure of her own particular worries came rushing upwards. 'Our Phyllis! You're not going to do anything silly?'

'It all depends on what you call silly. An' don't say it that way.'

Sarah, getting up, went to Phyllis and pulled her round by the shoulders, peering into her face in the dim light.

'You're not going to live . . .'

'Yes, I am, but I'm goin' to marry him. I could have married him a month ago but I waited thinkin' that you would do something definite, stop being pushed around.'

'But . . . but you can't, our Phyllis. You just can't go down and live among the Arabs.' Sarah couldn't bring herself to say: live with an Arab, marry an Arab.

'Let me tell you somethin'.' Phyllis's voice was quiet now and her words deliberately slow. 'If half of them round these doors were as decent as them Arabs – not all, mind you, not all, I know that, I'm not daft – but taking them singularly and weighing them one against the other, this lot would lose hands down.'

'What's the good of cutting off your nose to spite your face?' Sarah was pleading now. 'You know what it'll mean going down there just to spite him?'

Phyllis shrugged herself from Sarah's hold, then, her voice still quiet, said, 'It was like that at first, but not any more. I like Ali and he can give me a home, and a decent one; they've got money.' She jerked her head up. 'His father runs one of them boarding-houses and Ali helps. It'll be his one day and a lot more besides. His father's a name down there, and they have their own kind of stuckupness . . . Do you know something? He and some of the others are not very keen about Ali taking up with me. I thought everybody looked upon them as scum. Even from the bottom end here they do; but let me tell you, them Arabs have their own idea of scum, and we from this quarter are pretty well at the top of the list. I've had me eyes opened this last few weeks.'

'He won't let you do it.' Sarah's breast was heaving nearly as much now as when she had scrambled up the stairs a few minutes earlier. 'He'll go to the polis.'

'He can go where the bloody hell he likes . . .'

'Don't swear, our Phyllis . . .'

'Well, he can, and as far beyon't because once it's been signed and sealed he can do very little about it – nowt in fact. I was eighteen last week, an' I know him; it'll be such a slap in his dirty face that he won't be able to wipe it off, an' he'll want to keep mum about it.'

'Then you are doing it just to spite him.'

'No, I'm not; I've told you. But I can hear him: "Aa'va washed me hands off her, the trollop!" Ooh!' Phyllis lifted her face to the low ceiling, and there was a twisted smile on it as she exclaimed in tones that held even wonder, 'Won't it be lovely to be a trollop and get away from here, and him, and everything?'

Sarah sat down again. She felt sick, really sick as if she could vomit. This was the finish – the finish of her, anyway. Phyllis would go, but she would stay because when David's mother heard that her sister had gone down into Costerfine Town way to live with an Arab – even if she were married to him – that would be the finish.

And Mrs Hetherington had been rather strange lately, cool at times. She, of course, wanted them to be married in the Baptist chapel. Sarah had learned one thing about David's mother during

55

the past weeks. She was a dominant, proud woman, proud of her family, proud of her station in the top end, of living in the best house – the only double house – in the whole place. When this knowledge of her future mother-in-law's character was added to that of her determination not to let David marry the girl Eileen, she appeared super-humanly strong. Sarah knew for certain now that if Mrs Hetherington hadn't been pushed for a substitute at a critical time she herself would never have got across the doorstep.

She swung her body round, straining it forward towards her sister, appealing with every fibre of it as she whispered, 'Wait till I'm settled, Phyllis; aw, wait till I'm settled.'

'I've been waitin', Sarah. I thought the way you started it was all going to happen in a rush, you'd be married and settled afore now. Well, you started like that.' She shook her head at the silent denial from Sarah. 'I can't wait any longer, there's a reason. I'm . . . I'm leavin' here a week come Monday, it's all settled. I'm to be married then.'

'A reason?' Sarah's mouth was hanging open and the lashes of her upper lids were lying flat against the smooth skin of her eyes. 'A reason?' Her voice had sunk into deep emphasis.

'Yes, and it's no good going off the deep end, it's over and done.'

'Oh, my God!'

'Mine too.' This flippant remark would have at one time caused them to giggle helplessly even while Sarah reprimanded Phyllis for treating the name of God with lightness; but now she could only stare at the slight boyish-like figure of her sister. 'How far?' she asked.

'Six or seven weeks. It happened after he gave me the lathering. Ali saw me face and weals sticking up above the top of me blouse and he was kind to me. You know what?' Phyllis shook her head. 'He nearly cried. Can you believe that, he nearly cried. Well, it happened that night, and don't think I'm sorry 'cos I'm not, but you can see I've got to get away. An' you know it'll be just like gettin' out of prison. I've never been inside but I'd like to bet me bottom dollar that this place is ten degrees worse than any prison. D'you know, I've had to come straight up here every night for weeks to get out of his sight, for his hands 'ave been itching to leather me again. He can manage me, you see; even if I kick and tear he can manage me. He couldn't you; that's why he's never started on you, only that once when you first went to work and that lad set you home. But me, I'm smaller than him, something that he can handle in the way he wants, and me mother's let him get away with it. She's putting her foot down now when it's too late 'cos she knows we can both skedaddle. She's as much to blame as he is. She could have managed him with her bulk, but now he's got her as frightened as he thinks he's got me. But he doesn't know he's made a mistake. Oh lass, I wish I could be in two places at once next week when I post them me news. An' you know how I'm goin' to end it?' She cocked her head up defiantly. 'I've been goin' over it in me mind for days. I'm goin' to say, after the bit about me being married, I'm goin' to say, "You can come to the christenin' if yer like, it'll be in about seven months' time".'

'Oh, our Phyllis!' Sarah lowered her head in a series of low swings until her chin lay on her breast.

'Listen!' Phyllis had raised her hand. 'He's goin' out. He's likely settin' the priest down the road, and on his way back he'll do a bit of his snooping on the courtin' couples. Oh, I wish some fellow would catch him at it and take him by the legs and swing him face forward against a coal hatch.'

Sarah put her fingers to her lips and stared at the tiny iron grate opposite her. Then, jumping to her feet, she asked, 'What time do you think it is?' She was standing at the foot of the bed buttoning her coat up now.

'About quarter to ten I should say. Where you goin'?'

'To see David. I've got to.'

'You goin' to the house?'

'Yes.'

'What will his mother say?'

'I don't suppose she'll be there. The grandchild . . . John's boy's ill, it's whooping cough, and bad. David said his mother was taking a turn over there tonight, but if she isn't I'll just have to make some excuse, I don't know what yet.' She was gabbling now.

'But how'll you get back . . . in I mean?'

'I'll take the back-door key and get me mother to leave the bolt loose. I'll sleep on the couch until the mornin'.'

'If he finds out he won't let you in.'

'I'll have to risk that; I've got to see David. I can't wait until tomorrow night, I'll go mad.'

'You're goin' to tell him you're going to be married in the Baptist?'

'No, no.' Sarah shook her head violently.

'What, then?'

'Oh, I don't know. I just don't know. I just want to talk to him.'

'An' tell him what a wicked girl you've got for a sister?'

'Aw, our Phyllis, I won't do any such thing, you know I won't.'

'I know you won't, Sarah. You're soft, our Sarah, soft. But go on. Go on and get back as quick as you can, I'll keep awake.'

Down in the kitchen Annie said, 'For God's sake don't make a noise when you come in.' She pulled the big key from the lock of the back door. 'I'll stay down as long as I can.' Then she added, 'What's got into you? Why do you want to go out at this time? Are you going to the top end?'

'Yes.'

'Is it about the priest?'

Sarah hesitated. She would have to give some reason for going, so she nodded abruptly before slipping out of the door.

There was a moon shining, caressing the grey slate roofs of the long street, casting deep shadows over the rows of small windows on one side and lighting them up on the other, showing them as elongated eyes in an elongated face of dirty reddy-brown brick. But the moon was kind. The streets were mellowed. The grimness of the poorer houses was dimmed, and where the streets began to improve the moon lent a touch of enchantment. In Camelia Street everything was bright and gleaming. The houses looked like smiling faces. The bow-windows were glistening eyes and the bath-bricked steps large white teeth sticking out of flushed faces. All the doors in Camelia Street were painted every year.

Sarah stood with her arm raised towards the knocker of number one, and before she grasped it she doubled her hand into a fist and punched her cheek as she asked herself, 'What will I say? How will I begin?'

It seemed to her that the knocker had hardly touched the door when it was pulled open, and there stood Dan.

'Why, Sarah, come in, come in. What are you after at this time of night? David said he had packed you off home because of your . . .' He looked down at her ankles. 'Because you were tired.'

'Is he in, Dan?'

'Yes, yes. He'd have been here waiting on the step if he'd thought you were coming back. Come on, come in.' He pulled her aside so that he could close the door; then, peering at her through the hall light, he whispered. 'Anything wrong?'

She did not answer his question but whispered back, 'Is . . . is his mother in?'

'No, she's over the road. The young 'un is pretty bad. There's only Davie and me in. His dad's over there an' all . . . Come on.'

When Dan opened the living-room door he pushed Sarah before him, saying, 'Look what the moon's flushed up, Davie.'

David was on his feet. 'What's the matter?' He was holding her hands now, looking into her face. 'Is anything wrong?'

'Yes. Can I sit down?'

'Can you sit down!' It was Dan who pressed her into the chair while David still held her hand. 'What is it?' David asked gently.

'Look, I'll be off to bed now, I'll say goodnight.'

'No, no.' Sarah looked up at Dan. Somehow she felt that Dan's cool head, his easy unaffected way of seeing things, might help. 'You might as well know.' She turned her face to David. 'I had to come straight away an' tell you. It's about our Phyllis. I know it's going to make all the difference, but I had to come and tell you. It isn't her fault really, but she's marrying an Arab . . . A week come Monday.'

When she felt her fingers slide from David's she cried wildly inside herself. 'Oh no! no! Hold me hands.' She turned her eyes from his startled face and looked at Dan. His face too was wearing almost the same expression as David's, and the two men were looking at each other now. David's lips were moving; it was as if he were saying something to Dan yet no sound came.

The thoughts flowing between the two men were like hot wires passing through her body, vibrating pain. She couldn't bear to look at them any more. She wanted to rise from the chair and rush out of the house, but she hadn't the strength; she hadn't even the strength to keep her body upright. It was bending over as if beaten. From her downcast lids she saw David's legs move. He swung a chair round and then his knees were touching hers and there was promise of life when once again her hands were in his and he was asking, 'When did you say she was going to be married?'

'A . . . a week come Monday.' Her voice cracked on the last word and she cleared her throat.

'There's not much time.' Dan had turned another chair round and he too was sitting, almost in a line with David and in front of her. 'Look, Sarah.' David was shaking her hands as if bringing her awake, and he began to talk rapidly, his words crisp, decisive. 'You won't countenance the Baptist chapel, and this business of your church is going to take weeks. There's only one thing for it: the registry office.'

The words jerked Sarah. It was as if the wires had twanged against a patch of fear, disturbing it, sending it flowing in all directions through her body.

'I know you don't want to be married in a registry office, and neither do I, but it's like this, Sarah. Well . . .'

He stopped and closed his eyes, and Dan, putting his hand out and gripping his knee, said, 'I'd better finish for you. It's his mother, Sarah. You know how things are, you're no fool. When this business of your sister's is made public, it isn't only God alone who will know what her reactions will be, we'll all know. She's a very proud woman is Mary, and she can be hard, unmoving . . . Now, what you've got to do is to create a *fait accompli*.' He smiled here, then went on. 'I mean, you've got to do the trick, get married. The thing is then done, achieved, and she'll have to face it. But, on the other hand, if she gets wind of your sister marrying . . . an Arab . . .' He wagged his hand at Sarah. 'I'm not saying that there aren't decent Arabs . . . they would be bad if they weren't as good as some of the whites; but you know how it's taken, don't you?'

Into the silence David said, 'Will you, Sarah? Will you get married in the registry office?'

Sarah stared into David's eyes. If she didn't marry this man in the registry office she wouldn't get the chance to marry him at all, of that she was certain. Between the pressure of the priest and the power of Mrs Hetherington, David and she would be torn apart, the battle would be too much for them. It mustn't be. Never again would she meet a man of David's standing, not one who would want to marry her. Not one so lacking in side, not one who was the antithesis of his mother, of all proud mothers. But that she would suffer if she was married in a registry office she also knew . . . Her immortal soul would be in jeopardy, and her actions would make her responsible for the souls of her children – the priest had said. Even so, she must do it. She must marry David, if not in the sight of God, then in the sight of man.

Thinking along these lines, she was surprised that she should openly show the extent of her relief in the way she did; for she cried, 'Yes. Oh yes, David . . . any place . . . any place.'

David pulled her hands up under his chin and held them there, and Dan rose to his feet with the comment, 'Well, now, we'll drink on that, the kettle's on. And don't let's waste any time. How soon can this thing be got through – in the registry office, I mean?'

'About a week.' David was not looking at Dan, he was looking at Sarah.

'Well, if you give the notice in tomorrow you should be able to do the deed in a week to a fortnight. And if you make it a Wednesday I can get the morning off. Look.' He turned round the teapot in his hand. 'I tell you what I'll do. I'll stand the wedding breakfast, eh?'

'Aw, Dan, man, there's no need for that.'

'No need? Of course there's no need, but I'll do it all the same. It'll be a bit of a wedding present. And look.' He came eagerly towards them, the teapot outstretched in the direction of the wall. 'The Macdonalds are moving on Friday, it couldn't be better. Everything will work out. And you can spend your honeymoon doing the place up. You've got a week to come, haven't you?' He now dug the spout of the teapot into David's shoulder, and David smiled up at him without answering. 'Well, there you are, everything fixed.' He was looking at Sarah as he spoke, his voice and manner sweeping away all obstacles. But there was one obstacle it was impossible for him to remove from her path, and it wasn't her religion she was thinking about now, it was Mary Hetherington. Her face straight, she looked at David and said, 'Your mother will never forgive me.'

'Oh yes she will. I'll take the blame.'

She moved her head in small jerks. 'She'll never forgive me. She'll even hate me.'

'Now don't be silly.' Dan was bending over her, his face on a level with David's. He spoke sternly as if to a recalcitrant child. 'That's nonsense. Get the thing done and stop shilly-shallying. I'm glad this has happened, you know, for you could both have gone on between church and chapel, between turning and not turning for the next two years and then finished up' – he straightened his broad shoulders, and spread his arms wide, the teapot still in his hand – 'not getting married at all.'

'You're wrong there, Dan. Sarah and me will be married whether it's next week, or next year, or the year after. But for my money it's next week . . . That's it, isn't it, Sarah?'

She was about to nod when the latch of the back door clicked and they all turned their eyes in the direction of the kitchen.

'What can I say?' She was on her feet whispering.

'Nothing, nothing.' David was patting her hands. 'I brought you in, that's all. We'd just come back.' That meant his mother had been out when he returned home.

When the living-room door opened and John entered their combined sigh brought his gaze from one to the other. 'Aye, aye! What's up here? You all look as if you'd been caught in the act of breaking and entering.'

Dan cast a quick glance at David, wanting to know whether he was going to confide in his brother and David answered him by looking at John and saying, 'A little crisis has arisen. Good in a way, in fact for my part I'd say splendid. Sarah and I are going to be married next week . . . in the registry office.'

John stared at his brother. 'Sudden!' he said quietly.

'Yes, it is. But things are better that way.'

'Mother know?'

'No, and I don't want her to.'

'Dad?'

'Nor him either. Nobody, only Dan here and you.'

'Do you want a best man?' His lips smiled.

'Would you?' David moved towards him.

'It's as little as I can do.'

'Thanks, John.' David thumped his brother's broad chest without causing him to move in the slightest. 'And Dan's seeing to the breakfast. I couldn't feel happier about it.'

'Well, she doesn't think she's going to get you without taking the rest of us on, does she?' John was looking over David's shoulder, holding Sarah's eyes now. 'She takes one, she takes the lot – the Three Musketeers, one for all and all for one, isn't that it, Dan?'

'You're a fool. Take no heed of him, Sarah,' said Dan.

'Well, we've always hung together, haven't we, against authority . . . politics, religion, and . . . women?' He smiled broadly as he said the last word. Then, coming towards Sarah, he held out his hand. She placed hers in it, and when he covered it with his other large square palm and said gallantly, 'But not – not this one,' she had the strange desire to fall against him, to put her arms around his thick neck and cry and cry and cry and cry.

This feeling, unheralded, springing upon her from nowhere, was as frightening as the hate which had attacked her in the bedroom a

61

short while ago, and again, as on that occasion, she was trembling, every pore in her body was moving. Her breath quickened; her neck swelled and the pain in it became so unbearable that it forced itself up the back of her throat and into her eyes. She closed them tightly to stop the flood escaping, but it was no use.

'Oh! Oh! Don't, don't, Sarah. Aw! What is it? Come now, come now.' Their voices were floating around her, exclaiming, soothing. Their hands were touching her, her arms, her shoulders, her head, patting, patting. Her feelings changed now into panic; she wanted to push them off, all of them, and fly from the house. It was only a momentary feeling; it was gone as quickly as it had come.

Through her blurred vision she put out her hands and grasped those of David. His hands were different altogether from anyone else's. She gripped them and turned her face into his shoulder, and the others melted away.

The room became quiet, there was only David and her. There would always be only David and her. The rage, the fears, the strange emotions, were things of the past. There came upon her spirit a quietness which even the thought of Mary Hetherington or the loss of her immortal soul could not dispel: she had David. Next week she would have him for life and she would know peace.

6

'Well, how do you feel?' Dan leant his big head across the table towards Sarah as he whispered the question.

'Fu . . . funny.'

'Not f . . . funny-daft, funny-nice, eh?'

'Stop acting the goat, here's the waiter.' David, the red veins on his cheeks seeming more prominent because his skin was a shade paler, pushed Dan upwards by the shoulder.

The waiter had a bottle in his hand which he presented to Dan as if for him to read the label, saying, 'All right, sir?'

'All right.' Dan nodded. The waiter tore off the lead cap, pulled out the stubby-headed cork and proceeded with practised art to fill the four glasses with the sparkling wine.

When the waiter had departed and they had the glasses in their hands David said under his breath, 'Either you're loopy or you've come into money . . . Champagne! You're daft, man.'

'Drink it up and stop your nattering . . . Here's to you both.' Dan held out his glass. It was on a level with John's, but John did not speak, he merely inclined his head.

The wine had very little taste, Sarah thought. Its only noticeable effect was the gas which pricked her nostrils. But it was champagne. Fancy her drinking champagne! Oh, Dan was kind. He was a nice man was Dan.

'This is the life.' Dan was sitting back in his chair beaming. 'Wednesday morning and me not at work. It's never happened before. Every Wednesday morning at this time' – he looked at his watch – 'quarter to twelve, in comes Mrs Flaherty, and we have the same performance, it never varies. If her old man's had the dole or not the programme is as usual. "What's your ham, the day, Mr Hetherington?" she says. Give her her due, she's about the only one that gives me me title. "Wan and two, Mrs Flaherty." I'm very deferential to her; we're both deferential to each other, and she has me talkin' the Irish as broad as herself.'

Dan was addressing himself solely to Sarah and she was smiling at him. She knew he was doing his stuff to put them at their ease . . . oh, Dan was nice.

' "Wan an' two, Mr Hetherington. Aw, dear God, Aa couldn't go for that, not this smorin'. An' what's your back?"

' "The short is a shillin', Mrs Flaherty, and the long is eightpence."

' "Begod! it gets dearer . . ." And us the cheapest shop in the town, cutting everybody else's throat.' Dan made this quick aside to David, and David choked on his drink.

' "What about a bit of collar, Mrs Flaherty?"

' "Aw, it's always too lean an' it kizzles up in the pan. Like the top of his boots he says it is; he'd throw it at me he would . . . collar!"

' "Well, I've some nice streaky here, now how about that? There, look, that's a nice lean piece, an inch or more running through its middle!" ' Dan held out the table napkin and Sarah could believe it was streaky bacon she was looking at. 'I tell you I'm talkin' as thick as she is by this time. And this happens every Wednesday in life.'

They were all laughing now, even John; and with the bubbles from another sip of champagne making her screw up her face, Sarah asked, 'What did she have in the end?'

'Pieces.'

Their laughter turned into a roar and they made individual efforts to stifle it while glancing round the half-empty hotel dining-room. And they were returning to normal when Dan finished laconically, 'Three pennorth.' His accent was exaggerated now into broad Geordie, the inflexion high on the last syllable. They were off again, unrestrained now, and Sarah thought wistfully, Oh, if we could go on like this all day right till the night, just laughing and carrying on.

There was no doubt in her mind that Dan could have kept them laughing for a week, but within the next hour or so she would have to face Mary Hetherington, and the prospect, when she let herself think about it, was terrifying.

The meal began with sole, and when the main course turned out to be duck, and this accompanied by another wine, David, looking at Dan, shook his head reprovingly, 'You shouldn't have gone to this, man.'

'Why not? You mind your own business and tuck in, that's all you've got to do.'

'Don't worry about him throwing his money about.' John was looking at Dan. 'It'll take a little weight out of the stocking leg and he's got stacks of them piled away, and not even Mrs Flaherty could get her big toe into one of them.'

Sarah, laughing with the rest, looked at John and realised that it was the first time he had opened his mouth since they had left the registry office. He looked slightly off colour, and his manner was not so boisterous as usual. He was not striding ahead as though the world were a football at his feet. That was how she saw John, this brother of David's, who was so totally unlike him. Perhaps she thought he was worrying about the child, but the boy was getting better now; or perhaps he'd had another row with his wife.

It wasn't until an hour later, when they stood in King Street, outside the hotel, that she felt she had been given the reason for John's quiet manner and him looking so off colour.

David had just said, 'I don't know how to thank you, Dan. Do we Sarah?' And she had shaken her head dumbly.

'Look,' said Dan, 'it's nothing. Anyway, it's only half your wedding present . . . I'm opening another stocking leg.' He thrust his hand out towards John on this remark.

David too had turned to John, and he asked, 'Where you going? You coming back home?'

'No,' said John, 'I'm off to the Labour Ex . . .' He bit sharply down on his lip.

'So that's it?' Dan was standing with his chin pulled in. 'I was wondering what was up with you. You're out?' His face was screwed up. 'When did this happen?'

'Aw, my big mouth. I was off me guard . . . Oh, for over a week.'

'For over a week? And you've never said anything?' David's voice held a reproach. 'Does May know?'

'No, nobody knows; at least they didn't.' John's head was wagging as if it had been snapped at the nape. 'I thought I'd be set on afore this, it's just one of those things.' His head bounced up now. 'Don't start being sorry for me, either of you.' His eyes were round and bright, his face and manner aggressive. 'Look, they're not getting me on the scrap-heap, I'll be in work next week.'

'What happened?' Dan asked quietly. 'I thought it would be the last place to pay off, and you the last one.'

'Well, there was no more orders for boats; big, little, tall, or small.'

'But your place only dealt with small craft. I thought there was still a market for them from the south, and for lifeboats.'

'Aye, well, so did everybody else, but they seem to have all the boats they need in the south. And nobody seems to be getting drowned now as there's fewer ships on the water so nobody wants any more lifeboats. And that's something to be thankful for, isn't it, nobody getting drowned?' He was grinning now, a false grin. 'Look.' He took them all in with a swing of his head. 'Don't let it be on my conscience that I've put a damper on the proceedings. Don't be sorry for me, for God's sake. I'm all right. For weeks ahead, I'm not broke, but I'm not going to let the blasted government get off with anything. No, by God, I'm going to get some dole out of them.'

'You won't get any for a fortnight, anyway; they don't recognise the first week and then there's three days lying on.' Dan was still talking quietly.

'Tell me something I don't know, man. Anyway, I told you I'll be at it again next week and I'll tell them what to do with their dole. But look.' His manner changed abruptly and his voice became serious as he turned to David. 'Don't let on to me mother, mind.'

'No, no, of course not. Although' – David was now smiling wryly from one to the other and his eyes came to rest on Sarah as he finished – 'I think it would be really the best time to tell her, for she'll be going at us two so much it'll pass over her head.'

His words were meant to reassure Sarah but they failed, and it was evident to the three men. Dan said briskly, 'It'll be all right, never fear . . . Well, I'm off to . . . Westoe.' It seemed as if the name had brought a self-consciousness to him, for his laugh was sheepish.

'Go on, you old roué.' Sarah could not understand this remark of John's. She did not know what a roué was but she could gauge that it was something not quite nice, for as Dan looked at her there was a pink tinge under his skin. The next moment he was holding her hand, saying, 'I wish you all the happiness in the world, Sarah.'

'Thanks, Dan.' Her voice had a cracked sound.

'And mind you, you make the best of those three days in Newcastle and when you come back I'll have one room cleaned out at least, if not papered . . . I'll put the big fellow on here.' He grabbed at John's arm. 'You know what he is when he gets started, skull, hair, and white-wash flying . . . God bless you.' The last was soft as a benediction and it was almost too much for Sarah. That is what the priest would have said, God bless you – at least Father Bailey would have said it.

Now John was standing in front of her. He did not touch her, not even to take her hand, but he looked deep into her eyes, past the worried surface of her mind, past the deeper level where lay the love she had for David, down, down, until his gaze reached a depth in her she did not know existed. She did not retreat from the return of the strange feeling, but wide-eyed watched his lids droop, the short black thick lashes creating a shadow on the broad high cheek-bones. She was married and safe, she had nothing to fear from strange

65

feelings or anything else . . . except perhaps David's mother.

'All the best.' It was an ordinary, trite remark, used on such occasions. It was intended to mean everything, it usually meant nothing. Again John repeated this as he now shook hands with David. 'All the best, man,' he said. And David, gripping his shoulder with his free hand, answered, 'Thanks, John, thanks.'

David now took Sarah's arm and turned her about and across the road to where the tram was, the same tram that had carried her part of the way home during all her working days. Now she would use it no more – not as Sarah Bradley, anyway. She was Mrs David Hetherington. She made an effort and forced her shoulders back and lifted her head. What could they do? What could any of them do? Her father, his mother. She was married, legally married . . .

Dan and John stood still on the pavement watching them until they boarded the tram, then they waved.

'Better them than me.' Dan's voice was low. 'Your mother's going to play merry hell. That lass is going to have a time of it. We'll all have to stand by her. Davie alone won't be able to screen her. You know what your mother is when she gets her fangs in, and she hasn't had a target for a long time. We'll all have to act as a buffer in one way or another, she's too nice to be nooled.'

'I can't see anybody nooling her.' John spoke as he looked ahead to where the tram was disappearing into the distance. 'I mean, I can't see anybody wanting to nool her. And me mother puts up with May.' John now turned and glanced at Dan, a quizzical smile twisting his lips.

'Yes, but May married you, she didn't marry Davie. The truth is, your mother didn't ever have any intention of anybody marrying Davie, at least that's how I figure it. She pretended to accept the lass knowing that the scales were weighed heavily against her, her coming from the bottom end and all that, and she was hoping that the weight would gradually tell on Davie – religion, background, the lot. Of course, I might be wrong.'

'You're never very wrong, Dan.'

Dan turned and looked at his nephew. There was six years between them, but this was in no way apparent, they had always looked and felt equal. Dan said now, 'You look off colour. Are you worrying about being out?'

'No, no, I told you . . . No, by God.' He turned his head round on his shoulder as if looking at someone behind him. 'No. They're not getting me to rot at the street corner. Don't you worry about me, Dan. I'll fall on me feet, I always have. Now, I'm off . . . And by the way, thanks for the meal. You went to town, didn't you, and it was decent of you. I thought about making them a dining table and chairs. I can get the wood at cost.'

'Oh, they'd be tickled pink at that; that's a good idea, John.'

'Well, I'll be off. So long, Dan.'

'So long, John. See you the night.'

'Yes, see you the night.'

Dan crossed the road, and John turned the corner and went in the direction of the station, his stride long and quick. He reached the yard and made for the urinal, and there with his body bent double and his hand against the wall he retched.

'You feeling bad, mate?'

John wiped his face with his handkerchief. The sweat was running in rivulets down from his hair. After nodding at the man he said, 'Eating too well . . . duck and champagne.'

'Aye, begod, you'll get sick on duck and champagne these days, on seventeen bob a week. Aye, you'll get sick on that. Sick for the want of a good feed. You all right now?'

The man's reaction to John's remark had been what he had intended, and after he had nodded at him the man went on, 'Duck and champagne. You'd have to be in Parliament to have duck and champagne these days. Even the mayoral banquets wouldn't sport that the day in case the smell got into the streets and sent people mad. Something should be done . . . it'll have to be done.' The man pointed his thin dirty finger at John. 'We'll have to hang together, that's the solution. The bloody unions will have to find out whose side they're on. Why aren't they up in London doing somethin'? There'll be riots afore long, you'll see.'

If the fool didn't shut up he would push him on his back. He turned away from the man and kept his face to the wall, and the voice coming from a distance now said, 'That's it, get it up. It's better out than in, whatever it is.'

Left alone, John again turned and leaned against the wall. 'Get it up,' the man had said. 'Better out than in.' But the man didn't know that he was sick in two ways.

A mixture of sauterne and champagne and duck had been too much for his stomach which had grown accustomed to the dull diets of an indifferent cook. But this was a kind of sickness you could get rid of. He wished to God the other could be vomited up in the same way. What had Dan said? They would all have to act as a buffer between her and his mother. That was funny that was, damned funny, for Dan didn't know that from the minute he had seen her that night in the front room he had wanted to act as a buffer between her and the world.

Before he'd had May he'd had his practice. He knew all about women. From when he was fourteen and looked seventeen, and the lasses had made a bee line for him, he'd had them; he couldn't help but have them, for they had tripped over themselves to get him to touch them. He'd had his first lass when he was fifteen. His mother would have had a seizure if she had known. Yes, he knew all about

67

women, but he had never loved any of them. Wanted them? Oh, aye, wanted them until he couldn't bear himself. Lusted after them was the phrase. He had wanted May but he hadn't loved her, but he had taken her and she had seen that he damned well paid for that bit of frisking. She was the only one, at least to his knowledge, whom, as his mother would have said, he had got with child. Paul had been born prematurely. He had laughed at that. He wondered if the midwife had laughed too. If she had, she hadn't done it in front of him or his mother. Everything that had happened to the child since had been put down to his premature birth. Did a child ever become aware that he had been born of lust and not love? He had told himself that as long as you had the other thing you could live without love. That's what he had told himself. Until the night he had walked into the front room to see the lass their David was going to marry. That night he had said to himself, Don't be a blasted fool, it couldn't happen as quickly as that. But the passing days had proved him wrong. He was known as the big fellow, he liked the title. But the bigger the weight the harder the fall, and by God his fall had been hard.

He pulled himself from the wall and wiped his face, then straightened his hat and buttoned up his coat. Well, it was done. Two hours ago she had become Davie's wife. If it had been anybody else but Davie, Dan even, he would have gone all out, full sails set, and caught her up like a demon of wind, all the magnificent size of her, all her unconscious, unaffected loveliness. He would have cried, To hell, let's get out of here. What did it matter about a wife and a bairn, about a mother who was so stiff-necked with pride and a sense of security it became painful at times for him to look, or listen, to her. He knew that if he had let himself sail before the wind of his passion, Sarah, whether she wanted to or not, would have been borne along with him. But it was Davie she had married, Davie she wanted. Or, did she? . . . Anyway, Davie had wanted her, and the only decent thing that had been in his life had been the love for his brother.

PART TWO

CHAPTER ONE

Sarah alighted from the tram at the Market Place and made her way to the ferry. Her step was light, for there was no swelling around her ankles. Three men, coming up the bank from the landing, turned their heads towards her and one of them whistled as he winked at her.

Cheeky thing. She moved her body slightly, expressing indignation that she did not feel. That's what new clothes did, she told herself, made men cheeky.

But as she bought her ticket the pleasure that the men's admiration aroused in her vanished, to be replaced with the feeling of being slightly ashamed, slightly anxious and apprehensive.

Before boarding the ferry, she thought, What if she hasn't turned up? Well, I'll only have to come across again. But she said the two-thirty.

She stepped on to the boat and moved quickly around the engine-house, and there in the bows, her back to the rail, stood Phyllis. In a moment they were together, their hands joined, exchanging smiles and gabbled greetings.

'I thought you weren't comin'. You got me letter?'

'Well, I wouldn't be here else, would I?'

'Don't be silly.'

They laughed at each other as they moved back to the rail, and Phyllis, leaning her side against it, examined Sarah, and her verdict was, 'By! You look bonny. I've never seen you look like this. All new things?' She flicked Sarah's coat with her finger.

'Yes.' Sarah smiled shyly. 'I've got two complete rigouts right through . . . But never mind me. What about you? Are you in trouble?'

'Trouble?' Phyllis drew her chin in. 'No, no. I'm in no trouble.'

'Oh?' Sarah paused. 'I thought when I got your letter . . .'

'I just wanted to see you. I felt I had to see you. An' I wanted to hear about me mother an' all.'

Phyllis turned and leant her forearms on the rail; and bending over it and looking down to where the water was beginning to froth as the boat moved from the quay, she added, 'I would have come up to see her.' She swung her head quickly up and sideways. 'I'm not afraid of that lot up there. They couldn't do anything to me. I'm not afraid of any of them, but it was him. I didn't want to run into him. You understand?'

Yes, Sarah understood. She, too, looked over the side of the boat, but without leaning her arm on the rail because it was grubby and would soil her new coat. She looked for some time at the waves dashing themselves against the bows before she said, 'I've missed you an' all, Phyllis. I've thought about you nearly all the time. I've wanted to write but didn't know where to . . . How's things?'

'Oh, fine.' Phyllis now turned her back again to the river, and, supporting herself with her elbows against the rail, she nodded slowly at Sarah as she said, 'An' it's the truth, things are fine, better than I thought. I can hardly believe it, mind.' She flicked her eyes downwards. 'Still, things isn't all jam.'

'He's all right to you?'

'Ali? Oh, Ali's all right! I've got him there.' She twisted the forefinger of her left hand around the little finger of her right. 'I can manage him. Course he's a bit rough at times.' She pulled a knowing face. 'You know what I mean.' Noting Sarah's flushed face she laughed, and said, 'Aw, our Sarah, come off it, man, you're married . . . An' when we're on, how's things with you? Is he all right?'

Sarah wanted to say wonderful, wonderful, but she felt that her enthusiasm might in some way hurt Phyllis. Yet she seemed happy enough. But still it might, so she answered almost flippantly, 'Oh, you know, could be worse.'

'You've got your own house?'

'Yes, next door. You know, the one I told you about. We've got the kitchen and one bedroom furnished and are getting at the front room now. John, David's brother, is making us some furniture.'

'I thought he was a joiner . . . a boat joiner?'

'He is, but he can do anything with his hands and wood, it's a hobby. And he's got plenty of time now, he's on the dole.'

'On the dole! . . . One of the Hetheringtons out of work?' Phyllis was evidently surprised. 'My! I didn't think it would touch them. Anyway, how you findin' them all?'

'Oh, they're lovely. At least . . .' She pulled a face at Phyllis. 'The male members are.'

'His mother still sticky?'

'Oh, Phyllis.' Sarah now covered her mouth with her hand and closed her eyes for a second. 'I don't think I'll ever forget the day we were married and we went back and told her. Honestly . . . You know she's a quiet woman, I told you; you wouldn't think she would ever lose her temper, all dignified like, you know. Well, you know something?' She leaned towards her sister, and it was as if they were on the bed again in the back bedroom. 'I thought she was going to hit me, I did, honest. I've never seen anyone get into such a rage. You know how Mrs Cartwell used to go mad and break things around the house and throw them into the yard. Well, she went on just like her. It was an eye-opener. I thought she would be stiff, and cold and on her high-horse, but I never dreamed she'd act like that. I think she shocked David an' all. He looked flabbergasted. He expected her to go off the deep end an' all but not in that way. It put the damper on our time in Newcastle, and she never spoke to me for a fortnight. I don't think she would have spoken even yet if David hadn't stopped going in; that made her come round.'

'Is she all right now?'

'She is, on the surface. But you know, Phyllis, somehow I think she'll never forgive me. I've got to be so careful. You see, when David stopped going in, the men started to come into our place, Dan, and John, and even the father; but now that things are all right – at least, as I said, on the surface – they still keep coming in . . . Oh, I like it.' She smiled at Phyllis. 'It's lovely to have them all there, and Dan's a lad, he keeps us in stitches. But the awful thing is now, she's started to knock through. You see, our kitchen fireplace and their living-room fireplace are back to back and she must have heard us all laughing the other night, for there came a rat-tat on the back of the grate. Oh, Mr Hetherington was vexed. I've never seen him so vexed. And you know, one night last week he said to me, "Can I smoke, Sarah?" Just like that, he asked me could he smoke. Do you know where he's got to smoke?'

'In the lav!'

'No. She won't allow it there; he's got to use the shed at the bottom of the yard. She's never let him smoke in the house. That's why David or Dan don't smoke. John does, in his own place. When he asked me I said, "Of course, fancy asking." And when he said to me, "I shan't make a habit of it, only now and again," do you know, I could have cried, Phyllis. I like him, I like him better than I did at first. The twitch in his eyes got on my nerves, but now I don't notice it.'

'Her and Ali's father would make a pair. He tried to put me there.' Phyllis pressed her thumb into the palm of her hand. 'But I let him see just how far he could go. He runs a boardin' house, you know, and he thought he'd got some cheap labour in me, but he found his mistake out. He's as mean as muck. But Ali's got ideas . . . What do'you think we're going to do, Sarah? . . . Start a shop. Oh, I wish this wasn't comin'.' She patted the front of her coat, and Sarah exclaimed, 'Oh, I'd forgotten. You're not showing, how are you feeling?'

'All right now. I felt lousy at first.'

'But this shop, what kind? Oh, it would be lovely if you could start a shop.'

'Well, it'll be a sort of café. There's money in it, 'cause even if it's only tea and buns people've got to eat. Eeh, the men that's out of work around us, from the boats, it makes you frightened. It's worse down here than our end was, and that was bad enough, God knows . . . That's why' – her voice was excited – 'I'd love a café, 'cos food's the most important thing in life. It is, you know; you've only got to see them looking hungry and you know damn well just how import . . .'

As the ferry bumped against the North Shields pier Phyllis stopped talking, and for the first time looked rather helplessly at Sarah and asked, 'What we going to do? Have you go to get back?'

'No, not until tea-time. Let's go for a walk and have a cup of tea somewhere.'

'Aw, I'd like that.'

In the murky half-light of the December afternoon they walked through the dull streets talking, talking, talking. When in the main thoroughfare they came across a café that looked a . . . bit posh, they went shyly in, and over the elegance of a set tea with toasted tea-cakes and cream buns they laughed and giggled with the excitement of two girls let out on their own for the first time.

It wasn't until the ferry was half-way across the darkened water nearing South Shields again that their chatter trailed away, and they stood silently side by side, their arms touching, looking towards the unseen waterfront picked out with meagre lighting along its jumble-scarred length.

'Look.' Phyllis was fumbling in her bag now. 'I want you to give this to me mother for Christmas.' She handed Sarah two pound notes, and Sarah said, 'All that? Can you afford it?'

'Oh, aye. I look after number one.' The remark sounded as if it came from a woman versed in the ways of handling men, or riddling pockets, of demanding pay packets. But Phyllis wasn't like that; she was still a young girl, at least so she looked to Sarah, a short pink-and-white, doll-faced young girl.

'She'll be grateful for it, Phyllis.'

'Tell her it's for herself, mind. I'd burn it if I thought he'd get his chaps on it . . . Do you know how much Ali gives me a week, just to run the house with odds and ends, because we mainly feed downstairs?'

Sarah shook her head now.

'Three pounds. He said once we get the café going he'll double it.'

'Three pounds!' Sarah exclaimed.

Three pounds for odds and ends. Why, David's whole wage was only two pounds seventeen and she had thought that marvellous. She said to Phyllis, 'By! You're lucky!'

In the darkness Phyllis turned from her towards the rail, and her voice had a flat far-away sound as she said, 'Yes, yes, I'm lucky. An' I'm all right, Aye, I'm all right.' It was as if she was confirming a statement in her own mind. 'There's only one thing I can't stand.' In the darkness she swung round to Sarah and caught at her hand, and her voice cracked as she said, 'I feel a beast, Sarah, a proper swine 'cos Ali's good. He's better than any of them up there. I know that, I do. But . . . but it turns me stomach up when we walk down King

74

Street or through the market. It's all right in our quarter, it doesn't matter, 'cos there's other white girls there. Some of them's tarts, but one or two's nice. One girl's from High Jarrow. So it doesn't matter there. But going down King Street I want to yell at them . . . people who look at me: "Keep your pity for yoursel', missus!" I want to say. You know something, Sarah? You know the Howards that live in Duxham Street, you know when all the schemozzle was on a few years ago about the girl having a bairn to her brother . . . well, she didn't know whether it was her brother or her father, you remember? Well, you know, I always felt sorry for her and I've always spoken to her on the road when we passed. Well, what do you think the bitch did? We were in the market and she cut me as dead as a doornail. Do you know, I almost threw me basket at her. I was so flaming mad.'

'Oh, Phyllis! Perhaps you imagined it. Oh, our Phyllis!' Sarah's compassion brought the tears into her voice.

'Don't be daft; you don't imagine things like that. An' the others told me they've all had to go through it. But most of 'em can go back and see their folks . . . Oh, Sarah!' She was holding tightly to Sarah's hands. 'I wish we could be together, or we lived nearer, so I could pop in.'

There was a new kind of pain tearing through Sarah now. She wanted to say wholeheartedly, 'Well, don't you be daft. Come whenever you like; you'll be welcome, you know that.' And if she was speaking for herself Phyllis would be welcome. She would have even let her bring the Arab with her – she couldn't think of the man as Phyllis's husband. But there was David to think of. No, it wasn't David she was thinking about – David had said everybody must do what they felt driven to do. He had added lovingly at this point that he had felt driven to marry her. No, it wasn't David she was thinking about, it was his mother. She had hurt his mother very much, she realised that. Deep within herself she felt guilty. She felt she had forced herself into her family, and Mrs Hetherington fed this impression. So she couldn't make matters worse at this stage by asking her sister into her house. If they hadn't lived next door to David's mother she would have managed it somehow, but asking Phyllis up would be like asking her into the Hetheringtons' living-room. She couldn't do it – but oh, she wished she could. She gripped Phyllis's hands as she said, 'Look, we'll get together, make a habit of meeting, and I'll bring me mother with me sometime. What do you say?'

'I'd love that . . . You know, Sarah, you can come to our place if you wouldn't mind. I've the two rooms at the top done nice. You'd be surprised at the things I've got. But . . . but don't come on a Friday.' It was as if Sarah had already accepted the invitation. 'Friday's their Sunday, you know. You wouldn't believe it, you talk about the Catholics being religious . . . Coo! They couldn't hold a candle to Ali's people. His father's a big noise in their kind of church

. . . they're Moslems. They're always prayin' all times of the day, you wouldn't believe it, an' yet the old devil – Ali's father, I mean – bleeds his own folk white.' She pushed at Sarah. 'That's funny, isn't it? Bleeding them white! . . . They want me to become a Moslem.'

Sarah was aghast, 'But you're not!'

'No, I'll not. Not that it makes any difference; I was never affected by our church as you were, it just slid off me. Hell fire if you missed mass on Sunday. Who do they think they're kiddin'! You know, Sarah, you learn a lot by mixin' with other people. Still, I'd have to learn a lot more afore I became a Moslem.' She was laughing now and punching Sarah on the arm. And her laughter began to rise until Sarah said, 'Be quiet, our Phyllis, you'll raise the boat.' She wanted to slap her sister to stop her laughing because the sound was painful, it wasn't real laughter; it was the kind of laugh you laugh to stop crying.

As the boat once again bumped against the quay she gripped Phyllis by the arm and together they walked over the gangway and up the rough road to the market-place.

As the clock struck five Sarah exclaimed, 'Eeh! David will be in and he'll wonder what on earth's happened to me. No tea ready.'

'You didn't tell him you were meetin' me?'

'Yes, yes, I did.' Sarah made the lie sound convincing. 'But you know what they are for their tea. There's the tram in, Phyllis, I'd better catch it.'

They stood peering at each other in the dim light; then, their arms around each other, they held together tightly for a moment before turning away without further words . . .

All the way home Sarah wanted to cry. She kept saying over and over in her mind. Oh, our Phyllis. Oh, our Phyllis.

When she alighted at the bottom of the street there was David standing waiting for her. He came forward at a bound, saying, 'Where on earth have you been? I've been worried stiff. Look, it's quarter to six, the house all in darkness. Where've you been?'

'Oh, I'm sorry I am, David. I'll get your tea directly.'

He had her by the arm hurrying her up the street. 'It's not my tea I'm worrying about, woman.' He shook her. 'You've never been out before and there was no note or anything; I didn't know what to think.'

Sarah suddenly felt warm, wanted . . . she belonged. She dropped her head on to her shoulder and hunched it up against him as she said, 'Don't worry, I'll never run away.'

He patted her cheek before saying, 'But I do worry . . . and about you running away.'

'You're joking.'

'No, no I'm not.'

They were at the front door now. 'But you must be, David.'

76

'Get yourself in.' He pushed her playfully from behind. Then when the door was closed and they stood in the black darkness of the passage he groped at her and, pulling her into his arms, kissed her. It was a long hard kiss, and when he was finished he said, 'Always leave a note, will you?'

'Yes, David.' His deep concern at her absence puzzled her, she couldn't fully understand it. If he had been a little irritable, or chastised her in a jocular way, or even sulked, not that David would ever sulk, but if he had taken any of these attitudes she would have understood it, but that he was really frightened that she wouldn't come back was something that she couldn't take in because it put value on her beyond her worth, at least the worth she placed on herself. Now if the boot were on the other foot and she was concerned about him walking out on her, well she could have understood that plainly, because she knew that compared to David she was very ignorant. She wondered sometimes how he put up with her ignorance. She was doing her best to improve, she had even asked him to get her books, but she could never see herself conversing with David other than on personal topics. She would never be like May, able to hold her own, even argue with John or Dan about unemployment and politics. Yes, she could have understood it if the boot were on the other foot.

When the gas was lit in the kitchen it showed the fire banked down and almost out, and she hurried forward, saying, 'Eeh! I'll never let this happen again. I don't know what I was thinking about.'

'Don't worry.'

'But I am. And no tea ready for you. The time just flew.' She straightened her back from the fire, and turning to him, said, 'I haven't told you where I've been.'

'It doesn't matter.'

'I've been to see our Phyllis.'

He swung round towards her. 'You've been into Costerfine Town . . . to the house?' His voice held concern again.

'No, no, I got a letter from her by the second post. She asked me to meet her on the ferry. We went across to North Shields. I didn't know whether to tell you or not.' She drooped her head. 'I thought if I did you might stop me, and I wanted to see her because . . . because she's a good girl really. She's not bad, our Phyllis, she's only a child yet.'

'Oh, Sarah.' He was enfolding her again now. 'I wouldn't have stopped you. The only thing is I hate you going around the lower docks and that quarter on your own. It's pretty rough round there, you know, at all times, and' – he pummelled gently round her chin with his fist – 'you're an eyecatcher in any port.'

'Oh, David, I'm not. You stretch it.' She laughed, raising her brows at him. 'You forget I've been going back and forwards into Shields since I was fourteen.'

77

'Perhaps, but you didn't look . . . well . . . like you do now . . . happy. You're more than fetching, Mrs Hetherington, when you're happy.'

'Am I?' She slanted her eyes up to the ceiling as if thinking. 'Well, I'm not to blame, it's all your fault . . . Oh, David. Darlin' . . .'

They sprung apart as if cleaved by a chopper when there came a voice from the backyard and a knocking on the back door. 'Are you in?'

As David withdrew the bolt Sarah applied herself madly to the fire. No fire on, no tea ready . . . his mother would have to come in at this minute.

'I've been round three times this afternoon. You've just got in?'

Sarah turned from the fire. She was still wearing her outdoor coat and she muttered hastily, 'Yes, yes, I was held up.'

'She's been looking round the shops for Christmas boxes, got fascinated with the bargains and forgot the time.'

Mary Hetherington was looking at the table covered with a chenille cloth and no sign of food on it. Then, looking at the fire, she remarked coolly, 'It'll be some time before you'll get anything going on that; the tea's still on the table indoors, you'd better come in and have it.' Then, looking at David she added, 'I suppose you're ready for it with not a bite since dinner-time.' On this she went quietly out.

Sarah and David exchanged glances, and as Sarah saw him make a gesture towards his mother's back that meant refusal she quickly raised her hand, then called, 'We'll be in in a minute.' She pushed at David as she whispered now, 'You go on. I'll just put some sticks on and get it going. I'll follow you.'

'No, no, I'll see to it. I'm not going to be . . .'

She swung him about and pushed him out of the kitchen, saying, 'Go on. Go on.'

When she had closed the door on him she stood with her back to it looking towards the dead fire, but she felt as warm as if it was ablaze and its flames were lapping the heat towards her. If David had to choose between her and his mother there was no doubt which side he would be on. She knew that when a man married the cord was not always cut between him and his mother, and if the wife went to snap it she was in for trouble. But in this case it was his mother who had snapped the cord. Yet there was a part of her that felt sorry about the severance. She didn't want any upset. She didn't want David to have to take sides. She wanted him to want his mother; not as much as he wanted her, but to want her nevertheless. She wanted them all to be happy and jolly together because she was happy. Life was being wonderful to her, and, oh God, she was thankful. As her mind uttered the word God she turned her glance quickly round the kitchen as if to reassure herself she was alone, then, dropping quickly on to her knees by the side of David's chair, she buried her face in her hands and began to pray, asking God, as always, to overlook her past sins and to recognise her marriage. She followed this up with a prayer of thanksgiving, praying in her own way, her words bereft of any supplication. She made no pleas for future happiness, she only thanked God for giving her David.

And as she rose from her knees she thought of Sunday morning and muttered aloud, 'I'll go to Jarrow mass, early. They know nothing about me there.'

Only once since her marriage had she been to Tyne Dock church and she had come out feeling like the scarlet woman herself, and she knew that she couldn't sit under the gaze of Father O'Malley ever again.

She turned down the gas and was about to move out of the kitchen when she stopped and looked around. It had been a funny day. Funny things happened to people, perhaps they always had. But as you got older you became more aware of them. She had been to North Shields with Phyllis and walked countless streets, talking, talking, talking. David had met her off the tram and had nearly carried her into the house and had wanted to make love to her in the passage. Her body shivered deliciously at the thought. And then his mother had come in and brought with her bleak condemnation. And just a minute ago she had gone on her knees and prayed. She had never gone on her knees in the day-time before, unless she was in church . . . Yes, it had been a funny day.

She locked the door leading into the yard, and when she went to open the back door into the lane it was pushed inwards and she was confronted with John's broad back. He swung round towards her, his bulk only discernible in the reflection of the lamp from the bottom of the lane. His body stood within the shadow of the wall, but she could make out the chair he held in front of him.

'I've just finished this one,' he said.

'Oh, I've been out. There was no tea ready. Your mother came round and said we must go in for tea. I've locked up; will I let you in?' She was gabbling.

'Well, I'll only have to take it back, I'm not leaving it in the yard. Don't you want to see it?'

'Oh yes, yes, John.' She rushed back up the yard, unlocked the door and held it open for him, and he moved past her into the kitchen and placed the chair by the side of the table.

'There, what do you think?' He was looking at her.

'Oh, it's lovely.' The words were slow in admiration. 'I've never seen any like it, with a carved back.'

'Sit in it and see how it feels.'

She sat down and moved her ribs into the curve, then wriggled her body in the seat. 'It's lovely, and so comfortable. Oh, thanks, John. But you shouldn't go on wasting your time making these. You've

79

done us the table, that's enough.' She got to her feet and put her hand on the top rail.

'I don't think it's a waste of time.' He was looking at the chair. 'Chairs are the most difficult things to do, more so than a table. A chair knows it's going to be sat on; it's a personal thing, a chair.' He touched its back and moved his fingers across the grained wood to within an inch of hers.

'Nice feel wood, hasn't it? Clean, nothing underhand about wood.'

She looked at him. He was waiting for her eyes. They hadn't been alone together but once since she was married. She felt nervous, even slightly afraid, of what she couldn't say. There came to her the memory of the night when she had wanted to fall on his breast and cry. She moved quickly and said, 'Eeh! I'll have to be getting next door or I'll be in the black books. Are you staying?'

'If you don't mind.' His eyes were still on her.

'Have you had your tea?'

'Yes, I've had my tea, but I'll stay until you come back. I want to have a talk with Davie. But don't let on to the old lady I'm here.' He smiled. 'It wouldn't do, would it?'

She shook her head. They were like conspirators now. She moved towards the door, but felt compelled to turn and look at him again. His eyes never seemed to have left her. She said quietly, 'Thanks for the chairs, John.'

'It's nothing,' he said. As she turned away again his voice came at her. 'You know what I'm going to do when I get me dole this week?' She looked over her shoulder waiting. 'I'm going to get blind drunk. I'm going to bust the lot, every penny, and I'm going to roll in next door and lie on the couch snoring.'

She couldn't laugh. She knew that he wouldn't get drunk on his dole. She knew that he would never lie on his mother's couch snoring, as much as he might want to. He just said these things, he said them to her often, these things, apropos of nothing that had gone before, to hold her attention, to keep her looking at him. At first she had not known how to meet these moods – they were like the tantrums of a precocious child – and she had remained silent and embarrassed on the spate of his words, but on this occasion she put them in their place by saying, 'A raw egg in tea is a very good thing for a hangover.'

She was closing the back gate as she heard his laugh. It was high and mirthless, of the same quality as Phyllis's had been on the ferry.

It had been an odd day.

CHAPTER TWO

'Have you tried Palmers' lately?' said Dan.

'Aye.' John lowered himself further into the couch by letting out a deep breath.

'No good?'

'No good.'

'I thought since the N.S.S. had taken it over things had looked up. I heard they had a number of ships ordered.'

'Aye, they have; and they've got a number of men to do the work and they're sitting tight. They'll drop down dead on the job before they'll take a day off sick, that's what fear will do to you . . . But, look, don't worry about me, Dan. Stop, it, man, will you?' John hoisted himself up straight again. 'You're like an old hen. Isn't he, Sarah?'

Sarah was working at a side table, her arms deep in a batch of dough, mixing, turning, kneading. She looked relaxed, completely at ease. She turned and smiled, not at John in particular but at the three men sitting around the fire. Her eyes coming to rest on David, his long legs stretched out on the fender, her smile widened, and he said to her, 'Are you ready for more water?'

'No, I've got enough, I don't want to drown the miller.'

'You can't kid me,' said Dan, 'you're worried. Why not admit it and stop acting the big fellow. It stands to reason, everybody's worried. Even with the Palmers' little boom on, people are not spending like they used to, they're frightened. And who's to blame them? You know, some of them on the dole are spending as much on groceries as those in work. I had a talk about this to a woman, a Mrs Robinson – she's been a customer of ours for years. She admitted it. She said they were clearing up the rent and clubs and things because when the next bad spell comes they'd be able to run up again. But if they didn't pay up now they'd get short shrift if they ever wanted tick again. And, as she said, you may be sure they'd want it again. It's an awful look-out, you know.'

'Don't,' said John bitterly now. 'It makes me want to go berserk. We're back a hundred years ago, man. There's riots breaking out all over the country, and fellows being jailed. Nothing changed in a hundred years. The men marched from Hebburn and Shields to Jarrow in those days to be at a Trade Union meeting and what happened? Seven of 'em were sentenced to death. It was changed to transportation. Lads who were God-fearing, peace-loving individuals, Primitive Methodists . . . Not that I carry any flag for Primitive

Methodists, but all they and the others wanted to do was to work and eat.'

John was sitting forward now addressing Dan loudly as if this young uncle of his was the cause of all the past and present trouble. 'Young lads under twelve kept at work for twenty-four hours at a stretch they were then.'

'But that was in the pits . . .' Dan began, but was shouted down again by John crying, 'Pits or shipyards or steel mills or puddling mills, what does it matter on a twenty-four hour-stretch? It shouldn't 'ave been tolerated. And it's as bad today in a way. How do they expect a man to live? Twenty-six shillings to keep three of us. Two shillings to keep a child! Did you ever hear anything like it? And if I hadn't been working full time these last years I wouldn't be getting that. How about the poor devils who haven't had thirty contributions on their cards in the last two years or so. I tell you it's a bloody scandal.'

'Look, John, calm down and fight your own battles for the moment. As you stand now you could be off for seventy-four weeks and still get benefit . . .'

'Seventy-four weeks! My God, man, do you want me to land up in the loony bin in the Institution . . . Look, Dan. Don't you start talking as if they were being kind to me. Every man Jack of us is up afore them every eleven weeks and our money could be stopped like that.' He cracked his thick fingers and the sound was like the meeting of drumsticks. 'There's a clause called "the not genuinely seeking work clause". Have you heard of it?' His voice was sarcastic. 'You want to get into that queue, Dan, and hear just how those boys behind the wire grids with their smug gobs can manoeuvre it.'

'They're not to blame, John. They're just doing their job.'

They all turned and looked at David now. He was speaking quietly, his eyes directed towards the fire. 'Phil Taggart in the Exchange said he would be out of it tomorrow, but it would just mean him standing on the other side of the grid.'

'Phil Taggart!' John's voice was scornful. 'He's just one; you want to see the attitude of most of those swine. They look at you as if you'd just crawled up the wire. "Stand aside." "Come back this afternoon." "What did you say your number was?"' John's voice had taken up a haughty tone. Then it changed abruptly back as he said, 'There'll be riots I tell you, men can only stand so much.'

Yes, there would be riots. If all the men were like John there would be riots all the time, Sarah thought as she turned the dough over for the last time. Lack of work, resulting in enforced idleness, broken only by miles of tramping in search of the elusive job, had taken the spunk out of most of the men. She remembered the men two or three years ago standing at the corners, talking loudly, protest oozing out of them, aggressive against misfortune. Now they still stood at the corners, but they were more quiet, their talk intermittent. Some of them walked slower. Their faces had a pale-yellow tinge. They hoarded Woodbine ends in small tin boxes. Some of them pushed home-made barrows down to the tip at the bottom of Simonside Bank and scraped there for cinders and came around the doors selling them; a shilling they would ask for a barrow-load. She always bought a load. There were six buckets to the barrow. They were burnt-out cinders and wouldn't burn on their own, but they did all right for banking down. One man had called twice last week. He did not ask her to buy the second time, he just stood looking helplessly at her. She hadn't wanted the second load but she had taken it and said, 'Would you like a flat cake? It's just out of the oven?' 'Oh, missis!' was all he had said, but his lips became soft with saliva. It was the first time she had been addressed as 'missis', and it made her feel married and very adult.

Then there was David. David worried about the unemployed. He always had apparently, but now his concern was centred around John. He was very fond of John. He didn't agree with half he said and argued with him, but nevertheless she knew from the way he talked that he thought a lot of his elder brother. He said John was the last person on earth who should be out of work, it would do something to him. Unemployment was like a personal insult to a man of his calibre. John, he said, would die protesting. He was made like that . . .

Tomorrow was New Year's Eve, the last day of nineteen twenty-nine. She had decided to get her baking done tonight so that tomorrow she would only have the cleaning to do. Everything must be polished and shining with an extra brightness to greet the New Year. Everybody everywhere – to her everywhere was a synonym for the North – cleared up for New Year's Day. She wanted to be all done before tea-time because they were going to spend the evening next door. Apparently they had a lot of jollification on New Year's Eve, and also apparently without getting drunk. But this was the one night, she understood, when David's mother allowed wine in the house. Also for this night she brewed a batch of home-brewed beer, the recipe for which she would tell no-one, and which had a kick Dan said that was better than any Burton and as good as some whiskies. She was a strange woman was David's mother, Sarah thought, and a frightening woman in some ways. She had decided on one thing: she wouldn't sing tomorrow night, not even if they pressed her, because she knew that her mother-in-law didn't like her to sing – not on her own. She had gone out of the room when she had sang last time. It was 'Where my caravan has rested', and they had all praised her – all except David's mother.

As she put a cloth over the dough David rose from his chair and lifted the heavy earthenware dish down on to the fender. John

83

was still at it; he was thrusting his finger at Dan now and saying, 'We'll be marching from here, you'll see. It's the only way to get things done. The Scots did it last year, they're not the blokes to sit down under injustice. They've been marching and protesting since nineteen twenty-two.'

'The N.U.W.M. got up the national march last year, don't forget that,' said Dan. 'You don't have to be a dour Scot to get things done. They made the Tories consider the "Not genuinely seeking work clause" that you're on about; they didn't get it abolished but they got another year's grace. And it was prophetic that only a few weeks later the Tories were out . . .'

'Well, for all the good the change has done they might as well have stayed in, for Ramsay MacDonald and Snowdon are still carrying on the same policy; they make my belly heave. Once the Labour Government got in it was going to play hell with a big stick. And it's done bug . . .' On a warning look from David, John just suppressed the adjective and substituted 'damn all' in its place.

The little incident caught at Dan's sense of humour. The heat of the discourse, the added colour that rose to John's face with the suppression of the word bugger was too much; he put his head back and let out a bellow of a laugh.

'You . . . you big stiff!' John's great arm knocked Dan sideways on the couch. 'You can laugh.' But now John's laughter had joined Dan's. And Dan's finger came out and wagged itself in John's face while with the other arm he gripped himself around the waist to ease the pain that his merriment was causing. The next moment the two men were locked together sparring like irrepressible schoolboys.

'Give over, give over, you fools!' David was standing above them. 'You'll break the couch, the pair of you.' He jumped aside as they fell sideways on to the floor and there, locked together, they lay panting and still laughing.

'You pair of fools!' David, himself laughing now, was staring down at them where they both sat with their backs to the seat of the couch, their legs stretched out on the mat.

'That takes us back some years.' John had his head turned to Dan, and Dan, rubbing his wet face with his hand, said, 'By! It does that. We used to have some fun and games, didn't we?' As they hitched themselves back on to the couch, Dan took a fit of coughing which caused him to press his hand across his chest.

David, turning now to where Sarah was rubbing fat into flour preparatory to making pastry, and herself laughing at the antics of these men acting like young lads, said eagerly, 'What about us throwing a bit of a party, eh, Sarah?'

Her hands stopped their rubbing. 'A party! Oh, yes. Oh yes, I'd like that. When?' They were all looking at her. 'What about Thursday?' she said. They continued to look at her but no-one spoke. John was

84

the first to look away. He cast his eyes sideways towards Dan and then said on a small laugh, 'Well, what about Thursday?'

Dan got to his feet, pulling his coat straight, saying as he did so, 'Not Thursday, Sarah.'

'Oh no.' She nodded her head. She had forgotten, Dan always went to stay with a friend of his on Thursday. She could understand Dan having lots of friends. She had never seen this friend. Apparently he lived at yon side of Westoe village. Perhaps he had a wife, she didn't know. David hadn't seemed to know much about it when she had asked him about Dan's friend some time ago. Impetuously she said now, 'Why don't you bring your friend along, Dan? Shouldn't he, David?'

Dan's head came up quickly. He had been dusting the legs of his trousers and now his hands were held outwards as if the question had fixed him in one position. There was a look of perplexity on his face, until he turned his gaze full on David and smiled at him. Then, moving towards the scullery door and coming abreast of Sarah, he said quietly, 'Make it Friday and we'll have a night of it.'

When the door closed quietly John turned to David, and speaking below his breath, he said, 'Do you mean to say you haven't told her?'

'I didn't see the need.' There was an unusually sharp note in David's reply.

John turned his head and looked at Sarah now, and she looked at him as he said, 'Well, she's a married woman and she won't faint, and, being Sarah, she'll understand, won't you, Sarah?'

'Understand what?'

'About Dan. You see . . .'

'I'll tell her, John. If it's necessary, I'll tell her.'

'All right, have it your own way, but it would have saved an embarrassing situation if she had known already, wouldn't it? But that's you.' He brought his fist in a quick flick past the end of David's nose. Then he screwed his face up at him and moved across the room. 'Goodnight, Sarah.' His voice was quiet now.

'Goodnight, John.'

When the back door had closed, Sarah, scraping the flour and fat from her hands, looked over her shoulder and asked, 'What was all that about, about Dan? Is there something wrong?'

'Really it's none of our business, it's Dan's business.'

'Did I put my foot in it in some way?'

'No.' He caught at her floured hand and pulled her towards him, pressing her down into the big leather chair at the side of the fireplace. Then, seated himself on a cracket close to her knee and looking to where the rising dough was pushing against the cloth, he said, 'Dan's got a woman.'

Dan with a woman! Sarah couldn't believe it. Dan the kindly, jocular, nice man, carrying on with a woman! He wasn't the type.

85

She made David look at her as she said, 'I just can't take that in.'

'It's true. But it's his own business; it's Dan's own life and he can do what he likes with it.'

'Yes, yes, I know, David. Yes.' She was quick to agree with him. 'But somehow – well, Dan just doesn't seem . . . Is she married?'

'No.'

'She's not? Well, why doesn't he marry her?'

'It's very difficult to explain.' David took hold of her hand again. 'It sounds a bit fantastic, but you know different people think in different ways and some people think for themselves. Dan does, and apparently this woman does too. She's a widow and as far as I can gather she's glad to be a widow, as she had a pretty rough time during the six years she was married to her husband. He was killed by a lorry and the firm was found to be at fault and she gets a small pension. Perhaps this is a bit of the reason for her independence. Well, anyway, she doesn't want to marry and neither does Dan.'

'Dan doesn't want to marry her?'

'No, nor nobody else. I mean Dan doesn't want to marry anybody. Dan's been serving in a shop since he was twelve. He started running errands then and he's had a sort of education against marriage through listening to women . . . at least that's how he laughingly put it to me. But he just doesn't want to marry. Anyway, he met this woman. How, I don't know, he never told me; I only know that she's got a decent kind of house and that one night in the week, Thursday night – it has never varied over the last four years – he goes and sees her.'

'But your mother . . . ?'

'Oh! There was the devil to pay. Being Dan, he was quite straight about it. But fancy having to tell a thing like that to my mother; imagine the scene; especially when she looked on him almost as a son and not a brother. You see, she had the business of bringing him up when her own mother died. Anyway, he gave her the option; he was quite willing, he said, to go and get lodgings elsewhere. He emphasised to her that he was not going to live with the woman, only see her that one night a week. Lord, he had some pluck. It all sounded fantastic and I can see how my mother thought he was going up the pole. But, anyway, she didn't tell him to get out and take his life of sin with him. And for two reasons. First, she's a saver, and a very careful housekeeper as you have gathered. She's nearly always had twice as much coming in each week as what she's spent. She could teach Micawber a thing or two.'

'Micawber?'

'Oh, he's a character in Dickens. I must get you Dickens, you'll like him . . . And then there was the fact that if she ordered Dan out he might, although he said he wouldn't, go and live with the woman, whereas if she kept him under her eye she might manage to convert him from his sinful ways. But up to date she hasn't made any impression on him. The atmosphere in the house on a Thursday morning is always painful.'

'But it's fantastic. I can't see . . . well, I can't see Dan doing it. And if he's living with her part of the time what's the difference, why doesn't he live with her all the time?'

'Don't ask me, Sarah, I just don't know. Dan has arranged his life and he has found someone to arrange it with.'

'I liked Dan.'

'Don't say it like that in the past tense, Sarah. Surely this won't stop you going on liking him. Dan's a fine fellow.'

'But it's a bit of a shock. Dan doesn't look . . .'

'You can never tell by people's looks, Sarah. And see here.' He tilted her chin upwards, his voice holding a note which she had never heard before. 'You are not going to make any difference to Dan, I mean in your manner; I wouldn't like that, Sarah.'

'No, no, of course not.' She smiled at him now. 'It was just . . . well, just as I said. I . . . I couldn't see Dan doing anything like that. But don't worry, I'll be the same to him. And why should I make any difference?' She shook her head. 'I've got no room to speak. Look at our Phyllis. And she's nice and all. I've always told you our Phyllis is nice.'

'There you are then.' They were smiling at each other. He leant towards her now. 'And you're nice, too, Mrs Hetherington. Very, very, very nice. Do you know that, Mrs Hetherington?'

The niceness was inside her, she could feel it. David could make her feel that she was nice. She felt a different person when she was with David, soft inside, even refined. Yes, even refined. She had always longed to be refined, to know what to say, to know what to do. She had always felt she would never reach this desired pinnacle, not only because she was ignorant but because she didn't look refined, at least her body didn't, it was too big – the word was voluptuous. She had looked that up in the dictionary David had bought her. He bought it for her the very next day after she had told him she had always wanted a dictionary. He had seemed very pleased that she had wanted a dictionary.

David was looking at her now. She knew the look and she became quiet. She remained quiet when he rose swiftly from the cracket and went and put the bolt in the back door. She hitched her hips to one side and made room for him when he returned, and he lay with his head on her shoulder, his fingers slowly outlining her breasts. Her lips dropped apart; they were trembling slightly and moist. 'I've got the bread to do,' she said in a whisper. 'I've got all my baking to get through.'

He opened her blouse, and, supporting the large cup of her breast on the palm of his hand, he said, 'I wish all men joy because of you.'

87

She felt more than nice; more than refined, she felt wonderful, honoured, like a queen must feel.

CHAPTER THREE

New Year's Eve was typical, the day being made up of a number of small busy-busy issues leading to the climax. But when Sarah looked back on this particular day she saw that everything she had done had a bearing on what was to come. Like threads of a tapestry, on which was worked the outline pattern of her life, they began to work inwards to the central point.

It was when she finished scrubbing the scullery and had returned to the snug warmth of the kitchen that she thought, I wonder how me mother is. I should slip across, it being New Year's Eve. She'll feel it, being all on her own. And he'll be out this morning, signing on. Yes, I should slip across.

Ten minutes later she locked the scullery door and went down the back-yard and out into the lane. The back lane was clean and empty – you very rarely saw the women of Camelia Street standing gossiping at their back doors; it was a sign of their raised status, that any gossiping they did was over a cup of tea in the afternoon after they had . . . got the men off.

The morning was biting cold; there was a high wind blowing that spoke of snow. Sarah felt she could smell it. She pulled the collar of her new coat up around her ears and kept her gloved hands up under its warmth as she walked. She loved this coat, she had never had anything like it; it was David's Christmas box. He had paid five pounds ten for it. She had played war with him. It was dove grey, trimmed with brown fur, and it fitted her as if it had been made to measure.

Perhaps it was because her life was now spent between the sparkling cleanliness of her mother-in-law's house and her own home, that the streets through which she was now passing seemed dirtier than she had ever noticed them before, and the houses, although the same size as those in Camelia Street except for number one, looked smaller.

There were three men standing at the bottom of Howard Street and they looked at her but seemed shy of acknowledging her, until she remarked breezily, 'By! It's a stinger, isn't it?'

'Aye, aye, it is that. How are you getting on, Sarah?'

'Oh, fine, Mr Prideau.'

'That's the ticket, Sarah. You're looking well . . . Bonny.'

She turned her head as she passed them, smiling widely on them. People were nice, people were kind.

'Happy New Year, Sarah. Happy New Year.'

The combined voices turned her head towards them again and she called back, her mouth wide and laughing, 'Happy New Year to you an' all. Happy New Year.'

Mrs West from number seven was doing her windows, and Mrs Young was doing her step. It was late to do steps this time in the morning; still it was New Year's Eve and all the work was topsy-turvy.

The two women stopped what they were doing and waited for her approach. 'Hello, Sarah. Goin' to see your mother?' Mrs West nodded her head at her.

'Yes.' She nodded back, then turned to Mrs Young. 'Hello, Mrs Young.'

'Hello, Sarah, lass. By! Isn't it cold!'

'Freezing.'

'How's things going?' Mrs West was poking her head forward, speaking in a confidential whisper.

'Oh, fine, Mrs West, fine.'

'You like it up there?'

'I couldn't help but, could I?'

'No, I suppose not. Anyway, I'm glad to see you've fallen on your feet. Your mother can be proud of you, at least.'

Sarah turned from Mrs West again. She would have to say that, digging at their Phyllis. She said quickly, 'How are you keeping, Mrs Young?'

'Fine, lass, fine. But I won't say I wouldn't be better if they were at work. Still, you never know what the New Year'll bring, do you?'

'No, Mrs Young.' Sarah knocked on the front door, and as she heard the steps approaching on the other side she said, 'I wish you a Happy New Year in case I don't see you again.'

'The same to you, lass.'

'A Happy New Year, Mrs West.' She nodded to the other woman.

'The same to you, Sarah. The same to you.'

Annie was surprised to see her, but the light that spread over her face showed her pleasure. 'Why, lass, I didn't expect you across the day.' She spoke as if Sarah was in the habit of visiting every day. She went before her through the front room and into the kitchen, talking quickly. 'I've just made a cup of tea, I must have known you were comin'. I haven't done me baking yet, I was just about to start. Sit down, sit down, lass. By! You're looking well. Is that a new coat? It's bonny . . . a beauty.'

'David brought it for my Christmas box.'

She hadn't seen her mother since three days before Christmas when she had given her Phyllis's money and a pound of her own.

Sarah watched her mother pouring the tea out. Her hands were shaking slightly, and she spilled the tea into the saucers, exclaiming

89

on her awkwardness as she did so. Sarah glanced around the kitchen. Everything looked clean but not with the sparkle of her own house. She said, 'You're all done, I see.'

'Yes. Yes, I thought I might as well get it over with. Yet I ask meself, what for?' Annie sat down suddenly opposite to Sarah. Her hand was still on the teapot. She looked at her daughter for a long moment before saying, 'Oh, I'm glad to see you; I felt the house would be empty all the day. You notice it more on New Year's Eve and I was dreading twelve o'clock. We always sat up, didn't we, me and you and Phyllis, and saw the New Year in. But it'll be different this year.'

Sarah felt a lump rise to her throat. Yes, it would be different for them both. As her mother had said, they had always seen the New Year in; their father never sat up. Not given to drink or merriment of any kind, he saw no point in it. His logic on the matter had always been: it's just another day so why kid yourself? And he had usually left them with this sentiment, but slightly more embellished.

She said to her mother now, 'Are you going to sit up?'

'Well, I always have, lass. It's like a habit. Mrs Young has asked me next door but I don't think I'll go.'

'Why not? Go on.'

'I like me own fireside. You know what it is on a New Year's Eve. Everybody should be at their own fireside.'

Sarah hesitated only a moment, then she said, 'Why don't you come across to us? You've never been. You'll have to come some time. Come on.' She leant forward and caught her mother's hands.

'Ooh, no, lass, no, I wouldn't dream of it. I don't know them.'

'But you've met David that once, and you said you liked him.'

'Yes, yes, I do. I think he's a fine fellow. But no, no, lass. But mind' – she nodded her head at her daughter – 'I'm glad you asked me, and I won't forget it. But don't worry about me.' She straightened herself up in the chair. 'I'm all right now that I've seen you.'

'I tell you what.' Sarah's voice was eager, her attitude like that of an excited child. 'Are you sure you're going to sit up?'

'Yes, lass, yes, I'll sit up.'

'Then I'll come across about half-past twelve and wish you a Happy New Year.' Their hands were joined again. It was as if some great problem had been solved. Their hands still holding, they got to their feet and Sarah said, 'That's what I'll do.'

'But, look, you haven't drunk your tea.'

'Oh no.' Sarah took up the cup.

'Oh, I'd love that, lass. Do you think you'd be able to get away?'

'Oh yes. David will run over with me.'

In the middle of the front room Sarah stopped and, turning to her mother, asked quietly, 'But what if he stays up the night, you being on your own?'

'There's very little possibility of that, lass. But if he does, well . . .'

She looked around as if searching for a solution. Then she said quickly, 'Well, if he's up or if we're in next door – he was asked an' all and you never know with him – well, if that happens I'll leave the front room blind up. All right?'

'All right.' They nodded at each other then moved towards the door, but there stopped again, and Sarah, looking down at the handle round which her fingers were curved, said, 'I do miss our Phyllis. With everything I've got I still miss seeing our Phyllis . . . Oh, I'm sorry.' She looked at her mother's bent head. 'I shouldn't have mentioned her again.'

'Aw, lass, I'm glad you did. I think of her all the time. And you know what?' Annie thrust her head forward. 'In the New Year I'm going to start going out, I'm going to take trips into Shields.' She spoke as if Shields was a long distance away instead of three miles to its centre. 'And then I'm going to look in on our Phyllis. I don't care, I'm going to look in on her. He needn't know anything about it. But now and again I'll look in on her.'

'Oh, Mother, I'm glad. Oh, I'm glad of that.'

'Well, something must be done, she can't come up here.'

'No, no, that's true. Oh, I'm glad you're going to see her.' She leant quickly foward and they kissed and clung together, not close, just holding each other's arms. Annie was crying gently now, and Sarah, fumbling with the lock, lct herself out and hurried down the street. She felt sad and happy at the same time, and overall a feeling of relief. Her mother was going to see Phyllis and she too was going to see Phyllis. Yes, she would in the New Year on the quiet. She would tell David. Oh yes, she would tell David. He wouldn't stop her, but she must do it on the quiet. His mother would never forgive her if she knew she was going into a house in Costerfine Town . . .

The second thread was the arrival of Dan through her back door around twelve o'clock, long before his usual dinner hour. His face looked peaked and his voice was husky as he said, 'Oh, I'm glad you're in, Sarah. I wouldn't have known what to do with this except put it in your coalhouse.' He pulled from the inside pocket of his coat a flat flask of whisky. 'It's about the only sure cure for this.' He pointed to his chest. 'It's settling here. If I have this hot and stay by the fire for half an hour or so it'll do the trick. You don't mind?'

'No, no, of course not.' She looked hard at him. But she was not seeing him as the man whose goings-on had shocked her last night in spite of her denial. She did not see him as the man who was keeping a woman, and in a very odd way. He was just Dan, who was nice. She said, 'Sit yourself down, I'll get the fire going. You've had this cold coming on for nearly a week, why haven't you done something about it?'

'Oh, Mary wanted to put me to bed, but I thought I could work it off. I hate to be away from the shop. Young George is all right, he can carry on, but the girl and the lad are new to it. Just started this past month, and Friday and Saturday are our busiest days. But I felt I had to come away this morning, I thought I was going to pass out. I told the old man.'

'You should be in bed.' She was bustling around filling the kettle, bringing in a mug and sugar, putting more coals on the fire. 'Take your coat off,' she said, 'and I'll fill a bottle.' She bent down to the bottom cupboard and brought out a stone water-bottle.

'No, no, Sarah, I'd better not get too hot. I'll be all right. If I'd had a hot whisky going to bed each night it would have done the trick. But you know Mary.' He sighed. 'And yet the stuff she brewed yesterday is more deadly than raw Scotch.'

She was pouring the boiling water on to the generous portion of whisky when the back door opened and a voice called, 'Are you in, Sarah?'

'Yes, yes.' She glanced quickly at Dan. 'It's May.'

'Oh, May's all right.' Dan smiled wearily.

May stood within the kitchen door. She looked smart, yet cool and distant as always. She wrinkled her nose as she said, 'What's this? Whisky?'

'Help yourself,' said Dan, pointing to the bottle. 'I had to get something for this stinking cold.'

'Well, well.' May came and sat down by the table, and, lifting up the bottle, she looked at it. 'I won't say no.' She glanced at Sarah and smiled.

It was rarely May smiled and that was a pity, Sarah thought, because she looked attractive when she smiled. And softer, oh so much softer. She said, 'You really want a drop?'

'Yes, of course. Why not? We often used to have a toddy when we were first married, late at night . . . so the smell wouldn't carry . . . How you going to get over that, Dan? She'll smell it off you.'

'I brought some mints . . . Provided for everything.' He smiled weakly.

As Sarah watched May pouring herself out a good measure of the whisky her mind lifted to the room on the other side of the fireplace and it came to her with a strange feeling of sadness that Mary Hetherington was ruling an imaginary world. Within the confines of her four walls she dictated and claimed obedience, and was satisfied, at least apparently, that her family were subject to her. But did she guess, even faintly, that all of them threw off her domination once they crossed the threshold into the street? Dan with his women and his whisky – he likely had his whisky when he was with her; John with May and their toddies at night. This was only a small thing, the bigger issue there was the separate turbulent life that John and his wife led away from the narrow confines of number one. Then there was David. David most of all, she thought, had moved away from his mother's domination. Although he was still nice to her, gentle with her because that was David's nature, there was a part in him that had been set free when he had taken herself from the bottom end and married her. The only one who could not escape was the father. Yet even he tried. Yes, she could see that her mother-in-law was ruling a world that existed only within her own mind, and a part of her was unhappy for the dominant, self-satisfied woman, for this woman who would never like her.

An exclamation from May broke the trend of her thoughts and brought her eyes to the kitchen window and the dark shadow passing it.

'It's the big fellow himself, he must have smelt it.' May sniffed disdainfully, and as John entered the room she looked at her husband and said, 'Altogether like the folks of Shields. Did you smell it?'

John did not answer his wife but looked to where Dan was crouched over the fire. 'You've got it bad,' he said. 'You should be in bed.'

'This'll put me right.' Dan held up the mug.

'It'll do no such thing unless you can sweat it out of you. You'll be a damn sight worse drinking that and then going out into the blast. Have some sense, man; go on, get into bed.'

'Yes, it's the wisest thing,' said May. 'He's right. You should get yourself to bed, Dan.'

'What! On a New Year's Eve and the jollification coming up? What'll they do without me?' He grinned and inclined his head towards the back of the fireplace.

'Aw, you think too much of yourself,' said John. 'You won't be missed as long as there's Davie to play the piano. That's all that she'll want. That's all that'll be necessary.'

Dan, taking the remark the way it was meant, said, 'True, true. But all the same, I'm not going to bed. I've never been to bed on a New Year's Eve yet and I'm not going to start now. And' – his grin widened – 'what do you think I am, to miss the home brew and the port at three shillings a bottle, mind you. You must think I'm barmy!'

As they laughed, Dan, thumbing the whisky bottle, said, 'Help yourself; I'm bringing another down later. I've got to have them in flat halves so they won't bulge my coat. You never know, she could have run into me coming round the back way.'

The air of conspiracy was again to the fore. The feeling was always strong when the family were together – outside the parents' home.

May, like a practised hand, threw off the last of her whisky, then, looking up at Sarah, said, 'I just popped over to see if you would have Paul this afternoon. I want to go over to my mother's and it's too cold to take him, crossing the water and all.'

Before Sarah could reply John put in, 'I'll stay with him, I told you.'

'You're doing nothing of the sort, you're coming to my mother's.

93

You never show your face there from one year's end to the other; in fact my family . . .' May now looked from Sarah to Dan. 'My family don't believe I've a husband.'

John's head was lowered in a bull-like attitude. He was biting on his lip but he said nothing.

Sarah said quickly, 'Oh, I'd love to have him, May. Oh yes, leave him with me.'

May rose to her feet. 'Thanks.' She smiled at Sarah. 'He likes coming over here. You wouldn't believe I found him up the back lane the other day. He was crawling on his hands and knees over Mrs Barrett's step. He had gone to the wrong end, but he knew the house was near the end . . . Come on, big boy.' She pushed her husband sharply on the shoulder. 'Finish that up and get on your feet.' She spoke to him as if he were drunk and incapable; her tone held a deriding note. It made Sarah think, Why does she do it? She could handle him if she didn't use that voice and manner.

She watched John rise to his feet as if obedient to his wife's summons. She could not see the expression in his eyes, for his lids were lowered. He nodded towards Dan, saying abruptly, 'You look after that cold or it'll mean trouble.' Then he followed May out. He had not, Sarah noticed, said one word to her, neither hello nor goodbye. He must be in a state inside, she thought. It wasn't only not having a pay packet; it was, as David said, John needed to work.

Dan was laughing now, and his voice cracking, he said, 'That's a funny remark, you know, and everybody makes it. Take care of that cold, they say, as if it was something tender to be cherished. People say funny things.' Then, turning his body half from the fire, he asked quietly and abruptly, 'David tell you about me last night?'

The suddenness of the question took Sarah aback. She blinked and moved her head, then she made a gesture with one hand as if flapping something aside and answered, 'Yes, yes, Dan, but that's all right.'

'You weren't shocked?'

'No, Dan, no. That's your business. As David says, it's your business.'

'Aye, David says that, but what do you say?'

'Well' – again her hand flapped outwards – 'if you want it that way, and it's good for you . . . well then.' She paused and finished inanely, 'It's your life.'

'Yes, it's my life.' He turned towards the fire again. 'And I've arranged it as I want it. Though, let me tell you . . .' His voice was cracking more now. 'Eva wants it like that too. I'm not taking any young lass down, believe me, nor wrecking a home or spoiling a married woman's life. She's a widow, a very quiet sort, and wants no ties no more than I do.'

'All right, all right, Dan, now don't get upset. Look, it's like John said. I should go to bed if I were you.'

94

'I'll be all right, I'll be all right.' He lay back in the chair holding the stone water-bottle to him and closed his eyes. Sarah stood looking at him. His face looked drawn and weary, but still there was about him an attractiveness. She could understand any woman going for Dan, but she couldn't understand her not wanting to marry him. All the Hetherington men had something about them, in different ways. Yet Dan wasn't a Hetherington, was he? His name was Blyth.

A few minutes later, when the back door opened again and David entered the house, she was scrambling round setting the table. The dinner, a hotpot, was already in the oven. She greeted David in the scullery. They held each other for a moment while they kissed, and then she whispered swiftly, 'Dan's inside. He's not well, he should be in bed. It's his cold.'

When she entered the kitchen with the dish in her hands Dan was saying, 'It's only a cold, don't worry your head. I'm sweating it out. Look, it's running down me. I've got over half an hour before I need go next door, I'll be all right. Help yourself.' He pointed.

David did not reply. He just continued to look at Dan and shake his head. Then, turning to the table, he picked up the bottle, went to the cupboard and got himself a glass and poured himself out a measure of the whisky.

She hadn't known David drank whisky. Again her thoughts turned towards the woman in the room behind the fireplace, and again she felt sad for her, sad in a strange inexplicable way.

The jollification had begun. It had got on its way around ten o'clock. Besides the family there were additions to the party. Mr and Mrs Riley from number fourteen. Mr Riley was one of the two men who worked under Mr Hetherington. And there was Mrs Riley's sister and her husband who had come down from Hartlepool for the New Year. Then there was Mr and Mrs Ramsay from next door to Sarah. The sitting-room was crowded, and laughter filled the house, and the passage between the front room and the living-room was as busy as Newcastle station.

Already Mary Hetherington had doled out the first taste of her brew, and as usual it had been acclaimed with high praise and requests from the visitors to know the recipe. But, 'Ah! Ah!' said Mary. No-one was getting that, it would die with her. No, not even her husband knew how the brew was concocted. Nor did her brother either. Her mother had passed the recipe on to her; men had never had anything to do with it. There was high laughter at this point.

Sarah was in the kitchen beating up tinned salmon with mustard and vinegar to make up another batch of sandwiches; the first lot had vanished quicker than snow under the sun. She lifted her head from her task, her face bright and flushed with happiness, and looked at her mother-in-law who was entering the room. Mary Hetherington's face too was bright and flushed, and for the first time since she had come to know her, Sarah saw her smiling, really smiling. She looked relaxed and happy . . . in her element, as Sarah put it to herself. She said to her, 'These won't be a minute, I've got all the bread buttered.'

'That's good of you, Sarah. May could have given you a hand, but no, May's not like that.' There returned to her face a reflection of the primness that was usual to it, and then it was gone as she asked, 'How did you like my ale?'

'Oh, I thought it was wonderful, lovely. I've never tasted anything like it. I'm not going to ask you how you make it because David said it was a secret, but oh, I wouldn't mind a drop of that every day.'

'No, no.' The tone held laughter. 'It's not for every day, it's just for special occasions. I make it once a year as my mother did, and her mother afore her. You know, my mother was a farmer's daughter from near Blanchland. Lovely country that, lovely. It was a big farm, quite an estate. She took me once to see it when I was a little girl. She knew lots of country secrets did my mother, and . . . well, my ale is one of them. I could tell anyone what I put in it but they couldn't make it. It's just wheat and barley and hops and horehound, and odds and ends, but it's the quantities and how you use them. It's like cooking; some cooks can turn cream sour.'

As if she had uttered a great witticism they both laughed. Then their laughter stopping suddenly, they looked at each other, and Mary Hetherington said, 'Don't you think it's about time you had a name for me, Sarah?'

'Oh! Oh!' Sarah wagged her head in embarrassment. She had always addressed this woman as 'Mrs Hetherington', she had not dared say, 'mother'.

Mary Hetherington turned away and began to transfer mince-pies from a tray on to a plate and her hand moved swiftly and her words kept pace with it as she said, 'Mam would be nice I think, don't you? We can't go on for ever being addressed as "Mrs Hetherington", can we? Yes, I think mam will do.' Her hand and her voice halted abruptly and she turned her head and looked at Sarah.

Sarah remained very still as she said softly, 'Yes. Oh yes, I'd like that.' It was as if an honour had been bestowed on her.

And Mary Hetherington, acting in the manner of one who had bestowed the great gift, inclined her head downwards. Then adding one more mince-pie to the plate, she said, 'Well, that's that settled,' and left the kitchen.

Sarah sighed. A smile spread slowly over her happy face; she felt her ears moving backwards with it. Wouldn't David be tickled to death. Oh, his mother . . . Mam . . . should make her brew every week. Oh, she should! She'd had a glass or two, that was evident, she was a different woman the night. Sarah gripped the bowl with her two hands and had the desire to throw it towards the ceiling. Then her body shaking with inward laughter, she applied herself frantically to the sandwiches. It was a lovely New Year's Eve, lovely.

Sarah had become conscious that David had stopped playing the piano some time before she took the two plates of sandwiches into the room. As she pushed at the door with her hip, John, standing behind it, pulled it open and, relieving her of one of the plates, whispered, 'The old man's on his feet.'

Sarah looked to where Mr Hetherington was standing on the hearth rug, his back towards the blazing fire. He had a glass in his hand and was motioning with it down to his subordinate Mr Riley, saying, 'It's true, you'll endorse it, Bill. Hope can be as dead as a doornail, but come this night and it's injected with a spark of life. Even those who have been out for years, the night they'll be thinking next year's bound to be different. Am I right?'

Mr Riley made a deep obeisance with his head. 'Yes, you're right, Stan.' There followed a rustle through the room, then silence again as they all looked towards their host. And Stan went on, 'New Year's Eve, as I said, is not an ending, it's merely a day afore a beginning, a day when you clean inside and out, a day when you see your assets mounting. This affects every man Jack the same up till the moment the clock strikes twelve. You know, nobody, at least no northerner, can be without hope on New Year's Eve; we've proved it again and again, haven't we?'

His thin chin thrust forward, Stan looked around the company and was greeted with, 'Yes, you're right there, Stan. Aye, aye, never a truer word spoken.' And then they waited once again for him to go on as if they were enjoying it.

It seemed to Sarah as if Mr Hetherington was doing a turn. She looked towards David, but he was looking at his father. She looked quickly towards John, and John was looking towards her and he indicated with a swift downward glance the bottles on the sideboard, and Sarah, picking up his meaning, nodded and smiled, then turned to listen to her father-in-law again.

'The North is a separate world, you know, and it breeds a separate kind of man.' Stan was waxing eloquent now. 'Men who are anathema to men of softer tones, to men whose egos are of a normal size and who argue only with knowledge . . . for let's face the facts, we are an aggressive pig-headed lot. And I say thank God for it . . . What do you say?'

'Hear, Hear! Stan. Hear, hear! Carry on. Carry on.'

'Well, as I was saying, the Tynesider, right back to Bede, has had to push himself up through the mire for both bread and learning, and always on this particular night he dons the cloak of hope, and he throws his head back and looks to the coming year, to the set number of days, days in which he sees himself working hard, eating well, and sleeping soundly. And why not, why not?'

97

At this point Stan dramatically raised his glass, crying, 'Let's drink to the Northerner!' There was a rising to the feet and cries of 'Well spoken, Stan!'

John, turning to Sarah, whispered loudly, 'He should have been in Parliament, he could give MacDonald points . . . That's if me mother brewed every day.'

Their laughter was lost amidst the noise and chatter now filling the room, and Sarah, looking towards her father-in-law, thought, It's funny to hear him lead off like that. He must think that way all the time. He's like David, or David's like him. They both think alike, but it takes the drink to bring it out. And his eye has hardly twitched at all the night.

'It happens twice a year,' said John, still whispering. 'New Year's Eve and Armistice Day. He generally gets blotto then, on Armistice Day.'

'Really!' This surprised Sarah.

'It's a kind of protest against the War and . . .' He moved his finger unobtrusively towards his eyes.

Sarah couldn't imagine Mr Hetherington getting really drunk, but she remembered back to Armistice Day just a few weeks ago when he had been in bed for two days with a cold. She smiled to herself, and shook her head. Funny the things you didn't know.

'Look, it's three minutes to. Get the glasses filled there, Mary.' Mr Hetherington was addressing his wife as if he was master in his own house, and obediently she went to the sideboard and began refilling the glasses. She looked proud and happy.

Sarah was standing with David now, an arm around each other. They were behind Dan, who was sitting to the side of the fireplace, and they each had a hand on his shoulder. Dan, Sarah thought, was in a bad way, he should be in bed.

David bent down towards Dan, pulling Sarah with him as he said under his breath, 'Why don't you go up, man?'

'I will as soon as it's in.'

Sarah and David raised their heads, then looked at each other and for a moment pressed closer together. The room became full of bustle. Mr Riley, who was to be first-foot, had left by the back door laden with coal and bread – Mary Hetherington had never added a bottle to the ritual as was the rule – and now as many of the company as could manage it were in the passageway.

The ship's hooters were blowing. The church bells were ringing. The whole world outside of the house seemed to be alive with sound. In contrast the house appeared quiet, almost empty for all the voices had died away. Each member of the party was waiting, all touched in this moment with a feeling of awe, touched with the elemental feeling of mystery and of sadness. One woman, Mrs Riley's sister-in-law, was crying quietly. All the expressions were touched with tenderness. It was as if the essence of this quality had been brushed swiftly over them all. Not one of them at this moment held within himself bitterness or anger. Not one of them remembered past grievances. At the death-bed of the year their souls shone out from their eyes.

The wind was blowing high and hard and it brought the first booms from the clock in the centre of the town right to the door itself, and the sound split them apart. The faces returned to normal, mouths opened and cried in different ways: 'It's here. It's here.' As the clock struck for the twelfth time the rapper on the front door banged, and borne in on the wind came Mr Riley.

'Happy New Year. Happy New Year.'

'Happy New Year. Happy New Year.'

They shook hands; they embraced each other, they all pressed back into the sitting-room, still shaking hands, still embracing. Sarah found herself being held by her father-in-law.

'A Happy New Year, a Happy New Year, Sarah. And I mean that, I mean that.' He leant towards her and his moustache pressed tight against the side of her mouth.

'Happy New Year,' she cried. 'Happy New Year . . . Dad.'

At this Stan let out a bellow of laughter and for a moment they hugged each other. Then she was standing over Dan.

'Don't kiss me unless you want this cold. Happy New Year, Sarah. Oh, that's what I wish you, a very Happy New Year. Indeed I do.'

'The same to you, Dan. The same to you.' They were holding hands, shaking them up and down like children.

The three strange men kissed her, great smacks on the side of her cheek.

She stood before May for a moment exclaiming a Happy New Year, then such was the power of this night they leant swiftly to each other and embraced.

And Mary Hetherington kissed her. Her lips touched her cheek, and she said, 'A Happy New Year, Sarah.'

'A Happy New Year, Mam.' Again they laughed together.

People were passing from one to the other, and then she was standing in the passage opposite John.

'A Happy New Year, Sarah.'

'A Happy New Year, John.' They looked at each other, but they did not even touch hands. He smiled, and his smile still held something of the gentleness of the moment before twelve. He said again, 'A very Happy New Year.'

When he passed her and went into the room the laughter slid from her face for a moment; she felt slightly disturbed, even slighted. Then, tossing her head up, she almost ran into the living-room. That was John – she never knew how to take him. And now she began whipping up plates of mince-pies, and rice loaf, and bacon and egg tart, on to a large tray. As she turned to leave the room May came into the kitchen, saying, 'Dan wants a strong cup of tea.'

'I'll make it for him in a jiffy.'

'No, you carry on with what you are doing. I'll see to it.' May sounded pleasant, nice. Everybody was nice . . .

And then it was quarter-to-one.

David was playing the piano. Everybody was singing. Sticking to her decision she had refused to be persuaded to sing alone; nothing must mar the new-found harmony between herself and her mother-in-law. It was at this point she thought, I must slip across now. As she went from the room she whispered quietly to Mary Hetherington, who was still busy at the sideboard, 'I'm just going to slip across to wish me mother a Happy New Year.'

'Will you be all right?'

The concern was warming, heartening. She nodded briskly. 'Yes, yes, I'll be all right.'

May was standing near the door and she touched her arm, saying, 'You're not going across there on your own, surely?'

'Oh, I'll be all right, I'm used to it.'

'Well, I wouldn't take a gold watch and go through the streets at this time of the morning.'

'There'll be plenty of people about.'

Oh, everybody was nice. Fancy May being concerned about her.

May followed her into the passage, saying. 'You should have somebody with you. Tell Davie.'

'No, no. It will spoil things, they want him to play. I'll be all right, May, honest.'

'Wait until John comes back, then; he's just gone over to see to the fire, and he's going to look in on old Mrs Watson next door. He won't be long.'

'No, I won't wait, May. I'll be back before you know I'm gone. You see' – she smiled broadly – 'I'm used to going about the streets in the dark. I had to do it every night for years coming from work.' She nodded at May, then hurried into the living-room, and from a cupboard under the stairs she took out her coat and wrapped a scarf around her head, then went out of the kitchen door.

It was as she entered the back lane that she bumped into John. He gripped her arm to steady her and peered at her in the dim light from the lamp at the bottom of the lane, saying, 'Where on earth are you off to?'

'Oh . . . oh!' she laughed. It was a nervous laugh. 'I'm just going to run across and wish me mother a Happy New Year. I won't be long.'

'You're not going on your own? Where's Davie?'

'He's playing, I didn't want to stop him.'

'Well, you're not going across there on your own at this time of the night, I'll come along with you.'

'No, no.' She was standing stiff, talking stiff. 'I'm all right I tell you. There's no need, I won't be a minute.'

'A minute or half an hour, what do you think I am? What would Davie think if he knew I let you go across the streets, especially at this time, on your own? There'll be drunks all over the place; it doesn't take much to knock them out these days.'

'No, no.' She was protesting now, with her eyes closed.

'All right then . . .' His voice sounded sulky. 'If you don't want me to go with you come back in and get Davie, but I'm not letting you go over there on your own. If anything was to happen to you, what would they say? Fancy him doing that, letting her go across there on New Year's morning by herself.'

Yes, she knew. That's just what they would say. But nothing was going to happen to her and she didn't want him to come with her. She didn't. She didn't. She felt herself jerked around. He had hold of her arm, laughing as he pulled her forward, but his voice was gentle, very gentle as he said, 'It's New Year's Day, Sarah, New Year's Day. Everybody's nice to everybody on New Year's Day, remember?'

They met the full force of the wind as they came out of the lane and into the main road.

'By! It's blowing itself in all right. And look at that moon riding up there. It looks as if it's training for the Derby.'

Sarah looked up through the scudding clouds. David said it was the clouds that moved not the moon, at least not quickly. David had learned her lots of things . . . Eeh, that was one of the things he had taught her, that nobody can learn you, only yourself. They teach and you learn, David knew more than John, at least about some things, about the nice things. John was eaten up with politics and such . . . Eeh! The exclamation burst from her now as her hand was gripped and she was forced into a run.

John was running against the wind like a great lolloping bear. She tried to shake herself free, but his grip was like iron, and she could do nothing but run with him.

'We'll race him.' He was yelling like a lad and pointing upwards. He was daft. Mad. They fled past two groups of people all singing, and mingled laughter and song followed them on the wind.

'J-o-h-n . . . stop!' She pressed her body back from him and strained at his hand, and gradually they came to a stop, just three streets from her own. She leant against the wall now, her two hands under her breasts pressing against her ribs. She was gasping and laughing. It was either laugh or get into a temper and this was a New Year's morning.

'You . . . You are a fool, John. You're mad.'

'Perhaps I am. But have you never raced the moon afore?'

She shook her head at him. He was standing with the palm of one hand against the wall, the arm straight; the coat sleeve touched her shoulder. His face, looking upwards, appeared young and boyish. As he turned his head towards her the moon disappeared behind a bank of cloud and she could no longer see his face. As she pulled herself from the wall, she said, 'I'm all out of puff, I've never run like that since I was at school.'

'You've missed something then.' His voice was even now, and his tone ordinary. 'Up to the last few years I used to run every morning before breakfast, I was in the harriers. Six miles sometimes, and more; and then I cycled to work. And on a Sunday a hundred miles with the Cycling Club was nothing. I felt fit in those days.' His voice trailed away and they walked a few steps before he said, 'Is this your street?'

'No, the last one.'

Everything seemed very ordinary. He was David's brother. Why had she made such a fuss about him bringing her over? He was just like a young lad. He might be older than David in years but in his mind he was younger. That was because he did sillier things, and said sillier things; and although at times he was surly, he had, she thought, something of Dan's sense of fun. She turned to him now, saying, 'This is it. Look, I won't be more than five minutes. I won't keep you waiting.'

'Stay as long as you like, I'll do some skipping until you come out.' He lifted his big frame from the ground with a lightness that surprised her and began skipping in an imaginary rope.

'You are daft, you know.' She was laughing freely. Then; 'I won't be long,' she said again, and hurried from him.

When she reached the house and found the blind up she felt a sense of disappointment. Her mother had gone to Mrs Young's then, or perhaps to bed. No, she wouldn't have gone to bed. She must have gone next door to bring the New Year in. There came to her the sound of laughter and voices from the Youngs' kitchen and as she turned away she thought, 'Well, I'm glad she's having a bit of enjoyment.'

'By! That was quick.' John was standing against the wall, not jumping up or down any longer.

'She's not in. She's next door, by the sound of it. Anyway, we'll get back all the sooner.'

She had turned to walk down the road when he said, 'Let's cut down the back end, we'll escape the wind that way. We won't have it in our faces then.'

'All right.'

They went across the road and through Walham Street. 'We can cut through Fanny's Alley here,' he said.

She turned to him, her mouth wide. 'You know Fanny's Alley?'

'Of course! Why do you sound so surprised? I know every bit of the streets.'

'I didn't think you'd know about this end, and Fanny's Alley.'

'Why?' There was a slight argumentative note in his voice now that put her on her guard, and her tone was placating when she answered, 'Oh, well, you know, the top end never came down to the bottom end . . . that was until Davie came for me.' Her voice was soft as she finished speaking.

They had entered a cut between two houses, Fanny's Alley. He went first and they came out on to a piece of wind-torn waste ground that had on it a number of corrugated iron huts – the tool sheds of the allotments. They were in the black shadow of the gable-end wall of the last house and the first of the sheds when he turned on her bringing her to a halt, saying fiercely, 'Don't talk like that . . . humble . . . Why must you eat humble pie all the time? What's the matter with you?'

'What do you mean? What are you on about now?' She sounded both surprised and frightened.

'I'm on about you bending the knee so much . . .'

'I don't.'

'Yes you do, and you know it. My God! Where do you think you've landed, anyway? In Lord Redhead's or with the Percy family? Look, Sarah, get it into your head that you're still in the Fifteen Streets. We're in the Fifteen Streets . . . we're all in the Fifteen Streets. I tell you it makes me flaming mad to see you acting as if somebody had picked you up out of the gutter . . . And when you're with my mother . . . oh my God!'

He stopped, and in the darkness she felt his arm going up as he put his hand to his head, and she retreated a step from him. She was shivering inside with a feeling which his words were forcing into life, the feeling that had come unbidden into her body when she had first looked at him. She fought it now in the only way she knew. She said, 'Don't be silly, going on like that; it's the beer you've had.' She laughed nervously.

'Beer! Huh! It might knock them over, but it doesn't touch me. It'll take something stronger than that. I've had very little the night. Look, don't evade the question. I've been wanting to get at you about this for some time . . . Sarah.'

She felt her body jerk upwards as his hands came down on her shoulders covering them like clamps. 'Don't you realise your worth, woman? They . . . I mean our family isn't bestowing any honour on you; you're doing the honours, if it comes to talking about honours. Aye, you've given them life. You've brought the old man alive. You've made Davie into a man, and you've done something for Dan . . . aye, Dan, who doesn't need any lessons. Don't you know what you've done, woman?' He was shaking her now. 'Don't you know what you've done?' His voice was a hoarse whisper. His words were sending gusts of hot breath over her face. He still had hold of her shoulders, but his elbows were bent now, his body touching hers, but lightly, just their clothes.

'Sarah! Sarah!' The wind was whirling her name about her head. 'You know what you've done to me, don't you? You know it, that's why you've kept out of my way . . . Oh my God, Sarah.'

'No! No!' She thought she was screaming, but the scream was only inside her. Her words came out on a low hiss. 'No! No!' And then she was lost between his body and the corrugated iron hut. Through the thickness of their clothes she felt him, every inch of him; his knees, his thighs, his belly, his breast, they were all picking out the counterparts in her and she was gasping under the pressure of them.

'No, no, leave go of me. You're mad, mad . . . David!'

'Aye, David.' His mouth was against her ear; his words dropping into it like molten lead, burning her. 'There's David. You've got no need to remind me there's David. If it wasn't for David I would have tipped you up from the start. Didn't you feel it the first time we met in the front room? I knew then, in an instant.'

'Let me go! I tell you let me go! What if David found . . .'

'Don't worry, he'll not find out.'

'I'd rather die than hurt David, do you hear? Do you hear?' She was speaking through her teeth. 'Let me go.'

'Just a moment longer. Let's be like this a minute longer. It might have to last a lifetime. Oh, Sarah, Sarah.' His mouth was covering her ear.

She screwed her head into her shoulder and struggled with all her might to free herself from his arms, but he held her fast. As big as she was, he held her as if she were a child. Then with a suddenness that made her feel sick she felt her body go limp against him and she spluttered as she cried, 'I'm happy, I'm happy, leave me be, don't spoil it. I've never been so happy in me life, it's all I want, Davie and the house . . . A place of me own.'

'You're not happy. You don't know what it means. Davie rescued you. He was the first plank thrust out to the bottom end and you grabbed it, and now you're breaking your neck with gratitude.'

'I'm not, I'm not.'

'How does he love you, eh? How does he? Gentle, considerate, kindly, as if asking a favour? He doesn't take you, he couldn't.'

'Shut up, you! David's good . . . good.'

'Aye, he's good. Davie's a good fellow, a fine fellow. I'm his brother. Aye, aye, I'm his brother, and I wouldn't hurt him for the world either, so you have it, you needn't worry, but he hasn't got it in him to love you. Not like this . . . and this!' He jerked his loins into her. His mouth almost covered the lower part of her face and for as long as it took her to realise that he was right, every word he had said was right, she submitted to him, and then she was thumping and pushing and kicking his body from hers.

104

They were standing apart now, breathing like two great animals lost in the wind and darkness, still alone in a world that had been created when she had submitted for an instant to him. It made no difference that there was no contact of flesh, they knew each other as if they had sported stark naked on an open moor.

Then her limbs became weak, all strength left her and she had to lean against the shed again for support. Her whole body was shaking as if with St Vitus's dance. Her bones seemed to be strung on jangling wires. She had no power to move, nor did she want to; she had no urge to get away from him. No desire to run, nor did she wish she were dead, or that he had never been born. The only coherent thought in her turbulent brain was that David must not be hurt.

So close were they at this moment, even spiritually, that he picked up her thought and said, 'Stop worrying.' His tone was flat now. 'Davie won't be hurt. You would never hurt him, not with your sense of gratitude. And I don't want to hurt him either, I've told you . . . But I'm not in a position to hurt anybody, am I? You don't say "Come fly with me and be my love" when you're on the dole, do you? But everything apart, this is between you and me, so don't worry. Me madness is under lock and key and I'll try to see it doesn't break out again. Not in that way, anyhow . . .' He groped now and found her hands, and she did not resist him and he said softly and sadly, 'But, by God, how I could have loved you, Sarah.'

When she heard her voice answering him it sounded strange to her, she couldn't recognise herself, for it was a woman who was speaking, speaking the thoughts of a woman, slow and flat, 'It all depends on what you call love. David's kind of love takes in even me feet, and they aren't lovely. They swell and go shapeless and look like big white puddings, but he takes me shoes off and pulls me stockings away from me soles after I've walked back from the docks, or shopping. He's even washed me feet in hot water and soda – you wouldn't do that, would you?'

Except for their heavy breathing, which was caught and whirled away by the wind, there was no sound between them for some minutes, then he said, 'What you talking about? . . . I was talking about loving you.' His voice was hoarse and there was a note of perplexity in it.

'Loving me?' She experienced a weird urge to laugh, long and loud. She was afraid of the feeling. She was afraid of herself altogether at this moment, and she was actually shocked at the rawness of her next words, but still in that slow flat grown-up woman's tone, she said then, 'I know your kind of loving, you'd take me clothes off but not me shoes . . . Oh, I know, I'm no fool . . . Leave go me hands.'

She was shaking herself roughly, violently, to try to get away from him when with his voice, urgent and tender, now he appealed to her, 'Don't shut me out, Sarah . . . don't. And don't be frightened of me, ever. I won't do anything, try anything, I promise you. Just let me talk to you now and again and look at you. Give me this much . . . Say something to me, at times, something kind, Sarah. I need kindness, I do. You just don't know what it's like to be without kindness. And you're kind. The first minute I saw you, I saw your big heart shining from every part of you . . . You're big, Sarah, in every way. You're big and kind . . .'

Normality was rushing back into her body, the normality of fear, fear against the softening effect of his pleading. She almost whimpered now, speaking as if to herself. 'If I bring trouble on the house I'll kill meself, I will, I will. I couldn't bear it . . . Your mother . . .'

It was as if the mention of his mother's name broke the spell, for now he burst out, 'Oh, for God's sake! I've told you to stop being afraid of me mother, and of any of them. I think that's about the only thing that could make me really mad with you. It drives me crazy when I see you bending before them. And when May, the upstart, looks down her nose . . .'

'M . . . ay?' she put in stammering. 'M . . . ay? May looks down her nose at me?'

'Can't you see it? And she's not fit to wipe your shoes. May's a prig; a cold, bloodless prig. She's got as much of a woman in her as Leslie Waters next door, and he doesn't know what he is. But you've only yourself to blame, you're so damned humble . . . humble and kindly. Kindly, that's you, Sarah, when you should be haughty and proud, because you've got something to be proud of . . . You're beautiful. My God, you're beautiful . . . your face . . . your body . . . everything . . . Oh, it's all right, don't worry; I'm not going to start again.'

Above her own gasping breath she could hear the quick intake of his as if he were sucking it in and out through his teeth. They stood quiet and without words for some minutes, and then he asked, 'Is it a deal?'

There was another moment of silence before she said, 'What do you mean?'

'That you'll not ignore me, not push me aside as if I didn't matter. I won't ask anything of you, I promise you, and I mean it . . . Mind, I wouldn't say I'd be talking like this if there wasn't somebody like Davie with a claim on you. But that's the throw of the dice. It is Davie and that's that . . . Come on.' He pulled her sharply from the support of the shed and, holding her arm, he said softly, 'Stop trembling. You can't go in like that. Come on, walk briskly.' He led her forward, supporting her, and she walked like someone slightly drunk.

They went across the waste land above the bottom ends of the streets until they came to Camelia Street back lane. Neither of them had spoken since they started to walk, but now she halted and with her head down she muttered, 'You'd better go on, I'm going in our house for a minute.'

He went to take her hand again, but she pulled it aside, saying under her breath. 'Don't! My God, don't! Not here. You don't know who's out the night.'

He stood looking at her bent head for not more than a few seconds, then, without further words, he turned abruptly and walked down the back lane.

She stood, with her back arched, leaning against the wind, and not until she heard the dull thud of the back door banging did she go down the lane, and through her own back door and up the yard.

Once in the kitchen she didn't light the gas, but, crouching down on the mat beside the fender, rested her arm on the seat of David's chair, and twisting her hands together, she stared into the dying embers of the fire, crying, 'Oh, David! Oh, David! Oh, David!' Then jerking herself around she enfolded the chair in her arms as if it was the kindly gentle loving David himself. And her mind kept reiterating, Oh, David! Oh, David! Oh, David! and she told herself that she only wanted David, and David's kind of loving. She didn't want that other kind, not John's kind. No, no, she didn't want that, she didn't.

She became still, quite still, her body and her mind, and in the stillness she recaptured again the moment of terrifying intensity when she had grappled and strained and writhed to answer his body's demands and now she extended it. She could feel them struggling together like two savages, their bodies joined at every point possible, striving towards a climax of unearthly rapture, receiving and inflicting pain that created laughter, and the laughter did not escape from them but flowed back and forth through their beings as if through one body. The chair moved under her across the line and its motion brought her heaving body to stillness again and her mind to the present.

She became aware for the first time since entering the kitchen that they were still singing next door and she turned her face slowly towards the fireplace and whispered aloud, 'I can't help it. It wasn't my fault.' And it was as if in answer Mary Hetherington came walking through the wall and stood before her, saying, as she had done on the day of the wedding, 'A mixed marriage is bad enough, but to have it unsanctified in a registry office . . . Well, I only hope some good will come of it.'

Then she saw her mother-in-law joined by the priest, and Father O'Malley said, 'I told you mixed marriages have their penalties and this is only the beginning.'

Her greatest fear from a mixed marriage had been the loss of her immortal soul, but now even the phrase seemed meaningless. It was something that might or might not happen, something that wouldn't be proven until she was dead. What had come upon her tonight was something of the now – and it was tangible, this thing, this other love.

'No, no, I don't love him.' She was on her feet, speaking her denial aloud. She pressed her hand over her mouth and stood looking through the dark towards the wall. Then, heaving a great sigh that swelled and deflated her body, she said helplessly to herself, 'You'd better get in.'

They'd be wondering next door and they mustn't wonder, they mustn't ask questions. Nothing had happened, nothing ever would. As she had said, she would die rather than hurt David. David had pulled her up out of the mire . . . All right, what if he was a plank, he was a plank that she was going to cling to all her life. She would manage this thing, this wild-beast thing. She would have to. She straightened her shoulders, gulped spittle into her dry mouth, pulled the bolt out of the door, and went into the yard.

CHAPTER FOUR

Sarah came quietly down the stairs and into the living-room. Mary Hetherington was sitting in the armchair near the fire, her eyes closed, and as Sarah tiptoed past she opened them and said, 'I'm not asleep.'

'Oh, I thought you might have dropped off. You should, you know, you're worn out. He's asleep now; it seems sound, not like it's been.'

'I've made some tea. Would you like to pour it out, Sarah?'

Sarah poured out two cups of tea and took one to her mother-in-law, then sat near the end of the table drinking hers.

Mary Hetherington sipped at her tea, then, looking down into the cup, she said, 'It's been a time, hasn't it? All that jollification on New Year's Eve and since then we've never stopped running, three weeks of it.' She looked up and towards Sarah, and added, 'You've been very good, Sarah. I don't know what I'd have done without you. May is very little use in sickness, and she hasn't the lifting power of a mouse.'

'Well, I'm about twice her size. And she's been very good with the shopping and getting the medicine and that.' Sarah felt that she had to defend May, as if she owed her something. She didn't like this feeling and the only way she could ease it was to say something nice about May.

'I don't know what we'd have done if John hadn't been off work. Everything has its other side, hasn't it? He's been so good sitting up too, because David and his father couldn't have kept it up. With having to go to work they need their sleep . . . Ah, well.' She took another sip from her cup. 'He's past the worst but I never thought he'd get over it.'

'Nor did I.' Sarah shook her head. No, she never had thought Dan would get over it. His cold had resulted in double pneumonia and he had at one point seemed almost sure to die.

'Oh!' The cup wobbled in the saucer as Mary Hetherington brought herself upwards in the chair and, leaning towards Sarah, said, 'I'm awfully sorry, I forgot to tell you. I hope it isn't important, but your father called round this morning to see you. It was when you were out.'

'Me – my father!' Sarah screwed her face up in disbelief. 'My father called here?' Her lips were spread wide from her teeth.

'Yes.' Mary Hetherington's voice was soft. 'And he was very nice and civil. He asked if you were in and I told him you had gone out shopping for me. He said he was very sorry to hear about my brother. He asked if he could do anything.'

'My father!'

'Yes, your father. Now you mustn't be vindictive.' Mary Hetherington's Christianity was to the fore at the moment. 'Although I'd be the last person to tell you to encourage him, you mustn't bear malice or bitterness. It's never worth it. As I said, he was very civil and he looked very clean and tidy.'

'Did he say what he wanted?'

'No, no, he didn't say.'

'Perhaps my mother isn't very well?'

'I shouldn't think so. He said he called at the back door one or twice last week but got not reply; he wondered if you were all right.'

Again Sarah's face screwed up, but she said nothing this time. Her father calling on her? What was he after? Likely on the cadge. He was having to stump up his dole now that her mother hadn't got Phyllis's and her own money coming in. Yet he was no fool was her father, he knew the feeling that existed between them. He had never asked her for any money in his life, he had just taken it – that is, everything he could get his hands on. But was it likely that he would come cadging from her now? She couldn't understand it. Still, she would likely know what he was after when he turned up again. She said now, 'I'll take the washing round and put it in soak while there's still light.'

'No, no, no, Sarah, it's far too much; you've done it for weeks now. I'll get Mrs Watson to come in. She used to, you know.'

'There's no need when I can do it. I'm doing our own, and I'm as strong as a bull, anyway.' She flexed the muscles of her arm and smiled, and Mary Hetherington returned the smile, saying, 'Well, have it your own way.'

Sarah went out of the scullery and down the yard into the washhouse, and, gathering up the dirty linen from the poss tub, made it into a bundle and carried it next door, and placed it in her own washhouse.

In a way, if she could put it like this, she felt grateful to Dan for being ill. It had helped her to be of use to Mary Hetherington, really of use, and it had broken down some of the older woman's reserve . . . it had also given herself less time to think.

She began now to carry buckets of water from the tap at the bottom of the yard and fill the poss tub, then she placed in the ice-cold water all the white linen, sousing them, with her arms up to the elbows, until they were all wet. They would be ready for her early start in the morning.

The twilight was deepening when she went into the kitchen, but she didn't light the gas straight away, she was practising economy. Over the past three weeks she had learned more of the running of a house from her mother-in-law than she had in all the first weeks of her marriage. Mary Hetherington had unbent enough to give advice, such as, 'You can save so much by doing a thing the right way; you needn't be mean, you know. For instance, if you riddle your cinders every day you'd save a bucket of coal a week, four buckets a month and fifty-two a year. Reckon that up; the saving would buy you something for the house, wouldn't it? And then there's the men's clothes. Now when I buy a new shirt I always cut three inches off the tail straight away. This piece will give you a new collar and cuff facings later on.'

Yes, Sarah was learning a lot, and she had already started to save and with an object in view . . . she was going to get David a second-hand piano. She hadn't told anyone about this, not even David, and certainly not his mother, for she didn't think the purchase would be looked upon favourably; it would mean that David wouldn't be such a frequent visitor next door. Not that she minded him going to his mother's, but she knew that he would like a piano of his own.

But with regards to saving through economy Sarah found it was difficult to economise on food, because she and David went down to Shields Market on a Saturday afternoon. When they had first married it had been a sort of hilarious excursion and they had come back laden. That was, until the day they passed the men standing in the roadway, when one of them, looking at the top-heavy baskets, had remarked with sadness but without envy, 'By! That's a sight for sore eyes. There's not a better sight in the world than a basket laden with grub.'

On that Saturday David had said, 'We mustn't buy so much altogether, we'll just get what we need for the weekend and you can get the rest in the middle of the week.' So she did that, but she found it was dearer buying in bits and pieces.

After she had set the table for the tea she sat down for a moment by the fire, in the now darkening room. She had had little time to sit in the past three weeks and that was just as well. Sometimes she thought that what had happened in the wind-maddened first hour of the New Year was a figment of her imagination, and she could at times actually believe this, for neither by look nor sign had John reminded her that he had been party to the madness . . . the instigator of the madness. If there was any noticeable change in his manner towards her it was evident in an unusual gentleness of manner, like the gentleness he used towards Dan, but in Dan's case the gentleness was charged with power, and authority even to ward off death. John had literally fought with death to keep Dan alive, seeming almost to breathe for him when this became almost an agony. Only once had she seen the old John come rearing through this new gentleness. It was one evening down in the living-room when May said, 'Why don't you put in for a job of male nurse? They're going at Harton, you'd be in your element. They are always wanting them on the mental block . . .'

When she heard the knock on the front door she thought, Oh dear, somebody selling something again. But she was half through the front room when she remembered Mary Hetherington saying, 'Your father called.' She stopped for a moment. What if it was him?

Her approach to the door was slow, and when she opened it her face was set, almost grim, and it didn't change when she saw Father O'Malley standing below her on the pavement.

'Good afternoon, Sarah.'

'Good afternoon, Father.' They stared at each other.

'Well, aren't you going to ask me in?' This was no jocular request, it was made in the form of a command.

Without answering, Sarah stood aside and the priest moved past her and into the passage, where he waited for her to close the door. She seemed to take some time over this, but when she at last passed him she said, 'Will you come this way, Father. I'll light the gas.'

After the gas plopped and fluttered, then filled the mantle, its rays, through the pink porcelain globe, softened both their expressions. The priest was looking round the room and his gaze moved from the low-backed oak chairs to the legs of the table that had a stretcher joining them; then his hand going slowly out, he turned one of the chairs away from the table and without an invitation sat down.

'You've got this very nice.'

'Thank you, Father.' Sarah remained standing and he looked up at her, saying, 'Sit down, sit down; we'll talk more comfortably then.' He was entirely in command of the situation . . . and her. She could have been the visitor. His features moved into what was for him a smile, but it didn't lessen the agitation that was filling her.

The priest began drumming his fingers in a rhythmic beat on the corner of the table, and he looked at them for a full moment before saying, 'You are going to tell me that you are very happy?'

Her body was stiff, yet her chin trembled as she answered, 'I can say that, Father, and it's true.'

'The days are young yet, your life hasn't begun. It would be disastrous at this stage if you found yourself unhappy.' He paused. 'The awareness of conscience is a slow processs.'

'I've got nothing on my conscience, Father.' Her voice was trembling now, her agitation visible.

'Well, that's a matter of opinion, and time will prove which of us is right or wrong. God works in strange ways, sometimes through a series of disasters.' The priest turned towards the fire as if he were actually seeing the events passing before his eyes. 'Sometimes by withholding His hand until the eleventh hour, His ways are strange and it is not for us to question them . . . But it is our duty . . .' Now his voice was stern and his eyes were riveted on her, and he repeated, 'It is our duty not to bring His wrath upon us, not to aggravate Him too much.'

Sarah swallowed. At least she made an effort, for she felt that she was choking. She felt as she had done when a child, that God was a man who lived up in Newcastle, a big pot of big pots. Someone who could order you, through the medium of the priest, to be condemned to hell. Hell to her then was the blast furnace, the blast furnace that illuminated the sky all over Jarrow when the residue was poured on to the slag heap. That was hell: hell was fire, and hell was in Jarrow, administered from Newcastle . . . such were the narrow boundaries of her world. She had been twelve before she could grope with the fact that hell was not directly connected with Newcastle, nor yet the blast furnace. But she still believed in hell, then, and now, and she still believed it was administered by God. And she still believed that people paid for their sins. But at the same time she knew that she didn't want to believe it, and it wasn't only since she met David that she had kicked against these beliefs. Her rebellion had begun to stir much earlier . . . yet not against her religion. No, it was against Father O'Malley's delivered conception of God and of his own vindictive power that she had dared set her puny mind.

'Why haven't you been to Mass, lately?'

'I have, Father.'

The priest's eyes narrowed. 'I haven't see you, nor has Father Bailey.'

'I go to Jarrow, first Mass.'

'Why to Jarrow? All your life you have attended my church, so why to Jarrow?'

She wetted her lips and cast her eyes downwards but did not lower her head because the thoughts in it tended to thrust her chin out and upwards. She didn't go because of him. She didn't go because they all looked at her. The girls she had gone to school with, their mothers and fathers, they all knew she had married a Protestant; and if that wasn't bad enough, she had got married in a registry office. So to them she wasn't married at all. That's why she didn't go.

'It wouldn't be because you're ashamed of what you've done?'

'No, I'm not ashamed.' She was on her feet now, 'I've got nothing to be ashamed of, Father. I've married a good man, a very good man.'

The priest slowly drew himself upwards; he buttoned the top button of his black coat, took from the pocket his black gloves and put them on before saying, 'You know as well as I do, Sarah, that in the sight of God and His Holy Church you are not married, in fact you are living in sin . . . Well, I'll leave you with that thought, I'm always in the Presbytery any time you want to see me to make arrangements for the ceremony.' He turned and walked into the dark room, and from there he said, 'Tell your husband I've called.'

She heard him fumbling at the front door, but she could not go to his assistance.

She heard the door open and then close, and slowly she lowered herself into David's chair. 'I'll see you in hell first.' She did not recognise the sound of her own voice; it wasn't a young girl's voice, it was again the voice of a woman, the woman who had spoken to John on New Year's morning. He was cruel, cruel. She was married, she was. He was a pig of a man, a swine. She shuddered at her daring, at the blasphemy of calling a priest a pig, a swine. Well, she didn't care, she didn't care if she was struck down dead this minute . . . he was. He was a priest, a Christian, and he had sat there prophesying disasters, wishing them on her; yes, wishing them on her to prove himself right . . . The awareness of conscience . . . God works slowly.

She leaned back in the chair, feeling faint of a sudden. The fight seeped out of her. She felt funny, odd, and she asked herself was she frightened. Yes, she supposed she was. He had the name of being able to put the fear of God into anybody. Yet this was an odd feeling she had, a sickly odd feeling. She found that her stomach was acting in a strange way.

She wished David was in, just to look at him, to feel his hands holding hers, to know that she was secure. She lay with her eyes closed and gradually the feeling passed. It was funny to feel like this, weak . . . she had said to David's mother she felt as strong as a horse. Well, at this moment she felt as weak as a kitten, like a baby. The word brought her sitting straight up in the chair, a great question mark filling the room. She looked round as if for the answer. Then her eyes slowly came to rest on her stomach. She put her two hands across it and stroked it slowly, then whispered aloud. 'Oh . . . oh . . . but I'd better be sure before I say anything . . . Yes. Yes. I'd better. It might only be fright through him . . .'

When David came in, even before he changed his shoes or sat down and had a cup of tea, he took her in his arms. He looked at her, he kissed her. Then, holding her at arm's length, he said, 'Hello, Mrs Hetherington.'

It was a game, a playful routine, but it was also something that set their marriage apart from other marriages. Marriages, everybody knew, sank into mundane ordinariness after a wedding. Life became a routine. Even a battleground of wills, of warring temperaments, of hitherto unrevealed personal habits, irritating, maddening personal habits which became obnoxious to the other party. Sarah knew all about marriage from this angle. She had witnessed the process around the doors. She had heard it discussed among women in the kitchen. She had seen it enacted between her mother and father. Their first flush of love had not reached even the pale pink tinted stage before reality had hit them. Terms such as, 'Anybody seen that old cow of mine?' were thought funny and even a sign that a man loved his wife. That's how marriage went in the bottom end. And people and attitudes weren't all that different in the top end. Sarah was coming to this knowledge painfully. The upper stratum was only a bath-bricked step from the lower stratum. John had been right there.

But her marriage was different. She had been married for weeks now and David seemed to get more loving and gentle every day . . . John had been right there too . . . Damn John! Damn the priest!

'I said hello, Mrs Hetherington.'

'Hello, Mr Hethrington.' She rubbed her nose against his.

'What's the matter? You look peaked. Are you all right?'

'Yes, yes, I'm fine. Of course, I'm all right.'

'Have you been washing, doing all the lot? I told you last week that you hadn't to do it, Mother can get Mrs Watson. She's had her before . . .'

She had her fingers over his lips. 'You're wasting your breath; I haven't been washing, I've been sitting most of the afternoon with Dan.'

'Well, that's not good for you either. You've been up there too much. You've got no colour in your face . . . How is he?'

'Oh, much better. He seems to have improved a ton today.'

He turned from her now and, going to his chair and sitting down to change his shoes, he said, 'I want to talk to you, Sarah, about Dan. You know what I told you about his friend . . . the woman down Westoe?' He cast his eyes at her and she nodded. 'Well, he hasn't seen her for over a month, and on New Year's day, as bad as he was feeling, he wrote her a note, but he's received no reply. He wrote another after he got over the crisis, and when he had no reply to that either it dawned on him that they hadn't been posted; my mother just hadn't posted them. Naturally he was worried. He didn't know what she'd be thinking. From what I can gather – he did some talking to me when he wasn't quite himself – things haven't been running too smoothly lately in that direction. Surprisingly, he has asked her to marry him and she won't. Anyway, to ease his mind I wrote to her and told her what's happened. And I've talked the matter over with John, and he says that she should be allowed to come and see him if she wants to. It would likely get Dan on to his feet quicker than anything, for he's very low at present and it's not like him – he could joke with a gun at his head, could Dan.'

Sarah, her mouth hanging slightly open, said. 'Her come up here? Your mother would go mad.'

'Yes, if she knew, but she needn't. Dan's likely to be confined to the house for weeks yet, so we thought that if Mother could be persuaded to go to the chapel meeting as usual on Wednesday afternoon the woman could come in here, and when mother's gone she could slip next door for half an hour, no-one would be any the wiser.'

'But, David, what if your mother didn't go out?'

'Well, that would be just too bad. But look.' He reached out and grabbed her hand. 'There's no need to get worried. We're not planning a bank robbery or anything like that.'

'A bank robbery would be safer. What if she was to find out?'

'But she won't. Nothing will happen if she doesn't go to the chapel meeting, that's all there is about it. But don't you see.' He pulled her towards him. 'It would please Dan, and I want to please Dan. He's a good fellow is Dan. I've always known that, but I didn't realise how much I'd miss him until I thought he was a goner. Come on, come on.' He shook her hands. 'Don't look so frightened. If me mother found out, and she wanted to kill anyone, it would be me or John.'

Sarah looked down at him in silence. She made a small motion with her head but she did not reply, except to herself, and she said, 'No, no, she wouldn't kill either of you, it would be me she would kill.' And the knowledge brought a feeling of dread into her being.

CHAPTER FIVE

Sarah liked the woman from the moment she opened the door to her, but at the same time she wondered what Dan saw in her. She was quite well-dressed and she spoke nicely. Her manner was shy, quiet. She had about her a quality of refinement, but the impression she imparted to Sarah almost at once was that she looked nooled. Perhaps this was because she'd had a disastrous marriage, but still, that was over and she had Dan now and Dan wanted to marry her. And there was a timidness about her; she was like – Sarah searched in her mind to describe what the woman was like and, when the thought came to her . . . she looks like a superior mouse. She was pleased with herself because it was an indication that she was learning, that she was picking these things up from David.

The woman's name was Mrs Mount, Eva Mount. Sarah addressed her as Mrs Mount. She offered her tea and biscuits and tried to make conversation, but it was hard going.

'Are you sure it's convenient?' The woman asked for at least the third time since her arrival, and Sarah assured her that it was, or it would be. 'My husband did explain to you about his mother?' She said this gently.

'Yes, she did.' Mrs Mount's voice was small, high. She spoke in monosyllables most of the time. Only once more did she break away from yes, and no, to ask, 'Dan has told you about me?' And Sarah answered, 'Yes.' And added, 'Dan's nice.'

Following this there was another silence, and Sarah, glancing at the clock, said, 'It's half-past two. She's likely gone now, I'll go in and see.'

Mary Hetherington had gone. John was in charge in the bedroom, and when she entered he looked quickly towards her and said, 'All set?'

She nodded, but towards Dan, an older-looking much thinner Dan now, and he smiled at her and said, 'You're like a lot of conspirators. By! If this was to come out it would be the end of the world.'

'I'll go and get her.' As she turned away John said, 'I'll make myself scarce an' all. I'll go over home for an hour. I'll be back.' He punched the air in the direction of Dan, and for answer Dan smiled weakly, saying, 'Thanks for everything. If ever a war comes they'll make you a general.'

'Roll on a war.' John was coming down the stairs behind Sarah now, and he added, 'That's what we want, a war.'

Sarah wanted to say, 'Don't be silly.' But, as always, she prevented herself from making any retort to John's provocative remarks. She didn't want to get him going in any way, she told herself. Like a dangerous dog, he was better left sleeping.

They were in the living-room now, alone, and as she went to pass him she looked at him because he willed that she should. She was an arm's length from him and for a second or so they stared at each other until he asked quietly, 'Not mad at me any more, Sarah?'

And just as quietly, even gently, she replied, 'No.'

'Good.' He turned abruptly and preceded her into the scullery, and as he opened the door to let her pass he said. 'You'd better tell her to keep it to half an hour, just in case.' And as he closed the door on them he said under his breath, with a laugh that was both sad and bitter, 'The things we do for love.'

Then they went down the yard and parted in the back lane without looking at each other again, but she was trembling. He could always make her tremble.

Almost moving on tiptoe, Sarah led the woman from her house and into Mary Hetherington's. She never thought of her mother-in-law as mam although she now called her by this name; she thought of her as she, or David's mother.

As she opened the kitchen door the very house itself seemed aghast at the act she was perpetrating. She said hastily to the woman, 'Give me your coat and hat. You'll need them when you go out, it's so cold.'

But the woman said, 'I'll keep them on, if you don't mind.'

Without further ado Sarah led the way out of the room and up the stairs. Then, tapping gently on Dan's door, she went in. She smiled at him, let the woman pass her, then went quickly out and down the stairs again.

As she stood in the living-room looking at the clock her heart began to beat uncomfortably fast. Just supposing what would happen, just supposing she walked in that door at this minute. Just supposing! . . . She gave a violent shake of her head. Why was she so frightened of her mother-in-law? John was right: she shouldn't be frightened of anybody. She was big and strong enough to face ten Mary Hetheringtons, yet . . . She looked at the clock. Only five minutes gone. She wished, oh, she wished somebody would come. Oh, she'd better be careful and state her wishes precisely, else who knew but his mother herself might walk in the door. She wished John would come back. She didn't feel half so afraid when he was about; not of other people anyway, only of him, but that was a different kind of fear.

She filled the kettle and set Dan's tea-tray. She took the chenille cloth off the dining-table and put on the lace-edged one, the second best, and set the table for two.

She looked at the clock again. The woman had been up there twenty minutes. Oh, she wished she had said a quarter of an hour instead of half an hour.

There were two pairs of shoes by the door with mud on them; she cleaned them. The woman had been upstairs now twenty-seven minutes. She gazed up towards the ceiling, and as if her anxiety had prised through the floor she heard footsteps walking towards the bedroom door. She heard it open and close, then she herself moved towards the living-room door. She was two steps from it when the key turned in the front door and she let out an agonised exclamation that was also a prayer. 'Oh God in Heaven!' she groaned.

The woman was on the last stair but one when Mary Hetherington saw her. She had the door in her hand, but she didn't close it. Slowly she pushed it behind her and slowly she walked forward. She brought her eyes for a second from the woman to Sarah's red and agitated face, then looked back towards the woman again.

'Who are you? What are you doing here?'

The woman opened her mouth to speak, then, glancing fearfully at Sarah, she closed it again, and as she did so Mary Hetherington looked over her head towards the top of the stairs and the bedroom. Then, speaking below her breath, in a voice so deep that it seemed to be that of a man's, she growled, 'How dare you! Get out of here.'

'I've done nothing. Wh . . .'

'Get out of here!' Mary Hetherington seemed to leap backwards towards the door and, pulling it wide, she pointed dramatically towards the street.

The little woman, very, very like a mouse now, a trembling pathetic mouse, gave Sarah one piteous glance, then made her exit on the point of a run. As Sarah watched her scrambling ignominiously down the steps into the street, the reason why Dan had taken up with her became clear: it was because the poles of the earth were not more apart than she and his sister. In spite of being brought up under the domination of Mary Hetherington, he had survived and had become a man with a mind of his own, but Mary's dominance had coloured his choice of a woman.

As Sarah watched her mother-in-law come towards her she said to herself, Stand up to her, don't let her frighten you. But the admonition did not prevent her retreating into the living-room, where she stood at the far side of the table not daring to look into the outraged face before her. She had only seen this woman in a temper once before, that was on the day she and David had returned from the registry office, and, as she had told Phyllis, she had been frightening. During that particular scene she had raised her voice – if she had not actually shouted she had talked loudly – but now her voice was not raised, it was very low and it made her much more frightening than any wild burst of temper could.

'You . . . you knew about this, didn't you?'

'No, I didn't.'

'You arranged it.'

'No! No, I didn't.'

'You're a liar . . . a big blowsy, lazy liar.'

The attack widened Sarah's eyes. This was how the women of the bottom end talked. Moreover, this was an attack on her. It had really nothing to do with Dan or the woman, it was directed against her. She felt it. She knew it.

'Dan would never have dared, he knows how far he can go. But you . . . do you know what you've done?' She had her hands flat on the table and the edge of it was pressing her clothes into her thighs, her stomach, surprisingly large for one so thin, was covering inches of the table, and she was leaning at an angle that brought her head and shoulders half-way across it. 'You've wrecked my home, that's what you've done.'

'You don't know what you're talking about. I've done nothing. It wasn't me who . . .'

'Shut up! You could talk until you're black in the face and I'd never believe you. You're sly, cunning . . . using your lumps of flesh . . .' She released one white-knuckled hand from the table and flicked it within an inch of Sarah's breasts. 'You don't need any sign outside the door saying "All men welcome", you've just got to show yourself

. . . You – you young hussy – setting your cap for my menfolk! And you've taken them, haven't you . . . my menfolk. That's what you've done. And you meant to, didn't you?'

'I . . . I . . . What are you talking about? You must be mad!' Sarah shook her head slowly. Her mouth hung open and her tongue hung slack on her teeth with amazement.

'Go on, play the innocent, first David and then Dan. Oh, he has his woman on the side but he can't keep away from your kitchen. And then my own husband . . . what did you do to him? Encourage him in . . . "You can smoke in here, Dad" . . .' She was mimicking Sarah's voice. 'You think I don't know your little game. I wasn't born yesterday. And John, running round making your furniture when he won't knock a nail in for me, or May either.' She took a great intake of breath now. The beads of sweat were ringing her upper lip. She straightened her back, breathed hard again, then with her eyes still riveted in patent hate on Sarah, she went on, 'You should be in Costerfine Town with your sister. There's not a pin to choose between you. I must have been crazy to think that you were the lesser of two evils. Ellen said I'd be paid back, and how true her words have come. But I realised it from the beginning. And it wouldn't have happened if you hadn't sneaked off to the registry office. There are worse things than a taint of insanity. Well, God has punished me. Sure enough. He's punished me. I've lost a good friend in Ellen, I've lost a girl who'd have been a daughter to me, and what have I got? . . . You . . . who've split my family apart.'

'It's not true.' Sarah was standing straight now, her breathing sharp. 'Not a word you've said is true. I've never asked any of them into the house. If they come next door it's not to see me but for a bit of peace, do you hear? Do you hear that? For a bit of peace!' Although she was still trembling, still afraid of this woman, there came to her aid retaliation born of a sense of injustice. This feeling came boiling up in her when dealing with her father, or the priest, and it now enabled her to thrust back at her mother-in-law the truth, the truth that was going to sever their connection for all time. Her voice spitting out the words, she cried, 'And if they do come into my house who's to blame them. What is there for them here?' She flung one arm wide. 'Is there any real comfort or happiness? This isn't a home, it's your show-place, and you're the big boss. Dan is the only one who has kicked over the traces, but it's a wonder to me they're not all regular visitors at Maggie Conaman's . . . There, you've asked for it, and you've got it . . . You never intended I should have David, did you? No, you didn't. As you said, it wouldn't have happened if we hadn't sneaked off to the registry office. Well, you were foxed, weren't you? I've got David, and I'm going to keep him, and you can't do a thing about it. Now you've really got something to get your teeth into, so bite hard. You can't hurt me, do you hear? You can't hurt me.'

She turned away from the livid countenance and went out of the house, not rushing, just walking, walking steadily. Although fearful at her temerity and amazed at her daring, she was possessed of the knowledge that she was indeed a woman, all of her and for ever. The girl in her was gone completely.

Maggie Conaman was a notorious character of the docks and Sarah would have denied any knowledge of her existence if the question had been put to her, but now she had used her knowledgeably and thrown her into her mother-in-law's chapel-going sanctimonious teeth.

A few minutes later, as she stood in her own kitchen, her hands above her shoulders gripping the mantelpiece as she stared down into the fire, she seemed to see there her values being melted and reshaped. What were this family, anyway? What were they? They were no better than those at the bottom end. When she thought of the family she was not including the men. There was one figure only who represented the family: her mother-in-law. She had talked and gone on like any woman from Baxter Street or Poltar's Row. And only yesterday she had said one mustn't bear malice or bitterness. That was funny, that was. Anyway, who did she think she was, anyway? WHO? She grabbed at the poker and rammed it into the fire, stirring it vigorously, sending the ash over her shining black-leaded hob. A big, blowsy, lazy liar. She dropped the poker with a clatter on to the hearth, then, throwing herself into David's chair, she turned her face into the corner and began to cry, slow painful tears. There was always someone or something to spoil things, always, always.

'Don't worry yourself.' They both said it at once, John and David. They were standing in front of her and she looked up at them as she said, 'You're wasting your time. She blames me for it all. So let her go on thinking that. You're not going to make things any better by telling her the truth. In fact you'll make them worse.'

'We'll see about that.' David nodded his head down sharply at her. 'Come on.' He beckoned to John. 'This is one thing we can get straightened out and waste no time about it.'

'Have your tea first,' she said.

'Tea be damned!'

That was the first time she had heard David say damn; he was very upset for her. As she heard their combined footsteps going down the yard she joined her hands in her lap and sat waiting. Within a matter of minutes she heard the sound of voices, low and muffled coming through the wall.

Five minutes later she raised her eyes towards the kitchen door as she heard the back door open. She was surprised to see John coming in alone. 'I've left him,' he said, jerking his head towards the fireplace, 'pouring buckets of oil on the troubled waters. Not that it will do much good. You were right.' He came close to her, and, bending towards her, his hands cupping his knees, he asked quietly, 'Did you say we should all have gone down to Maggie Conaman's for diversion?'

She dropped her eyes from his and after a moment said, 'Something like that.'

'Good for you.'

She looked up at him. His eyes were twinkling, his face twisted into a wry grin. 'You certainly rent the temple asunder with that salvo. And the funny thing is, you know' – he wagged his finger slowly in front of her face – 'many's the time I nearly did just that.'

She lowered her eyes again and looked down at his feet. They were an extra large size. His boots were highly polished; he always took pride in his appearance. She liked that about him; he would never look down and out if he was out of work for ten years, she thought. She was wondering why she was thinking this way at this particular moment when his voice came at her again, saying, 'You know, some people think your church is the last word in domination. Well, it might be, but with it neck and neck at the post are the Baptists, ones like my mother. Humbugs who condemn drinking yet make a brew with a kick in it . . . Oh, I know I said it didn't affect me, but then I can stand a good deal . . . You know, I once believed in God. But no smoking, no drinking, no swearing, no taking the Lord's name in vain, no reading books on a Sunday other than . . . the Book; no playing the piano on a Sunday unless hymns, these things changed my opinion pretty early on about God, and chapel, and living the good life. And if they hadn't, the face of the bolster atween her and Dad would have done it in any case.'

'What?' She did not quite follow him. 'A bolster?'

'It's a fact. After Davie was born no more of . . . THAT, she said. I wasn't five at the time, but I remember as if it was yesterday, and getting out of bed because something disturbed me, I didn't know what, and opened the bedroom door. There she was standing on the landing in her nightie saying, "I want no more of that." The word THAT stuck in my mind for years. I was about ten when I discovered what THAT was and just turned thirteen when I learned about the bolster. It was the first of Dad's Armistice celebrations. You know, he always gets tight the day before Armistice Day and he told me – he was crying just like a kid – and he told me. "Fighting all through the War," he said, "and I had to come back to the bolster. It's unnatural, isn't it?" '

Sarah lowered her eyes. She felt embarrassed, as if somebody had told her a filthy story. She had never liked filthy stories.

'She's a cruel woman is me mother; narrow, and cruel, and like all such women, bitchy. May is bitchy, but she's not narrow in that way.

You know something, Sarah?' He was still bent towards her with his hands on his knees and she looked at him again. 'You've struck a blow for all of us the day. Every single one of us . . . Dan, Dad, Davie, and me. Oh yes . . . and me. For how many times have I wanted to say to her just what you said the day. You know, it's funny. We've known about the doors as a united family, yet each one of us hates her guts in some way . . . aw, don't let it trouble you, don't look so sad. Come on, cheer up. You've stood on your two feet today so you shouldn't look sad.' He took his hand from his knees and bent over her, and his tone dropped to a whisper as he said, 'I worry when you look sad. I do, I do . . . Sarah.' His hand came out to touch her cheek when she pressed herself away from him, saying under her breath, 'No, don't, don't. Don't, don't.'

'All right.' He straightened up and stood looking down at her for a moment before turning abruptly from her. 'I'll be seeing you,' he said.

She lay back in the chair. Her heart was pounding against her ribs. Why must he do it . . . touch her? Everything would be all right if he didn't touch her. When the beating subsided she thought of what he had said. She had struck a blow for all of them. Yes, she had struck a blow, and smashed the house. Very likely if she had kept her mouth shut this business would have died down and a veneer would have covered the real feelings of them all and they could have gone on with the daily business of living amicably – but never again. The blow she had struck had severed the lives of the two houses; and in her own house there stood David, Dan, and John, with her father-in-law astraddle the wreckage. But standing alone in the rooms of the other house was Mary Hetherington; bereft of her menfolk. This knowledge brought no feeling of triumph to Sarah, only awareness of the hard bitter woman's pain.

CHAPTER SIX

Sarah felt dreadful. She longed to go in to Dan to help as usual, to see to him, but she knew that even if she had the courage to walk up the next yard she would find the door bolted against her.

She had tidied upstairs. She had done her kitchen and dusted the few bits of furniture that were in the front room. She had prepared the dinner far in advance of its time. And now, taking up some socks of David's she sat down near the fire. She didn't feel well – she supposed it was the upset of last night – she felt all to pot. She said to herself, Get up and make yourself a cup of strong coffee – coffee was David's innovation. He liked it. He liked it better than tea. She wasn't very struck on it herself, but David said it bucked you up.

As she snapped off the wool from the sock there was a flick of shadow against the left-hand pane of the kitchen window. This meant there was someone at the back door. She was in the scullery before they knocked, and when she opened the door her mouth did not drop open into a gape of surprise, it clamped closed, her lips losing their full shape in a tight line. 'What do you want?'

'You were always civil, weren't you?'

'I asked you what you want?'

'Just a word.'

Her tongue drew a quick line over her upper lip before she said, 'Get it out then.'

'Well.' He moved from one foot to the other; then rubbed his thumb under his nose and brought his eyebrows close together before saying. 'It's a bit private like, I don't think I'd do me talking out here.'

She stood staring at him. She wanted to bang the door in his face. She remembered that he had been trying to see her before this. Without a word she pulled the door wide to give him plenty of room to pass her, she had never liked getting close to him – there was a smell about him, a body smell. Even when he had washed himself down there had still been that smell, a smoky, sweet, funny smell.

In the kitchen she kept her distance from him. She did not ask him to sit down but stood looking at him, waiting. He was looking about him, a smile on his face. When he looked like this she could understand anyone thinking he was a quiet, inoffensive little chap.

'You've got it nice . . . grand. Did well for yourself, didn't you?' He was still smiling as if in approbation. 'I'll sit down a minute, off me legs. I've been to the doctor's with me back . . . I'm on the sick. They stopped me dole.'

So that was it. He had come cadging. He had a nerve. She repeated the words in her mind, slow, deep, and emphatic. By! Yes . . . he had a nerve all right. Then, as she had guessed, it came.

'I was wondering if you could spare me a few bob to tide me over.' He had not said, us over, which would have meant he wanted the money for the house.

Her face was hard, her voice equally so, as she rapped out, 'I haven't any money to give or lend.'

'No?' He shook his head slowly.

'No, not now or any other time.'

'But your man's doing all right, he's got a permanent job. From three pounds five a week they get in the dock office, I understand.'

'It doesn't matter what they get, or what you understand, I've got no money to give you; it takes me all my time to manage. And now you'll have to go. I've got to go out.'

He sighed here, then leant his short body forward until his elbows

123

were resting on his knees, his hands hanging idly downwards, his whole impression one of relaxation. 'It's a pity.' He sounded sorry.

She was puzzled by his reaction. She had expected him to bounce to his feet and tell her what he thought she was, a bloody upstart. Instead he started talking about David.

'Nice fellow, that man of yours. Did he tell you I had a word with him on the road the other day?'

David hadn't told her.

'He asked me how long I'd been out and he gave me a bob.'

Oh David, David, what a silly thing to do. But that was David.

'I should think he was a chap in a thousand, straight like; no side to him. I was talking to some of 'em at the dock gates and they said he was the civilist fellow in the office.' He lifted his eyes upwards looking at her under his lids. 'You've been lucky, you know. You fell on your feet. It'd be a pity if you were knocked on your back now, wouldn't it?'

Her brows came together. 'Knocked on me back? What are you getting at? Look.' She did not go near him, but she bent her body towards him. 'I don't know what you're yammering on about or what you're leading up to. I only know one thing: coming from you it won't be any good.'

'Well, it's all how you look at it, isn't it? A thing is good or bad how you look at it, that's what I say . . . The mother's a bit of a tartar.' He jerked his head towards the wall. 'Thinks herself somebody, I hear. Never out of the Baptist chapel they say. Narrow as they come. No understanding. Now our lot can booze and whore and think nowt of it . . .'

'I'll have none of that talk in my house.'

'Well, I was just explaining, no offence. But you know yourself we're all human, you should know that better than anybody.' He was smiling again, nodding at her now. 'But what a Catholic would laugh off a Baptist would hang you for.'

Sarah was standing straight now, stiff and tall, her hands gripped in front of her waist. There had come upon her a terrible feeling of apprehension. It might only be imagination, she told herself, but the smell from him seemed to be filling the room. She felt faint, sick with it. He was staring at her, not speaking. She told herself not to let him see that she was agitated. That's what he wants, she said. Stand up to him like you did to her yesterday . . . go on. She took a deep breath, then said, 'Look, if you've had your say you'd better go because I'm going out, I've told you.'

When he still did not answer but continued to look at her with his unblinking red eyes she withdrew one hand from the other hand, and, putting them behind her, supported herself against the edge of the table. And as she did so he said quietly, 'It's a pity the big fellow hadn't been single an' all, you'd have had your pick then.'

'W . . . w . . . what?'

'I said . . .'

She was away from the table now, standing over him, shouting, 'I heard what you said.' She glanced at the wall. She would hear her next door if she went on like this. Her voice dropping, she hissed at him, 'Don't think you can frighten me with anything your sewer mind can make up. All David's family come in here, his uncle and his father.'

'Oh?' He turned his eyes up towards her and his voice sounded almost childish. 'I didn't know they all came in, that's nice. But it wasn't that I was meaning. You see . . .' He pushed his head back as if to get a better view of her. 'About New Year's morning. You know the Collins, me cousins down Bogey Hill way, well, they asked me over for first footin'. I was a bit surprised like but I went, but didn't stay long, and on me way back Aa was took short.' He stopped at this point and Sarah closed her eyes and waited, her breath suspended, her whole life suspended. She waited.

'I went in one of the huts, you know, the end one on the waste land, and then I heard this coughing. Well, you know, there's always couples around there. I bumped into two or three on me way up, making the best of New Year's morning. Well, this couple began . . . well, they began to talk. At least he did, an' Aa was a bit surprised like. Well, you see what I mean.'

Sarah, her eyes open now, was pressing herself against the table; then her body, arching itself upwards, shot forward and she was hanging over him and words, each borne on a spurt of rage, came frothing from her mouth. 'You devil! You dirty, evil devil! It was nothing . . . nothing. I tell you it was nothing. Nothing happened.'

'No?' He seemed to be untroubled by her rage, and his voice still held a childish innocent note and he shook his head as if in perplexity.

'You dirty-minded swine!'

'Now, look, Sarah.' He got slowly to his feet. 'I don't want to quarrel with you. There's no reason. An' it wasn't my doings, was it? I just happened to be there, and there I had to stay. You wouldn't have liked me to show me face, now would you? I had to stay put for over ten minutes, you know.'

Oh God! Oh God! Oh God! Sarah bowed her head deeply.

'I couldn't close me ears, that's why I said it was a pity, a pity the big fellow's married, for he seems clean gone on you . . . Mind . . .' He moved his head slowly. 'I don't blame him, but it's awkward, isn't it? It's an awkward situation all round, I mean with your man being such a nice bloke an' his mother being such a tartar an' all that. And then the big fellow's got a bairn, hasn't he, and a wife that's a bit of a spitfire too as far as I can gather . . .'

'Shut up! Shut your evil mouth. I tell you, nothing happened, noth . . . ing, do you hear? Noth . . . ing.' Spurts of frothy saliva came from her mouth with the last word. A voice was going mad inside her now, urging, directing, yelling. Stand up to him. Don't let him get you. Tell him to go to hell and do what he likes . . . But he wouldn't go to hell. She would, she would be plunged into a living hell. If she hurt David in any way that would be hell. But what she could do was to take the wind out of this slimy devil's sails by telling David what had happened . . . And turn him against John? No, no. She could never do that. Then she must tell John . . . What, and have him murder this little reptile! Whatever road she tried to take out of this mess was blocked, she could see that. If she made a move in any direction she'd bring disaster on them all, the disaster that Mary Hetherington had prophesied, that the priest had prophesied. She remembered Father O'Malley's words: God works in strange ways, sometimes through a series of disasters. Her whole being trembled. It was as if he had known what was going to happen, as if he had a hand in the plan.

'I wouldn't take on like that, there's no need to upset yourself. I just thought I'd tell you and put you on your guard like in case you got careless.'

Her eyes were closed again. She could not bear to look at him in case she sprang on him and beat her fists into his face. Her mouth opened twice before she said, with eerie quietness, 'There was nothing happened, he was drunk.'

'Aye, I can believe that. Yes, New Year's morning, lots of funny things happen in drink. Meself, I've always steered clear of it, but there it is . . . Well, I just thought I'd pop in and tell you an' see if you had a couple of shillings on you. That's all I want, a couple of shillings until you see your way clear . . . anyway, what's five bob a week to keep everybody happy, eh? I ask you now.'

She was going to be sick. She was going to faint. She had never fainted in her life, but she wanted to faint now, to pass right out, for if she didn't she would do something to him, she knew she would.

She found herself at the cupboard next to the fireplace where she kept her bag, and, groping blindly in it, she found her purse, and, taking from it a two-shilling piece she threw it with a backward movement on to the table. She heard it bounce twice; then from the corner of her eye she saw him stooping to pick it up from the floor.

'Thanks. Thanks, lass. Now don't worry, there's nothing to worry about. I won't tell your mother so you needn't worry, 'cos it would upset her, you know. She lays great store by your being up this end. It sort of makes up for the other one and the Arab like. There's nobody need know anything about this only you and me . . . and them concerned . . . Well, so long. Aa'll be seeing you. Aa'll pop over now and again. So long. Aa'll see meself out. Don't you bother.'

When she heard the door close she stood with her back pressed against the cupboard shelves. She would go mad. This would drive her mad. What could she do? She staggered to the table and gripped its edge until her nails broke. Then she was leaning over it, her stomach heaving. It seemed to turn over and rush upwards. The next moment she was standing over the sink vomiting.

She was still sick when David came in at dinner-time. 'What is it?' he said. 'Have you eaten something?'

She hung on to his hands tightly with both of hers, and she made herself smile when she gave him the news, 'I'm going to have a baby I think,' she said.

At two o'clock the following morning Sarah awoke screaming from a nightmare, and when David held her, trying to assure her that she was awake and safe, she grabbed at him. 'I was in the mud. Everybody was in the mud, but they dragged me to the middle. I had it in my mouth and I was choking . . . Oh, David, it was awful, awful. I'm frightened, David.'

'There's nothing to be frightened about, darling; it was only a dream.'

Yes, it was only a dream. Her body slowly unwound against him. 'But it was worse than usual.' She said, 'It was worse than usual, much worse.'

'You've had it before then?'

She nodded against his breast. 'It started with an overdose of cough mixture my mother gave me.' She felt a tremor of laughter go through his body. 'Well, that's put paid to cough mixture.'

They lay silently, their bodies close, breathing almost the same breath, until David whispered, 'Don't let anything frighten you, dreams or anything else. And as long as you've got me I'll see to it that nothing does, not even . . .' He pressed his finger into her backbone and the pressure spelt 'mother'. 'You understand, love?'

Yes, she understood. She also understood that his words meant the exact opposite from what he thought. They meant, for as long as she had him she would know fear, the fear of her little world, her new superior little world exploding.

PART THREE

CHAPTER ONE

'I think there's going to be a march,' said John.

'Where to?' asked David.

'London, of course.'

'It'll likely be the same as the one in Seaham Harbour when you met Ramsay MacDonald. Tea and soft soap and the promise that Jarrow would be kept in mind. That's three years ago.'

'We'll get results this time or else . . .'

'Or else what?' said David. 'Riots?'

'Aye, if necessary. But they don't want it to be like that; everything's going to be orderly, at least from our end. Ellen's coming with us.'

'Oh, that woman!' May's thin voice broke in on the men. 'My godfathers! You would think she was a priestess; I'm sick of the sound of Ellen Wilkinson's name.'

'Shut up!' John turned on her, spitting the words at her. 'You haven't got the list to lift a hand to help anybody, and you haven't a good word in your belly for those who do.'

May raked John with her cold glance before rising to her feet and saying, almost listlessly, 'Lift a hand? You've been lifting hands for years now, the great John the Baptist, and where's it got you? What's it got us?'

'As much as it's got anybody else in this town – a place the dole queue. If we hadn't fought, you and the likes of you would now be in Harton, that's if you could get in. You'd more likely be lying on the salt grass, as they did not fifty years ago, dying on a bit of sacking.'

'Oh, for God's sake! Let up, will you! I've heard it so often it's got whiskers.' May moved round the table, past Sarah, who sat silently sewing, and made her way towards the staircase door, saying, 'I'll call Paul down.' But before she reached it David spoke to her quietly, 'But he's right, you know, May. If it wasn't for the likes of John here and people like Alfred Rennie and Drummond . . .'

'Oh, David, don't you start . . . please. And tell me something I don't know. I'm sick of listening to the virtues of Drummond and Riley and Rennie and Thompson and the rest. Oh yes, and the Virgin Mary herself, Miss Ellen Wilkinson. But tell me, David . . .' She stepped back into the room, 'What have they done? All this cafuffling and what have they done?'

Before David could answer John was on his feet crying, 'They just keep men sane, that's all. Keep reminding them that they're men, that they might be down but not bloody well out. They're trying to feed their minds. At least, put into them as much as their depleted systems will allow them to take, so that when we march into London it won't be a band of ignorant numbskulls they'll be talking to, and that's what they take us for down there, a lot of bloody brainless numbskulls. And they're not alone in thinking along those lines, are they, May dear?'

They glared at each other for a moment. But just as May was about to speak John put in quickly, 'You won't come up to the rooms, will you? No, because you'd have to swallow your words. And, what's more, you might learn something . . . Oh, but you don't need to learn, do you? No, you know it all, don't you? Like them up there. Well, as I said, they'll get an eye-opener when we march in.'

'Da-di-da, da-di-da; tra-le-la-la.' May gave an imitation of blowing a bugle, and as John took a step forward David, catching his arm, said quickly, 'Now then, now then. Stop it, you two.'

'I'll make some tea.' Sarah rose from her chair, and, pushing the little dress she was smocking on to the dresser, went out into the scullery, while John, looking towards May again, said bitterly, 'One of these days I'll land you one and you'll not get up again.'

'Try it on.' She smiled at him as she rolled her head tauntingly on the back of her shoulders. Then, going into the passage, she called upstairs, 'Paul! Paul, do you hear me? Come on. We're going over.'

There was some laughter and chatter from the room above, then a bouncing step on the stairs and a boy of about eight years old followed May into the kitchen. He was tall for his age and thin, and he looked like neither May nor John, but there was a suggestion of his father in his mercurial manner. With a flicking movement of his eyes he looked from his father to David and said, 'You'll never be able to make her spell, Uncle, I bet you won't. She can read long words, but she can't even spell cat.'

'What should I do with her? Bray her?' David made great play of rolling up his shirt-sleeves, and the boy laughed a high tinkling laugh. 'I can see you doing that, Uncle David. But you being a good speller and knowing about words, you'd think she could spell, wouldn't you? She's over five.'

'Yes, you would at that age.' David shook his head sadly at the boy, causing him to laugh again.

May, pushing at her son, now cried, 'Get going. It's a shame to waste two houses between you and her.'

'Aw, let's have a minute, Mam.' The boy swung away from her and went quickly round the table to where John sat moving cardboard letters with his finger.

'You playing Lexicon, Dad?'

'Do as your mother bids you.' John did not raise his eyes.

'You playing Lexicon, Uncle David?'

'Do you want to get shot, Paul Hetherington?' David looked into the boy's grinning face.

'I want to watch you play. Why are you always messing about with letters, Uncle? You should have been a teacher. Have you always messed about with letters, like when you was a young lad?'

'Yes, Paul, always. They've always fascinated me.'

'Did you hear me?'

'Yes, Mam. Just one minute, only one minute. Go on, Uncle Davie.'

David looked at May and shook his head.

'Why do they fascinate you, Uncle Davie?'

'Well, I suppose it's because a few lines differently arranged can tell you so much.'

'But they're not lines, Uncle Davie, they're squibbles and things.'

'No, they all start with lines. Look.' David took from his pocket a piece of string and, cutting it into lengths with his pen-knife, he placed one piece before him, then he bent another in two, and, sticking it in the middle of the first piece, he said, 'There you are, one straight line, another straight line, bent in two, stick them together and you've got K.' The boy nodded and David went on, 'Then you take another straight piece, put it next to the K and you've got I. Now I is the most important letter in the alphabet; it not only means I, it means ME.' David thumped his chest in a number of places, 'It means all of ME. I've always thought the letter I was an amazing letter. You think of that straight line and then you think of what it means . . . you see?'

Paul nodded again, his eyes bright and twinkling.

'Then you want an S, so you take your straight line and you bend it like that . . . there.' He pointed. 'You've got an S.' He did the same again, then said, 'Look, another S, and what have you? Kiss.'

Paul thumped his uncle in the arm and laughed his high laugh. 'Do some more.'

'Oh no you don't. Come on.' May grabbed her son by the collar, swung him round and marched him out of the room.

In the scullery, protesting but still laughing, Paul grabbed at Sarah's skirt as he was hustled past her and cried, 'Goodnight, Aunt Sarah. She's not asleep. I bet you a shillin' she starts howling in a minute.'

'Goodnight, Paul. She'll get her bottom smacked if she does.'

'What you havin' for supper?'

This question brought May to a halt, and, turning towards Sarah, she said, 'Do you know something? I think he's got a tapeworm – I'm serious.' She nodded at Sarah. 'The minute he got in he had a basin of stew left over from the dinner. That was half-past four. When I went next door' – she jerked her head towards the scullery window – 'he was sitting up having a full tea with his grandad. Chips . . . the lot. And then I come over here and finds him scoffing again. And look at him.' She shook his collar. 'There's not a peck of flesh on his bones, people think he's starved. I tell you, he's got a tapeworm.'

Sarah smiled. 'Well, he never ails anything, does he?'

'Ail anything?' He hasn't got time, he's always eating.' She gave her son another shake, then pushed him out into the yard, saying, 'Goodnight then.'

'Goodnight, May.'

The door had hardly closed behind her when it was opened immediately and May, her face in the aperture, said, 'Tell him to get over home before twelve, will you? I hate to be woken up in the middle of the night.'

She was gone before Sarah could make any retort, but if she had thought of one she would not have been able to voice it. She stood for a moment looking out into the dark yard. What did she mean by that? May knew that she herself went up to bed and left them downstairs talking until all hours. She had likely meant nothing. What could she mean, anyway? But May was deep. No-one ever knew what May was thinking, you couldn't get to the bottom of her.

'Mammy! Mammy!' The cry came from almost above her head and she turned and, picking up the tray of tea, went into the kitchen.

David had half risen from his chair. 'I'll see to her,' he said.

'No, it's all right. Leave her to me.'

'She'll keep you going. She'll have you up there until dawn.'

'It's all right.' She put the tray on the corner of the table and went out and up the stairs, and when she entered her daughter's bedroom the child was sitting up in bed waiting for her.

'Paul didn't read me a story, Mammy.'

'Well, he was helping you with your spelling, wasn't he?'

'He wasn't. I was reading to him and when it was his turn Auntie May called.'

'Come on, lie down. What do you want?'

'Oh.' The child snuggled down into the bedclothes. 'Henny-penny and Cocky-locky and the sky is going to fall.'

Sarah pulled a chair towards the bedside, and, reaching out, picked up a thick-backed nursery book from the table. She had no need of the book, she knew the story word for word, but she flipped the pages over until she came to the story of Henny-penny and Cocky-locky going to tell the King the sky was going to fall. But before starting on it she cast a smiling glance down on her daughter and the child smiled back at her. Every now and again during the reading they would do this. Sarah would lift her head and look at the child and they would smile at each other. Almost from the day she was born it had been like that. They would look at each other and smile and become one.

134

Every time Sarah looked at this child of hers she knew she was the luckiest woman alive, for she not only had the child, she had its father. In this tiny world of hers she had everything, everything to make a woman happy. Was not David one of the few men in work? They had four meals a day, they owed no-one, they had everything, everything that made for joy . . . that was David's phrase. He had said to her, 'I just can't understand about you having nerves, honey, you're not built like that. And we have everything, haven't we? Everything that makes for joy. Is there anything you want? Tell me. Tell me, is there anything in the world that I can give?' And then he had added quickly, 'That's a silly question on three pounds fifteen a week.'

On that occasion she had thrown herself into his arms and assured him with all her heart that he had given her the world. Then why had she got nerves? Why had the doctor said she was suffering from nerves? The doctor had said he thought she was worrying about something . . . What was she worrying about?

Again she had reassured him that she hadn't a worry in the world. Perhaps, she had said, something had happened to her when she was carrying Kathleen, for it was from when she was first pregnant that she had felt this way.

Yes, David remembered it was from the night she had the nightmare, the night following the day she had told him about the baby coming.

She came to the end of the story.

'There now, go to sleep.' Sarah closed the book.

'I haven't said my prayers, Mammy.'

'Yes, you have. You said them before you got into bed. You know you did.' She patted the plump cheek, then, bending over, she laid her mouth to it and was imprisoned by two podgy arms.

'Mammy.'

'Yes, darling.'

'Paul says he loves you.'

'Does he? That's nice. I love Paul too.'

'Paul says that when he grows up he's going to have a house with fifteen rooms and a big car.'

'Oh, I'm glad to hear that; we'll have to go and stay with him . . . Leave go, darling.'

As Sarah disengaged herself Kathleen said, 'I want Nancy, Mammy, to keep me warm.'

'Oh, Nancy's too hard, you might roll on her and hurt yourself. Have Peter, he's soft.'

'He kicks me, Mammy.'

'I'll tell him not to.' Sarah went to the corner of the small room and from a shelf attached to the wall she took from among numerous toys a dilapidated velvet rabbit, and, holding it at arm's length as she walked to the bed, she said, 'If you kick Kathleen, Peter, you'll get your bottom smacked in the morning.' She placed the rabbit in the child's arms, kissed her once again, then saying as she put the light out, 'I'll leave the door open,' she went from the room and down the stairs.

Dan was in the kitchen now, sitting at the table shuffling a set of dominoes. He turned his head at Sarah's entry. 'Hello, there, how's it going?'

'Oh, all right, Dan.'

'Is she asleep?'

'Yes, she'll be off in a minute . . . I hope.' She smiled at him.

'You go to the doctor's today?'

'Yes.'

'What did he say?'

'Oh, nothing fresh, but he gave me a different bottle, it's very bitter.'

'That'll be for your appetite.'

Sarah picked up her sewing from the dresser again and seated herself in David's leather chair to the side of the fire and continued with the smocking. The dominoes clicked, and the two brothers and their uncle, all looking of a similar age now, played their nightly game. It had become almost a ritual, this gathering together each night from seven o'clock onwards. If, as they sometimes did, David and she went to the pictures, they would find Dan and John sitting at the table on their return. The key was always kept in the wash-house in between the legs of the poss stick which stood in the middle of the poss tub.

And Dan played on a Thursday night too now.

Sometimes they played Lexicon, or cards, but for the most part it was dominoes, and it was seldom that the evening did not end in some form of discussion. That their discourse kept clear of heated argument was due entirely to David's even temper and Dan's humour.

The only reason why David played games, Sarah thought, was to keep his fingers moving, for he missed his piano-playing. She had tried in every way she knew to persuade him to continue his practice, but his answer was always the same. When she was welcome next door he would start practising again. She had learned in her six years of marriage to David he could be stubborn, and it was surprising to her to realise that he could carry this stubbornness to great lengths. She knew that neither Dan nor John would have been so tenacious with regard to his principles. Although David still visited his mother his visits were short and they had become shorter with the years. The reason for this, Sarah knew, was that Mary Hetherington had not taken to her granddaughter. Although David had not put this in actual words, she knew that he was aware of it.

David's voice now brought her attention to the table, and Dan, as he said, 'What's up with you the night, Dan? That's the seventh game you've lost, and you've doubled twice. That means you owe me . . .' He consulted a piece of paper in his hand, then looked up and laughed. 'Four pounds seven-and-sixpence. I'll let you off with the sixpence.'

'Will you have it now or wait till you get it?'

'I'll wait till I get it.'

'Aw.' Dan scraped his chair back from the table, and, lifting his thick hair from his scalp with his spread fingers, he said, 'To tell you the truth, me mind's not on it, it's miles away . . . in the shop.'

'In the shop?' John looked up from shuffling the cards. 'Anything wrong?'

'Well, yes and no. It's like this.' Dan leaned forwards his forearms on the table again, and looked from John to David. 'The old man made a proposition to me today and I don't really know what to do. It's like this. He's up against the wall now, like all the others; four shops have closed in the last month down the street and our books are so full of tick there isn't any margin left. One of the main snags is that some of them when they've any money go elsewhere, down to Shields Market or some such place. I've said to them, "Look, you can have what tick you like as long as you bring your little bit of ready in." Some of them do, but you just can't keep going on the few. Well, he called me upstairs this morning, and there was the wife sitting. I tell you it was awful, but he put it to me plainly. He said he would have to shut up unless he could find a bit of ready to meet the bills. He's a proud old devil you know, but straight as a die. He's got his faults, but he's honest, and there he was, near tears. And the old woman, she was in tears. And he said to me without any palaver, "Well, Dan, what about it? What have you got left of your winnings?" "Well," I said, "I've got just over four hundred."'

Sarah's hands became still, the needle poised, and involuntarily she repeated, 'Four hundred?' And Dan, turning and looking at her, said, 'Yes, from me winnings. You know, out of *John Bull*.' Then, jerking his head round to David and shaking it, he muttered, 'Don't tell me you never told Sarah about it?'

'No, I never told her. There was no need. It's years ago you got it. I've never thought about it.'

'That's him.' Dan was looking at Sarah now, smiling. 'Yes. I won six hundred in *John Bull* . . . Fashions, you know.'

'Really?' Sarah smiled. 'Fashions?'

'Yes, I was a dab hand at fashions. I knew absolutely nothing about them, so I came up . . . Well, there it is.' He looked at the men again. 'The old boy's offered me a partnership if I'll put

137

me money in the shop. But he warned me, mind, that it might be like throwing it down the sink. If things don't turn in another year, well, we'll be like the others, we'll be shut up. But the other side of it is that if I don't go in with him we'll be shut up in any case and soon, and I'll be out of a job. And if I don't get another I'll have to live on the four hundred, won't I? They won't give me dole with that gold mine in the bank, not likely. So it's really as broad as it's long. What do you say?' He looked from one to the other.

'You could start up on your own on four hundred,' said John.

'Oh no you couldn't, except in a huxter's shop; not a place like Campbell's. It's a well-established shop and it's got a licence too, you see. He's had that place thirty-eight years; in nineteen twenty-one he could have retired, for he was sitting pretty then. And there's another thing that needs thinking about. He said that if we can keep the place going he'll leave it to me, that's if his wife goes before him. If she doesn't, then I'll have to make her an allowance, but in the end it would be mine . . . It's not to be sneezed at, is it? What do you say, Davie?'

'I think it's worth taking a chance on, Dan, for in the long run you've got nothing to lose. Anyway, you've already made up your mind, haven't you?'

Dan's hand came out and he pushed at Davie, saying, 'Aye, I suppose I have. But I wanted to know what you think.'

'Go ahead,' said David. 'And all the luck in the world. You won't sink. I couldn't imagine you ever sinking.'

Shuffling the cards, John put in quietly, 'If you want an errand boy remember charity begins at home, I'm ready any time.'

Sarah, rising from her chair, looked at Dan. 'I'll make a cup of tea, and we'll drink to it,' she said, smiling.

'That's the ticket, Sarah. And look . . .' He grabbed at her arm. 'When I have me . . . me chain of shops running from Shields Pier to the Swing Bridge in Newcastle, you know what? I'll buy you a car and a mink coat.'

'Thank you very much.' She was laughing now. 'But I'd rather have a wireless set.'

'Oh, but you're getting a wireless set; John's making you a . . .'

'Your big mouth!' John slapped out at Dan, and Dan said, 'Aw, I'm sorry.' He turned to Sarah. 'It was to be a surprise.'

Sarah looked at John. He was dealing out the cards now. She did not say 'Thank you' immediately, but, turning to David, she asked, 'Did you know about this?'

He nodded at her and she said, 'And you let me go on talking about wirelesses . . . Oh.' She ruffled his hair, then, glancing towards John's still bent head, she said, 'I didn't know you could do wirelesses. Thanks, John.'

'That fellow can do anything,' said Dan, laughing. 'Anything he puts his hand to. He is a blooming genius.'

Sarah's words had sounded grateful, but as she went into the scullery the thought in her mind was, Why had he to be the one to give her things? He had made nearly all their furniture, except for the bed, the couch, and the armchair. And what would May say about this? Very likely nothing, but she would think and look all the more.

As she put the kettle on she found herself feeling sorry for anyone who had to live with May, and she dared now to say to herself, I'm sorry for him. Every day for the past six years she had suffered because of John. There were times when she hated him and her feelings would come out in her attitude towards him. And most of the time she was on her guard in case she would say something to him that would bring comment from David. Yet besides all her submerged feelings concerning him, she was sorry for this big, bustling, bumptious, and frustrated individual. And he was frustrated in so many ways. Unemployment to him was a disease that was eating into the very core of his being, and it wasn't lightened by the fact that his father, his uncle, and his brother were all in jobs. He was the one that could least suffer unemployment. There were times when, seeing him in the depths of depression, she had wanted to put her hand out and touch him, to give him comfort, but the fear that accompanied this desire almost paralysed her body, and she was thankful that it did. There had been one particular occasion during the past few years when she had been grateful, yes grateful that she was being blackmailed because of him; for if anything could prevent her softening towards him it was this weekly trial on her nerves. The situation had arisen when one day John had returned hungry and tired from a fruitless workers' march, to be greeted by May and her barbed tongue. He had come over into the kitchen here – she had been alone in the house and he rarely came in when she was alone now – and with the sadness of an aged man, he had asked, 'Can I rest awhile here, Sarah? I'm dog-beat and May's playing hell.' She had made him a meal, and then he had fallen asleep in David's chair, and it was as he slept that there came on her an almost uncontrollable desire for her hands to touch him. And she had flown upstairs and stayed there until David came in . . .

As she made the tea she thought, Him always making things for me, David must be blind. Then she attacked the suggestion with, Well, you don't want his eyes opened, do you? Oh, my God! No, no, never that. Rather the nauseating sight of her father, the parting weekly with the precious five shillings, and her visits to the doctor for her nerve tonic. But how much longer could it go on? She could see her nerves as worn wires, and the strength of a wire at its weakest part. What was her weakest part? There was no answer to this, and she mashed the tea and took it into the kitchen to drink to Dan's success.

CHAPTER TWO

Over the years Sarah and Phyllis had met once or twice a month. If the weather was fine they took a ride on the ferry across the river. At other times they would walk down towards the sea. They had never reached the sands, for the time they spent together as the years went on grew shorter. Phyllis had now three children to see to, and Sarah always wanted to get back home to be in when David returned from work. Neither of them visited the other's home. Their homes were rarely mentioned. Sarah's decision, years earlier, had come to nothing. She had too much on her mind.

On this Saturday morning Sarah stood in the shelter of a doorway in the Market Place looking over the stalls in the direction of Waterloo Vale where Phyllis was now living. They, as a rule, never met at the week-ends – week-ends were for the family and were a busy time – but this morning was an exception and it was Sarah who had written to Phyllis making the appointment.

The market was almost deserted except for the stalls and their owners. The cutting wind was carrying on it a thick rain almost like sleet, and it was only early October.

When she saw Phyllis moving rapidly with her light step across the cobbles towards her, she went to meet her. After both exclaiming about the wretchedness of the weather, Phyllis said, 'Let's go in here and sit down.'

'Here' was a working-man's café, and when they had taken their thick cups of dark-looking tea from the counter they sat in the corner of the dismal and almost empty room. After sipping from the steaming cup, Phyllis, holding her hands over it, said, 'Do you know any more? Have you heard anything?'

'No, nothing, only what's in the papers . . . Phyllis.' She leant towards her sister. 'Do you know anything about it?'

'Me?' Phyllis pressed herself against the back of the chair, repeating, 'Me? No. No, I don't, but by God I wish I'd thought of it years ago. Is he going to live?'

'I don't know. I just saw me mother for a minute yesterday. We hadn't got the paper on Thursday night, I knew nothing about it until she came in; she had just come back from the hospital. She said he was in an awful state.'

'Hell's cure to him. He's got what he's been asking for for years. Some bloke likely caught him snooping and beat him up. I only wish the polis hadn't come across him so soon; if he'd lain out all night he might have died from exposure . . . that's what they said in the paper an' all.'

Sarah bowed her head. The feeling of guilt lifted from her for a moment; she hadn't been the only one to think along these lines. But she doubted if Phyllis had prayed for him to die. She herself had prayed every minute since yesterday morning that he wouldn't regain consciousness.

'The paper says his arm's broken and he's got injuries to his head. Oh' – Phyllis took another quick sip of her tea – 'if anybody's got their deserts he's got his. It said in the paper a pair of binoculars were found near him that he used for bird-watching. My God, that's something . . . bird-watching. Birds all right. You wouldn't think a reporter would be so daft as to put it in. Him! A man like him bird-watching. But me mother told them that. She said she had to say something because of him going round with a spy glass. I wonder where he got the money from to get it because he hadn't got the guts to pinch. But what made you think I'd 'ad a hand in it?'

Sarah's head was lowered. She knew where he had got the money from, only too true she knew. She looked up quickly, saying now, 'Since he was found near Redhead's Docks down East Holborn way I thought . . . well, to tell you the truth, Phyllis, I thought you might know something about it.'

'No, no, I tell you I don't; but mind, if I'd known he was in the habit of coming down that way, take it from me I'd have done something about it. There's one or two blokes down there who'd beat up their mother for a pint. But he chose the wrong place to use his spy glass when he chose Holborn. It's as Ali says, he was likely watching a couple. But somebody was watching him, and they lathered him. And good luck I say, good luck to whoever it was.'

Yes, good luck to whoever it was. She endorsed that, oh, she did. She only wished they had done the job properly. Eeh! If only she could stop thinking like that . . . She finished her tea, then asked, 'How's the children?'

'Oh, I've got Jimmy in bed again, he never seems well. I've had the doctor. He just says, well, nothing's wrong with him really; give him plenty of fresh air and feed him well, he says. I can do that all right. He gets his grub, he's luckier than some. I thank God for the café every day of me life. Getting things at cost, it means a lot.'

'How is it going now?'

'Oh, just scraping along. In fact hardly that, nobody's got anything.'

'It's worse up in Jarrow.'

'Yes, I know. I went up there the other day. It's dead. I was glad to get back. While I was waiting for a tram there was a fellow talking to a group of them; they all looked as if the smell of a pot of stew would

141

knock them over. But the way this fellow was talking! Like a lawyer. And something he said stuck with me. It isn't very often I listen to the blah-blah-blahing. But it was true what he said. He said Jarrow had been raped and it had given birth to twins, hated twins, hunger and idleness. That's what he said.'

'He's right too, in a way, at least. Only I don't know so much about the idleness. All the men up there are trying to do something. John is forever helping to organise things. It's funny.' She smiled. 'He said the other day that a lot of the fellows have received an education through being on the dole, and when your stomach isn't full he says you can always think better.'

'I saw him in the market last Saturday afternoon. He was with a woman; she was youngish, but she looked a snipe. Would it be his wife?'

'Yes, that sounds like May.' Sarah nodded. 'Small, thin. And she's a snipe all right, you never know how you have her.'

Sarah now gathered her bag and gloves towards her, saying, 'I'll have to be moving, I've left Paul looking after Kathleen and they'll have the place turned upside-down.'

It wasn't until they were on the pavement that Phyllis turned towards Sarah, saying, 'Are you still wanting a piano for David?'

'Yes. You know I do. But I can't manage the money now.'

'This one's only four pounds. Ali says it's a bargain. You know, he said he'd keep a look-out for you. He takes adverts for the café window, it always helps, and he got this one for the piano. He even went and had a look at it. It's just off Fowler Street and the people are in straits. Ali says it's being given away.'

'But four pounds! I haven't got it, Phyllis. I've got about thirty shillings put by and that's the lot.'

'I could lend it to you. Oh, I'm not on me beam ends, don't you worry. I keep slipping a shilling or two into the old tin. Look, Sarah, you can have it and welcome.'

Sarah looked through the slanting rain over the market place towards St Hilda's Church and she thought that the morning had lightened, her future had lightened. She saw through the rain a space ahead without the dread of the tap on the back door on a Monday morning. Perhaps weeks, months of respite, perhaps a lifetime of release . . . If he should die. Oh, dear God, let him die . . . There she was again. It was dreadful to keep going on like this, wishing somebody dead. But he deserved to die; he was wicked, horrible. She felt at times she could embrace a reptile easier than she could look at him . . . And then there was Phyllis offering to lend her money for the piano. Yes, the morning was lighter.

'Look, will I tell Ali to put five shillings on it, then you could go and have a look at it yourself, eh?'

'Yes, yes, Phyllis.' Sarah was nodding enthusiastically down on Phyllis. 'Yes, I'll come down on Monday, eh? What's the address?'

'Oh, I can't remember it off-hand. It'll be in the shop.' They looked at each other in silence for a moment, then Phyllis asked softly, 'Won't you come round to the house, Sarah? You've never been.'

'You've never asked me.' They smiled shyly at each other.

'It's seven, Waller Place.'

'Seven, Waller Place. All right, I'll come, Phyllis; I'll come in the afternoon after I've dropped Kathleen into school. About two, eh?'

'About two. But mind, don't expect too much. Although' – Phyllis's chin went up – 'I'm not ashamed of our place, I've got no reason to be. It's a damned sight better furnished than some of them at the other side of the town. I can tell you that.'

'I'd love to see it, Phyllis.'

'Well, Monday. So long, Sarah.'

'So long, Phyllis.'

They touched hands quickly, shyly, then went their separate ways, hurrying as if to get rid of their embarrassment.

It was as the tram came to a stop at the top of Stanhope Road that the thought sprang into Sarah's mind: 'I'll pay a visit.' And just as the bell rang for the tram to move on again she jumped off and crossed the road and went down the gentle slope towards the church.

The church was empty and quiet. She blessed herself with holy water from the font, then went down the side aisle, past the pictures of the Stations of the Cross to the front pew before the altar of the Virgin Mary; and as always when she came to this church she felt in a strange way as if she had come home. But she hadn't been in the church for years, and over the past four years she had rarely seen the priest. Father O'Malley had apparently given her up as a bad job, but since Kathleen had started at St Peter and St Paul's school Father Bailey had been to see her twice. He was nice was Father Bailey, and he thought the world of Kathleen.

She began to pray. The Our Father, the Hail Mary. Then she repeated parrot-wise, 'Come, Holy Ghost, fill the hearts of thy faithful and kindle in them the fire of thy love. Send forth thy spirit and they shall be created and they shall renew the face of the earth.' All the set prayers of her childhood. And then she was talking to God, talking rapidly, beseechingly, asking Him of His mercy to take her father, to make him die. She bent her back until her buttocks were resting against the seat, and her head bowed on the back of the seat in front of her; her forearms at each side of her head brought her hands clasped above her hat, and she talked to God as if He was before her, as if she was clutching His garments. Take him, O Lord, take him, because I'm frightened. I nearly hit him last week. Take him, O Lord. I can't bear the sight of him, he's evil, I'm afraid of what I might do. I've thought of doing just what this man's done to him, O Lord. I've thought of following him on a dark night, O God forgive me. Take him, Lord; please take him. And for no reason she could think of she found herself now repeating the seven capital or deadly sins. Pride, covetousness, lust, envy, gluttony, anger, and sloth.

'Sarah.'

She sprang back on to the seat, crouching against the pillar to the side of her, staring up at the hand that had touched her shoulder and the face above it.

'Are you all right, Sarah?'

'Y-e-s, Father. Oh, Father, you gave me a fright.'

'I'm sorry, Sarah.' The priest slowly sat down on the edge of the pew a few feet from her and he asked quietly, 'Are you in trouble, Sarah?'

She swallowed and moved her head as if in denial; yet its very action was an affirmative answer, and Father Bailey said, 'What is it? Can I help you? Dry your eyes.'

She fumbled in her bag for her handkerchief and dried her eyes and blew her nose, and then dried the fresh tears that were flowing down her cheeks.

'Is it your husband?'

'Oh, no. No!' The denial was emphatic. He's wonderful to me, Father. Believe me, no-one on earth could be better. No. No.'

'It isn't the child, is it? There can't be anything wrong with Kathleen. I saw her yesterday.'

'No, Father, Kathleen's all right.'

'Wouldn't you like to tell me, Sarah?'

'Oh, Father.' Her whole body slumped against the pillar. Could she tell him. Not a living soul had she uttered a word of the cause of her mental anguish over the past years. Everybody thought she had nerves, and indeed she had nerves now. But oh, the relief to be able to tell someone, to know that someone would understand, and this priest, this good priest, would understand. She wondered why she hadn't thought about it before. But then she remembered she had thought about telling it in confession and dismissed it. She lifted her eyes wearily to his now and asked quietly, 'Could you hear me in confession, Father?'

'Certainly, Sarah.' He held out his hand and raised her to her feet as if she was a sick person, and to him she was a sick person. Then he turned from her and moved out of the pew and up the church towards the confessional box, and he went into one door, and she into the other.

When she was kneeling on the kneeler, her face to the wire mesh, she whispered, 'Will I start as if in confession, Father?'

'Yes, Sarah.' And so she began formally, 'Please, Father, give me your blessing for I have sinned' – this opening had always struck her as comical, for it seemed you were asking the priest to bless you because you had sinned – but not today. She went on, 'It is nearly six years since my last confession. I have only missed Mass a few times, but I have never been to Communion or my Easter duties.' She paused here, thinking of all the venal sins she had committed. Bouts of temper. Thinking unkind thoughts. Missing her morning and night prayers. All her small sins she told him, and then she paused again before saying, 'My main sin, Father, is wishing someone dead. It's about this I want to tell you.'

'Go on, Sarah, I'm listening.'

And so she told him. She told him exactly what happened on that New Year's morning, and she told him of the morning her father had visited her and his weekly visits since. Of the five shillings a week she paid him, and of the terror rising in her of late in case she would do him an injury. And lastly she told him of feeling glad, in fact joyful, when she heard he had been beaten into unconsciousness.

When she had finished, the priest made no sound and she remained still, waiting. And then he said a surprising thing, he said, 'Do you love this man, Sarah, your husband's brother?'

'No, no, Father.' Her reply was like rapid fire.

'In no way, Sarah? You haven't encouraged him to take a liberty with you?'

'No, Father, no. I was a little afraid of him because I think I knew what he was feeling.'

'And there was no answering response in you to this feeling?'

She waited before answering, and then said falteringly, 'He's a very attractive man, very virile. He's . . . he's unhappy with his wife, I know. I've felt . . . well, sorry for him at times. At times I wanted . . . I wanted to be kind to him. But no, Father, I've never encouraged him and . . . and I don't love him.' She could not say to the priest that there was some part of her that called to her husband's brother and made her ashamed that this part would rear up like a wild animal at times, and these times usually occurred with the gentle loving of David. It was then that this part of her would long for a different loving, a wild, frenzied, mad loving, a kind of loving she sensed on the New Year's morning when locked in John's embrace. No, she could not say this to the priest because she was only barely conscious of it. The thoughts in your head while your man was loving you, and the thoughts that filled it for the rest of the day and night belonged to two separate beings. But when these two beings attempted to merge, as they sometimes did in the light of day, she was overcome by a feeling she had to flay, and flay it she did. She flayed it with her happiness, the happiness given to her by David. She flayed it with the gratitude she owed to David. She flayed it with the passionate love she had for her child.

The priest was talking now. He was saying, 'You have been very silly, Sarah. You should never have given your father money in the first place.'

'I couldn't help it, Father. I knew he would have told my husband, and although David wouldn't have believed him, not really, it would have caused a difference between him and his brother, and he's very fond of his brother, they are very fond of each other. And then there was his mother. His mother doesn't like me, and I knew that if she heard about this, life would be unbearable for us all. Then there was my sister-in-law, John's wife. She's an odd type of girl. Well, what I mean is, Father, she seems quiet, but she's quarrelsome, hard. You see, I just had to keep my father quiet.'

'When he comes out of hospital – you must stop praying that he won't come out, Sarah, do you hear me?'

'Yes, Father.'

'Well, when he comes out you must tell him that you're going to give him no more money, and if he becomes nasty you must tell him you are going to the police.'

'But, Father!'

'Listen, Sarah. You must tell him that. You must frighten him off. Whether you go to the police or not is up to you, but blackmailing is a serious offence and they'll soon put him in his place. What you've got to realise is that he is undermining your health. You've lost a lot of weight, haven't you?'

'Yes, Father, two stone.'

'Well, you can't go on like that. You know what you should do, but you won't do it. But I feel that your husband should know about this. What I have seen of him he is a very reasonable man. I like him, Sarah.'

'Thank you, Father, but . . . but I couldn't tell him.'

'Well, leave it for a time until your father comes out of hospital, but in the meantime think about it seriously, think about confiding in your husband. Bring him down to me if you like and we'll talk it over.'

'I couldn't, Father. There are too many complications.'

'Well, you must do what you think best. And remember, Sarah, I'm always here if you should need me.'

'Thank you, Father. I feel better now.'

'Make a good act of contrition, Sarah.'

She came out of the confessional box and waited a moment and then the priest joined her; he walked with her to the door of the church and there, taking her hand in his, he said, 'Nothing matters if your conscience is clear . . . Make that your aim in life, Sarah. Keep your conscience clear.'

'Yes, Father.' She inclined her head towards him. 'Goodbye, Father, and thank you, thank you very much.'

'Goodbye, Sarah.'

She walked quietly down the steps of the church, past the station, and down the Dock Bank. The Bank, as usual, was black with men, some talking in groups, some standing silently against the rails, just looking out of the hungry present into the hungry future. No longer were they on the lookout for the gangers with the hope of being set on a boat, because the gangers, too, were standing staring. Gone from the Bank was that notable measured stride of the burly, proud captains; the noticeable bearing of the arrogant chief engineers. No longer were there strings of coolies shopping on the Bank, their bass bags swelled with fish, their bare knees pointing upwards as their seemingly unbending feet left the ground. The colour, the excitement, had gone from the docks.

Sarah cast her eyes towards the Dock offices as she passed them. David was in there. She knew where he would be sitting, the exact spot, to the right of the main door where you went in, and her glance towards the grimed window next to the door was tender.

David was lucky; he was one of the envied ones, he was in work. As long as the docks were moving at all he was secure, and she was secure. But David didn't give the docks credit of his security, he gave it to Mr Batty. He had once said to her when talking about the office, 'He feels he's tamed me . . . training me he would call it, so if there is any security in the job at all it's that, just that. He hasn't made life unbearable for me like he has for some. I feel he holds me up to himself as part of his success.'

'And you don't mind?' she had said to him.

'No.' He had smiled at her. 'Why should I? It pleases him and it doesn't hurt me.'

That was David, the gentle way every time. Oh, she thanked God for David. She felt lighter, happier. Why hadn't she gone to Father Bailey before. Oh, she wished she had.

It had stopped raining, so she decided to walk home, it would save the bus fare. She crossed over the road to the path that led under the dock arches. The arches were dark and dismal, the brickwork was as black as a singed bloater, and the water dribbled down the walls in rivulets of slimy green. But the arches left no impression on Sarah; they were part of the dismal whole, unseen, except on rare occasions, because of their familiarity.

The pavement bordered by the actual dock wall curved round by the bottom of Simonside Bank, the Bank which led into . . . the country, to the nice houses and Hedworth Hall and the Robin Hood and places like that. She hadn't been up into the country for years. As she looked up the steep incline of the bank she said to herself, 'I must start and take Kathleen for walks up there, away from the streets.'

They could do it on a Sunday afternoon; she would speak to David.

She was turning her gaze away when it was pulled back again. A man had just rounded the bend. He came striding down the road, his step quick and purposeful, and as she watched him raise his hand quickly then break into a run she turned her head away and groaned inside. Oh, no, no, not this morning. Then fear came upon her. She would have to walk all the way home with him. What if her father . . . She closed her eyes. She had forgotten, he was in hospital. The relief scuttled the fear from her being and she turned and looked towards John as he came running up to her.

'Fancy seeing you . . . Here, give me your bag.' He took the bag from her hand.

'There's nothing in it,' she said.

'No, there's not.' He shook it up and down. 'Well, where've you been then?'

'To see Phyllis.'

'Oh, oh!' He was walking by her side now, suiting his step to hers. 'How is she?'

'Oh, she's fine.'

'I've been up to see Ted Cobber. He lives up near Jarrow cemetery, but I wanted a walk so I came back the country way . . . getting in training. Him and me, we were mates for years. He's a bit cut up, he wasn't picked for the march.'

'Is he oldish?'

'No, no, same age as me about. But he didn't pass the doctor. We all had to go through an examination, you know. It's a wonder that he found two hundred fit among us when you take everything into consideration.' His voice was quiet, and Sarah nodded. 'Yes, it is a wonder,' she said.

They walked in silence for some minutes, and each second of each minute Sarah was aware of the man by her side. It was always like this when she was alone with him. She wanted to break the silence but couldn't, and was relieved when he said, 'I went up to get a loan of his ground sheet; he used to do a lot of cycling at one time and sleep out.'

'But you won't have to sleep out?'

'No. No. It's all been arranged in different town centres and places, but we'll likely have to sleep rough on the boards. But you can use a ground sheet to cover you in the rain, you know.'

He was excited about the march on Monday, the march from Jarrow to London, the march of protest against starvation, and he had talked of nothing else for weeks. She had become almost as familiar with the names of those chiefly concerned as May was. David Reilly, Councillor Paddy Scullion, and Councillor Symonds; Councillor Studdick, the Conservative agent, and Harry Stoddard, his Labour counterpart. She knew that these latter two, political men from opposing sides, had been sent ahead – and together – to prepare the reception for the marchers in places like Harrogate, Leeds, Barnsley, Bedford, Luton, and other towns.

But the name mostly on John's lips was that of Ellen Wilkinson. Sarah had never seen Ellen Wilkinson. She didn't think of her as a woman, not an ordinary, normal woman. A woman who could lead men on a march to London could not be an ordinary, normal woman. In fact any woman who was in Parliament could, of course, not be ordinary. As for being normal, well, women had their place, hadn't they, and it wasn't really their place to yell their heads off among a lot of men in Parliament. So thought Sarah.

But John was quiet now. He was not talking at high speed about the arrangements and the arrangers, those for and those against. He wasn't wanting to wipe the floor with Bishop Hemsley Henson, Bishop of Durham, or worship at the feet of Bishop Gordon of Jarrow – his homage of the latter having nothing to do with the man being a churchman.

As Sarah glanced at him she was surprised at the unusual expression of sadness on his face; she had never seen him looking sad before. Aggressive, bitter, cynical, jolly, rollicking, but never sad. He was looking ahead as he said, 'There's going to be a short service in Christ Church for the marchers afore we leave.'

'Oh, that'll be nice.' Her answer sounded inane, but it was all she could find to say. And then he asked, 'Would you come, Sarah?'

She flashed her eyes towards him. 'To church, you mean?'

'Yes.' He was still looking ahead.

'Yes . . . yes, all right, John. Yes, I'll come. May could call for me . . .'

'May's not coming, nor is me mother. Neither of them, but for different reasons. My mother wouldn't put her foot inside a church if it meant saving her life, or anybody else's for that matter. As for May, she neither believes in God . . . or man.' He stressed the last word. 'She says it's a lot of damned hypocrisy, the men going to church before the march, for ten to one there hadn't been a man Jack of us inside a church or chapel for years . . . and I suppose she's right in a way. But you know, this isn't just an ordinary march, at least I don't see it that way. They're marching from Scotland and Cumberland, and Yorkshire and Wales, and Durham, but ours is different somehow. Runciman's said that the Government could do nothing for Jarrow, that Jarrow must work out its own salvation – well, that's what we're doing in this march. Some of us might never make it; it's a long way on two feet and mended shoes.' He looked down at his boots, and Sarah looked down at them too. They were newly cobbled. On each boot were two bulging patches of leather, but the boots were shining. As always John was tidy.

There came over her body now a softening, an enervating wave.

149

Again, and almost unconsciously, her body and mind were forgiving him for all the trouble he had caused her. She even forgot for the moment that a short while ago she had knelt in an agony of mental suffering in the church. At this point there came into her mind what she termed a silly thought. I wish I was his mother, she said to herself. She seemed to see inside the big aggressive bulk of him to the everlasting little boy who needed someone to turn to, someone who would always listen to his prattling and who would push the black hair back from his brow as he talked . . .

'Keep your conscience clear. Make that your aim in life, Sarah. Keep your conscience clear.' The priest's words were loud in her head and she exclaimed to herself, Oh God! But I've done nothing, said nothing. She was throwing denials back at her mind now. It was just that when she was alone with him she felt something, a sympathy; it was nothing else, just a feeling of sympathy. He made her feel like this, as if he wanted her protection . . . Protection. John needing protection . . . huh! Don't be so daft. She threw scorn at herself. What he wanted was to bear her to the ground and crush her into it with love. Oh, she knew, she knew what John wanted. Her body told her what John wanted, and there she was talking about being a mother to him. She hadn't been honest with the priest . . .Oh, she had, she said; she hadn't thought like this when she was with the priest, it was only when she was alone with John that she thought like this. Oh God, she wished she was home. And why had she said she would go to the church on the Monday morning and neither the one or the other going. She herself had more than one reason why she shouldn't go. It was forbidden that a Catholic should partake of a service in another church; it was a sin, she knew that, yet she had said she would go. And after Father Bailey being so kind to her. Oh, she wished she was home.

They were walking in step silently, both looking ahead. Then John, picking up where he had left off a few minutes earlier, said, 'It's as if every one of us was going on a private mission. Not a man of us but wants everything to be ordered and who wants to thrust the word rabble down the necks of those that say that's what it'll be. I don't think there's been anything so well organised as this march for years. Nothing has come out of the North so well organised, I'd like to swear on that. That petition will be handed over to Parliament by men, not a rabble. And for the few that's against us we've got the majority with us. All Tyneside is behind us, and the Lord Mayor of Newcastle, Alderman Lock, is with us all the way. He's not standing aside and saying every man for himself, Jack. He says, and these are his very words, "Jarrow's troubles are our troubles", and . . . and you know, Sarah' – he turned his face fully towards her now – 'what a lot forget is that it's us the day, but it'll be them the morrow if the canker isn't stopped.'

150

When she didn't answer he waited for a moment before saying, 'Are you all right?'

'Yes, yes. It's just the damp gets into you with all this rain.'

Again he was looking ahead, and again he was silent for a time until he said, 'Have you been to the doctor's this week?'

'Yes.'

'What did he say?'

'Oh, just that I must eat more.' She forced herself to smile at him. 'And I told him I didn't mind losing weight, it was fashionable to be thin.'

He kept his eyes on her now as he asked quietly, 'Sarah, has your worry anything to do with me?' He put out his hand quickly towards her, exclaiming with concern, 'Look . . . look, don't jib away from me like that, I'm not going to take anything up; and I can't do anything, can I?' He moved his head round to indicate the open space of the Slacks and the broad daylight. 'It's only that I get worried at times. Aye, yes, I do.' He nodded his head quickly at her. 'I get worried about you because you never seem to have been right since . . . well . . .' He flung his head round on his shoulders and muttered through his teeth. 'Since that New Year's Eve. If it's about me you are worried you can put your mind at rest, it won't happen again, I've told you . . . There now.' He swung his head sideways once more. 'Well, is it me that's worrying you . . . I'm asking you?'

She was sweating now; she could feel it running down between her breasts and from her armpits. Never before had she wanted to pour out the truth to him. Hadn't she done enough pouring out for one morning? The distress in her was like froth in a bottle, and she knew that once it was released it would be difficult to stop the flow. One thing was sure: if she told him she would have no more trouble with her father. He would scare the daylights out of him, perhaps finish the job that the other fellow had started. She shivered on the thought . . . But there was another thing she could be sure of too. If she were to answer his question truthfully they would be drawn together, held together by ties stronger than those they would have created through any physical means. She could not explain to herself this knowledge of John's reaction, except that in fighting her father for her he would unconsciously cloak himself with moral righteousness. Moreover, he would glory in holding some part of her that was not David's.

She made herself aggressive both in voice and manner and used it as a screen behind which to hide as she cried, 'Why must you bring that up? And what makes you imagine you have anything to do with the way I feel? You've got a nerve, you know, John.' Her eyes were blinking, her chin was thrust out at him, and her step became uneven as she quickened it with an effort to move away from him.

'All right, all right.' His voice was calming. 'I only wondered. But don't take on. When you act like that you sound like May.' His voice was still calm.

She paused in her stride. 'I'm not like May.'

'No . . . no, you're not.' He was looking at her, his eyes soft, his whole expression tender. 'I'm sorry, I shouldn't have said that. No, thank God, you're not like May.'

Again they walked in silence. They were approaching the streets now, and when she turned into Camelia Street he turned too. He did not say, 'So long, I'll be seeing you.' Nor did he say, 'You don't mind if I drop in for a moment?' He just accompanied her home.

As they approached the front door they heard high laughter, and after she had knocked on the rapper there came a scurrying through the front room and the door was pulled open. And there stood Paul and Kathleen, their faces bright with careless childhood.

Kathleen was about to cry, 'Oh, Mummy!' when she saw John. Then, literally leaving the ground, she jumped from the high step into his arms, shouting, 'Uncle John! Why, Uncle John!' It was as if she hadn't seen him for days.

John walked through the front room with her legs straddled round his waist, his arms supporting her shoulders as her head dangled beyond them.

Paul, walking by Sarah's side into the kitchen, said under his breath, 'We've broken a cup and saucer, Auntie.'

'You didn't.' Kathleen was looking from her upside-down position towards Paul and she waved her arms at him now as she cried, 'You didn't, I did. I threw it at him, Mammy.'

'You what! Let her down, John.'

John, with a lift, planted the child on her feet, and Sarah, looking down at her daughter, said, 'You threw a cup and saucer at Paul? Why did you do that?'

Putting her hands behind her back, Kathleen sauntered towards the fender; then sat down on it before she answered, 'Just 'cos.'

'Never mind just 'cos.' Sarah's voice was stern. She turned to Paul. 'Why did she throw it at you, Paul?'

'He likely deserved it.' John gave his son a gentle push that landed him in David's chair, and the boy, looking at Sarah, said, 'We . . . we were just playin'. I . . . I was teasing her.'

'You weren't, you were telling lies. You were . . . you were.' The little chin was thrust out at Paul. 'He said, Mammy . . .' She looked at Sarah now. 'He said you loved him better than me. So there. That's why I threw the cup and saucer at him. It hit the fender.' She looked down and pointed with her finger towards the brass rail that rimmed the steel fender, and she continued to look at it as she ended, 'And you don't, do you?'

'I was only teasing, Auntie.' The boy spoke with his head down, and Sarah turned her eyes away from him, away from her daughter,

152

and away from John. She could not please her daughter by saying, 'Of course I don't,' because that would hurt the boy, and the boy was John's. What she did say was, 'You'll get a skelped behind, me lady, one of these days.'

Then she fell back on the old stand-by that helped her through trying moments and over little obstacles, and big obstacles too. She said, 'I'll make a cup of tea . . . we're froze.'

On the Monday morning Sarah stood outside the Jarrow Town Hall and watched the mayor review the men. Two hundred shabbily dressed, freshly shaved, tidy, thin men. She followed them as they marched to Christ Church, and as they entered a man stopped a boy in front of her from going in by saying, 'It's only the wives and mothers, lad.' For a moment she hesitated, but the man accepted her and she passed into the church and sat in the back row. The Mayor and Corporation were seated at the front, and Bishop Gordon took the service.

Sarah had never been in any but a Catholic church in her life, but she did not find this service strange, as she did not follow it. Her mind was elsewhere, for she was overcome by a feeling of deep sadness. Yet at the same time she was experiencing a sense of exhilaration, and she was wishing that she too could march with them. Oh, she wished she could. Oh, she told herself, she did.

The service over, they filed outside, and John came to her side. He had a groundsheet in a roll slung across his shoulders. He looked big and gaunt, yet he too looked elated.

'Well, this is it.' It sounded like the goodbye of a man going to war. She looked at him, but she could not speak. Sadness had excluded all other feelings. A couple to the right of them were enfolded in each other's arms; all about them people were embracing, wives, mothers, children, all clinging to men as if they were about to march to their deaths.

She should say something, but she could not translate her thoughts into words; her mind was a jumble and full of pain, as was her body. It was a strange pain, unlike anything she had experienced before. As the tears welled into her eyes, John's face moved before her like a reflection beneath rippling water. She heard him saying, softly, 'Sarah, Sarah. Oh, Sarah.' He had hold of her hand now. 'Thanks for coming. You can't believe what it means. Goodbye, Sarah.'

She could not even say his name or bid him goodbye. But her mind, still in a turmoil, was creating a force which was driving something through her body, something that was beyond the voice of conscience, that could not be held in bounds by discretion, discretion that would have enforced propriety. There was only inches between them, yet the distance seemed immense; it was as if she had to leap to reach him, but reach him she did. Her mouth rested against his hard jaw line just to the side of his lips. After a second of hesitation, when she thought he would not touch her, his arms came about her, and he held her in a vice-like grip. Then she was standing shaking and blind among the other women, and he was on the road, somewhere in the ranks.

With the pad of her thumb she swiftly wiped the tears from her cheeks, and over the head of the throng she saw him clearly. He was looking towards her. He did not raise his hand in a last salute, he just looked at her and held her gaze. She watched him turn his head away, and it looked like that of a conqueror.

A small woman to the side of her was crying. She sniffed and blew her nose loudly. 'There they go,' she said; 'the skeletons of Palmers. It'll be fruitless, the march. The shipyard's dead an' it can't never be brought to life again.'

A woman standing behind Sarah said harshly, 'Well, they'll have a damned good try. It's a good job everybody doesn't think alike. When that lot gets to London they may look like skeletons, but what they lack in flesh they'll make up for in spirit. By the livin' Harry they will that.'

The little woman, now apparently aiming to make up for her despondency, looked at Sarah, and said, 'But your man'll be all right; he's big and tough looking, he'll stand it. His name's Hetherington, isn't it . . . John? I've heard me son on about him. Have you any bairns?'

Sarah's mind was working now. Like a juggler, it was tossing words here and there. Before she had time to stop herself she said, 'I've one, but he . . . he isn't my husband.'

'No!' There was surprise in the exclamation.

'He's my . . . my brother . . .'

'Oh.' The woman smiled as she put in, 'Aye, Aa should have gathered that, you're both the same build like, big strappin'.' Her smile became wider.

Sarah turned slowly about. The marchers had disappeared; some of the crowd had moved with them; the people about her were breaking up into groups. She nodded farewell to the little woman, then she found herself confronted by the woman behind her, who was looking at her through narrowed eyes, her whole expression one of close scrutiny, and she stopped Sarah's passage with her voice, saying quietly, 'Aa did washin' for Mrs Hetherington for years, it's the first time Aa knew she'd a daughter.'

Sarah took a great intake of breath and stammered, 'I didn't mean b-brother, I meant brother-in-law . . . but the woman' – she motioned her head towards the roadway where the little woman was now standing – 'she . . . she cut me off.'

'Aw, Aa see. Yes.' The head moved with each word the woman spoke. 'How is Mrs Hetherington these days?'

'Oh, she's quite well.'

'Tell her Hannah was askin' after her.'

'I will . . . goodbye.'

'Goodbye.'

Sarah knew what the woman was thinking as plainly as if she had yelled the words at her. 'Where's his wife then? Why couldn't she come?'

She did not take a bus from the town but kept walking, walking quickly as if this would enable her to get away from the condemning voice in her head which kept reiterating, 'You're mad, you're mad, you're mad, you're mad.' She had walked almost halfway home before she rounded on it. 'But I love David, I do.'

'You proved it, didn't you, to do that in the open in front of everyone, to kiss him in the open.'

'It was nothing, I tell you, it was nothing. He looked so lonely. He is lonely. He hasn't got anybody.'

'That woman thought different; that woman knew he has a wife . . . And she knows his mother, think of that. You're mad, I tell you, stark staring mad. Now you won't only have your father on your tracks, you'll have the gossips. You could see by the look of her she was a talker.'

Just beyond the Don Bridge she stood for a moment looking down at the slimy banks of the river, between which the narrow stream of dark water made its way to the Tyne. She felt beaten, tired, and her mind was weary, too weary to erect any façade, too weary to cover up for John, or for herself. He's like a magnet, she thought, drawing badness from me body, from some black depths of me.

Father Bailey had said: Keep your conscience clear.

Kind Father Bailey.

But Father O'Malley had said no good ever came out of a mixed marriage.

Clever Father O'Malley.

But what do you say? The question seemed to rise from the black mud lining the river bank, the mud with which she was familiar in her nightmares, the mud which sucked her closer towards its middle each time she dreamed of it. But it was a challenge she could face in the daylight. Yet the voice which answered it was still weary. 'I'll never hurt, David,' it said. 'Never.'

She turned away and walked home, and the journey seemed never ending, like the years ahead.

PART FOUR

CHAPTER ONE

'This is the best place for you.' David touched Sarah's hair with his fingers as he leaned over the bed. 'If anybody should knock let them knock, I've been in and told Dan that you would be upstairs, and he's going across the road' – he motioned his head in the direction of the window – 'to tell our John that you're all locked up for the night. I've got my key, so you stay put. Do you hear?'

She nodded up at him and raised her mouth to his as he bent to kiss her.

When he withdrew his lips from hers he did not straighten up immediately but said, 'Of course, if there's a warning you'll go into the shelter; that's different.'

'Yes, if there's one I'll go in.' She put her hand out now and gripped his arm. 'You'll be careful?'

'I'll be careful.' He smiled down on her. 'But whatever's on, as soon as I go on duty the night becomes as dead as a door-nail. I've been firewatching now for two years and never put out as much as a candle. They just don't come my way . . . scared of me that's it.' He straightened up now but did not move from the bed. Instead, he sat down slowly on its edge and, taking her hand in both of his, he looked at her for a long moment before saying, 'I wish I knew what's worrying you.' It seemed almost as if the word scared had prompted this question.

She moved her legs quickly and looked away from him as she answered, 'That's simple. Isn't everybody worried about the War dragging on like this?'

'I don't suppose you would have worried so much if they'd taken me.'

'Oh yes I would.' She was gazing up into his face now. 'I should have gone mad without you.'

'Look, Sarah.' He tapped her hand gently. 'I'm going to ask you something and I don't want you to get annoyed. It isn't the day or yesterday that it's been in my mind, it's been there for a long time, and somehow I've got an idea I'm right, because when our John's on leave you're as edgy as a foal.'

She had actually stopped breathing. She was staring at him, her eyes stretched wide.

'Now tell me, Sarah. Has he ever said anything to you . . . tried anything on?'

'No, no . . . No.' She was shaking her head rapidly, emphasising the denial of her words.

'Now, now, don't get yourself agitated. It was just an idea I got because, you know, you've never really been nice to our John. You're not snappy by nature.' He touched her cheek lovingly. 'But you've snapped at him, time and again, I've noticed it. And then this week, when he's been on leave, he's never been out of the house. And him drinking like a fish . . . well, I thought . . . perhaps he might have . . .'

'No, David, no.'

'All right, all right. Mind you' – he pointed his finger at her – 'I'm very fond of our John, but if I thought he'd ever said a wrong word to you I'd have him on his back as big as he is, and that would be the finish. As brothers go we've been close, very close, but there's some things I wouldn't stand, not from him or anyone else. I was for going for him last night, acting the goat like he did following you round . . .'

'Don't . . . don't quarrel with him, David, please. It's just that when he's on leave he goes a bit mad. I suppose it's understandable, him being stuck away in the far point of Scotland for months at a time, it . . . it must get him down. He's lonely there, and he's lonely here I think, and May . . . well, she . . .'

'Oh, May! May's the cause of his trouble, if you ask me. She's only got one thought in her head and that's the lad. There'll be trouble in that quarter, you'll see, for, as quiet as Paul is, he's got a will of his own, that boy. And if she brings her ruling hand down too heavy on him . . . Well. Of course the trouble with Paul too is that he's too fond of you. That gets under May's skin; it's evident.' He stopped speaking for a moment and stared at her, his head slightly to the side, his face wearing its usual gentle expression. And then he said softly, 'You've never liked our John, have you, Sarah?'

Her lids flickered just the slightest before she closed her eyes and brought her chin into the deep white flesh of her neck.

'It's all right, it's all right.' His voice was urgent yet consoling. 'I understand. And I'm glad in a way because John's always been a devil with women. You know me, don't you? I've never talked about him, or Dan, or their affairs. Dan, as far as I know, had that one woman and that was all, at least to my knowledge, but our John . . . aw, one was never any use to him. But I must say he steadied up after he married May. Then came the hard times afore the war and he hadn't any money to toss around, but since he joined the Air Force, I understand from Dan he's gone the whole hog again and that's why I didn't like the idea of him acting the goat with you, especially as you objected to it, as I could see you did without uttering a word.'

Sarah kept her eyes closed. Up till a moment ago her whole body had been full of fear; now, to it, was added pain. For days she had feared that John, with his boisterous drink-created hilarity, might go too far, might say something that would open David's eyes to this thing that was between them, this undeveloped thing that had been stunted in its growth, but which was nevertheless still alive. Twice during this past week she had thought, If he hurts David he'll cook his own goose, he'll kill whatever is in me for him. But David must not be hurt. She would do anything to save David from hurt, mental hurt. This gentle creature, whose love had lifted her from the mire of the bottom end – this man without fire. This docile man. Docile, even at times to the point of boredom, yet who had brought her love for him almost to the peak of adoration. Nothing or nobody must hurt David, because David was gentle, kind and incapable of hurting any living thing.

Yet there was room in her for pain of a dimension equal to that of the protective fear. It was the pain of degradation and humiliation, as if her body had been assailed. The pain would have been understandable had she been John's wife, or even his woman, and heard he was carrying on with someone else. But as she was neither, why should such news, news of which she was already aware, hurt her so deeply? She couldn't really understand herself.

'Aw, don't be upset.' David was bending over her again, enfolding her in his arms. 'I don't mind how you feel about our John, believe me. In fact, to tell the truth I think I'm glad you feel that way. As long as you love me that's all I care about.'

'Oh, David, David.'

'There now, there now. Look, I've got to go. I should be there now. Old Butler's a stickler for time; that's what comes of being a sergeant in the First War. You know' – he smiled at her – 'some of them enjoy it, I know they do . . . There now, give us a smile, come on.'

She smiled at him; she put her arms about him and held him fiercely to her; and then they stared at each other for a moment before he pulled himself up from the bed.

'Go to sleep.'

'Goodnight, darling.'

'Goodnight, my love.'

He was at the door when she whispered, 'Look in on Kathleen, will you, and see her blackout's all right? She's a devil with that blind.'

'I will. Goodnight, love.'

Sarah was not asleep when at a quarter-past ten the siren sounded. It lifted her out of bed and to the bedroom door, and, pulling it open, she called quickly, 'Kathleen! Kathleen!' She had begun dressing before its wailing died away. She called again, 'Are you up, Kathleen?'

'Yes, Mam, I'm nearly ready.'

As Sarah hurried to the landing Kathleen came out of her bedroom, dressed in a siren suit and with an eiderdown over her arm.

She was tall for fourteen and big-boned. In this way she took after Sarah, but her face held little resemblance as yet to her mother's, or yet her father's. If she resembled anyone it was her grandfather Hetherington, yet the resemblance to Stan stopped here, for her manner, unlike his, was quick, vivacious, even boisterous. She ran down the narrow stairs with the fleetness of a hare, crying up to Sarah behind her, 'I'll get the flask 'cos Uncle Dan will likely come in. Will I bring some cake?'

'Leave that alone' – Sarah's voice sounded unusually sharp – 'and get yourself over. I'll see to the flask and things. Go on now.'

'We'll both do it and we'll get there quicker. I'll put the kettle on.' She was flying into the kitchen as if partaking in a game.

'You know what your father said, we haven't to play about. Come on, let's get settled in, I can come in later and get the tea.'

'It won't take a minute . . . O-oh! Mam.'

The sound that cut off Kathleen's voice was a force that lifted her off her feet and sent her staggering against the wall.

Sarah found herself on the floor by David's chair. She was gripping handfuls of the mat. The house seemed to have stood on its end for a moment and was now settling back. As the gas flickered twice, then went out, she cried, 'Kathleen! Kathleen! Where are you? Are you all right?'

'Yes, yes.' Kathleen's voice was very small. 'It's a bomb somewhere . . . somewhere near, isn't it?'

Sarah pulled herself to her feet. There was cold air coming into the room and she said, 'Be careful, the window's broken. Where are you?' She groped forward until she found Kathleen's hand, and, pulling her towards her, she whispered, 'Let's get into the street.'

The front door was stuck, and as she tried to pull it open it was pushed from the outside and a voice out of the darkness said anxiously, 'Are you all right, Sarah?'

'Yes, Dad. Yes, we're all right. I thought the house was down . . . Where did it drop?'

'It must have been at the bottom end. We . . . we only got the blast.'

'The . . . bottom . . . end?' She repeated the words slowly, separating them. David was at the bottom end, that's where the post was. Her mother was at the bottom end too, but that didn't matter so much. David . . . David was on duty there. She gasped out now, 'Dad! Dad! David . . . he's on duty.'

'I know. Now keep calm, it'll likely not be anywhere near the houses. You go into the shelter . . . or, better still, come into ours.' His hand found her arm. 'Mary'll be glad if you'll come in. I know she will. It's hard for her to give in, she's made like that.'

'Yes, all right, I'll come, but later, Dad. Yes, yes, I'll come in later, but I must see if I can find David . . . he . . .' She stopped

162

talking. A moment ago she hadn't been able to see Stan, and now his face, grey, thin, and pinched, was outlined before her and it was covered with a rosy glow.

'Fire. There's a fire, a big one.' She made to run from him when he caught her by both arms, crying, 'Now be sensible, Sarah; he's got his job to do. Be sensible. Get inside and I'll go and see how things are. Dan's already gone down.'

'No! No! . . . And there's me mother, it might be our street.' She pulled away from him. 'Look, Dad, take Kathleen in, I'll just go and see, I'll be back in a minute.' She grabbed Kathleen and pushed her towards her grandfather.

'But, Mam . . .'

'Do as you're told and stay where you are.' On this she turned from them and ran round the corner. The red glow was brighter here, shot through with flashes crossing the sky. It showed up the main road and lorries and moving shapes. There was a constant rattle of anti-aircraft fire, and from the distance there came two more dull thuds, heaving pressing thuds. She was half-way to the bottom end when her running was jerked to a stop and a voice said, 'Where are you off to, missis?'

She gasped and her head wobbled back and forwards on her shoulders before she could bring out, 'Howard Street. Me Mother . . . and me husband's on duty.'

'Take it easy, missis. Take it easy; get your breath . . .' He paused a moment before saying, 'I'm afraid the bottom end's had it; they must have been trying for the factory beyond. Four of the streets are like matchwood, at least as far as I can gather. Best keep away, you'd never get through, anyway.'

'But me . . . me . . . hus . . . husband. Hetherington's the name.'

'Oh, Hetherington . . . David. Oh, aye, I know David, missis. Well, look, let me take you back home now, come on.' His voice was gentle and he turned her about, but she jerked away from his hold.

'I've got to see if he's all right; the post is up that way.'

'Look, lass, you couldn't do anything; the place is a shambles, fire and all that, you can see for yourself.' He pointed upwards.

'I've got to go. I must find out. Leave go, please.'

He was gripping her by the shoulders, his voice harsh now. 'They've got their work cut out as it is, getting people out, them that's left. You'll know sooner or later. I only know the post has gone. But that doesn't say your husband's not all right, he could have been any place.'

Perhaps it was because he didn't expect any further resistance that he found himself stumbling back against the wall. Sarah was running like the wind now, gabbling over and over again in her mind, 'David! David! Oh, don't be dead, David!'

She was stopped before she reached Dudley Street or where Dudley

163

Street had once been. There were a group of men frantically pulling hoses from a fire engine, and she fell headlong over a length of hose and on to her face. They picked her up, and one said, 'Steady, missis, steady on. You're going the wrong way; you must get out of this.' Another asked, 'Are you from here?'

She was standing on her feet supported between them; she was shaken with the fall and it rocked her words into a drunken mutter and she stuttered, 'Da . . . vid. I want Da . . . vid . . . my husband. Fi . . . fire-watching. He . . . he was f . . . fire-watching at the post.'

One of the men said something gently to her, but it was lost in the noise of the guns pop-popping overhead.

The older man shouted to someone and a woman came running. 'What is it?' she asked.

'Take her to headquarters.' He lifted Sarah's hand like that of a child towards her and the woman, who scarcely came up to Sarah's shoulder, put her arm around her waist and led her away. And she allowed herself to be led away from the burning tortured jumble of bricks, wood, and bodies. But when they reached the main road she said quietly to the woman, 'I'm going home, I live in Camelia Street.'

The woman still had her arm around Sarah's waist when they reached the front door.

CHAPTER TWO

It was three o'clock the next afternoon when they brought David home. John and Dan carried him in and laid him on the bed, and he still looked alive. He was unmarked except for the brick dust that covered him. They had found him in a pocket of beams. He had not died by being crushed, or by a blow, or yet by fire, he had died from shock. The heart that had stopped him passing for the Army had given up.

Sarah, alone in the room with him, knelt by the bedside. Gently she lifted up his hand, his long thin hand. It felt cool, not cold or clammy. He's not dead, she thought. He could be in a coma; they should do something. If he was dead she would be crying, wouldn't she, and she couldn't cry. She could only keep moaning, Oh, David, David.

Not until she laid her face against his did it get through to her that he was really dead, and with this knowledge was born a strange weird feeling. It worked itself up from the core of her being. She felt its approach even through the subconscious layers of her mind, and when it burst the surface she screwed her eyes tightly shut for a moment against the black light of the startling truth it presented to her . . . She was relieved, she was glad that David was dead.

Oh, NO! NO! NO!

But yes, she was. Her mind, rocking from the impact of this knowledge, steadied itself and spoke to her with frightening calm reasoning. He'll never be unhappy through you now, it said. It couldn't have gone on; look at last night. There was a rift opening between him and John and because of you. He knew how John felt about you; he never said anything, but he knew. What he didn't know was how you felt. He died thinking you perfect; be glad of that.

Yes, she was glad of that. He had gone on loving her wholeheartedly to his last breath, and that was what she had prayed for, wasn't it? But it couldn't have gone on much longer, not if John had remained in England, and had kept getting leaves. She thought at times lately that she must tell David, she just must tell him why her father came so often when he got no welcome, when she even showed her hate of him. David had known that she gave him money, but he took it for granted that it was to help her mother, and she had not disabused him of this idea.

But now it was all over, the fear and the worry . . . and the love. She would never be loved again as David had loved her, never. Nor would she ever love again as she had loved David . . . She would never love again, except Kathleen. But that was a different kind of love. In a way she was free. Her mother was dead, her husband was dead . . . and her father was dead.

There came a gentle tapping on the bedroom door. She made no movement or sound, but she knew it was May who had entered the room.

'It's Mam, she's coming up.'

When Mary Hetherington entered the bedroom her eyes went straight to the figure lying on the bed and she moved slowly towards it; she did not look at Sarah or say any word to her.

On the older woman's approach Sarah had moved back from the bed, and now she stood looking towards her mother-in-law. She hadn't looked at her for years, not in the face. Mary Hetherington did not seem much older than on the day they had faced each other across the table in the living-room; the only difference about her was that her face looked sharper and harder. But this woman was David's mother, she would be sorrowing too. She was his mother and had loved him the best – more, oh, much more, than she had loved John, or even her husband, for that matter. She must remember that; she must remember that she was suffering at this moment.

When Mary Hetherington turned from the bed without having touched the figure that lay there, Sarah, making a valiant effort through compassion towards reconciliation, whispered brokenly, 'Will you help me to see to him?'

Mary Hetherington paused and she brought her eyes from space to look at her daughter-in-law, and she kept them on her for a full minute while Sarah waited for her to speak. Then she turned her gaze away and with it her body. She did it with a measured timing that was an insult in itself, and with this timing in her step she went out of the room.

Sarah's lower jaw was trembling. When she tried to control it by clenching her teeth their chattering became loud in her head. It wasn't possible that anyone could keep up hate like that, and particularly at a time like this, but she had, David's mother had. Her face had been full of it. She had looked the picture of fury, as a female god might have looked, a jealous god . . .

'I'll give you a hand, Sarah.' May's voice was gentle, and Sarah, her throat swelled to bursting, murmured, 'Thank you, but if you don't mind, I'd . . . I'd rather see to him myself.'

'Very well.' May inclined her head, then went out, closing the bedroom door quietly after her, and Sarah set about the task of doing the last service she would ever do for David.

Two hours later Sarah sat in the kitchen; she felt drained and empty, yet filled with grief and still that strange, unwelcome sense of relief. Kathleen was standing on one side of her and Paul on the other. Kathleen was crying and Paul was not far from it. Sarah had hold of Kathleen's hand, and when Paul muttered, 'Oh, Auntie Sarah', she took his also.

The boy bent his willowy length towards her. He looked older than sixteen, he could have been eighteen, even nineteen, and he spoke like a man now as he said under his breath, 'Don't worry, Aunt Sarah, don't worry about anything. I'll see to you, I'll always see to you and Kathleen.' He flicked his eyes to the tear-drenched face of the girl who had always been his playmate. 'You'll neither of you want for anything, I'll see to that, I will.'

Sarah looked at the boy. He was a nice lad, a fine lad. Yes, she could imagine him meaning what he said, at least about Kathleen, because he was more than fond of Kathleen. He had never attempted to hide his feelings in that direction. But youth changed, all that was in the future. She could think of the future at this moment, at least for them, but there was no future for herself; she could see only a wilderness, a vast wilderness, in which she would walk until one day she met up with David again. It was funny how the habit of religion caught up with you when you were amidst death. She realised that the latter thought in her head could have been David speaking. He had said wise things had David.

Oh, David, David. How was she going to bear being alone, for from now on she would be entirely alone. Oh yes, there were the others. John. She shuddered on the name. If only it had been he who had died. And then there was Dan. There would always be Dan. Dan was good and thoughtful and kind. He was like David was Dan, only different, more carefree, more careless, at least about things in general, but so good, oh, so good. Yes, there would always be Dan. And in the background, her father-in-law. But close, close to her there was Kathleen and Paul. Yes, Paul was close to her, closer to her than he was to his own mother. But why was her mind thinking like this, for it didn't matter who she had when she hadn't David.

She heard May's voice now coming from the room. It was low and murmuring. She was talking to Dan and John about something, likely the preparation for the funeral.

There came a knock on the back door and Paul said, 'I'll see who it is.' He hurried away through the scullery and she heard the murmur of voices. Then filling the doorway and pushing into the room were three figures. Two of the men she had not seen before, but the man they were supporting between them was her father, and the sight of him changed her world yet again. As she looked at the dirty, bedraggled, undersized man her body became charged with a force that brought her to her feet and sent the chair spinning backwards across the room. She felt her body and her head swelling into gigantic proportions; she had the idea that her expanding flesh would push the walls apart.

One of the men, looking at her across the kitchen, said, 'They thought he was in the rubble but he just got the blast. He's been wandering about. He says you're his daughter, so we brought . . .'

'GET HIM OUT!'

'But, missis.'

'GET HIM OUT!'

'But he's got no place to go . . .'

'What is it?' She heard Dan's voice behind her, then she heard John's voice saying, 'My God!' She saw him move forward to her father. 'Well, you were lucky,' he said quietly.

Sarah glared at them, the big figure of John, the small wizened figure of her father. Because of these two men she was thankful, unnaturally thankful that her man was dead. Her body was swelling, swelling; her lungs were pushing her ribs out, there was pain all over her. She screamed again, 'Get him out, I tell you!'

All the faces were turned towards her, and when no-one moved, her hand, darted with the swiftness of a panther's paw, grabbed the teapot from the table, and, lifting it high, went to hurl it at the man who had seemingly come back from the dead.

In a flash, almost as swift as that which had enabled her to grab up the teapot, John reached her. With his body pressed against hers, his arms stretched wide, muscle to muscle, they stood outlined like a crooked cross for a second; then, as the teapot crashed to the floor, she heaved the gigantic structure that her body seemed to have become, and, like a wrestler throwing off an opponent, she hurled him from her. This was the second time she had been prevented from hitting her father with a teapot.

She could see the room once more. The two strangers had gone, her father with them. Dan, too, had gone. She could hear his voice from the yard exclaiming angrily, 'You'll just have to find some place but not here. Can't you see?'

There were only May and John left in the kitchen, and Kathleen. Kathleen was crouched in the far corner of the room, fear written all over her. It was the sight of her daughter's fear that seemed to pierce the swelling in her body. She felt herself running down like a deflated balloon as it were, and when she was her normal size again she looked from one to the other, from Kathleen to May, and then to John, and for the first time in her life she hated him, hated him at this moment almost as much as his mother hated her. Groping her way to David's chair, she dropped on to it, and, turning her face into the corner, she began to cry, tearing, agonised crying that knew no end.

PART FIVE

CHAPTER ONE

They left the tennis hut, their shoes and rackets swinging from their hands. They walked down by the wall of the workhouse, down Talbot Road and into Stanhope Road, and they never stopped talking, first one and then the other.

Paul at nineteen was half a head taller than Kathleen. His hair was dark and his eyes brown and his overall expression intense, yet attractive. His body had remained thin; unlike his father, he had no bulk.

Kathleen, on the other hand, had bulk; her body was just a younger edition of her mother's. She was not quite as pretty perhaps as Sarah had been at her age, but happier looking, freer.

Kathleen turned her bright gaze up to Paul now as she said, 'Don't you feel furious about having to do your National Service first? Why don't you go and tell them that you'll do it after you finish at Oxford? Some people do. Renee Patten said her cousin did it.'

'Don't talk dizzy. Renee Patten!' Paul gave an exaggerated sigh, and, turning a solemn countenance towards her, raised his free hand, and in a voice of a bishop intoning a blessing, began, 'My dear child, I do not intend to try to penetrate your dim wits again. After attempting, and having failed on several occasions, to get the facts through your thick skull that my future hangs on a small matter of a small amount of money, small being a comparative word, I am dismayed . . . indeed I am dismayed, dear child . . .'

As she hit out at him with her racket he skipped aside into the road; then they came together again and went on down the street laughing.

'I know you've got to have money,' Kathleen began once more, stressing each word with deliberation. 'But I meant that if you were to put it to them they would give you the money to go up first and then you could do your National Service after.'

Again Paul sighed, another deep exaggerated sigh, and staring ahead, he said, as if reading from a letter now, 'My dear His Majesty's Forces. You know that I intend to serve you with all my brain and brawn for two years, and in return – I hope – you are going to feed me and fend for me during my stay in a certain celestial city. But would it be too much to ask if you would reverse the process and put off my sojourn with you until I have my fling in the said celestial city, while probing, of course, during the said fling, deeper into English Literature, so that after three years, when I gladly join you, a cross between a neologist and a paleographer – trusting by that time to have achieved this distinction – you will understand how much more valuable I will be to my brothers in the barracks should they ever be lost for words . . .'

Again Kathleen's racket swung out. 'You think you're clever, don't you? You're swanking all the time. Neologist! Paleographer! I hope when you get to the British Museum they'll stuff you.'

Paul threw his head back and laughed, and in this action he took on a semblance of John.

'Yes, you can laugh, but listen; it's funny, isn't it, about you going in for words all because of Dad.' Her face had a thoughtful look now.

'Yes, it is funny when you come to think about it. And funny isn't the correct word but we'll skip it on this occasion.' He glanced teasingly towards her. But his flippancy didn't bring her to attack him with her tongue or racket, and picking up her mood, he went on. 'No, I don't suppose I'd ever have thought about words if it hadn't been for Uncle. I remember the first time he told me all words were straight lines. I didn't believe him. Even when he showed me, I didn't believe him, I wanted to argue with him. I suppose it was this feeling that years later made me get that book on Chinese writing. I remember thrusting it under his nose with a triumphant feeling and saying, "Straighten those out, Uncle David." He did laugh.'

'It's three years ago,' said Kathleen softly, 'and I still miss him. He was lovely was me Dad.'

They were walking down the bank now towards the church, quiet for the first time since they had left the tennis court, and when they came to the foot of the steps Kathleen stopped and said, 'I'm going to pay a visit.'

'OK.' He turned with her and walked up the steps.

At the church door Kathleen stopped again and, looking at him, said, 'Do you think you'd better. Me Aunt May will go for you.'

'She's not to know.'

'Well, it's odd but she has ways of finding out. You remember what she said a while ago: she said she could smell the incense off you.'

'That was sheer imagination. Anyway, I've always come in with you and I'm not going to stop now. Come on.' He pushed her forward into the dim porch.

The church was cool after the reflected heat of the pavements. Kathleen led the way down the side aisle to the front pew opposite the Lady altar. This was the pew her mother had always sat in when she came to church as a young girl. She prayed daily that she would one day return to it. She genuflected deeply before she entered the pew, then knelt down and, bowing her head, covered her face unself-consciously with both hands.

Paul had not genuflected; nor did he kneel down, he just sat back on the seat and looked quietly about him. He had told himself a number of times that he didn't quite know what the attraction was about this place. It certainly wasn't the beautiful structure of the church, nor yet its interior decoration, for the stencils, to his mind, were horrible. Kathleen said the lads from the club usually did most of the decoration and everybody thought it was lovely; well, it certainly was a matter of opinion. Nor was he attracted by the statues, for they appeared crude to him, glaringly crude except perhaps the face of the Virgin, whose expression, he had the idea, seemed to change from time to time. No, he couldn't quite lay his finger on what drew him to this church. Was it because Kathleen loved it? Perhaps. He glanced towards her, her face still buried in her hands, and a feeling of exquisite tenderness flowed through him. She was lovely was Kathleen; everything about her was lovely, her face, her figure, her simplicity. She tried to be clever – he smiled inwardly – oh, she tried hard, but he hoped she would never be clever because it was that inbred simplicity and her uncluttered way of looking at things that he loved. She was like her mother in that way. His Aunt Sarah had the same qualities, an uncluttered way of thinking. But his Aunt Sarah never tried to be clever. She was one of those women who didn't need to be. He remembered his father saying that. He loved his Aunt Sarah, that's why he loved Kathleen, he supposed, because they were one. He would soon have to speak to his mother about Kathleen, and it wasn't going to be easy. She didn't like Kathleen, nor his Aunt Sarah. Why, he didn't really know. But then she liked so few people, so he supposed it wasn't so strange. But his father would welcome the idea of Kathleen as a daughter, for he thought the world of her. His mother had taunted him once by saying that his father thought more of Kathleen than he did of him, but it didn't matter; he was glad his father loved Kathleen . . . Yet he was getting away from the question uppermost in his mind, his attraction towards this church. Mr Rogers, his Sixth Form master, had had a pet theory. 'If you cannot control your thinking before you are twenty, then you'll never control it or anything else.'

He looked towards the High Altar. He liked the High Altar. Perhaps this was the main attraction, the High Altar, where, Kathleen had told him a long, long time ago, the priest brought Christ alive every day. He had laughed his head off about that at the time and teased the life out of her, and yet now, when he knew so much more, when for years he had been delving back into the strange history of language, where myths and magic were realities, he laughed no longer. But still he couldn't understand why, with his extended knowledge, the idea of a daily resurrection had become more credible to him. 'As the hart pants after the foundations of water so does my soul pant after thee.' He had read these words in Kathleen's Prayer

Book, and as they came to his mind now he felt strangely disturbed, as if he was being hurt by beauty.

Kathleen raised her head, blessed herself, then turned her face towards him and smiled. He rose to his feet and went out of the pew, and she followed him. He paused for a moment as she dipped her fingers into the holy water in the little font, then, watching her bless herself and genuflect again towards the main altar, he pushed open the door and let her pass out.

'Oh, wasn't it cool in there!' She drew in a deep breath, took a flying leap down the first flight of stairs, laughing over her shoulder at him as she cried, 'Oh, I always feel wonderful after I've been into church.'

He took the steps two at a time and caught up with her as she stepped on to the pavement, and they both bumped into Father Bailey.

'There you go, dunching into everybody.' The priest was steadying her, laughing down into her face.

'Oh, I'm sorry . . . I'm sorry, Father.'

'And so you should be, knocking poor old men over, going round wrecking joints.' He now stooped and stroked his knee.

'Wrecking joints?' They repeated the priest's slanging quip on high laughter.

'It's nothing to laugh about.' He wagged his finger at them. 'It's another joint I'm referring to . . . the tennis hut. Who broke the seat, eh? Who broke the back off the garden seat?'

'Oh, Father,' Kathleen put her hand across her mouth, and glanced at Paul. 'We were having a bit fun, a bit carry on.'

'A bit carry on!' He nodded at her with mock sternness. 'As far as I can gather there were ten of you having a bit carry on, and I want two shillings from each of you, understood?' He looked from one to the other, and Paul, nodding his head once, replied, 'Understood.' He did not say Father.

As he looked at the young boy the priest's expression changed, the smile which lifted his cheeks up into pouches under his eyes had a seriousness to it. 'I'm to congratulate you, Paul, I understand. Oxford? Now isn't that wonderful . . . a scholarship to Oxford! When do you go up?'

'Oh, not for some time, sir.' The sir came out naturally. 'I've got to do my National Service first.'

'When did you have your interview . . . I mean for Oxford?'

'Oh, before last Christmas.'

The priest nodded. 'You must have done well, you must have impressed them, indeed you must, to have got a scholarship.'

'Oh no, sir.' Paul's eyes narrowed and his mouth took on a humorous twist, and with a facetiousness of youth he went on, 'I was just dead lucky. The English tutor who took the interview happened to be a dialectologist, and, hearing my Geordie twang, he said, "By, lad, y'just watt Aa'm lukin' for. Aa can de aall the dialects but Aa get stumped wi' the Geordie. By, yo're a God-send, lad!"'

They were all laughing again, the priest heartily, and when Father Bailey laughed heartily the tears ran out of his eyes. 'Go on with you. Go on.' He pushed at Paul, then as he dried his eyes he exclaimed, 'Oh, I wonder if you're any good at languages . . . translating? Do you know any Spanish?'

'Spanish? No.' Paul shook his head. 'I'm sorry.'

Father Bailey drew a piece of paper from his inside pocket and, after looking at it, he handed it to Paul, saying, 'Well, take a look at that and see if you can make anything of it.'

Paul took the paper on which was written the following:

Si Senor, Derdago, Forte Lorez Inaro.
Demainte Lorez Demis Trux,
Foolacoos Andens Andux.

Slowly he read aloud, 'Si Senor, Derdago.' Then looking at the priest he said, 'No, sir, I can't make head or tail of it . . . sorry.'

The priest shook his head solemnly. 'Well, if you can't read that it's a poor lookout for you up at Oxford,' and taking the paper from Paul he pointed his finger to each word translating, as he went, by splitting up the words. And what he read was:

Si Senor, der dey go, forty lorries in a row.
Dem ain't lorries, dem is trucks, full of coos and hens and ducks.

Paul and Kathleen looked at each other, then at the priest, then together they let out a howl of laughter, and again the tears ran from the priest's eyes. 'I had you that time . . . the last one's on me.'

'Oh, Father, you old twister!' Kathleen was pointing at the priest, and Paul through his laughter was crying, 'You wait, sir, I'll have my own back on you.'

'Any time, any time.' The priest was moving away from them now, waving his hand at them. 'Goodbye, goodbye.'

'Goodbye, Father.'

'Goodbye.' They called together.

Then, half running, half walking, in their laughter and excitement they went past the station calling to each other as if yards apart, 'Dem ain't lorries, dem is trucks, full of coos and hens and ducks.'

'Isn't Father Bailey lovely?'

'He's all right.' Paul was non-committal, mainly to tease her.

'He's not all right, he's lovely.' She swung her racket at him again in an upward movement, and he caught her arm and they struggled together until of a sudden Kathleen became still, and her face, losing its merriment, she whispered hastily under her breath, 'Give over, there's me grandda behind.'

Letting go of her, Paul glanced casually back up the road, and there, walking as always with his hands in his pockets, was the little man who Kathleen called grandda. Whenever Paul saw this man he would remind himself that there was no blood relation between his Aunt Sarah and Pat Bradley, and he was glad, even relieved. He would have hated to think there was anything of this man in his Aunt Sarah, or Kathleen.

They walked on quickly now, sedately, a space and silence between them. Kathleen said quietly, 'He gives me the creeps.'

'Don't let him worry you.'

'He worries me mother. He's started coming round again. He hasn't been for months. He's been living with his cousins, but they've had a row and now he's in digs and he doesn't like them. He wants to come and live with us.' She glanced towards Paul. 'I think I would die if he lived with us. I couldn't bear him in the house. But, anyway, I needn't worry about that, for me mother can't stand the sight of him. She's warned him time and time again, but he still comes. There's some people think we should have him because we've got room. Betty Lawson said last term when we had a quarrel that everybody knew that my mother was hard because she wouldn't give her own father house room after the blitz that time. The quarrel was nothing to do with Mam or anything else, it was about netball, but she brought that up. So people think that Mam is hard. She isn't, is she?'

'Aunt Sarah, hard? Good Lord, no. She's too soft, if anything. Don't you take any notice. People only get half of the story, then they make up the other half. Aunt Sarah's got reason to hate his guts because he led her and your Aunt Phyllis a life of it when they were young. Dad told me all about it.'

Kathleen said now, 'Let's get the bus. I want to get home. He might catch up on us. Look! There's one coming in, we'll just make it.'

Simultaneously they began to run, and they caught the bus.

Fifteen minutes later, laughing again, they came up the backyard and burst into the kitchen on Sarah and Phyllis.

'Oh, hello, Aunt Phyllis.'

'Hello, Kathleen pet; been playing tennis?'

'Yes, Aunt Phyllis.' She threw her racket and shoes on to the armchair, and Sarah, turning from the table where she was rolling out pastry, said, 'Now get those off there, Kathleen. I've told you before.'

'OK, Mam. OK, Mam.' And picking up the racket and holding it at arm's length and dangling it from her fingers, she asked innocently, 'Where'll I put it, Mam?'

Sarah and Phyllis exchanged glances, and Sarah, trying to suppress a smile, said, 'Wherever you're going to put it you'd better get it there and quick!' She turned round sharply, her hand extended to give her daughter a wallop across the buttocks, but Kathleen, leaping past Paul and towards the scullery, cried, 'Save me! Save me!'

'Save yourself, you're big enough.' With manly indifference Paul sauntered to the hearth and, jerking his head at Phyllis, exclaimed in throaty tones, 'That's telling 'em.' Whereupon Phyllis let out a bellow of a laugh. Sarah too laughed, but as she trimmed the pastry from the edge of a large plate she said without looking at Paul, 'Your mother's been across, Paul. She wondered if you were back.'

'Oh.' The laughter slid from Paul's face and again he said, 'Oh,' then added, 'I'd better be getting over.'

'Where you going?' Kathleen was entering the kitchen again.

'Over home, of course . . . I have one, you know . . . a home.' He thrust his head down to her.

'I didn't say you hadn't, there's nobody arguing with you. I'll come over with you.'

Before Paul could make any reply Sarah put in quietly, 'No, Kathleen, I want you for a moment. Let Paul go over home.'

'But . . .'

'Never mind any buts. Go on, Paul.' She smiled at the boy, and Paul, returning her smile, said, 'Be seeing you.' He made a small swipe with his racket in Kathleen's direction then went out.

'What do you want me for, Mam?'

'Never you mind, that can wait. You haven't been in the house five minutes.'

'Do you want me to do something?'

'No, I just want you to stay put for five minutes.' She turned, and, looking down at her daughter, smiled at her. And Kathleen, as always, returned her smile, but pursing her mouth and grinning now, her expression saying, 'Anything to humour you.'

'Well, I must be off, Sarah.' Phyllis rose to her feet.

'Oh, wait a minute, I'll make a cup of tea before you go.'

'You'll not. I've had two lots of tea since I've been in. You'll drown me in tea. It's a wonder your stomach's not poisoned. How many times do you have it at work?'

'Oh, only twice. In the morning and afternoon break.'

'When are you going back?'

'Monday, I suppose, if he'll sign me off. It seems daft to catch a cold, weather like this, doesn't it? It's sweltering. But they're worse in the summer.'

'Will you be able to come down at the weekend?'

'Yes, I'll likely be at the market; I'll look in.'

'Bring Kathleen with you.' Phyllis looked towards her niece, and added quietly, 'You don't often look in on us. The lads love you to come. Young Dick said to me the other day, why weren't there any girls in our family, and I said to him the doctor thought I could look

177

after boys better; he said me hands are too hard for braying girls with.'

Kathleen just smiled at this quip, she did not laugh, and Phyllis, turning abruptly away, said, 'Here's me for the road. Bye-bye, Kathleen.'

'Bye-bye, Aunt Phyllis.'

Clapping her hands over the board, then drying the remainder of the flour from them on her apron, Sarah followed Phyllis into the passage.

When they reached the door they stood for a moment looking down into the street, and Phyllis said, 'She's bats about Paul, isn't she? How's it going to work out?'

'Oh, it'll take its course.'

'What if they want to get married?'

'I hope they will.'

'You do?'

'Yes, why not?'

The sisters looked at each other, and Phyllis, her head drooping, said, 'Nothing, I suppose. There's not so much pressure against cousins marrying the day.' Then, glancing quickly up, she asked, 'You really want them to?'

'Yes.' Sarah was now staring out into the street. 'It's about the only thing I do want.'

'Why don't you marry again?' Phyllis's voice was gentle. 'You could, you know. You're bonnier now than you were at twenty, being thinner, except for your bust . . . you're stuck with that.' Sarah pushed her and they both laughed. Then Phyllis ended, 'Well, you wouldn't have to go to the factory day in and day out if you did.'

'I prefer the factory.'

'Well, I suppose you know your own road best, like us all.' She paused here before asking, 'How long are you going to keep Kathleen at school?'

'As long as she can stay. She'll never reach Paul's standard. But that doesn't matter; the main thing for her is an education so there won't be so much difference between them.'

'You've got it all cut and dried, haven't you?' Phyllis was smiling her understanding smile. 'Well, that's how it should be. I wish I could do the same for even one of my four, but they haven't a pennorth of brains atween them, except for making money, that is, and Ronnie isn't bad on the piano.' She laughed. 'Oh, they'll make out all right, the money way. You'd think our Jimmy was seventy instead of seventeen. And do you know that it was him who discovered ice-cream?' She pushed her fist into Sarah's arm. 'Yes, ice-cream hadn't been heard of until our Jimmy struck it. Anyway' – her laughter was high now – 'he's making money out of it, so good luck to him.'

As Phyllis's loud laugh floated into the street Sarah glanced towards the door that was only a few yards from her own, and she made a warning sign to Phyllis, and Phyllis, clapping her hand over her mouth, drew her head into her shoulders. 'Sorry,' she whispered. Then, looking towards the other door, she asked, 'No sign of a thaw?'

Sarah shook her head. 'I don't want any thaw now.'

'It would drive me round the bend. Do you mean to say she still doesn't open her mouth to you?'

'Not a word, and when we pass in the street she could be blind, she doesn't even see me. But there it is.' Sarah gave a small smile. 'It doesn't matter, it doesn't matter any more. You know, I forget she's there. For days on end I forget she's there.'

'Does the old man still pop in?'

'Oh yes, once or twice a week, mostly at the weekend. And Kathleen goes in and out.'

'If she was mine I wouldn't let her darken the door. If they wouldn't have me they damn well wouldn't have her.'

'No, I would never stop her. After all, she's her grandmother.'

'Well, as I said, better you than me. I couldn't put up with it. I must be off . . . Well, see you at the Assizes.'

To this macabre but colloquial parting Sarah laughed and replied, 'Yes. See you at the Assizes.' Which saying they were to recall within a matter of hours. 'My love to the boys,' she added softly.

'I'll tell them. So long.'

Going back through the front room, Sarah thought, It's odd what Phyllis thinks she couldn't stand, and her standing the stigma of the Arabs for years and still keeping her flag flying . . . Phyllis was a good lass. Yes, she was indeed. And she had spunk. By, she had that!

'I'm not going down to Aunt Phyllis's on Saturday, Mam.' Kathleen was waiting for her when she entered the kitchen.

'All right, all right, there's nobody forcing you.' Sarah's tone was tart.

'Well, I can't help it, Mam; I've tried.'

Sarah was at the table again, her back to her daughter and, her voice quiet now, she said, 'I know you can't. We'll not go into it, it's all right.'

Kathleen sat down in what had been David's chair, and she bowed her head as she said, 'I like Aunt Phyllis, I do. She's nice, and she's a good sort . . . but the boys, and Ali . . . Well, somehow . . .'

Sarah turned from the board. 'It's all right, dear.' Her manner was soothing. 'I know how you feel, so don't worry. But all you've got to do is to remember that the boys can't help looking like Arabs and that they're nice boys, they are.'

'I know.' Kathleen was mumbling now. 'But it's since Iris Bannister got to know about it and she told the others. And just before the

179

holidays, just as recently as that, Peggy Crofton, the sneaky little cat, came up to me and said, "It isn't true, is it, that your auntie lives among the Arabs?" I could have smacked her face. I nearly did.'

'Coloured folk are marrying white folk all the time now and it's only ignorant people who make something out of it. You've got to look at it like that. And those girls ought to be ashamed of themselves. And them with their education an' all.'

'Education!' Kathleen sniffed. 'Iris Bannister lives in Westhoe village. Their house – I've seen it – it's not much bigger than this, but because she lives in Westhoe she thinks she's the last word, and she's always telling you about the private school she went to before she came to the High School. Betty Chalmers says it was a potty little place, just a house run by two people, old maids, who hadn't even been teachers, but of course they were very . . . very refeened, and they talked like this.' Kathleen screwed up her nose and lifted her upper lip into a point showing two large white front teeth, and as her mother burst out laughing her face fell into its natural lines again, and she too laughed as she said, 'Betty Chalmers can do it wonderfully, she'd make you scream.'

'Oh, dear, dear.' Sarah, still laughing, shook her head at the tragedies of youth, but when Kathleen, rising from the chair, said, 'I think I'll go across to my Aunt May's for a bit,' Sarah stopped laughing and answered quickly, 'No, I wouldn't. Your Aunt May doesn't see much of Paul and you know he'll be gone soon.'

'Well, that's why . . .'

'But you must think of your Aunt May, Kathleen . . . Oh' – Sarah tapped her brow with the knuckle of her thumb – 'I forgot to tell you. Lorna MacKay called in this morning. She wanted you to go and hear her new record.'

'Oh, bust.'

'But I thought you liked Lorna?'

'I do, I do, but then Michael will likely be in.'

Sarah smiled. 'You used to like Michael, too, at one time.'

'Yes . . . well, I suppose I did. He's all right but he's always asking me to go out now, to the pictures and places.'

'Well, you go to the pictures with Paul, don't you?'

'Yes, I know, but that's different. But that's what he said too: I went to the pictures with Paul.'

'And what did you say to that?' Sarah was smiling quietly as she worked away at the table.

'Oh, I said . . . well . . .' Kathleen paused and gave a hick of a laugh. 'Well, I said, you let me go with Paul because he was my cousin, but you thought I wasn't old enough to go out with him.' Her voice became smothered with suppressed laughter.

'You little monkey!' Sarah was looking at her daughter, her eyes bright. 'Anyway, I would go up and see Lorna.' It was an order put gently over.

'Oh, all right. It'll be an educational afternoon,' she sighed, 'interposed with a running commentary on . . . our Michael.' Here she mimicked Lorna's voice and attitude. 'Our Michael's earning sixteen pounds a week and him only nineteen, and when he gets to the coal face he can make over twenty pounds a week, he can.' She waggled her plump, adolescent body, and Sarah said, 'Now don't be catty.'

'Well, she's always on about the money their Michael's making. Always getting a dig in that Paul won't be making any for years. She even said that her mother said that Paul would be twenty-three before he earned a penny.'

'Did she now?'

'Yes, she did.'

'Well, Paul has got something money can't buy, you tell her that.'

'I have; and I really don't believe that Michael makes sixteen pounds a week, do you?'

'Oh yes, they can make that at the pits now doing overtime. And I shouldn't be surprised that he reaches twenty when he gets to the face. Coal is like gold now. And long may it last for them, they've had it rough long enough.'

'I'd hate to marry a pitman.' Kathleen was sauntering to the door as Sarah said, 'Well, don't.'

'I won't.' And once again they looked at each other and once again they laughed.

'I won't stay long,' said Kathleen.

'There's no need to hurry. If Paul comes over I'll come up and knock for you.'

'You will?' Kathleen's face brightened. 'OK. Bye-bye.'

'Bye-bye, my dear.'

Paul, Paul, Paul; Paul all the time, waking and sleeping. Would she change? She was only sixteen, she might. But no, Sarah shook her head at the thought. She was held fast. Although Paul did not look like his father, there emanated from him the same virile attraction. No, Kathleen wouldn't change. She prayed to God she wouldn't, anyway, because if she did, well then . . . Sarah's hands became quiet on the board and she looked at the wall opposite. All her efforts, all her self-denial, all her trying to do the right thing would have been in vain, wouldn't it? Still staring at the wall, she saw there the day of her choice. It happened six months ago in this very kitchen. John had been out of the Air Force for eighteen months then and was doing well in his wireless business. That's how he had started, talking about the shop. 'I'm on to something here, Sarah,' he had said. 'You'd never believe the money that's in it.

Joe's opening another shop in Wallsend and I'm going to keep on with the Newcastle one and see to the workshops. And if we can get a likely enough fellow we'll open one down here in Shields. Everybody is wireless mad. And you know another thing that's going to boom . . . television. I bet you a shilling before ten years is out everybody'll have a television in their own house.'

'Television? Just what is television?'

'The pictures, that's what it is, the pictures.'

'And in your own house?' She had laughed as one would at a tall story.

He had shaken his head solemnly at her. 'It's a fact, Sarah. Fellows have been working on this long before the War and now they're getting pictures from London. I'm telling you, it's no fairy-tale. And we're in on the ground floor, Joe and me.' He had looked away from her at this point and said, 'That's one good thing that came out of the Air Force anyway, Joe and me stuck in that godforsaken hole planning what we'd do together after the War. Joe was to do the talking and the buying, and I was to do the making, wirelesses and that, and see to the production end. And that's how it has worked out. When I think of those years on the dole . . . years . . . my God, it was an eternity! I can't believe this is really happening to us . . . I've bought a car, Sarah.'

'A car?' Her eyes screwed up at him.

'Yes, a dandy. I got it as a snip. It's second-hand, but it was lying up all through the War. A nineteen thirty-eight Rover, a beautiful job, like a Rolls-Royce, it is, honest.'

'Oh, John.' She had looked at him softly and smiled. She was pleased for him. Success would ease the turbulence in him, part of it at any rate.

He had said, then 'I made plans at the end of the War, Sarah, not only with Joe, with meself. I said, I'll make money, real money, and then I'll buy me out, so to speak, and I'll do what I've longed to do for years.'

Her body had become stiff, rigid, but she had remained silent as he went on, 'I've had enough, a bellyful if anyone has. I'm not God's gift to woman, I know. Oh, I know, nobody better, but that's over. I've got money now and I'll have a hell of a lot more before I've finished. But I'm determined on one thing . . . May's not going to wallow in it. No, by God, I'll see to that. I'd rather give it to all the whores in the town.'

She had exclaimed aloud at this and he had cut in abruptly saying, 'You don't know what it's been like, Sarah. She's me mother all over, only in a different way. A damned sight worse if you ask me. No, I've made up me mind.'

She had said at this point, in a voice she could scarcely hear herself, 'Aren't you forgetting about Paul?'

'No, I'm not!' he had barked back at her. 'Paul will know where he's going in a few months' time. He'll have to do his National Service, anyway, and once he leaves the house he'll be on his own and my life sentence'll be finished.'

She had looked at him then and stated flatly, 'Paul is in love with Kathleen and she with him.'

His mouth had dropped open and he had gaped at her; for a full minute he had gaped at her before he said, 'But they're just kids; they've been brought up together.'

'It's more than that, at least I think so. Anyway, I'll have to wait and see.'

He had taken a step towards her, crying, 'Look, Sarah!' but with her outstretched hand she had stopped him. She had not touched him, she had just put her arm out towards him, her hand raised vertically.

'I'm waiting,' she said. 'Kathleen is the only thing that matters to me, you've got to know that.'

'I do know it, but I'm willing to take a chance, I'm willing to take what's left.'

She had her head bowed on her chest when she murmured, 'There's time enough for that.'

Again he looked at her for a long, long moment, and then characteristically he spoke the truth. 'There might be for you, but not for me. I'm at the end of my tether, Sarah. I'm made that way . . . There's got to be somebody . . . For years and years I've wanted it to be you.'

'I cannot help you,' she said. Her head was still lowered.

At this he had turned and walked out. It had all been comparatively quiet and orderly, the arranging of their future lives.

Sarah brought her attention back to the table. She gathered the scraps of pastry up, pressed them together, then rolled them out. As she lined an oven plate she saw Dan come in from the back lane and her face brightened.

When he entered the kitchen he sniffed, saying, 'Coo! That smells good. What is it?'

'Oh, just odds and ends; they're always hungry.'

'They are? You mean Paul. If you were to be paid for all the food he's eaten here you'd have a tidy sum.'

'Oh, that.' She gave an impatient toss of her head. 'I've got to bake, anyway. She can tuck it away like a young horse an' all.'

'By! It's hot.'

'I'll make you a cup of tea.'

'No, no, I won't be staying a minute.' Yet as he spoke he sat down by the side of the table.

Sarah looked at him. 'But it's Wednesday; you're off, aren't you?'

'The shop's closed.' He nodded at her. 'I'm off that far, but I'm going up again; the old lady wants some rooms turned round.'

He bounced his head. 'She's got an idea, and she's working on it. She thinks I can't see it . . . She wants me to go and live up there.'

'Really!'

'Aye. She's lonely since the old man went. I've known this has been coming for some time, and' – he wagged his finger at Sarah – 'it wouldn't be a bad thing, it wouldn't at that, for she's a dear old soul. I'm more than a bit fond of her, and, as she says, the place'll be mine some time . . . You know.' He rested his elbow on the table and pushed against a glass bottle lying on its side, and Sarah exclaimed quickly, 'Look, you'll get flour all over you.' As she lifted the bottle out of his way, he said, 'That's a cute idea, using a bottle for a rolling-pin. Where'd you find that?'

'Oh, in a magazine. It works an' all. You fill it with cold water and it helps to keep the pastry firm.'

'Well, well, I wonder what next. But as I was saying. You know, Sarah, there's kind people in the world, and those two have been pure gold to me, and not a drop of blood between us. Strangers can be kinder than your own, don't you think?' He did not wait for her to comment on this but went on, 'I did meself a good turn the day I put that four hundred into the business; they've paid me back a thousand-fold . . . Well, not quite,' he laughed. 'But you know what I mean. And now this changing round of rooms. There's six of them, you know, fine big ones at that, and well furnished. Oh, aye, they've got some nice pieces, and she's been on about making two flats of it for some time now. She keeps saying two people could live here amicably and not get in each other's hair . . . Poor old soul! I've known what she's been driving at, but I've never let on. You see, it's going to be difficult, I mean leaving next door.'

'Yes.' Sarah nodded down at him. 'That is going to be difficult. I don't think you should do it, Dan; she would be lonely without you.'

Dan stared at her for a moment before saying, 'You know, you're a remarkable woman, Sarah. I've always thought that.'

'Oh, don't make game, Dan. Remarkable, huh! I know just how remarkable I am.' She was nodding her head slowly at him.

'I'm not making game, not on this matter, I'm not. I know what I think. Here you are trying to persuade me not to leave her because you think she would be lonely. She's got Stan, she's got John and May across the way, she's got two grandchildren, and you say she'll be lonely. After the way she's treated you, you can still feel sorry for her.'

'She's not a happy woman . . . inside. That's what I mean. And unhappy people are lonely. We are all lonely in a way, but unhappy people are more lonely.'

'Yes, I suppose you're right there. But there's another thing against it, but I suppose you wouldn't notice. I wouldn't be able to pop in here every day.'

'Oh, I'd notice that all right, Dan.' She stood with her hands resting on the table, her body leaning towards him. 'I just don't know what I would have done without you, Dan. I've . . . I've never said this before, but I think that at the beginning I would have gone clean off my head, really off my head, if it hadn't been for you. Oh, I know what it would be like if you stopped popping in.'

Dan stared at her, his eyes holding no vestige of humour now. Then, pushing his fingers through his thick greying hair, he rose abruptly and went towards the fireplace and stood looking down into the empty grate. And Sarah stood by the table, her hands moving nervously and without purpose until he said, 'Have you talked to John lately?'

'John?' The name said like that jerked her into stiffness and she twisted her head over her shoulder and looked towards his back. And again she said, 'John?'

'There's going to be a bust-up there and it's a pity. He should let the lad get settled first. Although in a way I don't blame him, he's had it rough since he came back. It was bad enough before the War.'

She watched him turn slowly towards her now and he held her gaze when he spoke, 'He's going to leave May.'

There was a pressure in her throat as if from the point of a bone; the feeling would not allow her to swallow. Yet this was not news to her, she had known it was going to happen.

She heard him say, 'What are you going to do, Sarah?'

'Me? . . . Me?' She moved her head from side to side in one wide startled sweep. 'Nothing, nothing. Why . . . why should I?' She sounded indignant. But she could not keep her eyes on his and her lids dropped over them; then her head moved downwards. She felt him coming towards her, and when he was near he said, 'I'm glad of that, Sarah, I'm glad. I'll tell the old lady that I won't be moving up there, at least not for the present. I'll be going now. So long, Sarah.'

'So long, Dan.'

She waited for him to move, and when he didn't she looked up. She looked into the kindly face of this man – this man who had about him the gentleness of David and the virility of John. It was a strange attractive combination, seeing that he was also the brother of her mother-in-law. When he put out his hand and touched her cheek gently it was as if David had come alive. He turned from her and went out.

As Sarah watched him go down the backyard, pausing to turn off the dripping tap before going into the back lane, she did not think of him, nor yet of John, nor yet of David, but she thought of the woman next door who was mother and sister to these three men, and the words she had once spoken resounded loudly through the kitchen: 'You have taken my menfolk.'

Her head drooped again and she supported her brow with the palm of her hand. Then, blinking rapidly, she said to herself, 'I'll make a cup of tea before I clear.'

As she sat drinking her tea she thought of what the years had done to her, of what loving a number of people had done to her. She had loved David . . . Oh, yes, she had. But she had passioned for John. Without loving him she had wanted him. She realised that. During the first month of her marriage her body had in a way become a university for her natural desire, but she had learned so quickly in this direction that her tutor was left far behind on a plane from which he had not the power to propel himself. David was not ruthless enough, not brutal enough, not selfish enough. John in this particular field would have been all three.

She pulled at the neck of her blouse to give herself air. She felt as if she was going to suffocate, the room was stifling. She rose and went to the window and pushed it further upwards, and as she did so there walked in through the back door the thin wizened figure of her father. He saw her almost at the same moment as she caught sight of him, and to prevent the door being locked in his face he sprinted up the yard.

Breathing heavily, Sarah turned to the table. It was no good rushing into the scullery, he'd be in by now. The next moment his voice came from behind her, not placating as it was once, but surly. 'You would have shut me out, wouldn't you?'

She did not answer him for a moment, and then she said in a voice so unlike her own that it was impossible to imagine herself speaking, 'I've told you not to come here. Can't you take a telling?' But she knew that she became an entirely different being when confronted with this man.

'Aa've got no place else to go, Aa've been turned out.'

'It isn't the first time, you can find other lodgings.'

'Aa can't, not on my money; only place is a hovel.'

'It's of no interest to me where you stay, I've told you before. Now get out.' She still had her back towards him.

'Folks is talkin'. You with a room goin' beggin' and me on the street. You'd see me in the workhouse.'

'Yes, I would.'

'Well, you won't then, I'm comin' here.'

She turned towards him now, her eyes wide. 'You're what? You'll come here over my dead body. You've blackmailed me for years, but now, as I told you before, the only one I was afraid of you hurting has gone. And you can say what you damn well like now, it makes no difference. Go on, get on with it; shout about all you think you know.'

'You're speaking out of turn, you should think a bit afore you open your mouth so wide.' He was speaking slowly, quietly.

She narrowed her eyes at him. She couldn't follow him. What did he mean? What was he alluding to? He had got something else into that warped, twisted mind of his. 'What are you up to now?' she said from between her teeth.

He peered at her through his bleary eyes. There was a trickle of saliva running from one corner of his mouth. He asked again, 'Aa y' goin' to give me that room? You'll be sorry if y' don't, mind. Aa'm tellin' you, you'll be sorry.'

'Get out!' she took a step from the table, a threatening step, but he did not move.

'Y' could handle me if y' liked. It would be worth your while, Aa'm tellin' you.'

'Get out!'

'Aye, aall right then. If y' want it that way, Aa will. An' Aa'll find those two an' tell 'em.'

Her face screwed up. 'Those two? What two? Who you talking about?'

'The bairns.'

'The bairns?' she repeated.

'Aye, that's what Aa said, the bairns. Do Aa need t' name 'em. Aa'll tell 'em they'd better go careful.'

Her face was slowly stretching. She mouthed the word 'careful', but without a sound.

'They were carrying on together down the station bank, rolling about; they're ready to jump into bed any minute, and they can't, can they?' He stared into her wild, startled face. 'Y' mustn't let that happen, must you? It'd be unnatural, wouldn't it? After you given' 'em the same faather an' all . . . Well, didn't you? She was born practically nine months to the minute from one o'clock on that New Year's morning on the waste land, where you and the big fellow were neckin'. An' that's putting it mildly, isn't it? If there'd been nowt in it, do you think you'd have paid up all these years . . . You had somethin' to hide all right, an' y' still have.'

Once before she had experienced the feeling of her body swelling to explosive point; the feeling was with her again only more intense, more terrible. She felt her rage lift her off her feet. She swung round to the table and grabbed up the first thing that came to hand, which was the rolling-pin bottle filled with water, and she hurled it at him. As he turned his face from the onslaught it caught him full on the temple and he dropped like a stone.

She was standing, her back to the table, hanging on to its edge. She was aware that someone was in the yard, but she didn't know who; her body was still swelling, her head seemed to fill the room. She could feel her eyes stretching to snapping point as she watched

187

the blood flow over the lino. The bigger her body grew, the quieter she became inside, it was as if she was being carried away into a great silence. Even when she saw May burst into the room with Paul by her side she made no sound. She watched May kneeling on the floor, she saw her raise his head up, then put her hand inside his waistcoat. May looked more human in this moment than she had ever seen her before. 'He's dead,' she said.

Sarah knew he was dead. She knew as soon as the bottle had hit him that he had died. She was glad he was dead. Oh, she was glad he was dead. He could never hurt or terrify her again. He could never hurt anyone again. He could never hurt Kathleen now . . . that was the important thing, he could never hurt Kathleen. Kathleen was safe, safe, safe. And Paul too; yes, Paul was safe too. They were both safe.

CHAPTER TWO

Time was only in the mind. David had said that. He had read it some place. He had said how true it was . . . Time was only in the mind. She herself knew how true it was now, for time had almost ceased to exist for her. Soon she knew that time, as the mind knew it, would end altogether, but it wasn't worrying her. Her mind had rejected time as it had all other things. If it thought about anything clearly it was that it wished . . . it . . . was all over. She wasn't afraid of the end; she had even said so to the priest. At times her mind came back into the present sufficiently to answer questions if it considered they needed answering. When the priest spoke to her of God she almost laughed; the thought of God was ludicrous to her now, really funny. When her mind was on this other plane she was amazed at the credulity of all the people who believed in this thing called God, this thing that had become an . . . it, to her. Her mind admitted to this 'it' being alive, yet at the same time she saw it as inanimate because it was without feeling for the human being. She felt a malicious desire now to bring her thoughts from this far-away plane and hurl them at the priest, hurl 'it' at the priest. But the priest was Father Bailey, and he was kind was Father Bailey. But he kept repeating one thing to her, trying to drag an answer from her, a response. 'You've got to tell them, Sarah,' he kept saying. 'And today. It'll be your last chance. Tell them that he blackmailed you for years. Tell them. Do you hear me, Sarah? Sarah.'

She bowed her head before his pitying gaze. He could no nothing. Being a priest, his tongue was tied. And she would do nothing, because if she opened her mouth she could only tell them half the truth. She could say: My father blackmailed me because he thought I had been with John and I hadn't. But would they believe her? No. No. They would say, those clever ones in the court, they would say, Then why did you pay him to keep silent? And then it would become complicated. She couldn't begin to tell them why at first she paid him to keep silent, it was all too far in the past. Even if she could explain it would bear no weight. She alone knew the thing that would bear weight. Her father had known it and now he was dead. He was dead because he had created it . . . this thing, this thing that she alone knew now and must hide. And it was a lie this thing, the biggest lie of the lot, but nevertheless she must hide it because if she once showed it the light everyone would believe it. There was never smoke without fire, they would say. Yes, yes, that's why she had paid up all the years, they would say. Then they would look at Kathleen and Paul and remember they had been inseparable since they were babies. They would remember that John loved Kathleen like a father . . . But, she needn't worry, they wouldn't remember, for they wouldn't hear the lie spoken, the lie that would help her to live. It would die with her. Kathleen would be safe.

The priest went away and the warders came, two of them. One of them had a nice face, she had a kind voice too. She was about Sarah's own age and she took Sarah's hand and patted it before they mounted the steps. But when she sat down beside Sarah her face looked cold and remote . . .

Sarah looked around the court-room, her head moving slowly as if with an effort. There was Phyllis, her face filled with two great compassion-filled eyes. Dear Phyllis. And next to her was Ali and Jimmy . . . They were nice, Ali and Jimmy.

There was Dan, his eyes waiting for her. Something in her stretched out towards him and said, Don't cry any more; don't cry any more, Dan. And next to him was Kathleen, her face like paste, and her eyes like great dark pools, pools full of pity. The thing inside her stretched out to Kathleen, it leaped to Kathleen and said, 'Oh, my dear, my dear! Don't worry, you'll be all right.' And then there was Paul. Paul's head was down and he was not looking at her, he never looked at her. A voice from the far-away plane cried out to Paul, 'Look at me, Paul, I'm not bad. Please look at me.' But Paul refused to look at her. Next to Paul sat May, and May was looking at her. But what was May thinking? No-one ever knew what May was thinking. There was a man sitting next to May but Sarah did not look at him, or say his name to herself, for it was because of him, because he had been born, because the desire of his body was the ruling power in his life, that she was sitting here now . . . I'll see you at the Assizes . . . I'll see you at the Assizes.

Her mind slipped away on to the distant plane again, and from it she heard faintly the voice of the prosecuting counsel, the man who seemed to hate her. He talked as if he had known her from birth and as if she had never done a decent thing in her life. Why was he talking about her like that? He also seemed to hate the nice man who was defending her. He said nasty things to him, spiteful, sarcastic things, and they always referred to her. Her counsel was now speaking to the judge, asking to bring forward another witness. Time passed and then she was looking at a man in the box. She couldn't remember ever having seen him in her life. Of course that was natural because he had just said he lived in Wallsend and she didn't know anybody in Wallsend. He said his name was James Ballast and that his brother had once beaten up the deceased man.

'Why did your brother beat up the deceased man?' asked the nice man.

Because the deceased was always spying on courting couples, the man said. He had been spying on his brother, and his brother laid a trap for him, then beat him up.

'Where is your brother now?' asked the nice man.

'He's dead,' said the man in the box. 'He died in the War.'

The cool voice from the high bench cut through the examination, saying, 'What is all this? This has no bearing on the case at all.'

'I'm just trying to show, my lord,' said the nice man, 'what kind of man the deceased was.'

'We are not here to deal with the dead man's character,' said the cool voice. 'We are here to prove or disprove murder. Why have you raked up such a witness?'

'The man offered himself as a witness, me Lord. He thought he could help the accused.'

'And apparently you did too?'

'Yes, me Lord.'

People were kind. It was as Dan always kept saying, people were kind . . . all except the prosecuting counsel. He was standing in front of the jury now, telling them how bad she was. He even remembered to tell them about the day after the big raid when she wouldn't give her father shelter and had screamed at him and had gone to throw something at him.

People had long memories, May had a long memory. It was she who had told them that bit when she was asked if she had ever seen her raise her hand to her father before. May had a lot in common with the prosecuting counsel.

Then the nice man was talking to the jury. He was telling them what she had gone through in her childhood, how she had feared the deceased, how he had beaten her and her sister . . . Phyllis had told them all about that, and Phyllis had been fearless. Phyllis wasn't frightened of anybody. She had said to them, 'I always wanted to kill him and many a time I said I would, and I would if I'd got the chance.' The judge had told her to stop talking, and when she wouldn't he had warned her she would be put out of the court. He had warned her twice because she was always jumping up and down in her seat.

Now the jury filed out of the benches and went into a room and the warders took her downstairs and the kind one squeezed her shoulder, but she said nothing. They wanted her to eat and drink, but all she wanted was a cup of tea. And then it didn't taste like tea, not her kind of tea.

She sat staring ahead, waiting, her hands joined in her lap. Time passed. She supposed it was hours, she didn't know. Everybody seemed restless. The policeman came and spoke to her; even the stiff-looking ones spoke nicely. Then they went and talked in the passage outside. She heard a voice say, 'Well, he didn't find her insane, did he? And he examined her long enough. She's just withdrawn herself. They do, you know. She'll likely be like that until near the end . . . if there's an end.' 'Ssh!' said somebody else. 'Ssh!' and the voice answered, 'It's all right, she doesn't take it in.'

And then of a sudden they took her upstairs, and there they all were in their places as if there had been no long interval. And one man from the benches stood up and the judge asked him a question, and he said, 'We have found the prisoner guilty of manslaughter, my lord. Because we are agreed that there was no premeditation to kill.'

Her mind began to race now, flying away to reach the plane, the safe plane, where the voice of the judge couldn't follow, but even when she reached it she couldn't shut the voice out. Two sentences came floating to her. One was, 'The jury have agreed your act was unpremeditated.' But for some reason she got the impression that he didn't agree with the jury's verdict. The second sentence was: 'Nevertheless you have killed a man and been found guilty of manslaughter; therefore I sentence you to prison for fifteen years.'

Her mind was shot from the plane and into her head again. She wasn't to die, she wasn't going to die. She was surprised, amazed. Then her mind whimpered, but fifteen years! Fifteen years! Then she heard Phyllis screaming: 'It's monstrous! Cruel! He should've been dead years ago, the swine! I wish I had done it myself, I tell you. Oh, my God! Sarah, Sarah! Fifteen years! God Almighty!' Phyllis's voice trailed away as they pulled her from the court.

Just before she was led downstairs she glanced towards her family. They were all standing as if petrified, looking at her, all with the exception of John. Perhaps it was because he was not looking at her that her eyes went involuntarily to him. His head was bowed deep and his face was covered with his hands.

CHAPTER THREE

The day was dull, the world was dull. Everything was crazy; he was crazy. At times he thought he was going stark staring mad. Everybody had changed since the trial; everybody and everything had changed . . . But some of them had changed before the trial. Paul had. What was up with the lad? Just look how he was treating Kathleen.

In three rapid strides John was at the window looking down into the yard seeing Kathleen going through the back door and across the lane into her own backyard. Because it was still her own backyard, she had refused to budge. But she was no longer a young girl skipping and gay; she had grown up overnight, as it were, and the transition had left her dazed. She wanted help, comfort, and the one who could give her the most comfort was turning his back on her. Why? Why? Well, he would find out; he would have something to say to that young squirt, he would that.

As he turned from the window about to stalk from the room, Paul entered, and John stood aside and let him reach the fireplace before he started: 'Look, what's the matter with you these days? We've all had a shock, but the one that's troubled most is Kathleen and she needs your help. And what have you done? You've kept clear of her for weeks as if she's got the mange. I don't like it.' John's face screwed up, his lips leaving his teeth. 'I don't like the trait in your character that makes you shy off when you're most needed. Even if your Aunt Sarah has done something wrong, and that's a matter of opinion, you cannot hold Kathleen accountable for it. But that's what you're doing. Every time she walks in the door you go out. Now look here, let's get this straight.'

'I want to talk to you.' Paul's voice was quiet, cold and quiet.

'Then talk. Fire ahead.'

John looked at his son and waited, and when he did not begin he said brusquely, 'What's holding you up? I thought you wanted to . . . ?'

'I'm going to become a priest.'

The silence in the room was like sound amplified; it penetrated through the cries of the children outside in the back lane, through a man calling a boy's name, through the high cry of a baby.

'Say that again.' John's tone sounded ordinary.

'You heard what I said.'

'Aye . . . aye, I thought I did. I thought you said, "I'm going to become a priest." That's what I thought you said.'

'And that is what I said.'

192

John pulled his chin into his neck, pushing out the flesh that looked tough and thick like a reddy-brown hide. 'You're going to become . . . ? Look, lad, have you gone barmy?'

'No.'

'But you said a priest . . . not a minister, or a curate, but a priest?'

'That's what I said.'

'A Catholic priest?'

'A Catholic priest.'

'You trying to make me do something – hit you, knock you out or something?'

'It won't make any difference what you do.'

'It won't, eh? Get out.' John swung his arm in a half-circle motion indicating the door, but as Paul turned towards it he sprang across the room barring his way, crying, 'No begod! What am I saying? You'll not get out of here until I hear you talk sense . . . Priest! You're going to become a priest . . . Over my bloody dead body you will. Now sit down.' He pointed to a chair. 'Sit down and let's hear what all this is about.'

The boy moved with seeming quietness towards the chair and sat on its edge and waited; and John, towering over him, demanded, 'Well now, get going. Since when have you had the idea you're going to be a priest?' His voice was sneering.

Paul turned his white face up to his father's. 'Since the day my Aunt Sarah killed her father.'

The answer nonplussed John and it brought his shoulders back and his head up. It brought the lids of his eyes together, and he asked, puzzled, 'But what has that to do with this business? There's no connection that I can see.'

'You can't?'

'No, I can't.'

'I happened to hear what her father said before she hit him.'

'But you said . . . you said you didn't hear anything. You told them in court . . . only a babble of voices, you said.'

'I know what I told them.' Paul now thrust out his arm as if pushing his father aside, and, getting to his feet, he moved a few steps backwards, putting distance between them before he spoke again. 'The old man said Kathleen and I were acting like a courting couple and we shouldn't because . . . because you had fathered us both.'

The telling silence took over again until John whispered, 'I had what?' He brought his hand up to his chin, the forefinger pressing below his lower lip, and as if coming out of a daze he repeated, 'I had what? God Almighty!' With a movement of his leg he flicked the chair across the room, and as it crashed against the fender he cried, 'He said that? Well, let me tell you, son, and I'm swearing it on God's oath, it's a bloody lie . . . a bloody lie. Do you hear?' His voice was high now.

'Yes, I hear, but I also heard the old man remind my Aunt Sarah of the night Kathleen had been conceived. It was on New Year's morning nineteen and thirty on the waste ground . . . Kathleen's birthday is on the fourth of October.'

John stood as if someone had hit him a resounding blow, a blow that should have felled him to the ground. He swayed slightly, his hand moving now round his face, his eyes blinking; he had difficulty in speaking and when he did his voice had a note of pleading in it. 'Paul . . . listen, Paul boy. It's not true. Your Aunt Sarah and I did stand round there that night, and we talked. We talked because . . . Oh, my God! What does it matter now? I loved your Aunt Sarah, but nothing . . . ever . . . happened between us. You've got to believe me. Your Aunt Sarah's a good woman.'

'If nothing happened, then why did she let her father blackmail her all these years?'

'Blackmail her?' The word sprung John's brows upwards. 'What are you saying? Have you gone barmy?'

'No, I've not gone barmy, and you know I haven't. She'd been paying him money for years to keep quiet about that night.'

'Christ alive!' Slowly John turned his gaze from his son and going towards the fallen chair he picked it up, and when it was righted he sat down, gripping the seat with his hands as if to support himself. His mind in a blinding turmoil, he was seeing a picture which covered the years; Sarah's nerves, her tenseness, her terror of being left alone with him. Aye, she had been terrified, and with what reason! God Almighty! . . . God Almighty! 'Paul.' He put out a shaking hand towards his son, and his lips moved, trying to form the words that would establish his innocence in the boy's mind, but they were ineffective when they came. His tone held no conviction, he was too dazed to be convincing. 'There was nothing, Paul, nothing, nothing, between your Aunt Sarah and me. That swine of a man must have heard us talking that night and held it over her. She loved your Uncle Davie. There was only one person for her, she could see nobody but your Uncle Davie. It was likely because she didn't want trouble, and didn't want to hurt him, that she paid up. But, my God . . . !' His hands dropped to his side. 'My God! What she must have gone through.' Now his voice roughened and strengthened. 'You should have spoken up and told them, it would have helped her.'

'Would it? Would it have helped if they had thought she was carrying on with you and that you were Kathleen's father? Would it have helped her?' Paul's voice was accusing.

John shook his head. 'No. I suppose you're right. But, Paul . . .' He leant well forward from the chair. 'You've got to believe me, and you've got to make things right between you and Kathleen.'

Paul moved to the side of the table and he looked down at it before he said, 'That's over. We were like brother and sister, anyway. We were brought up too close.'

'But you're not brother and sister, or half-brother and sister. You could get married.'

'No.' The boy's voice was so harsh it could have been John himself speaking. The tables seemed to be turned; it was the boy who had the strength and John who was the weaker in this moment. 'I'm going through with this. I know now it was what I wanted to do all along. I was always attracted to the Catholic Church.'

'Oh, my God! Don't talk, boy, don't talk.' John's head was bowed forward, his hands supporting his brow.

'I've got to talk, and now. In six days' time I'll be in the Army . . . I've been taking a form of instruction from Father Bailey, a very preliminary form. He has told me of all the obstacles that are in my way, so you won't be the only one who will try to put a spoke into the wheel. I've got to convince them that I'm serious. I've got to see the Bishop, Bishop McCormack, and Father Bailey wouldn't make the appointment until I'd told you everything.'

'That's bloody kind of him.' John was rearing now. 'I'll have something to say to this Father Bailey, and one thing will be that you can't do a damn thing about it. I've got the idea that you're under my jurisdiction until you're twenty-one.'

'I know all about that, we've gone into that. You can get a Court Order to prevent me from becoming a priest. You can also prevent me turning a Catholic while I'm a minor, but I'll be twenty-one before I come out of the Army, and until then you or no-one else can stop me reading and learning. I'll be getting myself ready . . .'

'For Christ's sake! Shut up, will you! Be quiet, before I do something to you . . . And' – he paused – 'where does the university come in in all this?'

'I won't be going to Oxford. I can take my degrees while I'm studying. I'll likely go to Ushaw College near Durham.'

John bounced to his feet. He still looked dazed, but he sounded more like himself when he cried, 'Ushaw College, be buggered! I'll see you in hell first before I'll let you go through with this. You're mad. This business has turned your brain. As for those bloody cunning priests, wait till I get my tongue round them . . . and my hands.' He doubled his fist and shook it towards Paul. 'You know something? I'd rather see you dead than let you go through with this. Now get out.' He turned his back on his son and looked into the fire, and Paul moved slowly from the table and went to the door and opened it, and his intake of breath brought John's head round quickly to see May standing in the doorway. There was no need to wonder if she had heard anything; her face told him that there was nothing she hadn't heard; she must have been there all the time.

As Paul hesitated and looked at her she said evenly, in the ice-rimmed tone that was natural to her, 'Go on out, I'll see you later.' Then she went into the room and closed the door.

May stood with her back to the door, not leaning against it; she did not look in need of support, her small compact body was rigid with the white heat of hate. 'So!' she said.

'Aye. So. Well, you heard what he said.'

'Yes, I heard what he said, but I lay no stock on that. I understand my son where you never did. A priest indeed! He means that as a girl would mean it – if she said she was going to be a nun after being let down. I'll see to him presently. It isn't him I want to talk about now, it's you . . . and her!'

John's lips met in a straight line, the corners pulled in as if he was sucking.

'That's it, get ready to do battle. Get ready to lie your way out.'

'I've got no need to lie about anything and I'm not going to, so don't worry your head on that score.'

'Yes, I loved your Aunt Sarah.' She was mimicking his tone now, her face spread into a mirthless leer. Then as if a switch had changed her expression, her face was straight. The muscles tight and her eyes flint-hard as she spat at him, 'There was a pair of you. The big fellow and the big, fat floppy-breasted bitch.'

As she watched him silently writhing, she taunted him, 'Why don't you say something? At least defend her and say she wasn't a floppy-breasted bitch, she was beautiful. Aye, like a sow on her side she was beautiful all right.' She paused again. Then her voice dropping deep into her throat, she muttered, 'There could be another killing this very minute.'

'Aye, there could. So look out, I'm telling you.' His words sounded thick and fuddled as if he were drunk.

'I'm not frightened of you and your bulk, and you know it . . . To think that all these years, you and her . . . I could spit on you.'

'You're barking up the wrong tree as usual.' John moved his head slowly. 'It's true what I said and I'm not going to deny it. I was in love with her, and still am if you want to know, so coat that with your venom and burn it through . . . But there's been nothing between us, not a damn thing. That first New Year's Eve I tried to kiss her coming back from her mother's, but that's all that happened – she soon put me in me place. And I'm going to tell you something, right now I'm going to tell you something. If it hadn't been for our Davie the tale would have been different, for I would have taken her – and I could have – and I'd have left you high and dry. Twenty years I've sat like a mute under your tongue, but now it's finished. So you know.'

May was standing within an arm's length of him. She looked up at him, her thin face wearing a twisted smile, and her voice sounded

196

deceptively normal when she said, 'That's where you're wrong, John. Things are only beginning; you forget about Kathleen.'

'You can do nothing there; Kathleen isn't mine.'

'Can you prove it?' The smile slid from her face. 'If you went on your bended knees at this moment I wouldn't believe you, nor would anybody else. You've always been very fond . . . fond, that's a light term for your feeling for Kathleen, isn't it? You liked her better than you did your own son. You've never had much use for Paul, have you? Oh no. But Kathleen looks like her mother, doesn't she, and she takes after you, doesn't she? There's nothing of Davie in her, but you stick out a mile. Helter-skelter, never stay still. That's Kathleen . . . just like her father, eh?'

'I tell you you're barking up the wrong tree.' John's voice, although loud, sounded weary.

'I don't think so. In fact, I'm sure I'm not.' May was talking in a conversational tone now. 'If your dear Sarah had nothing to hide, why didn't she bring this all out at the trial; it would have helped her, she would have gained sympathy, a woman who had been blackmailed for years. But no, she was frightened because she knew that if she opened her mouth the cat would be out of the bag. As Paul said, Kathleen's birthday is on the fourth of October. You haven't to do much counting up from the first of January have you?'

'Look!' He was bawling now. 'You can talk until you're sick and you'd still be wrong. I tell you . . .'

'You can tell me nothing. Now you listen to me.' May's tone changed yet again; her face was tight, bitter. 'As I see it, your dear Sarah took a longer stretch than she need have done just to save Kathleen knowing the truth. Well . . . now listen hard, big fellow, because if you make a mistake it'll be a pity. If you think you're going to wait for her coming out you're mistaken, because if you as much as go and visit her, just once, I'll go across that back lane and I'll tell our dear Kathleen who her daddy is. You know, there are more ways of killing a cat than drowning it. And just think how Dan would take this bit of news . . . and your Dad. Oh, you wouldn't care what your mother thought, in fact you'd like to hit your mother with this, but not the other two. Oh no, you'd like to keep their good opinion, wouldn't you? All men together.' She stepped back quickly as John advanced towards her. 'Don't try it,' she said. 'Don't try it, I warn you.'

They stood staring at each other, the hate like molten lead between them. It was May who moved first. She turned from him, showing her disdain by giving him her back, and as she reached the door she looked over her shoulder towards him and said evenly. 'The way business is going we want a better address, don't you think? I'll look for a place down Westhoe in Shields, it's nice down there. And by the way, if you should get the idea into your head to let the business go flat to spite me, remember it would be a pity to think that your dear Sarah had sacrificed herself in vain, wouldn't it?'

When the door had closed on her, John turned slowly and went to the window, and, looking out across the back lane, he gazed down into Sarah's yard, into Sarah's kitchen window, and he said aloud: 'All this because of those few minutes that night. God Almighty! First her going through it, and now me. But I'm not Sarah. How long can I hold out? God Almighty!'

PART SIX

It was nineteen-fifty seven and Dan's birthday, and he was fifty-seven years old. He stood appraising himself in the wardrobe mirror. He was still upright and his figure hadn't fattened. He patted his flat tummy – he was too much on his feet to get any flesh on there. His hair, although quite thick, was a grisly grey, and there was no bright twinkle in his eyes now. They had a serious look, as had the whole of his face. He remarked to himself on the seriousness of his expression and thought, You've got to feel light inside. What you feel like inside always tells. But the mirror presented him with a smart, well-set-up man, a prosperous man. But what, he asked himself, was prosperity if there was nobody to share it? Well, things would be different within a week. Yes, the week ahead would be a very telling time. Now he must get going; he did not want to keep Kathleen and the Sunday dinner waiting.

He went out of the bedroom and stepped into a large carpeted hallway. He walked across it and into a sitting-room. It looked an extremely comfortable, and well-furnished room. He put a wire guard round the fire, went to the window, and looked down into the main street for a moment. It looked utterly deserted, as a shopping thoroughfare always does on a Sunday. Unconsciously he arranged the velvet curtains; then with one last look round the room he went out into the hall again, took his overcoat out of an oak wardrobe standing near the door, adjusted his trilby hat, and picked up a pair of fur-lined leather gloves from a small table. Going out, he locked the door and descended the carpeted stairs to the street, and there, getting into his car, he drove the two miles to the Fifteen Streets.

There was another car parked outside of the house he now thought of as Kathleen's. He drew up behind it, but when he alighted he did not go into Kathleen's, but went around the corner and into the back door of number one.

Mary Hetherington was setting the table for the dinner. She turned from a sideboard drawer with some cutlery in her hand and, looking casually at Dan, said, 'You're early.'

'Yes, I am a bit. Stan out?'

'He's next door.'

Dan stood with his back to the fire. He held his hat and his gloves in his hand and watched his sister laying three places at the table – May always came over to dinner on a Sunday now.

She went into the scullery next and filled a glass jug with water, and when she returned and set the jug on the corner of the table, and straightened the knives again, she said, 'Well?'

'Well, what?'

'Well, what have you arranged? You know what I mean.'

Dan remained silent, looking at this woman as he had looked at her over the years wondering how he ever came from the same source. She was seventy now and still upright – her tightly-laced stays helped here. But there was no help for her face; her skin looked like old Chinese silk that had cracked here and there where it had been folded. Her eyes still held the alert quality; that had never diminished, for it had been fed continuously on bitterness.

'You're not bringing her back here?'

'Where else can she go?'

'I don't care where she goes, you know that, but I'm warning you not to bring her back here.'

'Her home's next door, her daughter is next door, you seem to forget that.'

'I forget nothing, nothing.'

'No, you don't, Mary, you forget nothing. Forgiveness isn't in you, and the odd thing about it is that she had never done a damn thing to you.'

'What! What do you say? And, by the way, I'll thank you not to swear in my house. And as to her not doing a thing to me, how can you stand there and say that? You know she ruined this family. She broke it up.'

'She did no such thing.'

Mary Hetherington drew herself up. 'I'm not going to argue with you, you've always been soft. But I warn you, if you bring that woman next door it will mean trouble. You wouldn't want Kathleen's life to be broken, too, would you?'

'There's no fear of that.'

'Just you wait and see.' She nodded warningly at him. 'They should never have let her out of a sudden like this, she should have been made to do the full fifteen years.'

Dan pulled the rim of his hat through his hands, then, moving from the fireplace, he walked past her. He did not exchange any form of farewell, and he went out, closing the door none too gently.

No sooner had he gone than Mary Hetherington was out of the room and up the stairs and into the back bedroom, and there she stood to the side of the curtain watching him crossing the lane to May's back door. She saw him go up the yard and into the house, and as she stood waiting she glanced at the little clock on the mantelshelf. When he came out she looked at the clock again. He had been in there nearly fifteen minutes. She smiled to herself, a tight, satisfied smile, then went out of the room and down the stairs.

*　　*　　*

Meals at Kathleen's were never talkative or boisterous affairs. Kathleen had lost the art of laughter ten years ago, but today's meal was even quieter than usual. Dan sat opposite to Kathleen, and to her right sat her husband, Michael, and to her left, in a high chair and close to her, was a two-year-old baby girl.

Kathleen was nearly twenty-seven but she looked older, she looked a woman well into her thirties. Her face over the years had taken on a resemblance to Sarah's, but she had not Sarah's expression. There was a solemness about Kathleen's face now, an innate sadness printed on it. The look had been there for years. At first it had not been permanent; the day it became permanent was the day that Paul had been ordained a priest. That was over three years ago. Three months from that particular day she married Michael MacKay.

Michael, Dan thought, was a good fellow, and in a way Kathleen was lucky. Feeling as she did, and acting at times as if she wasn't aware of anybody, it said a great deal for him that he never lost patience with her. It was well for her that he had loved her for a long time – ever since he was a lad, in fact. At the same time Dan thought it was a bit hard on him.

From the day they had taken Sarah from the house to the magistrates' court at Clervaux Terrace in Jarrow Dan had made it his home and for over six years he had looked after Kathleen, right until the time Michael took over. On that day he had moved to the shop. Braving Mary Hetherington's tongue, he had taken his belongings and gone up to his new home. And now he held pleasant memories of two peaceful years with Mrs Campbell. But since the old lady had died over a year ago he had lived on his own. He didn't like living on his own and he had for some time now been hoping to change this state of affairs. But, like everything else, the outcome of this hope remained to be seen.

The meal over, he sat with Jessica on his knee making her laugh while Kathleen and Michael washed-up the dinner things. Then Michael took the child upstairs to bed, and Kathleen and he were alone together. Having so much to say, they said nothing, each waiting for the other to make an opening. Kathleen busied herself in putting the room to rights, placing the modern dining chairs, with the different-coloured leather seats, under the table, pushing the G-Plan armchairs into different positions. There was not a piece of the old furniture to be seen throughout the house. The whole place had been re-decorated and re-furnished.

At last Kathleen came and sat down by Dan, and, putting her hands between her knees, she looked at him as she said, 'How do you think it will work out, Uncle Dan?'

'We'll just have to wait and see, Kathleen, that's all.'

'I'm terrified.'

203

'What is there to be terrified about? She's your mother, remember that, and a good woman. A good woman, Kathleen. I've told you again and again, Sarah is a good woman.'

'If I only didn't believe . . .' Kathleen's head dropped down to her chest.

'But you've got to believe it, Kathleen, because it's the truth, I believe it. I know your Uncle John, I know him inside out. I tell you he almost went on his bended knees to prove it to me. You know he was fond – oh, more than fond of your father; there was a strong tie between them, a strong, strong tie, and your Uncle John admitted that if David hadn't been your father he would have gone off with your mother, but . . . well, he, in his own way . . . well, he loved your father, he couldn't bring himself to hurt him . . . David was your father, Kathleen.'

She looked at him, saying quietly, 'You know, Uncle Dan, I think I could be happy now if I could just believe it. I've tried, but I keep remembering . . . I keep remembering my Uncle John and . . . and him always being over here, and how he used to look at her . . . and Aunt May's jealousy, and her not liking me.'

'Look, Kathleen, we've been over all this before, it's old ground; but I say again, what your Uncle John felt for your mother we all felt in one way or another. She was a very fetching woman and she didn't go out of her way to attract anybody. She wasn't smart-tongued like your Aunt May, or clever in any way; she was just nice and kind . . . loving, sort of. And then the way she looked . . . you look like her, you know, Kathleen.'

Kathleen was on her feet. 'Don't say that, Uncle Dan.'

'I'm going to say it. And don't take that tone, Kathleen, it's a compliment.'

Kathleen turned from him and walked to the kitchen window, and from there she said, 'About Wednesday – will you pick me up? I'm leaving Jessica with Michael's mother. I'm not telling Grannie I'm going, she'd go mad.'

'I've got it all arranged. I'm picking up your Aunt Phyllis at half-past nine, that should get us there in time.'

Dan was standing behind Kathleen now, with his hand on her shoulder. 'Don't worry, my dear; things are going to turn out all right. Believe me.' His tone was emphatic. 'Just believe me. And try and remember that she'll be in a state too. She's been away for ten years, she'll be changed. She's likely as fearful of coming back as you are of her coming.'

Kathleen did not reply to this, but said, 'That tea. I suppose it's kind of them to want to welcome her back like that, but having a tea in the street and putting flags out, because that's what they'll do down there. You would still think they lived in the ramshackle houses the way they go on. And when me grannie knows she'll be wild . . . wild.'

'Well, there's nothing we can do about that, it's their way of expressing their feelings.'

'But she didn't know hardly any of them from the bottom end, not for years.'

He patted her shoulder, saying, 'It'll all be over this time next week. Everything will have settled down by then. You'll see, you'll see.'

'This time next week.' Kathleen muttered the words to herself as she looked up over the chimney-pots and into the sky. She had tried to readjust her life, she had tried to close the wound, but on Wednesday, between her grannie, her Aunt May, and her mother, the wound would not only be torn open again – she would be rent apart.

CHAPTER TWO

Before she had done a month of her sentence Sarah's mind came down from the plane to which it had escaped: time had a different meaning now. She got up with it early in the morning, in the mornings that always seemed like night, and the daytime was broken up into pieces of time; pieces when she ate colourless food, when she walked round a square; when she worked in a laundry; when she ate again, and worked again, and ate again, and then went to bed while it was still day. Nevertheless she longed for this time when she could go to bed, not to sleep or rest but to be by herself.

That was the most difficult thing: getting herself used to time, time being used in a different way from that in which she had used it before. Everything inside was connected with time; everybody was doing time. But she found you can get used to anything; so she got used to using time. She had to, as she had to get used to not being nauseated with the smell, the smell of urine. In the block it permeated the air; even in the laundry, where there was soap and water, the smell still hung around some of the women. She liked few of the women; there was one, but she went out after six years. Her name was Gladys and she had liked reading. She had looked after the library. It was because of her that Sarah had got the job helping in the library for an hour after tea. So for over six years she had accepted time. It would be thought she hadn't much choice, yet some didn't accept it, and for them life was a living hell.

But her acceptance ended one visiting day when Dan had said to her from across the table, 'Kathleen is going to get married.' Her heart had come alive at that moment. But she didn't know for how short a time. Kathleen hadn't been to visit her for four months, and she had written her only short, terse letters. She was at work and she couldn't get off, she had a cold. Then Dan, his head bowed, had said,

'I've got to tell you this, Sarah. She's marrying Michael MacKay.'

She had mouthed the name without a sound, then asked gropingly, 'Why, Dan, why?' and he had to say to her:

'Paul has become a priest.'

'A priest!' It was the first time she had heard anything about Paul and the priesthood. She had been hurt sore that he had never been near her, nor yet had written her a scribe of the pen, she couldn't understand it. But then there were lots of things she couldn't understand, such as Kathleen's aloof attitude. Her daughter seemed to have turned against her . . . This was torture.

Her mind dizzying as it had been wont to do, she asked again, 'But why, Dan, why?'

He had been forced to tell her the truth, the truth as Paul thought he had heard it, and, thinking she might as well know the rest, he went on to tell her of John, how he had left May and gone to live in Newcastle. But he did not tell her that he was living with a girl young enough to be his daughter, he couldn't tell her that. Nor that on the day he had broke away from May she had gone over to Kathleen's and told her why Paul was becoming a priest. There are things you cannot get the tongue to speak.

But Sarah had not been concerned at what was happening to John or May, she could only think of Kathleen and Paul. Paul a priest! It was unbelievable. Just because he had heard what was said that day, that terrible but fading day. Why was God doing this to her? Perhaps he was answering Father O'Malley's prayer and wreaking more vengeance on her. Perhaps, she thought, it was meant that she should go through all this just so Paul could become a priest. But no. No. She wouldn't think like that. She had given up thinking like a Catholic, she was no longer a Catholic. She was no longer anything that was connected with a God. She was just no longer anything. She didn't want to go on. She was finished. Paul a priest! A Protestant, with his mother and father bigots. Paul a priest! And then it had penetrated through her mind, the real reason – half-brother and sister, Oh, Kathleen! Oh, poor, poor Kathleen! It was all crazy . . . mad, mad. Who was causing this to happen, anyway? God? . . . God was mad.

It was from this time that she spent three months in the prison hospital, but she could not die. Her body, although thin and a shadow of its former self, would not give her up. Her mind was ready any moment, and it did its best to force her release, but it failed. And when she left the hospital they did not put her back into the laundry; her time was spent between the sewing-room and the library. And through this change she got to know, and in fact become friendly with a warden called Peters. Her life was now lived on a level plane, orderly, monotonous. Until one day, without any warning, she was told she was going to be released.

* * *

It was seven o'clock on a Monday morning when Sarah stood with one foot outside the prison gates. The officer said to her, 'Will you be all right? I think you should have told them it was today.'

Sarah shook her head. 'I would rather it was this way.' She spoke in an undertone as if afraid of disturbing someone.

'Goodbye, Mrs Hetherington, and good luck.' The officer was smiling and holding out her hand, and Sarah took it. 'Thank you,' she said. 'You've been kind.' Then she turned away.

She did not feel the strangeness of being in the open for the first moment because she was thinking . . . Mrs Hetherington, she was . . . Mrs for the first time in years. She was Mrs. Then she looked across the road. The other side looked far away. When her legs began to tremble she said to herself, It's no different to walking inside, and she kept on. The clothes that she was wearing felt strange, loose, as if she had no body to support them. She looked down at herself. She was so thin now. All except her bust. Her bust hadn't altered so much. The officer had joked with her and said she had a figure like Marilyn Monroe. Were people looking at her? No, no, they weren't. She passed a woman and glanced at her, but the woman was looking ahead. She felt surprised at this. Wasn't there some kind of a stamp on her to tell people where she had come from? When she reached the corner of the road she had the desire to run back and bang on the prison gates. She felt frightened; she was by herself and she hadn't been by herself for a long, long time. She wanted someone near, not to touch, oh no, but just to know that they were near . . . But yes . . . yes, she did . . . she did want someone to touch, a hand to hold. She had been silly, telling them it was Wednesday she was coming out. She should have told them it was today. But she couldn't face a street tea, anything but face a street tea and a sea of curious faces. She had told the warden that and the warden had understood. Dan said people were kind and this was their way of showing their kindness. Perhaps . . . but she didn't want this kind of kindness. Doubtless they had deluded themselves into thinking that in getting up a street tea and a jollification for her coming home they were doing her a kindness, but what they were really doing was giving themselves a bit of cheap sensation. She was not surprised at her own insight into human nature, for, as the idleness of the dole years ago had turned many a man towards self-education, so had her years of confinement and daily dealing with books tutored her mind a little, at least, to a certain stage of analytical reasoning. It had happened unobtrusively, so unobtrusively that she was unaware of the change. And yet she knew she was different, her way of thinking was different. She felt that she would never know fear as she had known it before; in a way it had overstepped itself. But being afraid, and facing a table full of laughing faces and questing eyes set out in the open street, was a

207

different thing. If it were to rain they would hold it in the factory hall; they were prepared for all contingencies. But wherever it was held they would have provided the opportunity to gape and question . . . 'What's it like in there, Sarah? What did they do to you? Did you ever get solitary? Come on, woman, open up, you're among friends.' And she was not exaggerating in imagining the trend the reception would take. She knew what some of them at the bottom end were like, and it would doubtless have been these very people who had proposed the welcome home tea, and their every probe would be in good part. Oh yes, everything would be in good part; it was a favourite cover-up for curiosity, the term, good part. And if she didn't take everything in good part, she would be damned . . . She couldn't have stood it . . .

The officer had told her the way to the station. She turned right down the street, then left, and left again, across a square, up another street, and there it was, the station. She didn't remember seeing it before, but she must have seen it, at least once, when they brought her here from the magistrates' court in Jarrow. 'You are committed in custody to await trial at Durham Assizes.'

The man at the ticket office said, 'What do you say, missis? Speak up.'

'A single to Newcastle.'

'A single to Newcastle . . . there you are.'

She put the change in her bag. It was funny having a bag hanging from your arm, it felt awkward. She thought people must think how stiffly she held her arm with the bag on it.

She had the carriage to herself all the way to Newcastle, and she did not stand up and walk from one window to the other taking her fill of both views, but sat quietly in the corner, her back straight, her head turned towards the changing scenery. The trees looked bonny, oh so bonny. The sun turned their browning leaves to glittering gold and bronze. She realised she was looking at colour. She had missed colour; oh yes, she had missed colour. She had always kept her home colourful. Cushion covers made from cheap remnants, curtains with patterns on, never Nottingham lace curtains . . . How would the kitchen look? She turned her mind deliberately from the kitchen, saying to herself, One thing at a time. You'll get the bus outside Newcastle station, it isn't likely that the stop will be changed; and then you'll get off at the corner . . . One thing at a time.

The bus stop was changed. 'Which part of Jarrow do you want to go?' said a man in a peaked cap.

'The Fifteen Streets,' she said.

'Oh, down that far? Oh well then, you can get either the one that will take you the Robin Hood way, or there's the other that goes straight through the town. The town one, I think, that's the one you want. And it's in, look, over there.'

208

Sarah thanked him; then boarded the bus, taking a seat right up at the front.

'Which part of the Fifteen Streets do you want?' the conductor asked her. 'It's a long walk if you get off at the wrong end.'

'The . . . top end?' She put this as a question and he replied, 'Oh yes. Well, I'll tell you when to get off.' Evidently he thought of her as someone who didn't know where she was going.

And from Hebburn onwards Sarah saw that she didn't know where she was going. The immediate landscape had changed; the places which she had last seen as open stretches of flat land were now covered with houses, dozens of houses, hundreds of houses. Here and there, she would think to herself, Yes, I remember that; that is the way to the ferry; that is the way to the church near Dee Street. We should be nearing the church bank now, and the park, and the quay corner.

At the quay corner she saw the church of St Paul. It looked so much smaller than she remembered; it looked lost, forgotten. She felt akin to it. Then the bus conductor came up to her and said, 'This is your stop, missis.' She followed him down the bus without looking to see where she was and the next minute she was on the main road. From the pavement she looked up at him puzzled, and he said, 'This is the top end, the top end of the Fifteen Streets . . . All right?'

She nodded her head slowly at him, and he rang the bell and the bus sped away. But he paused a while to look at her.

She stood looking across the road. He had put her off at the wrong end, he had put her off at the bottom end. But it was a different bottom end from when she had last seen it. Then there had been an open space where the four streets had stood before the night of the raid. Now before her were stretched not only four streets but street after street of new houses all with little gardens in front and bigger gardens behind. She walked slowly across the road, and she was at the end of the first street. There was a fancy board supported by two stout wooden pillars at the corner, and on it was written: Churchill Street. She began to walk past the corner of the streets going in the direction the bus had taken. The second street was called Eisenhower Avenue. This was about where they had lived, she thought. The following street was Montgomery Terrace, on and on; Wavell Avenue, Laurence Street, all new streets, all named after men of war. Here and there, there were children playing in back gardens, but except in the distance she saw no adults. Being nearly two o'clock, the men had returned to work and the women were taking it easy for an hour, things seemingly hadn't altered that much. On and on, slowly, towards the top end she went. And then abruptly the new houses ceased and she could see ahead four of the original streets, and the contrast gave her a shock. Like beggars lying at the rich man's gate the four streets lay at the foot of the new estate, and they looked dirty, old, and shrunken. Her step became slower.

She knew now why the bus conductor had put her off at the other end of the streets. The situation of the place had turned a complete somersault; the top end had now become the bottom end. Yet among the people in the new houses were those who still thought along the lines of street teas. Places, she realised, could be altered or renewed in a week, a month, a year, but not people. It took the accumulated years of a generation and perhaps another to alter people, turn them from their inbred ways. The Fifteen Streets would be the Fifteen Streets until this generation died, that was certain. It was only the status of the Streets themselves that had turned the somersault.

The sight of Camelia Street staggered her. This was the place she had once invested with royal status. Here she had lived in the glory of exclusiveness. For years she had thanked God at night in her prayers for depositing her at this end.

In the middle of the street two motor-cycles leaned against the kerb, their new brightness forcing its way through the shadow cast by the dismal houses. There were also three cars standing in the roadway, one of them outside her own door – she still thought of it as her own door. The car would be Michael's. Fancy him having a car; fancy anybody who lived here having a car.

She was standing at the door now, her hand half-raised to the knocker. But before she touched it she gripped the front of her coat and shook herself. Now then, steady, steady . . . take it easy, one thing at a time.

When the door opened, there stood Kathleen. Sarah watched her mouth drop into a loose gape, then close on a gasp: 'Wh . . . why,' she stammered. 'I thought . . . What brought you? Who's brought you?' She shook her head wildly, and then, pulling the door further open, she added, 'Come in.'

It was as if she were bidding a stranger enter, and, like a stranger, Sarah walked into what had been her home, for immediately she crossed the threshold the change sprang at her. She would have had to be blind not to take it in in one glance.

Kathleen walked sideways along the little passage through the front room and into the kitchen; she had her hand extended as if for guidance, but she didn't touch her mother.

In the kitchen they stood looking at each other, Kathleen with her hands joined at her throat. The action was painful to Sarah, for it gave away Kathleen's distress.

'You said Wednesday.'

'Yes, yes, I know, Kathleen, but I . . . I couldn't bear them making a tea and all that.'

'Oh.' Kathleen jerked her chin up as if in understanding, and then she said, 'Sit down. Why, sit down.' She pulled a chair hastily forward. It was one of the coloured-seated dining chairs and Sarah looked at it before she sat on it.

'I'll tell Michael. He's on night shift, but he would be getting up shortly.'

'Don't wake him, there's plenty of time.' Sarah was still speaking in that peculiar undertone she had come to use over the years.

'Oh, I'll tell him, I'll tell him.'

Kathleen almost ran from the room and she went up the stairs calling loudly, 'Michael! Michael!'

Sarah listened now to Kathleen's quick steps overhead. She heard the murmur of her speaking rapidly, warningly, and she bowed her head. How was she going to bear it? . . . One thing at a time, one thing at a time. Once today was over it wouldn't be so bad. She reminded herself that she was sitting in her own kitchen, she was home. But was she? She raised her head and looked about her. There wasn't a stick of furniture that she could recognise as hers. She experienced a new kind of pain.

When Kathleen came down the stairs there were footsteps behind her, and Sarah turned her head to look at the man entering the room. He was dressed in trousers and shirt; his sandy hair was ruffled, and his eyes still full of sleep, but she recognised Michael MacKay. He hadn't changed much. He was older of course.

'Well, hello, there,' he said.

'Hello, Michael,' she answered.

'We weren't expecting you the day. You should have told us, coming all that way by yourself.'

He was trying to be kind, not to show his surprise, not to let her see that he was put out in any way. 'Have you had a cup of tea?' he said.

'No, not yet.' She smiled towards Kathleen.

'We'll make one in a jiffy,' he said and went into the scullery.

Yes, Michael was nice. As Dan said, Kathleen could have done a lot worse. But Michael wasn't Paul . . . Oh, Paul . . . Paul. But she mustn't think of Paul . . . One thing at a time.

'How's the baby?' she said looking up at Kathleen.

'Oh, she's fine, she's asleep.' She made for the door again. 'I'll bring her down.'

'Kathleen.' Sarah's voice halted her. 'Don't . . . don't disturb her, there'll be plenty of time.'

'Yes, yes, of course.' After a pause Kathleen came back towards the table, and, standing before her mother, she said, 'Take your hat off . . . take your things off.'

Sarah reached up and slowly she removed her hat. Then, standing up, she took off her coat. As she put her hand up to smooth back her hair in which there was still not a thread of grey Michael entered the kitchen. He had a tray in his hand and he stopped dead for a moment and looked at Sarah. He saw a woman so like his wife that the resemblance startled him. When she'd had her coat and hat on he hadn't seen it so clearly, but now he was seeing them together. It was a strange experience. The only difference was that the older woman had a better figure and a softer face. Yes . . . yes, he had to admit that to himself. Even after all she had gone through, and she must have had a packet, she didn't look hard or bitter. Not that Kathleen looked hard or bitter; but there was a set look about her face that didn't show in her mother's. He sighed and smiled. Things wouldn't be too bad. Better than he'd thought. Now that her mother was out Kathleen might forget about the past. He hoped to God she would, anyway. 'There you are.' He placed the tray on the table. 'Nothing like a cup of char.' As he poured out the tea he looked at Sarah and said, 'We'll have to get your room ready, but that won't take long, it only needs the bed putting up. We can take the cot out any time.'

'But' – Sarah shook her head – 'the little boxroom will do me. Don't move anything.'

'There isn't a boxroom any more.' Kathleen was looking at the fire. 'Michael made it into a bathroom.'

'Oh!' Sarah glanced at Michael. 'That's nice. Oh, it's nice to have a bathroom.'

They were sitting, the three of them, drinking their tea when silence attacked them, the awkward horrible silence that yells aloud, and Sarah was just about to break it, she was just about to say, 'Don't worry. I won't be in your way. I'll get a job and then perhaps I'll find a little place of my own.' That is what she was going to say when the back door opened and Kathleen jerked out of her chair as if she had been shot.

There was the sound of steps in the scullery. The kitchen door opened and Mary Hetherington entered the room, and perhaps for the first time in years she was caught off her guard, and it registered on her face which showed utter and blank surprise.

Sarah's heart was beating wildly. This was the moment she had dreaded more so than entering her old home again and the meeting with Kathleen. Yet she had never imagined herself being actually confronted by her mother-in-law. Being passed by her in the street, yes; ignored, yes. At the same time being made vitally aware of her hate and loathing, but she had never imagined her walking into the kitchen like this. She had come in as if she were used to coming in . . . Yes, undoubtedly she was used to coming in.

Michael, trying to smooth over the tense moment, said, 'Come and sit down, Gran. I've just made some tea. Have a . . .'

Mary Hetherington, indicating with a swift movement of her arm towards him that she wished him to be quiet, he became quiet. His voice trailed away and he looked sharply at his wife, but Kathleen was looking at no-one. She had her head down. It looked as if she were rejecting something, something shameful.

'So you've come!' Mary Hetherington's voice was thick, like some-one who was gone in drink. 'How soon are you going?'

Sarah did not rise to her feet nor did she make any retort, but she sat, her stomach sick, looking up at this old woman, and she saw that she was old, and her hate was old, but strong still, stronger if anything. Sarah could see it all clearly. This hate-filled woman had taken Kathleen under her wing, not with the desire of protecting her, but of separating her from herself, from contamination with herself. That's how she would think of it.

'Look, Gran.' Michael was tentatively appealing again, and again he was silenced by a more violent wave of the hand now as Mary Hetherington repeated, 'When are you going? I asked you a question.'

Sarah had got out of the habit of talking. You didn't talk in there, you listened, and you only spoke when you were asked a question. She had been asked a question and now she forced herself to answer it. She said softly, 'I've come home . . .'

Before Sarah's lips settled on the last word Mary Hetherington charged in, crying, 'Home! This is no longer your home. You gave up this home ten years ago.'

Sarah, her voice still level, her words still spoken in that peculiar undertone, said, 'The rent book's still in my name. Dan said . . .'

'Dan said! Dan said!' There was scorn in Mary Hetherington's voice. 'I know what Dan said. What he doesn't know is that Michael had it transferred to his name two years ago. And look round you. Is there a stick of yours here? No, not so much as would fill a matchbox. Your home! Now again I say to you . . . When are you going?'

'Gran . . . Gran, stop it. I tell you, stop it! Leave her alone; it's my affair, our affair.' Kathleen was confronting her grandmother now, swallowing between each word, daring to oppose this woman who had imposed her rule on her.

'You leave this to me, Kathleen. Unless you want your life ruined and Michael in trouble . . . because let me tell you—' The old woman leant towards Kathleen and wagged her finger at her. 'As sure as God's in heaven she'll have Michael. She'll have your husband; no man is safe within a mile of her. They're never too old, they're never too young. I'm speaking from experience.'

Sarah rose to her feet, not hastily; she just rose from the chair, as if she were being pulled up by a mechanical device. She was trembling all over. She had a desire to cry, but she could neither cry nor speak; she could just stand, her hands on the table looking towards this hate-corroded being.

'You don't believe me?' Mary Hetherington lifted her eyes from Kathleen and brought them to Michael. 'I'll bet all I own this moment that within a few weeks, yes, within a few weeks she'll have set her cap at you and you won't know where you are.'

'Now look, Gran, stop talking like that. Let up. There's a limit.' Michael was obviously embarrassed and he wagged his head, his gaze directed towards the floor.

'You want proof . . . I'll give it to you.' The old woman swung round and, snatching at the curtain, lifted it into a loop, and as she did so Kathleen cried, 'No, no, Gran . . . don't bring Aunt May over . . . please!' She went to pull the curtain from her grandmother, but the old woman pushed her aside.

'Far better bring May across than have your home broken up. Leave it alone, I want May here. This woman took your Aunt May's man . . . my son, when she was only married a few weeks to my other son. She takes everything . . . everything with trousers on.'

Years ago Sarah would have thought, She's talking like one of the women at the bottom end; now she could only think, I'll have to go . . . I'll have to go . . . I can't bear it. Something will happen if I don't get out. Oh, my God!

She turned her head wildly now in the direction of the couch where lay her hat, coat and bag, and then her head was jerked back with startling suddenness to her mother-in-law again. Mary Hetherington was glaring at Kathleen and saying, 'She deprived my son, my David, of fatherhood. I've told you what she did, but you only half believed me. But let May confront her with it; yes, let May con . . .'

'Be quiet! You evil creature . . . be quiet!'

They were all looking at Sarah now. A different Sarah. Not the Sarah that Mary Hetherington remembered, nor the Sarah that Kathleen remembered as her mother, nor yet was there any connection with the Sarah who had sat so timidly before them only a few minutes earlier. The tall, pale, wide-eyed woman before them had a majestic bearing, a towering majestic bearing; there was no aggressiveness in her attitude, yet it held them all still. She stared at her mother-in-law for a full minute in silence before she began to speak again.

Her voice too was different now, the tone strong, the words crisp, yet quiet. 'I'm not going to let you get away with this. Oh, no, not with this. From the day we met you've hated me; you've sent your venom and your spleen through that wall there at me' – she pointed – 'until the very bricks were tense with the atmosphere you created. You hated me because David loved me; you hated the idea that I could make him happy. Me!' She pressed her finger gently into her breast. 'The scum from the bottom end. That's how you thought of me, wasn't it? And you couldn't bear the thought that I'd brought your favourite son alive; you couldn't bear the thought that in my kitchen your menfolk found peace from your nagging. That's all they came in here for, just to get away from your nagging. They were sick of listening to the gaffer of God.' She did not fire a barbed shaft here by adding, 'That was David's name for you' – but went on, 'From the moment I came into your life, you have tried to ruin me; every bit as much as my father did, you tried . . .'

'How . . . how can you stand there and speak the name of your . . .'

Sarah cut Mary Hetherington's words off with an uplifting movement of her head: 'I dare speak his name. I have paid for what I did . . . I'm free . . . and I dare speak his name. He doesn't trouble my conscience, he never has. Let that horrify you.' She paused for a second before going on. 'But that's beside the point . . . As I said, there's one thing you're not going to do. You're not going to burn that last lie into my daughter's mind.' Sarah now switched her eyes to Kathleen, and her voice had a ring of command in it. 'Kathleen,' she said, 'listen to me . . . listen closely to me. I never once went with your Uncle John . . . you understand? NEVER ONCE. Not once . . . Your Uncle John loved me. Once he kissed me, once on New Year's morning, nineteen-thirty, near the bottom end. I'd been to first-foot my mother. He came over with me because everybody else was joining in the jollification, and he kissed me and we talked. That was all. And my father heard what we talked about. Well, you know all about that part of it. The next time was the morning he marched to London with the hunger marchers. Neither his wife nor his mother would go to see him off; he asked me if I would, and that morning I kissed him . . . on the cheek. That, Kathleen, is the story of the vileness between your Uncle John and me. And that, when you sum it all up, is what I've done time for.'

Kathleen was looking at Sarah, staring up into her face. As they once used to look at each other and laugh, now they were looking at each other, but there was no laughter between them. As Sarah stared into the sad pleading countenance of her daughter she knew that she had to do something to give the seal of truth to her words. Her eyes flicked from Kathleen's face to the wall. There, hanging on it was a modern version of the picture of the Sacred Heart of Jesus. Like everything else, it was new.

It was the only holy picture in the room; likely it was Michael's choice, for he was a strong Catholic. She had never hung holy pictures in the house during her married life, but she remembered a similar one to this hanging in the kitchen when she was a child. The picture, although in a plain modern frame, held the same face of Christ, the same head and shoulders with the hand across the chest, palm up holding on it his bleeding heart, the blood dripping down through his fingers. She no longer believed in God or Jesus, or in any other symbol of the Catholic Church, but Kathleen did, and always would. With a swift movement she stepped to the wall and, lifting the picture by its string, brought it to Kathleen, and, laying it flat on one hand, she put the fingers of her other hand at the centre of the heart. But before she spoke she turned her eyes from Kathleen and fixed them on Mary Hetherington, and it was to her she said, 'I swear by the

Sacred Heart of Jesus that what I have said is true.' Then, looking at Kathleen again, she said, 'David was your father, Kathleen.'

Sarah imagined she saw a cloud lift from Kathleen's face, leaving it a shade lighter. She turned from her now and hung the picture back on the wall. Then once again she looked at her mother-in-law. It was evident that Mary Hetherington had received a setback, but it was also evident that she wasn't beaten, and she showed this by renewing her attack almost immediately. With a deriding mirthless laugh, and addressing no-one in particular, she cried, 'Well! You can take that bit of acting for what it's worth, and from where it comes. The Sacred Heart of Jesus . . . Huh! But the Lord isn't mocked . . . Let me tell you, the mills of God grind slow, but they grind exceeding small.'

'The mills of God!' Sarah repeated, shaking her head slowly as she looked now almost pityingly at the old woman. 'Though the mills of God grind slowly, yet they grind exceeding small; though with patience he stands waiting, with exactness grinds he all.' Sarah sensed immediately that her mother-in-law had never heard the second line of the quotation, and in this moment she felt a strange feeling of superiority over her . . . Prison life had done something for her after all. It had introduced her to the library, from where she had gathered a small amount of knowledge, small because her need in this direction was small, for she had never aspired to education – not for herself; all she had aspired to was to talk properly, as she put it to her herself, to be able to pass herself. She had always had this desire. Hadn't she longed for a dictionary when she was a girl just so that she could pass herself in conversation?

Her voice held an authoritative note as she repeated now, 'With exactness grinds he all. But not all . . . oh no, because you know what? He's blind, your miller, blind and vindictive. Indiscriminately doling out pain and agony, that's your God. Well, all I hope is that His groping hands don't find you, for even now I don't wish you your just deserts. I just pity you. I always have, you know . . . So there, you have it.'

With her bearing upright and dignified, she turned from the bitter face to the couch, and, picking up her coat, she put it on. And as she did so, Kathleen cried, 'Where you going? Oh, Mam, where you going?'

'Don't worry.' She smiled a sad faint smile at her daughter. 'Don't worry,' she said again. She put on her hat and picked up her bag. Then once again she turned, and, looking her mother-in-law straight in her eyes, she held her gaze for a moment before leaving the room. But she had just reached the in-between door when Mary Hetherington's voice sent its last bolt at her: 'And leave our Dan alone,' she cried, 'Him and May's going to be married. He spent enough years looking after you and yours, so let him do what he likes with the remainder of his life. Do that one decent thing at least.'

Her words halted Sarah, but only for a second. She went on through the front room into the passage. But when she reached the door Kathleen was behind her, and her hands on her Mother's shoulders, she turned her round and looked into her face for a moment before enfolding her in her arms, crying through her tears, 'Oh, Mam . . . Mam.'

'There, there. Don't upset yourself.'

'I believe you. I want you to know I believe you.'

Sarah remained quiet, and they clung together for a moment longer.

'Where you going?'

'Down to Phyllis's.'

'Look.' Kathleen was whispering now, her face close to Sarah's. 'We want to get a house away from here. We'll get fixed up, and you can come with us then. I would like it. Oh, I would, I would.'

'We'll see, we'll see. Don't worry.' Sarah opened the door, and Kathleen stood on the top step clinging on to her hand, saying, 'Oh, Mam. Oh, Mam.'

When there came to them from the kitchen the sound of raised voices, Sarah knew that May had arrived. She couldn't face May, she had stood all she could from them all. She knew she was going to break down, but she didn't want to upset Kathleen any more. She said hastily, 'Pop down to your Aunt Phyllis's when you can. Goodbye, my dear. Goodbye, my dear.'

Once again Kathleen had her arms around her; once again they clung together. Then Sarah was walking quickly away.

She could restrain the outlet no longer. When she reached the main road the tears were raining down her face, and she walked with her head down. The road between the Fifteen Streets and the New Buildings at East Jarrow was practically empty, but a woman who had passed her came running back after her, saying, 'What's the matter, lass? Are you in trouble?' Sarah did not look at the woman but shook her head. And the woman, walking by her side now, said, 'Can I help you, hinny?'

She raised her eyes to the woman and managed to say, 'No, thank you.'

As the woman looked at her her face crinkled slowly with recognition, But Sarah stopped her making any exclamation by waving her off with her hand; then she said, 'I'm sorry, just let me be,' and hurried on, leaving the woman standing on the pavement looking after her.

It was as she neared the New Buildings that the car drew up alongside the kerb. Michael had only a coat over his shirt and his hair was still ruffled. He said softly, 'Get in.' And she got in, still with her head bowed, the tears washing down her face.

Michael sat in deep embarrassed silence looking at her before starting the car, then he muttered, 'I'm sorry.' After a short while he asked quietly, 'Do you know the house?'

'It's in Laygate.'

He went through Tyne Dock, cut through the Deans, and they were in Laygate before she spoke again. 'She's an old devil.' He kept his eyes on the road as he spoke. 'I've had a job to keep me tongue meself. She's always trying to dominate Kathleen. I was goin' to try and get a job away last year in one of the Durham pits so we could move, but then things got a bit shaky. They're closing some pits down, so you've got to stay put. But I'll get a place out of it now. I told her afore I left just what I thought about her.'

There was an audible groan inside Sarah now. If Mary Hetherington wanted anything to confirm all she had said, Michael turning on her would have proved how right she had been about her daughter-in-law. She said now under her breath, 'It's the ice-cream café on the right.'

He helped her out of the car, then followed her into the shop.

Behind the counter stood a tall youth with Arab features and a fairish skin. And talking to him was a woman, a shortish, fat woman. She turned at the approach of customers, then her mouth springing open, she cried, 'Sarah! Why, Sarah! The day? You've come the day?' She was round the counter and they were holding each other. With tears running down her cheeks Phyllis kept repeating, 'Sarah! Oh, Sarah!' She held her at arm's length. 'Oh, lass, lass, am I glad to see you!' Becoming aware of the interest of the only two customers in the shop, she cried, 'Come on, away up out of this.' She went to pull Sarah forward; but pausing, she looked at her son, shouting to him as if he was streets away, 'You remember your Aunt Sarah, don't you?'

The young man smiled shyly. 'Yes . . . yes. Hello Aunt Sarah.'

'Hello . . .' Sarah didn't remember this one's name, and Phyllis cried. 'He's Joss, the youngest. Look at him, he's twice my size. But come on, come on . . . Come on, Michael.' Her arm extended, she drew Michael after them towards a door at the end of the long café. And leading the way up the stairs and into a large living-room, expensively if not artistically furnished, she turned again to Sarah. And now like a child she stood in front of her and laid her head on her breast. 'Oh, Sarah, lass! Oh, Sarah!' she said softly.

Sarah was overcome with emotion. Here indeed was a welcome. In the home of her sister who had married an Arab, a man who had always slightly repulsed her. Though Ali had always treated her with kindness, she had never met him but she had thought, How could our Phyllis do it? But she knew that Ali too would welcome her, warmly, sincerely. Life was strange. Oh, indeed, life was strange.

'Here, let me get your things off.' Phyllis was now pulling at Sarah's coat. 'We'll have a slap-up meal the night. I had it all prepared, in me mind that is, for Wednesday. What happened?'

Briefly, Sarah told her.

'Aw well, I see your point.' As Phyllis nodded it was evident to Sarah that she didn't quite see eye to eye with her in the matter of a street party. If Phyllis had spoken the truth she would have said, 'Well, I think it was jolly decent of them to think of such a thing.'

'Sit down, Michael. Sit down. And we'll have a cup of tea . . . Oh no we won't.' She raised her arm in a Hitler-like salute. 'We'll have something stronger to begin with, we will that.'

'Not for me, thanks all the same.' Michael smiled widely at her. 'I'm driving. And I've got to get back. In fact, I'd better be going. But I'll look in again.' He nodded his head quickly.

'Oh . . . Oh, all right then.' Phyllis didn't detain him, she wanted Sarah to herself.

'I'll be seeing you.' He was speaking to Sarah now in an under-tone. 'I'll bring Kathleen down.'

'Will you, Michael? Oh, that's kind of you.'

'The night, if you like.'

'Please. Oh, thanks, Michael, thanks.'

'Don't you worry.' He nodded his head down to her. 'Things'll pan out, you'll see. Now don't you worry.' He stood looking at her sympathetically for a moment before going to the door where Phyllis was waiting. And as he passed her he motioned to her with his head, and Phyllis, picking up the signal, turned to Sarah and said, 'I'll just see him down the stairs in case he breaks his neck. They're a bit dark. Go in the kitchen and get that tea under way. Make yourself busy, for if I know you, you'd rather tea than anything else.'

The sisters smiled at each other. The years seemed to have slipped away. Phyllis went out and closed the door, and Sarah went into the kitchen.

Here again everything was expensive and overcrowded. An outsize fridge, an electric washing machine, an electric food mixer . . . the lot. And Sarah was glad, glad that Phyllis had the things that stood for success.

She had made the tea and had it in the living-room before Phyllis returned. Phyllis's face was straight as she entered the room, and, looking across at Sarah, she said quietly, 'Michael's told me . . . You just got in about two? God, what a reception!' She came and stood close to Sarah, looking up into her face. 'But, anyway, you'd have likely got it on Wednesday, so it's over you. She's a sod. She's a sod of a woman if ever there's one. Sit down, lass, sit down and let's have a drink.' She pressed Sarah gently into an armchair. 'Will you have a drop of something in yours?' She pointed to the tea.

'No, Phyllis, no. Just a good cup of tea, that's all I want.' She smiled. 'I've longed for a real good cup of tea.'

Phyllis turned from her, and going to a cocktail-cabinet that stood in the corner of the room, she brought out a bottle, saying as she did so, 'I could go up there and pulverise that old bitch. I could that, this very minute.' She came back to the table and poured a generous measure of whisky into her own tea. Then, sitting down, she raised her cup to Sarah, saying, 'Here's to us, lass. Here's to us. We'll never be parted again. At least not if I can help it. You can stay here until you die. You can have a job if you want it, or you can leave it alone, it's all up to you. You've got nothing to worry about, not any more.'

'Oh, Phyllis.' Her sister's kindness was almost as painful as her mother-in-law's attack. She said again, 'Oh, Phyllis.'

Phyllis took a long drink from her cup; then, putting it down on the table, she wiped her mouth with the pad of her thumb, and, looking across the room towards the window, she said, thoughtfully, 'What I cannot understand is this business about Dan and May. Michael's just told me. I would have thought he had more sense.' She looked towards Sarah. But Sarah's head was bowed; she was staring down into her teacup. Then, lifting the cup to her lips, she took a long drink, as if something warm might soothe the new pain that had entered into her . . . Dan and May. Well, why not? Dan deserved happiness; Dan had been so good to her; pure gold Dan had been all through. He had been so kind and attentive that she had come to think of Dan as her main support; she had imagined him supporting her, at least morally, through the first strange months of her release. She remembered the time when he had told her that Paul had become a priest and that Kathleen was going to marry Michael. She had given up then, yet all the time a hand had been holding hers . . . Dan's hand, and it was this hand that had pulled her back into existence. Whatever happened there would always be Dan. He had even said those words to her, time and again, time and again. When he had come to visit her he had said in some way, 'You've got me; you'll always have me; I'll always be there, Sarah.'

Phyllis was saying, 'I'm beginning to see the light. She wouldn't give John a divorce, not for years. That lass had three bairns to him; she was likely in a stew in case he'd walk out on her. You could never tell with a bloke like that. But he did try, I'll say that much for him. He tried again and again to get May to agree to a divorce, but she wouldn't bite. But then, just about eighteen months ago, she tells him to go ahead, and early on this year it went through. And now he's married at last. Aw, Sarah!' Phyllis put her fingers over her mouth and shook her head slowly. 'This doesn't hurt you, does it, to know this?'

'No . . . no, Phyllis. Don't worry. Ten years is a long time; you have time to think in ten years. If you haven't got to worry about eating, or the rent, or firing, or light, you've got to put your mind to work in some way. I set mine the task of straightening up my thinking, and learning not to be afraid of being afraid.'

Phyllis lay back in the corner of the couch and her eyes narrowed as she looked at Sarah. And she said quietly, 'You've changed, you know; you've changed, Sarah.'

'I hope so,' said Sarah.

'Oh, I don't.' Phyllis was bending forward, her hand touching Sarah's knee. And Sarah covered it with her own as she said, 'Come on, it's your turn. Tell me about the family.'

'Oh, you know all about them; I've kept you informed over the years. Things are just the same. They're all set in the cafés. We did think about taking another, but Ali's biding his time; things are not as bright as they were a few years ago, you know. Oh, by the way, Ronnie's in Newcastle with the band this weekend.'

'Oh, is he? I'd love to hear him play.'

'It's funny that, isn't it?' said Phyllis. 'I mean how he became a pianist . . . all through that old four-pound piano. You remember?'

Sarah remembered . . . the day that she had kissed John, before he had marched off to London. And that dinner-time, to take her mind off things, she had told David that she was going down to see a second-hand piano, and to her amazement he had put his foot down and said he was having no piano in the house. 'Don't you see, it will only make matters worse,' he had said as he inclined his head towards the wall. She had written and told Phyllis. And Phyllis had written back to say it was all right, and that, anyway, Ali had bought the piano himself, he thought it would do for the bairn. And it had done for the bairn. Her second eldest son had become a first-class pianist.

'I would never have thought about a piano for meself, or any of us,' went on Phyllis. 'But there, it's fate; we had to have that piano because playing the piano is the only thing Ronnie lives for . . .'

For the next hour they talked, as they always had done when they were together; they talked until the light went. Phyllis was pulling herself to her feet, saying, 'What about a little light on the subject,' when a voice called from the foot of the stairs, 'Mum! Mum!'

'What is it now?' Phyllis went to the door and, opening it, cried, 'What is it? Can't you manage without me for five minutes?'

'There's someone to see you. It's Mr Blythe.'

'Dan?' Sarah rose to her feet. Of a sudden she felt nervous, uncomfortable. For the first time in her life she didn't want to come face to face with Dan.

Dan paused in the doorway a moment, then came swiftly forward, and, taking her hands in his, said, 'Why, Sarah! You silly lass, you silly lass. You should have told me.'

'It's all right, Dan. It's better this way.'

'Better?' He withdrew his hands from hers, and his face became solemn, almost stern. 'Not from what Michael told me on the phone. That woman will go off her head one of these days . . . But perhaps it's all for the good . . . I mean you coming today, Sarah.'

'Yes, perhaps, Dan.'

He was standing away from her, looking at her now, his attitude slightly uneasy, and Phyllis, quick to sense this, jumped into the awkward breach by exclaiming loudly, 'Well, you'll stay to tea, Dan. Now, I'm not taking no.' She flapped her hand at him, although he had made no sign of refusal to her offer. Then going to the sideboard and taking out a cloth, she spread it over the dining-table, talking all the time.

'Well, this is a get-together, the first of many, I hope . . . and how's business, Dan?'

'Oh, pretty fair, you know, Phyllis, pretty fair.'

He was sitting to the side of Sarah now but not looking at her. He kept his eyes on Phyllis as he talked, and it would seem that the state of business at the moment was all that concerned him. 'We've all been making hay in the last few years, but it looks like the harvest's over. The dole circle's enclosing the Tyne again, I can feel it. I bet you can an' all in your weekly returns.'

'Well yes, you're right there, Dan. I won't say they're as shining as they were a couple of years ago.'

'No. And they won't be for a long time again. A grocer's shop is a money thermometer; I've seen it again and again. And what have we now? Unemployment, getting worse every week. It's bad when it hits the young 'uns, the lads just out of their time. Just the twenties over again: they do their apprenticeships and then they're stood off.'

'Still, you're not in the workhouse yet, Dan.' Phyllis was smiling at him.

And he returned her smile with a laugh. 'No, not yet, Phyllis. On the doorstep, like, looking through the gates as it were, but not quite in.'

They both laughed together, and Phyllis asked now, 'Well, what about a mixed grill? I've got some nice chops and sausages. What about it?'

'Not for me, Phyllis. A cup of tea and a toasted tea-cake. Now I wouldn't turn my nose up at that.'

'How about you, Sarah?'

'I'll just have the same. No grill, Phyllis. Not yet, anyway.'

'Well, you're customers that's easily served. And I bet you don't leave a tip . . . Mean lot!' In mock indignation she stalked into the kitchen. And they were left alone.

Dan, turning fully round in his chair, now looked at this woman who had never, in his eyes, changed one iota from the first time he had seen her across the tea-table on her first visit to the house.

And Sarah was looking at him, at his kindly face, still hand-some, but perhaps not so jolly looking as when he was younger. And the more she looked at him the more she ached inside. She was feeling more lost at this moment than she had done since the prison gates had closed behind her.

'How you feeling?'

'Oh, all right, Dan.'

'You're not. You can't fool me. Look.' He leaned forward and gripped her hands. 'I've got something I want to say to you.'

She closed her eyes for a second; then forced herself to open them and look at him and wait. Dan deserved to be happy.

She watched his lips move two or three times before they formed words, and then he was speaking hesitantly.

'I wanted to give you this gradually, not spring it on you. I wanted to do things gently, take perhaps a week over it. Not because I wanted to wait a week. No, but because I wanted to give you time to settle in. Time to think. Not feel you were forced to do anything you didn't want. But now, what Michael told me on the phone has altered everything. I could go up there and slap her mouth for her, I could really . . . Saying that me and May . . .'

'It's all right, Dan.' She was holding his hands now, and she was looking down at them. 'It's all right, I understand.'

'Oh no you don't. You don't. That's what I'm getting at; that's what I'm trying to say. Look, Sarah, I'd have to be damned hard up for a woman and gone in the head before I'd go within a mile of May. All the way down in the car coming here, you know I really felt frightened. I can see it all now: Mary's plans. And May's an' all. The divorce and everything, after she had sat tight for years. And then her coming up to the shop and wanting to do things upstairs. I cooled her off there, but I still didn't guess, and I kept on going across on a Sunday to have a word with her – I always have since John left. But my God in Heaven! Men are infants! That's all we are, infants . . . Sarah . . . oh, lass, don't cry.' He put his hand up to her face and wiped away the tears.

'It's all right, Dan, it's all right.'

'Can I go on?'

'Yes, Dan, yes.'

He looked down at their joined hands now, and with his voice scarcely above a whisper, he said, 'I've waited a long time. Every day of ten years I've waited, knowingly waited, knowing what I was going to say to you the minute you came out. I've waited with hope these last ten years. And you might as well know it. I've waited from the first minute I saw you, but without hope . . . Mary was right about one thing, you know, Sarah: you did take us all. But not from her, because she never had us . . . Now don't get upset. Aw don't, you could no more help the lot of us coming to you than a flower can help itself opening to the sun. Anyway, I've thought and planned what I would say to you. Sometimes, especially at nights, I got worried. I'm not young any more; I'm ten years older than you; and whereas, as you hardly look – and I mean this, Sarah – with all you've gone through you hardly look a day older than when I first saw you. I could even say you were better looking, if that is possible. Well, what I was going to say to you after you'd got your breath was . . . Will you have me, Sarah?' He waited. Then in a small voice: 'Will you?'

'Dan. Oh, Dan.'

He slipped from his chair on to his knees by her side, and his arms going about her, he waited. 'Will you?'

She nodded slowly.

His head was on her breast now, as Phyllis's had been, and she laid her cheek on his hair. She did not ask herself if she loved Dan; she didn't, not as she had loved David, and again not as she had loved John. But this was a new kind of feeling, a feeling of warmth, of tenderness, a feeling without fear, without worry, a feeling that expressed laughter because she couldn't see herself living with Dan and not laughing.

It was as if Dan had read her thoughts, for he said, 'I'll give you everything I have, Sarah. There'll be no fifty-fifty, you can have all I've got. I've enough money put by to see us out comfortably. I've got enough to enable us to laugh.' He raised his head and looked at her. 'You were made for laughter, Sarah, laughter and jollity. But you've never had it; it's always been damped down one way or another.'

'Oh, Dan. . . Dan.' She was gazing at him, but she could see him only through a thick mist.

'I love you, Sarah.'

The tears still running, she smiled at him.

'And now I'm going to do something I've waited a long time to do.' And on this he bent forward and kissed her. His lips hard and firm; he kissed her full on the mouth. Then, getting to his feet and holding out his hands, he pulled her upwards and into his arms.

Holding close, they looked at each other. Then through her tears Sarah laughed. She laughed haltingly but freely for the first time in years. And she said to him, her voice cracking, 'How's Mrs Flaherty? Is she still alive?' She was giving him a lead to make her laugh, more and more, more and more.

Dan's head was back now, his laughter filling the room. And so he stayed for a moment before bringing it forward again to look at her and say, 'Alive and kicking. Oh, the things I'll tell you about Mrs Flaherty! You'll split your sides.'

But what he said to her now about Mrs Flaherty was: 'You know, over all the years when she was reduced to twopennorth of bacon scraps she would always say, "God's good. Aw, God's good." She hadn't a thing in the world to be thankful for, but always she would say that . . . God's good. Well, here's me. I have everything at this minute to be thankful for, and I say with Mrs Flaherty, God's good.'

No recess in her mind questioned Dan's conception of God, nor yet the God of Mrs Flaherty who had inspired faith even through

224

hunger. Perhaps there were millions of gods. Perhaps every man had his own god, and as he saw him in life so he found him in death . . . Gods like Mrs Flaherty's, gods like Dan's . . . and David's, who weren't acknowledged, only lived. Gods like Father Bailey's. Then there were the gods of the Father O'Malleys, and the gods of men like her father and the gods of the Mary Hetheringtons, and these gods were all blind millers. These were terrible gods, and their followers could be terrible people.

Phyllis came from the kitchen now, crying, 'I couldn't leave the toast. What are you two la . . . ?' She brought herself to a halt and looked at them for a full minute before flinging her arms wide and rushing at them. And as they entwined her in their embrace she lent her head once again on Sarah's breast, and between laughter and tears she too said, 'Aw, lass, God's good. When all's said and done, God's good.'

Though the mills of God grind slowly,
Yet they grind exceeding small;
Though with patience He stands waiting,
With exactness grinds He all.

THE END

KATE HANNIGAN

AUTHOR'S NOTE

The characters in this book are entirely fictitious and have no relation to any living person.

Although the setting is Tyneside and several actual place names have been used, 'the fifteen streets' are entirely imaginary.

Owing to difficulty in comprehension by the uninitiated, the Tyneside dialect has not been adhered to.

CONTENTS

THE BIRTH

'I shall want more hot water, and those towels there will not be enough.'

'Glory to God, doctor, you have every towel there is in the house!'

'Then bring sheets, old ones, and we can tear them.'

'Old ones, and we can tear them,' mimicked Dorrie Clarke to herself. 'New brooms sweep clean. By God, if they don't! Old Kelly would have more sense, drunk as he might have been. The way this one's going on you would think sovereigns were as thick as fleas and there was a father downstairs to welcome the brat.'

'There's no more sheets, doctor,' she said, rolling her already tightly rolled sleeves further up her fat arms. Speak to her like that, would he! She'd been bringing bairns into the world when his arse was still being washed! For two hours now he had said: 'Do this, do that,' as if Kate Hannigan on the bed there was the Duchess of Connaught, instead of a trollop going to bring a bastard into the world; when it made up its mind to come, which wouldn't be for another couple of hours. And here she'd been hanging around since tea-time; and it was Christmas Eve and all, and not a drop past her lips; an' couldn't get away for this young swine saying: 'Lend me a hand here, Mrs Clarke,' 'Let her pull on you, Mrs Clarke,' 'Get that damn fire to burn, Mrs Clarke!' . . . Yes, he even damned her. Now Doctor Kelly, rest his soul, could be as drunk as hell, but he'd never swear at you; more likely to say, 'Have a drop, Mrs Clarke; you need it.' There was a gentleman for you. This one wouldn't reign long; but he was reigning tonight, blast him! and get out for a wet she must, or die.

Into Dorrie Clarke's agile brain flashed an idea; she'd trade Sarah Hannigan a pair of sheets for the chiffonier downstairs; she'd always had her eyes on that. Begod! she'd get the best of this bargain, and get out of this young upstart's sight for five minutes.

Her fat, well-red face rolled itself into a stiff, oily smile. 'There's not a rag in this house but what's in the pawn, doctor; but I've a pair of sheets of me own that I'll gladly go and get this minute, for I couldn't see this poor thing want.' She nodded pathetically down at the humped figure on the bed.

7

The doctor didn't raise himself from his stooping posture over the bed, he didn't even raise his head, but he raised his eyes, and his eyebrows shot into the tumbled, thick black hair on his forehead. And his black eyes stared at Mrs Clarke for a second in such a way that she thought: 'Begod! he looks like the divil himself. And he might be that, with his black eyes in that long face and that pointed beard; and him so young and handsome. Holy Mother of God, I must have a drink!'

Whether it was she slipped, or it was the doctor's remark that momentarily unbalanced her she couldn't afterwards decide; for she was stamping down the narrow dark stairs, in a rage, when her feet . . . just left her, as she put it, and she found herself in a heap in the Hannigans' kitchen, with Tim Hannigan sitting in his chair by the fireside, wearing his look of sullen anger, only more so, and not moving to give a body a hand up, and Sarah Hannigan, with her weary face bending above her, saying: 'Oh, are you hurt, Dorrie?' She picked herself up, grabbed her coat off the back of the kitchen door, pulled a shawl tightly around her head, and, with figure bent, passed out through the door Sarah Hannigan held ajar for her and into the driving snow, without uttering a word. She was too angry even to take much notice of the pain in her knee.

She'd get even with the young sod . . . Begod! if it took her a lifetime, she'd get even with him.

'Mrs Clarke,' he had said, 'I don't allow intoxicated women to assist at births. And, if you bring the sheets, we won't tear them. They will only be a loan, Mrs Clarke.'

Dorrie Clarke suddenly shivered violently. And it wasn't a shiver caused by the snow as it danced and swirled about her; it wasn't a cold shiver at all. 'Jesus, Mary and Joseph! How did he know? He could have heard I take a drop, but he couldn't have known about the sheets. My God! it's what Father O'Malley said . . . The divil walks the earth, he has many guises . . . He's the divil! Ah! but as Father O'Malley would say, he's got to be fought, and, begod! I'll fight him!'

Back in the bedroom of 16 Whitley Street Doctor Rodney Prince stood with his elbows on the mantelpiece. He had to bend down a considerable way to do this as it was only four feet high and merely a narrow ledge above the bedroom fireplace. He kept pushing his hands through his hair with a rhythmic movement . . . God! but he was tired. Wasn't it ever going to come? What a Christmas Eve, and Stella likely sitting in a blue stately fume, cramming herself with pity . . . the beautiful, talented, brutally treated (he gave a soundless laugh at the thought) and neglected wife of a slum doctor! Well, he had telephoned her and told her to go on to the Richards. And he had also telephoned the Richards and told them; but they had said, 'Well, you know Mrs Prince! She won't come without you.' Clever Stella; playing the part of the dutiful wife, awaiting her husband's return

8

with coffee and sandwiches and a loving smile. Clever Stella . . .
Oh, my God, where was it going to end? Four years of it now,
and perhaps ten . . . fifteen . . . twenty more . . . Oh no! If only
he didn't love her so much . . . Christmas Day tomorrow; she would
go to church and kneel like . . . one of God's angels, somewhere where
the choirboys could see her. Poor choirboys! He knew the feelings she
would send through them. How could they think of the Trinity? sing
their little responses? when the great God Nature, he who gave you
concrete proof of his presence, was competing against the other God,
who, as far as they understood, wasn't introduced to them until they
were dead . . . Oh, Stella! What was he thinking? He was so tired.
If only he could go home after this was over and find her there, soft
and yielding, wanting something from him . . .

'Doctor! Doctor!'

He turned swiftly towards the bed and gripped the hands outstretched to him. 'There, there! Is it starting again? Try hard now.'

'How much longer, doctor?'

'Not long,' he lied; 'any time now. Only don't worry; you'll be all
right.'

'I don't mind . . . I don't mind.' The tousled head rolled to and
fro on the pillow. 'I want to die . . . I hope we both die . . . just go
out quietly . . .'

'Kate, here, don't talk like that!' He released one of his hands from
hers and brought her face round to look at him, his palm against her
cheek. 'Now, we want none of that nonsense. Do you hear?'

Her great blue eyes looked up at him, quietly and enquiringly, for
a second. 'What chance has it?' she asked.

He knew she wasn't enquiring after the child's chance of being born
alive, although about that he was beginning to have his doubts, but of
its chance to live in her world, handicapped as it would be. 'As much
as the next,' he answered her. 'And more,' he added, 'seeing it'll be
your child.'

Now, what had made him say that? For, if it inherited her beauty
and was brought up in these surroundings, it was doomed from birth.
How the feelings of kindliness made one lie, made one tactful and
insincere! Only when you hated someone did you tell the truth.

He pulled up a rickety chair and sat down, letting Kate, in her
spasms, pull on his arm . . . Where the deuce had that drunken
sot got to? . . . The room was cold; the fire that had glowed for
a little while had died down under its heap of coaldust . . . If that
old hag didn't come back he'd be in a nice fix; the mother downstairs was less than useless, scared to death of her man, and of this
event, and of life in general . . . If that Clarke woman didn't come
back. But why was he harping on about her not coming back?
She was a midwife . . . of sorts; it was her job. But he had had
a little experience of her during these last few months, and he had

9

come to recognise her as a fawning leech, picking her victims from among the poorer of her own kind.

'Oh, doc . . . tor! Oh, God!'

Easing the bedclothes off the contorted figure he moved his hands quickly over her. Then he covered her up again and banged on the floor with his heel. In a few seconds the door was opened quietly, and the mother stood there, clutching her holland apron in both hands.

'Has Mrs Clarke come back yet?'

'No, doctor.'

'Then will you kindly get this fire to burn? Put wood on it.'

'There's no wood, doctor; there's only the slack.'

'Can't you break up something?'

She looked at him helplessly; her lips twitched, and her tongue seemed to be moving at random in her mouth. He couldn't meet her eyes. He thrust his hand into his pocket and handed her a sovereign. She looked at it, lying bright and yellow on her palm. Her tongue ran wild races between her teeth, but she made no sound.

'Get what's necessary,' he said gruffly. 'And perhaps a chicken; Kate will likely need it tomorrow.'

She nodded slowly at him, while her tongue, darting from side to side, caught the drops as they ran down her cheeks.

Kate was moaning; she could hear herself. The moans seemed to float around her, then rise up to the ceiling and stick on the mottled plaster. Most of them were right above her head, gathered together in the dark patch that formed the three-legged horse which had been her companion and secret confidant since childhood. He wouldn't mind having her moans; he thought all about her, her sins, the secret things she thought and was ashamed of, even her feeling sometimes that there couldn't be a God. It was, as she had once read, that people like Father O'Malley were only put there to stop people like her from thinking; for, if she once started thinking, she and her like wouldn't put up with things as they were. Jimmy McManus had lent her that book, but she had understood hardly anything at all of it. Yet, it was after reading it that she had gone and got the place in Newcastle, in the best end . . . Shields wasn't good enough for her. And it was after reading that very book that she had taken off all her clothes and had stood naked before the mirror, swinging its mottled square back and forth so that she could see every part of herself; and glorying in it as she did it, and knowing that she was beautiful, that she was fit to marry anybody. It was only her talk that was all wrong . . . But she would learn; she was quick at picking things up . . . Of course, she had suffered for this. Her conscience had driven her to confession, and, in the dark box, with face ablaze, she had confessed the greatest sin of her life. The priest had told her she must guard against the sin of impurity by keeping a close watch on her thoughts; and he went on to explain how a great saint, when sorely tempted by the flesh, had thrown himself naked into a holly bush, or was it a bramble? she wasn't sure now.

The moans floated thick about her . . . Where was John now? . . . Did he know he was soon to be a father? . . . Had he ever been a father before? . . . He wasn't a husband, she wasn't a wife; yet she was having a baby . . . It was all her own fault, she couldn't blame John; he had never mentioned marriage to her. Her inherent honesty had told her so a thousand times these past months.

'John!' she called out sharply as the doctor wiped the sweat from her face.

'It's all right, Kate, it's all right; it won't be long now.'

It won't be long now! It won't be long now! the moans said. John's baby, with his slant eyes and beautiful mouth . . . It was as near as yesterday when she had first seen him, seated in the Jacksons' drawing-room. Since two of the maids had been sent into town, she had been told that she was to serve tea . . . wee cakes and china cups. Something had happened inside her when their eyes had first met. She had been glad to get out of the room and into the coolness of the hall. He had been there only three days when he slipped a note to her, asking her to meet him . . . Oh, the mad joy! the ecstasy of love before its fulfilment! Even when she had given herself to him, it had not compared with the strange delight of knowing she was wanted; and by him, a gentleman who had travelled the world. Twice he had taken her; only twice; and both times within a month, on her half-day. Right up Lanesby way they had gone; and he had told her she was the most beautiful thing he had ever seen, that he loved her as she'd never be loved again, and that she'd always be his . . .

'Oh, doctor! Doctor!'

'It's all right,' he assured her, as he went out of the room. 'Mrs Hannigan!' he shouted to the frightened face, framed in the shawl, already at the bottom of the dim stairs, 'get me Mrs Clarke here at once!'

'I'm here, doctor!' cried a voice, 'an' I can't come up them stairs.' Mrs Clarke pushed Sarah Hannigan to one side, and stood glaring up at him. 'Something's happened to me knee with that fall I had down the bl–down the stairs. I'm beside meself with the pain of it. I don't know if I'll be able to get back home through this snow, the drifts are chin high.'

'Mrs Clarke, I've got to have help! You'll come up here if I have to carry you up!'

'Begod, an' I will not! Look at that!' she cried.

He bounded down the stairs towards her. She had pulled up her skirt and was disclosing her knee, already laid bare for inspection.

He looked at it . . . Well, that settles that. The damned woman, you would think she had done it on purpose . . . He thought a moment . . . 'Nurse Snell, that's it! She'll come. How can I get . . . ?'

'It's no use. She's in the heart of Jarrow this very minute after a case; I saw her go only a couple of hours ago.' Mrs Clarke was triumphant. 'It's nobody you'll get this night. Now, Doctor Kelly used to—'

'Be quiet, woman!' He glared at her, the point of his beard thrust out.

Begod, if she could only strike him down dead! Him to speak to her like that, and to call her – woman! . . . She that was looked up to and respected for her knowledge all round these black buildings, all fifteen streets of them. They had even sent for her from Shields and Jarrow to deliver, before today, and Doctor Kelly had said she was every bit as good as himself. Yet this young snot . . . with his big, new-fangled motor-car and his fine clothes, and his voice like a foreigner . . . would tell her to shut up! Even Tim Hannigan there, who put the fear of God into everybody in the fifteen streets with his swearing and bashing, when the mood was on him, even he had never dared to tell her . . . Dorrie Clarke . . . to shut up. Her blood boiled. She fastened the top of her stocking into a knot and rolled it down her leg to make it secure; she pulled her coat tighter about her and limped to the kitchen door, before turning to him. 'You may be a doctor . . . yet that's got to be proved . . . but yer no gentleman. You can strike me off your club; and I wouldn't work on a case where you are to save me the workhouse; I'm a particular woman. And take my word for it, you won't reign long!' The snow whirled into the kitchen as she pulled open the door.

'Keep that leg up for a few days,' he called after her.

'You go to Hell's flames!' was the rejoinder.

A fleeting shadow, that could have been amusement, passed over Tim Hannigan's face. Throughout the conversation he had sat immobile in the straight-backed wooden arm-chair dead in front of the fire, staring at the glowing slack which the good draught of the big chimney kept bright.

Sarah Hannigan stood near the bare kitchen table in the centre of the room, picking at her bass bag and her shawl alternately, and her pale, weary eyes never left the doctor's face. She watched him think a minute after Dorrie Clarke had banged the door, then swiftly wrote something on a piece of paper which he took from a notebook.

'I'm sending for Doctor Davidson, Mrs Hannigan,' he said, as he wrote. 'Perhaps your husband will get this note to him as soon as possible?'

'I'll take it, doctor,' said Sarah, breathlessly.

'No, you have your shopping to do, and you must get something to keep that room warm. Your husband can take it.'

She looked helplessly from the back of her husband's head to the bearded face of this strange doctor . . . He didn't know, he was so cool and remote; from another world altogether; didn't the sovereign prove that? If it got round he threw his money about he'd have no

12

peace. And him speaking to Dorrie Clarke like that, and now asking Tim to go a message . . . Oh, Holy Mary! . . .

'I'll go on me way, doctor . . . '

'Certainly not! Mr Hannigan,' he addressed the back of Tim's head, still immobile, 'will you kindly get this message to Doctor Davidson at once? Your daughter is a very sick woman.'

Only Tim Hannigan's head turned; his pale eyes, under their overhanging, grizzly eyebrows, seemed to work behind a thin film. They moved slowly over the doctor and came to rest, derisively, on his black, pointed beard. 'Hell's cure to her!' he said slowly. His upper lip rested inside his lower one and his eyes flashed a quick glint at his wife before he turned his head to the fire again.

'Sir, do you know that your daughter might die?'

Tim's head came back with a jerk as if he was silently laughing.

'Doctor, please . . . let me. Oh, please! I'll get there in no time.'

Sarah grabbed the folded note from his hand, and he let her go without a word. The back door banged again, and he still stood staring at the back of Tim Hannigan's head. He felt more angry than ever he had done in his life before . . . These people! What were they? Animals? That frightful, fat, gin-smelling woman, and this man, callous beyond even the wildest stretches of imagination. He would like to punch that beastly mouth, close up those snake eyes . . . Oh, why get worked up? He'd need all his energy . . . He turned and went back up the stairs, groping at the walls in the dark . . . As Frank had said, it was a waste of sympathy; for what little he would achieve he would not assist their crawling out of the mire one jot, ninety per cent of them still being in the animal stage . . . Not that he took much notice of anything his brother might say; but he had upset his family and dragged Stella to this frightful place . . . for what? To express some obscure feeling that came to the surface and acted as a spoke whenever he was bent on following a sensible course . . . at least sensible to his people's way of thinking. Had he followed the course laid out he would now have his London surgery and a definite footing in one of the larger hospitals, and at this minute he would have been at Rookhurst; likely just going in to dinner with the family. Oh, what a fool he was! He couldn't pretend to an ideal urging him on, or love for these frightful people. Obstinacy, his father called it; a form of snobbery was his mother's verdict; cussedness and the desire to be different, Frank said, with a sneer. Only his grandfather had said nothing, neither of approbation nor of condemnation; he had just listened. But there was a peculiar expression in his eyes when he looked at Rodney, which might have been mistaken for envy.

This room was freezing. If this girl didn't die of childbirth she would of exposure. Bending over Kate, he felt her pulse. Davidson should be here within half an hour, if he were at home; the sooner

13

they got this job over the better, for it promised to be an awkward job . . . He must try to do something with that fire.

Kneeling down on the small clippy mat, he blew on the pale embers. This resulted in his face and hair being covered with coaldust . . . Damnation! . . . He stood up and shook himself. Temporarily blinded, he stumbled towards the half-circle of marble, supported on a three-legged frame, standing in the corner and poured some water out of the enamel jug standing in the tin dish. He washed his face, and the yellow soap stung his eyes more than the coal dust had done . . . What a night! And likely his car was half buried by now; it had been snowing for hours . . . In the ordinary course he would have left his patient earlier, to return later. But this fresh fall of snow, on top of twelve inches already frozen hard, had warned him that this would have been easier said than done, and the condition of this girl made it imperative that he should be on the spot . . . Pulling the cream paper window blind to one side, he looked out, but he couldn't see down into the street, the window being a thick, frosted mass of snowflakes. He turned towards the bed and sat down on the chair again.

Kate was lying inert, breathing heavily. He looked around the room, ten by eight at the most; the three-quarter-size iron bed, adorned with brass knobs, the marble-topped wash-hand stand, and a large wooden box, end up, with a curtain in front and a mirror on top, was all the room held in the way of furniture; pegs on the door supported an odd assortment of clothes, and a patchwork quilt and two thin biscuit-coloured blankets covered Kate; the floor was as white as frequent scrubbing could make it, and the whole was lit up by a single gas jet.

Rodney Prince looked at this gas jet flickering on the turned-up end of a piece of lead piping. Its power was, he thought, about one-hundredth that of the chandelier above the dining-table at home . . . Home, to his mind, was Rookhurst, not the place he shared with Stella; that was 'the house'. He had a sudden nostalgia for all the things he had known and had taken for granted for so many years, but most of all, at this moment, for the dining-room at Rookhurst, for its dim, worn red and golds, for its long, wide windows, forming a frame for the sweeping downs beyond, and for the old furniture polished by time and handling to a delight for the eye. And there was a strange longing for his people; for his greying and stately, slightly cynical mother, whom, temperamentally, he resembled too much to be on good terms with, for the easy tolerance of his father, even for the jealousy of Frank.

It was Christmas Eve, and, in spite of all their differences, Christmas Eve had always been a gay day at home. But from ten o'clock this morning he had been trudging in and out of tiny houses, some clean, some smelly, but all seeming to be filled with the same type of people, coarse-voiced and wary. Then there was Stella. The row they had had last night might have been patched up tonight had he been able to take her to the Richards. As much as he knew she despised them, their flattery would have helped to smooth the plumage that he had so brusquely ruffled, and perhaps put her into a tender frame of mind. But wasn't she always tender? Dreamy and tender, that was Stella. Then how could she be the cold, outraged beauty? How could she make a man feel like a wild beast? Last night she had snuggled, and nestled, and purred like a contented kitten, while he fondled her hair, murmuring into it, telling her of the magic she cast about him. He had kissed her eyes and her ears, and had stroked her arms, and she had lain, docile and beautifully sweet, as if awaiting final consummation. And his mind had cried, 'Ah, now!' And then, as always, like a snowflake on a hot log, she had melted away from him.

'Stella,' he had cried to her . . . actually cried to her! . . . 'Don't! You are torturing me.' He had crushed her body under his, but she was far withdrawn. He had been furious that this should be happening again, and had renewed his efforts to solicit her affections.

Her voice had come as a whisper, which might easily have been a hiss, when she had said, 'Why must you always want the same thing? Why are you so beastly? We have had all this out before. I'm just not going to put up with it, night after night.'

'But, darling, it's nearly . . . it's so long . . . ' he had stammered, in his pain.

'Oh, don't be so coarse! You talk like . . . well, like one of these dockers.'

At that he had let her go, her long, white limbs in their crumpled chiffon whirling out of the bed and into the dressing-room. It was only when he had heard the key turn in the lock, and he knew that she meant to spend the night on the couch, that the torturing desire in his blood seemed to gather itself into one hard knot in his head, which beat with sudden hate of her. He was banging on the dressing-room door and hissing words he would never have believed possible. She made no answering sound . . . When he dropped into bed, shaking and limp, he had to bite into the pillow to stifle the tearing emotion that racked him.

Stella could reduce him to that because he loved her, because he could not stop loving her. She had the power to change in a flash his six feet of virility into a shamed, trembling heap. He knew the course he should have adopted long ago; but he could never see himself touching anyone but Stella. He had loved her from the age of five, when she had walked between Frank and him and had been the cause of their first serious quarrel.

This morning they had met at breakfast; Stella, a little white, but smiling and talking of the snow and the Christmas doings, in front of the servants . . . Stella was very well bred; she would keep up appearances in hell, he thought . . . He knew he had looked ghastly, the blackness of his beard accentuated the pallor of his face. He had

15

scarcely spoken and had eaten nothing, and, on the plea of outstanding calls, he had hurriedly excused himself after drinking three cups of coffee. Without looking at her he knew that her whole bearing was one of sad and gentle reproach.

What the servants had heard last night from their distant rooms didn't trouble him; he was used to servants knowing as much about his life and that of his family as they did themselves. He forgot to take into account that the servants of thirty and forty years' standing, who were like one's own friends, were a different proposition from chance maids of three months.

The knocker of the front door banged twice. It brought back Kate from far-away regions. She opened her eyes wide. 'Who's that?' she asked. Then, grabbing his hand, 'You're not having me sent to the workhouse?' She looked around wildly. 'Where's Mrs Clarke? Oh, don't send me! Please don't send me. I can easily pay you when I'm up.'

'What on earth are you talking about? Don't be silly, Kate! What put such an idea into your head? That is likely Doctor Davidson; Mrs Clarke can't help me, she's hurt her knee. There, now, lie down.' He pressed her gently back into the pillow.

The knocker banged again, quicker and louder this time. Rodney went to the stair-head. Surely that brute wasn't still sitting there and making no attempt to open the door! He heard the poker rattle against the bars of the fire. By God, he was! Of all the swine!

He ran down the stairs. 'Are you deaf, sir?' he shouted at Tim Hannigan's back, as he hurried through the kitchen and into the front-room, from where the front door led into the street. The knocker banged once more as he pulled open the door, letting in a whirl of snow.

'I thought you were all dead.' The big muffled figure was kicking his feet against the wall. 'Phew! What a night!' He stepped into the room, and Rodney closed the door without a word and led the way through into the comparative brightness of the kitchen.

'Oh, hello, Tim! You deaf?' The easy familiarity of Doctor Davidson surprised Rodney. He gave the big, bony man a quick glance; no annoyance showed on his face at being kept waiting; there was about it that lingering half smile that had so baffled Rodney on the few previous occasions when they had met . . . He had felt at first that Davidson was laughing at him; laughing gently, but nevertheless laughing. And he had thought, how dare he! He had soon learnt all about Davidson, who was the son of a Jarrow grocer. The grocer had made money, and had spent it on his son. And the son, instead of taking himself and his career to a far distant place, as far away as possible from Jarrow, had returned, bought a practice in the worst quarter, near the ferry, and married a Jarrow girl. They lived in an ugly house overlooking the muddy Don, where it poured its chemical-discoloured

16

water into the Jarrow slacks and so into the Tyne. But all this had not wiped that quaint smile off Peter Davidson's face. And, through time, Rodney had found that the smile was not for him alone; Davidson seemed to handle life gently and with that half smile; he never seemed to hurry, nor to be impatient. Rodney wondered what he was really like. He had felt Davidson would be worth knowing, but at the same time knew it was impossible; they met seldom in the course of their rounds and the only other way would be through social visiting. For himself, he wouldn't mind in the least, but Stella! Well, he couldn't imagine her and the Jarrow girl, somehow.

They were in the bedroom before Rodney spoke. 'I'm sorry, Davidson, I've had to ask you to turn out on a night like this; Christmas Eve, too.'

'Oh, don't let that worry you, it's all in the game. Hello, Kate!' he said, bending over the bed, with his hands on his knees. 'You're going to have a Christmas baby, eh?'

Again that tone of familiarity. Rodney watched Kate's face; she smiled as one would at a friend. Rodney felt a little stir of professional jealousy; she hadn't smiled at him like that; nor would any of his patients, he thought, treat him as they did Davidson. He had tried for three months to get below their wary surface; he had tried, indeed he had, to put them at their ease, little guessing that his voice alone put him in the category of 'The Class' and that, in their fierce independence, they resented the necessity for what they unwordingly thought his condescension.

With great reluctance he took off his coat and rolled up his sleeves; the chill of the room seeped through his fine wool shirt and vest. As he opened his case and picked out what he required, voices from below the window came to him like words spoken through a thick towel:

'Hello there, Joe! Merry Christmas.'

'Same to you, Jimmy. Same to you.'

'Coming for a wet?'

'Ee, lad, no; ah haven't been yem yet. The missis'll likely bash me over the heed when ah puts me nose in the door!'

Muffled laughter, then the thick silence from the street again.

Davidson was still talking to Kate, and a feeling of utter and absolute loneliness suddenly flooded through Rodney. He seemed divorced from every human contact and feeling; everyone he knew, his family, and Stella, all stood aloof and condemning . . . sending out their displeasure through the bleak stares of their eyes. He saw them all as a hillside covered with sturdy oaks, and himself a little stream at their feet, bent on winding his own way past them. They were so powerful, but helpless to stop his meandering. And he had wound his way into the valley where there were these people . . . those men in the street, this girl on the bed, this big, burly doctor who held life steadily by the reins; they were all one. He was in their midst, but he couldn't get near them either; and, oh, he wanted the touch of some friendly hand. He was lost in that vast, unknown and terrible continent of loneliness; it stretched on and on, very white and hopeless, and quite bare.

Good heavens! he thought, this won't do. I'm light-headed. No breakfast, no dinner; must have something as soon as this is over . . . He looked across at Davidson who was still talking to Kate. 'Well, there it is,' he was saying. 'If you want the place it's yours. Their own girl won't be leaving for a month, and it's five shillings a week. So there you are, Kate; you're all set up and nothing to worry about.'

Rodney nodded to him, and Davidson came round the foot of the bed to the wash-hand stand. 'Afraid it's going to be a bit of a job; I think it advisable to give her a whiff.' He handed Davidson a bottle and a pad of cotton wool. Davidson nodded and walked back to the bed.

'Two old boys nearly eighty and their sister about seventy, and only eight rooms. When they told me today their girl was leaving I thought of you right away, Kate; and it's a lovely little house, down Westoe. If you go there you'll be set up. Now just breathe steadily, Kate. That's it, th . . . at's it. Now we are all set,' he addressed Rodney. 'That'll have eased her mind a bit; the main part of their worry is to get into a good place. Poor little beggar! She's only a child herself.'

'Do you know her?' asked Rodney, pulling the prostrate form into position.

'Yes. Watched her grow up. Everybody knows Kate Hannigan; she was too beautiful to miss. By! she was a lovely kiddy. It always struck me as odd how old Tim Hannigan could have a child like her. I didn't know she had got into this mess until yesterday; it surprised me. Somehow she always appeared different; quiet, a little aloof, as if she didn't quite belong around these quarters. Didn't run round with the lads, either; kept them at their distance. And if she hadn't, old Tim would have . . . And now this. Poor Kate!'

Doctor Davidson gently lifted one of the long, nut-brown plaits off Kate's face with his free hand, while with the other he felt her pulse. 'Not as strong as it should be,' he muttered. 'How is it to time? Was it due?'

'Yes, as far as I can gather. But I couldn't get much out of her,' said Rodney. 'She didn't come home until the day before yesterday. She had been working in some lodging house in Newcastle; the mother thought she was still in service. She hasn't been home for months, having made one excuse after another. Then she turns up like this. Knowing that beast downstairs, you can't wonder at her being terrified to come home; but I should have thought the workhouse would have been preferable to facing him. Yet she seems to have a horror of it.'

The smile disappeared from Doctor Davidson's face as he asked, 'You don't know much about the workhouse, do you?'

18

But Rodney didn't answer, he had started upon his job. His hands moved swiftly; he braced himself and pulled, gently pressing . . . easing . . . He worked for some minutes, and Davidson, who watched his every move, thought: Good hands, no quivers there. Yet he's as strung up and as taut as a bow. Wonder what brought him this way . . . funny fellow. Why did he take old Kelly's place when Anderson's was going up Westoe end? Could have had a couple of titles on his books there. But still, apparently it isn't money he wants; old windbag Richards says he's got at least two thousand a year private income . . . Whew! Two thousand a year! . . . Davidson had a vision of a bright shining clinic, fitted with the latest appliances . . . Wonder what he does want; he's certainly not the welfare type. Whatever his aim, I bet it doesn't meet with his lady-wife's . . .

'No use,' said Rodney, raising his eyes to Davidson; 'it's wedged . . . I'll have to cut.' He nodded towards his case.

Davidson handed him an instrument. There was a sharp snip, snip, a quick dabbing of spirits, and his hands were once more pulling, easing, pressing. He was no longer cold; beads of sweat ran down his forehead, falling from his brow on to his hands. His chin was drawn in, his beard lying like an arrow on his shirt front . . . A little more, a little more, he encouraged himself . . . Ah, the head! . . . Now then . . . now then . . . easy, but make it quick. She can't stand much more; Davidson is anxious about that pulse . . . There, there . . . a little more . . . Oh, hell! don't say it's going to be obstinate now!

Pulling, easing, pressing, it went on. The sweat was running into his eyes now and his shirt was no longer white.

Davidson's expression became pitying . . . Poor Kate! It was practically up. Still, this fellow was good; if she were paying hundreds she wouldn't have had anyone better . . . But these things happened . . .

'A . . . ah!' It was an exclamation of triumph as much as relief. Rodney slowly withdrew the red body covered with silvery slime. For a second it lay across both his hands, a girl child . . . to be named Annie Hannigan, and who was to help make and to almost mar his career.

THE KITCHEN

The kitchen was bright and gleaming. From the open fireplace the coal glowed a deeper red in contrast with the shining blackleaded hob, with the oven to its right and the nook for pans to its left. It sent down its glow on to the steel-topped and brass-railed fender, where its reflections appeared like delicate rose clouds seen through a silver curtain. The fire glinted on the mahogany legs of the kitchen-table and on the cups spread on the white, patched cloth. It shed its glow over the red wood of the chiffonier standing against the wall opposite, and over the brass-knobbed handle of the staircase door. The hard, wood saddle, standing along the wall to the left of the fire-place, took on an innocent deception from the glow; its flock-stuffed cushions looked soft and inviting. Even the sneck of the door that led to the front room had glints of white along its black handle. But it was to the window that the fire lent its most enchanting grace. With its six red earthenware pots of coloured hyacinths, and framed in the dolly-tinted lace curtains, starched to a stiffness which kept their folds in perpetual billows, it looked like a startling, bright painting. Never had that window-sill upheld such beauty.

Hyacinths at any time of the year were things one just dreamed of. But at Christmas! and in her kitchen! they made Sarah Hannigan feel that life was changing, that it was becoming easier, and that before she was really old she would know peace . . . she didn't ask for happiness, just peace. And she asked herself, as she looked out over the bulbs to the tiny backyard and to the backs of the houses opposite, hadn't she had more peace this last year than she had had for the previous seventeen years . . .

She had thought life would become unbearable when Kate had come home like that last Christmas. And it was unbearable for nearly a month after Annie was born. But when Kate got that place in Westoe things had seemed to change. It wasn't only that Kate gave her four-and-six a week out of her five shillings and God alone knew what a difference that had made – it was that things had seemed to happen to keep Tim off her, that his eighteen years' persecution of her was easing at last.

First, the baby had been fretful, and for most of the winter she had

20

had to keep it downstairs in the warmth of the kitchen. So she had slept, thankfully, on the saddle. Then she had been covered with that rash, and the smell of the ointment the doctor had given her had been nauseating to Tim. He had sworn and raged, and she had thankfully left the feather bed and her husband's side for the hard comfort of the saddle again. But a rash doesn't last for ever, although she had lengthened its stay by weeks, until he had begun to get suspicious. When she had returned to the feather bed the old nightmare began again. Sometimes she would wait a week, or even two, until, blind with rage at his own impotence and the caducity of his passion, he would repeat the old cry, 'She isn't mine! Tell me, or I'll throttle it out of you. Is she? Is she? She's the artist's bastard, isn't she? Tell me!'

Sarah knew that it was only the fear of hell as painted so realistically by Father O'Malley that had saved her life on more than one occasion. Three times, when Kate was but a few months old, she had flown with her into Mrs Mullen's, next door. Things like that soon got around the fifteen streets, and one day Father O'Malley came and had a talk with Tim up in the bedroom, and an equally long talk with her down in the kitchen. The result, in her case, had been that she never went to confession again without a dire feeling of guilt, whereas, up till then, her great sin, as it would be called, had been something between God and her alone. She could not put it into words, for the result of it was the brightness of her life. But Father O'Malley's probing had reached her very soul, only some instinct, not yet beaten into submission, warning her to risk hell's flames rather than entrust it to any human, even though he be an agent of the Almighty.

The effect on Tim was to make him attend mass regularly, even Benediction on a Thursday night. He could get sodden drunk on a Saturday and beat her up, but he'd go to mass on the Sunday. There were worse things than having your eyes blacked and being kicked around the room, as Sarah knew; and when he was drunk, strange as it may seem, he made no futile demands on her.

So, taking things all in all, she didn't mind him getting drunk as long as she could get the money out of him beforehand for the rent. And he usually let her have that; for she knew he had the fear of being turned out on to the street and of having to go to the workhouse. To provide their food she could always do a couple of days cleaning or washing. She had managed somehow up till last year. But then things in the docks became worse; sometimes he would only get one shift in in a week. When he returned from his twelve-hour shift, his moleskins red and wet up to the thighs, she had it in her heart then to feel sorry for him . . . unloading iron ore all day, and only bone broth, thickened with pot stuff, to set before him. And the three-and-six he got for the shift had to go for the rent, not even twopence for baccy, let alone a pint. With Kate's four-and-six a week and what she could pawn they had existed. They hadn't yet gone on the parish, for they both knew that, before they could get a penny, they'd be told to sell the chiffonier, the saddle and the spare iron bed upstairs that was kept for Kate.

Her mind wandered back and forth over the past, as she stared out into the dark day. Eleven o'clock on Christmas Eve, and you really needed a light, the sky was so low and heavy. Christmas had always brought trouble; she had never known a happy one, and you always seemed to remember your troubles more at Christmas. She and Tim had been married in Christmas week. She couldn't remember why she had married Tim; perhaps because he was big and quiet. And she had taken his quietness for kindness . . . never had she been so mistaken. Or perhaps because she had wanted to get away from Mrs Marris's, where she worked for sixteen hours a day for seven days a week for the sum total of half a crown. She hadn't known Tim very well when she had married him; it was difficult to get to know a man when you had only half a day off a month. She was then eighteen and Tim twenty-seven. Now she was forty-two and he was fifty-one; and of all her life she'd had only three months happiness . . . stolen moments of ecstasy and terror; but no-one could take them from her . . . no-one. She'd kept them for over eighteen years; she'd manage to keep them till she died . . . And now things were changing, she could feel the change. It wasn't that Tim had been a prisoner upstairs for six weeks, or that there was a baby in the house; it was rather a premonition . . .

She'd better mash some tea and take him up a cup. And she'd ask Maggie in for one; they'd be quiet, he wouldn't hear. She turned from the window and put the black kettle on to the centre of the red fire. Then, with a preliminary rattle of the bars to cover her signal, she gave two sharp taps on the back of the grate. After a short pause it was answered by a dull thud. Sarah put the poker down and went to the cupboard at the right-hand side of the fire-place and took from one of its scalloped-edged newspaper-covered shelves the brown teapot. After placing it on the hob, she went quietly through the front-room and gently opened the door, leaving it ajar. She returned to the kitchen and, drawing up the wooden chair near to the clothes-basket at the side of the hearth, she sat smiling wanly down on the sleeping baby lying therein. Presently her gaze wandered around the kitchen. It was all beautifully clean for Kate's coming. Any minute now Kate would come in, and for a whole week she'd be here with her in the kitchen . . . No Tim; just her and Kate and the baby. Her hands, as they lay one on the other in the lap of her white apron, relaxed, her body relaxed, and she slumped, staring unseeing at Tim's armchair on the other side of the hearth. Never had she known such a Christmas Eve; there was nothing to dread.

Sarah started slightly when a little dumpy woman with grey hair and twinkling eyes stepped noiselessly into the kitchen from the front-room. Mrs Mullen came to the improvised cradle and nodded, smiling down on the baby.

'By! she's lovely, Sarah,' she whispered. 'How's he?' She jerked her head sharply towards the ceiling.

'He's just the same. I'm expecting doctor today,' Sarah whispered back. 'Sit down, Maggie.'

Mrs Mullen, making a wry face, refused the proffered arm-chair and pulled up a small cracket to the fire. 'This'll do me; I mustn't stay long. I've just sent the whole bang lot of them out to draw their Christmas clubs. They've got twenty-five shillings on their cards between the six of them; God knows what they'll buy. But I say, let them buy what they like, they're only young once. But it'll be hell let loose when they bring all their ket back; so I won't stay long, Sarah, for we'll have him' – she nodded again to the ceiling – 'banging on the wall and cursing like old Harry.'

'The kettle's boiling, I'll mash the tea now,' said Sarah. 'Tell me, what are you putting in their stockings?'

'Oh, all kinds. Mick's had a few good weeks. And the things he's bought! You'd never believe. Come in the night, when we're filling them, and see. By! you're all done,' she said, looking around the room. 'And don't your window-sill look grand! I've never seen owt like them flowers; they weren't in bloom when I was in last.'

Going to the window, Sarah lifted two pots. 'I want you to have these for a Christmas-box, Maggie. I can't give you anything else, but I'd like you to have these.'

'No, lass. No. Kate brought them for you.'

'Sh!' said Sarah warningly. 'Take them, Maggie; they're so little for all the kindness you've shown me.'

'Well, thanks, Sarah . . . I do like a flower. By! they're grand.'

'I'll take this up first,' said Sarah, filling a pint pot with tea, and adding four heaped teaspoons of sugar. She disappeared up the dark stairs, leaving Maggie Mullen sitting on the cracket comparing the seeming spaciousness around her with her own cramped quarters next door. Ten of them in four box-like rooms, and two of the eight children nearly young men; it was such a crush. But still, please God, give her her lot any day before Sarah's, with her four rooms for two people and a baby. By God, yes; any day!

Sarah re-entered the kitchen, closing the stair door softly behind her. She poured out two cups of black tea and handed one to Mrs Mullen.

'Thanks, Sarah,' said Maggie. 'By the way, did you hear Big Dixon's got her other one?'

'No! When?'

'Eleven o'clock last night. Another boy. That's the sixth; she'll be all right for money later on. By! the place won't hold her when they all start working; you can't keep her down now since she's got her Mary in place at the doctor's. Do you know she bought a gramophone only last week?'

'No!'

23

'Yes, with a horn on it the size of a poss tub; you'd think she'd have plenty noise with six wee'ns round her, wouldn't you, now?'

'Who has she got looking after her?'

'Oh, Dorrie Clarke, of course! She can't afford a gramophone and Nurse Snell!'

Here the two women chuckled and sipped their tea.

'Very few people are having Dorrie Clarke now,' continued Mrs Mullen. 'Can you blame them? She reeks of gin. And how she has the nerve to go to the altar rails every Sunday morning, God alone knows – and He won't split!'

'Oh,' whispered Sarah, 'don't make me laugh, Maggie.'

'Laugh!' said Maggie; 'I wish I could. I'd like to see you laugh until you split yer stays.'

Sarah's weary face took on a sudden glow, and she smiled across the hearth at her friend. 'I've got a funny feeling today, Maggie; as if life was going to change for the better. That is, as if something was going to happen . . . perhaps it's only Kate coming home; I don't know . . . Oh, here she is!'

The back-door opened and Kate came in, carrying a heavy suitcase. She put down the case, closed the door, and then stood looking at her mother and Mrs Mullen who had both risen and were staring back at her, with eyes wide and mouths agape.

Kate lifted her arms from her sides and smiled at her mother. 'Do you like them, ma?' she asked.

'Name of God, Kate, where did you get them clothes?'

'Do you like them?' persisted Kate.

'Hinny . . . you look . . . oh, Kate! . . . ' Sarah could find no words.

'Aye, Kate, you do look luvly. My, I've never seen owt like them before!' put in Mrs Mullen.

Sarah went to her daughter. They didn't kiss, but stood for a second cheek pressed against cheek. Then Sarah stepped back. 'Where did you get them, lass?' A trace of anxiety showed in her voice.

'Miss Tolmache gave them to me for a Christmas box. Aren't they lovely, ma?'

'Lovely,' murmured Sarah, 'lovely.'

'By! lass, you look like a real . . . ' Mrs Mullen had been going to say 'lady', but, on the face of what had happened last year, felt it would be a little out of place; so she added, 'toff'.

'Miss Tolmache had the costume and hat specially made for me, and she took me out yesterday and bought me the shoes. Look at the fur round the bottom of the coat?' Kate held up the bottom of the three-quarter-length mole-coloured coat for her mother to inspect the trimming of dark-brown fur. 'And feel how thick the material is, ma. And look at my hat; she had it made to match, and trimmed with fur too.'

24

For the moment Kate was not the mother of a year-old child, she was an eighteen-year-old girl, wearing the first new clothes of her life. 'She's sent you a Christmas box, ma, but you're not getting it until tomorrow. And material to make dresses for Annie; oh, and heaps of other things!'

'Ee, Kate!' was all Sarah could utter, for the tears were choking her . . . her Kate to be dressed so . . . like . . . like the class: and she'd never seen any of the class look half so lovely as Kate did. Oh, she was beautiful, beautiful . . . Thank God Tim was upstairs.

'You won't half make the tongues wag in the fifteen streets when they see you in the rig-out, Kate . . . I think you've fallen on your feet in that place, lass.'

'Oh, I have, Mrs Mullen! Miss Tolmache is wonderful; and so is Master Rex, and Master Bernard. But, here I am, ma' – she turned to her mother – 'talking about my clothes and forgetting all about Annie. How is she?' Kate knelt down by the clothes-basket.

'Now leave her be, Kate, and let her sleep, for she's the devil's own imp when she's up,' said Sarah.

Kate gazed down at the sleeping baby; the dark lashes lay upcurled from the pink cheeks, the silver hair gleamed on the pillow. A rush of feeling, so intense as to be suffocating, swept through Kate; her thoughts encircled her, shutting out all but her desire . . . John! John! If you could only see her; she's so like you. Oh, where are you? I must know whether you are at home. I won't make any claim on you, I'll never mention marriage; only I must see you, I must show her to you. I've got a whole week. I'll phone the Jacksons' today, they'll know if you're back; you said about eighteen months. And when you see me in my new clothes, and see how different I am in other ways, too . . .

'My God, listen to that!' exclaimed Mrs Mullen, in a hoarse whisper, as a hullabaloo sounded through the thin wall of the kitchen. 'Cowboys and Indians! . . . Oh, Sarah, hinny, I must be off. See you later, lass.' She patted Kate's shoulder as she hurried out.

'Come on, lass, get your things off and have a cup of tea,' said Sarah.

'Never mind the tea, ma,' said Kate, getting up; 'just look what I've brought. Clear the table.'

She took off her hat and coat, and lifted the case on to the corner of the table. When it was opened, Sarah exclaimed, in amazement, 'But, hinny, she didn't give you all that stuff?'

'She did, ma. Look! A chicken, tinned peaches, a tongue, a box of cheese' – Kate named each article as she took it out of the case – 'dates, a pudding, a cake . . . '

'You're sure she gave you them all, Kate?'

'Ma!'

'Oh, I'm sorry, lass. I know you wouldn't touch anything that didn't belong to you; it's only I can't imagine anybody so good.'

'Yes,' said Kate, stopping the process of emptying the case and staring, unseeing, at the picture of Lord Roberts hanging on the wall above the chiffonier; 'it took me a long time to get used to it. At first I couldn't believe that anyone could be so kind and not want something back. I feel terrified, ma, when I think they'll soon die; Miss Tolmache is the youngest, and she's seventy!'

'But the old gentlemen must be hale and hearty to look after greenhouses and grow bulbs like them,' Sarah pointed to the window-sill.

'Oh, yes; they are all very healthy, but some day they must die,' said Kate.

'Oh, lass, don't be so mournful. There they are, off to Newcastle to spend their Christmas in an hotel so as to see a bit of life, and you talk of them dying. Folk like that seem far from dying to me.'

'Yes, I suppose so; this is the tenth Christmas they've spent in that hotel. You know, ma, when I set them to the train this morning they waved to me just like three schoolchildren . . . Do you think money keeps you young, ma?'

'I don't know, lass; I only know that work and worry can make you old before your time. But, hinny, don't let's get doleful.'

Sarah looked hard at her daughter . . . There was something different about her Kate; it wasn't only that she was taller, it was her manner, and the things she said, and the way she said them . . . Kate gave her part of the explanation in her next words: 'I haven't told you, ma, but I've been having lessons.'

'Lessons?' queried Sarah.

'Yes, from Master Bernard. I've had an hour each night. He's teaching me English, how to read and write it, and how to speak it.'

'But, lass, you can read and write better than the next, and you've always talked better than them around these doors.'

'But, ma, this is different; I'm learning grammar . . . nouns and pronouns, adjectives and adverbs . . .'

'Adjectives and adverbs!' Sarah looked at her daughter in amazement. 'But what good is it going to do you, hinny? Don't let them put ideas into your head, lass . . . you've got to work for your living.'

'Oh, ma, don't worry.' Kate smiled tenderly at her mother, and touched her rough cheeks with her fingers. 'It's only that you can understand things better when you can read properly and when you know what books to read . . . Look!' She went to her purse and took out two sovereigns. 'One from Master Bernard with which to buy books . . . he says he'll know how much I've learned by my choice of books . . . and the other from Master Rex, who says I've to stuff myself with chocolates and to forget about the books.'

'Two pounds! Oh, lass!'

'Yes, ma; and here's one of them . . . that's my Christmas box to you, and I must keep the other to get the books.'

'Kate, lass, I'll not take it.'

'Don't be silly, ma; I don't want it. With all my new clothes and everything, there's nothing I want . . . And I've another bit of news . . . I'm getting a two-shilling-a-week rise next year!'

'No!'

'I am.'

Sarah sat down on the kitchen chair. 'You know, lass, all the good things are happening together. God's good,' she added. Then, as if to question the Deity, her thoughts swung to Tim upstairs. But even the thought of him could do nothing to dim her gladness this day; it even evoked a spasm of pity. 'Would you mind, lass,' she asked, 'if I bought him an ounce of baccy out of this?' She motioned to the sovereign in her hand.

'No,' said Kate, without looking at her mother. 'How is his leg?'

'Just about the same; it doesn't seem to heal up. The doctor said he should be in hospital; but you know he won't go because they'll send him to Harton. The doctor explained it wouldn't be the workhouse side, but it's no use, he just won't go.'

'Will he walk again?'

'Oh yes; the bone isn't broken; only the dirt got in, with him dragging himself home from the docks and having to wait until the doctor came.'

They both started slightly as a knock sounded on the front-door . . . 'That's the doctor, now,' said Sarah, running her hand over her tightly drawn hair and smoothing her white apron.

Kate stood by the table and watched her mother go through the front-room. She felt embarrassed and shy; she had not seen the doctor since a fortnight after Annie had been born, when she sat, swathed in a blanket, before the bedroom fire, and here she was now all dressed up.

The front-door opened and a voice said, 'Morning to you, Mrs Hannigan.'

Sarah answered, 'Oh, good morning, Father,' in a toneless voice.

The priest entered the kitchen, and the pin-points of his eyes through the thick glasses took in all before him in their slow movement from right to left. They saw the table laden with food, and not ordinary food; they saw the fur-trimmed coat and hat lying on a chair; and, in the centre of the kitchen, dressed in rich cloth and silk, with the fire-light playing on the shining coils of her hair, piled high in no respectable fashion, they saw a tall girl, who had sinned, and who, doubtless, by the evidence of his eyes, was still sinning. The thin lips parted . . . 'Well, Kate!'

'Good morning, Father,' said Kate, her colour rising slowly under his cold stare. Sarah had no need to look at the priest's face, or to hear his tone, to know what was in his mind.

'Do have a chair, Father, and have a look at all the lovely things Kate's mistress has sent us for Christmas; and look, Father,' Sarah

27

said, holding out Kate's coat and hat across her arms. 'Miss Tolmache had this costume made, and the hat too. And look at the shoes that she bought, and the blouse.'

The priest did not take his eyes from Kate. 'Your mistress bought you all these things, Kate?'

'Yes, Father.'

'She is indeed kind; a most unusual mistress. No, Mrs Hannigan, I won't sit down.' He motioned away the chair that Sarah held out. 'Is she a Catholic, Kate?'

'No, Father.'

'No? Then of what religion is she?'

Kate glanced from the priest's face to her mother's, then back to the priest's again. She straightened her back and lifted her head from its respectful droop. 'No religion, Father.'

There was a pause during which the priest and Kate stared at each other, and Sarah tried to signal Kate to silence by the entreaty of her eyes.

'No religion! An atheist! And you are content to work there?'

'They are very kind, Father.'

'So is the devil, when he sets himself out.'

'They are good, Father!' Kate's voice had risen. 'They are wonderful people; they are better than anyone I've ever known.'

'Kate means they are kind, Father,' Sarah put in anxiously; 'she means . . .'

'I know what Kate means, Mrs Hannigan,' answered the priest, without looking at Sarah; 'I know quite well. When were you last at confession, Kate?'

'Three months ago, Father.'

'Three months! Father Bailey and I myself will be hearing confession from six until eight tonight. I'm just giving you the times in case you've forgotten, Kate. Perhaps I'll see you at the altar rails at Midnight Mass, and I hope you will have a happy and holy Christmas . . . And now, Mrs Hannigan' – he turned to Sarah – 'I will go up and see Tim, for, with all his faults, it will be a great sorrow to him not being able to attend Midnight Mass.'

The priest opened the stairway door and his short, spare figure disappeared into the dimness. Sarah watched him climb the stairs, and when he reached the top she softly closed the door and turned to Kate, who stood now, with one foot on the fender and her arm along the brass rail below the high mantelpiece, staring down into the fire.

'Oh, lass!' said Sarah, 'you should have said you didn't know what religion they were; you know what he is. Now, if it had been Father Bailey, he'd have understood.'

'Classing them with the Devil!' muttered Kate. 'They're the kindest and best people on earth.' She turned to her mother: 'Mr Bernard talked to me about God one night, ma. And he said if I found faith

28

in God through the Catholic religion, I had to hang on to it with all my might; for the greatest disaster in life was to lose one's faith. And then, him a priest, speaking of them like that!'

Sarah stared at her daughter . . . Yes, Kate was changing; she was talking differently already . . . A little shiver passed through her, and she uttered a silent prayer that in the change her child would not drift away from her.

'Miss Tolmache said if I wanted to go to mass on a Sunday morning I could.'

'And have you gone, hinny?'

'No.'

'Ah, lass. And he never asked you that . . . he likely will when he comes down.' Sarah glanced uneasily at the stair door. 'Look, hinny; go on down to Shields and buy your books.'

'Ma, I'm not afraid of him; I can't imagine now why I ever was . . . I'll tell him I haven't been.'

'Oh, God in Heaven, don't do that! He'll tell Tim, and then . . . Oh, lass, go on out! I don't want any more rows.'

'But, ma, I haven't seen Annie yet.'

'Oh, she'll sleep for another hour, she was up at six. Go on, lass, and get your books; go on before he comes down.'

Kate looked steadily at her mother. 'All right, ma.' She picked up her coat and hat. 'But why should a man like that be allowed to scare the wits out of people? He's terrified me for years, in fact up to this last few months. After all, he's only a man, ma.'

'Hinny!' The horror in Sarah's voice conveyed itself to Kate, and she said, 'Oh, don't look so shocked, ma; I didn't mean anything.'

'He's a priest, lass,' said Sarah, with as much reproach as she could find it in her heart to use to her daughter.

'Yes, I suppose he is,' said Kate dully. She put on her hat and coat. 'But why should he have the power to frighten people?' she asked, looking at her mother through the small mirror hanging on the wall. 'All right,' she added, as Sarah clasped and unclasped her hands, 'I won't say any more; I'm going.' She turned, and smiled suddenly, a soft, illuminating smile, and, bending forward, kissed her mother swiftly on the lips. 'Ta-ta, ma; and don't worry, I'll go to confession and communion tonight . . . But I'll not go to confession to him,' she added, pulling a face.

From the front door, Sarah watched Kate go down the long narrow street; she watched her until she was lost in the muck and gloom of the day. Then, with a sigh, she turned indoors. There was all this food, she had a whole sovereign, she had a present that Kate wouldn't let her see until tomorrow, and she had Kate. It's funny, she thought, as she cleared the table, I had a surprise sovereign last Christmas Eve too.

* * *

29

Immediately Kate was outside, one thing, and one thing alone, filled her mind: how was she going to word her telephone call to the Jacksons. She turned into the main road from which the fifteen streets branched off; walked between the tram sheds and the chemical works, and came to the Jarrow Slacks, with the great timbers, roped together in batches, lying helpless on the mud like skeletons unearthed in a graveyard. She passed the New Buildings opposite, similar in design to the group she had just left, and walked on down the long road connecting East Jarrow and Tyne Dock, past the saw-mill, through the four slime-dripping arches, and into the heart of the docks. She passed the dock gates and stood on the pavement, waiting for a tram that would take her into Shields; and she wasn't aware of standing there, so familiar was the scene and so urgent was the need to make a choice of words for the telephone call. Trimmers stood in groups, a little apart, as befitted their superior position; men gathered in batches, awaiting the choice by gaffers for the unloading of grain or ore boats; strings of coolies, in single file, passed up and down the dock bank, bass bags, full of fish, swinging against their thin, shining legs; sturdy, brass-buttoned captains strolled, with conscious insolence, into the dock offices, or across the road to one of the line of public houses, that stood wall to wall, filling a whole street, even continuing up the dock bank; sailors of all nationalities pushed in and out of their doors; and Kate stood among this seething life, utterly unconscious of anything but her own great need.

Heads were turned towards her; remarks passed between men; women, some of whom knew her, stopped and stared . . . That's young Kate Hannigan. You know, her who got dropped last year. Look at the way she's got up! My God, like the Duchess of Fife! It must be a paying business . . . A chief engineer, catching sight of Kate as he crossed the road, changed his course and came and stood within a few feet of her, presumably waiting for a tram, his eyes devouring her hungrily.

Even when Kate reached the Shields post office, and had passed her money across the counter, and had waited until her call was through and was directed to the nearer of the two boxes which stood in a corner, even then she was still not clear in her mind what she would say. She was quite used to this wonderful invention, for Miss Tolmache had a telephone, and it was part of Kate's pleasant duty to answer it; whereas at the Jacksons the housekeeper had allowed no-one of the staff but herself to touch the instrument.

She heard a buzz at the other end, and a voice said, 'Hello! Who's speaking?' Kate was stricken dumb; it was Mrs Hanlin, the housekeeper herself. 'Hello!' the voice said again. 'This is the Jackson residence.' Alter your voice; try to speak like Miss Tolmache, said Kate, wildly, to herself.

'Hel-lo!'

'Yes?'

'Er . . . is Mr Herrington . . . at home?'

'Mr Herrington?'

'Yes. I mean, has he returned from abroad yet?'

'Oh yes.' Kate leaned against the side of the booth for support. 'He came home three weeks ago. Who's speaking?'

'I'm . . . I'm a friend of his. Is he at home now?'

'At home? Oh no. He's on honeymoon; he was married by special licence last week . . . Are you there?'

'Yes.'

'They've gone to America, where Mr Herrington is going to lecture . . . What did you say? . . . Oh, who did he marry? Why, Miss Scott-Jones, of course, they were engaged before he left for Africa, the year before last . . . Can I give his sister, Mrs Jackson, any message? Hello! . . . Hello!'

Kate hung up the receiver and walked out of the booth. An old woman in a long black coat and bonnet touched her arm: 'What's the matter, hinny? Are yer not feeling well?'

'I'm all right, thank you,' said Kate, and walked away . . . Oh, John! John! . . . Miss Scott-Jones! You never said; no-one ever said; and she was so ugly. Oh, Holy Mary, help me! He'll never see Annie now. He couldn't have even loved me, after all he said; not even when he . . . Oh, I must sit down . . .

She went into a café, and sat in a corner, with her back to the room, oblivious of the stares and chatter of the Christmas shoppers. She ordered a cup of tea and sat sipping it . . . The purpose had suddenly been taken out of living, and the sick hopelessness of the period before Annie had been born returned. Her efforts of the past year had been for nothing; for she admitted to herself now that there had been but one aim in her desire for knowledge; to be different; one aim that made her such an apt pupil and evoked the praise and encouragement of Bernard Tolmache.

She felt very young and helpless; all the magnificent feeling of the morning had fled. She wanted to cry . . . She mustn't cry here, she told herself, she must wait until she got home. But then, she mustn't give way there, either; for what would her mother think? She knew nothing about John. She had asked her only once who the man was, and, on her stubborn silence, had not pressed the point. And it was strange, she thought at this moment, that her da, of all people, had said nothing; only glared at her silently. And always his glance had left her and rested on her mother, with an expression for which Kate could find no words to define . . . No, she mustn't go home and cry, because it would upset her mother; and she had looked happier this morning than Kate had ever remembered her looking before. She'd have to wait until she was in bed . . . And then there was Annie. Gone now was the hope that she would have a da. This disappointment added to her own wretched

31

feelings, and she realised how much she had been banking on that.

She didn't buy her books, but instead took the tram back to Tyne Dock; the Jarrow tram terminus was within a few yards of the dock gates. A tram was in, and she hurried towards it, dodging the groups of men so carefully that she didn't know how she managed to knock the case out of the young man's hand as he, too, hurried towards the tram. Kate's apology was laughingly brushed aside, the young man saying there was certainly nothing to be sorry about. He sat beside her on the long wooden seat. 'Mild weather we're having for the time of the year,' he remarked.

'Yes, it is,' answered Kate.

'I like to see a bit of snow myself at Christmas; don't you?' said the young man.

'Yes, it's more seasonable, I suppose.'

'You're Miss Hannigan, aren't you?'

'Yes, I am Kate Hannigan.' She wished he would be quiet and would stop talking . . . It was with relief when she stood up and said, 'Goodbye, and a happy Christmas.'

He was a little taken aback at the coolness of her; he had not expected her to be so composed . . . After all, she'd no need to put on airs. Anyway, he'd made a start, and she'd likely be at Midnight Mass tonight . . . He stretched his five feet four inches, patted his bow tie, and pulled down his celluloid cuffs. Together with the interested spectators of the little scene, he watched Kate alight from the tram and, lifting her skirt, step lightly over the puddles in the road and on to the pavement.

Now, Kate thought, as she walked slowly up the street, I must say they hadn't the books I wanted, and that I've got a bad head; she'll believe that. But, whatever I do, I mustn't spoil her Christmas.

The front door was ajar. She pulled up abruptly at the kitchen door. Her mother was by the window, with Annie in her arms, and, standing near the table, drawing on his gloves, was Doctor Prince.

The last time Rodney Prince had seen Kate she had looked what she was, a very young girl, and one who had narrowly escaped death. Staring at her now, in unfeigned amazement, he vividly recalled that night a year ago when he had had to put up a stiff fight for her life, only Davidson's help preventing him from losing. How they had worked on her! Now he felt grateful to her for being the medium through which he and Davidson had become such firm friends. And he wondered how he would have got through the past year without Davidson and his wife and the haven the grim-looking house on the Don had become.

But this girl, Kate Hannigan; she looked amazing . . . and so utterly out of place in her surroundings . . . What was it? . . . Not only her warm, glowing face, or that hair . . . Of course, it was her clothes! Good Lord, she was got up in style; and good style at that! . . . But where? . . . A sadness crept into his eyes . . . What a pity! Oh, why couldn't some man take her and marry her? . . . Instead of that! She was so fresh, so unusually beautiful, and she looked . . . yes, unspoiled, in spite of the fact . . .

'Good day, doctor.'

'Good day, Kate!' He finished drawing on his gloves. 'You're looking well, Kate.' To himself he sounded pompous.

Sarah came forward; she hadn't missed the doctor's scrutiny any more than the priest's. 'She does look grand, doesn't she, doctor? And it's all thanks to Doctor Davidson for getting her that place; her mistress bought her that whole rig-out for a Christmas box.'

Rodney suddenly smiled. He had heard of the Tolmaches and their kind eccentricities from Davidson. 'You look very smart, Kate.'

'Thank you, doctor,' said Kate, walking to her mother and taking Annie into her arms; the child bounced and gurgled with glee. Kate knew why her mother had informed both the priest and the doctor so quickly of the source of her new clothes, and felt both hurt and annoyed . . . I'm not bad . . . I'm not, she thought. I could never do a thing like that for money . . . or anything, but . . . she couldn't even say to herself the word 'love'.

'She's a lovely child, Kate.'

'Yes, she's growing, isn't she?'

'Your mother has her hands full with her, haven't you, Mrs Hannigan?'

Sarah smiled. What a grand man he was! She had been a little afraid of him at first, but not now. And he loved children; he had even nursed Annie, here in the kitchen.

'She gave me some trouble a year tonight, did this little madam,' he said, bending towards the child and poking her playfully with his finger. Annie opened her mouth wide, showing six white stumps, and beat her fists delightedly on Kate's face. Then, with a swift movement, she bent towards the black head, so temptingly near, and burrowed her two hands in its depth.

'Oh, good lord, you little imp!'

Rodney eased his head towards her and put up his hands, trying to unclasp the tiny fingers.

'Annie, let go this minute, you naughty girl!' said Kate.

'Oh, my goodness!' cried Sarah. 'Who'd have believed she'd be so sharp. Oh, dear me! Pull her off, Kate!'

'No, don't pull her off,' pleaded Rodney; 'you'll hurt her hands.' He went nearer: 'Unclasp one hand at a time, Kate, and I'll hold it.'

As Kate's fingers moved in his hair they touched his, and he felt their cool firmness.

Sarah stood irresolute, her hands wavering . . . Not to save her life could she have touched the doctor's hair.

The three of them were so engrossed that they did not hear the knock . . . if there had been one . . . nor the kitchen door opening.

But when they heard a familiar voice say, 'I'm sorry, Mrs Hannigan, I'm sure; I didn't know you had company. I'll give you a look in later,' they turned as one.

Rodney screwed round his head to look at the figure in the doorway; his hands were covering one of Kate's. As she turned, their faces were within an inch of each other, with the laughing face of the child behind.

They stared at Dorrie Clarke; and she stared back, genuinely surprised at the domesticity of the scene before her . . . By God, she had stumbled on something now! Would you believe it? Carrying on openly like that . . . Jesus strike her down this minute, she never suspected it. No wonder the upstart had ordered her about. No wonder! . . . Canoodling openly in the kitchen here, brazen as brass the both of them! And look at the way she was got up . . . He could spend money on her yet he'd deprive another woman of an honest living . . . Big Dixon was the first case she'd had in months, and she wouldn't have got her if he'd had anything to do with it . . . Why'd this carry-on not struck her before? . . . By the God above, she'd make it hot for him! So damned hot he'd be sorry he ever crossed her.

'I'll see you later, Sarah.' Her eyes darted a malevolent glance at Rodney, and she withdrew her grim-lipped, fat face and closed the door.

In making Rodney the father of Kate's child, Dorrie Clarke did not dream that she was defeating her own object; for he would become, for the mass of the people, a lad . . . someone human; in spite of him being a toff and different he would be one of themselves; various sections of the poor community would view his action in different lights, but most of them would want his attendance on them . . . and the reasons would have horrified some of the more respectable of them had they faced the truth, in their minds; her scandal was to enlarge his practice as hard work would never have done.

'That was Mrs Clarke,' said Sarah lamely. She had an uncomfortable feeling, although she could not explain why. 'Are you all right, doctor? Would you like a comb?'

'No, thanks, Mrs Hannigan; I have one . . . And, yes, I noticed that was my friend, Mrs Clarke,' he laughed, as he ran the comb through his hair; 'but we're not on speaking terms. And it's all through you, madam,' he said, pointing the comb at Annie. 'You lose me a friend, then you pull out my hair . . . Well, I must be off.'

He took up his case. 'A happy Christmas to you, Kate. And to you, Mrs Hannigan.'

'A happy Christmas, doctor,' they both said.

As the door closed behind him they looked at each other.

'Isn't he a lovely man?' Sarah said.

'Yes; he seems very nice,' Kate replied quietly.

'I wonder what brought Dorrie Clarke here,' mused Sarah; 'she's no friend of mine.'

'Nor of him, by the look she gave him,' said Kate.

THE DRAWING-ROOM

A narrow lane off the rural Harton road led to Conister House; at least, to one of the walls which surrounded it. A wrought-iron gate in the wall led out of the lane into the lower garden, a long sloping lawn, studded with ornamental trees. The upper garden, which was also on a slight rise, was another lawn, with a lily pond in the centre and bordered by flower-beds. Shallow steps led from this to a terrace, on to which two sets of broad french windows opened from the house. But so gentle was the rise of the ground and so high the surrounding creeper-covered walls that nothing but the garden was to be seen from any part of the ground floor of the three-storied, red-brick house. This, Stella Prince told herself, was the only thing that made life bearable in this vile town. When they had first arrived in Shields there had been no suitable house vacant in the best end of the town. Some that were offered were open to the gaze of passers-by or of neighbours; these were not to be even considered. So, when she saw Conister House, although not actually in the upper quarter, she felt that, in all this cesspool of ships, coal mines, mean streets and impossible people, this was an oasis. Here, in the summer, she could sit in the garden and write, as undisturbed as if she were a thousand miles away from all this grimness; only the far-away sound of ships' horns penetrated the garden, the soot and smuts which dared to invade it and the house being soon dealt with by two gardeners and three maids. She was determined that if she had to live here it was going to be bearable.

Stella had spent a lot of thought and time on the inside of the house, but most of all on the drawing-room. The walls were of a delicate silver-grey, not a picture marring their virgin surface, and the woodwork was painted black. The windows were draped in long straight folds of dull-rose velvet, and the plain carpet, of heavy pile, was a tone darker. Standing on the carpet, one at each side of the bog-oak fire-place, were two superb Hepplewhite elbow chairs, and two occasional chairs, oozing preserved antiquity, rested nonchalantly at given distances. A Queen Anne walnut bureau bookcase stood against one wall, while a china cabinet of the same period stood against the other. The black wood of the mantelpiece lent a deeper lustre to the three Bow figures which had its long length entirely to themselves. A cabriole-legged settee faced the fire, and opposite the french window stood a seventeenth-century writing-desk.

The room at any time would have appeared unusual, but at this period of chair-backs, mantel-borders and heavy mahogany it was rebellious. Visitors to Conister House were impressed, as they were meant to be. The order of the room was rarely disturbed. If there were more than six people present, chairs were brought in from other parts of the house, to be removed immediately the visitors had departed . . . a little subdued at the splendour and more than a little awed by the creator of it all; for who would think a gentle, fragile creature, such as Mrs Prince, could arrange a house like that, and give such dinners! But of course, she wasn't just an ordinary woman, no-one who wrote poetry was.

Stella knew herself to be absolutely in line with the room; she herself had chosen each article in it, replacing the more homely pieces she and Rodney had chosen together at the beginning of their married life.

She sat now at her desk and read again the letter she had received by the mid-morning post. Her deep-set eyes glowed, and the creamy pallor, usual to her heart-shaped face, was tinged with the flush of excitement.

What would Rodney, who had thought her writing only a pose and who had no belief in her ability, say to this? At first he had called her his clever little girl and had treated her work as a joke, or, at best, as a hobby. But lately he had been absolutely hostile to it; even going so far as to say she spent too much time scribbling, and hinting that there were more useful occupations. She hadn't put the question, 'Such as what?' telling herself she was too wise to make that mistake; one of his answers might have been, 'Raising an adopted family.' She had enough to endure, she thought, without this horror. Of course, had she known that Rodney would insist on practising in these slums, she would never have married him; she had thought it would have been Harley Street at least, and then, perhaps, a title. Her sister had managed that for herself, and she had always been inclined to look down on Annabel. She knew she could certainly have done better for herself than she had done; but it had been the two Prince boys constantly fighting over her that had seemed so exciting at the time, and Rodney had appeared so romantic when he had returned from college with that beard. Still, Frank, she now realised, would have been the more sensible choice, especially since at that time she liked him nearly as much. She felt certain he would have been easier to manage, much easier; for one thing, he was staunch to his class, he had no revolutionary ideas; and for another, she couldn't imagine Frank being beastly in the same way as Rodney was . . . Frank was more . . . yes . . . more cultured; there was a coarse streak in Rodney. Still, she smiled inwardly, she had managed very well to avoid all unpleasantness, such as children. After all, men were such fools, and

Rodney, a doctor too, was no exception. In fact, the whole thing was laughable; it paid one to finish off abroad. Of course, the knowledge had been of little use to her there, for she wasn't inclined that way. But it had stood her in good stead since her marriage, and Rodney had never guessed. He had always underestimated her intelligence; it was just as well, in that direction, at any rate.

Hearing the 'chunk-chunk' of his car behind the house, she rose and went out of the drawing-room, across the hall and into the dining-room, opposite. A glance at the table told her everything was in order. She rang a small hand-bell, and when a smartly dressed maid appeared she said, 'Tell cook not to serve dinner for fifteen minutes, Mary.' She returned to the drawing-room, picked up the letter from the desk, and stood near the fire-place, waiting. As she listened to the side-door opening, she was at a loss to account for what she heard. Who on earth was he talking to?

'Here we are, then. Let me take your hat and coat off. What a fine young lady! Now we're all ready.'

When Rodney stood in the drawing-room doorway, holding by the hand a child, the most startling blonde child she had ever seen, her surprise could not have been more genuine had he appeared sprouting horns out of his black head.

'I've brought a little lady to see you, Stella.' He advanced across the room, suiting his steps to the child's.

'Who on earth . . . ?' began Stella.

'Now, Annie, say, "How do you do, Mrs Prince?" Go on; like Kate showed you.' Rodney squatted down beside the child, his head level with hers. Annie gazed at him, her green slant eyes full of trust and adoration; her flaxen hair, dropping straight on to the shoulders of her white, frilled pinafore, lay in little tendrils; her mouth was wide, and when she smiled two gaps showed in her lower set of teeth.

She turned from him, quick to obey his command, and, thrusting her hand up to the very clean lady, said: 'How . . . do . . . you . . . do!' in a soft voice, thick with the Northern accent.

'There! Isn't she a clever girl!'

As Stella's fingers touched those of the child, she thought, 'Of all the impossible incidents! What does he mean?'

Seeing the expression on his wife's face, Rodney straightened himself, and, under pretext of poking the fire, murmured, 'Just thought I'd give her a treat, Stella. Hope you don't mind me bringing her; she waits for me nearly every day at the end of the fifteen streets; it's pathetic. And if you could see where she lives! The surroundings are dreadful . . . '

'Who is she?'

'Kate Hannigan's child; you know, the one I nearly lost four years tonight . . . in fact, I nearly lost the pair of them.'

'Won't her mother miss her?'

38

'Oh, she's in service in Westoe; I told the grandmother I was bringing her.'

Stella looked at her husband in amazement . . . Of all the unorthodox, undignified people! . . . 'What do you intend to do with her, now that she's here? You can't let a child run wild around the house!'

Rodney's black brows contracted, and his beard took on a slight forward tilt. 'I intend to give her some lunch!' he answered, in what she termed his stubborn voice.

'Very well! I'll ring for Mary to take her into the kitchen.'

'She's not going into the kitchen.'

'You don't propose to sit her at table with us?'

'That's just what I do propose!'

'Doctor!' Annie was gripping the bottom of his coat and staring up at him, the laughter gone now from her face, her eyes timorous. She sensed the warning element; her granda's voice was sharp like that when he pushed her out of the way or frightened her grandma.

'It's all right, my dear. It's all right,' said Rodney, picking her up in his arms.

Stella's eyes were like pieces of blue glass. 'There is a hand-worked lace cloth on the dining-table; there is cut-glass and Spode! Why, even I wasn't allowed in the dining-room until I was ten, and then only on . . .'

'All right! all right!' he snapped. 'Say no more about it.' He walked out of the drawing-room, down the passage, and into the kitchen, forcing himself to laugh and chat to take the look of fear from the child's face. The look had wrung his heart, for he knew that she had had, and would have, many occasions for fear in Tim Hannigan's house; but that she should have it in his was unthinkable!

The three women in the kitchen were not unprepared for his entry, for they had stared, in various degrees of astonishment, some minutes earlier when they had watched him, from the kitchen window, lifting the child from the car. Mary Dixon had simply gaped . . . Kate Hannigan's bairn! . . . and him bringing it here! Dorrie Clarke mightn't be so far wrong with her hints and 'My, there are things I could tell you if I had a mind!' She hadn't taken much notice of her, for she was a bitter old pig, and a Catholic at that, so you couldn't believe a word of what she said. But now, when you put two and two together . . . and all the grand clothes of Kate Hannigan's . . . well, what a kettle of fish! . . . She looked at the doctor through new eyes.

'I've brought you a visitor, cook. Would you like to give this little lady some lunch?'

'With pleasure, doctor. With pleasure.' Mrs Summers looked at the dark and fair heads close together; she gave an apt description of them to herself . . . He looks like a kindly divil holding a wee angel. It's bairns that man wants; he'd be a different man if he had bairns. But he'll never get any out of that 'un. She's got ice in her veins; I don't need to have fallen seven times to know that. I bet that's what half the rows are over, too . . .

Annie's lips quivered as she watched the doctor back towards the door. 'I want to come with you.'

'I won't be a minute, Annie; I'm just going into the other room.'

'Will you come back?'

'Of course I will.'

'Now just look what I've got for you.' Mrs Summers took the situation in hand, and Rodney went out and into the cloakroom off the hall, and washed his hands . . . It had been a mistake to bring the child here, but she had looked so pathetic, standing at the end of that grim street, waiting patiently for him to pass down the main road. And on a Christmas Eve, too; Christmas was made for children . . . He had had a vision of himself playing with her on the rug before the fire, and perhaps Stella laughing down at them from her chair . . . the perhaps had obliterated the vision . . . Annie's childish love, born of his kindness to her, had struck an answering chord in him. He wished he could do something for her, make her lot easier without causing comment . . . In his disappointment at Stella's reception of the child he realised that his intention had been to arouse her interest. There was so much she could do; there were so many like Annie. If only . . . Oh, it was hopeless! Every move he made, every suggestion was tactfully turned aside . . .

When he re-entered the drawing-room Stella was still standing by the fire-place, her face like a cameo against the black bog-oak. She gave off an air of delicacy, which made him wonder anew at the strength of so fragile a creature . . . Why had things gone wrong between them? Right from the beginning their temperaments had warred; not only in their physical relations but in their mental and everyday relations there were jarring notes. He wanted children; she couldn't have any. Yet, after having had the necessary examinations, she had been found quite normal. He had seen to it that the fault didn't lie with him; but still, never a mention of one. He had wanted a home, a place where he could at least have a dog, but she had made this beautiful shell. He wanted someone to talk to, someone who could enter into the desolation that was himself, or bring him out of it by their sympathy and understanding. He did not want to be led into the realms of mental phantasy by description of even the most commonplace things, which was the turn any conversation with her took. He liked poetry; but his poets were of a nature, so beefy, or style so simple, as to bring laughing derision on them. If only he and Stella could agree to differ; but this would seem to be the most difficult task of all.

Stella, still holding the letter in her hands, was impatient to give him the news. But she could not do it effectively while the atmosphere of the silly incident still prevailed; so she prepared her ground. 'Rodney, I'm sorry, dear, but children are so awkward. It would have upset us both if she had spilt or broken anything. You would then have blamed yourself for bringing her . . . Don't you see?' She went to him and held up her face to be kissed. 'There! Am I forgiven for not wanting my Spode to be broken?' she said, laughing up at him. 'You're not angry with me any more? When you are angry you look like a black demon; it's a wonder children aren't afraid of you, instead of waiting at street corners for you.' She had succeeded; he even looked gratified at her playfulness. 'Come on!' she urged, tweaking his nose.

He smiled at her, hope rising in him, anew, and he began to clutch wildly at straws again. 'I'm sorry, dear, I was nasty. But if you could see how some of those children live; twelve to fourteen people herded together in four rooms. Annie's lucky, in a way, there are only three of them; but she's got a beast of a grandfather. I attended him for eight months when his leg was smashed up. I used to loathe the thought of touching him; he always gave me the impression of being a gigantic snake; it's his eyes, I think. I can never understand how he came to be the father of . . . '

'Look, darling,' Stella broke in gently, 'Mary's taking the dinner in, and I want to tell you my little bit of news . . . Read that!' She thrust the letter towards him, and stood, her hands behind her back, gazing up at him in a little-girl attitude while he read it.

'Why, Stella, I didn't even know you had sent the book away. Oh, I am glad.'

Guessing how much this meant to her, he tried to appear thrilled at the news, thrusting down the dread that it would create another milestone between them. Taking her into his arms, he kissed her. 'Congratulations, my dear . . . Well!' he said, reading the letter again while standing with one arm around her shoulders. 'And they would like another at your leisure! I say, you're famous!'

'Rodney, don't be silly!'

'But it's no easy thing to get a book of poems published. Stories, yes; but publishers are very wary of poems.'

'But they are so simple.'

'Simple or not, they like them.'

To Stella's chagrin, she realised that his amazement was not so much at her writing the poems as the publisher accepting them . . . Simple or not! he had said. Would Herbert Barrington have given that retort? Never. But in Rodney's estimation Herbert Barrington was an effeminate sop. He didn't know that it was on Herbert's advice that she had sent the book away, and that the publisher was Herbert's cousin. Were she to tell him, he would likely imply that influence was the main factor on which it had relied for publication . . . Hiding her annoyance, she smilingly led the way into the dining-room.

In an endeavour to hold fast to the new ground they were on, Rodney burst out, 'This calls for a celebration. Let's go somewhere tonight! We'll dash up to Newcastle; I'll order a table . . . '

'Rodney!' Stella's voice was patient. 'Do you really mean to say you have forgotten we are giving a dinner tonight?'

'Good Lord! So I had.'

'Even with your friends the Davidsons coming?'

'Now, now, Stella. No sarcasm.'

'But I'm not being sarcastic. You are for ever talking of them, so it surprises me that you have forgotten you invited them.'

'I had forgotten about tonight, but only for the moment. I wanted us to have a little fling to celebrate your success.'

'That's very sweet of you, dear, but we'll have to reserve it for another time. Tonight we entertain the locals' . . . all but one, she added to herself.

At her reference to the locals Rodney gave her a quick glance. Then he lapsed into silence; for he knew they were no nearer. Her success had made her more pleasant for a time, that was all, and had saved him from having another dose of her patient suffering that would have surely followed his latest indiscretion of bringing the child to the house.

Another of Mrs Prince's dinners was drawing to its close. Clara Richards, sitting at her host's right hand looked down the long, glittering table to where her hostess sat talking to that pasty-looking young man who kept flinging his hands about as though they did not belong to him. Mrs Richards was inwardly seething. At her last dinner, when the Princes were there, she had served seven courses; it had taken days to look up books and think out dishes. Now that china doll up there had served only five and had everyone exclaiming over them . . . her and her *hors d'œuvres*, and her finger-bowls and candles on the table. Who was she, anyway? Only a doctor's wife, like herself. And look at him, there, laughing with Peggy Davidson . . . Looking at Rodney, she wondered what it was about him that had trebled his practice within four years; he had more than half the Tyne Dock patients and all East Jarrow; and then that Lady Cuthbert-Harris sending for him right from yon end of Westoe. It was easy for Joe to say she was a neurotic and hoped to get a sensation out of his beard. Joe had lost quite a number of patients lately, mostly women; and why? Well, he certainly wasn't her idea of handsome. It's his la-la manners and haw-haw voice they go daft over, I suppose. Something would have to be done; but what? She didn't know. She certainly couldn't see her Joe mincing around women, and perhaps that was something to be thankful for. She had enough trouble with him, as it was; the money he spent on drink, and with three girls to bring up! Which brought her back to her hostess . . . It paid you to hold a candle to the Devil. Stella Prince had a sister married to a lord; not one of these newly made ones, either. She had looked up this particular one's lineage, and had been deeply impressed. They had visited here last year, and would likely visit again; and if her girls could obtain an introduction to a lord – well, everything has to start, hasn't it . . .

Across the table, Peggy Davidson was now listening to Doctor Richards's pompous voice and thinking, How soon can we leave? I hope the kiddies are asleep. But they won't be . . . they'll be playing old Anna up. Fancy having a dinner on a Christmas Eve! Oh, I hate leaving the house tonight; and I've got their stockings to fill. I wonder if we could go about nine o'clock. No, that would be too soon. And it would likely hurt Rodney; he's so anxious for me to be friends with her; but I can't. Still, I mustn't let him see. He sounds very gay tonight, as if he has been drinking. But he seldom touches anything. She cast a quick glance at him. It's all put on; he's not happy. And this house! It's like a showpiece. What he wants is a home. I used to wonder how he could be comfortable in our sitting-room, with the mess it's usually in, but I don't wonder any longer after having seen this.

The rather squeaky voice of the young man broke in upon her thoughts. He had risen and was holding a glass of wine in his hand: 'Ladies and gentlemen! I ask you to drink to the success of our gifted hostess. I don't know whether you are aware of it, but our hostess is the author of a book of very fine poems which is soon to be published.'

Rodney frowned. How dare he! Damn him! What right has he, anyway? And how does he know? . . . He came late. It's not likely she's just told him . . . The muscles in his cheeks worked rapidly.

Amid exclamations of surprise and congratulations, the toast was drunk. Stella sweetly acknowledged their congratulations, and playfully admonished the young man for giving away her little secret. While he was insisting that she read the poems to the company in the drawing-room, Rodney's voice broke in on her pleasure: 'Let's celebrate,' he was saying, looking from Peggy Davidson to her husband. 'What do you say, Peter?'

'Anything you like, Rodney. Suits me.'

'We'll do a show in Shields . . . there's a pantomime on somewhere . . . That's it, let's all go to the pantomime!' He looked round the table, like an excited boy.

Mrs Richards nodded laughing assent . . . Anything, she thought, is better than listening to that madam blowing her horn over a book of poetry . . .

'A little childish fun won't do us any harm,' said Doctor Richards, easing his stomach away from the table. 'If the ladies are agreeable, I'm for it.'

The plain young woman who had come with Herbert Barrington looked relieved, even animated for a moment.

Herbert Barrington looked at Stella, and she, striving to keep the signs of her anger from her face, looked down the table towards Rodney . . . How dare he! What did he mean? Breaking up her

43

dinner party like this! And to suggest celebrating her success by going to a pantomime . . . a pantomime of all things! . . . She took a small, cold vow to herself: She'd make him suffer for this, as only she knew how. Her time would come.

'I think we're too late for the pantomime,' she temporised.

'No we're not. It's just turned eight o'clock, and the first house doesn't come out until half-past,' said Rodney, without looking at her. 'If we go now we'll have plenty of time.' With the exception of Barrington, he took in the rest of the company in his glance: 'Don't you think so?'

There were murmurs of assent.

'I think we'll leave the decision to our hostess,' said Herbert Barrington, whose bulbous eyes were sending messages of sympathy and understanding to Stella.

Stella allowed a little expectant silence to pervade the table before graciously answering, 'By all means. If we are all of the same mind, let us go.'

'And you will read your poems when we return?' Herbert Barrington's long white hands hovered before her beseechingly.

Stella smiled at him: 'If you wish.'

The ladies got into their wraps, with the exception of Peggy who was wearing a plain grey coat. There were repeated warnings from Doctor Richards to wrap up well, for there was snow coming and he didn't want any of them on his books. Peter Davidson stood aside in the hall, looking on, the half smile playing on his face. He wondered about Rodney . . . Why this sudden burst of animal spirits? He didn't like it. If only he'd come out, and talk about things. Something was worrying him; that was evident.

The party divided themselves into Rodney's and Doctor Richards's cars, and drove off amid laughter. Within fifteen minutes they were in Shields and had parked the cars in some stables off the market-place. The big, open market was thronged with shoppers, a number of them, by the sound of the singing and laughter, three seas over; paraffin flares threw into relief the gesticulating chocolate 'kings', medicine-men and other 'auctioneers'. The party skirted the market and walked down King Street, and ran into a throng of people coming out of the theatre.

'Keep together,' called Rodney; 'first house just coming out.'

Stella shuddered . . . He was acting as if he were drunk. But she knew he wasn't drunk; he was doing this just to annoy her . . . well!

Having piloted the company to a comparatively clear corner of the vestibule, Rodney said, 'I'll see if I can get a box. Stay there!'

They stood together, awaiting his return, Peter and Mrs Richards keeping up a bantering flow of small talk. A little distance away a queue for the second house passed quickly in front of the ticket box

44

as the last of the first-house audience were leaving the theatre.

Rodney was near the foot of the staircase talking to the manager – who was assuring him he was very lucky; there was one box left, and it would be a pleasure – when a childish voice shouting 'Doctor!' made itself heard above the din.

Turning quickly, Stella saw the child who had caused her so much annoyance earlier in the day evade the detaining hand of a tall girl and dash towards Rodney.

'Oh, doctor,' cried Annie, hurling herself against his legs, 'I've seen the goose and all the great big eggs and the funny man and the beautiful ladies . . . !'

'Why, Annie,' said Rodney, 'you've been to the pantomime!' He took the hands held up to him: 'Who brought you? . . . Hallo, Kate!' he exclaimed, as Kate, accompanied by a stocky young man, pushed her way to his side.

'Good evening, doctor. I'm so sorry,' she apologised . . . 'You're a very naughty girl, Annie. Come along this minute!'

'Now don't scold her, Kate. Is it her first pantomime?'

'Yes; and she's been so excited we've hardly been able to keep her in her seat.'

Rodney's hands were cupping Annie's upturned face, but he was looking at Kate . . . It must be three years since he last saw her. She was much taller . . . How fine she looked . . . stately; and what a figure! She had been a lovely girl . . . She was lovely now, but in a different way, for she had an air about her . . . Yes, that was it, she had a strange air about her . . . 'How are you getting on, Kate?' he asked her.

'Oh, very well, doctor, thank you.' Even her voice seemed different.

'Still at the Tolmaches'?'

'Oh yes!' She hesitated and cast a swift, sidelong glance at the young man at her side.

The young man looked at her with a possessive glint in his eye, and seemed to stretch himself to reach her height, as he spoke: 'Not for much longer, though; you'll soon be leaving there . . . We got engaged today, we'll soon be married,' he said to Rodney.

Rodney looked from Kate to the young man with the aggressive voice, then back to Kate again. 'Congratulations, Kate! I'm so glad.' His hand went out and she hesitantly put hers into it. It was the second time her fingers had touched him, and he was conscious of the fact. Her deep blue eyes, with that soft kindness in their depth, seemed to float mistily before him.

The young man stretched his neck and moved his chin from side to side, and Stella, standing amid her guests watching the scene, was livid with fury. Twice today Rodney had made a spectacle of himself with that child, and now, to stand there in a public place holding that girl's hand! It was just too much. She guessed who the girl was . . .

'Doctor Prince has met some friends,' Mrs Richards remarked, to no-one in particular; the expression on Stella's face had not escaped her, and she was beginning to enjoy herself.

'She was a patient of my husband's, and, as far as I can gather, is a maid in Westoe.'

A signal look passed between Peggy Davidson and her husband: 'And a patient of mine, too; for one night, at least,' said Peter. 'You know, I always had my eye on Kate Hannigan; she's the best-looking girl in the county. And if it hadn't been for Peggy here getting her hooks into me . . . well, you never know!'

Peggy smiled broadly; only she knew how much this great, lumbering man was hers.

Stella looked at Herbert Barrington and slowly closed her eyes. 'Oh, these people!' her expression said.

'I must go and have a word with Kate. Excuse me just a minute.' Peter ambled over to the other group, hoping that his comments had made the scene before them appear more general . . . Rodney seemed to be storing up trouble for himself with every step he took tonight . . . 'Hello, Kate! Hello, Annie!'

'Oh, hello, Doctor Davidson.'

'How are you, Kate? But why need I ask! You're looking fine; and this young lady too!' He patted Annie's cheek.

'For which I have to thank you, doctor.'

'Me, Kate?'

'Of course. I should have never met the Tolmaches but for you.'

'They are grand folk, aren't they, Kate?'

'The most wonderful on earth.'

'Don't you think she's grown into a very grand young lady, Rodney?'

'Very grand indeed!' said Rodney, not taking his eyes for one second from Kate's face. 'And she's going to be married!'

'Married! And this the lucky young man?' said Peter, turning to the man, who now stood a little apart, uncontrolled jealousy burning in his eyes. 'I should know you, shouldn't I? You're a Jarrowite like myself, surely?'

Somewhat mollified by the personal note, the young man replied, 'Yes, Doctor Davidson; I'm Alec Moran. I'm the agent for The New London Insurance.'

'Yes, yes, I thought I should know you. So you and Kate are to be married. Well, I hope you'll both be very happy.'

'And what does my little girl say about all this?' said Rodney, stooping down to Annie. Annie's fingers traced themselves over the white scarf hanging from his neck, as she said, 'Santy Clause is bringing me a doll and a shop.'

'Have you got our box, doctor?' Herbert Barrington's voice broke in, with studied politeness.

'Be with you in a minute,' said Rodney without looking up, his tone expressing total indifference.

'This way, sir,' said the manager to Barrington; 'if you'll just follow me.'

Stella, with neither a glance to right nor left, passed the group at the foot of the staircase. Rodney looked up from Annie's glorified countenance to the cold beauty of his wife, whose displeasure was evident from the point of her fine kid shoes to the floating tulle on her head . . . Great lady, he said to himself; she couldn't be expected to speak to the common people . . . His eyes hardened.

Turning to Annie again, he said, 'That's not all Father Christmas is going to bring you. I saw him this afternoon, and what do you think he told me? . . . You don't know?'

Annie shook her head, her eyes, like dark green pools, adoring him.

' "Well," he said, "I'm away off now to Africa to see if I can get a black baby for Annie Hannigan!" '

'A black baby?'

'Yes, with curly hair.' Peter made accompanying sounds of delight.

'Doctor, it was most kind of you; it's really beautiful,' said Kate softly.

'Nonsense!' His eyes came back to her face again.

'We must go now,' said Kate hurriedly. 'Good night, Doctor Davidson. Good night, Doctor Prince. Say "Good night, and a merry Christmas" to the doctors, Annie.'

Annie suddenly flung her arms up and around Rodney's neck; her young mouth pressed on his, and then she laughed in high delight, 'Your beard tickles.'

'Good night,' said Kate again, forcefully dragging Annie away to where Alec, now glowering, awaited them from a distance.

Rodney and Peter walked up the stairs to the circle. Rodney was strangely stirred by the child's kiss; it opened the old desire, the ever-present desire for a child of his own . . . By God, he would have a child! He would make her have a child!

'Kate's quite a grand-looking girl, isn't she?' Peter remarked. 'The Tolmaches think the world of her. I heard old Bernard had ideas for her, but this marriage will knock them on the head.'

'He looks a surly devil; I can't see her being happy with him.'

'Oh, I don't see why not; the most odd-assorted couples generally make the best go of it. Anyway, it's the best thing for her, and he'll be a father to the child.'

A deep, inexplicable sadness enveloped Rodney . . . a new sadness, a new emptiness. For some time now he had felt that he owned nothing, possessed nothing, beyond his work; but it would seem there were still things which could be taken from him . . . 'He'll be a father to the child!' he repeated to himself.

THE RIDE

Peggy Davidson sat hunched up on a lop-sided pouffe in front of
the fire between her husband and the dark, sombre man who had,
in some strange way, become part and parcel of their joint lives.
The busy day was nearly over, and for the past two hours they had
sat, talking in spasms or sunk in companionable silence. But as the
time of quietude was almost spent and she must arouse herself to
get ready for her journey into Jarrow she returned to the attack she
had waged on and off all evening: 'Why be so pig-headed, Rodney?
You have no need to go home. Now, have you? You can telephone
Mrs Summers and tell her you are staying the night, and, as you are
coming to dinner tomorrow, doesn't it seem silly to go back to an
empty house?'

'Woman, won't you be convinced? You cannot talk me round,'
said Rodney. 'If I were to stay, old Peter there would miss Midnight
Mass, and there I'd be, sitting in torment, knowing I had imperilled
his immortal soul,' he laughed; 'and the face of Father O'Malley would
haunt me for weeks afterwards.'

'Isn't he a fool!' said Peggy to her husband.

Peter laughed at the seriousness of her thin face, and nodded.

'Don't be silly, Rodney; there are no Father O'Malleys in Jarrow
church. If you met Father Patterson, you'd change your mind about
priests,' said Peggy.

'Nothing will make me change my mind about one priest, at least.
Do you know, Peggy, I've had three cases of hysteria in children
during the past month. And I've traced it all to the fear of Hell
and Purgatory that damned priest has put into their little heads. Of
course, the parents are staunch Catholics, and they won't have that it
is anything to do with the church at all. It's no use trying to explain
even the weakest psychology to adults who are eaten up with fear and
superstition, which they call faith. That old fellow's got something to
answer for, if he believes what he preaches.'

'Now, now! I shouldn't have given you that last drink,' laughed
Peter.

'You know what I'm saying is true,' said Rodney earnestly, hoisting
himself from the deep, leather arm-chair and leaning forward. 'You

48

two are Catholics, and enlightened ones, at that, but can you honestly say that, at some time or other, the tenets of the Catholic faith have not scared you stiff?'

'No, of course not!' Peter said. 'You've been dealing with a type of person who would have hysterics in any case.'

'You know, Rodney, I've always found the greatest comfort in my religion,' said Peggy seriously. 'And, honestly, I've never known fear of a priest . . . just the reverse.'

'Well, tell me,' persisted Rodney, 'do you believe in Purgatory, as it is preached? Do you believe that some of the poor devils around these towns are to be made to suffer for a period of time after death for the actions they do, named sins, mostly the result of the squalor in which they live? I've yet to meet a delinquent of another religious body troubled by the same fear. It would appear that Catholics can commit sins, any sins, for which they will be forgiven if they obey the rules: mass every Sunday, and confession and communion at least once a year. But let them break the rules, and then comes the penalty – Purgatory, Hell! Their misery of the present is nothing to what's in store for them. I tell you, Peter, the majority are Catholics through fear.'

'It's a wide question, and neither of us knows much about it, but I admit you are right, up to a point,' said Peter, with urbanity.

'No, he's not!' put in Peggy vehemently.

'Yes, he is,' went on Peter quietly; 'but only up to a point. There are a number of people who attend mass mainly out of fear, and it's all to the good; that very fear is a preventative. For what control have the civil authorities over men like Pat Donovan, say? and Danny McQueen of Jarrow? or Micky Macgregor of Shields? and of Tim Hannigan of the fifteen streets? A priest can manage men like these, where a policeman would be knocked flat for looking at them . . . I admit it's the old fear of the supernatural; but if they had no fear of something, or someone, if they thought they would not suffer personally after death for their misdeeds now, can you imagine, Rodney, what life in these few towns would be like? Let us hope that education in the coming generations will erase the necessity for fear.'

'But the number of bad hats is few compared with the number of ordinary people; don't forget that, Peter!' said Rodney. 'And, anyway, I'm not concerned with men like McQueen and Hannigan, I'm concerned mainly with children. The religion is crammed into them, the fear is crammed into them; they don't stand a chance.

'You talk of education erasing fears; do you think it will ever be allowed to? When I proposed seeing the headmistress of the Borough Road school and the priest, because I had been called three times in one week to a child of eight who had had screaming nightmares of the Devil coming to take her to Hell, the mother almost had hysterics too, and said, oh, I mustn't go to the school; it was nothing to do with the school, or the church, for she had had the same spasms when she was young – it was her stomach! Stomach, yes; racked nerves playing on the digestive organs! Doesn't that speak for itself?'

'Christmas Eve,' said Peggy, 'and peace on earth; and you two having a theological discussion.'

'Sorry, Peggy. And you, too, Peter. It is very bad form of me, and at this time too. But you've yourself to blame,' Rodney said, wagging his finger at Peggy.

'Carry on, carry on!' said Peter. 'We'll convert you yet.'

'So that's your game, is it?' said Rodney, getting up. 'Well, I'm off!'

'Sure you won't stay, Rodney? The children would love you to be here in the morning.' Peggy made one last effort. 'Come on, do!'

'Temptress!' Rodney laughed down at her.

'By the way,' said Peter, 'speaking of the children, don't you buy my bairns more expensive presents than I can afford to give them. You have estranged their affections enough already.'

'Oh yes,' laughed Peggy. 'Do you know, Rodney, we listened to Michael and Cathleen talking? They were on about Santa Claus. Of course, Cathleen is well aware of his identity, but Michael is not quite sure; so he said to her, "What do you think Santa will bring us, Cathleen?" "Oh, I don't know," said Cathleen, "but I do know that Uncle Rodney will bring us something worth while. He's the only one who does!" . . . Now what do you think of that?'

'See what you've done? Made them mercenaries,' said Peter. 'And we'll have to watch him, Peggy,' he said to his wife, with mock sternness, 'or he'll be giving them talks on religion next, for they are two very scared children.'

'Shut up!' said Rodney.

'Have one more before you go,' laughed Peter, going to the sideboard.

'No more for me, I'm just right. I've had about as much as I can carry,' protested Rodney, 'and I've got to drive a car.'

'Here, drink that! You're too sober for my liking.'

'All right. But, you see, you are judging me by my legs only.' Rodney raised his glass: 'The very best in life to both of you. And thank you for all your kindness to me.'

Peter looked over his glass, his eyes crinkling with a warmth and affection. 'The boot's on the other foot,' he said.

'See you tomorrow, then,' said Rodney, as he got into his coat.

For a moment the three stood on top of the house steps; the sky was high and ablaze with stars, the light of a pale moon was reflected in the river below them. 'Look!' cried Peggy, 'it's started to snow, just the slightest bit.'

'It won't be much,' said Peter, sniffing the raw air. 'Good night, then, Rodney.'

'Good night. Good night. Happy Christmas.'

They watched him drive away; then turned indoors. 'Oh, I could shoot that woman!' cried Peggy. 'It's the second Christmas she's gone off and left him on his own. Her and her house parties and literary dinners! He's so unhappy, isn't he? Doesn't he say anything?'

'Not a word.'

'He looks as if he were burning up inside, and he's working too hard.'

'Well, he's got one of the biggest practices on the Tyne, and it's growing every day. He'll soon have to have help.'

They stood on the hearthrug, shoulder to shoulder, looking down into the fire. A silence held them. The shabby room, with its Christmas tree and paper-chains, was seeped in peace. 'You don't think he knows what they say about him?' asked Peggy quietly.

'Good gracious no!'

'But that's why all the women went daft over him.'

'Yes, maybe.'

'And you still think there's nothing in it?'

'Certain of it.'

'Does he ever speak of her?'

'Kate, you mean? No, never.'

'But he does make a fuss of the child, doesn't he?'

'So he does of Michael and Cathleen. So am I to understand you've misbehaved yourself?'

'Oh, Peter!'

He laughed, and pulled her to him gently.

'I often wonder, though, how he accounts to himself for his sudden popularity,' mused Peggy.

'I don't know,' said Peter. 'But it's certainly not because he's suspected of being the father of Annie Hannigan. And I shouldn't like to witness his reactions should he ever hear it. Of course, he never will.'

Rodney followed the road of the Don, around by St Bede's church, then past Bogie Hill, past the fifteen streets and the New Buildings, and along the stretch of the East Jarrow slacks. The tide was high and the lights were dancing on the ships at anchor in the narrow strip of the river Tyne, where it left the docks and meandered before expanding between Jarrow and Howden. Tram cars, on their way to Jarrow, clanked by him, full to the steps, and stray groups of people, loaded, inside and out, shambled on and off the pavement in their walk, all making their way to Jarrow. One man, with the coaldust of the pits still on him, clung to a lamp-post for support, a Christmas tree trailing from his hand into the dirt. Going in Rodney's direction were more orderly groups; Midnight Mass bent to the Borough Road or Tyne Dock church, he thought. It said a lot for Peter's argument . . . they had a goal of sorts, something to cleave to; at least it made Christmas mean something.

Conister House loomed up vividly before him. No Christmas tree there, no paper chains, no stockings in the morning. He felt a great reluctance to return, and was tempted to keep to the arrangements of a week ago, before the last row with Stella, and drive straight on to Jesmond; the party would be on until four o'clock at least, and he could drive back tomorrow. But that would mean meeting Herbert Barrington. No, it would be wise to keep away from that gentleman, feeling as he did; and if he were to go, naturally he and Stella would have to share a room . . . he thought with bitterness of the room she had prepared for herself across the landing. No, he wouldn't go. As long as he could bear it he wouldn't force himself upon her; he had made up his mind on that score, he told himself, adding whimsically that the mind hadn't much say in it at times. She was a devil, he thought, like some evil temptress, a mythological figure, beckoning, then rebuking with disdain . . . He prayed for strength for the next time she should beckon.

He had almost reached the Tyne Dock arches when he passed a lone figure, walking with a free stride, the skirts of her long coat swinging from the hips. She was walking in the shadow of the dock wall, but as she passed in, then out of the weak rays of a street lamp he knew she was Kate Hannigan.

Kate Hannigan and Christmas Eve! They seemed to be linked together. He didn't often see her, but when he did it seemed to be on a Christmas Eve. He would stop and speak to her. Why not? he questioned himself. Why not? She had not married that fellow, after all. Peter hadn't known why; something had gone wrong, but what? He was curious. Anyway, he hadn't liked the fellow. Of course he would stop and speak to her!

Pulling up the car to the kerb, he waited. He swivelled round in his seat and watched her coming towards him. She spoke first, without a trace of embarrassment: 'Happy Christmas, doctor.'

'Happy Christmas, Kate.'

'Thank you so much for Annie's present. But you really ought not to do it; she is being spoilt.'

'Annie being spoilt! Nonsense; you couldn't spoil Annie. Anyway, I get much more fun out of buying the toys than Annie gets in receiving them. It's a part of me that's never grown up. How are the Tolmaches, Kate?'

'Oh, quite well. Only Mr Bernard's had sciatica rather badly. But it didn't stop him from going away.'

'Where are you off to at this time of night, Kate, a party?'

'No; Midnight Mass.'

'Oh! Yes, of course. Well, jump in and I'll give you a lift!'

Kate looked up at him, perched above her. His black eyes seemed unnaturally bright. He'd had one or two, she thought, or he'd never have suggested such a thing. Imagine how the tongues would wag if

52

she drove up to church in a motor car, sitting beside the doctor.

'Thank you, doctor,' she said; 'but I've never driven in a motor car; I'm a wee bit afraid. And they make such a noise. Traps are more to my liking.'

'You've never driven in a car?' said Rodney. 'Oh, come on then, Kate; you must, you simply must.'

He drew up his long legs and stepped down on to the pavement beside her. 'Go on, up you get, Kate!'

'No, doctor, no.' She glanced back uneasily up the road. Dim figures were approaching, likely people from the fifteen streets. Anyway, people who would know them both; and it would not take much to set tongues wagging. Oh, why hadn't he just gone straight on? They'd be on them in a minute! . . . She was too wise to argue with a man who had had a few. If she persisted in her refusal he'd only stand talking. So she said, 'I'll go for a short drive, doctor, but not to church.'

'Up the Newcastle road then, Kate!' He helped her in; then swung the starting handle vigorously, and hurried around to his seat.

As the car swung out of the main road and up the narrow, steep incline of the Simonside Bank, Kate gasped. Rodney's dark eyes laughed at her. The moon, gleaming on the frost-covered road, reflected a pale light through the high glass windscreen on to her face. She looked dewy and warm, like a soft summer morning, he thought.

'Like it?' he shouted.

'I don't quite know,' she called back. 'Yes,' she turned her head and smiled at him, 'I think I do.'

'Splendid!'

On they sped; past the Simonside school and the little group of cottages, past the Maze Hall and into the open country; only a mile or so from the docks but seeming, in its rural spaciousness and neatly ploughed fields, to be in another world.

'The country looks different from a car.'

'What's that?' shouted Rodney.

'I said, the country looks different from a car,' called Kate, leaning forward eagerly. 'It looks so beautiful in the moonlight, but a little unreal. I feel I'm taking part in a fairy story,' she laughed gaily.

Suddenly Rodney stopped the car. She looked at him enquiringly.

'Kate, don't go to Midnight Mass!' he brought out with a rush.

'What!' Kate retreated into her seat.

'Let's drive on. Let's talk and laugh for an hour . . . will you?'

Something in his voice startled her; she leant back, tight against the leather, but said nothing.

God, he thought, what had made him propose that? She would get it all wrong. Hell! Well, why not? What harm was there in taking her for a drive? His wife would likely be sitting in a corner with Barrington at this moment, promising easy seduction, with her eyes. Damn Stella! But he must make it clear to this girl that it was a drive he was proposing, and nothing more . . . 'Don't misunderstand me, Kate,' he said; 'please don't misunderstand me. You see, I was going back to an empty house, and I don't think anyone should be alone on Christmas Eve.' . . . Heaven, he did sound sorry for himself, he thought. 'And there's another thing,' he went on. 'All these years I've known you, I've wanted to talk to you, but there's never been the opportunity up till now.' . . . He must be drunk, rattling on like this . . . 'You know, Kate, you've grown from a very young girl into . . . well, to say the least, a self-composed woman, and I've often wondered how it came about. Don't think me rude, Kate, please.' He looked closely at her. But her long, dark lashes lay practically on her cheeks, so he couldn't see the effect of his words. Lord, what a fool he was! This was Stella's fault, and Peter's whisky . . . What was she thinking? . . . He gripped the wheel: 'I'm sorry Kate, if I have annoyed you. I'll turn the car round at the next bend and take you back. I suppose you have the impression that you are riding to Hell with the Devil?'

Kate raised her eyes: 'I could be going there in worse company.'

'Kate, you're not annoyed with me!' He laughed in relief. 'Am I to drive on?'

She nodded. 'But I must be back in Tyne Dock by a quarter past one at the latest, doctor.'

'You'll be there on the dot, Kate.' He got out and did some more winding.

Kate sat up, as if throwing off a cloak. She watched him through the windscreen. He looked up, and their eyes met; they smiled at each other.

On past Jarrow, Hebburn and Pelaw the car chunked in a soothing rhythm. They sat, silent now, just looking ahead, relaxed against the seats, feeling knit together in an exciting warmth.

'Shall I stop on the top of one of the Felling Hills?' asked Rodney; 'where we can survey the world lying at our feet, as we talk.'

'Yes, if you wish,' replied Kate.

Presently he drew up on the brow of a hill. Far away, like a strip of shining steel, lay the river. To the right, the town of Felling, its streets of little houses clinging to the hillside, rested at peace under the moon.

Rodney brought the car off the road on to the grass verge of the open hilltop. 'Put this rug around you,' he said, lifting a heavy blanket from the back seat. 'There!' He leaned back and began to fill his pipe. 'We're all set for our talk, now,' he said, giving her a sidelong smile.

'What do you want to know?'

'Oh, Kate, don't say it like that. It makes me feel I'm being rude and inquisitive.'

'If you were inquisitive, you wouldn't be asking me now, you would know already all there is to know; you can't keep your life private in the fifteen streets.'

'No, I suppose not . . . Well, the last time I spoke to you, Kate, you were engaged to be married. Something happened?'

'He wouldn't have Annie,' said Kate; 'he wanted me to leave her at home.'

'Not have Annie?' Rodney's voice was incredulous.

'No. He wanted me to leave her with my mother . . . for good. But I couldn't give her up altogether, I couldn't do it. If it wasn't that it would upset my mother, I'd take her away now. But to leave her there, all her young life, while I was with someone . . . oh, you can see it was impossible!'

'Of course, Kate. And it's just as well you found out in time, isn't it?'

'Yes, and for him, too; for I wasn't being quite fair to him.'

She did not say where her unfairness lay.

'Couldn't Annie stay with you at the Tolmaches?'

'Yes, they offered to have her years ago . . . But it's my mother; she clings to Annie and . . . me.'

'Of course . . . Yes, of course, I can see that.'

'You know, doctor, if I hadn't had Annie I should never have met the Tolmaches, and I daren't think what life without them would have been . . . Annie, you, Dorrie Clarke and Doctor Davidson, all leading me to the Tolmaches.'

'Why give Dorrie Clarke credit for a virtuous deed?' Rodney queried.

'Because had she not hurt her leg you would never have sent out for Doctor Davidson, and had he not come I should never have learned about the Tolmaches. Some other girl would have got the place. He told me of it only to ease my mind; he is what Mr Bernard calls a psychologist.'

Rodney looked at her in silence for a moment. 'Mr Bernard gives you lessons, doesn't he?'

'Yes,' said Kate, her voice vibrating with a depth of feeling; 'nearly every day, except holidays, for six years, Mr Bernard has given me a lesson.' She clasped her hands on top of the rug and stared across the hilltop, through the sparsely falling snow, into the star-laden sky where it came down to meet the river.

Rodney, still staring at her, thought, And she has certainly profited by them. It seems incredible . . . 'Yes?' he prompted.

'Well, the first year was very hard work,' Kate went on, 'but I kept at it because I wanted to speak differently.' She cast a swift glance at him, half apologetic. 'Then followed a period during which I didn't want to learn at all. But Mr Bernard encouraged me, and the desire suddenly came not only to speak differently but to think differently. From that time life changed entirely for me. Nothing can affect me in the same way as it did before, nothing!'

'What does he teach you?'

'Oh, mostly English, and appreciation of literature. He was a lecturer in English at Oxford, you know.'

Rodney nodded, his eyes riveted on her face.

'I'm doing German now, and I've done quite a bit of French. I can read French works – Honoré de Balzac and . . . ' She turned towards him, her blue eyes darkly bright with excitement. 'You are the first one, doctor, I've been able to talk to about it, other than the Tolmaches. Can you imagine what it means to me?'

He didn't answer, but continued to stare at her, his pipe held within a few inches of his mouth.

'To leave the fifteen streets,' she went on, 'and live with those three people, day after day, to listen to them talking, to eat at the same table . . . Yes, I eat at the same table. Can you believe that?' Her face was serious and her voice questioning, but still he didn't answer. 'And I know of people like Edmond Gosse, the critic . . . well, more than I do of you and Doctor Davidson. Mr Bernard has promised to take me to the House of Lords some day. He is a friend of Mr Gosse, who is librarian there. Do you read his articles in *The Sunday Times*?'

Rodney shook his head.

'Then there's Swinburne and Robert Louis Stevenson, and Reade, men I'd never heard of. And I've read everything I can find of Steele and Addison. I've even read Gibbon's *Decline and Fall of the Roman Empire*.' She was excited now, her hands clasped tight. 'Every evening I read aloud to Mr Bernard; I'm reading Lord Chesterfield's letters now, Mr Bernard likes their style. But I think Lord Chesterfield would have been a very dull man to live with; he didn't like laughter, did he?'

'I don't know, Kate, I've never read him.'

'Do you know what we are going to do in the New Year?' she asked him eagerly. 'Read Shakespeare, the four of us. We are to take so many parts each. *King Lear* first; there are nice long speeches in that for Mr Bernard to get his teeth into. Then *The Taming of the Shrew*. I am to speak Katherine's part; I've already read it over and over again.'

'*The Taming of the Shrew*?' cried Rodney. 'Why, Kate, what do you remember? . . .

'I say it is the moon.' He made a dramatic gesture through the windscreen.

'I know it is the moon,' answered Kate, her face aglow.

'Nay, then you lie; it is the blessed sun,' said Rodney.

'Then God be bless'd, it is the blessed sun:

But sun it is not when you say it is not,

And the moon changes even as your mind.

What you will have it nam'd, even that it is;

And so, it shall be so for Katherine.'

They turned to each other, laughing like children, their bodies swaying back and forth.

'How splendid of you to be able to quote so pat, Kate! I played Petruchio when I was at college. Oh, that was good! But, Kate,' his voice lost some of its merriment, 'what are you going to do with all this learning? Stay on at the Tolmaches?' He didn't add, as a maid, which was in his mind.

The laughter died out of Kate's face. She looked soberly ahead again. 'That seems to be the trouble. You see, I'm not in the least ambitious. I'm quite content to go on as I am, cooking, and cleaning and learning. Mr Bernard wants me to take a course in teaching, but I don't want to be a teacher; I want . . . ' But she couldn't put into words what she wanted. Even as thoughts they were kept firmly in the background of her mind. Impossible to say to him, 'I want a home of my own, as near the Tolmaches as possible, and to see Annie grow there . . . and . . .' the deep, deep thought . . . someone to love and be loved by, someone who would think on the level of the three people she adored, yet would be young and warm and ardent, demanding of her all she had to give, freeing that burning that made her body restless . . . the feeling that could only be brought about by marriage; there could be no more Annies. No, no! That fear kept the thoughts in check and quietened the urgent demands of her body . . .

'What do you want, Kate?' Rodney asked quietly.

'Oh, I don't know,' she said, shaking her head. 'I only know I can't bear the thought of leaving them. They are all set on this teaching business because they think it is for my good, but in their hearts they don't really want me to go. You see, doctor' – she turned towards him again – 'if I left there now, I'd never go back. From a training college I'd naturally go on to a school. One, two, three years . . . and any one of them might die at any minute. This seems to be my daily bread, their dying . . . And Mr Bernard, what would he do if he hadn't me to teach? He'd still have his books; but he's taught all his life, and finding someone as ignorant as I was, and eager, and right to hand, was like new life to him.'

'I couldn't imagine you ever being ignorant, Kate.'

'Oh, I was. I am still.'

'I won't argue that point,' said Rodney.

'I have so much to learn,' said Kate, 'and time goes so quickly. Every week now a discussion takes place on what I must do. I tell them that I have no other ambition but to work for them. And they talk at a great rate and say how silly I am; and Miss Henrietta says I have the slave complex and that she must write to Mrs Pankhurst about me. Yet I know in their hearts they are glad . . . and, oh, how happy that makes me! You can't imagine how it feels to be liked by them; I seem to belong to them, I sing all day!' she ended, on a joyous note.

'Kate,' said Rodney, bending towards her, his knees pressing against the rug covering her, 'where did you get all your wisdom from?' He brought his face close to hers, in the dim light. 'You know so much not culled from books. It's in your eyes, a great kindliness enveloping all you look upon. You would have that wisdom without learning; no wonder they don't want to lose you.'

She made a little inarticulate sound.

'That's why I've always felt drawn to you. We must talk often, Kate; you make me feel the world is a good place to live in.'

She gave a start as though something had leapt within her; her eyes grew larger for a second as she gazed back in the black pools before her. In the silence of the hushed night they heard their own laboured breathing . . . She spoke suddenly, with a startling crispness, and he was aware of the rebuke in her voice: 'I have no wisdom, doctor; I want to stay there from gratitude to them. They took me in, knowing I had just had an illegitimate child.' She paused, as if to make him recall this fact. 'They treated me with kindness and courtesy from the very first moment I entered their house. If I work for them until I die I'll still be in their debt.'

'You're purposely misunderstanding me, Kate. Don't be alarmed or afraid of me.' He felt for her hands and gripped them, stopping their withdrawal.

'I'm not, doctor.'

'Yes, you are.'

She was silent.

'We could be friends, Kate.' The dark appeal of his eyes made her catch her breath.

'Doctor, that's impossible, and you know it is. I should never have come with you tonight.' She moved her head restlessly.

He gazed at her averted head, and found himself on the brink of a chasm, so full of warmth and loveliness that the desolation of his life appeared blacker than ever before . . . He would persuade her . . . But what of Stella? . . . Well, what of her? He didn't owe her anything. If he were drawn into the ecstasy of beauty that was Kate, what would it mean? Hole in corner? The term struck him like a cold douche; the fastidious part of him reared its head . . . No, he had always been against affairs of that sort; hole-in-corner affairs which had aroused his disgust in others, even while sympathising with them. He drew away and settled in his seat again. He was shaking slightly, and his voice betrayed it: 'You're right, Kate; and I'm sorry. But don't let us spoil this hour, it has been so good up till now. Tell me more of yourself; or Annie. Have you any plans for her?' He fumbled at relighting his pipe.

She didn't answer. And when he cast a quick glance at her, she said dully, 'I'd like her to go to a good school.'

'Are you going to send her to a convent?'

'No. You see . . . ' she hesitated; then went on, 'I'm even afraid to put my thoughts into words. I never have done yet . . . but . . . well, I want to take her away from the Catholic school.'

58

'Really, Kate!' Rodney stopped ramming his pipe in surprise. 'Why?'

'You wouldn't understand as you're not a Catholic. It's religion, religion all the time. Learning takes a second place, especially in the elementary schools. And then there's the fear . . . '

'Fear, Kate?' He seemed to have forgotten the personal issue of a few minutes ago, and was the professional man once again. 'You think that the religion frightens the children, then?'

'Well, not exactly the religion; because if all the priests were like Father White and Father Bailey and all the teachers were like Miss Cail and Miss Holden you couldn't imagine being frightened. But it's the priests like Father O'Malley and teachers like the headmistress of the Borough Road school who instil fear into you; and I don't want Annie to be afraid as I was.'

'Go on, Kate; tell me how it affected you. I'm very interested, as I've had a few cases of children being afraid of Hell this past month.'

Kate seemed relieved, and began to talk as if recently the beating of her heart had not threatened to suffocate her: 'That was my main fear, too. After my first confession, at the age of seven, I had the idea that hosts of people in Heaven were watching my every move and would report to God on all my misdeeds, and so I would be sent to Hell. I used to placate them, one after the other – the Virgin Mary, Joseph, St Anthony, St Catherine, St Agnes – and instead of getting relief by going to confession Father O'Malley made it worse, a thousand times worse. After being told I'd end up "in Hell's flames, burning", I had a nightmare. I dreamed that I was thrown into Hell, falling through layer after layer of terrible blackness, with things in it, not seen but felt, until I reached a red, gaping void. For years that dream recurred, and sometimes, even now, it comes back.'

'Are you still afraid?' asked Rodney.

'No, not really; although at times I am haunted by vague fears for which I have no explanation. Do you know, I have never prayed to God in my life until recently. The Tolmaches, who practise no religion, have really brought me nearer to a knowledge of God than I have ever been before.'

'Not prayed to God!' exclaimed Rodney. 'To whom did you pray, then?'

'The Holy Family, the saints, the martyrs.'

'But what about Jesus, Kate?'

'Jesus? . . . Well, Jesus was more frightening than the rest, for he was dead, dead and awful, so dead that no resurrection could ever bring him to life again. Every Sunday, in church, I sat opposite to him, a life-size Jesus, just taken down from the cross, his limp body trailing to the ground from his mother's arms, his blood realistically red and dripping from his wounds. He was naked but for a loincloth, and all his body had that sickly pallor of death. He was quite dead, and Easter Sunday could do nothing to bring him to life again.'

'Good heavens, Kate,' exclaimed Rodney, 'do you think the statues make the same impression on most children?'

'No,' said Kate. 'Some don't seem to mind. But I know I did, and I don't want Annie to suffer in the same way. So that's why I want to take her away from the school and the Borough Road church. But I'll still send her to a Catholic church, for they don't all have such gruesome statues as in the Borough Road church. But whatever I do it's going to be difficult, because as long as she's at home there's my da—father to contend with.'

'Kate, stick to the decision you have already come to in your mind,' Rodney entreated her. 'Don't let your father or anyone else turn you from it. I should hate to think of Annie's little mind being tortured like that. And if there's anything I can do to help you with Annie, Kate, you know I will; I'm very fond of her.'

'I know that, doctor. You have always been so good to her, and I am very grateful. But it's my father and Father O'Malley I'll have to fight. If only I could take her away; but I can't. I can't hurt my mother, she's suffered so much. Everything is so difficult.'

Rodney sought an answer to a question he was asking himself: 'Why were you going to Midnight Mass, Kate, feeling about things as you do?'

Kate considered a minute: 'Habit, I suppose, and . . . yes, because a part of me is attracted by the mass and, I feel, always will be. There is a lot of beauty in the religion, if one were allowed to look at it without its coating of Hell and sin. I have thought a lot about it, lately, and I think more care should be taken over the choice of priests. Quite a number of them lose more Catholics than they convert. But my real reason for going tonight was to keep the peace at home; it makes things easier for my mother.'

'Does she go?'

'No, her legs are so bad. What is really wrong with her legs, doctor?'

'It's dropsy, Kate.'

'Is it very serious?'

'Well, she needs a lot of rest; she should keep her legs up as much as possible.'

Kate sighed, and they were silent for a moment.

Rodney looked at his watch: 'Time's getting on, Kate. Let's get out for a moment and take a breather on the hill, eh?'

She nodded. He got down and came round the car and helped her to alight. As he touched her, back floated the warm, disturbing feeling. He stood near her, on the road, and looked at her face as she gazed up into the sky and inhaled deeply. His throat felt tight, his muscles gathered into knots in his arms, he moistened his lips; her face, pale and lovely, began to draw him, as if over a great distance. He was saying to himself, 'It's no good; I want her, and I'm glad I want her,' when her voice recalled him to himself: 'There's a car coming over the hill,' she said, with the crispness of tone she had used before.

He turned and looked at the oncoming car and sighed heavily. Then, taking her lightly by the elbow, he led her on to the hill.

Two of the occupants of the passing car watched Rodney and Kate, shoulder to shoulder, walk over the sparkling grass. They craned round until the figures disappeared into the shadows and blur of the hillside.

Mrs Richards was the first to speak: 'Upon my word! I would never have believed it if I hadn't seen it with my own eyes. At one o'clock in the morning! What do you make of it, Joe?'

Doctor Richards, the look of surprise still on his face, settled himself further into his seat. 'Well, what can you make of it?'

'That was the Hannigan girl, wasn't it?' said Jennie Richards, leaning forwards from the back seat towards her mother. 'The one Miss Tolmache dresses like a duchess.'

It's a question as to who dresses her, Mrs Richards thought; but she said aloud, primly, 'Whether it was or not, you keep your mouth shut, Jennie.'

'Oh, don't treat me as a child, mother,' said Jennie petulantly. 'Why, it's common knowledge that Doctor Prince is the father of her child! And he certainly makes no secret of it; he takes the kiddie all over the place in his car.'

To the peril of them all, Doctor Richards swung round in his seat, his head nearly colliding with his wife's.

'Look where you're going, Joe!' she cried. 'Do you want to kill us?'

Turning back to the wheel, he asked over his shoulder, 'Where did you hear that?'

'I heard Bella talking to cook . . . oh, ages ago . . . Mary, the Princes' maid told her.'

'Good God!' said Doctor Richards. Mrs Richards said nothing; she was thinking of two years ago tonight when they had all gone to the pantomime.

ANNIE

Annie opened her eyes slowly. She was surprised to find she had to open them, for the last thing she could remember was sitting up in bed, feeling very frightened after having shouted at her granda. Her mind cleared of sleep at once, and the frightened feeling returned; but not so badly, for it was morning now and she could hear her grandma moving about downstairs . . . Things didn't frighten you so much in the daytime as they did at night, and although she was always afraid of her granda, the feeling became a choking terror in the night when she heard his voice muttering and grumbling at her grandma. She had never before heard her grandma's voice from the other room until last night, and it was this that had made her shout out. Her granda's voice, low and terrible with menace, had come to her through the thin wall, causing the little body to stiffen on the bed; then her grandma's voice, thick and full of something that struck greater terror into Annie's heart, had cried, 'Don't! Oh, don't! I won't! I won't!' It was then she could bear it no longer, and she yelled, 'Leave her alone, granda! Leave her alone!' A terrible silence had followed, and she had sat, paralysed with fear, waiting for the door to open. And now it was morning, and it was Christmas Eve . . .

A little shiver of ecstasy passed through her, sweeping fear and all thought of last night away. Bringing her knees up, she curled into a ball and put her head under the clothes, a favourite position when she wanted to think something nice . . . Tonight she would hang up her stocking, and their Kate would be home today, and at half-past eleven she would see the doctor, and perhaps he'd have time to give her a ride . . . She gave a succession of shivers and hugged her knees tighter.

When her grandmother gently turned back the clothes, Annie's green eyes laughed up at her, her lashes curled like a dark smudge under the line of her arched eyebrows, her delicate-tinted skin flushed with her own breath. Her grandmother straightened out the strands of tumbled, silver hair that had escaped from one plait, and arranged, with little stroking movements, the fringe on her forehead: 'Come on, hinny; it's time you were up.'

'It's Christmas Eve, grandma!'

'Yes, hinny, it's Christmas Eve.'

'And Santa Claus will come tonight!'

'He will that, my bairn. But come on, get up now; and hurry.'

No word of last night, but the sight of her grandma with her sleeves down brought it all back to Annie's mind. She didn't expect her grandma to make any reference to it, for it was an unspoken understanding that granda was not mentioned in any way . . . Yet with her shouting out like that, she thought perhaps her grandma might have said something; and she couldn't remember seeing her grandma with her sleeves down before. But other strange things had happened like that after her granda had shouted at her grandma; such as the time when she wore a scarf for weeks in the summer; and there was the time, too, when her finger was bad, and she had kept it wrapped up; and when it had mended it was crooked . . . She looked searchingly into her grandmother's face, but the pale eyes, with little wrinkled bags beneath them, crinkled at the corners reassuringly.

Annie put her arms around her neck and kissed her: 'Have I to put my clean vest and bloomers on?'

'No, not until tomorrow, hinny. And come on, now, and hurry downstairs and get washed.'

When Annie was told to hurry downstairs and get washed it meant her granda was coming into breakfast at half-past eight from the long shift, and that she must be ready and have had her breakfast and be sitting quietly while he ate, or go out to play, or down the yard.

She washed in the bowl that stood on the backless chair in the two-foot recess between the kitchen door and the cupboard. Her grandma had given her hot water with which to wash, and she would have liked to play about, but she knew that she mustn't. Standing before the fire that held the big black frying-pan with her bacon and fried bread sizzling in it, she put on her vest and bloomers, her one calico-topped petticoat, her flannel one, her blue woollen dress and her white, frilled pinafore. Then she sat down at the table and said her grace.

When she had finished her bacon and had wiped up her dip with a piece of oven-bottom cake, keeping one eye on her grandmother while she did it, knowing that this was one of the things that Kate said she was not to do, and which her grandmother reluctantly enforced, she again said her grace and left the table. The fire looked inviting, and she would have liked to have sat before it on the fender and read one of her story books until it was time to go and meet Kate. But, again remembering last night, she hurriedly got into her thick reefer coat, pulled on to her head a red woollen hat with a pom-pom on the top, picked up her gloves, and kissed her grandmother.

'Keep on the dry parts, hinny,' said Sarah; 'and don't play with the snow, it's too dirty now. You must keep yourself clean for Kate coming, you know.'

63

Annie nodded and hurried out, down the yard and into the lavatory, just as the backyard door opened and her granda clumped up the yard. She gave a little sigh, shot the bolt and got on to the seat. And then the safe feeling crept over her, the feeling she always had when she was in here. No-one could get at you here; it was quiet, like a little square house, all red and white, and you were tight locked in.

The red bricks of the floor, the whitewashed walls, the white wooden seat extending right across the breadth of the lavatory and filling half its depth, was a place of sanctuary for Annie. There were rarely any bad smells here, for her grandmother kept it fresh with ashes down the hole, and daily scrubbing. The only time Annie got a violent distaste for it was when the men unexpectedly lifted the back hatch to clean it out with their long shovels. Then a revulsion for it would overcome her. She didn't like the scavengers, nor would she follow the cart with her companions, shouting:

> '*Cloggy Betty, on the netty,*
> *On a Sunday morning . . .*'

She never looked at the men, they were so filthy; but she felt pity for the bushy-footed horse, and had wild visions of herself unharnessing it and letting it away.

She heard a scramble of feet in the Mullens' yard, next door. Their back-door banged and her own opened, and a plaintive voice chanted up the yard, 'An-nie! . . . Are-ya-comin' out? . . . An-nie! . . . Are-ya-comin' out?'

Quickly scrambling out of the lavatory, she joined her friend, and marshalled her with unseeming haste out of the yard into the back lane.

'I didn't know yer granda was in, Annie,' said Rosie Mullen, apologetically; she hadn't asked for an explanation of the hustle; she knew all about Annie's granda, in some ways much more than Annie did, as her parents were outspoken in their comments on their neighbour. Rosie was two years older than Annie, but much shorter. She was a replica of her mother, being dumpy and fat, with small, bright eyes and a round face. Her dark hair stuck out in two-inch plaited points from behind her ears. She looked ugly and quaint and likeable, and Annie had a deep affection for her, for which Rosie was grateful, although she didn't know it; she only knew that Annie Hannigan was her best friend, and if the girls said things about her granda that made Annie cry she punched them in the chest or slapped their faces.

'I've got to take our Nancy out in the pram,' said Rosie, in disgust. 'That'll mean I can't go with you to meet your Kate.' Which would also mean she would miss either some sweets or a ha'penny.

'Oh, well, I haven't got to go till half-past ten, so we can take Nancy round to the shop and have a look in,' said Annie; and, with great intuition, added, 'and I'll keep you half of whatever our Kate gives me.'

Rosie grinned broadly, and, taking hold of Annie's hand, dashed with her into their backyard, seized the big dilapidated pram, in which a two-year-old child lay sucking a dummy, and pushed it out into the cobbled back lane, down which they hurried, the pram tossing about like a cork on the ocean, past seven back doors with their accompanying coal and oozing lavatory hatches, round the bottom corner, across a piece of waste land where children were already playing among mounds of dirty snow and wet, brown grass, and into the front street of the houses opposite their own. About half way up, one of the houses suddenly changed its pattern; above its window a large, yellow tin placard said, DRINK BROOKEBOND'S TEA, and a gay old gentleman, on another piece of tin, asked you to look at him to see how fit he kept on ALLY SLOPER'S SAUCE. The house window itself held tier on tier of bottles of sweets receding away from the gaze of the beholder to dim regions beyond, while, balancing on the front of every shelf, were boxes of hearts-and-crosses, sherbet dips, everlasting stripes, scented cachous and jujubes. In front of the window were large jars of pickled cabbage and pickled onions, and seven-pound jars of loose jam and lemon curd. Among these, at crazy angles, were placed Christmas wares of 'Shops with real scales', dolls in the minutest of gauze chemises, work-boxes, miniature boxing-gloves and tram-conductor sets of hat and ticket puncher. Paper-chains hung in loops from the ceiling, together with huge red and green paper bells, of a honeycomb pattern. From the chains and bells, held by fine threads, dangled swans, balls, dolls, ships and fairies, all in fine glass and painted a variety of colours.

Annie and Rosie pushed the pram against the wall and joined two other children, who were endeavouring to get a first-hand view by hanging on to the high window-sill by their elbows and sticking their toes into the wall . . . 'Ooh! ain't they luverly?' said Rosie, gazing in rapture at the display.

'I'm getting a great big doll,' said the taller of the two girls in front, jerking her head round.

'Oh, you! You are always saying that, Cissy Luck!' snapped Rosie, without taking her eyes from the chains and their dangling splendour.

'I am, ain't I, Peggy?'

'Yes, she is,' said her companion; 'and she's going to take me into their house to play, ain't you?'

'Yes,' said Cissy, pursing her lips, 'and she's going to play with my doll the morrer.'

There was a questioning silence while the two girls turned from the window and confronted Annie and Rosie. When no further remarks regarding the integrity of her statements were forthcoming, Cissy said to Annie, 'Whatcher getting in yer stockin'?'

Annie, whose eyes, like Rosie's, were fixed upon the magic array behind the glass, answered abstractedly, 'Oh, I don't know yet, not until Santa Claus comes; I've sent him a letter.'

Cissy and Peggy exchanged sidelong, incredulous glances. Then, suddenly throwing their arms around each other, they shrieked with laughter.

'You gone barmy?' asked Rosie, looking at them stolidly.

Annie smiled, feeling that she was the source of their enjoyment, but not knowing why.

'She says . . . she sent 'im a letter,' spluttered Cissy into her friend's neck.

'Well, what about it?' demanded Rosie, her square jaw thrust out. 'Ain't nowt funny about that.'

The other two suddenly turned on her, their faces aggressive with knowledge. 'She's a silly bitch! There ain't no Santa Claus; it's yer ma and da,' said Cissy.

Rosie blinked rapidly; she knew this to be the truth, but, glancing at Annie, something in her friend's face caused her to deny this statement hotly: 'You shut yer mouth up! There's a picture of Santa up there,' she pointed into the window. Then, grinning broadly at Annie, she said, 'That must be a picture of Cissy Luck's da!' This sudden piece of wit sent her off into loud guffaws, to which Annie joined her high-pitched laugh.

Cissy's face grew dark, her eyes narrowed, and her loose, lower lip pouted. She took a step forward, not towards Rosie but towards Annie . . . This Annie Hannigan, with her thick lashes and fair hair, her big top coat and her woolly hat with the red pom-pom, who was she anyway? She wanted to destroy her, punch her face, kick her, hear her yell; but there was Rosie Mullen, you had to be careful with Rosie Mullen! 'What you laughin' at?' she demanded of Annie. 'Laughin' about my da! You're the one to laugh, you are! You ain't got no da, like Santa Claus nor nobody else, so there! Me ma said so.'

The eyes of the four children darted from one to the other, following this startling announcement. Annie's face showed utter bewilderment. She made a mute appeal to Rosie, but Rosie was for once tongue-tied and hid her embarrassment by a sudden and violent rocking of her pram, to the delight of the youngest Mullen.

Annie's voice did not sound convincing to herself, when she heard it, for there were dreadful new fears attacking her, and, rising to the surface of her mind, hazy and troublesome impressions that weren't new: 'I have got a da, you know I have. I've got a da and a ma . . .'

'Don't be daft!' cut in Cissy. 'That's your grandma and your granda; we've all got grandmas and grandas. But you've got to have a ma and a da too, and you ain't got any.'

They stared at each other in silence; then Annie's head dropped slowly forward. A terrible emptiness was creeping over her, and a

66

longing to fly away and never see Cissy Luck or anyone else ever again, to hide for ever and ever. But where could she go? The new fears were growing bigger every minute, like the dream she had in the night of the lion going to swallow her up. The fears were like that.

Peggy put her arms round Cissy and whispered into her ear, and Cissy, after listening intently, seemed to grow with new power. Her next announcement brought Annie's head up with a jerk: 'Your Kate's your ma, so she is,' she cried.

Denial sprang to Annie's lips, but was checked by another fear, a fear that stripped Kate of wonder and made her into a ma. Her world was suddenly topsy-turvy; she must get away, fly from everyone. 'I've got to go . . . I must go . . . I'm going to the lavatory,' she stammered at Rosie. 'But I'll come back.' And, turning, she flew down the street, around the corner, up the back lane and burst into the yard and into the lavatory. When she had shot the bolt she didn't sit down, but stood with her back to the wall, her hands behind her, her bottom pressing her palms into the rough-edged bricks until she could feel the points through her woollen gloves . . . They said she hadn't a da; what could she do? Where was her da, then? Should she go in and ask her grandma about it? No. Some instinct told her that it would hurt her grandma. Then, could she ask Kate? . . . She dropped her head and stared at her shoes. A queer sense of shame, inexplicable, filled the lavatory, flowing over into the yard, the house and all the world of her knowledge. There was no place it did not penetrate. Great tears rolled down her cheeks, dropping heedlessly from her chin . . . She had no da; was that why her granda didn't like her, and never called her Annie, but . . . that one, or that funny name that sounded like . . . bedstead?

But you must have a da; Jesus had given everybody das; you couldn't be borned unless you had a da . . . And if Kate was her ma . . . But her mind switched away from Kate; Kate was mixed up with something so painful that it hurt . . . Where was her da? . . . She remembered Alec. No, he wasn't her da. He had been going to marry Kate, and she was glad he hadn't. No, he couldn't be her da . . . Well, who was?

She began to pray: 'Oh, please Jesus, tell me who my da is.' Raising her head, she looked up as if the answer would be found in the air above her, and she licked her tears, savouring their saltiness as she waited. But no answer came . . . It must be right, then, what they'd said, she wasn't like other girls. What could she do? Nothing! Nothing!

In fresh despair she turned to the wall and buried her face in her hands. Through long practice, she cried quietly, and when, eventually, she stopped, she sat on the edge of the lavatory seat wondering what she could do about this dreadful shame which had come upon her; for she had no doubt but that it was a shame. Then the solution came; like a streak of dazzling light it flashed into her mind, bringing with it the remedy. Although it would be only 'making on' it would be wonderful, for she'd have a da. Though her choice was already made she felt she must arrive at it by a process of elimination . . . She was going to 'pick' a da for herself! None of the other girls could do that, could they? Now, who did she know? There was Mr Mullen, next door; he was kind and nice . . . but he swore awful. No, he wouldn't do; and besides he was a da eight times already. Then there was Mr Todd, the coalman; he always heaped her buckets so full she could scarcely carry them into the yard . . . but he spat, didn't he? Of course, it was with sitting in the middle of the coal-cart all day that made him do it . . . but still, he spat! Then there was Patrick Delahunty, the big Irishman who had come to lodge up the street; he always stopped and spoke to her, and he sometimes gave her and Rosie a penny. Yes, he was nice, but . . . !

Then there was the doctor! She shivered, and joining her hands together, pressed them between her knees. She turned her head and gazed at the wall, a hot feeling of shyness sweeping over her because of the tremendous thing she was about to do. She sat lost in contemplation of the wonder of this new existence wherein the doctor was to be her da; so lost that had she heard Tim's heavy boots coming down the yard they had ceased to be a warning to her for flight. Only when he tried to open the door and, finding it locked, shook it with such violence as to nearly wrench it off its hinges did she start up, withdraw the bolt and, pushing open the door, sidle out.

A muttered curse and a quick movement from Tim lent wings to her legs. She was out of the yard and into the back lane in a flash. She looked about her like a startled hare . . . Had he been going to hit her? He put his hand to his belt . . . the leather belt with the big steel buckle which was part of her regular nightmare. Sometimes the buckle became a face, the face of her granda . . . She blinked her eyes and shook her head, as if this would dismiss it from her mind. It did; and she thought again of the beautiful, new 'make-on' game . . . And it wasn't all 'make-on', was it? she asked herself, for the doctor was a real person, the reallest person on earth and she loved him . . . better than God! Eeh! what had she said? Well, she did love him, as much as God. Wasn't it lovely to feel like this, all shivery and jumpy inside, because he was her da? And it was her secret, just hers; she wouldn't tell anyone. But what about Rosie? Surely she could tell Rosie.

While walking slowly down the back lane and into the next street she debated in her mind whether Rosie should be let into this secret. She couldn't quite understand why she was hesitating about telling Rosie, for Rosie was her friend, and she told her everything. But, somehow, she had the same feeling about it as she had with her grandma when they didn't talk about the things granda did.

The sight of Rosie leaving the pram to chase Cissy Luck and thump her in the back decided her. Rosie was shouting: 'Take that, you cheeky bitch . . . and that! You're as soft as clarts . . . and your ma's soft as clarts, and your da's soft as clarts!'

Annie dashed up to her and, taking her face between her hands, a gesture which always warmed Rosie, whispered, bending a little so that their noses nearly touched, 'I have got a da!'

Rosie drew back: 'What! Who?'

Annie pulled her forward again, 'The doctor!'

'The doctor?'

'Mm-m.'

Rosie again withdrew herself to a short distance from where she could look steadily at Annie . . . Annie didn't tell lies, but, the doctor her da! Well, of course . . . yes, that explained everything – the rides in his car, the sweets and fruit, right in the middle of the week, and then those great big presents at Christmas . . . Of course; he must be her da. Why hadn't she thought of it before? . . . But then, he wasn't married to Kate. Well, that was a thing she couldn't understand, but definitely he was Annie's da . . . only das brought you things.

'It's a "make-on" secret,' again whispered Annie.

But Rosie didn't hear this last confidence, or else she was conveniently deaf, not meaning her next course of action to be restricted.

Turning from Annie, she advanced halfway across the road again and addressed the now snivelling Cissy and her comforter, Peggy, on the opposite pavement: 'Think yer clever, doncher?' she yelled. 'Well, she has got a da, see! And a better one than yours. Her da's the doctor, if you want to know . . . there!' she said, jerking her head violently in their direction. Then, turning her back, she lifted up her clothes and thrust out her bottom at them, and, leaving them with this final insult, she grabbed the handle of the pram at one end, assigning the other to Annie, and led a triumphant march at a smart pace down the street.

It was just on ten-thirty, and Annie waited near the police-house, as she called the small dock police office that stood at the side of the big dock gates. She watched the men pass in and out of the docks with great interest. The policeman on duty had spoken to her, saying, 'You waiting for your ma again?' She remembered now he had called Kate her ma before today . . . so he had known. Everybody had known, except her . . . She nodded at him, shyly.

The tram from Westoe came rolling down the 'dock bank', and, when it stopped, Kate alighted and the conductor lifted her suitcase on to the pavement.

Annie paused a moment before running to her, savouring a feeling akin to that experienced earlier in the morning . . . this was her ma; and Annie realised for the first time that she was different from everyone around her . . . none of the women wore a beautiful

69

green coat and a big green hat and a fur with a lot of tails . . . the fur must be new, she hadn't seen it before . . . and none of them stood like Kate did, or walked like her; she stood very straight and, when she walked, her skirts danced. The women she saw every day wore dark, drab clothes, and stood hunched up, like the group which was waiting for the Jarrow tram now and had turned their eyes, like the eyes of a wolf pack, on her.

As Kate looked about her, Annie ran forward, and, as she heard herself say 'Hello, Kate,' as Kate bent to kiss her, she knew, with great certainty, that she'd never be able to call her anything else; it would always be 'Kate', never 'ma'.

Kate looked her over quickly, tenderly. She touched her cheek with the back of her hand before picking up the suitcase and crossing the road to the tram terminus. 'Have you been waiting long, dear?' she asked.

'No,' said Annie; 'and I've been talking to the policeman.'

'Grandma all right?' asked Kate.

Annie hesitated, thinking of the rolled-down sleeves. 'Ye . . . s. Yes, I think so. She's going to bake, she's making me a yule doo.'

Kate glanced down at her, swiftly, and sighed. Annie thought it was because the case was so heavy: 'Let me help, I'll take one side,' she suggested.

'No, of course not,' said Kate. 'Here we are, anyway, and there's the tram coming.'

They stood for a few minutes while the tram disgorged its passengers, some giving Kate a brief nod of acknowledgement and a long stare, others calling cheerily, 'Hallo there, Kate! Happy Christmas.' Annie noted it was the men who were nicer.

Kate pulled Annie's arm through hers as they sat together on the long wooden seat, while opposite sat a row of women. All the women seemed to have sat on the opposite side of the tram, Annie noticed; perhaps they wanted to look at Kate's fur; yes, that was it, for they were all staring at Kate; but Kate didn't seem to notice, for she was talking about Christmas and . . . What was she saying? . . . She was going to take her up to Newcastle in the train this afternoon? And they would go to the big bazaar where Santa Claus lived!

She pressed herself against Kate, against the green coat and the tails of the fur. There was a faint smell, warm and lovely. Her mind could offer no name for it; it wasn't scent, for Connie Fawcett, who was Kate's cousin and had been hers up till today but had now become in some way disconnected with this new relationship, she used scent. When Connie came from High Jarrow to see her grandma, her grandma always waffed her apron around the kitchen after she had gone to get rid of the smell; but you wouldn't want to get rid of this smell.

'Come on, dreamer,' said Kate softly, 'we're nearly there.'

Annie looked about her in surprise: yes, so they were. There was the first of the fifteen streets.

The tram stopped just before the first street. 'The stops've been altered,' explained the conductor; 'we only stop at each end of the fifteen streets now.'

Kate made a wry face at Annie; the case was heavy and she'd have to carry it past the breadth of eight streets before coming to her own . . . Still, it wasn't like walking past the streets in the late afternoon or evening when each corner had its special clique of loafers.

As she rested at the corner of the second street she noticed a woman running from the far end towards her; she carried her hat in her hand, from which a broken feather dangled, a coil of her hair was hanging on her shoulder, and Kate noticed, as she drew nearer, that the front of her coat was covered with soft filth, and that angry tears were running down her face.

'Why,' exclaimed Kate, 'what on earth's the matter, Jessie?'

The woman stopped and leant against the wall, gasping: 'It's them bitches, Kate. They did this to me,' she said, holding out her hat with one hand and pointing to her coat with the other. 'I'll have the law on them, see if I don't. They won't get off with it, I'll make them pay, every one of them. Dirty swine!'

Kate looked at her pityingly as she made this idle threat . . . Poor Jessie! . . . Had she really gone to school with this woman? Played with her? Knelt beside her at mass? It seemed impossible; she looked old and haggard now . . . spent. Could she be only two years older than herself?

'I was only goin' to see me ma, Kate, that's all, it bein' Christmas Eve an' all. Ooh . . . h! I wish I was dead.' Her head dropped to her chest, and she moved it from side to side in a gesture of despair that wrung Kate's heart.

Kate knew what Jessie's life had been. After a youth spent working in a laundry, ten hours a day, and the rest of her waking life at street corners or in dark recesses of shop doors, Jessie had married one of the boys from the fifteen streets, who, in the neighbours' opinion was much too good for her; which must have been God's opinion also, said the God-fearing members of the community, when, just a year later, he was killed in the pit. Jessie had a friend who lived next door and who was very kind to her during her trouble, to the extent of allowing her husband to do odd jobs for her. It was later brought to the friend's notice by kind neighbours that it seemed funny that her husband and Jessie had to go up to Newcastle on the same day, and that as soon as she went out to do her shopping her man was in with Jessie when he was supposed to be getting his sleep ready for the night shift. The result of this exposure had been a promise from the husband to have nothing further to do with Jessie. But he had counted without Jessie, for she had found someone at last who could satisfy her

71

physically, and she could no more leave him alone than she could stop herself wanting him. However, she moved to Shields to make things easier, and nothing the wife could do about it could loosen Jessie's hold on her husband; until nature took a hand. Aided, no doubt, by the wife's feverish desire to keep her man, it presented her with a child after eight years of marriage.

The baby was an enemy against whom Jessie was powerless, and the visits of its father became less and less, until they ceased altogether. Desperate, Jessie came to the fifteen streets, where she hadn't been for two years, supposedly to see her mother. This morning's visit was her third within a week, and some of the neighbours, seeing which way the wind was blowing, became self-constituted avengers, determined to protect the reformed husband against this shameless woman.

Most of this story was known to Kate, and the right or the wrong of it passed her by. She only knew that she felt a great pity for her one-time schoolmate. 'Why don't you get right away, Jessie? Go into service somewhere; you'll forget all about this. There are good places to be had . . . look at me. Why don't you try it?' she urged.

Jessie began to sob helplessly: 'You fell on your feet, Kate; there ain't many places like yours. And you've got your bairn, I've got nothing . . . Anyway, I only want him,' she added, with finality.

A gasp at her side brought Kate's attention from Jessie to Annie; she was staring wide-eyed at Jessie, and the tears were raining down her cheeks. Kate was about to tell Annie to run home when they heard shouts coming from up the main road, and there, pouring from the street next to her own, was a group of women, who were gesticulating and pointing towards them. There was no doubt in Kate's mind that they were bent on further destruction. 'Get away, Jessie, as quickly as you can! Look, there's a tram coming; you'll just get it!'

'I can't go on the tram like this, Kate,' gasped Jessie, desperately; 'I'll walk.'

'You must get the tram,' said Kate. 'The way they are feeling, some of them would likely follow you to the docks. Surely you know them by now.'

A stone hurtled past them, and Kate pulled Annie close to her. It decided Jessie. Sobbing afresh, she took to her heels and ran, boarding the tram just as the women came up with Kate, frustration and hate predominant in all their faces. They paused a moment, breathless, watching the tram roll away.

'Yer wanter give that'un a wide berth,' said one of them, turning to Kate, 'she's a real wrong 'un.'

'I'm surprised you speak to her, filthy bitch that she is,' said another, hitching up her enormous breasts with her forearms. 'She's shameless, bloody well shameless. If I'd got me hands into her hair instead of grabbing that hat I'd have let her see, the—!'

72

Kate looked at the last speaker coldly, an anger that was only stirred by injustice rising in her . . . How dare this woman whom she had known from childhood, and who had always shocked her with her obscenities, in spite of having been brought up under the specialised language of Tim! How dare she, who delighted in exchanging the filth of her mind with any man so interested, appoint herself judge of another woman! She was feared, and consequently fawned upon by most of her associates; she was Kate's idea of corruption; there was no tempering of judgement here. Mrs Luck was bad! Her mind was a sewer; she could defile by a look. She had eleven children alive, which made Kate shudder at the productive power of evil . . .

Kate's distaste and anger showed clearly in her face as she looked at the little crowd before her, and it wasn't lost on them. There was a moment of hostile silence as they stared back at her and the child, pressed close to her side. A moment ago they had felt protective towards her, warning against the contamination of Jessie . . . but now, with her looking at them like that, and her dressed up to the knocker like a goddam queen or somesuch . . . their attitude changed . . . and if all the tales were true she was a damn sight as bad as that whore just gone.

'I don't think it's for you to judge Jessie Daley, it behoves us all to mind our own business,' said Kate scornfully.

They gasped, speechless with surprise at her daring, and listened, fascinated by her tone, for Kate was unconsciously speaking to them much as Miss Tolmache would have done. 'You'll never right wrongs by the methods you are using. Can't you see you'll only make matters worse? A little kindness from one of you would have had much more effect than all your horseplay . . . but then, of course,' Kate's eyes swept them with disdain, 'you wouldn't have enjoyed it so much.'

As she stooped to pick up her case there was a murmur of, 'By damn, who the hell does she think she is? . . . We're coming to something now, ain't we?' but nothing really audible until she had passed through the midst of them, with Annie clinging to her hand.

She had walked a few yards ahead when the first voice reached her, which she recognised as Dorrie Clarke's: 'Birds of a feather, lasses!' Dorrie yelled. 'Only this one picks on professional blokes; they can pay more; look at her clothes. What did I tell you?'

Kate jerked to a halt as if a bullet had struck her in the back. She had no time to think before Mrs Luck screamed words that seemed to freeze her blood; all the hard-won beauty in her life was darkened from this moment, never to fully return to its previous brightness; her real misfortunes seemed to date from the moment Mrs Luck shouted: 'It's coming to something . . . by God it is! Who jer think yer talking to . . . brazen hussy! No wonder yer bairn brags in the street that the doctor is her da. She gets her barefacedness from the right one, you bloody upstart, you!'

73

All the terror Annie had known in her short life paled before this new terror. As she lifted her eyes to Kate's her heart seemed to leap from her body by way of her mouth, for she saw there something that chilled her and turned her stomach over as never Tim's look had done. Kate's face was white, and her blue eyes black and deep and full of that something that made Annie want to hide her face. But she had to go on looking up into Kate's eyes for they wouldn't let hers go. Slowly Kate turned her face away, and with it her body, and she was facing the women again.

The women were all quiet now, some a little awed at the length Nell Luck had gone, and growing uneasy . . . Why couldn't Nell keep her mouth shut? This Kate Hannigan wasn't Jessie Daley. Besides, having the doctor for a fancy man she was in with the toffs. Best keep clear of them, money was power; and most of the houses around here were owned by the Westoe toffs. You could be put on the street and never know the reason why . . . Well, why didn't she say something instead of standing there like that? She certainly was putting up a good bluff; but it had taken the wind out of her sails, she looked like a corpse, but not a frightened one . . . no, nothing frightened about her, she wouldn't run . . . Ah, she was going through, and without a word too!

They watched her turn and walk away, the child walking behind her, tearing the thumb of her glove with her teeth. No-one spoke. They were suddenly deflated; even Mrs Luck voiced no thought, merely rolling her folded arms tighter in her shawl. It was as if they were fed by one artery, so general appeared their sense of defeat. All at once they seemed to remember they were busy women and were wasting time. They dispersed in twos and threes, Dorrie Clarke and Mrs Luck together. 'Well, you showed the bitch,' said Dorrie.

Mrs Luck straightened her shoulders: 'Yes, I showed the bitch.'

'Nice way to spend a Christmas Eve! Who started this bloody business, anyway?' said one of the two remaining women.

'I think it was Dorrie.'

'Aye, it would be. But, if my Sam gets to know I've been mixed up in this, he'll bash me face in!'

'Did you see Kate Hannigan's face, Mary? D'yer think there could have been a mistake? . . . About the doctor, I mean. She looked so surprised.'

'No, there's no mistake; he's her fancy man, all right. But she was a damn fool to let the bairn know.'

When Sarah opened the door to Kate, the glad smile of welcome died out of her face. 'My God, hinny . . . what's happened? What's the matter? Are you ill?'

Kate said nothing, but walked past her. Annie followed, the thumb of her glove now a mass of tangled wool. Sarah closed the door and hurried after them into the kitchen, crying, 'Kate, hinny, tell me what's happened.'

Kate sat down heavily on a chair by the side of the table and leaned her head on her hand. Annie stood in the dark recess which housed the wash-bowl; her eyes gleamed out of the dimness in mute appeal to her grandmother, but when Sarah put the same question to her, 'What's happened, hinny?' she only dug her fingers into her lower lip and remained silent.

Kate looked up at her mother . . . 'She's been telling people the doctor is her da . . . They're all saying he's my . . . that I'm . . . '

There was a strangled silence in the kitchen.

'No, Kate!' Sarah's voice was horrified and incredulous.

'Yes,' said Kate dully. 'They were baiting Jessie Daley; I told them they should mind their own business, and they turned on me. It was Mrs Luck and her crowd. If they think that, others do . . . everybody must . . . '

'Dear God,' said Sarah, 'what'll happen if he hears? . . . Oh, and him such a nice man too . . . But how can they say that, Kate? You didn't know him, did you?'

To the question behind the question Kate replied, 'No, ma, I didn't know him; I never saw him before he came upstairs when she was born.'

'Oh, what made her say such a thing?' Sarah looked at Annie. 'What made you say it, hinny?'

Annie simply stared back, her eyes becoming wider, threatening to slip beyond the boundary of her face.

'Come here,' said Kate quietly.

Annie came slowly forward, and the look on her face broke the ice in Kate's heart. 'Don't be frightened,' she said, 'you won't get into trouble . . . Only tell me, what made you say it? Has anyone ever said it to you?'

Annie shook her head.

'You just made it up?'

Annie nodded quickly.

'But you knew it was a lie, didn't you, and it was wrong?'

'They said . . . ' whispered Annie.

'Yes?' prompted Kate.

'Well . . . they said I hadn't got a da at all, and I wanted a da, and I just made on the doctor was my da. And I told Rosie, and she told Cissy Luck . . . Oh, Kate, I was only making-on.'

Looking at her child, Kate realised the hurt and loneliness that must have preceded this game of 'making-on'. She was suddenly overwhelmed with the pity of it. She had done everything in her power to make up to Annie for the lack of a father, but it would seem nothing one could do would ever fill that gap. 'How long have you pretended he was . . . your da?'

75

'Just this morning, round at the shop.'

'You've never said it before?'

'No, never, Kate. I made it up in the lavatory.'

Kate looked at Sarah. 'It isn't something fresh they have just got hold of ma. They must have thought this . . . for a long time; I could see it in their faces. But, oh, the irony of it, that she should play into their hands by picking on him.' Great tears welled up into her eyes; she dropped her head suddenly on to her arms and sobbed.

Sarah stood mute, mechanically rolling and unrolling the corner of her apron. She had never seen Kate cry since she was a child . . . not even when she came home that time did she cry! And now the sound of her sobbing was more than she could bear. 'Don't, hinny, don't,' she pleaded; 'he can't know, and nobody would dare say anything to him; and you know it's all lies. Oh' – she turned to Annie – 'why did you say such a thing? . . . What made you?'

Kate put her hand out blindly and drew Annie's shivering body to her. 'Don't blame her, ma; please. She's not to blame.' She sat up and dried her face with her handkerchief, and unpinned her hat and put it on the table. Then, taking Annie's two hands in hers, she drew her close to her knees: 'Dear,' she began, 'now listen carefully to what I am going to say . . .'

Annie listened, but the softness of Kate's voice and the love and understanding in her eyes in no way eased the blow when it came. 'You are not to ride in the doctor's car any more, and you are not to wait for him at the corner . . . you understand? You must keep out of his way . . . If you can't avoid him, then you must tell him . . . well, tell him you are going a message, or you've got to hurry home. But you mustn't wait about for him. Now promise me you'll do as I tell you.'

No amount of blinking would keep the scalding tears from falling, or quick swallowing dislodge the lump that was choking her; nothing that could ever happen could be as bad as this . . . Not to see the doctor again, not to sit beside him on the beautiful leather seat in the front of the car and see him laughing down at her, and to watch his long brown hands coming forward to lift her down, and the thrill as he whirled her through the air . . . or not to stand at the corner and see him wave to her, when he couldn't stop . . . not to do any of these things, never, never again . . .

'Answer me, dear.'

Annie tried to speak, but couldn't. Kate suddenly pulled her to her breast and held her close. 'There, there, my dear, don't cry like that. Stop now!'

Sarah, too, had her apron to her eyes when the front-door knocker banged once. In answer to Kate's startled glance, she said, 'It's all right, hinny, it'll be the insurance man, that's his knock.'

'You won't ask him in?' said Kate.

'No, hinny.'

76

Sarah took some coppers from a cup in the corner of the cupboard and a book out of the chiffonier, and went through the front-room.

'Come on, dear,' said Kate to Annie, 'dry your eyes. We'll still go to Newcastle and . . . ' She got no further, the blood slowly mounting to her face as she heard the voice at the front door speaking to her mother . . . Surely she wouldn't let him in . . . He was in, in the front-room. She pushed Annie, who was staring, as if petrified, towards the door, to one side, and in the matter of seconds she made and reversed a decision . . . to escape upstairs; no, to see him and finish this thing once and for all. As the strands of the web are like steel bands to the fly so she felt the fine-woven strands of circumstance holding her to this fate, of which she would be free, for she saw nothing but disaster for all concerned and the fulfilling of the prophecies of the women of the fifteen streets . . . She would put an end to it and stop their evil tongues, and still for ever the desire that was eating into her. In that minute she realised how this could be accomplished. The decision surprised her, for she had scorned it before today. But she saw it now as the only way out of this enveloping tangle. She felt it was inevitable; these things had to happen; life was planned; do all you could, learn, try to be different, you were brought back to the path that was set for you the day you were born . . . And, if you happened to have made a mistake as she had done, you were dragged back. But anything was better than following the dictates of her heart . . . Goodbye to Mr Bernard, and Mr Rex, and Miss Tolmache . . . but, oh, goodbye to Mr Bernard and evenings of strange delight ! . . . Why should she be called upon to do this ? Why had he come into her life, when he could have no part in it ? And now she had to give up all she valued because of him. Hostility welled up in her, but died as she met his eyes as he stood in the doorway, looking at her . . . Why must he look at her like that ? He had no right to do it . . . She felt suddenly weak and sick . . . Oh, God, why had he come ? He, too, playing into their hands.

'Hullo, there, Kate,' he said. 'Happy Christmas.'

'Hallo, doctor,' she answered quietly.

He walked to the table and put down a long box he had under his arm, ignoring Annie as he did so, although he could see her standing close to the wall in the dim corner of the kitchen. He also ignored the fact, but for a different reason, that the three of them had been crying and that the atmosphere was strained. 'A certain young lady had an appointment with me at eleven-thirty this morning, Kate,' he said, 'but she failed to put in an appearance, although she knew I had been to see Santa Claus last night, and that I would have a message for her, if not a present, from him . . . This is the first time this young lady has let me down; I thought she must be ill.'

A strangled sob came from the corner. He looked towards Annie and back to Kate again. 'Is anything wrong, Kate ?'

Kate didn't answer him but turned to Annie: 'Go upstairs, dear,' she said.

Annie, her eyes lingering on Rodney, stood as if she hadn't heard. 'Annie!' said Kate again, sharply.

Annie turned away and made a dash for the stair door, fumbled blindly with the latch, then ran upstairs. They heard her footsteps overhead before speaking, and then it was Rodney again who asked, 'What is wrong with her, Kate?'

'She is getting out of hand; I'm afraid she's being spoilt.'

He laughed. 'You're always saying she's being spoilt. It's nonsense, you couldn't spoil Annie . . . no more than you could spoil . . . ' He had been going to add 'you', but withheld it and let his eyes speak for him.

'She needs control,' went on Kate hastily; her hands were joined together, the knuckles showing white. 'She can't get used to the idea of having . . . a father!'

Rodney's exclamation of 'A father!' covered Sarah's gasp of amazement.

'Yes, she doesn't like the idea of me getting married.' There, it was out; it was quite simple really, just a few words and everything was altered.

Sarah dropped quietly into Tim's chair. Rodney stared across the width of the table at Kate. Why was it, he thought, that her face always swam towards him; no matter what the distance, it seemed to bridge it until he felt it near his own, warming him with its radiance. She seemed more beautiful than ever today because she looked sad. It was only a week since he had seen her. He had tried to keep away from the Tolmaches' after his attendance on old Rex was no longer necessary, but it had been so easy to drop in to tea, once in a while, knowing that she'd be there. Only the once in a while had become a regular habit. Last week she had presided over tea. Sitting proudly beside Miss Tolmache, she had joined in the general conversation, and he had seen her in a new light, quite at ease, laughing and talking generally. She never wore uniform, but a grey dress with a white collar which gave her a Quakerish air. He had felt she was glad he had seen her thus, and had noted the pride with which old Bernard always watched her, and the tenderness in her eyes when she looked at old Bernard or cleverly turned some remark, purposely set by him to be parried . . . And now, what was she saying?

Kate thought, he's not listening to me . . . he's got to listen: 'Doctor, I think it would be better if you gave Annie no more presents.' She swallowed hard and forced herself to meet his eyes. 'It has been most kind of you, and I am grateful . . . But now . . . well, Patrick thinks . . . well, we won't be quite in the position to buy her these kind of things.' She pointed to the box on the table. 'Patrick says . . . '

78

'Yes, Patrick says,' said Rodney in a cold voice; 'go on.' His mind raced . . . what has made her do this? . . . Something has happened . . . Who is this Patrick?

Sarah looked from one to the other . . . Oh, what was this? . . . What was this? Why didn't Kate speak? Why were they standing looking at one another like that? . . . And it couldn't be true about Patrick Delahunty! Only last week she had laughed the idea to scorn. He had haunted the house for days, asking about her and when she was coming home. And look how often she had had to tell him Kate had gone back to Westoe, when she'd been sitting upstairs all the time. He'd been after her for a year now, and she wouldn't even look at him . . . her Kate and Pat Delahunty! . . . He was a nice enough fellow . . . but not for her Kate. Oh no!

'You were saying you were going to be married,' said Rodney, his words falling like tinkling ice; 'and Patrick says . . . What does Patrick say?'

His eyes were black and hard and were boring into her. A quiver passed over Kate's face. She couldn't carry it through, she couldn't, she couldn't. Why must he . . . ? It wasn't fair. And, oh, he looked so hurt! She dropped her head.

In the months to come she was to ask herself what they would have done had not Father O'Malley walked in the back door at that moment accompanied by her cousin Connie from Jarrow. The strident voice and loud, senseless laughter of Connie as she bid everyone 'A merry Christmas' might have slackened the tension if Father O'Malley had been the loving, trusting Christian that his cloth proclaimed. But he prided himself that he knew human nature and the baseness therein, and between Kate Hannigan and this doctor, whom he had grown to hate, having been forced to listen to his views across the table of the boardroom in the workhouse, he sensed baseness like a hungry dog.

If Sarah could have put into clear thought her intuitive knowledge of the priest she would have been astounded and not a little frightened, and he, if he could have read her mind, would have credited her with possessing supernatural gifts. 'Happy Christmas, Connie,' said Sarah to her niece; 'and to you, Father. It's well you've come at this minute, you're just in time to hear the news. Kate here . . . well . . . she's going to be married.'

'Married! Oh Kate!' yelled Connie.

'And who are you going to marry, Kate?' asked the priest, in a tone of polite enquiry.

Kate regarded him steadily. From now on he would think he had a tight hand on her life . . . 'Patrick Delahunty,' she replied quietly.

The pin-points of the priest's eyes widened through his glasses: 'Patrick Delahunty . . . well, well! I'm surprised at your common sense . . . A good, steady-going, God-fearing man; you've done well for yourself.'

Kate's head went up, a look flashing from her eyes, which the priest read only too well.

'I've never known him miss mass,' he went on; 'nor the altar rails on a Sunday morning for the three years he's been over here. He'll be a great influence on Annie . . .'

'Oh, are you going, doctor?' said Sarah. 'I'll show you out.'

'That's quite all right, Mrs Hannigan,' said Rodney. 'Good morning.' He inclined his head towards Connie, where she stood, strangely quiet since she had heard the name of the man Kate was going to marry. 'Good morning,' he said to her, and, looking at neither Kate nor the priest, he went out through the front-room.

Father O'Malley watched Kate's gaze follow him . . . Patrick Delahunty, he thought; there's something funny here. Why, I was talking to him at nine o'clock this morning and he said nothing to me . . . His mind suddenly switched to the doctor . . . That man's dangerous, I'm never mistaken; and this one, she's ripe for the Devil; and she's too strong for Pat, she'll have an influence on him. Well, God's will be done!

THE PATH IS MAPPED OUT

Sitting before the kitchen fire, at three o'clock in the afternoon, Kate reviewed the happenings of the past year, with not a little wonder at the change time and the simple personality of a man had wrought in her; her mind, compared with the turmoil it had been in a year ago today, was at peace. In a fortnight's time, when she was to marry Pat, her life would change completely. No longer did she dread the idea; in fact, there were times when she actually looked forward to it, for, once married, she would be safe; there would be no more 'wondering' at what might happen, no more mistrusting herself; married to Pat, she intended her sole aim would be to make him a good wife . . . Last Christmas Eve, when she had sent for him and told him she would marry him and that she had already told her mother and Father O'Malley, he had asked no reason for her lightning change of front, but had simply taken her two hands in his and pressed her palms against his face, and, in his soft Irish voice, had said, 'It's a miracle. He has answered my prayers. If you ever live to regret this day, Kate, may my death soon follow.'

She had been amused at what she termed his theatrical speech, but was to remember it vividly within the next few hours. Gentleness had been his keynote; he was big and lumbering, but not uncouth; he had thick brown hair and a ruddy complexion, and his temper and love of peace denied his nationality. That he loved her with a deep abiding love she knew, and she felt sure in her heart that . . . left alone . . . she would be happy and would find peace with him. The phrase 'left alone' was with her less now than at the beginning of the year; contrary to her usual procedure of facing up to things she had never dissected the phrase, had never asked herself what she meant by being 'left alone'.

Looking back now, she thought how grossly she must have exaggerated the emotions of last Christmas Eve, and on other occasions too, and how near she had become to making a fool of herself by turning kindly interest into something that even now made her feel hot inside. She excused herself with the thought that the evil-tongued women had unbalanced her and that, for a moment, she had seen things through their eyes. But she had silenced their tongues, she felt, and felt truly that she had them guessing and that they did not know what to make of the turn of events.

She had seen the doctor only twice during the past year, both occasions being during the past month when he was visiting her mother. His visits to the Tolmaches had seemed to coincide with her days off. When they had met in the kitchen he had been so ordinary and nice that she had thought to herself: How dreadful it is that one exaggerates things so much; the second time Pat had been with her, and she had chided herself for willing him to like Pat. But apparently he had found this quite easy, for within a short while they were talking, even laughing, together. He had wished them both every happiness. One awkward moment alone had occurred, when the doctor had asked Pat if, later, he would be allowed to pay court to his stepdaughter once in a while. Pat had laughed heartily at a joke he couldn't see, and Kate, looking at the doctor's face, had seen nothing but kindly interest and, perhaps, a little amusement. Pat had been loud in his praises of the doctor: 'There's a real gentleman, and a man, Kate . . . If it wasn't that I love Ireland I'd want to be an Englishman like himself.' Dear, simple Pat.

Yes, the year had turned out much better than she had expected. Her hardest task had been to tell the Tolmaches. They had covered their regret at their coming loss by taking an active interest in the preparations for her wedding. Miss Tolmache was providing all the linen, Mr Rex had bought them a carpet and Mr Bernard had given her a cheque for ten pounds. The unfailing kindness of these people was sometimes more than Kate could bear. That her marriage was not to cut her off entirely from them, she owed to Pat's understanding; for it was he who had suggested she should go to them at least two afternoons a week, and even to keep up her reading with Mr Bernard if she wished. Seeing with what bands of prejudice the women around her were tied to their houses, welded by the men's domination, she felt this augured good for their future together.

Their house was all ready for them; it was in the quiet corner of Simonside, only a mile from the fifteen streets but as distant as heaven from earth. It had four rooms and a garden, back and front. When Kate thought of the garden she thought of Annie; there she would grow and blossom, away from these filthy back lanes and streets. She had been worried about Annie, after the business of last Christmas Eve; she had lost the sparkle and eagerness of childhood and a sadness had settled on her. Remembering her own short memory at Annie's age, Kate felt there must be another cause other than that of not seeing the doctor for this continued staleness. Pat, through time, had won her round to laughter again, for he loved her already as his own. But still Sarah's reports of her were that she sat too long looking at nothing. Well, thought Kate, once she was married it wouldn't matter; she could let her see the doctor occasionally, if this were really the reason for her unusual behaviour. But not so much as before. No, that wouldn't do, she had been far too fond of him; but just now and again wouldn't do any harm.

She was feeling that everything would settle in its groove. What a fool she had been to worry so much . . . Her mind flashed back to last Christmas Eve . . . What would have happened had the priest and Connie not come in when they did . . . Now, she told herself, you've been through all that before. Stop dramatising things! Whatever happened was only in your imagination . . .

She looked at her mother lying dozing on the saddle . . . How old she looked, and ill. If only she could take her with them, away from this house and him. Her ankles overflowed over her slippers, the swelling seemed to get worse every week. Kate wished she were staying over Christmas, she would have been able to make her rest. But the Tolmaches had decided that, at last, they were too old for hotels. With the war being on, they had said, the hotel would likely be overcrowded and noisy anyway, and it would be nice to have Kate spend her last Christmas with them. So she was returning tonight; it was no hardship, she could never have too much of their company . . . only she knew how much her mother looked forward to this week alone with her . . . and then there was Annie.

As Sarah lay, she kept muttering to herself. It sounded, to Kate, like a single word, a name being repeated, but it was unintelligible. She's tired and worn out, thought Kate. I'll let her sleep as long as possible, there'll be no-one coming in before tea-time, unless Connie comes . . . The thought of her cousin aroused a slight uneasiness in Kate's mind. Why had she ceased calling these past two months? Her mother, who had grumbled that she was never off the door-step, was now wondering why her visits had stopped altogether. Perhaps, thought Kate, it's because I demurred about going to Peter's wedding . . . She and Pat had been invited to her cousin Peter's wedding, and when in an effort to evade what she knew would be a drinking bout, she had said she thought she would be unable to get off that week-end, Connie had caused quite a scene and accused her of thinking herself to be a cut above them all now. So she had gone, and sat in the packed front-room, watching whisky and beer being drunk in such quantities as to ensure that everyone was having a real good time. Her refusal to touch anything had only made Connie more firm in her belief that 'Kate was looking down her nose at them all'. It was in his endeavour to turn Connie's spleen from her that Pat had laughingly drunk all Connie had pressed on him, and, not being used to it in quantity, for as he was wont to say he could 'take it or leave it', he was soon quite befuddled, if not actually drunk. At four o'clock in the morning it was impossible for him to attempt the three miles walk home. There he had sat, smiling broadly at everyone and powerless to use his legs. Kate told herself she was glad she had seen him in drink and witnessed his reactions to it, and she was amazed, and not a little pleased, that he hadn't followed the usual course of his countrymen and become fighting mad.

The house had been full with the family alone, there being ten of them in the four rooms, so, when it was decided that they couldn't possibly go home until Pat had sobered up, Kate found herself sharing one of the two beds in the back room, lying between two of her young cousins. Pat, amid screams of laughter, had been assigned to a cupboard which ran under the stairs. Apparently this had often been used as a spare bedspace and a straw mattress had been made to fit it. Kate had rebuked herself for feeling disgust of her cousins, for, after all, she had told herself, they were her people, and had it not been for the Tolmaches she would have found them, if not likeable, at least amusing, but the only impression they left on her was disgust. After the wedding Pat seemingly thought as she did, for he blamed them for having made him drunk and spoke bitterly of drink, swearing he had tasted his last.

She had laughed at him, and although she was glad he intended to drink no more she thought he had taken the effect of his lapse too seriously, for in the weeks that followed he was at times openly hostile towards the Fawcetts as a whole, and Connie in particular, going so far as to walk out of the kitchen whenever she came in.

Kate could find no reason for this. Had he made a spectacle of himself when drunk she could have understood his attitude. Sometimes she thought that Connie did not like the idea of her marrying . . . She was five years Kate's senior and anything but attractive, being inclined to fat and, as her own father was wont to say, 'wore too much on her hat and not enough on her chest.'

Kate, in the quiet peacefulness of the kitchen and the knowledge of the home that was soon to be hers, in the love that Pat showered on her, and in the deep friendship and kindness . . . yes, and love of the Tolmaches, felt it in her heart to be sorry for her cousin and her vain, and all too obvious, attempts to attract the opposite sex.

Resuming the smocking on a frock for Annie, that she had laid aside when she had begun her reverie, Kate's thoughts wandered lovingly around her daughter and her future. She'd still have to be brought up a Catholic, but not at the Borough Road school, on that she was determined; and, although it would mean a two- or three-mile walk there, and perhaps back, every Sunday, she would take her to either Shields or Tyne Dock church; St David's in the Borough Road and Father O'Malley would see them no more.

A cry from her mother suddenly startled her; Sarah was sitting upright on the saddle, calling out a name. 'Stephen! Stephen!'

'Ma!' cried Kate, shaking her gently. 'Wake up! Wake up, dear!'

'Oh!' whispered Sarah, opening her eyes. 'Oh, hinny, Stephen's here.'

'You're dreaming, ma. There, lie down.' Kate pressed her gently back.

Sarah lay for some minutes staring up at her daughter. There was a look on her face that was new to Kate, a youthful, happy look; but, even as she watched, it died away and Sarah sighed.

'Yes, lass, I've been dreaming.'

'You were calling someone named Stephen. Who's Stephen? We don't know anyone by that name, do we?'

'Did I shout that name out?'

'Yes, you've been muttering for some time.'

'Dear God! Dear God!' The look of fear that was almost habitual returned to Sarah's eyes. 'It's because I've been thinking lately . . . been wondering what I should do. I've been thinking, hinny, that I'm not long for the top.'

'Oh, ma, don't talk like that! Your legs will get better, you only need rest . . . Please don't say that. Things will be different next year, I'll be able to come and help you. Oh, ma!' Kate stroked her mother's thin, grey hair, and her eyes looked anxious.

Sarah lay for some minutes in silence. Then she said quietly, 'Is anyone in? . . . Annie, or anyone?'

'No, dear. Annie's gone to the matinée with Rosie. There'll be no-one in till five o'clock . . . I hope,' she added.

'Then,' said Sarah, 'I've got something to tell you, lass . . . I never meant to tell you, or anyone, I meant it to go to the grave with me . . . But somehow, lately, the thought has come to me that you've the right to know . . . You're sure there's no-one about?'

'No, dear.'

'Then close the front-room door, lass, and slip the bolt in the back, and bring up your chair.'

Somewhat mystified, Kate complied. Taking her mother's hand in hers she waited for her to speak.

'I don't know where to begin, hinny.' Sarah's voice had the catch of tears in it. She gazed up at Kate, taking in the warm beauty of this child of hers, wondering vaguely how she could have been born of her. She licked her lips with the old, nervous habit. 'I think I'd better tell you straight out, if it's got to be said . . . Tim isn't your father, Kate!' Anxiously, she watched for some startling change in the face of her daughter.

The pressure of Kate's hand on her mother's remained the same as a moment before . . . She was conscious only of thinking, I hope Annie doesn't get wet, it is raining so hard. She heard the fire drop, and with it some of the glow faded from the kitchen . . . The gas would soon have to be lit . . . Her mother was looking up, searchingly, into her face. Kate knew she should say something . . . but what? She hadn't words with which to describe this new surge of happiness, what this revelation meant to her. For as long as she could remember she had hated the thought of Tim Hannigan being her father. But it had been something she was powerless to alter, like being blind or deformed. The very sight of him always made her recoil, and an early fear of becoming like him had not wholly vanished. But now! Oh, now! This blessed, blessed relief . . .

'Hinny,' said Sarah anxiously, 'you don't mind, do you?'

'Oh, ma!' Kate suddenly laid her face against her mother's.

Sarah put her hand on her hair. 'There, lass . . . there! Well, it's out . . . But, hinny' – she pressed Kate away from her – 'you'll never tell a soul until I'm gone? . . . promise!'

Kate promised, but at the same time the desire was in her to tell the world. For to know that Tim Hannigan had no part in her being, that her cousins in Jarrow were not really her cousins, was so uplifting to her spirit that she had the quaint urge to sing and dance . . . really frolic around the kitchen. She remembered short spasms of happiness she had experienced as a child; they had come unbidden, unannounced, called from some central pool of delight that supplied all children, at some time or another, whether they had cause for happiness or not . . . At these times her desire had been to run, to feel her feet just flicking the earth . . . And now this was the same feeling.

To her mother's surprise she suddenly stood up, flung her arms above her head, and pivoted rapidly two or three times, her full skirt billowing against the kitchen table. Then she flung herself on her knees by the couch and buried her head on her mother's shoulder. They stayed thus, in silence, for some minutes.

After a while Kate began to think more steadily about the matter; questions tumbled into her mind, and she sat up on the chair again, and held her mother's hands once more . . .

'Does he know, ma?' she asked.

'Yes, and no,' said Sarah; 'he's always been suspicious. When you were born you were so like your father that he tried to make me admit it . . . But once I had done that, I was afraid of what he might do to you. So I've always denied it strongly.'

'Who was my father?'

'He was an artist, lass.'

'An artist!' Kate's face lit up.

'Yes, hinny . . . He painted pictures of slums and docks and people like the blind beggar who used to sit under the arches, never anything pretty. He came to the back door there one stifling night in July and said someone had told him we'd a room to spare . . . Would we let him have it? Just for a few weeks? I asked him in; Tim was eating his tea, and I felt he was going to say no. But then he looked him up and down, and I could see he didn't think much of him; for he was rather short and slim and his hair was going

86

grey at the temples, although he wasn't forty. And when he offered to pay thirty shillings a week, that settled the matter, for thirty shillings a week was a fortune.'

'How long did he stay? . . . And did he know about me?' asked Kate, eagerly.

'He stayed three months . . . No, he didn't know about you . . . but he wanted me to go away with him.'

'Oh, why didn't you?'

'I had married Tim, hinny, for better or worse . . . Anyway, I hadn't the courage then. Had it been a few years later, God knows what I might have done. But then it was too late . . . It was too late eighteen months after.'

'Why? Did you hear from him?'

'I never heard from him after he left, but I had an address to go to if ever I wanted him. But he died . . . I saw it one morning in the paper, half a page was taken up with his paintings, and his picture was there too . . . but I daren't even keep that.'

'Oh, ma.' Kate stroked her mother's hand. 'Why didn't you tell him about me?'

'Because he would have come back, and there'd 'ave been murder; Tim and him had grown to hate each other in a very short time.'

'Did he love you, ma?'

'He said he did.'

Kate looked at her mother's grey hair, the weary eyes with the wrinkled bags beneath, the tremulous mouth, the nervous, twitching tongue; how old she looked! . . . It was hard to imagine her young and attractive, with an artist in love with her. But she must have been pretty once. And anyway, there was her disposition; he would have been attracted by that alone, thought Kate, for she was so sweet, so gentle, asking nothing, and giving all.

'I love you, too,' said Kate suddenly, bending above her, her eyes large and dark with tenderness.

Sarah blinked rapidly and shook her head, evidently embarrassed . . . Kate came out with the oddest things, putting into words thoughts that she would never dream of voicing, even if she felt them deeply . . . She supposed it was living with the Tolmaches that had made Kate like that, and yet it was good to hear her say what she had . . . How many years was it since she had heard someone say they loved her? Nearly twenty-six!

They both started as the back door was shaken with considerable violence. Their eyes flashed the same message . . . It can't be him, he isn't finished till five o'clock.

When Kate withdrew the bolt and saw Pat standing there, she sighed with relief. But the laughing comment she was about to make died on her lips as she noticed the expression on his face. 'Why, Pat, what's happened? Don't stand there like that, come in.'

But from the first sight of her his eagerness to get into the house was gone. He stared at her as if storing up for all time all his eyes could take in.

'Have you had an accident ? . . . Do please come in, and don't stand there!' she repeated. 'What on earth is the matter, anyway?'

He passed her and took a few steps backwards into the kitchen, never letting his gaze drop from her face.

Kate closed the door, thinking, Something, something dreadful's happened . . . Oh, and I was so happy . . . Why must it always be like this?

'Sit down,' she said quietly, 'till I light the gas. I thought you were working right through when you didn't call in at dinner-time.'

The gas lit, she pulled down the blind and turned to him. His eyes held a stricken look. She put her hand out in compassion and touched his arm, and found herself pulled into his embrace so fiercely and crushed so hard against him that her breath caught in a gasp and there was a surging in her ears. His arms, like steel bands, moved about her, pressing her, crushing her into him, and when his hand came behind her head and his mouth covered hers, in such a way as she had never experienced before, she thought dimly . . . Don't struggle, he's ill.

Sarah, her legs dangling over the edge of the saddle, looked on in dumb amazement. She was well acquainted with trouble, and she knew it was once more in the kitchen, but the form it was taking was unusual . . . He's in a way, poor lad, he's in a way, she kept repeating to herself. And oh, if he would only stop carrying on like that!

When Kate, after what seemed an eternity, felt Pat release her lips and the tenderness she was used to creep back into his touch, she gently pressed him away and sank down into a chair. She was breathless and a little afraid.

As he still did not speak, but stood looking so strangely at Kate, Sarah said quietly, 'What is it, lad? Tell us what's happened.'

After a silence that was painful in its length, he turned slowly to Sarah. He looked suddenly childish and forlorn. 'It's Connie Fawcett, ma! She's done this.'

'Connie!' Kate and Sarah exclaimed together. Then, 'What's Connie got to do with us, Pat?' Kate asked; while a rising fear told her that Connie, at this moment, had everything to do with them.

'Oh, me darling. Oh, me Kate.' Pat's long frame doubled up and he was on his knees in front of her, with his head in her lap and his arms around her once more.

Kate looked helplessly over his bowed head at her mother. Sarah, pink with embarrassment, for she had never witnessed anything like this, murmured, 'Oh dear! Oh dear!'

'Look, Pat,' Kate said, taking his head between her hands and raising it. 'You must tell me what has happened. What has Connie done that you should go on like this? I must know,' she said firmly.

His eyes roamed over her face, and he moaned aloud. 'Yes, you must know.' He lumbered to his feet. 'And I've got to tell you! I've been telling meself that for hours as I walked the streets. I've been saying . . . I've got to tell her! . . . Holy Mary, I've got to tell her . . . Well, I'll tell you; but I can't look at you and say what's got to be said . . . Don't go, ma,' he added, as Sarah got up; 'it's best you should hear this, too.' He turned and looked into the fire, and began to talk.

Kate and Sarah stared at his broad back and at his outstretched hands, clasping and unclasping the brass rod under the mantelpiece, and listened as he went back to the night of Peter Fawcett's wedding.

The pain in Kate's chest was like a tight band, constricting her breathing; her eyes and throat burned . . . She saw the cupboard under the stairs and the straw mattress. She saw Pat, roused from a drunken sleep, open his arms to a woman whom in his stupor he imagined to be her . . . It was over and done with, there was no going back . . . and the probable consequences, that had only too truly come about, had sobered him, and he had threatened to strangle her . . . The weeks had passed, and he had tried to forget it and what she might do. And then, last night, her father had come to him, together with Father O'Malley, and Father O'Malley had made him swear to marry Connie. He had made him give his word for the sake of the child.

'Do you hear, Kate?' Pat said, turning to her, tears streaming down his cheeks. 'I had to swear that I would marry her. But, as Jesus is my judge, I hate the very name of her. This also I swore, and on the altar, unknown to Father O'Malley, that she'd have me name but nothing else. I made sure of that this morning, for I joined up.'

'If you ever live to regret this day, Kate, may my death soon follow . . . ' His words of a year ago came back to her, and she had a horrifying glimpse into the future . . . As on a screen flung up before her mind's eye she saw his mangled body half buried in mud, unrecognisable but for the crucifix he always wore round his neck. She felt hot and sick; the kitchen receded. Her mother was standing close to Pat, begging him to do something . . . 'Forget your promise,' she was saying . . . as if he could; Father O'Malley knew how to seal an Irishman's oath . . . They floated away from her, and she felt herself falling gently into thankful blackness.

She came to herself breathing air that stung and pricked and made her gasp; and she realised she was sniffing smelling-salts, and wondered vaguely from where they had come . . . she hadn't any, there wasn't any need, for she rarely had a headache and she had never fainted before . . . This feeling of lying in between two worlds was pleasant, you didn't think here, not about new fathers or lost husbands, or anything. If one could just go on and on like this . . . She felt her head lifted and a glass put to her lips. She was comfortable and at rest in the crook of an arm, until a burning liquid ran down her throat. As she coughed, her mind flashed back once more into the throes of pain. Her eyes opened and she looked up into the doctor's face. She felt the tweed of his greatcoat against her neck and cheek, and his gay, woollen scarf dangled like a ladder on to her chest. His black eyes looked down into hers, and he smiled at her as he laid her head back on the saddle.

'That's what is meant by a doctor being on the spot, Kate,' he said. 'You faint, and I knock at the door.'

She neither answered nor smiled, but closed her eyes again. Her mother said, 'Is she all right, doctor?' And Rodney answered, 'Yes, she'll be all right; just let her rest.'

There was quiet in the kitchen. Kate felt the three of them looking down on her. Then a sob from Pat rent the silence, and she heard a thud as he turned away and flung himself into a chair, and the beat of his fist on the table.

She listened to Rodney's voice, low and questioning, and she listened to Pat's muffled replies. Then, from soothing tones to one of utter incredulity, Rodney's voice changed to low, bitter cadences: 'He can't do it, Pat! . . . Why, man, don't be a fool! . . . Come on, pull yourself together!'

There was a movement of the chair as Pat writhed in agony.

'See here, Pat! You don't mean to tell me you are going to let that damn priest wreck your life, and, what is much more important to you, Kate's? . . . You can't let him do it! He hasn't the power to make you marry anyone you don't want to; he has only the power you give him, through your fear of him.'

Kate thought, You don't understand . . . You're wasting your breath; you've got to be a Catholic before you can understand . . .

'Pat . . . go to him now; tell him you'll support the child; tell him that you were tricked into it . . . Look, Pat, I'll stand by you in this . . . You won't be without friends; let her take you to court.'

'You're a grand fellow.' There was the utterness of finality in Pat's few words; and they conveyed to Rodney the hopelessness of his appeal . . . But it mustn't be hopeless! Pat must marry Kate; he had got to marry her! She must be made safe, put out of reach . . . He didn't want that internal war over again, it had been hell. He had seen the danger signal last Christmas Eve . . . She must get married; there must be some barrier put between them . . . He started talking again, and no-one answered him.

The back-door latch clicked, and Kate opened her eyes. And when she heard her mother's surprised voice say, 'Father!' she thought, No, no, it can't be! This is too much . . . Her mother continued, 'We don't often see you.' And, realising it was Father Bailey, she relaxed.

'I've been to your lodgings, Pat; I've been looking all over for you.'

'Have you, Father?' said Pat, in a dead voice.

'I wanted you to know how sorry I am about all this, Pat.'

'I know it.' There was a soothing quality in Pat's words, as if he intended to lessen the pain of the priest's embarrassment.

'Sir, do you consider this is right?' Rodney addressed the priest without using the usual prefix. 'To trap a man, half demented with trouble, into marrying a woman he hates . . . ?'

Father Bailey, looking at Rodney sadly, broke in, 'We all have our own ideas of what is right and wrong, doctor. When a wrong is done someone always suffers, it's inevitable. And when it's the ones we know and respect it appears like injustice, and we see the enforcing of right as cruelty or wickedness. But,' he added wistfully, 'a lot, of course, depends on how it is enforced.'

'What right has Father O'Malley, or any man for that matter, to wield the power of fear to make another follow the course that he deems right? . . . Surely you would admit that such coercion is diabolical?' Rodney faced the priest, his beard stuck out in anger.

'I would admit that coercion by fear is diabolical,' answered Father Bailey calmly. 'But then, we have both to explain to each other what we mean by fear and by coercion. I think we view the former from different standpoints. It's a question I'd like to talk over with you some time, doctor, for it makes for lengthy discussion. And now, if you will excuse me . . . ' He turned once again to Pat: 'Would you care to walk part of the way home with me, Pat?'

Pat nodded dumbly, then made to go towards the saddle for some final word with Kate. But he changed his mind, and, with a violent shake of his head, he stumbled out of the back door.

The priest went to Kate and bent over her: 'You're not well, Kate. I can understand that; but try not to worry,' he said. 'I will see you later and have a talk . . . God is good, and the path is all mapped out for us; He knows exactly where we are going.' He patted her shoulder, then followed Pat, and there was silence in the kitchen once more.

The path is all mapped out for us! Kate shuddered. Why struggle? Why try? . . . The path is all mapped out . . . It always had been; she had tried to take a side road last Christmas Eve. She had seen herself as good and noble, and the spasms of happiness that had been hers this past year she had accepted as payment for her goodness . . . Pat, the buffer, had gone, and with him the cloak she had wrapped around her real feelings. She had not dramatised anything; she knew, as she felt Rodney standing over her, that it had not been her imagination which had played her false; she had played herself false and had clung to Pat, as a drowning man to a straw.

What lay before her now? . . . A struggle, or a giving up? . . . A delightful giving up . . . and involving what? . . . Scandal? Well, she had been scandalised when she was innocent. But the other person . . . what would scandal bring to him? . . . Disaster, finally! She sensed this more than she knew it, glimpsing the lengths to which his feelings would carry him . . . And what of her mother and of Annie? . . . and of the other Annies who might come? . . . No, she must fight it! But could she? . . . The path is all mapped out!

She suddenly began to laugh, and once more found herself in the shelter of Rodney's arm.

'Don't do that, Kate!' he said sternly. 'Come now!'

As she saw his free hand come up to touch her cheek, she burst out, 'Did you hear what he said? . . . The path is all mapped out!'

'Stop it, Kate! Do you hear?'

She laughed the louder.

'If you don't stop it I'll have to slap you!'

'The path is all mapped out!'

He laid her back and struck her twice on the face, two ringing slaps which made her head reel.

She stopped and lay still, then the slow tears brimmed her eyes and rolled down her cheeks. Her breath caught in her throat and she sobbed painfully and bitterly.

Rodney stared down at her, and gritted his teeth. Then, swiftly falling to one knee, he gathered her into his arms. His face pressed into her hair, he held her, and she clung to him in the paroxysm of her weeping.

Sarah leant against the kitchen table, listening in amazement to the endearments dropping from his lips; her hands, gripping each other, were pressed into her chest. She stared at them, her eyes fixed with anxiety and fear, praying, 'Don't let her do it . . . Oh, Mary, Mother of God, don't let her do it!'

THE BELT

Rodney opened the gate which led from the lane, and walked up
between the frost-painted shrubs of the lower garden and across the
glassy lawn of the upper to the house. How different it all looked after
only ten weeks! Different, but as formal; absence could do nothing
to soften its formality, either inside or out. The difference lay, he
thought, in his seeing it after a complete break; for nine years he had
merely felt it, without seeing it.

Mary opened the door to him: 'Why, sir, we weren't expecting
you. The mistress is in Newcastle; she went right after lunch, and
she won't be back till tea-time.'

'That's all right, Mary. I'll have a bath and something to eat in the
meantime . . . How are you?'

'Oh, fine, sir.'

Mary watched him as he walked up the stairs . . . Coo! he didn't arf
look funny without his beard . . . barelike! But the khaki suited him
all right. Well, that would mean another one for dinner tonight . . .
But cook wouldn't mind; fair daft about him, she was . . . be dashing
upstairs as soon as she knew, seeing her ladyship wasn't in . . . I
wonder if she'll be pleased! The thought brought an inward smirk . . .
See, what did I tell you! she said to herself, as cook hurried up the
stairs as fast as her lack of breath allowed.

Rodney called 'Come in!' to the knock on his door. 'Hallo, cook,
it's good to see you!' he said.

'Oh, sir, and it's good to see you . . . I am glad you're home for
Christmas, sir.'

'So am I, cook, and I'm as hungry as a hunter. Can you do anything
about it?'

'I'll soon fix that . . . Do you like the life, sir?' she asked.

'Oh, it's all right, cook; you get a bit bored at times, you know;
nothing much to do . . . likely to be more next year!'

She nodded. Yes, when we went over the water there would be
more, not arf there would. But she would see he had a good Christmas,
for her part, anyway; might be his last, you never could tell. He
wouldn't like it when he knew there was a high falutin' dinner
tonight, with that band of conchies! What else were they, with all

93

their palavering and reading parties, when poor lads were roughing it in the trenches and being knocked off like flies? . . . 'Well, I'm glad you're home, sir,' she said. 'And I'll have a meal ready as soon as you are; say half an hour?'

'Fine!' He grinned engagingly at her. 'I've missed your cooking.'

'Go on, sir!' she said, smiling back at him . . . Ah, it was nice to have him home; he was human, he was . . . 'I'll get Mary to light a fire, this room's like ice,' she said.

'Thanks, cook.'

'Look, sir, there's a good fire in the mistress's room. Why don't you dress in there after your bath, sir, till this warms up?'

'All right, cook; don't you worry. I'll pick the warmest spot. Trust me.'

Mrs Summers went out, leaving him strangely comforted, with the new sensation of being fussed over.

As he lay in his bath, luxuriating in the pine-scented warmth, he wondered what he would do with his seven days . . . Seven days with nothing to do! No bodies to examine, no feet to inspect. He'd see old Peter and Peggy a lot, that'd be good, and do a few shows in Newcastle . . . with Stella? No, he didn't think so. What was the good of putting on a front when things stood as they did; he had made his last and final effort a long time ago. What time does to one! he thought; it seems impossible to believe she can hurt me no more and that she hasn't an atom of power over me. I've been a fool all my life where she's concerned, but now I'm free . . . What had really brought it about? he asked himself. Kate? No, I was waking up long before Kate entered my mind. I suppose I saw her shallowness and devilry, for she is a devil. Oh, God, what it was to feel free of all desire of her! . . . He lashed the water with his feet for a moment; then became still, thinking of Kate . . . But was he free? Wasn't he chained to Kate with stronger chains than ever Stella had welded? Yes, he supposed he was. But with what a difference.

He thought back to last Christmas Eve, when he had given up fighting and held Kate in his arms, for the one and only time. He had known then that, had the mother not been there and they could have talked, she would have been his . . . She was his; he was convinced of that; as irrevocably as if they had been joined together by that damned, fear-inspiring priest. He had wanted her more than he had ever wanted Stella, the ache for her had persisted from the night he had taken her for the drive two years ago. But he also felt for her something he had never felt for Stella; a certain protectiveness, coupled with a deep admiration for the fight she had made to emancipate herself from the fifteen streets . . . he had wanted only Stella's body, her mind had irritated him.

When he had left Kate, on the sound of Tim Hannigan's steps in the back-yard, he already knew what he intended doing . . . He would

94

take a little house, perhaps a cottage, outside Newcastle, and install her
there, with Annie. No-one need know, and if they did what would it
matter? He could laugh at all their social codes which cloaked such
rampant immorality. He would be hurting no-one, the only hurt to
Stella would be to her pride . . . Over the holidays he had been excited
and on edge. When he had called and found that Kate was not on her
usual Christmas holidays, but was back at the Tolmaches, he had gone
straight there, feeling he had but to see her to hold her in his arms
again. His heart had pounded against his ribs at the first glimpse of
her; she had looked pale and tired, with a sadness darkening her eyes.
He had tried to catch her eye, so that a mingled glance would join them
together once again; but within a few minutes of his arrival she had left
the room without looking at him. The brothers and sister had discussed
the recent happenings with concern, being as troubled and worried as if
she were their own. His conscience had pricked him when, using Sarah
as an excuse, he had asked if he might go and speak to her about her
mother, as he had found her in a really bad state and was afraid she
would have to go into hospital. This, he comforted himself, was the
truth, but he had hated the idea of making use of it and of deceiving
these kind and trusting old people. He had felt sure that, frail as
Bernard Tolmache was, he'd have been quite capable of kicking him
out had he known the real reason for his desire to see Kate.

When he had opened the green baize door of the kitchen and had
seen her sitting by the table, her head resting on her hands, a deep and
protective tenderness had been born in him. Swiftly he had taken her
hands in his and had drawn her to her feet; but no further, for when
his arms would have gone round her she had whispered tensely, 'No,
no!'

'Kate, darling,' he had pleaded, holding her hands tightly against
his breast, 'you know it's no good, don't you? We have both fought
for so long. It's useless . . . Oh, Kate, my dear . . .'

'Please!' she had protested.

But he had gone on, in low, urgent tones: 'You know I am sorry
about Pat. There was no-one more eager than I that you should marry
him; for I was afraid of this very thing happening . . . I love you, my
dear . . . I worship you. Can't you see that? You can . . . you've
always known it. Oh, Kate, I need you so . . . Don't be afraid.'

She strained away from him, and turned her face to one side: 'Mrs
Prince!' The words had seemed wrenched from her.

'Kate, I can explain . . . Look at me! I must explain all that; when
can I see you? You need not worry about . . . Mrs Prince . . . She . . .
we . . . I can't explain here, there's so much to say. When can I see
you, Kate?'

'Doctor, I can't . . . I mustn't! Don't ask me.'

'Don't say doctor; Rodney, Kate.'

Kate had shaken her head desperately: 'It can't be!'

'You love me, Kate. Look at me . . . You do, don't you?'

She had remained silent as he forced her to meet his eyes. 'Even if you won't say it, I know you do; nothing can alter that.' They had stood tense, their eyes holding, hers dark with misery.

On hearing the drawing-room door open he had released her hands and whispered urgently, 'I will write you.' Then, with as much calmness as he could command, he had gone on and told her about her mother, while she had stood looking blankly down at the table.

He had written to her, making an appointment, but she had neither answered the letter nor kept the appointment. Desperate, he had written again and yet again, with the same result. It had been Sarah who had provided the opportunity for seeing her alone, for he had had to send her into hospital; he had taken the task on himself of informing Kate and taking her, by car, to the workhouse. Her genuine anxiety for her mother had silenced any appeal he had intended making. He had driven her and Annie back to the Tolmaches that night, after having met them near the docks; Kate had protested strongly when he had proposed coming to the house to collect them. Annie's delight in being near him and riding in the car again had been touching.

During the following weeks he had seen quite a lot of Kate, but never alone; there had always been Annie or the Tolmaches.

Sarah came out of the hospital and Annie had returned reluctantly home, and things took up their normal course again, at least on the surface. It was when he had decided that he could wait no longer, and that he must see her to explain his case, that he received the letter. He had opened it at breakfast, with Stella sitting opposite him . . . It had started, 'Dear Doctor,' and had ended abruptly, 'Kate Hannigan'. It had told him in concise terms that he had a wife and a career to think about, she had her mother and Annie; her mother was still ill and, she knew, was worried about her; she must give her no cause for worry; finally, she loved the Tolmaches, and it would distress her greatly if she had to leave them entirely; but this she would have to do and seek work elsewhere unless he could see her point of view.

No word of love, just an ultimatum; yet he was sure that she was his, as if every line had proclaimed it. Why was it, he had asked himself at that moment, that he, a man of strong passions, as he knew himself to be, should be incapable of having but one woman in his life? . . . First, and from boyhood, it had been Stella. He had married Stella when the torch of his passion was at its height, and she had quenched it swiftly and surely. He had been unable to do anything about it, for as long as he had loved Stella he had been incapable of taking from another woman what she had withheld. Now Stella was like the remains of a burn; the scar she had left would always be visible to him, but it didn't hurt any more . . . And Kate, this was something different, something higher than any feeling he had had for his wife, which, he knew now, had been all physical. But Kate had bound him as surely as ever Stella had, and he couldn't seek relief from her either. Nor did he want to, in spite of her ultimatum.

He had looked across the table at Stella, so beautifully calm and insolently sure of herself. Divorce had crossed his mind . . . non-consummation of conjugal rights . . . Yes, he could get it on those grounds; but would he? No, he knew he would never do it . . . But she could divorce him . . . Would she, if he gave her cause? Not unless it would suit her purpose; and she would have to want it very much, for she was as vain as a peacock, and the very fact of his wanting another woman would make her fight. The whole position had seemed impossible.

An easing, at least, of the situation had pointed itself out after days of mental strife. True, there were feelings of patriotism in the gesture, but it was more as a means of escape that he had enlisted.

Rodney got out of the bath, and was towelling himself vigorously when Mary's voice, following a knock, came through the bathroom door: 'Doctor Swinburn's downstairs, sir; would you like to see him?'

'Why, yes!' Rodney called back. 'Tell him to wait a second; I'll be right down.'

Swinburn had been his locum at one time, then, under pressure of work, he had taken him on as assistant. Now he was in charge and, thought Rodney, thinking himself no end of a fellow, I bet. He had found traits in Swinburn's character which had become evident only through time, and which he did not like; a certain meanness and lack of sympathy and an eye to the main chance were among them. Getting into a dressing-gown he went downstairs and found him in the study.

Doctor Swinburn, a lean young man of middle height, with dark-brown eyes and fair, crinkly hair, a sensual mouth, and a nose that could only be described as pinched, greeted Rodney effusively. They shook hands, and he offered Rodney a cigarette, and lit it for him. 'You're looking fit,' he said; 'although seeing you without your beard is a bit of a shock.'

'It was a bit of a shock to me at first,' laughed Rodney. 'I'm used to it now. Only it's this continual shaving that gets me down.'

'You'll have to let it grow before you come back on the job, or the ladies won't like it,' chuckled Swinburn.

Rodney frowned inwardly. That was the kind of chat that made him annoyed with Swinburn. 'How's everything?' he asked.

'Up to the eyes,' said Swinburn. 'Half the calls are damned un-necessary . . . such as Lady Cuthbert-Harris. I had a time with her after you left; she wouldn't believe you had gone, wouldn't have me near her; she demanded to know where you were every time I saw her, and said that you must come as you were the only one who understood her. Still I persevered, as one call on her equals a day's work around the docks. But it is hard going. I spend my visits answering questions about you, and tell her you send enquiries about her by every letter . . . '

'You've no right to say that!' broke in Rodney, somewhat sharply. 'That woman's got enough ideas in her head already.'

'Well, what can I say? We don't want to lose her.'

'We certainly shall if it depends on me visiting her, for I've intended passing her on to you for some time. I never could stand the woman.'

'What will you do when you get the socks? She's knitting some for you,' laughed Swinburn.

'Good God!' exclaimed Rodney.

'Still, it's people like her who keep the practice going,' said Swinburn smugly. 'You know, your books are in a heck of a mess. Some of these dockites haven't paid for as long as six years; I've been rounding them up.'

'I don't want them rounded up,' said Rodney stiffly. 'Some of them can't eat, let alone pay doctor's bills.'

Fool! thought Swinburn . . . Can't eat, indeed! No, but they can drink . . . Still, keep on the right side of him . . . 'Well, just as you say,' he said. 'But it's a devil of a lot of money you're out. I was only thinking for your good.'

'That's very kind of you, but don't press any of them.'

Swinburn looked at him with ill-concealed resentment . . . All right for him, with his damned private income; he can afford to talk big. Wonder how much that Hannigan girl has to do with his kindness to the poor? he asked himself. There's never smoke without fire; damn funny rumours going around about her kid.

'You know about old Tolmache dying, I suppose?' he asked Rodney, scrutinising his face for any confirmation of the rumours his words might evoke.

'No,' said Rodney. 'Which one? And when did it happen?' The very mention of the Tolmaches had brought a quickening of his pulse, but he showed nothing of it in his query, his tone implying professional interest only.

'A fortnight ago; the elder one, Rex. And the other two seem to have gone all to pieces lately, since they lost their girl.'

'Lost their girl?'

Swinburn noticed that although Prince's face didn't alter he pressed the cigarette he was holding to his mouth quite flat between his finger and thumb. 'Yes, she went home to look after her mother. It was either that or the workhouse . . . I had to put it to her quite plainly. The mother couldn't be left alone, with just neighbours popping in, she needs constant attention. I told her her mother couldn't last long, and if she went into the workhouse it would be to die. So she left the Tolmaches and went home.'

Staring at Swinburn with an expressionless face, Rodney thought, God, I thought he meant she was dead! But Kate, back in the fifteen streets! All day, every day, living practically in that kitchen, cut off from the Tolmaches and all they stood for . . . For a moment he experienced the pain that the wrench must have been to her. Sarah might linger on for months . . . years even . . . with care and attention. And Kate getting older, living alone . . . For he knew the Tolmaches had spoiled her for ever for the fifteen streets and the companionship that community had to offer. Mentally she'd be alone, and he could do nothing. Gone even was the chance of seeing her on this leave; he couldn't go to the fifteen streets, she would only be disconcerted, knowing that it would upset her mother.

He's not giving much away, said Swinburn to himself, but he didn't squash that cigarette for nothing. 'Well,' he remarked, getting up, 'I must be on the move again. I just called in to see if I could do anything for Mrs Prince.' His eyes flicked away and he turned towards the door; and Rodney thought, Good Lord, him too.

Rodney felt a sudden pity for Swinburn, for it seemed such a frightful waste for anyone to lavish affection on Stella; it was like falling in love with the statue of de Milo. 'I'll tell her you called,' he said. 'I'll be seeing you again; I'll look in at the surgery at the beginning of the week.'

'You'll see me tonight,' said Swinburn, continuing towards the front door, 'I'm coming to dinner . . . See you later, then, goodbye.'

Rodney returned upstairs. So there was a dinner tonight: Barrington; Tollyer, her publisher; that modern poet chap, with his hair on his shoulders; and Swinburn. For two pins he'd make a dash and get a train home . . . Then there'd be the question: Where was Stella? and 'It's just as I expected' looks from Frank. There was nothing for it but to stick it out.

He found his room struck cold, after the warmth of his bath and the room downstairs. The fire was alight, but as yet giving off no heat. So he took a change of underwear and a suit out of the wardrobe and went into the room across the landing.

Stella's room . . . her own, of which he had no part, the room she had made for herself after their final break. Funny, he thought, I haven't been in this room half a dozen times in three years. As he dressed he looked around; it expressed her perfectly, everything ice-blue and gold, all except the old walnut bureau that stood in the deep shadow of the recess. The sight of that simple piece of furniture brought back to his mind the day they had bought it . . . that had been one of their happy days, when Stella had given way to the excitement and thrill of furnishing a house. The bureau was one of the few pieces left of those they had chosen together; all the others had been gradually replaced. He thought of the young man

99

who had sold the bureau to them; he had sensed their excitement and added to it by betting them they would never find the secret drawer. Rodney had soon found the button which would release the spring, but he had kept the knowledge to himself, leaving to Stella the pleasure of discovery.

Looking down on the bureau now he felt a sudden sadness. Gone for ever was the wonder of life that had seemed to be opening for him when they had bought it. Gently pulling open the right-hand side drawer, he felt in the roof for the button. Pressing it, he watched the narrow top of the desk slowly rise, exposing two sets of two drawers, divided by a miniature cupboard, and he felt again the romance of the workmanship and ingenuity. He opened one of the tiny drawers and pressed another button. The door of the cupboard swung open, revealing an exquisitely panelled recess in satinwood . . . He could almost hear Stella's squeal of delight on that bygone day . . . such a faraway day, for now she apparently used the desk only as a receptacle for broken pieces of jewellery . . . Inside the cupboard was a square box, filling most of the space. He took it out and idly examined it. The lid was in a beautiful mosaic pattern of mother-of-pearl. Just as idly he lifted the lid; then stood staring down at the collection of tubes within. Two were full, but the majority empty and tightly rolled up. After reading the writing on one of the tubes, which was in both French and English, he stood staring fixedly at the box for some time. Then he opened the cylindrical box which was partly covered by the tubes.

Slowly the blood drained from his face. Like one in a trance, he closed the secret drawer and, taking the mother-of-pearl box, he returned to his room.

His discovery had given him the biggest shock of his life, and, for the moment, he was quite incapable of thinking; he could only feel. As he stood looking down into the frozen garden, some atom of respect that he still retained for his wife cried out . . . Don't let this be! She couldn't have done it . . . But, then, she had done it, and with what success!

He stared again at the box, and all that it implied rushed into his mind, searing it as with a hot iron. Right from the beginning, from the night of their marriage she must have practised this. From where had she obtained such knowledge? she was barely twenty at the time. She had deliberately killed . . . yes, that was the word . . . she had killed every chance of giving him a child from the word go, and he had never for a second suspected it. How could he? So gentle, so fragile, so . . . virginal a creature. She had fooled him, oh, so easily! How she must have been laughing all these years!

He could see her now, with that pathetic air, when he had spoken of children. So hurt had she looked that at times it had wrung his heart, feeling that she suffered the miss as greatly as he . . . Explained now, also, was the freezing attitude which could leave him distraught and the rages which his spontaneous love-making would bring about . . . there were the times when she had been unprepared. And all these years he had been duped by that delicate, gentle creature! Of how many sons had she deprived him? Had she withheld herself after having given him one son, how different life would have been! . . . His son. His mind conjured up a boy of nearly fourteen, bursting with vitality, eyes bright with the eagerness of life. He would be home for the holidays now, turning the house upside down, thumping up the stairs calling . . . 'Father! . . . where are you, father?'

Rodney listened. The cry of 'Father! father!' re-echoed from his mind through the stillness of the house. He shuddered violently and ground his teeth. Waves of hatred swept through him . . . Where was she? If he could only get his hands on her!

Recognising the strength of his emotion, a fear took its place and he realised he must not see her yet, but must get out of the house and try to walk this off, giving himself time to let the blow settle and rest among the many hurts she had dealt him. For he knew that, should he encounter her now, he would kill her as surely as she had killed his sons.

He locked the box in his suitcase, and put on his greatcoat and went downstairs. Mrs Summers hurried out of the kitchen: 'It's all ready, sir. I hope you enjoy . . . ' She stopped, taking in his outdoor apparel and, most of all, the change in him from half an hour ago. He looked ill, as if he had had a shock . . . But there'd been nobody in the house except Doctor Swinburn. Ah! perhaps that was it! He had found out about him and the missis. Although, what with them separate rooms an' all, you wouldn't have thought he'd have minded like this. But there was nowt so funny as men; just look at her Sep.

'I'm sorry, cook, I've got to go out.' His hands fumbled with his hat.

'That's all right, sir, that's all right,' she said gently. 'Perhaps you'll feel like it when you come back.'

'Yes. I may feel more like it when I return.'

She watched him leave. The straightness had gone out of his back, he seemed humped, somehow. She returned to her kitchen and sat down; and suddenly began to cry, without knowing the reason.

It had been three o'clock when Rodney had left the house. He had walked right through Shields to the sea. But there were soldiers everywhere, mostly near the sea, which he was wont to seek as a balm. He had walked back through the town, choosing the back streets and alleys like someone trying to escape, through Tyne Dock and East Jarrow, and on to the Davidsons. He had turned his mind from the fifteen streets as he passed them in the darkness of the early evening; Kate must not come into this pit of hate which no walking or reasonable thinking seemed to erase.

Peter and Peggy and the two children were having late tea when he walked in on them. In the enthusiasm of shaking hands and exclamations of delight at seeing him, they did not, for the moment, take in his weariness and the drawn, strained look about his eyes. He smiled on the children, but hardly spoke. Michael and Cathleen clambered about him, shouting, 'Where's your beard, Uncle Rodney?' until Peggy ordered them to finish their tea.

Having packed them off to the kitchen to Anna, she turned to Rodney: 'Sure you won't have something to eat, Rodney?' she asked looking hard at him.

He shook his head.

'Well, have a cup of tea then,' she pleaded.

'All right, a cup of tea then,' he said.

While he drank the tea Peggy and Peter exchanged bewildered glances. 'Anything wrong, Rodney?' asked Peter.

'No, no,' Rodney replied, twisting his mouth into a smile.

'How are you finding the new life?' Peggy enquired.

'Oh, all right, Peggy.'

'Glad you went?' Peter questioned.

'Yes . . . Yes, I'm glad I went.'

The almost monosyllabic answers, so unlike Rodney, both puzzled and alarmed them. They sat talking to him, covering up his silences. When he suddenly got to his feet they rose with him, deeply concerned. 'I'll have to go; I'm not very good company tonight. See you both soon.'

Peter set him to the door: 'What is it, Rodney?' he asked. 'Surely you can tell me.'

'Yes, I could tell you, Peter . . . Oh, I don't know,' he said, running his hands through his hair. 'I feel so boiled up with hate that I . . . Have you ever thought of killing a woman, Peter?'

Peter stared at him: 'You're not going home tonight, man,' he said quietly, putting his hand on Rodney's arm; 'you're staying here.'

'It's no use, Peter . . . I've got to go. I've got to see her; I'll not rest until I do. And there's a dam' dinner on!'

'What has she done?'

'She's . . . ' But he was unable to put into words what his wife had done to him. 'I'll tell you another time,' he said and was gone.

'What do you think I'd better do, Peggy?' asked Peter, some minutes later.

'Follow him,' she answered.

'But she has one of her dinners on,' he said, pointing to the clock. 'It's half-past seven now, they'll just be sitting down . . . He can't do anything with people there.'

'Never mind; you go. You can always pretend you haven't seen him, and say you heard he was home and called . . . He'll understand.'

'He's walking. I'll give him time to get there, and then I'll take the car,' said Peter.

The company had just finished dinner and settled themselves in the drawing-room, Stella, three other women and four men. The women, who were all unusually plain, were not the wives of the men, but were very pleased to be there in any capacity. The men were very glad to be there too; for what could be more pleasant than to eat one of Stella's dinners, and then to sit and look at her for a whole evening. For each of the men she had a peculiar charm. She spelt romance, and romance always beckoned. That the beckoning was becoming an irritation, Herbert Barrington was forced to admit to himself; he was heartily tired of promises. Only once had he experienced anything with Stella that could be given the name of an affair. And then it had been very disappointing, petering out to nothing, leaving him without the stimulus of his urge for her; quite a dead thing, yet full of live irritation . . . She had promised it would be better next time, but there had never been a next time. And now there was Swinburn, and she still kept him dangling on . . . promising . . . and he was unable to free himself.

He was thinking of all she had told him about her husband, and not for the first time a vague mistrust of what she had said entered his mind, when Rodney himself walked in. He watched Stella's eyes dart to him, and he knew her well enough to know she was uneasy behind her polished smile. He rose with the other men and joined his greeting to theirs. It wasn't until the ladies were introduced that Barrington realised that Rodney had neither spoken nor smiled, but had merely acknowledged the introductions by a nod.

They all sat down again, Rodney taking a seat opposite Stella. A strange silence, which no-one seemed to have the power to break, fell on the room. He's heard about Swinburn, Stella thought, and as usual is acting like a fool . . . she had heard from Mary of their meeting earlier in the day and of his rejected meal . . . He looks ghastly. But she felt the thrill of power rise in her with the knowledge that she could still make him feel like this. For lately she had been piqued by his indifference . . . She had got what she wanted, a life free from what she called his sexual pesterings, but it had turned out to be less satisfying than she had thought. Well, by the look of things, she could alter it any time. She smiled, and addressed him, for the benefit of the company, as if they had met but a short while ago, instead of nearly three months: 'We didn't wait dinner for you, dear; I didn't know what time you would get back.'

He made no answer, but sat looking at her, his face set.

Her poise began to slip away, she felt uneasy . . . He hadn't taken his eyes from her for a second. What was everyone thinking? . . . She turned to Herbert . . . you could always rely on him to keep the tone of the party just right . . . 'Will you begin reading, Herbert?' she asked sweetly.

But Herbert was being awkward too. 'You begin,' he said. 'Let us hear some of the latest prose poems.'

'Yes!' chorused the ladies, glad to hear the sound of their own voices, for since the husband had come in things had become decidedly strained.

Without further ado, Stella took up a slim volume from the table at her hand, settled herself in her chair, gave one quick glance at the company, and commenced to read:

> Let the beauty linger in my soul
> Of a rose just bursting into bloom,
> Of a bird in flight,
> Of the moon, new born into the night,
> Reflecting on a sea of gentle ripples.
>
> Let the beauty linger in my soul
> Of a winter morn draped in patterned frost,
> Of air like wine,
> Of sunlit snow on limbs of trees,
> Of black, brown trunks bare to the winds
>   that sweep the woods.
> Of drifts of crisp brown leaves,
> Swept, now here, now there, with the breeze.
>
> Let the beauty linger in my soul
> Of firelight in a darkened room,
> Of kindly words,
> Of lovers' laughter coming through the night,
> Until, at last, I know no greater peace nor
>   ease
> But to remember these.

The company was startled and shocked by a harsh sound; Rodney, his head leaning against the high back of the chair, was laughing. He stopped abruptly and bent towards Stella: 'I like that; so full of feeling; so much understanding of the simple things of life, especially that part: Of lovers' laughter coming through the night.'

Stella stared at him, anger and fear fighting each other in her face. The women looked distinctly shocked, and the men indignant. Swinburn stood up and impulsively took a step towards her. Barrington, watching him, thought, I would have done that at one time, and wondered why he did not do so now. His mind was suddenly distracted from the scene before him by steps on the gravel outside the french window. He was sitting close to the heavy velvet curtains, and when the sharp rap came on the window he started, as did the rest of those in the room; thankfully, it would seem, as the tension was unbearable.

They all turned towards the window, and Stella, gladly clutching at this distraction, said: 'Someone's knocking; who on earth can it be? See who it is, Herbert; but do be careful of the lights.'

Barrington stepped within the closed curtains and opened the window: 'Who is it?' he asked.

'I want Doctor Swinburn. I've been to his house, and they said he was here. I couldn't find the door, then I saw a bit of light,' the childish voice floated into the room.

'You'd better come in,' said Barrington, 'or the light will show.'

When Annie stepped through the velvet curtain she brought a sense of unreality with her. Everyone, including Rodney, sat or stood perfectly still, looking at her as she stared from one to the other, blinking in the strong light.

'Christ!' said the poet to himself. 'What a picture!' He looked at her hair, springing away from the crown of her head and floating down to her waist in sheer silver lines, at the deep fringe which curved inwards just above her dark eyebrows, and at her slanting green eyes, set in skin so delicate as to appear artificial . . . Here was beauty!

Annie's frightened eyes searched the faces before her, looking for Doctor Swinburn's. They passed over a face that seemed familiar; then darted back to it: 'Oh!' she cried, and ran towards Rodney at the same time as he stepped towards her. 'Oh, doctor!' She flung her arms around his waist, and pressed her cheek hard against his waistcoat. Rodney stroked her hair and held her close, oblivious of the incredulous eyes upon them.

'What is it, Annie?' he asked. 'What's wrong?'

'It's Kate,' said Annie, recalling the urgency of her errand and gazing up into his face. 'My granda hit her with the belt. He hit her and hit her, and the sharp prong stuck in her neck. And it won't stop bleeding, the blood's all over the place. Oh, come quickly!'

For one startled moment, Rodney looked down on her face, then turned and hurried out of the room. Annie followed him into the hall, keeping close on his heels. He was getting into his coat when Swinburn and Stella came out of the drawing room.

'You're not going!' said Swinburn. 'Surely I'm the person to deal with this!'

'Have you gone mad, Rodney?' asked Stella, with deathly calm. 'What will people say? And how dare you place me in the position of having to explain your behaviour to my guests! I think you are out of your mind . . . I'm sure you are,' she finished.

Without a word Rodney buttoned his coat; then slipped into the cloakroom off the hall and filled a small case with necessities from a medicine cupboard. When he returned he said to Swinburn, with studied politeness, 'I would like a word with my wife, if you don't mind.'

Swinburn, with compressed lips, went into the drawing-room.

Before Rodney could speak Stella said under her breath, 'What is this girl to you? How dare you insult me . . . for a maid, a common servant! . . . You shan't do it, do you hear? I'll have her hounded out of the town.'

'Will Barrington and Swinburn go with her?' Rodney asked calmly, as he picked up his hat and took Annie's hand. He felt quite calm now.

It was years since he had uttered a prayer; but when Annie had stepped into the room, she had appeared like an angel sent to stay his hand and calm his mind; and her arms, as they went around him, seemed to extinguish that blaze of hate which had urged him on to Stella's destruction; and he had offered up a silent prayer to a God in whom he had not believed.

Rage flashing from her eyes, Stella gazed at him. That she should be overlooked, in any capacity, for a maid was unthinkable. She turned her furious glance on the child . . . that's why he had always liked this child; the mother was his mistress . . . But for how long? Not so long . . . it couldn't have been. He had been all hers until three years ago, she knew that. Well, he would be hers again . . . Suddenly she wanted him back, wanted him as she had never done before. His charm, which had been dead to her, sprang to life again, and she saw him as he must appear to other women.

The anger died out of her, and she seemed to melt to a clinging softness before his eyes.

'Darling, don't go,' she pleaded. 'Or if you must, hurry back.' She touched his arm.

Rodney looked from her changed face to the hand on his arm, and laughed softly.

'Wait,' he said to Annie; 'I won't be a minute.'

Then to Stella: 'I have something for you. You'd better have it now, as I don't know when I'll be back.'

She watched him take the stairs two at a time, and return, hurrying still, with a box in his hands. She was looking at his face, thinking: No common slut will get the better of me, so she did not see his gift until he had placed it in her hands.

Slowly the blood drained from her face as she saw the familiar mother-of-pearl box. She raised her eyes to his, and for a moment they stood looking at each other. And in that time she knew he was gone from her for ever, and a destructive hate was let loose in her.

He left her without a word.

When they were outside, Rodney gripped Annie's hand.

'Can you run?' he asked. 'We'll catch a tram; it's no use me tinkering with the car, it hasn't been used for weeks. Come, keep tight hold of me.'

They ran down the garden and out into the lane.

'What happened?' he asked, as they ran.

'My granda said I had to go back to the Borough Road school,' panted Annie, 'and Kate said she wouldn't send me. He's been on about it ever since Kate came home . . . Oh, doctor, will she die? the blood was all over the place.'

Rodney gripped her hand tighter and increased his pace.

They were nearing the end of the lane when they almost ran into a figure.

Rodney gave an exclamation.

'That you, Rodney?' asked a familiar voice.

'Yes, Peter,' said Rodney, surprised. 'What are you doing here?'

'What are you running for?' asked Peter anxiously. 'Are you all right? . . . What's happened?'

The reason for Peter's presence flashed on Rodney, and he put out his hand and gripped Peter's arm.

'Nothing's happened, Peter. But thanks for coming, all the same . . . Have you got your car here? Something's wrong with Kate; old Hannigan has been beating her. Annie here came up to the house for Swinburn, and, incidentally, brought me to reason again . . . Will you run us up to the fifteen streets?'

Peter did not question why Swinburn wasn't seeing to the case, nor why Rodney should be so concerned about Kate Hannigan. Enough that he was himself again.

When they reached the end of the fifteen streets, he dropped them, not offering to accompany Rodney to see what the trouble was. Although he didn't believe for one moment that Rodney was the father of Annie, there was something here he could not understand, but something into which, he felt, it was not his business to probe.

So he left them, saying, 'Come up tomorrow, Rodney . . . come to dinner . . . Mind, don't forget ours is at one o'clock,' he added, laughing.

'I will,' said Rodney. 'Many thanks, Peter.'

And, taking Annie's hand again, he hurried off.

It was Mr Mullen who opened the door to them, peering at them in the dim light.

'Oh,' he said, 'it's you! You've been quicker than I thought.'

Then, on closer inspection, 'Begod, if it isn't Doctor Prince, himself! . . . Well, I didn't expect to see you, doctor; I thought you'd be across the water by now. But I'm glad to see you, all the same . . . Mind how you go,' he admonished; 'this place is in a hell of a mess.'

Rodney looked at the kitchen aghast. The table was end up near the window, the floor was strewn with broken crockery, Lord Roberts had been ruthlessly torn from his frame, and from his horse, which, with his black bodyguard, was now lying on top of a pile of brasses in the far corner of the room. The mantelpiece, which the brasses had adorned, was bare; the chiffonier door was splintered, as if a foot had gone through it; and the wall near the staircase was spattered with blood.

'Yes, just look at it!' said Mr Mullen. 'He should be put bloody well inside. I wanted to go for the bobbies. But would Sarah hear of it? No! Didn't want the disgrace of fetching the bobbies. But I told her that if anything happens to that lass, there'll be more than a bit of disgrace . . . he'll swing! . . . 'Bout time too, I say; bloody maniac!'

'Where is he?' asked Rodney.

'Oh, he's cleared out. He always does after a bout like this. You won't see him for days; goes to his sister's in Jarrow, I think. Hope he breaks his bloody neck in getting there. That's my prayer . . . Can you see your way?' he asked, as Rodney went up the stairs, and added: 'You stay here with me, Annie, and we'll see if we can get this place straight.'

Sarah, sitting beside Kate's bed, gave a start as Rodney entered the room, and her fingers went uncertainly to her mouth, and Mrs Mullen, looking up from the fire she was tending, exclaimed in surprise: 'Why, doctor!'

Rodney gave her a nod and bent over Kate, whose face was ashen except where it was spattered with blood. A towel, pressed to her neck, was red and wet.

He stripped off his coat.

'Come,' he said to Sarah gently. 'You must go to bed; you shouldn't be up, you know.' Whatever had to be done, he couldn't do it with her sitting looking at him, with that pained and frightened expression.

'Will she die?' asked Sarah, letting him help her to rise.

'Not if I can help it . . . you know that,' he added softly.

She turned to him at the door, looking up into his face: 'You'll not hurt my Kate?' she pleaded . . . 'Oh, doctor, don't hurt her.'

'I'll never hurt Kate,' he answered, after a moment. 'You can rest assured.'

She sighed and turned away as if satisfied. Mrs Mullen, taking her arm, put her own construction on the conversation. 'Of course he won't hurt her, Sarah. You know that. If anyone can put her right, it will be the doctor.'

'Pray God you're right,' murmured Rodney, as he set about examining Kate.

She lay quite still, her eyes closed. When he lifted up an eyelid he saw she was conscious, but she gave no sign of recognition.

He took the towel gently away from her neck and examined the wound, his eyes narrowing as he did so. What an escape! Another fraction and it would have been a jugular vein. As it was she had lost a lot of blood.

She was still in her clothes – what was left of them. Her blouse was torn in shreds, disclosing the weals on her breast and shoulders. The flesh was torn in places, and was now beginning to discolour. His jaw stiffened, even as his heart melted with pity.

'Can you help me, Mrs Mullen?' he asked, as she came back into the room.

'I'll do whatever I can, doctor,' she answered.

'That's good. Then just follow what I say and we'll get along fine . . . First get me some boiling water, and then we'll start.'

'You've missed your vocation, Mrs Mullen,' said Rodney, some time later. 'You should have been a nurse.'

Her homely face flushed at his praise.

'Never had no chance of being anything like that, in my time,' she said . . . 'Will I try to get her clothes off, doctor?' she added.

'No, her corsets are loose, so that's all right.'

'I'll sit up with her,' said Mrs Mullen. 'I'll just go and settle them next door, and I'll come back. She'd better not be left, had she?'

Rodney turned from washing his hands and picked up the towel and dried them carefully.

'No, she can't be left,' he said; 'but I'll be staying, Mrs Mullen.'

For a moment she looked her surprise.

Then: 'Very well, doctor,' she said. 'I'll get you some wood to keep this fire going.'

It was none of her business. She had heard rumours, which she hadn't believed for a minute; but now . . . well, he was a fine chap. But he was married and Kate was a Catholic, and these things didn't ought to be. Still, she had a family of her own, and God knew what some of them would come to. Look at her Michael, for instance, going after Betty Farrow, and her a rank Nonconformist. You see, you couldn't tell what'd befall your bairns. And with Kate being so bonny and that, it was harder for her. Well, she'd keep her mouth shut. Nobody would know owt from her . . .

'I'll bring you up a bite to eat, later on,' she said, and went out.

It was close on two o'clock when Rodney heard the carol singers. At first their voices were distant and thin. They were some streets away, he thought, and he hoped they would come no nearer and disturb Kate.

She was sleeping peacefully, after having had a light draught, and the deathly pallor had gone from her face. He felt he had been sitting there for an eternity; he felt no weariness nor any discomfort from the straight-backed chair. Had the choice lain with him of being whisked away to any place on earth at that moment, he would have elected to stay exactly where he was.

The room had changed since he had last seen it; the floor was now covered with linoleum, a chintz frill camouflaged the wash-hand stand, and a number of books stood upon a chest of drawers. These additions, together with the innovation of a gas mantle, had transformed the appearance of the room from that of stark poverty, which he remembered, and gave it an air of homeliness.

Kate had neither spoken to him nor looked at him, but he knew she was aware of his presence. He sat close to the bed, feeling more at peace than he had been for years.

The carol singers, suddenly giving voice a few doors away, made him start. Strong male and female voices rose to the heavens, crying:

> '*God rest you merry gentlemen,*
> *Let nothing you dismay . . .*'

He clicked his tongue with impatience, and was about to rise when Kate said, in a small voice, 'It's all right; I like to hear them.'

'I thought you were still sleeping,' Rodney said softly. 'Kate, look at me. How are you feeling?'

She opened her eyes slowly and looked up at him, as he bent above her, and her answer surprised him.

'At peace,' she said.

They stared at each other, in silence. Then she murmured, 'Do you believe in prayers being answered?'

Before Rodney could reply, she went on, 'No, you don't. You don't believe in God, do you?'

'Don't talk, my dear,' he said soothingly, his fingers on her pulse.

'I must talk. Don't stop me. If I don't speak now, I never shall . . . Rodney,' she whispered his name for the first time.

He caught her hand and carried the palm to his mouth.

'Oh, my love!'

'I prayed to see you before you went to France, and my prayers have been answered.'

'Beloved!'

The dropping of her defences was so unexpected that he felt light-headed. He sat down and pulled his chair nearer to her, and traced his lips over her fingers: 'Oh, Kate!'

'Nothing can be changed,' she whispered, 'only I wanted you to know before you went that I . . . I . . .'

'Say it, my darling.'

He remained still, her hand pressed to his mouth, waiting.

'I love you.'

Making a little sound like a sigh he laid his face on the pillow beside hers. His cheek couldn't touch her because of the padding around her neck. But she turned her head slightly, and they lay looking at each other in silence.

When she would have spoken he put his fingers on her lips: 'Not now, my beloved. Not now. Go to sleep.'

He gently stroked her hair, and the delight of touching it was overwhelming. 'You can talk tomorrow, and tell me all the things I long to hear . . . It's all right,' he assured her as a flicker of apprehension came into her eyes, 'nothing is changed; I know that . . . Sufficient to hear you say you love me. Sufficient for life, my dear.'

As she dropped off to sleep again, he thought of the strangeness of the past twelve hours; most of all, that she had to be beaten almost to death for her prayers to be answered, and that through her suffering he had been saved from himself.

'No, Annie; you're not going. And don't ask again.'

Kate went on kneading lumps of dough into loaves and putting them into tins.

'There's hardly any coal left, Kate. And Rosie and Florrie and Jimmy got a sackful of lovely cinders yesterday, nearly six bucketfuls . . .'

'I've told you you're not going!' Kate turned sharply on Annie as the back door opened. 'And don't ask again.'

'And why not, may I ask?' queried Mrs Mullen, coming in. 'It's going to do her no harm, Kate, going getting a few cinders.'

Kate sighed. 'She's not going, Mrs Mullen.'

' 'Tisn't any disgrace, Kate. They like it; it's a sort of game to them. And when they sit round the fire at night, it's their fire.'

'It's no use talking . . . she's not going.'

'You make me sick, Kate, so you do. You can't bring her up in cotton wool, not round these doors, you can't . . . And you can't burn the candle at both ends, either.'

Kate gave her a sharp glance.

'Ah!' went on Mrs Mullen; 'thinks nobody knows; but you can't sneak out of the house at midnight and come back in the small hours of the mornin', without anybody hearing you. You weren't back at three this mornin', for I listened for you . . . Now, don't you think it's better to let the child go and pick in the daylight than you to sit on the tip among a lot of men in the dead of the night?'

Kate arranged the loaf tins along the fender and covered them with a cloth.

'They are mostly women who are there, the few men are old,' she said.

'It's a disgrace that you should go at all,' said Mrs Mullen.

'But not that Annie should go?' questioned Kate sharply.

'No, that's different; she's only a bairn. Anyway, why doesn't that big lazy hulk do some picking? He's not working half his time. What's up with him?' Mrs Mullen felt she knew, without asking, what was up with Tim Hannigan. He was puzzled, as she was herself. He, of course, would know about Kate and the doctor being thick, and wondered why, consequently, money wasn't more plentiful. She wondered herself. She couldn't, somehow, understand it. It was usual to be in funds, under the circumstances, but Kate certainly wasn't. Hannigan, she thought, was suspecting Kate of withholding her money from the house, and was playing up, making his bad leg an excuse for staying off work.

'Leave the house without a fire for a few days, he'll soon get a sack on his back then,' she finished.

'There's my mother's fire to be kept going, and bread to bake, and food to cook. I'd rather freeze than ask him . . . you know that.'

'Aye, lass, I know,' said Mrs Mullen flatly. She patted Kate's arm. 'It's a hell of a life . . . What makes me mad,' she suddenly started, 'is that lot o'er there,' she indicated the houses opposite, 'getting pit coal for practically nowt and selling it for tuppence and tuppence ha'penny a pail, and not a roundie in it. The lot I got yesterday was all slack. Daylight robbers!'

Three faces suddenly appeared at the kitchen window.

'Is Annie coming?'

Mrs Mullen opened the door: 'No, she's not. Get yerselves away.'

'Aw . . . w!' They stood, shapeless bundles of old coats and scarves, each carrying a bucket and a raker, and Rosie with an empty sack slung over her back. 'Aw . . . w! Why not?'

'She's got chilblains,' said Mrs Mullen. 'Off you go now, and get a nice lot. And if we get a good fire going we'll have panhacklety tonight and ask Santa Claus to come and have a tuck in.'

'Ooh! Panhacklety and Santa Claus!' the younger ones cried, banging their buckets together.

They went off down the yard, yelling, 'At the cross, at the cross, where the Kaiser lost his horse and the eagle on his hat flew away . . . ' But Rosie followed more slowly, turning to the window to look at Annie, standing wistfully there.

'You're a fool, you know, but I suppose you know your own business best.'

Mrs Mullen opened the stair door: 'Anything you want taking up?' she asked.

'No thanks,' said Kate. 'She's had her wash and her breakfast. And, Mrs Mullen . . . you won't mention the tip?'

'Now what d'you take me for, a numbskull?' Mrs Mullen gave a toss of her head and went upstairs.

Kate turned to Annie: 'Look out and see if the postman's coming,' she said, glancing at the clock.

It was a quarter to ten. Surely he hadn't been . . . He'd be late, it was Christmas Eve. Oh, there must be a letter this morning; he couldn't have gone to France without letting her know . . . if he were still in England, he would have written . . . Over a week now and no letter; when every other day had brought a letter from him. What was wrong?

Annie returned: 'I can't see him, Kate . . . Do you want me to go any messages?' she asked.

'Yes, you'd better go and get some things.' Kate sat down and wrote out a list of groceries, pausing as she did so to consider whether the money would run to all she was putting down. She thought of the case of groceries which had come every Christmas from the Tolmaches and she experienced again that deep sense of personal loss for the very dear people who had provided them. It seemed impossible to believe that she would visit the house in Westoe no more, that the three people who had given her new life now lay, side by side, in the earth.

The brother and sister had seemed to wither away after Rex had died and Kate had left them. They had died in the previous summer within a month of each other, Bernard going first. In his will Bernard had left Kate twenty-five pounds of the hundred which was the total amount of his estate beside his books. Their generosity had amazed Kate afresh when she had learned that they had been living on annuities, not over-large for their wants, either. Yet there had always been an outfit every year from Miss Tolmache, and clothes for Annie, expensive books from Mr Bernard, and sly boxes of chocolates and a pound or two from Mr Rex. Oh, Kate thought, were there ever such people born, as they!

She remembered her last talk with Mr Bernard: 'Take happiness, Kate,' he had said, holding her hands. 'It's all that matters. To be happy and to make another supremely so is the reason for being. In all my life of thinking and pondering I have come to know this as an essential truth. I learned it a little late, more's the pity, but you, Kate, you can build your life on it . . . '

She wondered if he had known. She thought he had . . . dear, beloved Mr Bernard.

'Will I get the taties from the shop, Kate, or will I fetch them from the docks?'

'Potatoes, Annie!'

'Potatoes . . . I'm sorry, I forgot.'

'Get them from the shop; they are too heavy to carry from the docks. Here's the list, and that's a ha'penny for your tram back. And don't stop if a man should speak to you, unless you know him; you understand?'

'Yes, Kate.'

'Go on then.'

'Here's the postie, Kate,' Annie called from the front door . . . 'Postman, I mean,' she added.

'All right, dear, I'm coming. Go along.'

Kate waited tensely at the door for the postman's approach.

'Two for you,' he said, as he put them into her hand.

She looked down at their open flaps . . . Christmas cards!

Oh, Rodney, what is it? What's happened? . . . The anxiety was like a heavy weight bearing her down.

She returned to the kitchen and stood looking round her; the feeling of being hemmed in, chained for life within these four walls, returned. That was how she had felt when she had first left the Tolmaches, but Rodney, from last Christmas Eve, had lifted her spiritually out of this house and these streets.

The sufferings she had experienced that night had almost broken her spirit. The humiliation of cowering under the merciless flailing of the belt had affected her more than the physical pain, bringing with it a desire for death . . . And then he had come. From the moment he entered the room she knew that he alone could give her the desire to live, and she would fight against him no more.

After a week he had gone, leaving her still in bed, dazed with a strange happiness that demanded nothing but the knowledge that they loved each other. And then his letters had come, sometimes every day, at least every other day. They were like beams of clear light shining through the muck of her surroundings.

Only once had they met since . . . a few stolen hours taken from a broken journey when on his way to a remote corner of Scotland. He had wired her to meet him in Newcastle, and they had sat for most of the time in a restaurant, strangely tongue-tied, offering each other food which they neither wanted nor could eat. Her love on that day, as now, was no dazed thing, content with words as it had been earlier in the year. Her body had cried out to give him all that she knew he desired but for which he would never now ask. His love had taken on a tender quality that seemed foreign to the desire that emanated from him. It puzzled her and made her impatient. If only he would take her by force, would give her no time to be afraid or to reason, no time to think of the future, the time that would come for looking back, and around her at the living consequence of their union . . . this was what she dreaded, another child, who would perhaps say to her, as Annie had said, 'They said I hadn't a da.' Later, Annie might forgive her for having, in the ignorance of youth, created her, but would be ashamed of her for having knowingly created another . . . Her mind had repeated, 'She's right,' but her heart had cried, 'Nothing matters.'

Mrs Mullen came down the stairs and into the kitchen, breaking in on her thoughts.

'She's a bit brighter this morning, Kate.'

'Yes, she seems to have had a good night.'

Kate changed the loaf tins around on the fender.

'Well, I suppose I'll have to go and make a start,' Mrs Mullen sighed. 'It isn't a bit like Christmas this year. I've no heart to do anything. What with the war and our Michael I don't know where I am . . . I just can't get over him. He's never missed mass or benediction for years until lately. Our Peter used to scoff him and say he should be a priest, and now he wants to marry a Nonconformist.'

'She's a nice girl,' said Kate. 'I can quite understand him wanting to marry her.'

'There are plenty of nice Catholic girls, and you know, Kate, there's no good ever comes of a mixed marriage.'

'No, I don't,' said Kate sharply. 'I suppose it is better if they are both of the same religion, but if they love each other that's all that matters.'

'Love! Kate, you talk like a child.' Mrs Mullen was scornful. 'I'm surprised at you. When you start getting bairns around your feet there's not much time for love. It's quite hard enough when you're both of the same creed; but what's going to happen when he wants them to go to mass and she's bent on sending them to chapel?'

'If they care for each other they'll work that out.'

'I wish Father O'Malley thought like that.'

'Oh, Father O'Malley!' said Kate bitterly. 'He'll do more harm than good . . . Father O'Malley!'

'Aye, I've thought that meself, but I daren't say it. It was like hell let loose when he collared our Michael last week. Mike hadn't been to mass and had been keeping out of his way, and there he was, waiting for him when he came in to tea . . . The things he said! But it only seemed to make Michael worse. And then later his da started on him . . .'

'But why?' put in Kate. 'Neither you nor Mr Mullen go to mass, do you?'

'No. But we've always seen to it that the bairns go.'

'But why should you make them do something that you don't do yourselves, because you either can't be bothered or you no longer believe in it? If you went with them it would be different, and then Mr Mullen might be justified in going for Michael . . . Oh, what's the good of talking?' Kate ended.

'Aye . . . what's the good of talking? You're a new generation, and you've got new ideas. You're cleverer than us, you can talk it out . . . But still, in the long run, I can't see it's making you any happier. Well, I'll get away in,' she added. 'And by the way' – she turned from the door – 'don't you think it's time you got out for a blow? It's weeks since you've been across the doors . . . except at night,' she added slyly. 'If you feel like taking Annie around the shops this afternoon I'll pop in and see to Sarah.'

Kate smiled. 'Thanks, Mrs Mullen, it's very good of you. I'll see and let you know.'

Left alone, she thought: I can't go before four o'clock. I must see if there's a letter then . . . Could anything have happened to him? She wouldn't know if there had . . . she wouldn't hear of it until everyone else did.

She took his last letter from inside her blouse, where it lay close to her flesh, pricking her with each movement, a constant reminder of him. Sitting by the fire, she read it again, and it brought him near, into the room . . .

Beloved,

Let me kiss you. There! I feel better. I am sitting looking at you; your eyes are deep blue pools and they are playing their old tricks on me . . . My darling, it seems years since I really looked into them, but I have hopes that it won't be long now. Things are moving at last. In what direction I can't say, but undoubtedly they are moving; and not before time.

It is only the constant thought of you that has kept me sane these past months in this God-forsaken hole. Imagine, three times thinking that I should see you within a few days, and then leave to be cancelled! I felt I should go mad. Everyone is so fed up, and would welcome orders for France. I long for orders for anywhere so long as I can break my journey at Newcastle . . . Do you love me, Kate? . . . Let me hear you say it. Write it, darling; you don't write it enough, some of your letters are constrained . . .

Constrained! Kate gazed into the fire. If he were only here now she wouldn't be constrained, overboard would go every fear . . . Let there be a child! Let there be two, three!

She thrust the letter into her bosom and began to walk up and down the kitchen . . . The years she had wasted in fooling herself! Empty, empty years. Why had she let anything stop them from coming together? His wife, who was nothing to him, her mother, Annie, her religion . . . yes, even her religion, which said this beautiful thing was wrong, this feeling of life that he infused into her by his very presence was sin. How could anything so fine be bad? . . . She couldn't give herself where she didn't love . . . Yet they would say it was. Oh, if he were only here . . . Rodney! Rodney!

Annie came in, loaded down with her basket of groceries. She had an orange in her hand.

'Look, Kate!' she said. 'Mrs Clarke gave me this.'

'Dorrie Clarke?' Kate stared at her, apprehension in her eyes. 'What did she say to you? Did she ask you any questions?'

'She only asked me how I was getting on, and said I was getting a big girl. And she asked about grandma, and said she must come and see her.'

'Don't speak to Mrs Clarke unless you must,' said Kate. 'And never tell her anything about me or . . . anyone else. If she asks, say you don't know.'

'I wouldn't tell her anything, Kate,' said Annie, who still carried the memory of a certain Christmas Eve vividly in her mind. 'I didn't want to take the orange, but she made me.'

'All right, dear. Only be careful, she's not a nice woman.'

'Some of the shops are decorated,' said Annie. 'They must be lovely right down Shields,' she added wistfully.

Kate tweaked her nose: 'All right, I'll take you down later.'

'Ooh, Kate!' Annie put her arms around Kate's waist. They clung closely for a minute.

'There, now,' said Kate. 'Go up with grandma for a while, she must be lonely. Tell her I'll be up as soon as I get the bread in the oven.'

At half-past three Kate and Annie were dressed, ready to go out. They stood beside Sarah's bed.

'Sure you'll be all right, ma?' asked Kate, giving a final pat to the pillows. 'You won't be lonely?'

'No, lass, no. I'm glad you're going out for an hour. You're in too much; you're getting pale and thin.'

She put up her hand and stroked her daughter's cheek. Kate bent and kissed her.

'We won't be long, we'll be back about six. I've set the tea, and there's some fish cooking in the oven.'

'Don't you hurry yourself, it'll be all right. Maggie'll be up, she'll see to the tea.'

' 'Bye, grandma,' Annie kissed the blue lips. 'I'll tell you all about it when I get back . . . about all I see in the shops.'

Sarah smiled and watched them go out. She lay thinking, her eyes fixed on the bedrail . . . This dying took a long time. But she didn't want to go just yet . . . if only she could outlast Tim, so Kate wouldn't be left alone with him, even for a day. She knew the impossibility of her wish. Apart from his leg, which troubled him at times, he was as strong as a horse. She began to pray, but dropped off into a doze, which filled most of her days.

Standing at the front door, Kate said, 'We'll wait a few minutes for the postman.'

'There he is,' cried Annie, 'coming round the corner.'

'It's getting colder,' said the postman. 'Shouldn't wonder if we don't see more snow . . . There's nothing for you, they're piling up for tomorrow, I expect.' He laughed and passed on.

Something must have happened . . . but what? What? To know the worst that possibly could happen would be better than the sickening weight of this anxiety.

She walked into Tyne Dock, with only a small part of her mind listening to Annie's gay chatter . . . 'Would you, Kate?' Annie was asking.

'Would I what, dear?' Kate brought her attention back to her child.

'Would you come into the Borough Road church and see the crib? Rosie says it's lovely.'

'You want to see it?' asked Kate.

'Oh yes,' Annie said. 'Rosie says they've got real straw and a real cave and two new shepherds this year.'

'All right. We'll go before we get the tram for Shields.'

They took a short cut to the Borough Road church, and knelt on the stone steps of the Lady Altar and gazed at the crib, with its infant child and kneeling Mary and Joseph. The flickering candles seemed to endow the group with life.

Annie's lips moved as she said her rosary, and her face was rapt with the wonder of it all. But Kate knelt stiffly, uttering no prayer.

It was nearly a year since she had said a prayer of any kind, and she asked herself, would her prayers for him be answered? If she believed all she had been taught then the answer was no. For God gave you only the things which were good for your soul; such as poverty and pain! And, unless you made friends with these, life was impossible for her and her kind. Rodney would be considered anything but good for her.

But in spite of her reasoning her heart suddenly cried, 'Oh! Mary, Mother of God, don't let anything happen to him. Please, please keep him safe. Do what you like to me, for I know I deserve it, I know I am proud and vain of my knowledge, thinking I am above my own people, and I criticise my religion . . . but only keep him safe, and I will try to be better. I will do anything, anything . . . '

She suddenly stopped her wild plea, the bargaining side of prayer, which her reason had come to abhor, made her ashamed . . . never praying unless one wanted something. She stood up and turned to the main altar . . . 'Thy will be done,' she said, and felt better.

She sat in a pew opposite the statue she had described to Rodney on that faraway night, sitting in the car on the top of the Felling hills, and, when Annie, face radiant with mystical happiness, came to her, she drew her close and, pointing to the statue, whispered, 'Tell me, dear. Do you like that statue, or does it frighten you?'

Surprised, Annie looked at her. 'The statue of Our Lord frighten me?' she whispered back. 'No, Kate. But it nearly always makes me want to cry. Then I think, He was only like that for three days; 'cos He came Himself again on Easter Sunday, didn't He?'

Kate nodded, and realised that Annie would never be afraid of the things that had frightened her . . . except Tim. Christ had certainly risen for Annie.

'Which school do you like the better, the Borough Road or the one you are at now?' Kate asked, as they walked to the tram.

'Oh, the one I'm at now! It's a lovely school. But I don't like their church; I went in with one of the girls when there was a service on.

I didn't like it a bit; God didn't seem to be there . . . Oh, I love our church; don't you, Kate?'

Kate was not obliged to answer, for they boarded a tram. But she thought, some temperaments make good Catholics, others bad. Mine is in the latter category. But Annie will be a Catholic all her life, and I must never say or do anything which might spoil her faith. It is so beautiful and clean now, and, unlike mine was, without fear. If I have other children, will I bring them up as Catholics? . . . The question, involving so much not touching on religion, was unanswerable.

Her thoughts returned to Annie and her shining faith, and she knew that it would have hurt and puzzled her had she been told she had committed a sin through attending a service in a non-Catholic church. But it would not have really touched her faith, for she was one of those lucky people, born to believe without questioning. Kate wished she had been born that way too.

Her neck would carry a mark for life as a result of her stand in sending Annie to a protestant school, but her conscience, which had troubled her at times, was suddenly easy. She felt she had deprived Annie of nothing; the Catholic religion, she thought, would always be Annie's choice, and she had given her the best education possible under the circumstances.

It was dark when they returned home, and bitterly cold, with thin snowflakes lazily dropping here and there. Mrs Mullen was waiting for them at her own front door.

'Where've you been?' she demanded.

'What's the matter? Is mother worse?' Kate asked anxiously.

'No,' said Mrs Mullen, pulling Kate into the doorway. 'You, Annie,' she went on, to Kate's amazement, 'go on round the back way and sit with your grandma. And if your granda asks where Kate is tell him she's gone for . . . groceries, or meat . . . or anything. Go on now . . . don't stand there gaping . . . go on!'

Perplexed, Annie did as she had been told.

'Doctor Prince has been,' said Mrs Mullen.

'What!' Life whirled through Kate's veins; her head reeled with its force.

'Listen . . . There's not much time. He came about fifteen minutes after you had gone. Now he told me to tell you that he's leaving Tyne Dock station at a quarter to seven . . . he's for across the water . . . but he'll be at the station just after six.'

'For France,' Kate said dully, the new life ebbing away at the thought.

'Yes. Now get yourself off, it's twenty to six now. You'll be there by six if you hurry . . . Here, give me your basket.'

Kate turned without a word and ran down the street.

There was no tram in sight, so, lifting her skirts, she raced along the

road, her heart crying, 'Rodney! Rodney!' with each flying step . . .
Two hours wasted, and he going to France! . . . She heard a tram
coming, and stopped it. When she got to Tyne Dock she took another
to the station, arriving there just on six o'clock.

Rushing up the steep, narrow slope of the booking-hall, she found
her way momentarily obstructed by a tall fur-clad woman, with a
chauffeur in attendance. The latter, she noticed, had a club-foot, and
for a second she wondered how one faced life under such a handicap.
How one's thoughts flew off at a tangent, especially at times of greatest
stress.

Rodney was not in the booking-hall, but she assured herself he
would come, it was just six o'clock. She would get a platform ticket . . .
the respite would steady her.

She was turning away from the booking let when the chauffeur with
the club-foot spoke to the clerk. His question startled her, and she
stared at him. For he had asked, quietly, 'Has Captain Prince . . .
you know, Doctor Prince passed through here recently?'

The irritated clerk snapped, 'How should I know? Think I write
down the names of everyone who buys a ticket? . . . Damn silly
question to ask.'

Kate looked at the woman in the fur coat, and was more perplexed
still when she heard the chauffeur say to her, 'He left half an hour
ago, my lady. He caught the five-thirty to Newcastle.'

He seemed to hover over the woman, and, when she said, 'We'll
go to Newcastle,' he answered, 'Very well, my lady.'

As they walked away Kate noticed that, although he did not touch
her, he seemed to lead her down the long slope.

A car started up in the darkness beyond, and Kate guessed they
had gone . . . Who was she? Not Mrs Prince . . . His mother then?
No, she was too young . . . And why had the chauffeur lied?

She stood, perplexed at the situation, staring out into the night,
until a tall, lean, khaki-clad figure came striding towards her from
out of the blackness.

Her heart leaped, and she seemed to grow taller within herself. Then
he was there, close to her. Their hands met, and gripped. His dark
eyes glowed into hers. They stood for a second, caught up in ecstatic
silence, then, turning without speaking, they showed their tickets and
passed through the barrier. By mutual consent they made their way to
the far end of the platform, which was totally deserted . . . And they
were in each other's arms, without having spoken a word.

Their lips clinging, their bodies endeavouring to merge, they swayed
as they stood, holding this moment, willing it to go on for ever.

When at last he released her she leant against him, limp and
trembling. His lips continued to move over her face, kissing her
eyes and her brow, murmuring words which gave her an inward
glow. Presently she said, 'Darling, is it France?'

'Yes,' he whispered, still caressing her.

'Oh, why was I out?'

'Yes, why were you?' he asked. 'The bottom seemed to drop out of everything when I found you weren't there . . . Didn't you receive my letter, dear?'

'I've had none for a week.'

'What! But I've posted you two this week; the last one three days ago telling you about this move. I really expected to be here yesterday, but everything's been in such a devil of a mix-up.'

'It's the Christmas post,' said Kate; 'they must have been held up . . . Oh, darling, I've been so worried!'

'Have you, my love? . . . In a way, it makes my heart glad to know that . . . Let me look at you. Come here,' he said, drawing her into the weak gleam of a gas jet. 'How do you do it?' he cupped her face tenderly in his hands. 'You are more beautiful each time I see you . . . Oh' – he drew her into his embrace again – 'how am I going to let you go? Oh, Kate! . . . darling! darling! I love you . . . Oh, God!'

They clung to each other desperately, hungrily.

Then, in a little while, she asked, tentatively, 'Must you go tonight?'

'Yes,' he answered bitterly. 'We are to leave Newcastle just after eight . . . Christmas Eve, too! The men are in a devil of a way . . . We should all have had leave, but they've tried to tell the men that the unexpected seven days they got last Christmas was really embarkation leave, and that we should have been in France months ago. There's been a dreadful bungle somewhere. The few who managed dying mothers and wives got twenty-four hours! I had my business to set in order . . . Which reminds me, darling. Come, sit down here; if I hold you I can't talk sensibly, and there is something I want to say to you . . . Oh, wait . . . ' He again drew her to him. 'You're too sweet, you're too . . . Oh, I can't bear it! . . . '

The dark desolate station vanished, together with the cold and the falling snow.

'Oh, dearest; I'm sorry; I'm quite mad. You're like a heady wine . . . Come, sit down!'

They sat close together on the station seat. Her eyes moved over his face as he spoke, and her heart cried out, 'Don't go tonight. Don't! Don't! . . . I'm mad, too.'

'It's about money, dearest,' he was saying. 'If anything happens to me, you'll be all right; I've seen to that. But it's money for you to carry on with that I want to talk about. I'm going to make you an allowance, through my bank . . . I wanted to write to you about it, but it's so difficult to put these things into a letter. I've wondered how on earth you've managed this last year.'

Money! He was offering her money! An allowance . . . Money would buy coal and food, and extras for her mother, and clothes for Annie, who was growing so quickly that her things had to be lengthened and she had to cut down her own for her. Her own stock of clothes was rapidly diminishing. Soon there would be none to remake, which had worried her. But now, an allowance! The dreadful, soul-destroying burden of poverty would be lifted . . . No! What was she thinking? She couldn't take money from him . . . Money! That was the term in which the women of the fifteen streets thought; you gave so much and you got so much! . . . This was the only lovely thing in her life. She couldn't, she wouldn't bring it down to the level of their thinking.

'Please! Please, Rodney, I can't! Don't talk about it.'

'Why not, darling?'

'I can't explain. Only don't, please!'

'Don't be silly; you must! I have more money than I know what to do with; a great-uncle died some years ago, leaving me shares in a steel works. And now, with the war, the money's simply piling up . . . So, darling, you must let me do this.'

'No, Rodney. No! Oh, don't let us waste these precious minutes talking about it . . . You see, it's because I don't want to spoil this . . . our . . . oh, I can't explain . . . Darling, don't you see?'

'No I don't. I only know that you must be in need of money and that you're being silly. I'll send it to you whether you give me leave or not.'

'No, don't do that . . . Promise me you won't do that! How could I explain from where the money was coming? My mother . . . everyone would think that I . . . ' She shrugged. 'Well, what does it really matter what they think? It's what I think that matters. No, Rodney; whatever our relationship, I'll never be able to take money from you.'

'That's utterly ridiculous! . . . Dearest!' – he held her hands tight against his breast – 'I want to buy you things . . . clothes, furs . . . '

'Furs!' Kate broke in. 'Oh, Rodney, I forgot to tell you. Someone . . . a lady, was enquiring for you in the booking-hall, just before you came. Talking of furs reminded me.'

'Enquiring for me?' Rodney's mind flew to Stella. He hadn't seen her, she'd been out when he arrived; she was, he understood from Mary, on various committees. No letters had passed between them during the months he had been away, so it was hardly likely she had come to see him off. 'What was she like?' he asked.

'Tall and pale, with very large eyes. She had a chauffeur with her . . . he had a club-foot.'

'Good God!' Rodney exclaimed. 'That woman! to come to the station enquiring for me!'

'You know her?' Kate asked.

'Know her! She's a nightmare! She's Lady Cuthbert-Harris.'

He went on to tell Kate briefly about her.

123

'Why did the chauffeur lie, I wonder?' said Kate.

'Oh, Henderson knows how to manage her, and he's devoted to her, poor fellow. She's a dreadful woman, really. I should like to know, though, how she knew I was leaving here at this time . . .' He suddenly thought of Swinburn, who, besides the Davidsons, was the only other person who had known. But why should he tell her? What was his motive? Devilment, perhaps. It would need thinking about later. There would be time enough for that . . . But now:

'Don't let's talk about her. Look' – he pointed to his illuminated watch – 'we've only fifteen minutes, my dear, and I've so much to say.'

'Shall I come to Newcastle with you?' Kate asked eagerly.

He paused for a moment.

'You know I would like nothing better. But Peter and Peggy Davidson are meeting the train at Jarrow. They were determined to see me off . . . I could hardly say no; they have been such wonderful friends to me. But if you wouldn't mind . . . come, darling. They guess about you, anyway, I think.'

Kate shook her head: 'I won't come . . . I'd better not.'

For some seconds they sat quietly, peering at each other in the dimness, each aware of the other's sadness.

'You'll write often?' Rodney asked.

She nodded dumbly.

'Oh, I want to ask you such a lot of silly things . . . such as, that you won't look at another fellow, or ever forget me.'

'You don't need to ask me,' she said.

'But you're so lovely, and good. I'm afraid. Oh, I'm afraid . . . Put your arms tight round my neck and kiss me,' he suddenly demanded.

She laughed softly, and, as her lips touched his, he held himself still, not touching her . . . Then, 'That's what I'll remember always,' he said.

Putting his arms about her and holding her tenderly, he asked, 'What made you suddenly decide to marry Pat Delahunty, Kate, that Christmas Eve? I've always wanted to ask you, but kept putting it off, thinking you would tell me. It was something to do with me, wasn't it?'

'You know Pat's dead?' she asked.

'Yes, I know, and I was really sorry. I liked him, in spite of him loving you.'

'I sometimes think his death was my fault.'

'Nonsense! He would have been called up in any case . . . But why were you going to marry him?'

'To escape you . . . and because they were saying that I . . . was your mistress, and you were the father of Annie.'

'Kate! No!' He sprang up and drew her with him: 'No!' he repeated.

'Yes . . . ' A goods train puffed by them and they stood silent during its passage, Rodney gazing at Kate with knitted brows.

'Oh, darling . . . And you've had to put up with all this! No wonder you were afraid. Poor, poor dear . . . But what could have given them that idea?'

'I don't know; I can't tell . . . only that you made a fuss of Annie.'

Gently drawing her to him, he said, 'If only I had been Annie's father . . . I've always loved her. You see, I could love her when I couldn't allow myself to love you . . . I sometimes used to imagine I was her father. How funny! When they must have been thinking that, saying that, and watching me. What a queer world! And now they'll be saying, "What did I tell you! It's been going on for years." Oh, if only it had! Kate, I've such a lot to make up to you; life has been so hard for you.'

'Not half as hard as for some. I've had the Tolmaches . . . now I've you.'

'Oh, my love, you're so brave.'

'How much longer have we?' she asked.

'For ever . . . Don't let's look,' he said, holding her close.

Presently, taking two small packages from his pocket, he exclaimed, 'I almost forgot: here's your Christmas box, and Annie's. They're all I could get in the time. Now don't open them until you reach home.'

She stood looking down at them. 'Oh, Rodney; and I've nothing to give you, not a thing.'

'Don't talk nonsense.'

'You know,' she smiled at him, 'if there were time I'd resent being told I talk nonsense, that I'm ridiculous and that I'm silly. You have a very arrogant manner, Doctor Prince!'

'Oh, darling; do I sound arrogant?'

'You do.'

'Well then, do as I say, and I'll be like a lamb when I get my own way . . . Let me arrange about the money.'

She put her hand over his mouth: 'Seriously, dear, don't talk about it . . . the time is flying. Oh!' she exclaimed, 'I have something . . . but don't laugh.' Opening her handbag she took out a tiny, flat tin box which had once had an enamelled picture on its lid . . . 'It's my rosary. I've had it since I was a child. Will you take it? I'm still superstitious about it; I haven't done much praying lately, but I feel I must carry it with me. And, if you have it, it will still be with me.'

He held the tiny rosary in his fingers: 'Thanks, my dear. It will never leave me, because it is yours.'

Then he smiled: 'The only thing we want now is Father O'Malley's blessing . . . what?'

A gale of laughter assailed them; they rocked helplessly with it.

'Well, we've travelled some distance when we can laugh at the old fellow . . . What do you say, darling?'

Kate didn't answer. Suddenly he felt her face wet . . . 'Oh, my dear, don't . . . don't!' he begged. 'Look, only three more minutes. Come, smile. I want to remember you smiling and those eyes playing their tricks with me . . . Tell me you'll never forget me, darling. Say it.'

'I'll never forget you . . . Oh, Rodney, take care!'

He dried her face gently with his handkerchief. 'Good heavens, you'll be in much more danger than I shall be, stuck miles behind the lines!'

She turned swiftly: 'Here's the train! Oh, it can't be! It's early, but it won't stop a minute. Oh, my darling! . . . Oh, you can't go! I have so much to say . . . I love you, I love you.'

They held together as the train slowed down. Doors opened. Rodney dragged himself away, his face stiff and showing grey in the dim light from the carriages.

'Keep on loving me, dearest, always. There'll never be anyone but you. Goodbye, my love.'

He got into the carriage, the door closed and the train moved, and she was left on the platform, alone. It was as if it had been a dream and he had never really been there.

As the red light disappeared into the tunnel, she moved away, thinking, I never thanked him for the presents . . . such footling thoughts!

She walked all the way home in a maze of numbed pain, she was back where she was an hour ago, with anxiety lying heavy on her.

When she entered the kitchen Tim was sitting before the fire, his leg resting on a chair. The fire was blazing up the chimney, glowing bright with coal. She went straight upstairs, anger, for the moment, blotting out her anxiety . . . That would be the last of the coal, which she had been keeping to light the fires with . . . There was nothing she could do about it, nothing she could say . . . no word ever passed between them now.

Passing Sarah's door, she called softly, 'I'll be in in a minute, ma, when I've taken my things off.'

She sat on her bed and opened the little parcel Rodney had given her for Annie. It was a silver bangle, hung with tiny charms. Then she opened her own . . . She lifted out the gold wristlet watch. The face was small and exquisite, the strap of flat plaited gold. She put it on her wrist and held up her hand, but she could barely see it for the swimming of her eyes . . . How beautiful! how beautiful! But when could she wear it? In a few hours, Christmas Eve or no Christmas Eve, she'd be sitting on the tip.

Tears began to choke her . . . Rodney! Rodney! Why must life be like this? . . . She lay across the bed, sobbing, pressing the patched quilt against her mouth to still the sound . . .

Oh, Rodney, Rodney, come back!

THE FIELDCARD

Annie and Rosie stood one on each side of the clothes-basket as Kate put the things in: first, the sheets and pillow cases and towels, then the tablecloths, then the shirts and pants, the petticoats and pinafores, and, lastly, three silk blouses. She covered the whole with a cloth. 'Be careful how you carry them,' she said.

'How much have I got to say they are?' asked Annie.

'Three shillings.'

Rosie looked from one to the other. She wished Kate would smile or laugh like she used to, then Annie would be different. But whatever Kate did Annie seemed to do. Perhaps Kate'd stopped laughing because she had to take in washing, 'cos old Tim wouldn't work. Her da said old Tim was a lazy swine who should be hung, drawn and quartered. Sometimes he said that he wanted kicking from here to Hell and back again, for that was too good a place for him to stay . . . Oh, by heck, he was glad old Tim wasn't her granda!

'Hurry back,' said Kate to Annie; 'I want you to stay with grandma, I've got to go into Shields.'

Annie and Rosie picked up the basket and went out. The ground was hard with frozen snow and they walked warily, the basket swinging between them.

'Where's this lot going?' Rosie asked.

'To Mrs Beckett's at Simonside.'

'Coo! She's the one that gives you cake and sometimes a ha'penny, isn't she?'

'Yes, sometimes,' said Annie.

'By, it's a long way though! Let's count our steps from here to Simonside bank, eh? It'll make the time go.'

'I can manage the basket myself if you don't want to come.'

'Lord, what's up with you?' demanded Rosie, her small eyes snapping. 'Who said I didn't want to come? What's the matter with you, anyway? You've got a face like the back of a tram smash.'

Annie did not answer.

'Aw . . . w! Come on, Annie,' Rosie coaxed. 'Let's have a singsong, eh. Let's sing "Sam! Sam!" Come on.'

Breaking into a surprisingly strong, contralto voice she sang:

> '*Sam! Sam! The dirty man,*
> *Washed himself in the frying-pan,*
> *Combed his hair with a donkey's tail,*
> *Scratched his belly with his big toenail.*'

'Look,' she encouraged the still silent Annie, 'I'll sing "Sam! Sam!" and you sing "the dirty man". Then I'll sing, "Washed himself in the frying-pan," eh?'

'I don't want to,' said Annie. She had no liking for 'Sam! Sam!' at any time, but today he was revolting. Not wishing to hurt Rosie's feelings, however, she added, 'But you sing, I like to hear you. Sing "Venite adoremus" or the "O Salutaria".'

'Oh, all right:

> '*Venite adoremus, venite adoremus,*
> *Venite adore . . . emus . . .*'

Her voice rang out into the frosty air with power, causing passersby to smile at her. She smiled back, still singing.

As Rosie sang, Annie thought, If only the letters would come again; then Kate would be different. But they wouldn't come again, not now. For weeks there had been no letters. They had stopped when her pretty postcards, with the roses and mandolins worked in silk on them, had stopped . . . The cards had come from the doctor . . . the letters too had come from the doctor. She didn't know how she knew this, but she did. The doctor had been missing a long time . . . weeks. People said that when you were missing you were as good as dead . . . Kate didn't laugh any more, she hardly spoke. She said, 'Do this,' or, 'Don't do that.' But Annie thought Kate wouldn't have cared if she hadn't done this . . . or did do that. The only thing she wouldn't let her do was to go on the tip. But they bought less coal than ever now, because her granda sat with his leg on the chair most of the time. And, when he did go to work, he nearly always came home drunk. She had noticed, too, that he had taken to standing near Kate. Not to hit her, but just standing near looking at her, with his hand moving up and down his trouser leg. To see him thus had filled her with a nameless horror . . . Last night he had said, 'Go to the shop and get me half an ounce of baccy,' and Kate had come out of the house with her and stood at the back door until she came back.

But if only the letter would come again everything would be all right, she felt sure. Because there had always been her granda, and Kate had been taking in washing for a long time, but she had always seemed happy . . . But now she got tired when she was doing the washing, and sometimes stood, leaning her head against the wall. And also she seemed openly afraid of her granda; not that he'd hit

her, but . . . well . . . Annie shook her head in perplexity, the term
'Bad things' coming into her mind . . . Oh, she wished her granda
was dead . . . or missing!

Annie was recalled to Rosie's entertainment by a shake of the
basket.

'I don't believe you've been listening to a thing.'

'Oh yes I have.'

'Well, I've a new one,' said Rosie. 'Now listen.'

She performed her next number in two voices; one as near Father
O'Malley's as she could contrive, and the other a squeaky treble:

> *'Pray, Father, I've killed the cat.*
> *Ah, my child, you'll suffer for that!*
> *But, pray, Father, it was a Protestant cat.*
> *Oh! Then, my child, doesn't matter about that.'*

'Isn't it funny?' Rosie looked at Annie, hoping for a laugh, at
least a broad grin. But when she was confronted with a weak smile,
she said to herself, 'Oh, ta pot!'

When they returned to the fifteen streets Rosie left Annie with
the empty basket, in disgust . . . No ha'penny, no piece of cake!
Annie hadn't even got the money for the washing; the woman was
out and it had to be left next door . . . Annie had been worse
company coming back than going.

Annie put the basket in the washhouse and went reluctantly into
the house.

'What? you didn't get the money?' said Kate, when Annie had told
her the woman wasn't in. She sat down heavily on a chair and slowly
tapped her fingers on the table; Annie sat on the carpet and looked
into the fire.

I won't ask him, Kate thought. I'll do anything, anything rather
than ask him. She knew she was afraid, and she did not seem to have
the strength to fight against her fear.

Whatever money Tim had contributed to the household he had
been in the habit of throwing on the bed to Sarah, but these past
two weeks he had stopped this procedure and when Sarah had asked
him for the money he had replied, 'What'ja want it for? . . . Who's
keeping house?' and had gone and stood near Kate, handing her the
money without a word, but with his eyes playing over her.

She had taken it in amazement, and, seeing his look, a new fear of
him had come into being, making her sick with shame and terror.

Then, last week, he had waited for her to ask for the money, and
when she hadn't he had gone out and drunk it. He was waiting again,
and she hadn't a penny in the house!

She went upstairs to her room and, opening the bottom drawer of
the chest, she took out a small box. The wristlet watch was all she

had of Rodney beside his letters. She had hung on to it these months past, pawning everything belonging to herself except what she stood up in . . . and now it would have to go.

She touched it tenderly with her fingers . . . Rodney, Rodney, you're not dead, are you? . . . You can't be dead. You mustn't die.

Abruptly, she turned and took her coat and hat from the back of the door and went out of the room. If she began to think again she would be unable to go on, something would snap. And there was her mother and Annie to see to.

She put the box resolutely into the pocket of her coat, and went into Sarah's room.

'I'm going down to Shields, ma. I won't be long. Annie's downstairs, I'll send her up.'

Sarah nodded, speaking no word. Speech seemed to have dried up in her; the thing that was in the house now, stalking her Kate, had paralysed every emotion but fear. It stared out of her eyes continually; it was ever in her twitching tongue and plucking fingers.

When Kate had gone Annie went upstairs and sat near the window. Her grandma was asleep. She looked at the houses opposite with the grubby lace curtains and the rail of a brass bedstead showing between them. She looked up into the sky and down into the backyard with its sheet of grey ice strewn with cinders. Everything was grey and dull; there seemed nothing to smile or laugh about any more; nothing made you feel nice inside; there was a deadness in her and all around. Why had things changed so suddenly? Her grandma had been ill a long time, her granda had always been a bad man, Kate had always had to work, the houses opposite had never been different from what they were now. All these things had been happening when the doctor was alive, and she hadn't noticed them very much . . . But now he was dead they all seemed to matter.

She unplaited and replaited her hair. He used to like her hair, saying it was 'Fairy Queen's hair'. She examined it. The silver had turned to a pale gold. Sometimes she thought it was funny hair, no-one else seemed to have hair this colour. She looked at the bracelet he had sent her last Christmas. She was twirling it round her wrist when the door opened, startling her. Dorrie Clarke, in a bonnet and bead cape, her face red and bloated, tiptoed ponderously in.

'Couldn't make anyone hear,' she whispered, 'so I popped up . . . How is she?' She went and stood near the bed, looking down on Sarah.

'She's asleep,' said Annie.

'Ah, so she is! I'll sit meself here for a while till she wakes.'

Dorrie Clarke seated herself on a chair by the bed. Annie stood looking at her, stiff with apprehension.

'Growin', aren't you?' said Dorrie.

'Yes,' Annie said.

'Kate out?'

'Yes.' Annie thought, she knows Kate's out, or she wouldn't be here.

I'll not be able to do much with that young bitch watching me, Dorrie told herself. And I'll never have as good a chance as this again.

'Would you run a message, hinny?' she asked. 'Me leg's bothering me. Yer granny isn't the only one with bad legs, you know. Look, run round to the shop and get me a quarter stone of taties and twopennorth o' pot stuff. And there's a penny for yerself.'

Annie hesitated.

'Go on, hinny,' urged Dorrie. 'It won't take you a minute . . . Surely you don't mind going to the shop for me. You, with good legs on yer, and me, in the state I am.'

Annie took the money and the bag and hurried out.

'That bitch is as cute as a box o' monkeys,' Dorrie muttered to herself.

She listened until she heard the back door close, then she glanced down at Sarah . . . Not long for the top, she's not. No trouble from her . . . Now!

Hurrying out as softly as a cat, she made her way to Kate's room . . . Not much place to hide owt here . . . She made straight for the chest of drawers, and went through them. In the bottom one she found what she wanted . . . By God, there weren't 'alf some of them, too. Bundles of them, done up in ribbons . . . Well, well! Split yer sides, yer could.

She extracted a letter here and there, taking six in all, and she was back, sitting beside Sarah, within a few minutes.

The idea had first entered her mind some months ago, but when he had been reported missing there was no sense in doing it. But now . . . well, things were just as they were before, but she wasn't letting on.

Mary Dixon's brother had given her the idea. He was a postman, and he had remarked, 'That Kate Hannigan's bloke out in France does some writing; she stands on the doorstep waiting for letters every post . . . and she gets them. He must have nowt else to do.' And when Mary Dixon got her the job, mornings, at the doctor's, after their cook had left, she began to hear things, and see quite a bit, too. It was then the use to which some of the letters could be put had entered her mind.

It was another score she held against him, that she had to go out charring and cooking, and her a midwife. For never a case had she had in years, and all through him . . . and now she was working at his house! What would he say to that, if he knew? Her time would be short, she guessed. Well, he wouldn't know; he was nicely set for a long time yet. God blast him and keep him there!

She liked his wife no better than she did him . . . snotty bitch! And she was having a nice titty-fal-lal with the other doctor, wasn't she now. And another bloke in the offing, Mary said. Thinking this over, it had occurred to Dorrie that her mistress might find her husband's letters to another woman useful, should things become too hot for her with her couple of fancy men. And she would likely stump up a pretty penny to get them . . . by God, yes! She would stump up, if she had anything to do with it!

Ah! She sighed contentedly; she'd waited a long time to get even with him . . . but God was good.

She was sitting placidly on the chair, her hands folded in her lap, when Annie returned.

'That's a good lass. Now I'll have to go, I'm afraid . . . Yer granny hasn't woken up so I won't disturb her. Tell her I just popped in.'

As she went out, Annie thought, Oh, Kate will be vexed. But what could I do? I don't know whether to tell her or not.

It was late in the afternoon, and Kate was cleaning the brasses when Annie said, 'Dorrie Clarke came to see grandma this morning, when you were out.'

'What!' Kate turned on her.

'I couldn't help it . . . I couldn't stop her; she came into the bedroom without knocking.'

'You should have said . . . oh, you couldn't, I suppose.'

She put the candlestick down slowly on the table. 'How long did she stay?' she asked flatly.

'Not long, about five minutes . . . or ten.'

'What did she say?'

'Not much. Just how was grandma . . . and she said her legs were bad too. She asked me . . . ' Annie stopped. Should she tell Kate that she had gone a message for Dorrie Clarke and left her in the house with her grandma? No, she wouldn't; perhaps it would make her more vexed.

Kate looked at her sharply. 'Well, what did she ask you?'

'Only about grandma.'

'Nothing else?'

'No.'

Kate stood for a moment looking out of the kitchen window . . . What did it matter, anyway? Dorrie Clarke could do no more harm.

Saying to Annie, 'Will you finish these for me?' she washed her hands and went upstairs.

In her own room, she sat on the foot of the bed and leant her head wearily on the brass rail. She felt suddenly tired, not the exhausting tiredness that the end of each day brought to her body, but a tiredness that seemed to drain the very spirit from her . . . Why, oh why had she to go through all this? One thing after another piling up . . . no respite . . . The fact of Dorrie Clarke being in the house had created

132

another dread. But what, she asked herself, need she fear from Dorrie Clarke now? If he were still alive there might be cause to worry. She gripped the bedrail . . . But he wasn't dead . . . he wasn't! Oh God, don't let him be dead! she prayed. I'll do anything, anything. Jesus, save him! Do what you like with me, only don't let him die.

The old bargaining was in her prayer. She recognised it, but was too weary to scorn it. She slumped down, her hands dropping into her lap.

Was God paying her out for all her questioning, for all her probing? she wondered. No; God, as she saw Him now, wasn't that kind of a god. He said, 'I have given you a life and a conscience by which to steer it. Whether you arrive at your destination by way of the Catholic religion, the Protestant religion, or by way of no recognised sect whatever, as long as you recognise you are steering for me, that is all that matters.' She knew He understood all things, her sickness of heart now, her burning desire of a few weeks ago.

Was it only a few weeks ago since she had stood in this room, clasping Rodney's letter to her? It had said: Seven days, beloved . . . Seven days! In a short while, seven days. I can't believe it. We must spend every minute together. Arrange for someone to look after your mother and Annie; offer any sum you like, only get someone. Now don't be silly about this. I read your special letter every night. You'll never really know all it means to me . . .

Her special letter! The letter which had taken so long to write; hours of thinking and rewriting when a look would have conveyed all there was to say. There had been nothing restrained about that letter; her battered-down emotions had overflowed; and when his reply came the house had become bright with her singing and happy laughter, except when Tim was in.

She had set about preparing herself for their meeting; for nearly two years there had been no time to spend on herself. Each moment was taken up with nursing and work and with washing to eke out their existence. So she had feverishly tried to make up for lost time; her weekly bath had become a nightly affair, the work it entailed on top of the grind of the day becoming a pleasure. After the washing she would fill the boiler with clean water, and a dying fire would heat it sufficiently. The tin bath had to be carried to her room, then the water, bucket after bucket.

Years before she had swung the cracked mirror back and forth and had seen that she was beautiful. Now she swung it again . . . but more shyly, for she swung it with the knowledge of what she was searching for. It was eleven years since she had desired to see the reflection of her body. But, as she looked at it now, she knew it had much more to offer than when she was seventeen. It was firm, and moulded like live ivory. From her breast, over the curve of her stomach, down to the rise of her thighs, was a continued modulation. Her face was thinner, but still without a line, and her hair was alive and winging. Only one thing marred the whole, her beauty stopped at her wrists. Her hands were red and coarse – cinders and soda water had taken their toll of them. Nightly, before getting into bed, she sat and rubbed grease into them. In the morning they would look paler, but by evening they were white, with the skin crinkled into little folds. Then, freed from the water and pushing the flat iron, they would harden and redden once more.

Annie hurried into the room.

'The priest's downstairs, Kate.'

'Well,' answered Kate, shortly, 'he certainly knows his way up.'

'But it's Father Bailey, Kate.'

'Oh.' Kate rose and went downstairs.

'Hallo there, Kate!' said Father Bailey. 'I thought I'd look in and see your mother; Father O'Malley is laid up with rheumatism.'

'Oh yes, Father. Will you come up?'

She held the door open for him. Before mounting he turned and faced her: 'You're having a hard time, Kate, aren't you?'

She didn't answer; his sympathy was more unnerving than Father O'Malley's censure.

'Won't you come to mass and try to find peace that way?'

She shook her head: 'I can't, Father.'

'Why not, Kate?'

'I don't believe in any of the things I used to.'

He looked at her, long and steadily.

'You're passing through one of the bad patches, aren't you? And you think you're alone; you don't think anyone's ever been through your particular kind of misery before. But it happens to most of us . . . I know, for I've been through it.'

Kate looked at him in surprise.

'Don't let suffering make you hard, Kate. Let it rather be an academy of sympathy . . . No man dare look God in the face and say he has never doubted Him, Kate.'

'It isn't that I doubt the existence of God, Father . . . it's . . . oh, I can't explain it!' She put her hand wearily to her head.

'I know, I know. It's the Catholic way of looking at Him that you are doubting . . . Yes, if you think at all, that comes too, sooner or later. But if you'll only keep on praying, Kate, He'll put that right. Keep knocking and the door will be opened . . . He'll give you the faith to see clearly and to trust simply, and you'll find that the way He dictates is for your own good. If you rebel against life, struggle against the tide, time and again you will find yourself thrust into black despair. It is as if God wants you to work along certain channels, and either through obstinacy, misdirection of will, or fear, you will not allow yourself to be led. Kate, He knows what makes for your ultimate good . . . for the good of the soul, that must live on, if we believe in anything . . . Stop fighting, and come to mass, Kate.'

'I can't, Father.'

'What's made you like this, Kate? I've known and watched you since you were a child.'

She was about to answer, 'Priests and teachers have made me like this,' but then she thought, I would likely have come to this way of thinking in the end, in any case. So she remained silent.

He read her thoughts nearer than she guessed, for his patience, too, was tried daily. Sometimes he felt he was earning a saint's halo simply by living with Father O'Malley.

'God bless you, Kate,' he said, and went upstairs.

She stood biting her lip, the tears stinging her eyes; understanding made things worse, it made her ask herself about this question, Can I be right and millions of people wrong?

She thought of Master Bernard's words: 'If you find faith in God through the Catholic religion, hang on to it with all your might, for the greatest disaster in life is to lose one's faith.'

She was trying to follow the truth, as she saw it; and she had wanted life, full, pulsing life; she had been willing at last to barter all for life. But now she had neither life nor religion, and she was lost.

Oh, she couldn't think . . . Why bother to think! What did anything matter? The end was near, she felt; something must happen soon; she couldn't fight this unequal battle against poverty and fear much longer.

'I've finished the brasses, Kate,' Annie said. 'Can I do anything else for you?'

Kate looked at her, and, seeing the anxiety in her face, thought, I'm forgetting about her; I mustn't. I mustn't give in. What would become of her? It would be my early life over again. Place, twelve hours a day, ten if she were lucky, for there wouldn't be any Tolmaches for her . . . they happen only once in a thousand years . . . She stared at Annie fixedly, thinking, She's too beautiful, she'd be dragged under right away.

'Kate!' said Annie. 'Kate, what's the matter?'

'Nothing, my dear, nothing; I was just thinking.'

Kate shook her head and jumped towards the fire. 'Go on out to play for a while if you like.'

'Oh, all right. I'll go round to the shops for one more look before they pull the blinds down.'

Kate nodded, and Annie hurried out.

Christmas, and not a thing to give her! If only she could have got her some small thing . . . Oh, what was the use of thinking about it; she must conserve every penny she had received for the watch as there was nothing more left in the house which she could pawn. What she would do when the money was gone, she did not know. She would never ask him for any, and she felt she had imposed enough on Mrs Mullen. There were other neighbours, but she couldn't bear to think of their looks of satisfaction were she to humble herself to borrow from them . . . She would know what they were thinking . . . 'Lady' Hannigan, brought off her perch at last. She knew that was how they referred to her, and that not an action of hers escaped their notice. With the exception of a few here and there, it was as if improvement or difference in another bred hate in them. They were waiting for her to snap . . . There was a street near the docks where it was easy to make money . . . My God!

She was in a flurry as she set about laying the tea . . . God above, what had put that into her head? What had made her even think of it? Yes, she knew; it was what most of them were hoping would happen.

She had just finished getting the tea ready when Tim came in. She put the teapot on the table and went into the front room and busied herself there.

A little later, hearing his chair scrape, and thinking he had gone to wash himself and that she would be able to slip upstairs without having to pass close to him, she went into the kitchen.

But he was standing in front of the fire, his eyes on the door.

She hesitated for a second. Then, as she went to walk between him and the table, he held out his hand. In his palm lay a number of half-crowns. She stared at them, fascinated but unable to touch them.

He waited; then said gruffly, 'Go on.'

But terror filled her, and she could not move.

Swiftly, he took one of her hands and put the money into it, his fist closing over hers as he did so, and, as swiftly, his other hand moved and pressed hard against the front of her thigh.

She gave a scream and sprang back from him, letting the money fall to the mat.

He was standing staring at her, his lids drooping over his eyes, his hands working a slow movement up and down his trouser legs, when the stair door opened. He turned and gaped in surprise at the priest, having been unaware of his presence in the house, and Father Bailey saw the evil, raw and uncovered, that oozed from him, and the stark terror in Kate's eyes.

The expression on Tim's face fought between resentment and the look of penitence he was wont to keep for the priests, but something in Father Bailey's face showed him the uselessness of pretence. He gathered up the money from the mat, switched his cap off the back door and went out.

The priest stood looking at Kate pityingly for some moments, then, shaking his head in perplexity, hurried out after Tim.

Not a word had been spoken.

Kate sat down heavily, her legs refusing to support her. She was trembling from head to foot . . . Something must happen soon . . . Something had got to happen soon.

At half-past six Annie came in and asked if she could go to the Baptist Chapel hall with Rosie. The soldiers were there, and were giving a party and presents, and one was dressed up as Father Christmas. And Rosie said they'd get in because they didn't ask if you were a Catholic or not . . .

She suddenly stopped, and before Kate could answer said, 'Oh, it's all right, I don't want to go.' She saw that Kate looked very white and that the needle in her hand with which she was mending her socks was shaking.

She took off her outdoor things and sat down near Kate.

'The postman's doing a late round, he's loaded with parcels and things,' she said.

Kate looked at her, and Annie hung her head. She didn't know what had made her say it. 'I didn't mean to say it, Kate,' she whispered, her lip trembling.

'It's all right, my dear, but he won't be coming here.'

It was just then the knock came: rat-a-tat-tat, rat-a-tat-tat. They looked at each other, startled.

'I'll go,' cried Annie, and was through the front-room in a flash.

Kate stood, awaiting her return; the socks lay on the mat.

Annie came running back into the kitchen: 'It's a card, Kate,' she said.

Kate read the printed buff-coloured card. She read it again. She turned it over, and back, and re-read it.

She sat down in a chair: 'It's the doctor, Annie. He's safe,' she said in a voice scarcely above a whisper; 'he's a prisoner.'

Annie shivered. She had forgotten what it was like to feel that shiver of delight; the greyness went out of the day, out of all the things that made up her life; everything was bright and shining again.

'Oh, Kate!' she cried, and flung her arms about her. 'Oh, Kate, he'll be coming back! Oh, Kate!'

'Yes, my dear, he'll be coming back,' she said, pressing Annie fiercely to her and rocking her like a child.

Rosie Mullen opened the back door, unobserved. She stood for a moment wide-eyed before closing it again.

She ran into her own yard, calling, 'Kate and Annie's howling the house down, ma.'

'Oh, my, that'll mean Sarah's gone!' Mrs Mullen hurried out, with Rosie at her heels.

'Is it Sarah?' she asked, bursting in on Kate.

Kate shook her head: 'No, Mrs Mullen . . . it's . . . Look!' she handed the card to Mrs Mullen.

Mrs Mullen read it laboriously. 'Oh, lass, I am glad. A prisoner! Oh, I am glad. You'll be A1 again now.'

She put her arm about Kate's shoulder and pulled her head to her much-used breast: 'There, lass, there! Have a good cry, it'll do you good.'

Rosie watched her mother in bewilderment; she wasn't only telling Kate to cry, but she was starting to cry herself. Never before had she seen as much as a tear on her face; they weren't a crying lot, the Mullens; only the babies cried, and they soon had that knocked out of them. She didn't cry; not even at that time when her mother had swiped her lug so hard that she had turned a somersault and landed upside down in the bottom of the cupboard . . . She looked at Annie . . . she was howling awful.

Rosie began to experience a queer feeling, like pins and needles, in her nose, and a bit of brick seemed to have stuck edgeways in her throat. Her face crumpled up, and, try as she might, she was unable to straighten it out.

Mr Mullen came in, saying, 'Anything I can do, lass? . . . Is it Sarah?'

Mrs Mullen shook her head at him: 'No, it isn't Sarah . . . Kate's had a bit of good news, that's all.'

He stopped dead, gazing at the four of them. 'My God! Then what you all blaring for? Crikey! Did you ever see such a lot of bloody fools! I suppose if it was bad news you'd have a damn good laugh, eh? . . . And you' – he pointed to his daughter, the daughter who, he prided himself, was a chip off the old block, the male block – 'don't tell me you're piping too!'

'I ain't,' protested Rosie, endeavouring to straighten out her face, 'I ain't . . . it's me nose, it's stopped up.'

She managed to grin at her father, who grinned back. Then, turning to his wife, Mr Mullen said, 'I'm off for a wet, and I hope I get happy enough to have a damn good cry!'

After he had gone, they looked at each other in silence for a moment, then, one after the other, they began to laugh; Rosie, her face all wet and her mouth wide open, was saying to herself in relief, 'By, lad, this is better! Me da's a one, ain't he? I wish Annie had a da like him, she'd laugh more then.'

Kate lay and listened to the carol singers; the card was on the pillow, half under her cheek; Annie lay curled into her back, fast asleep.

'While shepherds watched their flocks by night . . .' the voices rose to her from the street.

'Oh, God, watch over him,' she prayed. 'Make the war soon end; bring him back safely . . . And, oh, thank You, thank You, that he is alive.'

> ' "Fear not," said he, for mighty dread has seized their
> troubled mind . . . '

'No . . . I will not fear. He will come back. I will fear nothing,' she said to herself, 'not now; not even "him".'

She had lain awake, waiting for Tim to come in, dreading his footsteps on the stairs. She had dragged the big box that had for years acted as a cupboard and placed it across the door, for she felt now that not even Annie was a protection. But he had not come. She wondered if he had gone to Jarrow . . . Had the priest said anything to him?

Long after the carol singers had gone from the street she lay awake, waiting. Everywhere was silent; there was no more shouting, no more drunken singing, not even the echo of the carollers from the distance, just that uncanny quiet that seemed full of sound. So, when the footsteps came up the street, she heard them, slithering over the ice. And when they stopped beneath the window she sat up, and, as the knocker banged, she was out of bed and had her coat on in a flash.

It couldn't be him; he always came in the back way. She opened the window and looked down on to a shadowy figure. A white blur was turned up to her, and a voice asked, 'This Hannigans'?'

'Yes,' she answered.

'Well, I've news for you. You'd better come down.'

Sarah called out, as Kate passed her door, 'What is it?'

'I don't know, ma. I'll be back in a minute,' she answered.

She opened the door, to find a policeman standing there . . .

When she returned upstairs and went into Sarah's room, she noticed that her mother looked strangely alert.

'What is it?' Sarah asked. 'What's the matter, hinny?'

'It's him,' said Kate; 'he's had an accident . . . he's in Harton.'

Sarah hitched herself up on her pillows, an effort she had stopped making months ago. 'Bad?' she asked.

'It's his arm and head . . . I don't know how bad; the policeman says I have to go down.'

'Yes, hinny. Go down. You needn't see him, only find out how bad it is.'

They did not look at each other, and Kate hurried out to dress. She felt light headed with relief; it would appear that good news attracted good news as bad bad.

From the moment Kate left the house Sarah began to pray. Not mumbled prayers . . . not the prayers that were for ever being repeated at the back of her mind, a jumble of entreaties and requests, but verbal prayers, said aloud into the room, each word distinctly spoken, rising into the air, filling the room with power. The faculties which had been slowly fading during the months past seemed to regain new life. Each word she uttered vibrated with terrible purpose. She went on and on, speaking words and framing sentences that were new to her. Nor did she stop until she was exhausted. Then she lay, wide-eyed, waiting . . .

When she heard Kate's step on the stairs her bloated body stiffened against the bed and her eyes fixed themselves on the door.

Kate came in panting; she had been gone only an hour and a half.

Sarah brought herself on to her elbow: 'Yes?' she asked.

'He's gone!' said Kate, unable to keep the joy and relief from her voice.

Sarah dropped back on to her pillows, a slow smile spreading over her face.

'Sit down, hinny,' she said; 'you're puffed.'

Kate sat on the side of the bed and took her mother's hand.

'How was it?' asked Sarah.

'They don't know, really. He was knocked down by a tram in Eldon Street. His arm was broken and he received a blow on the head which made him unconscious. But it wasn't serious, they said, and they could not understand him dying. When he came round and asked where he was, and they told him Harton, the nurse said he had a kind of fit, and died in it.'

'Ah!' exclaimed Sarah. 'Harton! . . . That's what he was always feared of, having to end his days in the workhouse . . . it's the only thing that ever worried him; he was mortally afraid of the workhouse . . . He died of fright, Kate.'

She lay silent for some time, her eyes roving gently round the room, a wondrous peace filling her, like that of carrying a child. It would vanish later, she knew, and there would be the throes of dying, but at present it was here and she hugged it to herself. She smiled at Kate: 'Do you think we might have a cup of tea, hinny, it's Christmas Day?'

ALWAYS FLIGHT

John Swinburn and Stella faced each other in the drawing-room. Swinburn's face was white and drawn, and his thin nostrils moved in and out in little jerks.

'Do you mean to say, Stella, you don't want to get a divorce . . . ever?' His voice was harsh, and deep in his throat.

'Must we have it all over again, John?' Stella made an impatient movement with her shoulders. 'I have told you already I have no desire to be a divorced woman . . . Anyway, if I were divorced, I shouldn't marry you.'

'You're a fiend, Stella, a heartless fiend!'

'Then why do you bother with me?'

'I don't know,' he said despairingly.

'John, don't act like a boy. I have told you things can go on just as they are . . . We can be together now and again. He'll live his life and I'll live mine.'

'I couldn't do it,' said Swinburn, turning away and beating a fist in the palm of his hand. 'I know how many different kinds of a swine I am, nobody better, and I have no love for Rodney. I think him a prig, but I couldn't work with him and have you at the same time . . . not the way I want you. I couldn't do it. He's coming home smashed up, and, after a year as a prisoner, he's not going to feel very bright . . . I tell you, I couldn't play that underhand game . . . I could go to him and lay my cards on the table and ask him to divorce you, but not the other way.'

'You'll do nothing of the kind,' rapped out Stella. 'Should you attempt it I wouldn't even look at you again.'

'But what about him?' Swinburn turned on her. 'What about the Hannigan girl? Have you thought about her? He may want a divorce.'

'He won't get it . . . And please don't shout,' she added coldly.

'How are you going to stop him living with her then, if he wants to? . . . Tell me that.'

'He won't live with her, I'll see to that,' said Stella, her lips folding into a thin line.

'What do you mean to do? What are you up to?' he asked.

141

'Never mind . . . He won't live with her! He will live here, and things will go on just as they did before he left.'

'You're a cold-blooded devil.'

'Really!' She raised her eyebrows, tauntingly, at him.

'Oh, you'd drive a fellow mad!' He made a grab at her.

'Please, John,' she commanded; 'not here . . . I have told you . . . not here!'

'Hell!' He turned from her and flung out of the room.

Stella listened to him stamping across the hall. The front door banged, and she went to the window and watched him stride away down the garden. She stood, biting her lip with vexation.

Something must be done, and at once . . . things seemed to be getting swiftly out of hand. Why had she gone so far with him, anyway? she wondered. Why had she started it? She had never intended it to reach this stage. In the beginning she had used him to play off Herbert, who was demanding too much. But she had found John wasn't like Herbert, she couldn't keep him in line at all. The week-ends they spent together were nerve racking and exhausting; she had been made aware that Rodney, even in his passion, had been tender; and now John was proposing divorce, and marriage to him . . . a struggling doctor, with not a penny behind him; it was ridiculous.

Stella admitted to herself that she had been foolish, very foolish, but whatever happened there must be no divorce. The Hannigan girl would have to be dealt with; she should have done it months ago, when that old hag had brought her those letters.

Her face stiffened at the thought of them, and jealousy rose in her like a corroding acid . . . To think Rodney would write letters like that to a maid! Of course, she admitted, she had herself to blame, she had played him too tightly.

She wondered if she could regain her lost ground . . . He would be sick, and would doubtless respond to sweetness. She would devote herself to him; it wouldn't be her fault if she failed to establish at least a friendly footing. She still hated him, and desired nothing but to humiliate him for his spurning of her that memorable Christmas Eve. Well, the opportunity might yet come. But, in the meantime, if she didn't want a terrific scandal and wished to keep her head above the social waters, then Rodney was her only hope. But the Hannigan girl must be dealt with at once, she must be placed out of his reach.

She went to her desk and unlocked a drawer, and took out a bundle of letters. She fingered them as though they scorched her flesh.

Why, she wondered, did that old hag hate Rodney so? She evidently did, to go to the lengths she had in stealing these letters; her tale that she had found them in the street was paltry.

Stella felt that she had made a mistake in paying for them. Yet the old witch had played her nicely, leaving her no other way of getting them. And, although she had dismissed her some time ago, she wondered whether she had seen the last of her. Still, she had provided the means of putting the Hannigan girl where she wanted her; and she must lose no further time in doing it.

Annie was playing at the corner of the street; she stood in a circle with other children, all hopping from one foot to the other to keep warm. A child in the centre stabbed a finger at each in turn, shouting:

> *'Iccle occle, black bottle,*
> *Fishes in the sea,*
> *If you want a pretty girl,*
> *Please choose . . . me!'*

Annie knew that the first stab could be regulated to choose whichever one you liked. The unfairness of the system did not trouble her; she felt gloriously happy . . . the sun was shining, the frost was sparkling, it was Christmas Eve and she was going to hang up her stocking, she had a secret present for Kate . . . and oh! oh! oh! the doctor was coming home, the doctor was coming home, the doctor was coming home . . . she beat out each word with her hopping feet. Everything was lovely and bright and shiny, Kate was lovely and bright and shiny. She sang all day. They both sang together in the kitchen at night, and Mrs Mullen knocked on the wall at them, and they laughed because they knew it was only in fun. Oh, they were so happy! They missed grandma at times, but she had been so happy before she died that you did not feel sorry for her now . . . it made you feel she had gone straight to Heaven like that . . . nice and happy. Oh, wasn't everything lovely! No granda, no more carrying washing for Kate went out to work now, most days, and the doctor, doctor, doctor was coming, coming back! She was still hopping when the circle broke up.

'Count a hundred before you look, mind, Jinnie Taylor!' a little girl was admonished. Jinnie turned her face to the wall and started to count quickly in a loud voice.

Annie dashed into the main road, she knew a lovely place to hide . . . It was then she saw the car. It was gliding slowly forward and the chauffeur was looking up at the names of the streets. A woman in the back leaned forward and spoke to him; and Annie stopped running for a second. Turning, she dashed back the way she had come.

Running up the street, she knew that the car had turned the corner and was behind her. It was almost upon her when she reached the door. As she thrust open the door the car stopped. She ran into the kitchen, whispering hoarsely, 'Kate! Kate!'

Kate was not there, so she dashed into the backyard and found her in the wash-house.

'Oh, there you are,' she said. 'I'm getting the steps to put the chains up, you can come and help me.'

'There's . . . there's a lady outside, Kate,' Annie panted. 'I think she's coming here.'

'A lady?' Kate asked, knowing that any of their usual visitors would have had the term 'woman' affixed to them. 'Do you know who it is?' she went on, straightening her dress, one of the faded and washed out Quaker-grey dresses she had worn at the Tolmaches, and smoothing her burnished hair up the back of her head with a sweep of her hand.

'It's . . . I think it's . . . ' But Kate was already in the kitchen, and Annie let her go through the front-room without adding, 'the doctor's wife.'

To say that Kate was surprised at the sight of her visitor was to say the least. She looked at this beautiful, magnificently-dressed woman, with the background of the car behind her, and found herself incapable of uttering a word.

'Miss Hannigan?' Stella asked.

Kate inclined her head slowly.

'May I come in? I should like to talk with you.'

Stella, poised and calm, felt she already had this woman at a disadvantage. She took in, at a glance, the poverty of Kate's attire, shutting her mind to the beauty that it clothed.

At the second motion of Kate's head she stepped into the front-room, and barely suppressed a shudder as she looked around at the horse-hair suite and the bamboo table standing on the bare wood floor.

Kate found her voice: 'Will you come into the kitchen, it's warmer there?' She led the way, and indicated Tim's chair to the visitor. To Annie, who was standing wide-eyed, she said, 'Go into the front-room, dear, and close the door.'

Stella experienced a sense of irritation at the sound of Kate's voice; she must, she conceded, be suffering a shock, yet her voice was strangely controlled and well modulated; there was none of the raucousness that, to her mind, accompanied the Tyneside speech. She remembered vaguely having heard that one of the old Tolmaches had educated the girl, which increased her irritation. But her voice was cool and level when she spoke: 'You wonder why I am here, Miss Hannigan?'

'No,' answered Kate surprisingly.

'Oh!' said Stella, slightly nonplussed. 'Then that does away with the need of an introductory opening . . . Sit down,' she spoke as if commanding a servant; 'you'll be tired before we finish, no doubt.'

'Thank you; I don't wish to sit down,' said Kate. She stood with one hand resting on the kitchen table and holding the middle button of her dress with the other.

'Very well!' Stella suppressed her annoyance with difficulty, for this attitude was unexpected. 'I shall come to the reason for my visit right away,' she said. 'My husband is, as I suppose you know, expected home any day now. I understand he is a very sick man and will need careful nursing for some time, as I expect the surgery was rough in a prison camp, especially with amputations.'

She was allowed a pause, while they stared at each other.

'He will,' she went on, 'need peace, and rest from worry . . . Whether or not he gets it will depend on you, Miss Hannigan.'

Kate did not answer, but her eyes widened slightly and became dark.

'I want you, Miss Hannigan,' Stella continued coolly, 'to leave the district, and promise in no way to get in touch with my husband. If you do this he will have a chance to get well and strong again, and to resume his career, which means so much to him.'

'And if I don't?' put in Kate quietly.

'Then, if you don't, he will not have a career to resume . . . for I will sue for a divorce.'

'There are no grounds for a divorce,' Kate said evenly. 'And anyway, divorce does not end a man's career.'

'To the first . . . I can prove there are grounds for divorce.'

Stella opened her bag and took out the bundle of letters.

'These are six of my husband's letters to you. In one of them, he speaks of "our beautiful Annie", and that he has loved her since the day he brought her into the world; in another, that to him you are more than a wife, and he makes reference to a week you are to spend together, which he refers to as "heaven".'

The button Kate was holding snapped across, making a loud twang in the silence . . . Her letters! . . . How? . . . Where? . . . Mrs Mullen? . . . No. Who, then? . . . Dorrie Clarke! Last Christmas Eve . . . Yes, sending Annie out so that she could search . . . Annie hadn't told her of that until after Christmas, knowing she was so worried and it would only have annoyed her to know.

Kate's voice trembled as she said, 'He's not Annie's father . . . you know he's not.'

'Whether I know it or not everything points to it. I can do my best to prove it. But I am not going on that alone . . . Rodney made no secret of his attachment to you; he never does when he has these strong attachments for women. You start, Miss Hannigan,' said Stella, with a smile. 'Surely you didn't think you were the only one. Dear, dear! I've had to straighten out these affairs all my married life. But that's beside the point.

'The Christmas Eve before last he spent the night here, and most of the following week. You don't deny that?'

Kate did not answer.

'Also, previous to that, you were seen in a field . . .'

'In a field!' Kate exclaimed in amazement.

'Yes. Somewhere near Felling. That was at Christmas time, too.'

The night of the drive! Kate thought; walking across the moonlit green hill . . . Oh, Rodney . . . But to put it like that . . . in a field! How sordid it sounded.

'Mrs Richards, Doctor Richards's wife, told me of this; she felt I should know . . . Candidly, I think she would like to see a divorce, and would help me to get it. Anything that would endanger Rodney's career would be beneficial to her husband's practice . . . Women are strange creatures, aren't they?' she said, smiling stiffly.

Kate just stared at her, at her beautiful unlined face and her eyes, as cold as the sea.

'You remarked,' continued Stella, 'that divorce does not end a man's career. But this one would. For, should I divorce him and he does not marry a certain lady . . . namely, Gwendoline Cuthbert-Harris . . . she will immediately bring up a case against him for seduction, when she was his patient.'

'You must be mad!' cried Kate. 'I don't believe a word you say.'

'It does sound mad, doesn't it?' said Stella calmly.

'Lady Cuthbert-Harris is a sick woman,' said Kate, 'she's neurotic. You know she is.'

'Aren't we all!' Stella retorted. 'Tell me who isn't suffering from nerves after going through this war . . . But she has asked me to divorce Rodney when he returns. She says that she's crazy about him, which, of course, I know, and so do most people. And, she states, he loves her, and that I am the only obstacle in the way of their happiness.'

'You're lying!'

'Why should I lie about such a thing?' Stella opened her bag again and, taking out another letter, she said, 'Please notice the crest on the envelope and also on the paper . . . Now, would you mind listening to this?'

Stella read the letter aloud, raising her eyes every now and again to Kate's white face.

It was the outpourings of a sex-ridden woman, and, as Stella had said, was asking her to divorce Rodney on the grounds of what had taken place between them.

Kate felt sick. She knew it was the letter of a woman who was mentally ill; but she also saw what could be made out of this letter if brought before the public notice. And whether it was or not depended on her . . . How was it, Kate thought, she had always sensed disaster would come to him through her? . . . And she fully realised that this woman before her meant every word she said. She was as dangerous as an adder; nothing would stop her reaching her object, and her object, Kate knew, was to have Rodney once more. And if she couldn't get him she would ruin him . . . Oh, God,

she cried voicelessly, is there no end to it? What must I do? . . .
But, even as she asked, she knew.

But first she would tell this woman that what she had said about
Rodney had no effect on her; it was what she would do to him that
was forcing her hand.

'You needn't continue!' she interrupted, her voice quivering. 'I
don't believe a word of it . . . No, not a word!'

'You don't?' Stella folded the letter carefully and returned it to her
bag. 'However,' she continued, 'whether you believe it or not, Miss
Hannigan, is beside the point. Should Lady Cuthbert-Harris bring up
a case of such a nature on top of my suing for divorce, and she will bring
up her case, I'll see to that, what chance do you think Rodney's career
will stand? The Medical Board is rather puritanical about the members of its profession, and, should nothing even be proved, Rodney
wouldn't be able to stand the strain of it . . . it would break him.

'I have the advantage in the knowledge I possess of my husband,
Miss Hannigan. His affairs were always numerous, but never serious
enough to damage his career; and his affairs were secondary things in
his life . . . his work came first.

'Have you realised, Miss Hannigan, that nothing matters to him so
much as his work? His one aim before the war was to specialise in
children's diseases and child psychology. Should you bring about the
end of his career, do you think you would be capable of replacing it
in his life? . . . Remember, once he is struck off the medical register,
that will be the end. Sex is not all a man needs. But perhaps you
have that to learn . . . You undoubtedly will learn it should you
force my hand, Miss Hannigan.'

'What if I refuse to fall in with your plans?' cried Kate, momentarily
driven to defiance. 'If I stay he will come to me, and you could do your
worst. You lost him years ago . . . Even if you get your way and you
share the same roof for the rest of your days you'll never have him; I
know that. You don't exist for him!' she spat out the last words.

Stella stood up, her face bloodless, and they confronted each other
in silence.

Then: 'How dare you!' Stella said between her teeth.

She fought to gain control, forcing a smile to her lips. 'Of course,
it's foolish to lose one's temper with people of your class. Your speech
at any time is apt to be crude . . . It only proves to me how soon Rodney
would tire of someone having nothing but the flesh to offer him.'

Kate remained silent, refusing to be goaded.

'Well, Miss Hannigan; you know my terms,' said Stella, hunching
her fur coat around her. 'Should you be here the day Rodney returns,
which will be in about a week's time, then I will not stay my hand
a minute. And you will be surprised at the number of people who
will come forward to help me obtain the divorce. I have found that
the people who dislike Rodney are equal in number to those who

like him. For instance, there's Mrs Clarke. It was she, incidentally, who found your letters in the street. It was careless of you to drop them, Miss Hannigan. She thought I ought to know; very good moral sense, don't you think?'

'Have you quite finished?' asked Kate.

'Nearly,' said Stella. 'You will need money for such a hasty withdrawal. Here,' she said, placing a roll of notes on the table, 'is enough to take you quite a distance from this county, and to keep you and your child until you find suitable work.'

Kate stared straight at Stella: 'Would you mind picking up that money?' she asked, with dangerous quiet.

'We don't want any heroics, Miss Hannigan; nor hypocrisy,' said Stella firmly. 'I am sure you know the value of money. You will no doubt need . . . '

She did not finish; for Kate's hand shot out, and, picking up the roll, threw it into the heart of the fire.

The effect on Stella was paralysing for a second. Then she cried, 'Are you crazy, you fool? Pick it out! . . . There's twenty pounds there, get it out!'

'It's your money,' said Kate. 'It's there for you to take.'

The bundle of notes was well alight. Stella made an effort to put her hand towards them, then drew it back. She lifted the poker and tried to flip them out, but only succeeded in fanning the blaze. She stood watching them helplessly, venomous rage consuming her . . . There was a swelling of flame, and they were gone. Pieces of black charred paper broke away and floated up the wide chimney.

It was not the loss of the twenty pounds, for it would have been a loss had Kate accepted, but it was Kate's spurning of it that infuriated Stella.

She turned a white, contorted face to Kate: 'You'll be sorry you did that.' She gave a short, bitter laugh. 'It was foolish of me to offer it. Why, I should have known; Rodney was ever generous where his fancy led him. Your great gesture has been lost, Miss Hannigan. But I am afraid from now on you'll find your source of income cut off. So I repeat, you'll be sorry you did that.

'I will take my leave, Miss Hannigan.' She waited for Kate to precede her through the room, but Kate stood stiff and staring.

Kate knew she dare not speak, a hate she had never experienced before was raging within her, and she was afraid of it. She wanted to throw herself on this woman and rend her; there was an overpowering desire to beat her fists into that cold, sneering face. She knew that if she spoke all the work of Bernard Tolmache would be destroyed in a second. One word would release this fury, and she would act worse than any woman of the fifteen streets; the self she had created through constant observation and study would perish in the flame of this hate. Not even Tim Hannigan had aroused such a destructive urge.

After waiting a moment, Stella raised her eyebrows and walked past Kate, so close to her that their skirts touched. She went through the front-room, passing Annie, who was standing with her hands up her sleeves, without a word. She found difficulty in opening the door, and Annie came forward shyly and undid it. Stella gave her no word of thanks; she did not even look at her, but stepped down on to the pavement and into the crowd of children who were surging around the car.

From the window, Annie watched the car drive away, with the screaming children hanging on behind. She watched the curtains being put back into place at the windows opposite and dark figures disappearing into doorways. She watched until the street became quiet again, for she couldn't go into the kitchen . . . the lovely bright, shining light had gone from the day. She did not want to look at Kate, for she knew that the light would be gone from her too. She stood trembling, cold inside and out.

Kate remained standing where Stella had left her; the feeling of rage was dying away and a terrible ache was taking its place . . . This had been bound to happen; why had she blinded herself all these months? What had she expected? That he would just come back? Come straight to her and they would live happily ever after, while she, his wife, would sit back and let it happen?

Stella, she realised, had not only the law on her side but she had Rodney in the hollow of her hand; that she could break him and that she would, rather than allow him to go free, was evident, and that she had struck the right note when saying that man needed something more than passion, Kate knew. Rodney loved his work, it had been his life for so many years, and, without it, he would be lost . . . and lost he would eventually become if she stayed here; for she knew that, no matter what Stella threatened, he would come to her, throwing everything to the winds . . . She leaned against the wall and beat it slowly with her fist.

Annie, hearing the dull thuds, crept to the kitchen door, and stood, horrified, watching. Kate made no sign, and Annie could not go to her. This crying, this sorrow was different from any she had ever seen; it frightened her and created a sorrow inside of her which was unbearable. She crept back into the room again.

Mrs Mullen let an hour elapse after seeing the car drive away, and she wondered if it would look nosey if she were to go in and see Kate now. She had been behind her curtains, like the majority of the women in the street, waiting to see the 'lady' come out. It was Doctor Prince's wife, Rosie had told her; everybody in the street knew who it was. Oh, poor Kate! . . . Poor Kate! She had been over the moon these past few weeks; and now what would happen? It should never have started in the first place, he was a married man. Kate should have known what she was letting herself in for . . . But there, these things did happen. God knew why! And the doctor was a fine chap, and he seemed to think the world of Kate. But he was a doctor, and he was married, and his wife was a big bug. And, after all, in spite of all her learning, Kate was only a working lass . . . Aw, but poor Kate . . . poor lass! . . . She would pop in now and see how things were; she would take in Annie's Christmas box, it would serve as an excuse.

Before she had time to get it there was a knock on the back door, and Kate herself came in, taking her utterly by surprise; for Kate rarely visited anyone . . . even her.

Mrs Mullen looked quickly at her, and away again . . . whatever had happened, it had certainly taken it out of her.

'Sit down, lass,' she said, awkwardly.

Kate shook her head. 'Willie's saving up to buy furniture, isn't he, Mrs Mullen?'

'Yes, lass,' answered Mrs Mullen, perplexed.

'Do you think there's anything next door he'd like?'

Mrs Mullen stared at her.

'I know the stuff's not much good,' Kate went on, 'but there's the chest of drawers, and one good bed and the lino. Then there's the saddle and chiffonier and kitchen table.'

'What are you talking about, lass?'

'Selling up,' said Kate, in a rush. 'I'm going away and I must have some money. I've only twenty-two shillings in the world. If I could get about ten pounds . . . but the stuff's not worth that, I know. Could you lend me a few pounds, Mrs Mullen? I'll soon get work and let you have it back.'

'Lass, sit down and calm yourself. What do you want to go away for like this? . . . Why, I thought . . . well . . . the doctor will be here any day now!'

Kate shook her head from side to side: 'I can't tell you why I'm going, Mrs Mullen . . . only I've got to go . . . Do you think Willie will take some of the things?'

'It's very likely; I'll ask him, lass, as soon as he comes in. But what's your rush? When are you going?'

'As soon as I possibly can. Only don't ask me any questions, Mrs Mullen. If I could tell anybody I'd tell you, you've been so good to me . . . but I can't.'

'But it's Christmas, Kate! You can't go rushing off at Christmas.'

'Christmas!' said Kate bitterly. 'Christmas is the very time for me to go. Anything that's going to happen to me waits until Christmas . . . I loathe Christmas! I hate it! Goodwill to men!'

She went out, leaving Mrs Mullen gazing at the kitchen door in amazement.

WAITING

Rodney stood leaning on his stick and looking out of the Davidsons' sitting-room window. Below, the river Don at low tide ran sluggishly between its slimy banks; to the right lay the Salt Grass, a barren stretch of mounds, bordered, in the far distance, by the houses of Jarrow. Of all the dreary views in the world, he thought, this was the worst. God! if only he could get away from it and never see it again.

Peggy Davidson came into the room, carrying a tray in her hand.

'Oh, Rodney,' she exclaimed, 'why will you stand about? Do sit down and put your leg up . . . Peter will be furious with you.'

'I loathe your view, Peggy,' he said, turning from the window.

'Yes, it is awful, isn't it? But I don't seem to see it any more . . . Do sit down, Rodney . . . Here; come on.' She patted the cushions on a long chair.

'You can live with a thing until you neither see it nor feel it, then?'

'Yes. Yes, I suppose so . . . Look here, I'm not going to become involved in one of your arguments at half-past ten in the morning. Sit down and drink this beef-tea. And remember, you induced Peter to let you come downstairs on the solemn promise that you would take things easy for another week or so.'

Rodney smiled at her and sat down. 'I wonder what would have happened to me without you and Peter,' he said. 'I often wonder that, you know.'

'God provides,' she answered.

'Oh, Peggy, you sound like an old Irish woman! You're a real Jarrowite, you know.'

'And I'm proud of it too.'

Peggy was relieved that his tone, even for a moment, could be bantering. She was worried, and Peter was worried, about him. As much as they loved him, they wished he would go away for a change. Nothing, however, would induce him to talk about it. A few months ago, when he had been at breaking point, he had gone to his people, presumably to stay the winter. But he had returned within a fortnight and had just escaped a severe breakdown . . . Oh, Peggy thought, if only she knew where that fool of a woman was! Why didn't she come back?

Rodney sat thinking . . . Peggy doesn't see this view because she's happy. Happy! . . . The word plunged him into weariness again, and his mind echoed the persistent cry, 'Kate, where are you? Why don't you come back? You must know that you can come back now.' Last night he had dreamed the same old dream again. He woke from it sure that she was lying beside him, and lay taking in the peace and ecstasy of her presence for some moments before realisation came, bringing with it its despair. He first experienced the dream after his foot was amputated. He had only to doze off and Kate would be with him, and he would wake up calling her name. The other fellows around made no comment; the calling out of names was a stage which most of them reached.

Being a prisoner was a hell at any time. But to lie helpless and to have them chopping away at you, knowing that nothing you could say would make any difference, was an indescribable hell. He did not know why they had not amputated his left arm too; they prepared him for it, and the thought of what it would mean nearly drove him mad. He looked at it now, lying practically useless by his side. Its delayed action irritated him beyond all words; to all intents and purposes it was off, dead. It gave him no pain at all, whereas the foot which was no longer there ached like mad.

The sight of a man striding down the street could fill him with envy; a work-stained drunk, rolling along, brought up the eternal 'Why?' He needed his arms and legs; they could accomplish so much that was good; yet he was left practically useless.

During these spasms of self-pity he would tell himself it could have been two arms and two feet.

When the terrible necessity of having to amputate both arms or both feet had been thrust upon him his mind had shut down on itself, his pity refusing to form thought. At such times pity could wreck you and those around. You used it only in subtle form; you laughed, you cursed; you swore and badgered; and it kept your hand steady. The German doctor, he remembered, neither cursed nor swore; he was polite, and cold and in a hurry.

What effect the happenings of the past year would have left on his enfeebled system if Peter and Peggy Davidson had not been at hand to sustain him he dreaded to think. Stella's changed attitude, on his return to England, was disconcerting; her sweetness and solicitude left him embarrassed and at a loss. She pooh-poohed the idea of a nurse and insisted on looking after him herself. Her constant attention and anticipation of his every need, far from setting a spark to his dead affection, created an uneasiness in his mind. No correspondence had passed between them until just before he embarked for England, when he received a most charming letter from her. Thinking along the lines that a leopard doesn't change its spots, he had asked himself the reason for her attitude.

He had been in a fever to see Kate, but being dependent on someone posting his letters he could not even write to her. So he laid the situation before Peter, who showed no surprise nor offered any advice, but said he would go personally to see Kate and fetch him word of her.

The news Peter brought was so alarming to Rodney that, against all advice, he was soon making frantic efforts to walk on his artificial foot. Stella did everything in her power to restrict his movements, only falling short of locking him in his room.

When Rodney eventually reached the fifteen streets Mrs Mullen made clear the reason for Stella's attitude and also for Kate's disappearance.

'She must have got work right away, doctor,' she said, 'for I got this letter yesterday, with the four pounds she borrowed. There's no address, as you can see, but the postmark's London.'

From Mrs Mullen's he had gone straight to Peter and asked if he could stay with him for a time, knowing that, feeling as he did, he could not cope with Stella. However, Stella showed no reaction to this move until she found that John Swinburn had come to Rodney, asking him to divorce her.

Rodney had not been prepared for Stella's visit. She was like the embodiment of white-hot lava; raging, she denied all Swinburn had said. Her cool poise was thrown aside and he saw a woman who, even with his knowledge of her, was new to him. She said she would ruin him, that he would never practise again. He had replied that it was doubtful whether he would in any case.

'There are other avenues in the medical line you will want to take up, remember?' she said. 'But I have the power to close them all to you. Apart from your illicit amours with a maid, which are the talk of the town, there is this!' And she showed him what she said was a copy of Lady Cuthbert-Harris's letter.

Rodney was shocked and visibly staggered.

'You know it's a lie!' he said.

'Of course,' Stella answered. 'And you'll prove it to be a lie. But only after I have made that mud stick so hard that you'll never be able to scrape it off.'

The contents of this letter and the talk it would arouse, should it be made public, had hung over him like a black cloud. When Stella mentioned the other avenues which were open to him she was drawing on her knowledge of the plans of which he had often spoken to her and which, she realised, he would be more likely to take up now that he was disabled. The plans concerned sick children, sick not only of body but of mind. Child psychology, he had recognised for some time, was more important to him than the attending of worn-out bodies held together by acid-encrusted bones. If he could prevent some of the children of today from becoming those dimmed and troubled people of tomorrow then he would achieve something. This was the avenue Stella could block.

Yet, in spite of her threats, he went ahead on the evidence Swinburn supplied and petitioned for a divorce. It was strange that he liked Swinburn at this time better than at any other time during their acquaintance; not because he was supplying the means of freeing him from Stella, but rather because he knew Swinburn to be under great stress and that he was trying to do the right thing, as he saw it. Swinburn said he could not help his love for Stella. Try as he might it was no use; his feeling for her swamped everything. His career meant nothing to him without her, and he proposed starting afresh somewhere abroad.

Rodney pitied him from the bottom of his heart. He knew Stella had nothing to give any man; what she offered was a mirage. But it had the power to drive a man mad, as he knew only too well.

That it drove Barrington mad was made tragically evident, for, although Barrington knew that he was supplanted by Swinburn, the canker of desire for Stella seemed to grow with the hopelessness of its fulfilment. It reached its climax when he visited her after reading the notice of the divorce proceedings. The result of this meeting which gave Rodney his freedom by Stella's death instead of by divorce shocked him so much that, for a time, he thought he too would lose his sanity.

At dinner-time Rodney spoke less than usual. Kate was filling his mind again. He felt tied to this place because of her; something beyond reason said it was to here she would return, even to the fifteen streets.

He was recalled to the effect his silence was having on the others by Peter saying, 'Do stop jabbering, Cathleen!'

Rodney roused himself: 'Good heavens, Peter! Don't keep her quiet on my account . . . Look here, don't you think it's about time you stopped treating me as an invalid? Go on, Cathleen.'

'Who said it was on your account? You flatter yourself, man. I've had a devil of a morning, and now I want a little peace while I'm eating my dinner. For her tongue never stops wagging.'

'Uncle Rodney doesn't mind, do you?' asked Cathleen.

'Of course not.' He smiled at her and winked his eye.

'Uncle,' said Michael, 'you should see the Meccano set working in a shop in King's Street in Shields. It's wonderful. They've got cranes unloading ships and filling wagons, and it's all set up in a miniature dock. Oh, it's great!'

'It sounds great,' said Rodney. He did a stage whisper across the table: 'What about asking Doctor Davidson to take us round that way in his car this afternoon?'

'Not on your life!' cried Peter. 'Oh, no. And me up to the eyes and you hardly out of bed!'

'O . . . oh, daddy!'

'It would be just what a sensible doctor would order,' said Rodney, 'a change of scene. And I'm sick of looking at your filthy river.'

'Be quiet you two,' shouted Peter to Cathleen and Michael. 'And if you want a change of scene, look out of the back window,' he said to Rodney. 'And, woman' – he glared at Peggy – 'if I can't have peace with my dinner I'm going to eat out.'

She smiled at him serenely. 'If Rodney wrapped up well, and we made him comfortable in the back of the car, these two could squeeze in the front seat' – she indicated the children. 'Then, I don't see why not. And, after all, it's Christmas Eve.'

'I have calls to make, woman.'

'Well, they wouldn't stop you; they could sit in the car and wait.'

'No, I just can't do it! If those two want to go to Shields they can take the tram. And as for you' – he nodded at Rodney – 'you should have more sense, man.'

They looked at him in silence for a few moments.

'Oh, all right then,' he said, his old smile breaking out. 'But I can't take you till after tea; I'm packed with calls in Jarrow this afternoon.'

The gaily dressed shop windows, the alive and teeming market-place, and the excitement of the children, lifted Rodney out of himself for a time. But only until he thought of what it would have meant to him had he been driving down here with Kate and Annie. However, he maintained an air of excitement in order to please the children and to allay any unrest in Peter's mind. But during the homeward drive to Jarrow he felt very tired and lay back in the car, feeling his strength seeping from him.

Half turning, Peter said: 'Do you mind if I make a call in the fifteen streets; there's a woman there I'd like to see? It might save me coming out later on.'

'No, of course not,' said Rodney. 'Don't worry about me. Go ahead.'

'I'll leave you here, on the main road,' said Peter, bringing the car to the kerb; 'the house is only a few doors up Slade Street.'

Cathleen slipped into her father's seat and was arguing with Michael on who would learn to drive the car first when Michael suddenly exclaimed: 'Look, Cathleen! Look at that old woman along there. She's drunk! She's hanging on to the lamp-post.'

'Oh, so she is! She isn't half drunk, too. And she's coming this way,' said Cathleen, peering through the windscreen. 'Look at the boys following her. Look, Uncle Rodney, she's nearly falling!'

Rodney bent forward. Then swiftly he leant back again as he recognised the figure reeling into the circle of light to be that of Dorrie Clarke. He prayed that she would pass on and would not come near the car; this was the woman who had read his letters. He could still hear Stella's voice quoting extractions from them and telling him how they came into her possession.

The children sat silent, watching the woman. She was harrying the boys. When she was abreast the car she stumbled against the radiator and let out an exclamation: 'God blast yer! Burn an old woman, would yer?' she cried.

Cathleen and Michael started to giggle, and Dorrie Clarke waved her fist at them shouting, 'You would laugh? That's a Christian for yer!' She brought her face close to the window and spluttered, 'Young upstarts, that's what you are.' Her head rolled round, nodding on her fat neck, and she stared into the back of the car.

Rodney, head bent, was pretending interest in a paper, but the light from the street lamp shone on him.

'God Almighty!'

Rodney did not look up, the children sat silent, their eyes wide with mingled amusement and fright.

'Ah, you can bow yer head,' cried Dorrie. 'Yes, bow yer head. Yes; go on, bow yer head. I've seen me day with you. By God, I have . . . I said I would, didn't I? And what Dorrie Clarke says she does . . . God looks after his own. You thought you were a doctor! Ha, ha! Why, you weren't fit to lick Doctor Kelly's boots! An' what are yer now? . . . Yer not even half a man!'

Rodney lowered the paper and sat staring straight ahead, his face pallid. Two women came out of Slade Street and, hearing Dorrie, hurried towards the car.

'Come away, you old fool,' said one; 'you'll get yersel' into trouble.'

'What!' she turned on them. 'Me get into trouble for tellin' that sod the truth? Take yer 'ands off me; I'm goin' to tell him some more . . . about his fancy piece.'

'Come away, woman.'

'Leave me alone! Get yer 'ands off!' She wrenched herself free and fell heavily against the car door. Steadying herself, she turned her face to the window again: 'Went off and left yer, didn't she? High an' dry! No half man for Kate Hannigan. An' yer put notices in the paper . . . God Almighty, it was a laugh!

'Come back to Erin, mavourneen, mavourneen,' she sang, beating time against the window with her hand. 'What would jer give to know where she is, eh? Yer other leg, eh? Dorrie Clarke could tell yer. Yes; I could tell yer. What d'yer think about that?'

Suddenly she was wrenched away from the car, and Peter was saying, 'Mrs Clarke! If this happens again, I'll put the police on you.'

He got into the car without another word and drove away.

Dorrie Clarke stood leaning against the wall where he had flung her. 'Another bloody upstart! Polis on me, indeed!'

'Ye'll get yersel' in the cart, Dorrie, mind,' said one of the women.

156

'Do yer really know where Kate Hannigan is?' asked the other.

'Of course she doesn't,' her companion said; 'it's the gin that's talkin'.'

'Gin is it!' yelled Dorrie. 'Gin is it! Yer think I don't know where she's gone! A . . . ah! A . . . ah! It's me that knows a thing or two.'

'The doctor'd likely pay a pretty penny to know, Dorrie,' the woman persisted.

'Me take his dirty money!' cried Dorrie. 'Not me. Why . . . if I was starvin', if I was crawlin' in the gutter for a crust, like this . . . ' She went to get down on her knees, and the women pulled her up, saying, 'Don't be such a damned fool, Dorrie!'

'If he was handin' me a plate of gold sovereigns, I tell yer, and going down on his one good leg to do it, I'd . . . spit in his eye! And he'll never get Kate Hannigan . . . never! 'Cos yer know why? . . . She's dead! Dead as a doornail!'

'Dead!' exclaimed the women.

'Yes, dead,' said Dorrie. 'Yer think I'm drunk an' it's the gin talkin' . . . but I can still use me head . . . She's dead this long while . . . Can't yer see? If she wasn't dead she'd've been back and snaffled him. But she's dead, I know for certain she's dead, an' in Hell, sizzling, where she should be.'

One of the boys who had followed Dorrie suddenly cried, 'Ee, look there!' He nudged the woman nearest him and pointed to the tram which had stopped across the road.

'My God!' she exclaimed. 'Well, of all the things that could happen!'

Dorrie Clarke blinked her bleary eyes at the approaching figures; her slack jaw wobbled from side to side and, as the tall woman and girl walked past the group, she slowly slid down the wall to the pavement.

THE RETURN

Annie lay staring into the dark, waiting for the alarm to go. For some mornings past she had woken up long before the alarm had gone and lain quiet, thinking about Rosie Mullen and the north. Early last Christmas Eve morning she and Rosie had been down to Jarrow slacks to gather wood; there had been a rough tide during the night, which always meant there would be wood and lots of other things, including rotten vegetables, lining the bank. It was funny, but she imagined she could smell the stinking cabbages now. Perhaps it was just the smell of this house, for, no matter how Kate cleaned it, it always smelled like old cabbages.

She had forgotten what Rosie Mullen's face was like. She could see her as a dumpy whole, but her face was never clear. Would she ever see Rosie again? she wondered. Always there was a sick longing within her for Rosie and all that she stood for, the docks, the slacks, the fifteen streets, the Borough Road church and the children . . . The children in this town of St Leonards were not like the children in the north. Apart from speaking quite differently, they didn't play the same games; and the ones who were supposed to be poor didn't look poor. A girl had taken her round an old part of Hastings, which was as close to St Leonards as Tyne Dock was to Shields, and pointed out the slums to her. The slums had appeared houses of moderate affluence and very quaint, some even beautiful. She couldn't see how those people could be poor, not poor, anyway, like the poor back home. She longed to be able to talk to Kate about it, but whenever she mentioned the north Kate turned the conversation. On her evening off, last week, when they stood on the promenade and watched the moon's reflection gleaming like molten silver on the water, Kate had remarked, 'It's very beautiful, isn't it?' And she had answered her by saying, 'Do you remember, Kate, the glow that used to come over Jarrow when the blast furnaces tipped at night?' Kate had not answered, and they walked on in silence. And that night she heard Kate crying; the quiet, still crying that often went on and on. She always pretended to be asleep when Kate cried, for Kate's tears formed a barrier of pain which she found impossible to surmount.

In that dreadful house where Kate worked in London and they slept

158

in the basement, and where people's feet were continually passing over the iron grating above the small window, even into the dead of night, Kate cried often, and her face always looked swollen. The basement was very damp, too. She remembered how ill she felt one night, and how she went to sleep, feeling a pain in her chest, and woke up to find herself in a ward with a lot of other children. When she was better, Kate had not taken her back to the house, but came here, to this house which smelt of cabbages and was so full of old furniture and pictures that you could hardly move.

Miss Patterson-Carey, who owned the house, liked to tell her all about the furniture and pictures; they had belonged to her grandmother and her mother. She said that if they knew she was reduced to taking in guests for a living they would turn in their graves. She had explained that when she was a little girl they lived in The Square and kept eight servants, and that her father drove his prancing bays up and down the front. But now she had been reduced to living above The Square, in this house which was called Wide Sea View. Which was very funny, Annie thought, since the only place from which you could view the sea was the attic window.

Miss Patterson-Carey told her all these things. She didn't tell Kate, because that would have kept Kate from her work, and she had the guests to see to and all the house. The guests were all old people, and seemed to wear a lot of clothes.

Annie didn't like Miss Patterson-Carey; she was mean and religious and was always giving her tracts to read. All the guests read tracts, too. Sometimes the house seemed to be full of all kinds of tracts. Miss Patterson-Carey had called her a naughty girl for reading comics; she said they weren't 'holy reading', and she didn't allow anything in the house that wasn't 'holy reading'.

Now it was winter and there weren't so many guests, Miss Patterson-Carey sometimes came into the kitchen at night and talked to Kate. But it was all about God and a thing called . . . retribution. Kate never answered her, which seemed to annoy Miss Patterson-Carey, who usually brought up the subject of how difficult it was to obtain a situation where you could keep a child.

The alarm gave a warning bur . . . rrr, but before it could get fully going Kate had switched it off; so Annie knew that she had been awake, too. Kate got up immediately and started to dress by the light of a candle, and Annie whispered, 'Kate, can I come down with you?'

'You should be asleep,' said Kate. 'And it's cold down there. Wait until I get the fire on.'

'I don't mind the cold, Kate. I don't like staying up here alone, and I could help you.'

'Very well,' Kate said. 'But be quiet, mind.'

Annie got out of bed and hurried into her clothes; she was ready almost as soon as Kate.

Leading the way down the bare attic stairs, Kate whispered, 'Be careful of the torn carpet on the second flight, mind.'

They crept past Miss Patterson-Carey's door on the first-floor landing and down the last flight into the kitchen. It struck icy cold, and Kate busied herself in cleaning out and lighting the kitchen fire.

Annie asked, 'Shall I do the sitting-room fire for you, Kate?'

'You'll never be able to light it, dear, there's hardly any paper left.'

'I've last week's comic,' said Annie. 'And, oh, I know where there's some paper, Kate. In the bottom of the vegetable basket; I saw it sticking through the slats yesterday, when the man left it. Shall I take the vegetables out and get it?'

'Yes, you can do that,' said Kate. 'I'll light the gas, and then you can get on with it. But try not to make a noise.'

Annie emptied the box and took out the folded newspaper. She picked up some sticks and went into the sitting-room and set about doing the hearth. She opened out the newspaper and crumpled it loosely, as Kate had shown her, and laid it in the grate. She was laying the sticks in a criss-cross pattern on it when a large black-printed word caught her eye. Something about it was familiar. She looked more closely. It said TYNESIDE. She knelt, her head bent sideways, drinking in the word. It was like a fresh breeze in this stuffy, cluttered room. She sat back on her heels, her head still bent sideways, and gazed at the word. She wondered, abstractedly, what the paper could have to say about Tyneside. She lifted two sticks away, and disclosed the word TRAGEDY . . . TYNESIDE TRAGEDY . . . Somebody had been knocked down, she thought; they always said that in the paper when anyone had been knocked down. She wondered who it was; would it be anyone whom she knew? Hurriedly she pulled away the sticks, and, lifting out the paper, smoothed it on the hearth. She was reading intently when Kate came in, saying, 'Oh, my dear, haven't you got it on yet? Get by, out of the way, and let me do it.' She pushed her gently to one side and crumpled the paper again.

Annie knelt for a second, as if dazed, watching her. Then she cried out: 'No, Kate! No! Don't burn it . . . Look at the paper . . . Look what it says.'

'For goodness' sake, child, be quiet! What are you yelling like that for? Do you want her to come down?'

For answer, Annie pulled the paper from Kate's hands and spread it out on the hearth again, and pointed to it . . . 'Look!'

Kate knelt back and read for a few seconds. Then her body jerked forward, and, with hands grasping each side of the paper, her eyes moved swiftly down the column.

She sat back slowly and turned to Annie. They stared stupidly at each other. Annie suddenly shivered, the inward shiver of delight. Kate took her hand, and they both rose to their feet.

'What are we going to do, Kate?' whispered Annie.

Kate just stared at her, with that dazed look still in her eyes. Then it seemed to lift like a curtain, taking with it the drawn, dead look that Annie had seen there for so long.

'We're going home,' she said.

'When?'

'Now. Now.'

'Now?'

'This minute!' cried Kate.

'Oh, Kate!' They clung together for a second, their arms gripping each other tightly.

'Come on. We'll get packed.'

They hurried upstairs, yet went softly, through habit; and in ten minutes they returned again, dressed for the street and Kate carrying two cases.

In the kitchen Kate said, 'I'll take her a cup of tea, it will lighten the shock.'

Annie, who still held the dirty newspaper in her hand, asked, 'Kate, can I keep this?'

Kate touched her cheek tenderly: 'Yes, darling; you can.'

As Kate hurried out, Annie opened the paper and read the report again. It was dated April 24th and read:

DOUBLE TYNESIDE TRAGEDY
ON DAY FOLLOWING DOCTOR SUING FOR
DIVORCE NAMING ASSISTANT AS
CO-RESPONDENT WIFE SHOT BY
FORMER LOVER

Stella Dorothy Prince, wife of Doctor Rodney Prince of Conister House, South Shields, was today shot dead by her former lover, Herbert Barrington, who afterwards shot himself. Only yesterday it was made public that divorce proceedings were pending between Doctor Prince and his wife, and naming Doctor John Swinburn, Doctor Prince's assistant, as co-respondent. Barrington called at the home of Mrs Prince, and, after heated argument, overheard by a servant, shot her. The servant, Mary Dixon, stated . . .

A blur of tears hid the print. It seemed awful that the doctor's wife was dead; although she wasn't nice she had been beautiful . . . But, anyway, they could go back home . . . Oh, they could go back home now!

Kate came hurrying into the kitchen. She took some money from her bag and laid it on the table. She had hardly done this when the kitchen door burst open and Miss Patterson-Carey entered, her hair under a high night-cap and an old dressing-gown draped around her angular body.

'You can't go like this!' she cried. 'You just can't do it!'

'But I can,' said Kate quietly. 'There is the money in lieu of notice that you say you require.'

'You're a wicked woman to leave me like this.'

'I have just read some news,' said Kate, 'which has altered everything for me, but had you treated me even once as a human being I should not have left you so suddenly. Anyway, you are neither old nor sick, and, as you have often quoted to me, idle hands are armchairs for the Devil. So it will be a change for him, in your case, to be made to stand this Christmas.' Kate picked up the cases and motioned Annie to the door. Then she turned and delivered her Parthian shot: 'This, Miss Patterson-Carey, is what is known as . . . retribution!'

Annie opened the door and they went out into the dark morning.

The long journey from St Leonards was nearly over. Kate and Annie, with the compartment to themselves, sat close together in one corner. The reaction from almost hysterical joy had set in, and Annie was sobbing, long, shivering sobs that shook every bone of her slight frame. Kate soothed her, saying, 'There, there. Come, darling; stop it. You'll only make yourself ill.'

'I can't help it, Kate, I . . . I keep thinking, if I hadn't seen that paper we might never have . . . '

'Sh . . . h!' said Kate. 'Just let's thank God you did see it. And there now; stop crying . . . Listen! We'll soon be coming to the tunnel. Remember the tunnel?'

In the dark of the tunnel they sat with their arms about each other, and Kate kissed Annie almost passionately.

When they got out at Tyne Dock station, Kate stood for a moment on the dimly lit platform and looked around her. She was home . . . home! For years she had longed to get away from the north and never see it again, but now she felt it held all that she wanted in life. She did not know where she would find Rodney; she might have to move on again in search of him; but she knew that she would return here eventually. For this was her home; the people here were her people . . . good, bad and indifferent, they were her kindred.

At the dock gates they took the Jarrow tram. And Kate felt she would not exchange the hard slotted seat for one in Paradise. After they got out of the tram at the fifteen streets, they passed a group of people standing at the corner of Slade Street, and Annie asked softly, 'Did you see who that was, Kate?' And Kate answered, 'Yes, I saw. But she can do nothing more to us.'

Kate's eyes were dry and bright, and her hand trembled as she knocked on the Mullens' door. It was opened by one of the younger children. He peered at them through the gloom, then darted away without a word, and they heard him yell, 'It's Kate and Annie Hannigan.'

Before they could cross the threshold Mrs Mullen was there. 'Kate lass! Kate! In the name of God where've you sprung from? Come in, lass; don't stand there, come in . . . Oh, lass . . . where've you been?' They were borne into the kitchen on her welcome and into a surge of the Mullens, all talking at once and clamouring about them. 'Sit down. Sit down, Kate,' cried Mrs Mullen. But before Kate could do so, she had gathered her and Annie into her embrace, and they all clung together for a moment, half laughing, half crying.

Annie turned to Rosie and they stood staring at each other, awkward and embarrassed, not even touching hands.

'Oh, Rosie!' was all Annie could murmur.

'Ee, Annie, ye've come back!' said Rosie.

'All the way across the country in one day!' Mrs Mullen was saying. 'Why, lass, you must be famished! I'll have you something to eat in a coupl'a shakes of a lamb's tail.'

Kate drew Mrs Mullen to one side: 'Where is he, Mrs Mullen? Do you know?'

'He's at Doctor Davidson's, lass; he's been there all the time.'

Kate stood silent a moment. 'Do you think I could have a wash and do my hair, Mrs Mullen? I won't have anything to eat, just a cup of tea.'

'Well, just as you like, hinny,' said Mrs Mullen. 'Aw, lass' – she squeezed Kate's arm – 'I'm glad to see your face again. And just wait till the father sees you,' she said, referring to her husband, 'he won't half get a gliff.'

Annie was saying to Rosie, 'We lived in a place called St Leonards, with an awful woman . . . She reads tracts.' Annie caught Kate's eye and they both began to laugh. Kate laughed as she had not done for a year, and in a moment the whole of the Mullen family had joined in. And Rosie thought, It's like that night in Kate's kitchen when we all cried and me da was funny and old Tim died.

Kate walked from the fifteen streets to the house on the Don. She had the urge in her to pick up her skirts and run. She felt her heart would burst through her flesh; her mind was crying, 'In a few more minutes I'll see him. In just a few minutes I'll be able to touch him.' She crossed the Don bridge, and thought, It all seems beautiful. But when she pressed the bell of the Davidsons' door she felt faint and weak.

The door was opened by Peggy, who said, 'Yes?' then stood staring in wonder at Kate. She had seen Kate only a few times before, but had never spoken to her.

'I'm Kate Hannigan,' Kate said. 'Could I . . . Could I see Doctor Prince?'

Peggy drew her inside and into a room off the hall before speaking. Then she exclaimed, 'Oh, I'm so glad you've come! Oh, you don't know how pleased I am to see you at this moment.'

'I never knew what had happened until this morning,' Kate said; 'Annie, my daughter, saw the report in an old newspaper.'

They appraised each other in silence for a moment; then smiled, as if each liked what she saw. 'Really, I can't believe it's true that you are here!' exclaimed Peggy. 'Excuse me a moment. I must tell my husband.' She darted into the hall and called, 'Peter!'

Peter's voice came from the sitting-room, saying, 'There! I bet I'm off again. Now do as I say, won't you? Go to bed, and I'll look in on you when I return.'

With a finger on her lips, Peggy motioned him to silence. She closed the sitting-room door which he had left open, and whispered, 'It's Kate! She's come.'

'What! No! Where?' Peter's eyebrows almost disappeared into his hair in surprise.

'Ah!' warned Peggy. 'In there.' She pointed to the door.

'Well!'

When Peter went into the room and saw Kate standing wide-eyed on the hearth-rug, whatever he had intended saying was never said. This was not the Kate he remembered; she had always appeared to him a very young girl, even when well into her twenties. But here was a woman, beautiful still, yet in a widely different way from the other Kate; more finely drawn, more poised, but strung up, at this moment, to breaking point, if he knew anything about it. His treatment of her was studiously casual: 'Where on earth do you think you've been?' He spoke as though she had left the house at seven o'clock promising to return at eight, and now it was nine.

She smiled faintly.

'Nice dance you've led everybody . . . haven't you?'

'Take no notice of him, Kate,' Peggy said. She turned to Peter: 'She found out about it only this morning from an old newspaper . . . Isn't it strange?'

'Strange!' said Peter. 'Of course not; you couldn't expect her to act like a sensible person and read the daily paper. Anyway, Kate, where have you come from now?'

'From St Leonards in Sussex,' Kate said. She understood what his off-hand manner was aiming to achieve, and his efforts were succeeding, for her tense nerves were easing, even as he spoke.

'When? Today?'

'Yes; we left early this morning.'

Peter's voice became softly sympathetic as he said, 'He's in the next room, Kate; but you'll find him somewhat changed. He's never given up hope that you would return.'

Kate said nothing. Now that the moment had come she wished she had more time, time to control the trembling of her body and the racing, whirling expectancy of her mind.

Peggy took her arm. 'Come, Kate,' she said, giving an intonation to the name, which brought a flash of gratitude from Kate. 'Let me have your hat and coat,' she added.

Kate took off her things in the hall, and Peggy, pointing to the sitting-room door, gave her arm a gentle pat and left her.

As she opened the door Kate did not know what she expected to find. But when she saw Rodney looking to all appearances whole she experienced a slight shock; she had not expected him to look whole. He sat lost in brooding thought, his head bent and his hands lying idle on his knees. At the sight of him all her senses seemed to rush from her body. In the second before he looked up she experienced the acute pain of incredulity that accompanies any feeling nearing ecstasy; she was alive to the overlapping of the emotions, for this joy which filled her was also suffering. He lifted his head, and the remark he was about to make to Peggy died on his lips as he beheld Kate standing with her back to the door. The air between them seemed to vibrate; emotion winged back and forth; but neither of them moved. He closed his eyes, and when he opened them again and Kate was still there he breathed her name . . . a small sound, so inadequate, expressing nothing of the wonder of this moment. He made a hasty and clumsy effort to rise, grabbing for his stick and knocking it out of his reach. His bad arm gave way under his weight as he tried to assist himself from the chair. He floundered back, despair and rage at his helplessness and inadequacy to meet this occasion tearing at him.

In the second that it took Kate to reach him, she saw that he wasn't whole, nothing about him was the same; his hair was grey at the temples and his face was unnaturally pale, with the bones showing prominent under the skin, and his body seemed broken.

She was at his feet, and her arms were around him, straining him to her. As only one arm returned the pressure she was choked by a rush of feeling, so poignant that no words could express it . . . Love and tenderness seemed small parts of its ingredients; there was a protective and maternal urge mixed with her passion for him; all so intertwined that they were inseparable. And, as his lips gropingly sought hers, her whole being was transported, even while her heart was rent by his tears which were wetting her face.

THE END